P9-AQC-095

3 4028 09198 6738

HARRIS COUNTY PUBLIC LIBRARY

SciFi Kratma SF
Kratman, Tom
Carnifex

$7.99

WITHDRAWN aqn501324018

Gotta love it u ... thought as he watc ... overhead carrying Oabaash's brigade north to seize the summit ... awaited; ... sources ...

Dista ... hundred ... moving ... *about w* ... *We'll la* ... *place has ever seen before.*

As the last navigation light from the helicopters was killed by pilots interested in survival, Carrera got in his vehicle and instructed his driver to take him to headquarters.

It was an odd thing, really, the drive back. They passed column after column of infantry moving up on foot. That wasn't the odd thing; that was simply part of the scheme of maneuver. No, what was odd was that the columns all stopped to cheer him as they passed each other. He waved back, of course, and held out his hand to shake whatever hands he could, but uncertainly and even with a touch of embarrassment.

Why should they cheer me? The bloody Sumeris did, too. Makes no sense. I am nobody but a nasty bastard out for revenge and using them to get it.

The driver provided half the answer. "The boys sure seem ready for another fight, sir."

The other half, or perhaps it was more than half, is that soldiers love a commander who leads them to victory. It has ever been thus. And that, at *least* that, Carrera had done. He felt his mind and spirit click into full battle mode.

CARNIFEX

TOM KRATMAN

CARNIFEX

This is a work of fiction. All the characters and events portrayed in this book are fictional, and any resemblance to real people or incidents is purely coincidental.

Copyright © 2007 by Tom Kratman.

All rights reserved, including the right to reproduce this book or portions thereof in any form.

A Baen Books Original

Baen Publishing Enterprises
P.O. Box 1403
Riverdale, NY 10471
www.baen.com

ISBN: 978-1-4165-9150-4

Cover art by Kurt Miller
Maps by Randy Asplund

First Baen paperback printing, November 2009

Distributed by Simon & Schuster
1230 Avenue of the Americas
New York, NY 10020

Library of Congress Control Number: 2007027929

Pages by Joy Freeman (www.pagesbyjoy.com)
Printed in the United States of America

CARNIFEX

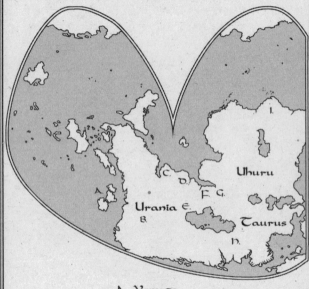

A. Yamato
B. Zhong Guo
C. Sind
D. Kashmir
E. Pashtia
F. Farsia
G. Sumer
H. Volgan Republic

Nova

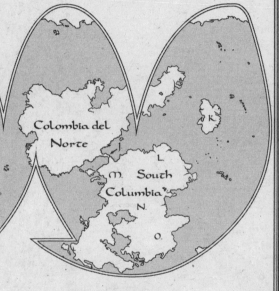

Colombia del Norte

South Columbia

M.

L.

N.

O.

K.

I.   Republic of Northern Uhuru

J.   Republic of Balboa

K.   Atlantis (UEPF Lodgment)

L.   Atzlan

M. Colombia Central

N.   Federated States of Columbia

O.   Secordia

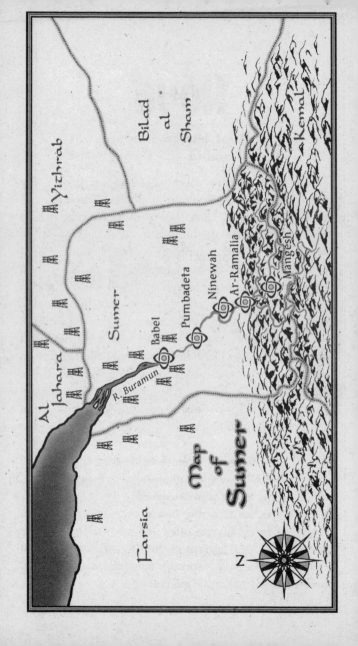

What has gone before
(Anno Condita –23 through 462):

In the year 2037 a robotic interstellar probe, the *Cristobal Colon*, driven by lightsail, disappeared enroute to Alpha Centauri. Three years later it returned, under automated guidance, through the same rift in space into which it had disappeared. The *Colon* brought with it wonderful news of another Earth-like planet, orbiting another star. Moreover, implicit in its disappearance and return was the news that here, finally, was a relatively cheap means to colonize another planet.

The first colonization effort was an utter disaster, with the ship, the *Cheng Ho*, breaking down into ethnic and religious strife that annihilated almost every crewman and colonist aboard her. Thereafter, rather than risk further bloodshed by mixing colonies, the colonization effort would be run by regional groups such as NAFTA, the European Union, the Organization of African Unity, MERCOSUR, the Russian Empire and the Chinese Hegemony. Each of these groups was given colonization rights to a specific area on the new world, which was named—with a stunning lack of originality— "Terra Nova" or something in other tongues that meant the same thing. Most groups elected to establish national colonies within their respective mandates, some of them under United Nations' "guidance."

With the removal from Earth of substantial numbers of the most difficult portions of the populations of Earth's various nations, the power and influence of transnational organizations such as the UN and EU increased dramatically. With the increase of transnational power, often enough expressed in corruption, even more of Earth's more difficult, ethnocentric, and traditionalist population volunteered to leave. Still others were deported forcibly. Within not much more than a century and a quarter, and much less in many cases, nations had ceased to have much meaning or importance on Earth. On the other hand, and over about the same time scale, nations had become preeminent on Terra Nova. Moreover, because of the way the surface of the new world had been divided, these nations tended to reflect—if sometimes only generally—the nations of Old Earth.

Warfare was endemic, beginning with the wars of liberation by many of the weaker colonies to throw off the yoke of Earth's United Nations.

In this environment Patrick Hennessey was born, grew to manhood, and became a soldier. As a soldier, he married, oh, *very* well.

Hennessey's wife, Linda—a native of the Republic of Balboa, was killed, along with their three children, in a massive terrorist attack on Hennessey's native land, the Federated States of Columbia. The same attack likewise killed Hennessey's uncle, the head of his extended and rather wealthy family. As his dying testament, Uncle Bob changed his will to leave Hennessey with control over the entire corpus of his wealth.

Half mad with grief, Hennessey, living in Balboa, ruthlessly provoked and then mercilessly gunned down six local supporters of the terrorists. In retaliation, and with astonishing bad judgment, the terrorist organization, the Salafi *Ikhwan*, attacked Balboa, killing hundreds of innocent civilians, including many children.

With Balboa now enraged, and money from his uncle's rather impressive estate, Hennessey began to build a small army within the Republic. This army, the *Legion del Cid*, was initially about the size of a reinforced brigade though differently organized. For reasons of internal politics, Hennessey began to use his late wife's maiden name, Carrera. It was as Carrera that he became known to the world of Terra Nova.

The legion was hired out to assist the Federated States of Columbia in a war against the Republic of Sumer, a nominally Islamic but politically secular—indeed fascist—state that had been known to have supported terrorism in the past, to have used chemical weapons in the past, and to have had a significant biological warfare program. It was widely believed to have been developing nuclear weapons, as well.

Against some expectations, the *Legion del Cid* performed quite well, even admirably. Equally against expectations, its greatest battle in the campaign was against a Sumeri infantry brigade led by a first rate officer, Adnan Sada, who not only fought well but stayed within the rules and laws of war.

Impressed with the legion's performance (even while loathing the openly brutal ways it had of enforcing the laws of war), and needing foreign troops badly, the War Department of the Federated States offered Carrera a long-term employment contract. Impressed with Sada, and with some of the profits from the contract with the Federated States, Carrera likewise offered to not only hire, but substantially increase, Sada's military force. Accepting the offer, and loyal to his salt, Sada revealed seven nuclear weapons to Carrera, three of which were functional and the rest restorable. These Carrera quietly removed, telling no one except a very few, *very* close subordinates.

The former government of Sumer had a cadre and arms for an insurgency in place before the Federated States and its allies invaded. In Carrera's area of responsibility, this insurgency, while bloody, was contained through the help of Sada's men and Carrera's ruthlessness. In the rest of the country, however, the unwise demobilization of the former armed forces of the Republic of Sumer left so many young men unemployed that the insurgency grew to nearly unmanageable levels. Eventually, Carrera's area of responsibility was changed and he was forced to undertake a difficult campaign against a city, Pumbadeta, held by the rebels. He surrounded and starved the city, forcing women and children to remain within it until he was certain that every dog, cat and rat had been eaten. Only then did he permit the women and children to leave. His clear intention was to kill every male in Pumbadeta capable of sprouting a beard.

After the departure of the noncombatants, Carrera's legion continued the blockade until the civilians within the town rebelled against the rebels. The former he aided to take the town. Thereafter nearly every insurgent found within Pumbadeta was executed, along with several members of the press sympathetic to the rebels. The few insurgents he—temporarily—spared were sent to a ship for *rigorous* interrogation.

PART I

CHAPTER ONE

But my dreams
They aren't as empty
As my conscience seems to be
I have hours, only lonely
My love is vengeance
That's never free
—The Who, "Behind Blue Eyes"

United Earth Peace Fleet Starship *Spirit of Peace*, 25/10/462 AC

The traditional Christmas orgy was in full swing on the hangar deck. Since it was supposed to be a time to celebrate universal brotherhood, even the proles were invited. Indeed, so universal was the sense of brotherhood implicit in the season that Lieutenant Commander Khan, the fleet's sociology officer, was lying, rear up and breasts down, on an ottoman with a prole at each end, one in each hand and short lines emanating in four directions. Khan's husband cheered her on, And why not? He had bet a month's salary on her performance for the night.

Sitting on a plain chair on an elevated dais, High

Admiral Martin Robinson, Commander of the United Earth Peace Fleet, watched through his blue-gray eyes without much interest. In truth, Robinson was bored silly by the whole thing. *It's as bad as a party back home. Same old faces, same old events . . . same old, same old. Bah. Never anything new.*

Robinson had reason to be bored. Though he looked to be in his mid-twenties, face unlined and back unstooped, the high admiral was a beneficiary of the best antiagathic therapy Old Earth could provide. His blond hair was untouched by gray and without any recession in his hairline.

On the other hand, Robinson had had better than two centuries in which to grow bored, two centuries of peace, two centuries of orgies, two centuries of . . . *Well . . . nothing, really. Nothing until I came here. This, at least, hasn't been boring. It's been frustrating.*

Frustration wasn't the half of it. Mixed in, and perhaps in greater quantity than the frustration, was fear; fear for his class, fear for their rule, and fear for his planet.

And there's nothing for it but to change the cesspool down below from a near cognate of Earth, as it was, into a perfect clone of Earth, as it is. That, or plunge the whole thing into a Salafi sect dark age. Either would be acceptable. Indeed, having the planet fall under the Salafis would probably leave my world safer. Let them be content to pray five times a day to a nonexistent god via a rock in a building in a nothing-too-much city. Let them keep better than half their people as cattle. Let them keep themselves poor and ignorant and, above all, incapable of space flight.

But if I fail, if the non-Salafi barbarians down below achieve interstellar travel, my home will be taken and pillaged, my class will be cast down, and my entire civilization will be plunged into barbarism. And Khan—here Robinson looked up to see that Khan was an easy half dozen partnerings ahead of her nearest competition—*Khan assures me that when a civilization like that meets one like ours, ours hasn't a chance. If they can get to us, they can and will ruin us.*

Unconsciously, Robinson lifted a thumb nail and began nervously to chew.

So I do what I must, dirty my hands, as I must, and fight . . . well, fight through others, of course; I can't risk the loss of my fleet. That, above all, I must preserve.

Robinson laughed at himself. *I must preserve it until it falls apart around me. Preserve it while the Consensus back home does nothing to maintain it.*

Dropping his thumb and shaking his head at the bloody damned frustration of it all, Robinson stood to leave the hangar deck. He'd call the captain of the ship, Marguerite Wallenstein, later, if he needed sex. For now he just needed to be alone.

Ahead of him, an oval hatchway dilated to permit the high admiral passage. As the hatchway leading off the hangar deck *whooshed* shut behind him, Robinson heard Khan frantically pleading for more.

Parade Field, Camp Balboa, Ninewa Province, Sumer, 25/10/462

The troops in the camp stood in ranks and sang lustily and in their thousands:

Abide with me; fast falls the eventide;
The darkness deepens; Lord, with me abide;
When other helpers fail and comforts flee,
Help of the helpless, oh, abide with me.

Patricio Carrera, commander of the troops of the *Legion del Cid* in Sumer and of their thousands of *compadres* in training back in Balboa, didn't join in the singing. Any other song and he might have. But this song, a favorite of his late wife, Linda, figured prominently in one of the recurrent nightmares he endured of her death, and of the deaths of their children. He just couldn't sing it. It was all he could do not to cry. Instead, his blue eyes, normally fierce, became indescribably sad as, indeed, did his entire face.

Carrera's closest friends stood or sat around his office, drinking Christmas cheer that had, until that moment, seemed very cheerful indeed. Yet the mood the song brought to Carrera instantly transformed the mood of every man and the two women in the place.

Two of those closest friends, Sergeant Major John McNamara and Legate Xavier Jimenez, both coal black, very tall and whippet thin, looked meaningfully at each other. *Note to the chief chaplain: next year that particular song does* not *go in the Christmas program.* The two women, Lourdes, and Ruqaya, exchanged glances as well. As much as the two blacks resembled each other, one could at least be certain they were unrelated, Jimenez being frightfully handsome and McNamara, well, the best one could say of him was that he looked his part, the quintessential grizzled sergeant major, his face heavily lined and never exactly lovely.

Lourdes and Ruqaya, on the other hand, might have been sisters, or at least close cousins. Both were tall and slender. Both had amazingly large and melting brown eyes. Skin color? About the same. Faces? Different, of course, yet each was in the range of symmetrical attractiveness that tended to resemble. However, whereas Mac and Jimenez had shared the same thought, the women's thoughts were only somewhat related. For Lourdes: *Poor Patricio.* For Ruqaya: *Poor Lourdes; having to share her man with a dead woman.*

Where is death's sting? Where, grave, thy victory? I triumph still, if Thou abide with me.

Carrera gripped one of his disgustingly small, distressingly soft, and nauseatingly dainty hands around a tall tumbler of scotch and drank deeply. *For the things I do,* he thought, *and the things I allow to be done, somehow I doubt that the Lord will abide with me.*

Hildegard Mises, Sea of Sind, 33/10/462 AC

The conex inside the ship rang with the helpless shrieks. It practically reverberated with them. The conex, soundproofed, also kept in the stench of voided bowels and bladders, and the iron-coppery stink of blood.

You wouldn't think one man could scream that much, especially with the tongue protector installed, mused Achmed al Mahamda, the chief of interrogations. Mahamda, quite unperturbed, casually munched a Terra Novan olive, the fruit of an odd palm with green trunk and gray fronds. The olive, itself, was gray and about plum sized. Its taste was similar to, but slightly more astringent than an Old Earth olive. Mahamda loved them, as did many of his people.

He put the olive down and wrinkled his nose as the victim, Fadeel al Nizal, lost sphincter control. The assistant applying electricity to Fadeel's genitalia looked over at Mahamda. *Should we clean him up before we continue? This is pretty vile.*

Genial seeming, a little fat, and—appearances notwithstanding— utterly ruthless, Mahamda had been an interrogator for the secret police, or *Mukhabarat*, of the old regime in Sumer. When that one had been tossed out the year before by a coalition led by the Federated States of Columbia, Mahamda had gone into hiding. Eventually, one of Sada's people had found him and offered him a job—with a raise, no less, and protection from the Coalition forces searching for him—working for some of the infidels. He'd had to give his family as hostages but, since he'd only gone back to work to ensure they were fed, this seemed not unreasonable.

Mahamda shook his head at the assistant's unvoiced question. His look said, *If you want to work in this line, you're going to have to learn to accept foul smells.*

Shrugging *you're the boss*, the assistant turned a dial to increase the juice. Impossible as it might have seemed, Fadeel's screaming actually increased. His eyes seemed ready to burst from his head as his teeth ground against the rubber bit installed in his mouth to keep him from biting off his own tongue.

It's a shame what we have to do to squeeze out the last little bit of useful intelligence and propaganda, thought Mahamda *But this is that kind of war. Let those who began it take the blame. And it's not like this sniveling wretch deserves any better.*

Once stocky, and even with a bit of midriff fat,

Fadeel was already beginning to waste away under the torture. Though near enough in appearance to the captive that they could have been cousins, Mahamda felt no pity. Fadeel was one of those who had begun and advanced the kind of terrorist war being waged in Mahamda's homeland of Sumer. His list of atrocities was long, the coating of blood on his hands deep, the stain indelible. Mahamda felt nothing but loathing for the Bomber of Ninewa, the Butcher of Pumbadeta.

While Mahamda sat in a comfortable swivel chair bolted to the floor of the shipborne conex, Nizal was strapped firmly to a dental chair, with an electrode stuffed up his anus through a hole in the chair and his penis firmly affixed into something that still looked much like the droplight socket from which it had originated. Nizal's body quaked with the electric jolts surging through it, wrists and ankles straining at the thick leather straps that held him in place. Helpless tears coursed down his face while an inarticulate "gahhhhhh" poured from his mouth.

Mahamda raised a palm, signaling his assistant to stop for the nonce.

"I warned you, Fadeel," Mahamda said, not unkindly. "*Any* failure to cooperate, any at all, will bring punishment." The interrogator *tsk-tsk*ed. "Why do you continue to doubt me? It isn't like we haven't broken you in every other particular. It isn't as if you haven't spilled cells and safe houses, armories and bank accounts. Do I have to bring your parents in, Fadeel? You *know* how you hate it when we bring your parents in."

In answer al Nizal only sobbed the more heartbrokenly.

Again Mahamda *tsk-tsk*ed. "Get his mother," he ordered the assistant.

That got more than sobs and tears from al Nizal. "Gnoo! P'ease . . . gnoo," he managed to get out around the rubber bit.

Since Fadeel hadn't offered more full cooperation, Mahamda said nothing to stop the assistant who then left, returning in a few minutes with a stoop-shouldered woman. He pushed her to a wall and began chaining her upright. She, too, sobbed.

"That won't do any good, madam," Mahamda said to the woman. "You raised the boy to be a terrorist. You are responsible. It's only right that you help him see the error of his ways."

Finished with restraining the woman, the assistant went to a table from which he retrieved a blow torch and friction igniter. She began to scream and plead with her son as soon as the blowtorch was lit. In a cage on the table, a brace of *antaniae*, or moonbats, the septic-mouthed, carnivorous, winged lizards of Terra Nova, likewise hissed in fear as the torch was lit. It was sometimes used to drive them toward the faces of victims.

"It's up to you, Fadeel," Mahamda said. There was no answer.

"Start with the toes," the interrogator ordered.

"Bwait!" al Nizal begged, between sobs. "'eave 'er . . . go; don' . . . 'urt her. I make . . . your fi'm." The assistant with the blowtorch knelt to bare the woman's feet but stopped, looking at Mahamda.

"I don't know," said Mahamda, doubtfully. Even so, he took a moment to ungag the terrorist. "We *did* give you a chance to speak the words we wanted spoken to the camera. You refused. Why should we not punish you for that?"

Al Nizal looked at his electricity-scorched penis and answered, "I think you've"—he sniffed—"punished me enough. I'll *make* your film."

Mahamda rocked his head from side to side, as if weighing the time that might be wasted against the advantage of more willing cooperation. He pointed towards the *antaniae*. "It will be really hard on your mother if you fail us again, Fadeel. The moonbats are hungry."

The terrorist's voice was full of an inexpressible hopelessness. "I won't. Just *please* don't hurt her."

The ship rocked more or less continuously. Nonetheless, there was one room on the ship, a conex, actually, that did not rock. This was set up on gimbals and so kept its perpendicularity. This was the camera room.

Inside the room, on a comfortable looking chair under a picture of Adnan Sada, Fadeel al Nizal sat, still chained, and answered questions from an interviewer. Mahamda did not play the part of the interviewer; it just wasn't his thing. Besides, he didn't want Coalition authorities to have any clue as to his whereabouts.

Beside the picture of Sada was a calendar, with the month opened up to show a date not too long after al Nizal's capture in Pumbadeta. The coffee table between him and the interviewer held a newspaper, the headlines of which screamed of the fall of Pumbadeta, an event which had taken place months prior. For all anyone who might watch it could tell, the interview was taking place in the recent past, a few days before the announcement of al Nizal's

execution and cremation. It was only for purposes
of this interview that Mahamda had kept the dentist
away from al Nizal's front teeth.

"What can you tell the audience about the suicide
bombers you recruited?" asked the interviewer.

Fadeel had been well rehearsed. He answered,
from the script he'd been given, "The first thing you
have to understand is that most of those foolish boys
are not suicide bombers. We load them down with
explosives, yes, or set them to driving automobiles full
of explosives. But we never tell them they're going to
be blown up. Instead, they go somewhere as couriers.
And when they're in a good place we set them off by
radio or cell phone."

"But they make films beforehand, announcing their
martyrdom," insisted the interviewer.

Nizal, still on script, laughed. "Oh, the films. When
we have them make those we tell them it's just in case
they're killed in action, so that the cause will still benefit.
I think not one in a hundred, not one in a thousand,
would actually blow themselves up if told to."

"So all they are to you are tools, mere drivers and
couriers?"

"That's about it," Fadeel agreed. "That, and fools,
ignorant boys who have no clue what they're getting
into."

"Those boys get a lot of press, though," cued the
interviewer.

"Oh, the *press*," said al Nizal. "Let me tell you
about the press."

"Do you mean our press or the Tauran and FSC
press?"

"There's really not much difference between them,"

al Nizal answered. "All of them shunt us money. All of them spread our propaganda. Any of them will help us bait an ambush, or will be happy to point out coalition soldiers to our riflemen. We wouldn't have a chance in this war without the press—"

"But your people have killed members of the press. Hamad al Thani, for example, was blown up not long ago. Aren't you afraid they'll eventually retaliate?"

Fadeel snorted, as required, and answered, "They wouldn't dare."

Ninewa, Sumer, 15/1/463 AC

While Fadeel al Nizal had not given up every cell, every bank account, and every cache of arms of which he knew—not *quite*, not *yet*—even of those he had given up not all had been turned. This wasn't because they could not have been, but because there were better and worse ways of destroying them. Better said, sometimes one really could kill two birds with one stone. And if one could not only destroy a terrorist cell but at the same time destroy the mutual confidence and trust between those who blew up children in markets and those who called them "freedom fighters," so much the better.

Only one of Terra Nova's three moons, Bellona, shone down on the scene.

"Come! Hurry, hurry!" insisted the keffiyah-topped rifleman to the reporter come to interview his chief. "Into the van before you are seen. The enemy has eyes everywhere."

Silently, warily, the news team approached the van. They were three. The reporter, who seemed to be in charge, was a tall, swarthy sort who gave his name as "Montoya," and said he was from Castile, in Taurus. The cameraman said nothing beyond his name, "Cruz." The translator introduced himself only as "Khalid." All three had brown eyes. None were quite white, though the cameraman was much darker than the other two. They seemed to be in rather good physical shape as well. On his shoulder, the cameraman easily bore an unusually large camera, which the translator said was a special model for direct transmission to the home station. All three wore the body armor that was de rigueur for nearly everyone in Sumer by this time.

As the news team reached the van they were each subject to a hasty but thorough search of their persons. Neither their cell phones, nor their armor, nor their large camera with its tripod incited any comment. With a nod from the searcher, their guide again said, "Hurry. Into the van."

Once inside, all three were blindfolded. "It's for your own good," their guide explained. "What you do not know you cannot be forced to reveal. And you know the enemy has horrible ways."

"Militaristic hyenas," said Montoya.

"Imperialist pigs," agreed Cruz.

"Infidel dogs," summed up Khalid.

With the news team blindfolded, the van sped off with no more wheel screeching than one would expect of any innocuous van in any major city in Sumer.

The drive was long, though it never left the city; the sounds of traffic told as much. After a period of time the van stopped. The news team could hear the driver open the door and get out. They heard what sounded like a garage door being opened by hand.

The driver returned, closed his door, put the van in gear, and drove forward into blackness. Once the van stopped he killed the engine, again got out, turned on a light, and closed the garage door behind him.

"You can take your blindfolds off now," said the guide.

"Have all the major chiefs come?" asked Montoya. Khalid, the translator, passed on the question.

"Only three," answered the guide, with a weary shrug. "You know how the streets are these days with the infidel swine. The others couldn't risk it."

"I understand," agreed Montoya. "Fascist beasts."

"Antiprogressive poltroons," added Cruz.

"Heretical blasphemers," finished Khalid.

"This way, friends," said the guide, more warmly, if still wearily. "The chiefs that *have* come are eager to see you."

"As we are them," said Montoya.

Clutching his rifle firmly, the guide led the team out of the garage and into a well lit, finished basement where three somber looking men awaited, each of them armed with pistols in high-fashion shoulder holsters, with rifles at their feet, and with a guard each standing by. The guards' weapons were loaded and ready, though they, themselves, seemed calm enough.

There are a number of ways of feeding ammunition to a weapon. The simplest is, of course, by hand, one round at a time. More complex is to use a magazine or belt. Magazines come in several varieties, single stacked, double stacked, and rotary, for example. There are also somewhat rarer approaches, notably helical and cassette.

✧   ✧   ✧

The guide made introductions. Ordinarily, this would have been done over food and drink. These were no ordinary times, however. It wasn't every day that the faithful were able to make a broadcast through a Tauran news network. Normally they had to settle for al Iskandaria. And there was no telling how quickly the infidels would be able to home in on the transmission. Best to be quick.

"Set up the camera, Cruz, quickly," Montoya ordered. "We must hurry; there is no telling what fresh atrocities the enemies of the people are planning."

"Yes, sir," answered the cameraman who went about doing just that, setting up the camera and fine tuning its angle of view. When finished, Cruz got behind the large camera and announced he was ready. By that time, two of the guards had taken position at the corners of the room behind the news team.

Meanwhile, Montoya hooked each of the three chiefs up with small microphones, then hooked himself up as well. As he did, unnoticed he pressed a small button. A radio signal immediately went out to the news team's backup. Then Montoya, himself, backed up to stand nearer the door.

Montoya looked at Khalid. Yes, he appeared ready, too.

Montoya smiled at the three Sumeri men at the table and announced, "Then, gentlemen, let us begin . . . *now.*"

The really tricky part hadn't been ripping the guts out of a new camera, nor even getting a weapon inside. The bitch, the absolute bitch, had been getting enough *ammunition*, with a reliable enough feed and ejection mechanism, inside the camera. No stacked magazine would do, they didn't hold enough ammunition. A belt required too complex a mechanism in the inner weapon. Rotary was invariably too fat.

This was where the close relationship between the legion and the some elements of the Volgan Republic came in. The latter had a new submachine gun, the Aurochs, which used a helical magazine containing sixty-four nine-millimeter rounds and which fired at a rate of just over seven hundred rounds per minute, ordinarily. The mechanism could be modified to spit out closer to twelve hundred, however. Moreover, it had been.

At the word "now" four things happened. Montoya and Khalid, whose real names were, in fact, Montoya and Khalid, pivoted and launched themselves at the guards stationed in the corners. At the same time, Cruz, whose real name was Cruz and who was really in charge, depressed a button on the handle of his "camera." The lens, which was a much thinner glass than it looked, immediately broke as a nine-millimeter bullet departed through it, followed quickly by another seven. All left the "camera" accompanied by great bursts of flame. Lastly, just as the first bullet left, a small panel in the side of the camera opened to allow a spent casing, followed by another seven, to depart.

The guard and guide standing behind the dignitaries were the first to go. With two quick bursts of eight to ten rounds each, these were slammed to the wall and their bodies simply *ruined*. (The legion tended to ignore the rule on frangible ammunition when dealing with its irregular adversaries.) After that, with

the chiefs just coming out of their shock to reach for
their own arms, Cruz simply held the firing button
down and swept across the table until the Aurochs
inside the camera clicked empty. The chiefs went
down like ninepins.

Meanwhile, Montoya and Khalid struggled with
the two guards at the corners. Neither really had any
advantage. All four were young men, fit and strong and
trained to fight. That didn't matter, however, as Cruz
now had his pick of weapons. He retrieved one, made
sure it was loaded, then went to stand beside Montoya.

"This is really going to sting, buddy," Cruz told the
struggling Cazador.

"Fuckthatjustkillthemotherfucker!"

Bang.

"Sorry about this, Khalid," Cruz said, as he placed
the muzzle against the last guard's head. *Bang.* Khalid,
member of Adnan Sada's underground, revenge-minded
men recruited to fight terror with terror, winced as he
was stung with muzzle blast and covered with flecks
of bone, bits of brain, and a wash of blood.

Once the "camera" had expended its ammunition,
there was no reason to keep it whole. Cruz flicked
a latch, split it open, and withdrew three small hand
grenades. *If only old Martinez could see me now,*
he thought. There had been a time when hand grenades frightened Cruz. That time was long past. *Just
another tool.*

Montoya and Khalid acquired arms the same way
Cruz had, from the bodies. They were just loading
them when the driver of the van burst into the room,
shouting and firing his rifle into the ceiling. The driver
lasted a very short time.

Montoya spoke into his microphone. "Mission accomplished. No back up necessary. We're leaving the same way we got here. We'll dump the van and walk home. Oh, and if you assholes think we're going to do this kind of fucking crazy shit again, then *you're* crazy."

They left Al Iskandaria and Tauran News Network calling cards on each of the bodies, each card bearing a handwritten note, "In the future, watch where you plant your bombs and who you kill. Hamad al Thani was our brother."

Before they left, Cruz and Montoya wired the bodies of the chiefs with grenades and set the camera to arm in five minutes and explode as soon as anything disturbed its integral motion sensor. Since the legion *wasn't* going to investigate, it seemed a safe bet for nailing a few more.

"Do you think they'll buy that it was a hit by the pressies?" Sergeant Montoya asked, as Khalid backed the van out of the garage. Khalid knew how to drive the madcap streets of Sumer better than did the two legionaries.

"They'll wonder, at least," answered Ricardo Cruz, Optio, *Legion del Cid*. "If we'd left by helicopter, if any kind of reinforcement had come by helicopter, or at all, then no, they'd know it was us. But as is?" He shrugged. "It looks enough like a private hit, a vendetta hit, to make them wonder and maybe chill press-terrorist brotherhood."

"Something must chill it," Khalid said.

Khalid was an odd case, though not so odd in relation to Adnan Sada's little corps of assassins. Initially, he'd been very much against the infidel invasion of Sumer, despite being a Druze rather than a Moslem (a fact he generally hid; Cruz and Montoya, for example, had no idea Khalid was a Druze and they'd been working together for quite a while). Yet he had seen just rule come to his home province for perhaps the very first time when one of his own people, Adnan Sada, had become governor. This had dampened his early enthusiasm for resistance. (For whatever their other faults and virtues, Druze tended to be fiercely loyal to their homelands, wherever those might be and whoever might be in charge, provided, at least, that the governments and people of those homelands did not threaten the Druze.)

It hadn't done any more than that, though, no more than to make him neutral. To turn him from neutral to committed partisan had taken the loss of much of his family. These victims—his mother, his little brother, the doe-eyed baby sister, Hurriyah, Khalid had doted on—had been butchered by a terrorist car bomb, a bomb that turned them into disassociated chunks of bloody meat as they shopped the local market. At that point, Khalid had been identified, sought out, offered the chance of revenge, and recruited.

His initial training had been sketchy, at best, and his initial missions simple. But, with time, with the development of newer and better courses of instruction, above all with his demonstrated propensity for assassination, Khalid's training and skills had much improved. Tonight he wouldn't add any black ribbons to the family picture he kept at his home, one for each terrorist he slew. He hadn't actually killed anyone, this mission, and the ribbons were for personal kills, personal revenge.

The chief of the *Legion del Cid*, Patricio Carrera, didn't know Khalid, personally. If he had, he'd have instantly recognized a kindred spirit.

"Where to from here, Khalid?" Cruz asked. "Montoya and I are back to our tercios, me to the First and him to the Sixth, after this mission."

"I've got one more mission, then it's off to Balboa, actually," Khalid answered. "Balboa for an immersion course in English—English! Allah, your fucking Spanish was strange enough!—and then Volga for some advanced training. After that, I don't know."

"Lucky guy," said Montoya. Then, thinking, *Yeah, Khalid's a wog, but he's a damned good man to have on your side,* he added, "Hey, I've got a sister you might like . . ."

Parade Field, Camp Balboa, Ninewa Province, Sumer, 11/2/463 AC

Two very unlucky men, not brothers, stood side by side on the carefully maintained and watered, very green parade field in the center of the earthen-walled base. One, a legionary of the *Legion del Cid,* had been accused and found guilty of raping a Sumeri girl. The other was her brother who had killed her afterwards to expiate the shame. The Sumeri wore a dirty dishdasha. The legionary had on the remnants of a uniform, all the insignia cut away, buttons stripped off, and the man's award for valor, the *Cruz de Coraje en Acero,* lying in the dirt nearby.

Both men stood on short, unpainted wooden stools, about half a meter high. Around their necks were hemp ropes, tightly wound into nooses and leading to a simple wooden frame with cross piece. Both trembled not so much in fear as in shame. This was going to be a hard and, especially, a *shameful* death, a kicking, choking, pissing and shitting your pants death, and both knew it.

The legionary's cohort was drawn up in formation before the gallows. Under some tranzitrees, planted for shade, the Sumeri's family elders stood witness as well, as did some of the clan's women. Nobody even thought to touch the beckoning fruit of the tranzitrees. Inviting green on the outside, luscious red within, the fruit of the tranzitree was poisonous to any forms of life with highly developed brains. Still, they provided good shade, were immensely hard to kill, and had pretty flowers.

While Sergeant Major Epolito Martinez, a fireplug-shaped, dark-skinned sergeant major with his hair in a severe buzz cut, harangued the cohort on the wages of sin, Major General Adnan Sada, Army of the Republic of Sumer, had some choice words for the family.

"I have consulted with my brigade chaplain," Sada said, "on the question of honor killing of raped females. Mullah Thaquib informs me—and he is an educated man, an Islamic scholar, who has studied in Yithrab—that there is not one word, not *one*, to permit or condone such a crime. He tells me that it is *un*Islamic, that it is murder. As such . . ." Sada turned and nodded to his own sergeant major, Na'ib 'Dabit Bashar, standing not far from Martinez.

"Epolito, time," the Sumeri sergeant major announced. Bashar was tall and rail thin and had but a single eye. He'd lost the other in the fight for Ninewa, facing, among others, Martinez's own cohort. It was just business; Bashar held no grudges.

"And furthermore," finished Martinez, "I'm *glad* to be hanging this son of a bitch who brought shame on all of us, and I'll be glad to do the same for any of *you*."

With that Martinez executed a smart about-face and marched a few paces to bring himself parallel to the Sumeri. There he halted a few seconds until the Sumeri said, quietly, "Forward . . . . march."

"Man, I hate this shit," Bashar said. His Spanish had gotten rather good over the last few years.

"Nothing for it," Martinez answered, "but it makes me sick, too." *But I deserve it. Who failed to train you to keep your cock in you pants, boy, who failed to train you not to rape women, if it wasn't me?*

At the base of the gallows, both noncoms stopped and placed one foot each on one of the stools. Together they looked toward Sada.

Sada heard one woman begin to wail. He supposed it was the mother who had lost a daughter and was about to lose a son. *Nothing for it,* he thought. *If you have more sons, woman, raise them better.*

He turned towards the gallows and raised one hand. When he dropped it both Martinez and Bashar tipped the stools over and backed up. The condemned men dropped less than six inches each. Their feet immediately began to flail in panic. The nooses hardly tightened at first.

It was going to be a very slow hanging.

Where there had been only one *Dux*, or *Duque*, when the legion had been created, now there were two. The increase was necessary to deal with the overly rank conscious officer corps of both the Kingdom of Anglia and the Federated States of Columbia. Of the two, Parilla remained in the rear, in Balboa, with the bulk of the troops. Carrera stayed forward with the one legion kept deployed. (*Dux? Duce? Duque?* The official title was Latin, Dux, Duce, but, troops being troops, they had dropped the Latin and used the Spanish cognate, *Duque.* Similarly, they had on their own stopped saying or writing *"legio"* and used the Spanish—and English—"legion.")

Patricio Carrera, aka Patrick Hennessey, *Dux,* or *Duque,* of that deployed legion of the *Legion del Cid,* forced himself to watch the hanging from the second floor window of his adobe brick office. Though no one was looking, he kept his face a stony mask, even while the two doomed men struggled and twisted at the end of their ropes.

For the slowly strangling Sumeri who had murdered his own sister Carrera felt no pity. *You stupid bastard. I'd have paid recompense money and moved her out of the country, married her off to one of my troops or maybe sent her to school somewhere. Even in your fucked-up culture there's such a thing as out of sight, out of mind. You didn't have to kill the girl. And I'd still have hanged the man who raped her.*

His own soldier was a different matter, for Carrera loved his Legion and loved the soldiers who composed it. Watching one of his own die slowly and disgracefully *hurt.*

Carrera sighed. *But what choice have I, boy? When one of you rapes a girl he drives up resistance and endangers all the others. And it wasn't like we didn't have whores available for you. There was no excuse. And if I loved you, son, I hate you, too, for what you've made me do to you.*

✦   ✦   ✦

The definition of a bad death could be said to be one in which two or more deadly factors race at a snail's pace to kill the victim. In this case there were three such factors. While gravity pulled the men down, straining their necks and threatening to break them, the ropes tightened slowly, cutting off air and blood to the brain, even while the combination of impeded blood flow and terror promised eventual cardiac arrest. All this the two men suffered until, finally, the Sumeri's skinny neck gave way. His legs thrashed once, twice, and then he went still except for the unconscious rippling of dying muscles and the steady drip, drip, drip of piss and liquefied shit off still wriggling toes.

The choking and gagging Balboan legionary had a tougher time of it. With his much more muscular neck there was no chance of breakage. Nor did the rope cut off blood to the brain or induce cardiac arrest. Instead, his thrashing and his weight gradually tightened the noose until there was no more passage for air. Only then, and even then not for some time, did he lose consciousness and, finally, die.

All this Carrera watched, unwilling that he should not witness what he himself ordered, however horrible. Only when it was over, when the doctor in attendance placed his stethoscope to the victims' chests and made the signal that they were dead, did the *Dux* step away from the window.

Even as he did, he could still hear a Sumeri mother wailing.

Ninewa, Sumer, 8/3/463 AC

An ambulance siren wailed in the distance, racing
to the scene of the latest bombing in the provincial
capital. They weren't as common here as they were
some other places in the country; yet they were far
too common still.

Carrera, Sada, and their respective military formations did what they could to aid the local police and
even to search vehicles themselves. It helped . . .
somewhat . . . sometimes . . . in some places.

They'd tried both high-tech and low-tech solutions,
from explosive sniffing machines to explosive sniffing
dogs. Both methods had faltered under the simple
terrorist expedient of sending forth small boys with
spray bottles to spray underchassis and wheel wells,
signposts and curbs with a solution containing various
explosive compounds in low dilution. To the machines
and the dogs, explosive was explosive. They were soon
alerting on nearly everything. When everything smells
like explosive nothing does. The machines were retired
and the dogs sent to other duties.

There had been some successes of course. Early on
in the campaign aircraft equipped to spit out every
imaginable cell phone number and every possible
radio frequency had overflown likely areas for bomb
construction. This had blasted a goodly number of
bomb manufacturers into the next world over a short
period of time.

Those who lived had reverted to using infrared
garage door openers to detonate their bombs. The
legion had not yet figured out a way to prematurely

detonate those until they were already emplaced, which was all too often all too late.

The bomb that had just gone off in a market had been detonated in just that way. Fortunately, something had warned the civilians nearby who had, for the most part, gone scurrying. Casualties were remarkably low and for those there were there was a catch all phrase, *il hamdu l'illah*, to God be the praise.

Now, to either side of that attack site and the few bodies it held, other groups waited for some special targets to show up to detonate their own little gateways to Hell.

It had been a hell of an argument really. After the assassination of their three local leaders by men purporting to be from the news media, the first assumption had been that it was the foreign mercenaries' doing. As one of the remaining terrorist chiefs, Faisal ibn Bahir, pointed out, though, "Really *not* their style. They never even searched the place for files. And they only took personal arms when they left and not all of those. No, I think it was a personal hit, maybe even because of that pressie that was blown up."

"But the infidel press has shown it's been on our side from the beginning," objected another of the leading terrorists, this one a representative of the Salafi *Ikhwan*.

"That's very true," agreed Bahir, with a serious nod. "And yet, does it not strike you as suspicious, my brother, that this same infidel press supports and advances the very things we loathe and fight against? Freedom for women, for queers, for atheists? Are they not the very essence of perfidy? Are they not the mothers of lies? Why then should we accept anything they say or do at face value? The only thing we can be sure of is that they take care of each other. And *that*, brother, is completely consistent with them assassinating, more likely paying someone to assassinate, our fallen comrades."

"But . . . if the infidel press is against us, what chance have we?"

"This is why we must strike them," insisted Bahir, "to let them know who their masters are. After all, the 'courageous' infidel press is brave only when not pressed."

"Should we assassinate then, or take hostages for ransom?"

This, Bahir contemplated. After a bit of deep concentration, he answered, "Nobody expects us to honor ransoms anymore, not since that Masera *houri* was fed feet-first into a wood chipper."

Giulia Masera, a progressive journalist from the Tauran Union, had volunteered to be a hostage for ransom early in the war. Her mistake had been in surrendering herself to Sada's boys, rather than the actual insurgents. These had taken the ransom, then murdered her for the cameras in just the way Bahir had said. This had had the salutary effect of stopping such voluntary hostage takings pretty much entirely.

"No," Bahir continued. "Let's pay them back in the same coin; kill a team or two and leave our calling cards on the bodies."

"Don't press too soon," cautioned the leader of the five-man bomber team. "Wait for the vultures to show up on their way to gorge on the meat from the bodies that lie dismembered in the market."

The bomber with the infrared switch in his hand smiled at the metaphor. *Good one, Anwar. What are the pressies, after all, but carrion feeders?*

They didn't have long to wait. Ambulances passed. Military vehicles passed. And then came the word from an observer a further half mile down the road, "Tauran News Network, yellow van, eye painted on the side."

Placing a hand, fraternally, on the shoulder of the bomber with the detonating switch, Anwar said, "On my signal, Brother . . . and . . . FIRE!"

Infrared, despite sending a signal at the speed of light, activated a mechanism that was much slower. Anwar knew the time it would take between sending that signal and his bomb exploding. He had mentally calculated the time, and done so rather well. The yellow painted van with the TNN eye on the side was only a meter or so past the bomb when it went off.

The explosion came in the form of a fiery dark cloud and the whizzing of hot chunks of steel. The bomb, itself, was of the concave directional type. It was mid-sized, and just perfect for sending a very heavy concentration of metal chunks in a fairly precise direction.

The rear tires of the van were blown off as the rear three-fourths of one side disintegrated under the steel hail. The van's tail was forced about ninety degrees from its direction of travel. Forward momentum, however, had not been lost. The van had no option, given the laws of physics, but to begin to spin along its long axis as it tumbled down the street. It crashed, finally, at a store front. Between the bomb and the wildly careening van, some numbers of innocent people were hurt or killed.

No matter; the bomber team was well sheltered and they emerged moments after the bomb went off, ignoring the dead and wounded and racing afoot for the van. Their faces were covered by their keffiyahs. Once at the van, rifles went into action, pouring lead into the stunned and bleeding men—*oh, and there's one woman, too. Infidel slut!*—inside the wrecked vehicle. One or more bullets must have found the gas tank, for the air quickly filled with the stench of gasoline. One terrorist carried a grenade. This he donated into a broken window. The van was soon blazing merrily and, based on the screaming, finishing off whichever of the infidel vultures had survived bomb and bullet.

Nodding satisfaction, Anwar gave the order, "Leave the rifles; plenty more where they came from. Now go and disperse. We'll meet at my house this evening."

As the men ran off they heard another bomb, and more rifle fire, coming from what sounded like about a mile in the other direction.

All three moons were up, Hecate, Eris and Bellona, when Khalid, representing Adnan Sada, met with Bahir in a walled in courtyard in a suburb of Ninewa. "That was well done," Khalid congratulated. "My *liwa* is pleased."

"He is pleased even over the twenty-three innocents we killed?" Bahir retorted.

"No . . . no, of course not," Khalid shook his head. "But there is always what the Balboan mercenaries call 'collateral damage.' If you had not killed the innocents then it would not have seemed as if it were an attack by the resistance. The question is whether the damage is less than there would be if we did not take the action. He thinks it was worth it, however regrettable it may have been."

And how am I different, then, from the people who blew up my family? Khalid wondered. *In this only: they blew up my family; I only blow up others' families. That is as much moral difference as can be.*

From inside his dishdasha Khalid drew several packages of Tauran money which he placed on a low table between himself and Bahir. "This is for your expenses. There is a bonus in there, as well, for a job—well, two jobs, really—well done."

"It was *three* jobs, including getting you the introductions and passes to bring your 'news team' to murder the chiefs."

"You were already paid for the first," Khalid insisted.

"I know. That isn't the point. But after three such jobs, is that not enough to earn the release of my father's son?"

Khalid sighed. "I have told you this before, Bahir. Your brother will be pardoned and released when the war is over, really and finally over. He hasn't been subjected to the *question* since he gave us your name. But until the war is over, you dance to our tune if you do not want your brother to dance to a very different tune."

Under the shadowless light of the three moons, Bahir scowled even as he raked in the money.

UEPF *Spirit of Peace*, 8/3/463 AC (Old Earth Year 2518)

From space, Hecate was up and appeared full as Captain Marguerite Wallenstein's shuttle touched down on the *Spirit*'s hangar deck. Robinson was there to meet her. He waited for the hangar doors to lock, and the air previously pumped out to be released back into the open space, before cycling the airtight doors. Even then, he didn't trust the green light that came on to signal that air pressure was adequate. Rather, he waited for the balloon visible from the porthole in the hatch to collapse.

The fleet needed things like the balloon. The ships were old, irreplaceable, and almost unmaintainable. Things went wrong. Things *were* wrong that simply could not be repaired without resort to drastic measures. He'd been on station for four Old Earth years and had had to order progressive cannibalization of some of his ships to keep others going.

Clever prole, who thought of the balloon trick, thought the high admiral, as he walked to the shuttle's hatch. *I wonder if I should have had him spaced after all as being* too *clever a prole. No, I suppose not. After all, it might be* me *he saves next.*

The symbol of United Earth—northern hemisphere at the center and southern exaggerated out of size, the whole surrounded by a laurel wreath—split as the hatch opened to either side. A small walkway emerged and down the walkway strode the blonde and leggy Captain Wallenstein, a pistol strapped to her hip and some black cloth held in her arms. Blue eyes flashed angrily. Wallenstein did *not* look happy.

"Never!" she shouted, throwing the black cloth at Robinson. "*Never* will I go down to that stinking cesspool again."

The high admiral smiled, letting the burka fall to the deck. A prole would see to it, later. "I gather then that Mustafa was his usual warm and friendly self."

Wallenstein's eyes were flame. "Warm and frien . . . *arghghgh*! Do you know that bastard made me dress in a sack? That he never spoke to me directly but made me talk through a *slave*? That he . . . ah, what's the use? Of *course*, you knew."

"Yes, and isn't he just *lovely*, my dear Captain? Can you imagine Terra Nova under him and his sort? We could all go home, Marguerite, with never a care that this hellhole could ever become a threat to our people."

"Yes . . . yes, I suppose so," the captain agreed. "Except that they can't win, Martin. It's just as you said, Sumer is lost. I saw that on my sojourn there. Oh, yes; the *Ikhwan* will likely drag it out. But they can't *win*."

Nodding sagely, Robinson said, "I don't care about Sumer. That's been a lost cause since the Balboan mercenaries showed they were more ruthless than the Salafi *Ikhwan*. Tell me about Pashtia."

An underling came up to take charge of Wallenstein's pistol. She unbuckled the weapon and gave it over, then said to Robinson, "Later, in your quarters."

"It's going to be a long, slow struggle to reopen Pashtia fully, Martin," Wallenstein insisted. "But Mustafa, the filthy barbarian, is making some strides. In particular they're doing well at rearming, at limiting the degree to which government control can be spread, and at training some of what I think will eventually be very good leaders. It's a race though, between how long they can keep the Federated States occupied in Sumer while building up in Pashtia."

"How long do you think before the war there kicks off with a bang?"

"I've been thinking of little but that," Wallenstein said. "I think . . . five years."

"So long? Damn!"

"It won't do to hurry," the captain insisted.

"I know," Robinson admitted. "But I keep thinking about what the engineering officer said. They might have interstellar flight in as little as twenty years . . . and he said that *six years ago*."

"It would help, Martin, if you went down and coached Mustafa. He won't listen to me, of course, but maybe you can push him to do the things he needs to in order to win."

"Which would be?" Robinson asked. In point of fact, he outranked Wallenstein through caste, not through military ability. It was, if anything, her superior military talent that would keep her from ever being raised to the highest caste. She was simply too dangerous in her abilities ever to trust, fully.

"He needs a thorough grounding in the principles of war," she said. "He needs to take control of his movement, not just to leave it entirely to individual initiative. He needs to wage a global war."

Robinson nodded agreement. Even as he did so, though, he started to chuckle.

"What's so funny?"

"I was just thinking about an individual who *is* waging a global war. Perhaps *he'll* teach Mustafa."

The Base, Kashmir Tribal Trust Territories, Terra Nova, 9/3/463 AC

Under the light of two moons, a tall and slender, bearded and swarthy man, Mustafa ibn Mohamed ibn Salah, min Sa'ana, purified himself with water, for water was plentiful here, though the desert began not far away. With the last drop of water Mustafa felt the last and least of his sins wash away as well. He then faced to the northeast toward Makkah al Jedidah. He uttered the words, "I take refuge in God against Satan the accursed," then knelt upon his small and austere prayer rug, and abased himself before his God.

Allah, Mustafa prayed, *thou art my God. None is your equal, none is your peer. Help me, Your humble servant, to do Your work. Aid me in Your righteous vengeance. Guide my hand, steel my heart, preserve my soul.*

Allah, this world is a place of wickedness, as You know well. Unclean men, who lie with men, prosper. Women, whom you created to be under men, assert their equality. Men, whom You created to be under You, make laws as they will, defying Your will. Forbid it, O Allah. Punish it, O Mighty One.

Though you permit to your followers the ownership of those under our right hands, the slaves, wicked men, knowing not your wisdom, would prohibit it. Though you have set the law for which women we may and may not know, women flout it and men permit that. It is an abomination.

I am but a man, O Allah, yet I am Your man. Others, likewise Your men, follow me. Use us. Help us. Smite the wicked. Crush the infidel. Destroy above all the Jews, as You promised us you would do.

Mustafa felt a sudden sharp pain emanating from his kidneys. They'd been getting progressively worse over the last several years. He added to his prayer, *O Allah, let me live only long enough to see your cause through to victory.*

Prayer finished, Mustafa again tapped his head multiple times to the prayer rug. Then he arose, and looked skyward. He had the eyes of an eagle, so said his followers. With those eyes he spotted, dimly and distantly, one of the spaceships of the Earth infidels.

Mustafa nodded and added to his prayers, aloud, "Smite them too, O Lord, but not before we have full use of them."

INTERLUDE

23 February, 2075, Shuttle 11, USSS *Harriet Tubman*, Cape Canaveral, Florida

The first major colonization ship had been built, unsurprisingly, in the United States. Also, unsurprisingly, it had been built by private firms to government specifications. While the European Union was still struggling to apportion widget production between England, Scotland, France, and Germany, and struggling with how much of it to have done in China to make up for the inflated wages demanded by European trade unions (which was another way of saying how much would eventually show up in government revenues, of course, given Europe's confiscatory levels of taxation), America simply acted.

Curiously, no one in the EU screamed, "Unilateralism." They had their reasons for wanting America to be first with practical, large scale, colonization capability.

"Large scale," in this case, meant twenty-five thousand colonists in cryogenic suspension or "deep sleep." Future ships would be larger, approximately twice as large, but—give the imperialist, revanchionist, capitalist, war-mongering, fascist American beasts their due— twenty-five thousand was a nice start. Besides, since the ship was going to be available for lease *long* before any Euro ship could be expected to be, the bureaucrats who ran the EU had every expectation that it could be, and would be, used to eliminate some of their excess and unwanted population.

Oliver Rogers' flintlock was safely stowed with the baggage. There were better weapons available for those leaving Earth, but none that he could be sure of feeding with ammunition or keeping in repair, on the new world. His animals—one bull, three heifers, two horses, five goats, seven sheep, half a dozen domesticated turkeys, two dozen chickens and a rooster, and two hundred and fourteen embryos, not counting eggs—had already gone up and been put under. Spare arms were up there too, for when his sons grew to manhood.

Rogers' three wives, two of them officially unofficial, and eleven children would go up with him. Perhaps more importantly, from the point of view of the charity that had paid for Rogers' rather extended family's extended trip, along with all those goats and chickens and whatnot would go an eventual fifteen conservative voters (more, really, as all three wives were quite young and very fertile). It was a bargain, from some points of view, even counting shipping their minimal household goods from Idaho to Florida.

"Oh, God, I'm scared, Ollie," said wife number one, Gertrude, as she leaned against her shared husband's arm. "I've never even *flown* before and now—"

"I know, Gertie," Rogers said, "I know. It's not easy to pick up and leave our roots. But our ancestors have been doing just that for four hundred years or more. A *lot* more if you count how they got to Europe in the first place, before they came here. It's worked out well enough, so far. And God will watch over his own."

"They used to say that God watches out for fools, drunkards and the United States, too," Gertie objected. "But he's turned his back on the USA."

"And so are we," said Rogers. "Especially since the Senate ratified the Gag Treaty and the President signed it. That was when the United States turned its back on us."

Whatever Gertie was about to say in reply was drowned out by the scream of Shuttle 11 coming in for a landing to board the colonists and take them to a new world and a new life.

CHAPTER TWO

Jest roll to your rifle
and blow out your brains . . .
—Kipling, "The Young British Soldier"

**24/8/466 AC, Isla Real, Republic of Balboa,
Terra Nova**

A solar chimney dominated the island's skyline, rising
several hundred meters above its highest elevation, the
otherwise unnamed Hill 287. From the base of that
chimney, a thick tube of reinforced concrete, ran an
extension northward, toward the equator, along the
side of the hill. This ended at one of the three largest
greenhouses on the planet, the other two also being
the foundations for solar chimneys. Fixed mirrors,
sighted to reflect the maximum amount of sunlight
into the greenhouse with the least expense and for
the least effort, sparkled on the hillside.

The greenhouse contained air heated by the local
sun. The air escaped along the tube that ran along
the ground and up the hill before making its final
exit at the top of the chimney. Along the way, the
wind thus created turned turbines that produced the

electricity needed for the island's twenty-one thousand
legionary personnel and their families plus the families
of the thirteen thousand legionaries deployed to the
war. Intended, eventually, to provide electricity for
almost twice that many, the chimney operated at less
than half capacity.

There was probably money to be made in connecting
the island's own electrical grid to the larger grid of
the host country, the Republic of Balboa. Moreover,
there had in the past been murmurings from the
mainland about forcing the owners of the island, the
Legion del Cid, to do just that. The response of the
legion, having several times the coercive power of the
Republic, to the idea of being forced into anything was
silence containing a heavy admixture of wry contempt.

Still, in a spirit of "one enemy at a time," the
Legion had instead constructed another solar chimney
on the mainland, one which it continued to own and
the electricity from which it sold. There were plans
for a third and fourth, and vague interest in building
a fifth through fifteenth, though these would really
be more than the largely agrarian Republic needed.
Still, one never knew when a couple of extra terawatts
might come in handy.

On the other hand, at nearly seven hundred million
FSD, Federated States drachma, each, solar chimneys
were not cheap. Even with the money saved by running
significant portions of the chimney along the ground
and up mountains, the cost remained very high. It was
especially high in land as individual Balboan landhold-
ers parted with their patrimony most reluctantly. After
that initial capital investment, however, fairly abundant
electricity, in the range of two hundred megawatts

per tower, was available more or less continuously for no more than the price of occasionally replaced turbines, and the personnel who oversaw them and kept the jungle at bay.

Contemplating from his office window the vapor cloud at the top of the island's chimney, Patricio Carrera wondered if the effort and expense were worth it. *On the other hand, what price is too high to be free of energy blackmail by the Salafis?*

Toward that end, the legion had also funded, and made some profit on, a number of thermal depolymerization plants about the Republic. These took waste—mostly agricultural waste but also human sewage and even old tires—and converted it into oil at a rate of about two and a half to three barrels per ton from the best feedstock. Not every stock was of the best, however. The average yield was much less. Even so, the TDP plants, too, had gone a long way toward getting the legion's host, Balboa, out from under the Salafi thumb.

And that is always worth doing, Carrera thought with satisfaction. *And even if Sada—no Salafi, he—were able to supply us with oil someday, the supply would still be in others' hands. Though, I suppose, with us taking whatever sewage and garbage can be shipped in from some of the larger cities of South Columbia and Colombia del Norte, our supply is still partially not in our own hands.*

Carrera had aged much more than the seven years that had passed since his family's murder in the great terrorist attacks that had begun this war. Hair once black had gone mostly gray. The sun and wind and rain had begun turning his face a tough leathery brown.

Only the eyes, a bright and clear blue like the sky on a cloudless summer day, remained youthful, and even those were framed by crows' feet at the corners.

The intercom on his desk buzzed. "Tribune Esterhazy is here, *Duque*," announced Carrera's aide de camp.

"Send him in," said Carrera, looking up at the heavy, locally manufactured, mahogany door to his office. The door had been ornately hand-carved with military scenes at a factory, the *Fabrica* Hertzog, a couple of hundred miles up the coast and a bit inland. There was a contract between the legion and the factory for a certain number of discharged legionaries to be apprenticed there, with the legion picking up the tab of their training. The door had been made by these apprentices.

The scene-carved door opened, held by an aide. In walked Matthias Esterhazy, formerly a major in the Airborne Assault Engineers of the Army of the Federal Republic of Sachsen on the continent of Taurus, later an investment banker with SachsenBank, most recently comptroller and chief of investments of both the *Legion del Cid, SA* and Carrera's own family's corporation of Chatham, Hennessey and Schmied. He had other duties, as well; most significantly, Esterhazy was the direct representative of the legion to the War Department of the Federated States of Columbia.

About Carrera's height, five-ten or so, Esterhazy's appearance, like his name, indicated a heavy admixture of Magyar along with his predominantly Sachsen heritage. He was, by nature, darker than Carrera. The natural dark could not easily be seen, however, except in the eyes. Contrasted to Carrera's icy blue, Esterhazy's were hazel.

The Sachsen's skin was only slightly olive in tone.

While Carrera's had tanned to a dark finish to match his office door, as one would expect with someone who spent nine months in ten under the pitiless sun of the Sumeri desert, Esterhazy had paled under the weak sun and indoor lighting of the metropolis of First Landing, the largest city in the Federated States.

Carrera shook hands over the desk and indicated a seat with the other hand. He pushed aside a map. Had anyone looked, the map would have shown a one to two-hundred-thousand scale topological view of Pashtia, a half mountainous-half desertified half-failed state south of Kashmir and north of the Islamic glacis states along the border of the Volgan Republic. There was a war going on in Pashtia, a sister campaign to the one being waged in Sumer.

"Good news and bad news, Patricio," Esterhazy began, after seating himself. Carrera noted that Esterhazy's Sachsen accent had almost disappeared under the influence of seven years of living in the Federated States.

"Bad news first."

Esterhazy had anticipated that. "In a few days the Progressive Party is going to win the next election in the Federated States. Yes, it will be close but they're still going to win. Their most likely candidate for SecWar is James Malcolm. I have spoken with Malcolm, at a fund raiser. The legion's contract for Sumer will not be renewed. No possible campaign contribution, or even outright bribe, that we could offer will change that. I have also spoken with your family senator, Harriet Rodman. She says that getting it renewed is beyond her power and that it doesn't matter what you pay her; it would still be beyond her power."

Carrera shrugged. "I expected that. The campaign in Sumer is pretty much over, anyway. That Harriet can't help is . . . disappointing. But she's always been up front with me and if she says she can't then she probably really can't. Pity. And the good news . . . ?"

Esterhazy, uninvited but welcome, took a cigarette from a pack on Carrera's desk. Lighting and puffing it to life, he continued, "Financially, you can continue to support the force you have, and even expand it to the full fifty thousand you want to. But that is all; you don't and won't—not with anything low risk that I can do, investment-wise—have the means to continue the war at the current level. At least you won't be able to continue it indefinitely."

"Details?" Carrera asked, likewise reaching for a cigarette and leaning back to put his feet up on the desk.

"I've been conservative, as you wished me to be," Esterhazy cautioned. "Right now, legionary assets are on the order of fifty-two billion FSD. The income from this, after adjusting for inflation and the limited tax we pay, is about two billion FSD per year. This pays for the force but for almost nothing else. It absolutely will not pay for maintaining a full legion of over thirteen thousand men deployed and at war without invading the corpus. In the long run, that is death."

Carrera thought, *In the long run, we're all dead anyway.*

"There is," Esterhazy continued, "a way to substantially increase the amount I have to work with, if you are willing."

Carrera's eyes narrowed. Whenever Esterhazy used the phrase "substantially increase" it always meant "risk." Carrera was not particularly risk averse, in most respects. Risking money, however? *That* went against his family's grain. Besides, he understood the kind of risks *he* took willingly. Those were military risks. He didn't, quite despite upbringing, really *understand* finances.

"Go on," he said warily.

"Well . . . you need to start making your own money," Esterhazy announced. He hastily added, "Not money for street commerce. I mean—and I've thought on this a *lot*, Patricio—that you can increase your assets by converting some of it to precious metals and then offering precious metal certificates, PMCs, for x quantity of gold, silver, platinum, palladium and rhodium to people—rich people—who feel the need to have escape money or even just a hedge against inflation or economic collapse. There are a lot of people like that in the world, you know. There are, for example, something on the order of half a trillion FSD"—Federated States drachma—"out of circulation around the globe, many—perhaps most—of them held for just those reasons. All the inflation on that money represents profit, risk-free profit, for the Federated States."

"So where would our profit come in?" Carrera asked.

"In two ways," Esterhazy answered. "As it is very unlikely that everyone in the world is likely to ask for their precious metals all at the same time, we can sell a lot more of the certificates than we actually have precious metals on hand. Equally important, I can play the market, buying up certificates and metal when the value of, say, gold is down and selling them when it's high. This is all really just playing the market, but with the added features of leveraging a smaller amount of metal and ourselves becoming something like inside traders. I am *good* at what I do, Patricio. I *will* make you money."

"And how much of our fifty-two billion would you like to put into this?"

"Ideally all . . ." Esterhazy was stopped by Carrera's vigorously shaken head. ". . . but I know you won't go for that. How about twenty percent then?"

"How about five percent and we'll see how it works?" Carrera countered.

Esterhazy sighed. "With a mere two and a half billion, Patricio, I can't exercise the kind of leverage that would really generate a profit. How about that amount over and above what I need to generate sufficient operating expenses for the full force . . . say . . . five billion?"

Carrera considered quietly for a few moments. "I could accept that amount . . . maybe. But see, Matthias; I am not really worried about our being unemployed for very long."

"But I just told you . . ."

"Never mind that," Carrera interrupted, reaching for the map he had earlier pushed aside. "The FSC's War Department may not want to renew our contract for Sumer. I can hardly blame them. But there's still a piracy problem at the edges of the Islamic and Salafi world and the old *Venganza*"—a Great Global War era aircraft carrier the legion had purchased for a song—"is about to be recommissioned . . . though we still haven't got a name for the ship. I think they, or somebody, may hire us for that. Moreover, they're going to need a good infantry division for Pashtia here," his finger indicated the map, "before too very long. More specifically, the FSC is going to need a good infantry division capable of operating with very constrained logistics. We're the only ones who fit that bill, the only ones on the planet."

Esterhazy contemplated that. He had good reason to trust Carrera's military judgment. He had no reason to trust his financial instincts, however.

"Patricio, if you are that certain of a renewed contract, why not take the greater chance on the PMCs?"

Carrera's eyes narrowed as he glared at Esterhazy. "Sneaky fucking Magyar."

"With Magyars for friends you don't *need* enemies," Esterhazy quoted. "Still, I *am* your friend and this *would* be a tremendous opportunity."

"You want to put ten *billion* FSD into metals? Ten *billion*?"

"Patricio, I can use that much and triple it."

Carrera sighed, deeply. Yes, he *was* that sure of a new contract for Pashtia. He just couldn't be quite sure of exactly when.

"Two and a half billion now," he offered. "I'll double that in six months if it's working out. When I get a contract for Pashtia I'll go for the rest. Fair enough?"

Esterhazy nodded, shallowly. If it wasn't quite fair or quite smart, he could still work with it.

"Good. Do it. By the way, when's your flight back to the FS?"

"Tomorrow morning. Airship from Herrera Airport direct to First Landing."

"Excellent. Dinner with my family, then, tonight. Say . . . nineteen hundred."

"I'd be honored, Patricio," Esterhazy answered. "By the way, who did you leave minding the shop back in Sumer?"

"Sada."

"You trusted an *Arab* to be in charge?"

"Matthias, *everybody* trusts Sada," Carrera answered warmly. "He's as reliable as the moons and as strong as the sun. Has he got his own agenda? Sure; he wants to run the country. And, to the extent I can, I intend to help him do just that. If everyone over there were like him—"

Esterhazy didn't know Sada very well. They'd only met a few times, those rare occasions when Carrera sent Sam Cheatham on leave and let the Sachsen-Magyar come out and fill the duties of legionary chief engineer. He did, however, know Carrera very well.

You need Sada, Esterhazy thought, *don't you? Not just because he's a fine soldier and a better politician than you. You need him because he's your proof to yourself that you haven't gone all the way over the edge, that you're not a genocidal maniac, that you can humanly and humanely distinguish between enemies and those who just share some form of a religion.*

"Speaking of being over there," Esterhazy said, "what do I have to do to get the fuck out of First Landing and do another tour?"

Carrera thought on that. At length, he answered, "I don't think you do another tour, not in Sumer anyway. I *do* have some things I need a competent engineer to look at for me in Pashtia, though."

Sharan, Pashtia, 27/8/466AC

With the relative positions they were in, Terra Nova's three moons cast shadowless light. Cautiously, not least because of the lack of shadow, Noorzad the one-eyed crept forward. Another man might have been nervous. Another man's heart might have pounded. Noorzad was *ice*.

He was followed by seventy-seven of his men, most of them, unlike their chief, at least apprehensive. This was only a large fraction of the force Noorzad commanded. The rest of his company had stayed behind, guarding the pass through which the group would escape after completing their mission. That pass led to theoretically enemy—but, at least along the tribal lands by the border, in fact, allied—Kashmir, a state caught up in internal conflict between Salafism, more moderate versions of Islam, secular democracy and secular fascism.

In some ways, and while it certainly irked Noorzad and his followers to have only halfhearted support from Kashmir, and even that only from certain elements acting unofficially, overall the arrangement had this much going for it: the boundlessly evil infidel, the despised Federated States of Columbia and their Tauran lackeys and Balboan mercenaries, were content with Kashmir's shadowy status and never crossed over the border openly in order to avoid embarrassing their "allies."

The infiltrating guerillas of the Salafi *Ikhwan*—based, trained and supplied from the Kashmiri side of the border—felt no such restraint.

"Restraint," Noorzad muttered, as softly as a butterfly landing on silk. "We'll show them some restraint."

A regular army unit would probably not have had its leader on point. Sometimes, too, Noorzad felt comfortable ordering one of his platoons to lead out. In action, though, a leader of the Pashtun in war had little choice but to go first, and to leave last. There was no other way to gain and keep the respect of the men who followed him. They were, after all, *Pashtun*, the freest men on this world. Even the Arabs in the company, volunteers from far-off lands, were no different in that. They followed where they would, and no one could make them do otherwise.

There were a lot more Arabs, Noorzad knew, ever since the war to free their lands had gone so badly against the faithful in Sumer. Their fighters killed, their support chains betrayed; the Arabs no longer even had a decent way into Sumer, let alone a way to prosper and succeed there. So instead they came—eyes all aglow with the hope and expectation of martyrdom—to where there was still a chance, to where their brethren still fought with some success. They came to Kashmir and then to Pashtia, or sometimes to Pashtia directly.

There was a glow ahead, as if from a small fire. Noorzad stiffened, his eyes searching and his keen nose sniffing for signs of the enemy. Satisfied that the enemy were neither dangerously close nor expecting him, he continued forward to a low, rock-strewn ridge between the source of the glow and the column he led. The guerilla leader stooped lower as he closed on the ridge. A few meters from it he got to his belly and crawled forward, still as soft and silent as a kitten's breath.

It *had been* a fire, wonder of wonders. In similar circumstances Noorzad's men would have gone cold, eaten cold food, rather than reveal their positions like that. The Tauran troops—he could see they had Tauran vehicles in the glow from the fire—had been spoiled, it seemed, by no contact this far into Pashtia in years.

That was about to change.

Carefully, Noorzad counted his enemies. *Six vehicles, all soft skinned. Thirty-eight men, near enough . . . soft hearted and weak as are all the Tauran infidels. Fools do not even keep their weapons to hand. Am I some soft woman that they should not fear me?* As carefully as he had counted the enemy, he marked firing and assault positions in his mind.

Still careful, still as quiet as a cat, the guerrilla leader backed off from the ridge and, in hushed tones, issued last-minute instructions to his chief subordinates.

Noorzad pointed with a finger at a tall, aesthetic-looking fighter. "Suleiman, take your RGLs"—rocket grenade launchers—"that way. There's a rock outcropping and some low bushes. They're progressivines, I think." The progressivines were one of those few species, like the tranzitree, the bolshiberry, and the septic-mouthed *antania*, or moonbat, that the Noahs, the unknown others who had seeded Terra Nova with life from Old Earth, had set down, possibly to interfere with the development of intelligent life on the new world.

"You can engage the whole encampment from there," Noorzad continued. "Remember, concentrate on the vehicle with the most antennae *first*. We don't want them calling for artillery or air support. Your signal to open fire will be when I fire. The signal that the assault is beginning is 'Allahu akbar.'"

Suleiman nodded—he rarely spoke much—and turned to collect his seventeen men and eight RGLs. These were all that the company owned. Noorzad waited until that part of his column was underway before laying a hand on the shoulder of his next subordinate, Malakzay. To this one, in charge of all three of the company's machine guns, he gave similar instructions, differing only in that the low ridge Noorzad had just vacated was to be their firing position.

As Malakzay and his gunners and their assistants began to creep forward as quietly as their chief had crept back, Noorzad went and picked up the remainder of his organization, the forty-four riflemen that he would lead personally. He led them back, then down into a draw that led almost to the enemy encampment. From there the men crept forward in single file, behind their leader. No sentry barred the way.

Stinking amateurs, Noorzad cursed. *Hardly worth the bother of killing.*

At what he judged was a distance of about one hundred and twenty meters from the edge of the encampment, Noorzad halted. There was a substantial boulder, half the height of a man, perched precariously on the lip of the draw. It was this, as much as the nearness of the enemy, which caused the guerilla to stop. From there he sent half his men left, the other half right. They, like their leader, crept on cat feet.

Noorzad himself stayed in the draw until the last of the men had gone out to form the assault line and the word, "Ready," had come whispered back. Then he, too, silently scrambled up and posted himself, crouched low, behind the boulder.

Risking a peek out, Noorzad saw that his enemy had heard and seen nothing. *Just pitiful*, he subvocalized. *Tsk.* He gave a last look left and right, just to confirm that his men really *were* ready. Then he drew his own rifle to his shoulder, drew a bead on a silhouette outlined by the fire and began to squeeze the trigger.

The shot came as a surprise, as most good shots do. Noorzad's surprise was as nothing though, compared to the surprise of the Taurans when eight rockets streaked from the darkness and caused three of their wheeled vehicles, including the command vehicle, to explode in flame. To this surprise was added the shock of several score, then several hundred, tracers ranging through their camp as the guerilla machine guns joined in within half a second after the first rocket.

Watching from his boulder, Noorzad saw the enemy knocked on their asses by exploding RGL rounds and sliced down by the searching machine guns. One target, in particular, drew a smile from the way it danced as two guns chopped at it from slightly different directions.

Satisfied after a minute's steady firing, and by the lack of any return fire, Noorzad stood and in a voice that carried even over machine guns and rocket launchers shouted "Allahu akbar! Kill the infidels!"

On command his men stood up and began running forward, firing from the hip as their fathers and uncles had learned to do during the Volgan invasion and occupation of their land almost a generation before. Still there was no return fire. Indeed, as Noorzad drew closer he heard the wailing of women, infidel women he was certain, coming from the enemy camp.

His men must have heard it, too, as they slowed their fire and picked up the pace.

The camp's denizens were not soldiers. Rather, they appeared to be civilians, about two thirds men and the remainder women. Nor were they all dead. Many screamed and moaned. A few seemed to be begging for help. The pleas cut off one by one as Noorzad's followers killed the men. They seemed less eager to kill the women, though some of those were shot as well.

Malakzay arrived at the burning encampment leading his band of gunners. "What do we do with them?" he asked. "What were they?"

"Non-Governmental Organization types, I think," answered Noorzad. "Hand wringers and bleeding hearts. Kill the men; they're just infidel dogs. As to what we do with the women?" He smiled. "Fuck 'em. Then kill the ones who look like they won't make the march back. The rest we can sell back in Kashmir. Might raise enough to get a few more heavy weapons."

"But first we can fuck them?" Malakzay asked again, the eagerness in his voice palpable.

In answer, Noorzad raised his voice to carry to all his band. "As the Prophet commanded, 'Go and take a slave girl.' These women are your fields; plow them as you will."

Isla Real, Balboa, 34/8/466 AC,

At first, and for some years, the legion had raised its own beef on the island. Little by little, though, the cattle fields had given way to casernes and training areas. They still kept cattle, but only in small numbers and only for dairy. Carrera watched the dairy cows at work through the glass door that led from his office to a railed, tiled and partially shedded roof. The orientation of the roof was at ninety degrees from the window facing the solar chimney. Much like watching tropical fish in a tank, the cattle gave a sense of calm. This was important to a man with great responsibilities who also happened to be in a very bad mood.

There was a tapping on the glass below. Carrera looked down and saw *Jinfeng*, his late wife's pet trixie tapping impatiently. He'd brought the bird out some years prior, leaving her in his current wife's, Lourdes', care. Trixies were smart though, as smart as a grey parrot, and *Jinfeng* had quickly learned the way to his office. She showed up most mornings that he was actually on the island, rather than in Sumer, looking for a handout, or just to be skritched atop her head.

Carrera and the bird had never been more than tolerably friendly before Linda's death. Afterwards, when the bird had no one else, she'd warmed considerably. As soon as Carrera opened the door, she gave a loud screech and stepped into the office, boney tail scraping the stone floor and claws from her partially reversed big toes click-clacking as she walked.

Carrera bent to pat the proto-bird, raising a more contented call. He then walked to the intercom on his desk. "Do we have any—"

"I'll bring it right in, sir," his aide answered. *Jinfeng* and her appetite had become well known at the headquarters.

Terra Novan ecology was a very mixed up thing, courtesy of the Noahs—aliens about whom nothing was known and whose very existence was only inferred, albeit very strongly inferred. After all, someone, some*thing* had to have brought to the planet the life forms from Old Earth, sometime in the impenetrable mists of prehistory. *Jinfeng* and her increasingly rare kind were but one example of what the aliens had brought. Besides the trixies, archaeopteryxes, in the air, there were carcharodon megalodons at sea, the great carnivorous birds, phorohacos, on land, and thousands upon thousands of other terrestrial species, most long extinct on the home world.

There had once been more species but, man being man, many of those which had been saved by the Noahs and gone extinct on Old Earth tended to be driven to extinction on the new once man put down roots.

Besides those living relics of Old Earth, other species, plant and animal, were either native to Terra Nova, or had been transplanted from some other world or worlds by the Noahs, or were even the product of genetic manipulation. Some of these appeared to have been created expressly to prevent the rise of intelligent life on Terra Nova. The septic mouthed, winged reptiles called "antaniae," or moonbats, were one example. More sinister still was the fruit of the tranzitree. Very sweet, tranzitree fruit contained a toxin that was deadly to beings with highly developed brains. Moreover, the toxin built up in the flesh of food animals. Eat a steak from a cow that had been eating of the tranzitree fruit, or its kin the bolshiberry and progressivine; die in shrieking agony, brain inflamed and swelling until it seemed it would burst from your skull.

These were clever traps and might have been sufficient, on their own, to prevent the rise of intelligent life on Terra Nova. They had proved generally ineffective against *colonization* by intelligent life, however.

The archaeopteryx ate greedily, beak scraping on a metal tray on the floor. Carrera continued to pat it while looking out the glass door. Off in the distance, he saw a mid-sized airship winding gracefully through the air on its way from somewhere in Colombia del

Norte down to Southern Columbia. An airship had been the instrument of the murder of his Linda and their children, so he always looked at the things with feelings, at best, mixed.

Every feeling I have, he thought, with a sigh, *is mixed these last seven years.*

He stood, leaving the trixie to eat, and walked the few steps to the window that overlooked the solar chimney. *Am I doing right,* he wondered, *trying to bring Balboa into the fifth century? After all, the Oil Yithrabis have been spending money right and left to try to do the same there, while keeping the culture of thirteenth-century Old Earth. Hasn't worked for them for beans.*

The difference, he thought, *between Balboa and, say, Sumer or Pashtia . . . or even Yithrab, isn't one merely of religion, but also one of degree. The Arabs and Pashtun put family above all except religion . . . so do the Balboans, and only to a somewhat lesser degree. Breaking them of that . . . well . . . difficult. I have not succeeded yet, and I may never entirely succeed. Even in the legion . . .*

Even in the legion there were connections that mattered. He'd combated that, or tried to, in a number of ways. It was perhaps the only armed force on the planet that insisted on a complete family tree for four generations back before enlistment, and *that* only to organize cousins out of the same units to prevent them from taking care of each other to the detriment of the organization as a whole. He'd had leaders turned out and even shot for preferring cousins and brothers over better, but unrelated, men. Even then, it still popped up, this preference for family, or amoral familism. And even the appearance of it was dangerous.

More dangerous is that even I *am infected with it,* he thought. *My only saving grace is that the number of people whom I will favor for familial relation is very small: Lourdes, and the children. Of course, I was infected with it as a boy, when my parents and their friends tried to turn me into a cosmopolitan, too.*

Which helped explain his bad mood and his need for the cows to calm him. Lourdes, his second wife and arguably the reason he retained as much sanity as he had, had spoken to him the night prior to try to get him to help a member of *her* extended family. Her cousin, Marqueli—Carrera had met the girl once, beautiful little thing—was married to one of his soldiers. That soldier was on the medically retired list which, in the legion, only meant that he was given some other duty out of his normal regiment. In Marqueli Mendoza's husband's case, those duties for the last several years had been going to school, at legion expense, at the university to earn his baccalaureate.

Jorge Mendoza, former tanker in what was then the Mechanized Cohort, *Carlos Martillo*, was blind and missing both legs, the result of enemy action in the Sumeri city of Ninewa, early in the war.

The boy—well, he was only twenty-two or three— wanted to continue his studies. His wife, Marqueli, had spoken to Lourdes, apparently, and Lourdes to Carrera, about giving Jorge Mendoza some special help with that.

He *wanted* to help the boy, of course, anything to help one of his legionaries and especially one who had given up so much in the cause. But he hadn't a clue how to do that, consistent with his principles, and the Mendozas were due at his office any minute.

✧ ✧ ✧

Actually, though Carrera didn't know it, the couple was already there, sitting nervously in the anteroom while Carrera's aide de camp waited for the time to tick away until their last minute appointment was due. They were both very nervous.

Jorge Mendoza showed it. Marqueli didn't, even though she was more nervous for her husband's sake than he was for his own.

"It's a good idea you have, Jorge," she insisted, placing a warm and comforting hand on his arm. "*Duque* Carrera will see that; I'm sure of it. My cousin was sure of it, as well. She agrees it's a wonderful idea and that her husband will support it."

"Maybe," Mendoza admitted just as the AdC looked up and said, "Time, Candidate."

Into the speaker box on his desk he announced, "*Duque*, Warrant Officer Candidate and Mrs. Mendoza are here to see you."

Barring exceptional circumstances, Carrera would have had tossed from his office anyone who brought his wife along. Mendoza, legless and sightless, was such an exceptional circumstance.

Can't criticize a man who suffered as much as he has in my service just for bringing along some help. Besides, she's awfully easy on the eyes.

The door opened, allowing the Mendozas to enter. *Yes, she's just as pretty as I remembered. Poor Mendoza, that he can't see that. Then again, he's a fine-looking boy, too. I can see why the girl was drawn to him.*

Instead of meeting them at his desk, Carrera stood and indicated a couch for the couple, then took for himself a well-stuffed chair opposite. Mendoza's artificial legs whined slightly as they bent to allow him to sit.

"You want to continue your studies, I am informed," Carrera began.

"Yes, sir," Mendoza answered, turning his head to face Carrera. His eyes remained unfocused. "I had thought to take up teaching at one of the military schools when I finished. But it hit me when I was reading a book that there was something more, something better, I could do. Actually, Marqueli was reading the book to me," he amended.

Note to self: Library, Braille, pass on to Professor Ruiz to investigate the possibilities, Carrera thought. *Even if not worth it to us, maybe it will be good public relations for the legion.*

"Something better?" Carrera asked.

Marqueli pulled a paperback from her purse. Carrera saw that it was one he had had printed by the publishing house he'd had set up under Professor Ruiz's propaganda department. He saw, too, the title: *Tropas del Espacio* and the letters, "RAH."

"How'd you like the translation?" he asked Marqueli.

"It was so-so, I think," she answered. No one but Carrera and Ruiz knew that Carrera had personally translated the first third or so of the book.

Both deflated and wryly amused, Carrera sighed. *Oh, well, can't win 'em all.*

"But the original thoughts," Marqueli continued, "well . . . tell the *Duque*, Jorge."

"*History and Moral Philosophy, Duque.* There is a need for such a book, a need all over this planet. Balboa needs it as much as anyone."

Ohhh, so that's his idea. Not bad. Can I tell myself

with a straight face that I am doing this, if I do, for one of my soldiers and not for a man married to my wife's cousin? For my adoptive country and not for a relative? For the world and not for nepotism? That would help.

"And you want to write this book, Candidate Mendoza?"

"I do . . . but it will take time. That, and more education than a baccalaureate."

"In English," Carrera said, "Ph.D. stands for 'piled higher and deeper.' Still, I see your point."

Carrera then went silent for a while, unconsciously leaving the Mendozas to squirm. *If I do support this will I be breaking my own principles? No, I am doing it for one of my troops which is absolutely consistent with my principles. But . . . even worse, maybe I'll look like I'm breaking my own principles. But what if . . .*

He smiled broadly. *It's such a joy when the answer just jumps out at you.* "Candidate Mendoza . . . Mrs. Mendoza. I think your idea is a fine one, especially if you broaden it to the question of which one should place first, family or nation or civilization or religion." *It's a question to which I need an answer myself.* "There is a new program for the legion." *Damned straight it's new since I just thought of it.* "It's so new we haven't even had a chance to advertise it yet. Actually, we haven't even yet worked out the application procedures. But we are going to offer, annually, a half a dozen scholarships for higher education to deserving veterans of the legion. There will be a battle- or service-connected disability preference."

Am I quick on my feet or what?

"You'll have to apply and be interviewed by either myself or *Duque* Parilla and a board we will designate. At that board you will have to make a presentation of your intended project. The first board will meet in about six months. I suggest you have your presentation ready by then," he finished, standing to indicate the interview was over.

Marqueli, too, stood, followed by Jorge once he felt her lift from the couch.

"Thank you, sir," Mendoza said. Until Marqueli nudged his right arm he was uncertain as to whether to offer his hand to a superior and could not see that Carrera had thrust his own out. At the nudge he did offer his hand, which Carrera took and shook warmly enough.

The tiny Marqueli waited until the handshake was done, then launched herself at Carrera, wrapping her arms around his torso and pressing her lovely head to his chest.

"Thank you, *Duque*," she said, tears of gratitude shining in her eyes for the favor she was certain had just been done her husband. "Thank you."

Ninewa Province, Sumer, 15/9/466 AC

The farmer plowing his field waved at the passing column of legionary infantry. Newly promoted centurion, junior grade, Ricardo Cruz, taking up the rear, waved back. Curiously, the farmer kept waving, even after Cruz had returned it. Cruz's eyes narrowed and he looked more carefully at the farmer. Yes, the man's wave was definitely exaggerated.

"Thank you muchly, Mister Farmer," he muttered.

"Platoon leader," he said into the earpiece-cum-microphone he wore. It was a minor modification to a civilian system, a short-range wireless that ran through a longer ranged one. The Legion had adopted the communication system, or comsys, because it was cheap, effective, and available almost immediately.

Almost immediately a voice answered, "Centurion Arredondo. What is it, Cruz?"

"That farmer we just passed. I think he's trying to give us a warning, boss."

"Maybe," Arredondo answered. It was even likely. As time had passed and the insurgency weakened, more and more civilians had proved willing to help both the legion and the Sumeri National Forces to flush out more of the enemy. As more of the enemy had been flushed out, more civilians had become willing to help. The guerillas were really on the ropes over most of the country. Worse, they knew it and so did the civilians among whom they tried to operate.

It could easily have gone the other way, had certain things not come to pass some years before.

"Did he give you any specific indicators?" Arredondo asked, then continued, ". . . Ah . . . never mind. The pooch's already alerted. They're in the wheat growing to our left front."

Cruz couldn't see the attached scout dog from his position in the back of the platoon, but did see the men sinking to their bellies along the dirt road that led between the irrigated fields. He joined them.

"Artillery?" he asked Arredondo over the comsys.

"No . . . no. I don't want to fuck up the farmer's crop; be a damned poor way to repay him for trying to help. What's available for air?"

Air support was well out of the range of the com-sys, which were, by design, limited to no more than a mile in range. Cruz turned to the chief of the forward observer team, bellying down beside him.

"What can we get from the air?" Cruz asked.

The corporal made an inquiry over his longer-ranged radio. A few minutes later he answered, "We can have a brace of Turbo-Finch Avengers"—crop dusters reconfigured for the close air support role—"in about twenty minutes, or there's an armed Cricket recon bird we can have in five. The Avengers are carrying some flechette rockets and a gun pod each. Mostly they're carrying bombs though."

"Can we have both?" Cruz asked. *After all, we don't necessarily have to use the bombs.*

"Don't see why not."

"Get 'em both. We'll let the Cricket flush them and use the Avengers to help us pursue. Rockets and machine guns only though." He passed the same on to Arredondo via the comsys.

"That's fine, Cruz," Arredondo answered. Cruz then heard him say, "O Group," or orders group. All four squad leaders immediately answered with their ordinal numbers, "First . . . Second . . . Third . . . Fourth." Fourth was also known as the weapons squad.

Cruz himself announced only his name, and that only to let the squad leaders know he was there and listening.

"Here's the deal," Arrodendo announced. "I think we've got a group of guerillas up ahead in the wheat to the left. They probably know they've been spotted by the fact we took cover. That's okay. We're going to kill them anyway.

"We've got air inbound in five . . . no, about four now . . . minutes. Once that's overhead, we're going to start moving forward by bounds, by squad. Second Squad will bound first. Once we take fire we'll return it and develop the situation a bit. I want to flush them into the open where the air can kill them. Questions?"

"First, negative . . . Second, no questions, Centurion . . . Third, roger, out . . . Weapons, no sweat."

"Centurion, this is Cruz. The machine guns can range the wood from the road and can see it, too."

After a short pause to think, Arredondo said, "Right . . . keep weapons by the road, Cruz. You stay with them to control the air. Now, good hunting, gentlemen. The war's been dull of late. This should give the boys a little much-needed excitement."

The Cricket was heavily muffled. Cruz didn't see or hear it until the pilot came up on the radio to announce he'd arrived.

"Keep out of light missile range," Cruz cautioned. "We're going to try to flush them out of cover."

"Wilco," answered the pilot. "Hey, Cruz, that you?"

"Montoya?" Cruz asked in return.

"'Oh, Cazador Buddy,'" Montoya answered.

"I didn't know you were going to flight school."

Montoya sighed over the radio. "I didn't do well enough in school"—he meant Cazador School, a miserable exercise in starvation, sleep deprivation, danger and sheer hard work; it was also the legion's *sine qua non* for leader selection—"for them to actually trust me as an officer or centurion. So I hung around the Cazador Tercio until someone came to talk to me about becoming a pilot. So it's Flight Warrant Officer Montoya now."

"Good job," Cruz answered, and meant it. Unlike most armed forces the air component of the legion was a part and parcel of the whole; treated like crap the same as everyone else, rather than as spoiled children with too many privileges. There was, therefore, quite a bit more affection between ground and air than was true of most armed forces. The air loved the ground because they were the honorable edge of battle. The ground loved the air because there was none of this "our pilots are too precious to risk" and "but we need our crew rest" nonsense and because they'd always be there when needed, even at the cost of pilots' lives.

"Yeah," Montoya agreed. "Besides, I'm a better pilot than I was a grunt. I'll be standing by and watching," he concluded.

The enemy opened fire first, at a range somewhat long for the rifles and light machine guns they carried. From the road, about twelve hundred meters away from the wood, the legionaries had no trouble returning fire with their excellent .34 caliber machine guns. Three medium guns, belting out three to four hundred rounds per minute, sustained, between them, and coupled with return fire from the infantry squads closer in, were more than the insurgents really felt up to dealing with. They began to run.

"Cruz, Montoya; I see them and I'm on it."

"Get some, Montoya."

For the first time that day Cruz heard the *thrummm* of the Cricket's engine as Montoya gunned it to close to range. Then, mere moments later, he heard the steady sound of cloth ripping as the dual machine gun mounted to side-fire from the Cricket opened up. He couldn't see if they hit anything, as the enemy was running away. He could see the rest of the platoon rise to their feet and begin to run forward, firing from the hip, urged on by Arredondo's wide-carrying shout.

"Cease fire! Cease fire!" Cruz ordered the weapons squad and then began to trot low from gun to gun, making sure the crews had heard.

Idly, Cruz wondered if there would be prisoners. *Hopefully so; this is enough excitement for the day.*

Then the brace of Turbo-Finch Avengers swooped in like eager hound dogs. "Where you want it?" they panted. Their lives had been a bit short of excitement over the last year, too, and it showed.

"Save it," Cruz answered, "but thanks for stopping by. This party's about over."

"Fuck!"

Over the radio Cruz heard Montoya laugh. "What? You guys think me and *my* Cazador *Compadre* are going to leave anything for the likes of you."

"Tell 'em, Montoya," Cruz added, with a snicker.

"Hey, Cruz, I got a postcard from Khalid in Taurus a few months back. Nothing too personal but he says he's doing well."

"Good old Khalid," said Cruz.

Westminster, Anglia, Tauran Union, 21/9/466 AC

The small brass placard above the mailbox said, "Mahrous ibn Mohamed ibn Salah, min Sa'ana." That name and address matched his briefing packet was no particular surprise to Khalid. This was his fifth hit in two years and, so far, there had never been a mistake in identity. What he would do if he ever was called upon to make a hit that turned out to be a mistake, Khalid didn't know. At this point, he suspected, he'd probably yawn, then go to a café and read the paper. He'd grown a steel shell, had Khalid, these last five years.

Unlike the previous four, this target was "hardened." This is to say that his house was detached, with broad lawns around it and a wall around them, that his sedan—sedans, rather; Mahrous kept four Phaetons—was armored. He had bodyguards, mostly veterans of the Royal Anglian Army's Special Operations Directorate, or SOD. He was believed to wear body armor of the very highest caliber, religiously. Moreover, Mahrous rarely traveled the same way from his home twice in a week.

If the swine wasn't so paranoid, thought Khalid, *I'd have offed his ass months ago.*

For those months Khalid had considered and discarded one option after another. Shoot him from a distance? *No way; nothing elevated hereabouts and no really good firing positions. Besides, I'm a good long-range shot, but not a great one. We Arabs rarely are; I don't know why.* Shoot him close up? *I'd never get through the bodyguards who are, let's admit it, first rate men.* Bomb the house? *No way to get close enough with enough material.* Bomb the office? *Similar problem.* Bomb the Phaetons? *Which one. How do I get to it? No way.*

He'd even considered leaving a small bomb with a chemical agent in it but . . . *It wouldn't surprise me a bit if those SOD types carry atropine and nerve agent antidote.*

In the end, Khalid had gone for something simple. There was a sewer that ran the length of the street Mahrous lived on. That sewer had one manhole cover not far from the driveway to Mahrous's residence. Khalid had simply made a radio control detonator from parts obtained at a local hobby store, then manufactured—as he had been trained to do in Volga—about fifteen pounds of PETN, pentaerythritol tetranitrate, in his apartment in the city. "Factor P for *plenty*," the Volgan instructor had said. Fifteen pounds of PETN was more than plenty. An electric blasting cap he lifted from a poorly guarded construction site.

A visit to the local courthouse had given Khalid the map for the sewer system. A couple of visits to three different uniform shops had given him a fair simulacrum of a sewer worker's uniform and accoutrements. A used automobile dealer provided the van and a paint shop changed the van's color to green to match those used by the public works authority. A few telephonic complaints to the PWA had given him, after a bit of figuring, a schedule and therefore a time frame in which there would be no sewer workers down below.

Making a package of the PETN, descending into the sewers— *Blech, that stank!*—and finding the right manhole cover had been easy.

And so, now, Khalid waited and watched the road and the manhole from a café not far from the manhole cover. He'd been waiting for four days. If Mahrous didn't soon use the road that led by the bomb, Khalid would have to think of something else. You just couldn't leave a bomb lying around indefinitely. And if it was found, if Mahrous or his bodyguards got wind of it, their paranoia level would go, oh, *way* up.

"Which would be saying something," Khalid muttered, as he sipped his coffee.

As Khalid put down the cup, he spied a long, black Phaeton easing out of the barred and guarded gate that fronted the driveway from Mahrous's house. He didn't tense; he seen the same thing three times already, since planting his bomb, and three times the Phaeton had gone in a different direction.

Ah, but Allah smiles upon those who wait, Khalid thought, with a smile of his own. *Now let's see if the wretch doesn't turn off before he reaches the manhole. And . . . bingo. They might stop outright, but there are no good turns before the bomb.*

Judging the speed of the Phaeton, Khalid carefully timed his reach into the side pocket of the jacket he wore. His hand curled around a small transmitter, his finger caressing the detonator button. At precisely the right moment, he pushed that button and smiled.

The explosion went off directly under Mahrous's ample posterior. Besides cracking the street around the manhole cover, sending chunks of asphalt, concrete and rebar flying, it lifted the cover straight up at an amazing rate of speed. The cover cut right through the Phaeton's transmission and then cover and transmission together mashed Mahrous' anus into his brain, forcing the resulting mix right through and out of the Phaeton's armored roof.

The blast was also sufficient to kill the ex-SOD driver and guard, both seated in front, as well as Mahrous's eldest son, sitting beside him.

Knocked over by the blast, as was nearly everyone else within two hundred feet, Khalid stood up, forcing an artificial expression of shocked disbelief onto his face. Like other people, he ran forward to try to help the injured. Khalid, however, merely wanted to confirm results.

He saw that all four tires had been blasted off the torn and twisted wreckage of the Phaeton, and that it was burning merrily. Since there were no screams coming from inside, despite the fire, he was reasonably confident that his hit had been a success. Once a sufficient crowd had gathered to cover his withdrawal, Khalid simply melted through it and was away.

I love my job, he thought. *Where else could I get both revenge and excitement in these quantities and to these qualities?*

War Department, Hamilton, FD, Federated States of Columbia, 29/9/466 AC,

Fuck, this sort of "excitement" I can live without, mused Virgil Rivers, waiting impatiently, and even nervously, at the office of the secretary of war for the Federated States. Rivers, a tall, slender, café-au-lait colored general officer, could not be said to be handsome. He had, however, a friendly manner and infectious grin that most women found very attractive. He'd married well as a result of it.

Ron Campos was gone as SecWar, gone with the outgoing Federalist administration. Truth be told, nobody much missed him. That is, nobody missed him *yet.* Virgil Rivers suspected a lot of people were *going* to miss him, to miss him badly and soon. The new

SecWar, James K. Malcolm, Progressive, was Campos's match in arrogance, in Rivers' opinion, but lacked both the former SecWar's patriotism and his determination. Indeed, it was widely believed that, given a choice between advancing the interests of the Federated States, or looking out for the interests of his childhood summer home, the Gallic Republic, Malcolm would always choose Gaul. Nonetheless, Malcolm was one of a very few Progressives with any military background at all. Thus, he had been a seeming natural for secretary of war in the new administration.

He's a natural buffoon, Rivers thought, *a natural gigolo, a natural panderer and an unnatural citizen. On the other hand, his goddamned tan is just a little too orange to be natural. Well, what can one expect from a natural fake.*

Rivers' collar sported the two stars of a major general now. He'd always known he'd rise at least this high, even as a little boy. *Thank you, Daddy, for training me as well as you did.* The only question was would he rise any higher. He considered it no better than even money that he would. Rather, he *had* considered it no better than even money. With Malcolm as SecWar, he would now have given long odds against.

Still, I've had a good run, a damned *good run for someone who's great-grandpappy retired as a master sergeant in the horse cavalry.*

Rivers ported a laptop under his left arm. It contained the SecWar's daily briefing on the ongoing war. Briefing the secretary was so unpleasant, however, that it had quickly become a rotating duty. Today was Rivers' day and he was not looking forward to it. He'd already been kept standing in front of the secretary's desk, rudely ignored, for almost ten minutes while Malcolm pretended to be busy with a file. It was another five minutes before the secretary closed the file and looked up. He didn't bother to rise or offer to shake hands.

Just as well; I'm pissed enough right now that if he did I'd probably do or say something that would move my chances of another star from dismal to none.

"Have a seat, Rivers," Malcolm ordered.

Rivers sat next to the desk, opened the laptop and faced it toward the secretary. The outside of the computer's top had a smaller screen that showed the same images as the main one. Rivers controlled the images with a small device he retrieved from his shirt pocket. He pressed a button on the device. A color map of the Republic of Sumer, highly annotated, appeared on both screens.

Malcolm looked the map over briefly. There wasn't much to see; the war in Sumer had been steadily winding down for two years. While the first three and a half years had cost the Federated States an average of just under one hundred men a month, killed, this had dropped down into the low double and occasionally single digits.

Rivers had been told not to offer commentary; that the secretary, being a lawyer, liked to direct the briefings like cross examinations in court.

"I see the Balboan sector has almost no incidents, General. To what do you attribute that?"

"They started off well and were able to enlist a great deal of Sumeri help early on," Rivers answered. He did not add, though he considered adding, *and they're so ruthless almost nobody in their sector is willing to cross them.*

"And we're paying for that?"

"Yes, Mr. Secretary. Under your predecessor we had an arrangement whereby the Balboans fielded, or sponsored the fielding of, combat capable forces, for a price that was originally about fifty-five percent of what the same force would have cost us. In addition, we had to provide medical care equivalent to what we give our own, but in Balboa. The price has slowly crept up as the cost of living rose in Balboa in response to all the money they earned from us. Right now it's about two thirds of our equivalent cost. That's still a bargain, since the blood is theirs, not ours."

Malcolm frowned. He'd known about the Balboans and had mostly negative feelings. Many of these feelings stemmed from rumors. He'd heard the Balboans used torture with gleeful abandon, though no one had ever provided proof. It was said they were conducting an international campaign of terror and assassination against both the common enemy, the Salafi *Ikhwan*, and any critics of their legion; though, here too, they covered their tracks well. In a sense, it didn't even matter if the charges were true; the international and progressivist press believed they were true and acted accordingly. There was very little criticism of the Balboan force in the newspapers or on television.

He knew they'd put to death a number of international journalists for spying, war crimes and generally aiding the enemy; they made no secret of any of that. Neither did they make any secret of their penchant for enforcing the laws of war in the most forthright and barbaric fashions. Indeed, they made it a point to broadcast those reprisals.

They did not *broadcast* reprisals taken against family

members though that, too, happened. So it was said and widely believed, in any case.

"How large a force do they have?" Malcolm asked. "How much does it cost us? How big a force could they field?"

This information Rivers had at his fingertips. He'd been, in a partial and roundabout way, instrumental in the Federated States' hiring his old friend Patrick Hennessey, now going by the name Carrera, and the force he had raised. He'd kept up on developments. After all, Hennessey had always been entertaining.

"In theory, Mr. Secretary, they have four divisions. They call them 'legions,' which is a little confusing as the overall organization is called "the legion." Then again, we call the Army 'the Army' even though we have eight 'armies' under it.

"Of those four, one is forward deployed in Sumer. That's the only one that, officially, we pay for. The other three are back in Balboa in varying states of training and manning. The forward legion usually numbers around twelve to thirteen thousand men. The total active force is about thirty-three or thirty-four thousand and rising. There is also a reserve force but they are very tight lipped about that. We don't think it's as large as the active force . . . yet. They could probably double or triple their force if they wanted to. So far they have given no indication that they do want to. What they have raised, so far, costs us on the order of seventeen billion drachma a year."

Malcolm's eyes bugged. "We pay *seventeen billion drachma* to some pisspot North Colombian city state?"

"Actually, no, Mr. Secretary. We pay it directly to the legion. They give a portion, a very small portion, less than a percent, to the government of Balboa. But they're only a nongovernmental organization, sponsored by that government. They are not controlled by it. They're not controlled by *anybody.*"

"Oh, *really?* We'll just see about that."

Goodbye, third star.

"No, Mr. Secretary," Rivers answered forcefully. "*Don't* see about that. They're quite capable now, financially, of continuing the war on their own for quite a few years, if not quite indefinitely. If you try to control them you'll just find you've let slip any control we have for a control we can't have. I know their commander. *Don't* try to control him. It just won't work."

Isla Real, Quarters #2, 31/9/466 AC,

I think the thing I like about this, thought Lourdes, on her knees with her head bobbing and her tongue working, *is the control it gives me, not just over the sex, but over Patricio. But then,* she thought as her husband pulled her head off, stood her up and pressed her back to the wall, *but then he doesn't always let me keep control.*

Despite having borne two children, a boy and a girl, Lourdes' body was unmarked, well shaped and still very firm. Tall, almost as tall as her husband, she was quite slender except in those places a woman should be more full. If anything, her breasts had improved from her pregnancies.

Cupping one of those breasts, Carrera bent his head to tease the nipple of the other with his tongue. Lourdes loved that, he knew.

She let him continue in that for a long while, moans

of sheer desire occasionally escaping her lips. When she couldn't stand it anymore she pulled his head up to kiss more intimately.

Balancing her back on the wall, Lourdes arched her hips forward and reached down to guide. A small gasp escaped her lips as Carrera thrust up and forward. The gasp became a long moan as he filled her fully.

And, for a while, she didn't think of much of anything.

"Do you really have to go so soon?" Lourdes asked Carrera, later as they lay in bed. "You only come home about five or sometimes six weeks a year. Are you so anxious to leave me?"

Carrera sighed, then answered, "I take more leave than the troops get."

"Yes," she conceded, "but they only spend one year away for every three years they spend here."

"That's only now," he countered. "Most of the leaders have been gone half the time since the war began."

"And you've been gone eighty percent of it."

To that Carrera had no really good answer. He went silent, thinking, *They don't carry the curse I do, the obligation to destroy those who murdered Linda and the children.*

After a short time he offered, "You were with me there until you came up pregnant with the second child. Besides, the war won't last forever."

"It will last too long; long enough for me to become a dried up old prune."

"Never happen," he answered, adding, "You're one of those women who will keep her looks into old age. I can tell."

Lourdes shook her head, doubtfully. "I'll age, the same as anyone. And you'll grow tired of me."

"Never happen," he repeated, wrapping an arm around her and pulling her head onto his shoulder. "For one thing, you're a lot younger than I am. By the time you're a wrinkled up old lady, I'll be using a walker, too old to get tired of anything except pissing myself."

She giggled at the image. "Now *that*," she said, "will never happen."

"Yes it will." *Unless I'm lucky enough to be killed before it does.*

"Speaking of the future, what's on for tomorrow?" Lourdes asked.

"Mass review of the Corps of Cadets at *Puerto Lindo*, then rechristening of the old HAMS *Venganza*. Want to come watch? The boys are bussing in from all over."

"No . . . no. I'm not comfortable with turning fourteen-year-old boys into soldiers."

"I love you for that, too," Carrera whispered, "for that among many other reasons."

Lourdes never asked if her husband loved her more than he had his first wife, Linda. She was much, much too afraid of the answer.

INTERLUDE

15 May, 2077, Munich, Germany, European Union

The first thing Martin Hoyer the Third noticed about the envelope was that it was pink and flowered on the outside. *How like the government to send bad news in such bright packaging,* Hoyer thought. *Perhaps if grandfather had not been such an untalentierte teilzeit schmierfink we would have had enough money of our own not to have to rely on the state's largess to see us through our old age. Instead he wasted his life writing books no one would read . . . even in German.*

Not that Martin or his wife, or their one—unemployed—child, were particularly old. He and she were only fifty-seven and had been drawing on the state's pension scheme for a scant two years. The boy, Martin Hoyer the Fourth, received unemployment compensation, despite never having worked a day in his life. But even in two years they had seen the system go from penny-pinching to outright miserly.

At least we haven't been reduced to eating dog food. Yet.

He opened the envelope and began to read:

Dear Sir or Madam:

> *In accordance with the European Union Directive 2076/015 for the preservation of the public fisc and extra-planetary colonization, you and you spouse have been identified for reduction of benefits or transportation, with assets, to the planet of New Earth.*

Hoyer took a quick glance at what "reduction of benefits" meant in concrete, Euro, terms and thought, *dog food.*

> *You and your spouse have thirty (30) days from the date of this letter to decide. Thereafter, should you decline transportation, on each anniversary of this letter you will have another thirty (30) days to change your minds, transportation schedule permitting.*

Hoyer read the missive through, sighing frequently. He put it down and called for his wife. As he waited, he went through the rest of the mail.

Interesting that there's a letter too for our lazy-as-dirt son, he thought.

CHAPTER THREE

From Baen's Encyclopedia of New and Old Earth, Terra Novan Edition of 475 AC

The Helen (H): that amount of beauty required to launch one thousand Achaean ships of approximately eight tons empty displacement each, or approximately eight-thousand tons of shipping, and to destroy one city.

The milliHelen (mH): a more convenient measure than the Helen, that amount of beauty required to launch one ship and burn down a single house.

The Linda (L): a more up-to-date measure; that amount of beauty required to launch eight-thousand tons of shipping in a single ship and destroy a city.

Dos Lindas: (ex-*Venganza*) an antique aircraft carrier of sixteen-thousand tons unladen displacement, restored and recommissioned to take part in the war waged against Salafi terrorists and their supporters by the *Legion del Cid* (qv). Destroyed cities: TBA.

Academia Militar Sargento Juan Malvegui, *Puerto Lindo*, Balboa, 1/10/466 AC,

The original port had been raided and burned by pirates almost three centuries before. Its crumbling walls, what remained of them, huddled at one corner of the rectangular bay, held up in places by nothing but friction, gravity and the binding, green and brown tendrils of jungle that interwove among the stones. Shacks, too, sat within the ruins, sometimes surrounded on three sides by the chewed walls.

Outside that original town, or the ruins and shacks that remained of it, a certain amount of newfound prosperity could be seen; new houses, some few stores with bright glass windows, paved streets. This was to be expected when one trebled the population of a not very populous place, and considerably more than quadrupled the average income of an otherwise rather impoverished place. The new population and the new money had come from two sources. The first of these was the Academy, especially its fairly well paid (by local standards) professors and military cadre. The second was the shipyard built to refit the old aircraft carrier—the ex-HAMS *Venganza*—the legion had purchased for a song, albeit at three and a half million FSD a rather pricey jingle, one step ahead of the breakers. There were other ships in port waiting for the shipyard's attentions.

Carrera had made some efforts to keep the old town as it was, buying up properties to fix and preserve the ruins. He'd wanted the boys of this first military school to have the lesson always before them: This is defeat; avoid it. (Another school sat on the other side of Balboa, right next to the equally ruined Balboa *Antiguo*, also sacked and burned but by Old Earth's UN. That one, the *Academia Militar* Belisario Carrera, was sited by the ruins for much the same reason as was the Juan Malvegui.)

The school itself was on the other side of the bay from the town, near the bay's mouth. When the fog was not heavy or the rain was light, the boys could see the ruins from the battlements of the old stone fortress—*Fortaleza San Filipe*—that dominated the bay, the school, and the old town.

There was no rain and only a very light fog as Carrera's staff car wound through the street. It was both preceded and followed by armed and armored vehicles. There was a battalion of Castilian troops at Fort Williams, not so far away. Relations between the legion, on the one hand, and the government of Balboa and the Tauran brigade of which the Castilians were a part, on the other, were, at best, strained. Moreover, the Tauran dominated Cosmopolitan Criminal Court had a standing warrant for the arrest of Carrera and his nominal chief, Raul Parilla, for various alleged crimes committed by the Legion during the initial campaign in Sumer.

I know we're going to have to fight them, eventually, Carrera admitted to himself. *But I want that fight to be on our terms, not brought on by well-meaning troops trying to save Parilla or myself from incarceration. So . . . best not to tempt the Taurans . . . yet.*

Though no one but Carrera knew it for a fact, the boys of the Brigade of Cadets were part and parcel of the plan for meeting and defeating the Taurans when the day came. Some others had guessed some of that plan. Aleksandr Sitnikov, in particular, was, as commander of the cadets, well aware that the boys spent two days a week training on strictly military subjects, that the three schools thus far built had their buildings connected by tunnels, and that those tunnels led off the school grounds to well-concealed spots in the jungle. Sitnikov knew, too, that the three schools still building shared these features. Lastly, any fool with a map could see that four of the six schools were well sited to serve as springboards to attack into the Taurans' base area, the ten-mile wide strip through the country that contained the Balboa Transitway, an above sea-level canal. Of the other two, one was in excellent position to defend the country's main airport, west of the capital, from ground or airborne attack, while the last was near enough to the former—and future—military base at Lago Sombrero to effect the same purpose.

Sitnikov kept his insights to himself. He had few qualms about using fourteen-year-olds as soldiers, and none whatsoever to using fifteen- through eighteen-year-olds.

Formerly a colonel of armor in the army of the Volgan Republic, and before that in the Red Tsar's Guards, Sitnikov had been sent to Balboa early on, to train the new legionaries in the complexities and nuances of Volgan-built tanks, as well as their techniques and tactics. He'd come over, liked what he'd seen, liked the larger paycheck on offer for switching nationalities, and so had elected to stay. That had been more than five years ago.

He'd been as bald then as he was now. Nor had he aged otherwise. Everything in Balboa agreed with

Sitnikov, from the weather to the work to his new Balboan wife, a smoky beauty from this very town. The work especially agreed with him. His lifetime's ambition had been to command a division—tank or motorized rifle; it mattered not—in war. He was reasonably certain that, under the table, Carrera had given him the first half of that ambition, the division in the form of what was soon to be nearly thirteen thousand cadets. The other half, the war, was almost certainly coming.

Sitnikov and his key staff met Carrera at the base of the terreplein over which had been erected a reviewing stand. Behind the reviewing stand stood the fort's massive stone walls.

"At ease," Carrera ordered, after casually returning the mass salute.

Sitnikov led the group up a smooth granite stairway, then along the grassy terreplein to the stand. There were already some dozens of spectators; one of them, Carrera was surprised to see, the Castilian colonel commanding the Tauran battalion at Fort Williams.

Idly, Carrera wondered if Colonel Muñoz-Infantes was here as a spy or perhaps in sympathy. He didn't know enough about the man.

Note to self: Muñoz-Infantes, check into, task for Fernandez.

Slowly Carrera walked the line, shaking hands, patting shoulders, smiling. When he reached Muñoz-Infantes he was somewhat surprised to see the Castilian colonel brace to a stiff attention, click his heels, and announce, "Legate Fernandez intervened with Legate Sitnikov to invite me to this ceremony, *Duque.*"

"Did he indeed?" Carrera searched into the man's

face for some insight. No use, it was as blank as a stone slab. "Well . . . welcome, Colonel. Enjoy the show."

"Fernandez thinks he can be turned," Sitnikov whispered later, once he and Carrera were seated. "Muñoz-Infantes is a Falangist. He hates the Tauran Union, hates the wogs, hates the Gauls, hates the World League, hates United Earth, hates cosmopolitan progressivism, hates—"

At that point Sitnikov was interrupted by a fanfare of trumpets, emanating from both sides of the reviewing stand. This was joined a few moments later by massed drums on the fort's *parade*, below the terreplain.

Then came the singing. From three gates to the northeast the six thousand—soon to be over twelve thousand—boys, aged at this point fourteen to seventeen, marched onto the parade singing the theme song chosen for the youth:

> *"Think, boys, think on all that matters most:*
> *Your homeland, the Legion, your flag and*
>   *your faith.*
> *Hold them holy, holy in your hearts*
> *Pure as the morning light.*
>
> *Juventud adelante, cantando feliz*
> *Si hay sol o si llueve*
> *Juventud adelante, cantando feliz*
> *A muerte o victoria*
> *Assaltamos el mundo con pasos fuertes . . ."*

"Is there anything he likes?" Carrera asked.

"Huh?" Sitnikov looked puzzled.

"Muñoz-Infantes; is there anything he likes?"

"Ah. Yes . . . according to Fernandez. They include Castille, the Spanish language, the Catholic Church, the Castilian Army . . . and, apparently . . . us."

The ceremony concluded, the boys were still singing as they marched off the field.

> *"Juventud adelante,*
> *No camino tan duro.*
> *Gritamos "Ave Victoria!"*

"We've laid on a little reception, partly for ourselves but mostly for guests and the families of the boys transitioning to senior status next year," Sitnikov announced. "Perhaps you might want to chat with Colonel Muñoz-Infantes . . ."

Carrera thought on it briefly before answering, "No . . . I would if I could but I can't. The *Dos Lindas* is supposed to be recommissioned tomorrow morning and I have another speech to rehearse in my mind. You feel free to feel him out, though, Sasha. Just don't commit to anything and don't let him send anyone to snoop around our facilities."

"I understand, Patricio," Sitnikov answered.

Carrera was reasonably sure that the Volgan understood *perfectly*.

Most of the tonnage of the legion's not-so-very-small fleet was, for the time being, here at *Puerto Lindo*. Besides the aircraft carrier, which dominated all the others, there were five ex-Volgan Suvarov-class cruisers, purchased from a scrap dealer for a total of eleven million FSD, along with thirteen more former Volgan ships, one destroyer, two submarines, six obsolete frigates, one mine-countermeasures ship, and three corvettes.

The Suvarovs had been out of commission and slated for scrapping for over a decade but, in the confusion attendant on the collapse of the Volgan Empire, no one had ever gotten around to actually scrapping these last five. They were virtually scrap anyway, all but one of them, or possibly two. That best one had been kept up longer than the rest to serve as a flagship. Carrera thought that still something might be done with the rest. The one that was in fair shape was being restored in a somewhat desultory fashion. The others? Even if scrapped for their steel, the gun turrets, five dual six-inch mountings each, might be emplaced on concrete pads around the *Isla Real's* perimeter.

The other warships were newer and in better shape. Among these were even two titanium-hulled submarines, formerly nuclear but in fact as dead as chivalry with the reactors and anything to do with them torn out. Carrera didn't actually know to a certainty what he would do with any of them, but the price had been right. Nobody wanted Volgan ships, not even Volga.

There was a second carrier out there, also an ex-His Anglic Majesty's Ship, the *Perseus*, the legion had an option on. It was in truly awful shape though, since some light scrapping had actually commenced before the legion bought its option. It might, at best, serve as a stationary training ship. It was certainly never going to sail again; it would have to be towed to Balboa to be any use at all.

Though Carrera didn't know what he was going to do with most of the hulls he'd bought; he *did* know what he was going to do with the *Venganza*.

We're going to commission it.

The ship had started out as a bargain. Purchased for three and a half million FSD, and needing about twelve times that in overhaul, it had seemed like a relatively cheap, and potentially highly profitable, way of transporting aircraft to the war zone and perhaps even suppressing Salafi piracy in various areas of the globe that had fallen under it. Then the cost of Yithrabi crude had hit eighty FSD a barrel and an oil powered ship had seemed rather less of a bargain. Just moving the ship, slowly, halfway around the globe used about six and a half million FSD worth of diesel. And there was no guarantee that the price wouldn't go up. There wasn't even a guarantee of an adequate supply. Nor were the thermal deploymerization plants—built or building—so far in Balboa really up to more than domestic consumption. Indeed, they didn't even cover most that that, yet.

Someone suggested nuclear. But it was not that big a ship, at about two hundred and twelve meters in length and twenty-four in beam, measured at the waterline. Oh, sure, this was much larger than some of the nuclear submarines in use by the Federated States, Volga, Zhong Guo, Anglia and Gaul. But the submarines didn't have to account for a flight deck, or fuel for aircraft. In any case, no one except the Volgans was willing to sell a militarily capable nuclear reactor to a private military organization for an essentially private warship. It just wasn't going to happen. As far as the Volgans went, they had lots of redundant reactors from their rusting fleet, but nobody really trusted their reactors.

I wonder if the FSC or Anglia would have been more

cooperative if they'd known the legion was already *a nuclear power,* mused Carrera, standing by the dock.

Enter the Republic of Northern Uhuru, which had a new design for which they needed money. This design used tennis ball-sized spheres of mixed graphite and uranium instead of the more dangerous, expensive and difficult to dispose of uranium fuel rods used by others. The RNU was willing to sell. Even better, since the reactor design was modular, and not all that large, it could be constructed inside the ship. Hooray!

Except that even one miserable module provided more than five times the power the ship needed. Worse, each module cost about one hundred and twenty-five million FSD. *Talk about cost overruns.* The RNU went back to the drawing board, coming back some months later with a much smaller design, costing about seventy-five million, and producing only twice the power actually needed. Carrera had been offered two of the things for one hundred and thirty million so perhaps that one Suvarov-class cruiser might someday sail again, after all.

"But that's still twice as much as we need," Carrera had railed at the design team.

"Yeah, Duque . . . but . . . see . . . there are things we can do with the extra power. Lasers."

"Laaasssers . . ." the ship's redesign team had echoed when their chief said that.

"Lasers?"

"Oh, yes. Lasers. Shoot down incoming missiles . . . aircraft . . . cruise missiles . . . even shells. Lasers."

✧　　✧　　✧

And so the ship had been fitted with three high-energy lasers; one each bow and stern on projecting mounts, plus one over the superstructure, or island. Add another seventy-five million to the cost. Then, once one has a ship into which one has sunk some hundreds of millions of dollars, one starts to give a lot of thought to protecting one's investment. Guns it had. The lasers helped, too. Armor was right out. That left maneuverability.

"You want me to spend what *on this new drive?"*
"But it only makes sense, Duque. *The electric, podded, variable azimuth drive would make the ship turn within its own length. And we can get substantially increased speed, too."*

After that, the twenty thousand spent for a bronze figurehead of his lost Linda, with her breasts demurely covered, had seemed pretty cheap to Carrera. In the end the thing had cost just over a quarter of a billion, not counting aircraft. All that just to get eighteen helicopters (three of them equipped for anti-submarine warfare), twelve light attack aircraft modified from crop dusters, eighteen *slightly* lengthened and widened, and substantially upengined, Cricket light recon birds, eight remotely piloted aircraft, and a demi-battalion of light infantry into some littoral area where they could raid.

Even with that light an aircraft load there had been problems. None of the older Volgan helicopters that were suitable, available, and affordable fit both the hangar deck's 5.3 meters of height and the dimensions of the elevators. Conversely, none of the more modern helicopters produced by the FSC or Tauran

Union were capable enough or affordable enough, although they fit the hangar nicely. In the end, they'd decided—rather, the legate of the *classis*, Roderigo Fosa, had decided, since Carrera had simply given him a budget and said, "*You* figure it out"—on a newer Volgan helicopter, the Yakamov YA-72 that was offered for sale for surprisingly little.

Little was not, however, nothing. The twenty-two YA-6s purchased had still run nearly fifty million FSD, with spares.

It is *a fine chopper,* Carrera thought. *But still; fifty million . . . And it doesn't mesh logistically with the IMs we already have . . .*

Sighing at the cost, Carrera approached the ship's bow. Fosa, as the legate commanding the *classis*, or fleet, followed, leading Mrs. Parilla, who had been selected to do the honors for the rechristening.

Let's hope somebody hires us to use it.

UEPF *Spirit of Peace*, 2/10/466 AC (Old Earth Year 2521)

One might have thought that a figurehead on a starship would have made little sense. Nonetheless, United Earth had for centuries had hundreds of thousands of otherwise unemployed and unemployable "artists." Some of them were even capable of more than flinging dung onto a canvas and calling it "art." Of those, some numbers had been commissioned to create figureheads for the Spirit-class of UE starships.

Spirit of Peace had been assumed to be a representative of all Earth's peoples, for only a joining of all the people could hope to bring peace. Thus, her figurehead had been a mixed race beauty. It looked quite a bit like the figurehead for the *Dos Lindas*, for that matter.

Which is decidedly ironic, thought High Admiral Robinson, sitting in his quarters, half turned from his desk. His uniform trousers were partly undone since he was being fellated by his fleet sociologist, Lieutenant Commander Iris Khan.

Khan, despite having one distant ancestor from the region of Pakistan on Old Earth, was blonde and blue-eyed. Kneeling between Robinson's legs, her eyes stayed upturned, intent on the high admiral's face, even as her mouth worked diligently to give the high admiral the quality of service to which his position entitled him.

Normally Robinson used the captain of *Peace*, Marguerite Wallenstein, for his physical needs. The captain, however, had duty at the moment and Khan had been otherwise unemployed. She would do.

Indeed, she does very well, Robinson thought as he reached out a hand to force Khan's head down and his penis into her throat moments before ejaculation. She stayed that way, her lips against the root of the high admiral's penis, even when a yeoman entered the quarters with the fleet's morning report. In the UEPF there was no shame in servicing one's betters. Only after the yeoman had left did Khan back off to lick away the still leaking residue. By that time the high admiral's face was blocked by the report.

"That will be all, thank you, Iris. I'll call you if I need you," was all Robinson had to say.

A few last licks and Khan closed the admiral's trousers, refastened his belt, stood and turned to go.

Just before she exited the cabin, Robinson ordered, "Send your husband to me. I want to go over some developments down below with him. It seems the local mercenary chief isn't content with merely having a ground army. He's got a major warship now. I wonder what's next."

Obras Zorrilleras, *Cuidad* Balboa, Republic of Balboa, 3/10/466 AC,

Cheapness was a watchword for the legion. Let others pay the expense of being on the cutting edge of military and scientific research; the Legion didn't need that. Instead, the *Obras Zorrilleras*, the research and development arm of the *Legion del Cid*, concentrated on stealing, reverse engineering, modifying, and occasionally—after evaluation—outright purchasing of technology. Even so, they did some original work, too.

They'd had some successes. The modifications for the *Dos Lindas* had come from OZ's naval bureau. They'd had a strong hand in the remanufacture of several smallish nuclear weapons captured in Sumer half a decade before. The small unit tactical communications system, or comsys, was likewise their design, modified from a wireless cell phone system in broad use around Terra Nova.

The big projects now were stealth, something the Federated States had a near monopoly on and which they would not share even with very close allies like Anglia.

Carrera had some potential uses for stealth, in the air, at sea and under the sea. That made it an OZ priority.

"We've got three things for you, *Duque*," the chief of OZ, an immigrant named Pislowski from the Jagielonian Commonwealth, said. "Two of these are the same basic technique but applied differently."

Carrera, Pislowski, and three others sat at a cheap conference table deep inside the main building for OZ. The researchers hadn't thought to provide refreshments. Instead, three models stood atop the table.

How refreshing, Carrera thought. He loathed briefings, meetings, and all the rest of the modern world's bureaucratic time-sinks. Refreshments tended to make it worse, not better, since they invited people to stay too long and talk too much. On occasion, Carrera thought of enacting a regulation requiring all meetings and briefings in the legion to be conducted standing and in the rain.

Pislowski smiled, pointing a finger. "It was that bloody Volgan's idea."

The Volgan—his given name was Pyotr—smiled back. He then picked up one of the models, a strangely proportioned aircraft. "As my friend has said, it was my idea. Technically. Better to say I was the one who pulled together some things I'd seen and read over the years. Some of that came from Jagielonia. This is a glider we've nicknamed the Condor.

"They build many gliders in Jagielonia," Pyotr continued. "Their interest goes back many decades. Even when I was doing design work for the Volgan Empire, it occurred to me that a glider has many advantages over an aircraft, even for combat purposes. It is fuel efficient. It is easy and cheap to maintain, even if it has an engine, as some do. It is quite easy and cheap to train people to fly a glider. Because a glider is so cheap and easy to fly, there is no great reason to require that the highest caliber men be chosen as pilots. Ground support requirements are only a tiny fraction of what is needed for a high performance aircraft. A glider is also relatively difficult to pick up on radar.

"Still there are disadvantages," Pyotr admitted. "A glider cannot carry much of a load. It is slow and not very maneuverable. It must be raised to a considerable height by some means, most commonly another aircraft. It depends upon natural updrafts in the air to keep going. With an auxiliary engine many of these disadvantages can be at least partially overcome. But with an engine, the glider becomes much easier to acquire, either on radar or by infrared from the heat of the engine and exhaust. Georgi and I have an answer to that."

Georgi, the senior of the two Volgan designers, spoke up. "Sir, do you know anything about radar?"

Carrera answered, "Assume not."

"Yes, sir. Radar is microwave energy, traveling through the air. It can also travel through other things, ground and water, for example, but with less range and accuracy. When the energy reaches something with a density different from air, it reacts. In effect, it radiates back from whatever it hit that was different from air, if the material it hits is capable of radiating back. Some materials radiate back poorly or not at all. These change the microwave energy into heat. Is the *Duque* familiar with the Federated States Air Force's P-71?"

"I know of it as a name. I've seen pictures."

"Here's a picture you didn't see," Georgi said,

handing over an eight-by-ten black and white of a remarkably odd-looking aircraft.

Carrera took it and looked at it carefully. He asked, "What's that dark ring around it?"

"Bats," Georgi answered. "Hundreds and thousands of stunned, crippled or dead bats. They couldn't see the plane and flew into it, usually killing themselves. You see, bats use sonar which is, in some ways, similar to radar. The P-71 presented no surfaces to bounce back the sonar signals to the bats. So they couldn't 'see' it and flew into the plane. The P-71 presents a very small radar, or sonar, cross section. Too small for bats to see."

Pyotr took up the briefing, once again. "There are three primary factors that affect an aircraft's radar cross section. These are size, materials, and shape. Although it is the least important factor, if two aircraft have exactly the same materials and shape, but are of different size, the larger will have a greater radar cross section. These gliders will be quite small. For shape, the important things are to have no sharp edges, no flat surfaces pointed toward the radar. For materials, there are two . . . oh, tricks, that we can use. The first is, construction wise, the tougher. Radar notices the change in density of an object in the air. To the extent that that difference is tiny, radar is apt not to notice. We plan to build gliders based on a spun carbon monofilament and resin shell. The shell itself can be made 'lossy'—"

"Glossy?" Carrera interrupted.

"No, sir. Lossy. It's a chemical property that refers to the conductivity of a material. Simply put, we can make the shell to absorb much radar energy and convert it to heat."

Carrera sat up. "Won't that give the glider away?"

"No, sir. The radar energy is small so the amount of heat produced in the shell is quite small and the polyurethane outside of it is almost the best insulator known. A plane might pick up the heat; a missile will not lock on very well.

"But we were discussing radar. By itself, the lossiness of the carbon monofilament is not enough. So outside of that, we shall build up polyurethane foam of decreasing density. The dielectric constant of the outermost polyurethane will be—"

Interrupting, Carrera asked "Dielectric constant?"

Pyotr reminded himself that he was dealing with a soldier, not a scientist. "Air has a dielectric constant of 1. The outermost polyurethane will have a DC of 1.01, near enough. At that difference, only an immeasurable amount of radar energy will radiate back. Not enough for a receiver to notice. As the radar penetrates the polyurethane, each increasingly dense layer will also radiate back a small amount; again, not enough to notice.

"The polyurethane itself will be reinforced by carbon fibers in the mix, which tend also to absorb radar energy. Inside it will be suspended a great many tiny metalicized chips. The chips will be curved to disperse radar energy outward on one side, or focus, and then disperse it, on the other."

Seeing Carrera's lack of comprehension, Pyotr explained. "The mix being sprayed on, the chips will be in random positions within the polyurethane. In almost all cases radar that hits them will be bounced away from the radar source. For those chips—and remember; they'll be tiny—that point directly toward the source, the radar will hit the convex or concave curves and be scattered so only a small portion of the energy is returned. These chips will also decrease in size as they near the outer surface. Where the P-71 has precisely calculated facets to insure the smallest possible surface pointed toward a radar, we will let random nature do much the same thing for us. Being random, it is possible that more than a desirable number of chips may reflect in the same direction. But the mathematical odds are plainly on our side. We can ground test each glider for particularly vulnerable areas, and use those with unsatisfactory chip alignment as something like a throwaway cruise missile, or as drones on recon missions. I believe you mentioned an interest in throwaways?"

"Yes." Carrera gestured for the Volgan to continue.

Pyotr nodded vigorously. "However, we cannot count on the plastics—the polyurethane and the carbon monofilament—to completely defeat the radar. Even the chips will only do so much. Inside the glider will be several objects that could give back quite a large radar cross section. The engine and the control package are problems. Even the pilot's skull will give back some radar energy. We plan on encasing the engine and control package in small, faceted, flattened domes of highly lossy material. These are much cheaper and easier to design and build than a full airframe like the P-71. They will reflect radar either down or straight up, and away from the radar source. The pilot, too, will be similarly covered although only on five sides, plus a partial—he has to see, after all.

"We have still to determine the best materials and composition for the propeller and wings. We might even go to a small jet engine. Likewise, we are arguing about the pilot's canopy. Neither of these problems appears insurmountable. For a guidance package for use as a drone we think it is possible to use a fairly simple computer and cheap, civilian model, global locating system. We would have to subcontract that out, however."

Carrera stopped writing in his notebook. "Range?"

Georgi answered, "Up to thirty-seven hundred kilometers, about twenty-three hundred miles, without a pilot, with maximum fuel, and a payload of over one hundred kilos. That is, if it doesn't have to expend fuel getting airborne."

"Maximum payload?"

"At twelve hundred kilometers, three hundred kilograms with pilot. Self lifting. These are approximations."

"Cost?"

"Under three hundred thousand FSD per copy. Possibly as little as two hundred and fifty. That doesn't count R and D costs. We will need thirty or, better, forty million to begin real development."

"Thirty days. Present me a budget." Carrera paused, then continued. "What's the rest?"

Pislowski pointed at the largest of the models on the table. It looked to Carrera much like the *Dos Lindas*, but with somewhat different lines.

"The same basic idea for stealthing the gliders can be used to stealth a ship. That is the aircraft carrier you have been restoring. We can create slabs of the polyurethane, carbon fiber, chip composite and—"

"No," Carrera interjected, holding up a restraining hand. He was already frustrated beyond belief with the cost of the carrier. "I've spent enough on that bitch. It's not intended to stand in line of battle again anyone who really counts. At this point, stealthing it is not necessary."

Shrugging, Pislowski pointed toward the third model, this one midway in size between the aircraft carrier and the glider. "We've taken to calling this a Megalodon. It has nothing like the stealthing features of the gliders; the material would not survive the pressure. Instead, we stole the idea from someone down in the Federated States."

Carrera noted mentally that the Megalodon model was facetted, just as had been the P-71 in the picture shown him by Georgi.

"Bounces sonar instead of radar, doesn't it; just like the bats in that photo?"

"Correct, *Duque*. The submarine itself is plastic . . . acrylic, actually." Pislowski removed the top of outer facetted fairing with his hands. "Inside, it would use either a hydrogen peroxide system, or some other air independent system, for propulsion. Extremely quiet."

Carrera looked long and hard at the model. Under the fairing was a cylinder that bulged out to a larger cylinder in the middle. Noticing his finger edging toward the bulge, Pislowski said, "That's where the torpedoes will be housed, in a rotating carousel turned, probably, by hand. It's only a thought, though."

The diving planes on the model were outsized, almost like wings. Pislowski explained, "The ship can glide forward as it rises or sinks. We have an idea for pumping out the ballast tanks by heating and cooling ammonia inside a flexible, condomlike, sheath. The ammonia would expand, displacing water from the tanks, or contract, allowing it in, and all fairly silently."

"Costs?"

"We have *no* idea, Legate. It depends on too many things that are out of our control. Will the Sachsens sell us peroxide systems? We don't know. Will the Anglics sell us the machinery to make thick acrylic cast tubes seven meters in diameter? Not if they know what we want it for. We can assume these will be expensive, though, especially if we have to develop them for ourselves. I am guessing here; maybe two hundred million each."

"All right," Carrera conceded. "That's a bit high for us. But I do like the idea. Send us a budget request for R and D only."

Pislowski nodded: "There is one other thing, *Duque*. We are getting into the realm of things which countries might classify as top secret. I . . ."

"You think you need a more secure location than the city," Carrera supplied. "I agree. It will take about a month to prepare things but at the end of that time I want those working on your more . . . mmm . . . let us say your more *clandestine* projects to move to the *Isla Real*."

Isla Real, Quarters #1, 4/10/466 AC,

The evening breeze cooled even as it kept off the mosquitoes. In the distance could be seen the lights of half a dozen merchant ships plying their trade between the Federated States, Atzlan, and Secordia, at one end, and the various republics-in-name-only, at the other. Still other ships pulled into and out of the Transitway.

"You really think it's going to come to a fight with the Tauran Union, Patricio?"

Carrera sighed and looked at his host. Parilla was short, stocky and dark. Pushing seventy, his hair y still mostly the jet black of the indians and mestizos who made up much of his ancestry. Only a distinguished frosting of gray at the temples betrayed his age.

"Eventually, yes, Raul," he answered. "We might be able to hold it off for a few years. But, in the long run, they're here for the purpose of confronting us, of supporting the civil government in confronting us."

"But why? I don't understand. We're fighting the fight they should be fighting. We're protecting *them*. It doesn't make any sense."

Carrera reached for the bottle of scotch sitting on the table between the two as he answered, "That's an interesting question. I thought for a while that it was the Gauls. After all, they've never quite forgiven the FSC for building the Transitway after they, themselves, failed to. And the Gauls are vindictive, make no mistake about it. But *that* vindictive?"

Parilla held his own tumbler out to be filled. "Okay, maybe not the Gauls. But they *did* send their troops here. They did entice the rest of the TU into sending their troops here."

"All true," Carrera conceded. "But think about the TU: how do they see themselves except as an organ of the World League. And what is the World League an organ of? What do they see as their spiritual foundation?"

Both men looked skyward to where the United Earth Peace Fleet mixed its lights with the stars beyond.

UEPF *Spirit of Peace*, 4/10/466 AC (Old Earth Year 2521)

High Admiral Robinson looked drearily from the window of his cabin at the green and blue planet spinning below. The planet spun in both senses, objectively, around its own axis, and subjectively, from the spinning of the ship around its axis to produce a practical artificial gravity. On the whole, the image would have made Robinson ill even if what went on, what had gone on, below hadn't already sufficed to do so.

So frustrating that I've lost in Sumer. Ah, well. At least I haven't lost the war, Robinson thought. He then amended the thought, *Yet.*

Robinson turned from the window onto space and looked instead at a map projected on the main screen of his cabin, a local product that—maddeningly, infuriatingly—came from a factory in Yamato, down below. "*Kurosawa Vision Solutions,*" was written in small letters across the silvery frame of the screen.

The map was of Sumer, one of the many wretched, little nation-pustules that dominated the globe below. Once again Robinson played out in his mind the reasons he had decided to assist a group of radical barbarians to confront the major power—some below said the "hyperpower"—of Terra Nova.

We are stagnant on Earth. In one hundred years, or maybe as few as twenty years if Peace's *engineering officer is to be believed, the Novans will be able to launch ships and do to Earth what Earth did to Terra Nova; colonize it. The big difference being that TN wasn't occupied by people and Earth is. Our system couldn't resist and won't survive. I could nuke them now; we still have some capability. And that knocks Terra Nova back five hundred years so that when they come looking for us in five hundred and twenty they'll have blood in their eye. And this fleet won't be here to stop them because if I nuke Terra Nova the Federated States of Columbia will nuke this fleet to ash. But Earth's Consensus won't build another fleet to replace the one lost here. They won't even pay to keep up what we have; for that I am reduced to selling art and, sometimes, slaves.*

Robinson sighed deeply and wearily. He had upon his shoulders the whole burden of protecting his civilization and the class, his own class, which ran it. It was a crushing load.

We sell art. We sell slaves, the refuse of Earth's sixth class. And that just to keep my ships running and my crews and their families fed, paid and clothed. Must I run drugs next?

I had hoped to wear down the hyperpower below with a series of costly and indecisive wars. The problem with that is that they appear to be winning. Who would have imagined a single nation-state with that kind of sheer . . . ooomph? Formidable swine. What they lack themselves they can buy.

At the thought of the Federated States being able to buy what it needed, Robinson's thoughts turned to the soldiers the FSC had bought. Most were wretched, of course, or, if not, banned by their government from doing anything that might lead to casualties. The FSC paid for the upkeep and deployment costs of these, but nothing more. It got about what it paid for, or perhaps a bit less.

But then there are the others, those little brown Latin mercenaries. Those the FSC pays top drachma for and gets full value, too. I wonder how the war in Sumer would have turned out without that ruthless mercenary legion. Better; of that much I am sure.

Robinson thought back on the extraordinarily clever

scheme Captain Wallenstein had come up with whereby
sympathetic citizens of Tauran states had given themselves up as hostages to force their governments to pay
ransoms to the insurgents in Sumer. It had been clever,
but it had ended when someone started kidnapping
Taurans for ransom and then feeding them feet first
into wood chippers for the nightly news, even after
the ransoms had been paid. The supply of volunteers
had dried up very quickly after that and even real
hostages had not been bargained for anymore. He
was reasonably certain that the mercenary legion had
been involved in all that.

But there's never any proof. *Bastards.*

And then there was the humiliation inflicted on the
cosmopolitan progressives of Terra Nova by the legion,
from torture stings to simply ignoring the Kosmo press
no matter how loudly it howled.

Never mind, I must think to the future.

"Computer, change display," Robinson commanded.

"To what, High Admiral?" the artificial and vaguely
feminine voice answered.

"World view. Show me incidents over the last thirty-
five local days."

The image changed. Robinson studied.

*Nice to see that things are taking a turn for the
worse for the FSC in Pashtia. And the piracy along
the western coast of Uruhu is encouraging . . .*

"Computer, connect me with the intelligence office."

A male face appeared in one corner of the screen.
A male voice answered. "Lieutenant Commander Khan
here, High Admiral. Did you want me, sir, or my wife?"
Iris Khan's husband meant, *do you need another blow
job or do you actually require intelligence support?*

He wasn't offended or judgmental about the matter, either way. The UE was very casual about both sex and marital relations. Moreover, it was considered bad form to use someone's wife for sex and not at the same time watch out for the husband's career.

"Khan, tell me about piracy on Terra Nova."

"Yes, High Admiral." Khan played with his computer to bring up some data. "Though piracy exists all over Terra Nova, there are four main nexus for piracy down below. One is the islands and coasts on both sides of the Republic of Balboa. This is mainly concerned with retail robbery of yachts and then reusing those yachts for drug smuggling, along with occasional kidnapping for ransom. A second is the eastern shore of Uhuru which, because of the nature of the trade there, tends to take entire ships and cargo. Ships plying that trade are smallish. A third is the Straits of Nicobar, which is not generally concerned with drug smuggling or theft of cargo but more with ship's safe robbery and kidnapping for ransom. There is some religious element to the Nicobar piracy, at least in the sense that a bare majority of the pirates are Islamic and seem to use Islam as a justification for piracy. They would still be pirates if they worshipped Odin. The last nexus is around the area of Xamar, on Uruhu's western coast. This is not new but has grown substantially over the last several years. Xamar piracy is also, officially, Islamic in intent though, once again, they would be pirates even if they were pagans."

Khan, the husband, pulled up more data from his screen. "Officially, piracy costs the economy down below about twelve to sixteen billion FSD annually. It is believed, however, that the actual incidence of piracy is understated by a factor of about twenty . . . though it is doubtful that the costs are quite that understated."

Robinson scratched his head. "Interesting. Thank you, Khan. Tell me, did your wife enjoy our session?"

"She says she did, Admiral, but wishes you had pinched her nipples more and come in her mouth rather than her throat. She likes that sort of thing."

"I'll remember that for next time. In the interim, I want both you and her to look into the long-term potential for both squeezing funds from and ruining a large-scale economy through unchecked piracy. Robinson, out."

Xamar Coast, Western Uhuru, 5/10/466 AC

"This is becoming tedious, *sayidi*," said the Helvetian banker representing a Tauran shipping firm, the Red Star Line. The banker looked rather like a gnome, short and stout and bearded. It was his job to negotiate the release of a dozen merchant sailors taken from a Red Star Line refrigerator ship two weeks prior. The sailors, bound and filthy, lined one corner of the sparsely furnished office near the center of the city.

Within the office tea and dates were served by tall, slender women with amazingly large, dark eyes. The women, some of them slave girls, likewise set out a tray of thin bread made from the flour of the chorley, a non-Old Earth species that resembled a sunflower that grew just above ground level, accompanied by local *shoug*, a mix of ground peppers ranging from "Holy Shit" to "Joan of Arc," with a *very* small admixture of "Satan Triumphant."

Of the women, the eyes were all that could be seen, that, and the seductive swaying even their robes could not conceal. They didn't matter though; the gnome had little use for women.

"Indeed," agreed the formidable, even fierce, looking *Hawiye* tribe chief seated on a cushion opposite the banker. Like the women, the chief was tall and quite slender, despite his years. "As I have told you many times, retrieving your people from these thugs costs me. It costs in money; it costs in arms; it costs in favors and in influence. I would prefer to put our relationship on a more formal and regular basis. But you people . . ."

It was all a polite fiction. The *Hawiye* chief, Abdulahi was his name, didn't actually ransom anyone himself, nor did he have the slightest objection to groups of his underlings seizing infidel shipping. In fact, he sent them out to do so and then maintained, for form's sake, that he was only acting as an intermediary for the return of the crews. This face-saving arrangement was workable, but far from ideal.

"I know, *sayidi.* And I have spoken to my superiors at length on the subject. They've finally agreed to a more . . . regularized, arrangement."

At last, thought Abdulahi. *Protection money. Or "Danegeld," as my instructors in Anglia would have called it.*

"Here is what I propose," said Abdulahi. "Your firm will inform me in advance of when it will have a ship passing within this area. You will pay me an amount based on cargo—"

"The displacement," interjected the Helvetian. "My principals are not going to accept allowing your people aboard to inspect cargos. Besides, we could not really be sure they even *were* your people without you meeting every ship."

"Fair enough," Abdulahi agreed. "Displacement. That can be checked objectively. Moreover, it has a direct, if uneven, relationship to crew size, and therefore ransom potential, as well as docking fees, which likewise bears on money carried in the ship's safe. This is fair and simple enough."

"In any case," the *Hawiye* pirate lord continued, "You will pay a reasonable fee—yes, we will have to agree on what constitutes 'reasonable'—in advance. I will use the money to pay off the pirates who infest our coast."

"They will, of course, be free to attack the ships of other firms," added the Helvetian. *Which is absolutely necessary to us or those firms will be able to ship cheaper than we can.*

"Naturally."

"The question remains, however, *can* you control the pirates?"

Abdulahi simply laughed.

Zioni Embassy, *Ciudad* Balboa, 6/10/466 AC,

The Jewish Brigadier, Yonatan Bar El, laughed aloud. "Yes, *Duque*," he answered. "I *do* rather understand the problems inherent in the legion using Zioni equipment in Arab lands. Even your friends—and we in Zion are amazed at some of the friends you've made—wouldn't, just as you say, know whether to support you or shoot at you. Still, you must admit, our Chariot is a tank infinitely superior to the Volgan dreck you've been using."

"The Volgan stuff is better than you admit, Yoni,"

Carrera replied. "After all, don't you use every piece of Volgan equipment you can get your hands on, after a quality rebuild?"

"We do," the Jew admitted.

"Well, we have a substantial, if not quite controlling interest, in the Kirov tank factory. They do a quality initial build. We're pretty happy with our equipment, with a few exceptions."

"Which exceptions?" the Zioni inquired. Maybe there was a sale to be made after all.

"Lighter but longer-ranged artillery would be nice. Small arms are acceptable but . . ." Carrera shrugged eloquently.

"But the Volgan Bakanovas don't really have the range you would like."

"They lack range," Carrera admitted. "They lack penetration—"

Lourdes, wearing a long, silk sheath dress interrupted. "Patricio, Mrs. Bar El asked me to her family quarters. Do you mind if I slip out for a few minutes?"

The other half of the sales team, Carrera thought, answering, "Not at all, *miel.* I'll still be here when you return."

Lourdes pecked chastely at Carrera's cheek before turning to sway away. Yoni Bar El's eyes followed for just as long as politeness permitted, while thinking, *Yum.*

"We have a new small arms system in Zion . . ." he said, once he could tear his eyes away from Lourdes' seductively swaying posterior.

"I know. We've looked at the SAR-47. Not interested."

"Yeah . . . our troops don't like it either." It was Bar El's turn to shrug. "Though I expected them to like the grenade system that goes with it."

"Now *that* looked to have promise," Carrera agreed. "But what we really want is something that takes advantage of all the recent developments in small arms: super fast burst rates to make burst fire practical— the Bakanova has that, but only for two rounds—a cartridge firing a bullet with really superior ballistics, combustible casings, electronic ignition, integral limited visibility sights."

"It's funny, isn't it?" the Zioni observed. "There really *are* a number of major . . . oh . . . possibilities out there, and nobody seems interested in pursuing them. You would think that the FSC—"

"That much I don't really understand myself," Carrera said. "I served in the FS Army for quite a long time. The rifle my troops were last issued wasn't any better, really, than the rifle I'd been first issued. And it was a twenty-year-old design then. But they don't seem able to come up with a new one. This would be fine if the old one were great. But it wasn't."

"In any case," Bar El said, "we've blown our small arms design budget on the SAR-47 and we're stuck with it. And it's not a bad weapon, really. But now, we've got our designers reduced to making oversized pistols for Columbians with penis envy."

It was Carrera's turn to snicker. Then he turned serious. "You know, Yoni, I still do have money for small arms development. Maybe we could arrange something."

The Base, Kashmir, Tribal Trust Territories, 15/10/466 AC

"A superb arrangement, Abdulahi," said Mustafa ibn Mohamed ibn Salah, min Sa'ana. The news was enough to launch Mustafa up from his usual misery to something like hope, maybe even happiness.

The years had been unkind to Mustafa. Naturally tall and vigorous, disaster heaped upon disaster had shrunk him, even as a lingering illness weakened him. With good news so hard to come by, the news brought by Abdulahi was welcome indeed.

Communications for the movement were never secure. The only way to be certain of a secret was to carry it in person. Even the infidel press could not balance out that inferiority, though they tried. And using couriers, too, had its problems, as any number of mujahadin grabbed without cause or warrant from airplanes and airports around the globe could have testified. It was infuriating, and—Mustafa had to admit—unexpected, for the infidels to fail to follow their own rules. It was worse when the Kosmos weren't able to shriek, scream and nag their own governments into compliance in their own suicide.

"It *is* superb, Sheik. And it can only get better. This one heathen shipping company will be off limits, for a good price. But that doesn't reduce our righteous plundering. It only means we can concentrate on those who have not yet agreed to pay this maritime *yizyah*. This will increase the pressure on them to come to an arrangement with us. And each one that does submit increases the pressure on those who have not. One by one they will bow."

Abdulahi laid down a thick briefcase and opened it. Inside, Mustafa could see, were stacks of large denomination bills; Tauran lira, Federated States drachma, masu of Yamato, Volgan gold rubles, Helvetian escudi . . .

Mustafa felt tears begin to form. Abdulahi turned away, feigning not to notice.

"When here, in our darkest hour, you come to our rescue . . ." Mustafa began.

"Sheik, when my homeland was torn and my tribe starving, who came to our aid? You did. When the infidels occupied our land, who gave us the means and the encouragement to resist them? You did. Who built for us schools and hospitals? You did. This is a small repayment . . . with the promise of much more to come."

Later—after Abdulahi had been presented with a recently captured Tauran slave girl to take back with him to Xamar; a small token of Mustafa's appreciation and esteem—Mustafa had sat in his quarters for a long time stroking his beard and looking at the case of money while thinking upon the uses to which it could be put.

It's not that much really, a few million, five at most. I could almost weep for the days when the Ikhwan commanded hundreds of millions of FSD and thousands upon thousands of fighters.

This money is a start. It is also a suggestion. Along with the Xamari, I must think upon how to direct the seaborne mujahadin of Nicobar. Then again, they do not owe me as did Abdulahi and his people. Is it worth my time and effort to try to direct the Nicobars? Perhaps not. Can I make it worth their time and effort to support me? Perhaps so. It must be thought upon.

For now, I have the fight in Pashtia to worry about. And, even though I am a son of the Prophet, peace be upon him, I find I must worry, that I must not leave everything to Allah.

What a strange thought that is. The filthy Nazrani say that "God helps those who help themselves." How odd that this seemingly impious notion should infect me, and yet it may be so. I must set the mullahs to searching the Holy Koran and the Sacred Hadiths to see if this idea may be religiously supportable.

In any case, if it is not supportable, I do not know what is. Allah has turned his face from us everywhere we relied upon him too heavily. In Pashtia we were slaughtered in weeks. In Sumer, the holy warriors could not face the infidels. Millions have gone over to them, keeping only the shell and shadow of the Faith and none of its meat and drink. Perhaps Allah . . .

Mustafa sipped at *qahwa*, unsweetened coffee brewed from beans still green, and filtered through a piece of hemp rope stuck in the spout. There was a thought there, an important thought that had gone skittering away. *Perhaps Allah . . . what?*

Perhaps this is another test of our faith in him? Perhaps. But . . . Aha! There is the thought. What if it is as much a test of His faith in us?

A serving boy, a slave but not a Tauran, bent to refill Mustafa's cup. The emir of the *Ikhwan* stopped the boy by covering the cup with his hand.

"Go," he said. "Find and bring me Nur al Din, the Misrani, and Abdul Aziz who helps manage the accounts. Bring me, too, Mullah al Kareem, that we might use his insight into the holy words. When that is done, brew more *qahwa*. It will be a long night."

Training Area Thirty-Five, *Isla Real*, 16/10/466 AC

Leave was never quite "leave" when Carrera returned from the war. Rather, it was his opportunity to observe, direct and correct the training and administration taking place behind him.

There was only one moon up this evening, Eris, but she was full, casting sharp shadows on the ground. At that, Eris only provided perhaps twenty percent of the maximum illumination possible from Terra Nova's three moons.

Under that moonlight, battle-dressed and wearing night vision goggles, Carrera watched an infantry platoon from Fourth Tercio going through their paces in setting up a night ambush. It looked professional; it looked well-oiled. Yet something bothered him about it and he wasn't sure quite what.

"What's wrong with this, Jamey?" he asked Soult.

Soult shrugged. "No clue, boss. It looks fine by me."

"Yeah . . . yeah, that's it. It *looks* fine. How does something look that fine? When does real war ever *look* that fine? Let's go trip into the objective rally point, shall we?"

The two were challenged by the team left behind at the objective rally point, or ORP, with the platoon's rucksacks. That was fine, too, but not in a way that bothered Carrera.

"Don't tell anyone I'm here," he told the sergeant in charge. "I just want to watch for a bit."

The sergeant was obviously not happy about that. If his tribune, Cano, came back and found *Duque* Carrera waiting for him without his having been warned, there'd be hell to pay later on.

Carrera understood that. "Jamey," he said, "stick with the sergeant so that when his tribune comes to rip his balls off he can plead superior orders *and* no opportunity." Soult went and stood next to the sergeant while Carrera walked to the side of the ORP nearest the ambush and waited. With his goggles on, he could just make out the ambush position, though not the men in it who had all gone prone. He continued forward until he could make out the waiting legionaries, then stopped and went to one knee to watch.

Mannequins joined to each other and suspended from a cable strung tightly between two trees began to enter the kill zone, in single file, pulled by someone off to the right, somewhere. Carrera saw them move across at a walking pace, a pace a group of Salafis might well take up when they thought they were safe but had to get somewhere.

The target mannequins—there were twelve of so of them, Carrera thought—were fully in the target area when the entire scene was brightly, if momentarily, lit by the flashes of two directional mines. Carrera ducked his chin onto his chest against the backblast and the fragments.

There followed rifle and machine gun fire; dozens of weapons sending out streams of tracers into the jungle downrange. Mannequins began to drop to the ground as bullets found the inflated balloons within sandbags that held them to the cable overhead. The bullets pierced the balloons, collapsing them and letting them and their sandbags flow through the harnesses, detaching them from the overhead cable.

This continued for a minute before there was a *whoosh* as a star cluster launched into the sky. The ground was suddenly lit in a bright magnesium light. Carrera heard a whistle and then voice commands. Men began to move rapidly across the kill zone, shooting every mannequin once more in the head as it lay on the ground. Special teams searched the "bodies," collecting documents of intelligence value, communications devices, and weapons. The documents, cell phones and one radio were turned over to the platoon leader. A pile was made of the captured weapons, which pile a two-man team prepared for demolition.

At some point—Carrera presumed it was when the intel collection team reported to the platoon leader that the bodies were clear— another star cluster was launched. Men began to scurry back to the ambush line, even as the demo team shouted "Fire in the hole" and pulled the igniters that led to the charges they'd placed on the arms.

Once the demo team had cleared away, there was another whistle blast and, once again, the rifles and machine guns poured lines of death into the jungle opposite the ambush line. Voice commands followed and, by ones and twos the ambushing platoon began to form up to fall back to the ORP.

"It's *too* smooth," Carrera whispered.

Cano was *pissed*. Being taken by surprise, ambushed himself by the *Duque*, was just too fucking much. Bad enough that—

"Relax, Tribune," Carrera said, not urgently. He was actually impressed with the kid. "I just have some questions. It was a *good* ambush. Really. What bothers me was that maybe it was *too* good. Why do you think it was so good?"

Cano didn't relax. Sure, he wasn't a signifer anymore; he was entitled to tie his boots in the morning without tying the left one to the right one. Even so, this was the bloody *Duque*. He was a bastard; everyone knew it. Cano could just see his career flying off to parts unknown and unknowable. He could—

"I asked a question, Tribune," Carrera reminded.

"Oh . . . sorry, sir. I was . . . I just wasn't expecting you to—"

"I *asked* a question, Tribune."

"Yes, sir. Sorry, sir. Well . . . sir . . . we've done this ambush here maybe a dozen times just since *I've* been leading the platoon. The boys know what to do and, then again, we drill the shit out of it . . ."

Aha.

"Jamey! Call the Chief of Staff, the I and the Ia. I don't give a shit if they're asleep. Get 'em up."

Main Officers' Club, *Isla Real*, 17/10/466 AC

Normally, in every day life, Carrera was a surprisingly gentle sort. He wasn't particularly aggressive, or vicious. He'd probably never done a deliberately cruel thing, outside of line of duty, in his life.

In line of duty, however, or especially in action, he changed. The change wasn't like that of a man turning into a wolf; that kind of transition, even in myth, took time. Instead, for Carerra, there simply came a moment when stress impended and he changed.

It was something like a click.

"I'm *so* glad you could all make it," Carrera hissed to the assembled senior officers and centurions of the legion.

As a single man, they thought, *Oh, shit, we're in trouble.*

"You people suck mastodon cock," Carrera began, with his usual fine sense of tact. "Where the *fuck* did you get the idea that your job is to train people to follow formulae, rather than training them, mentally and morally, as individuals and as units, to solve unique problems? You've been fighting for *five* fucking years now. When did you all forget that war is always *different*?"

His face was livid as he continued, "Can anyone answer me; when did Cazador School begin training leaders to be robots? Hmmm? No takers? I see. Did it creep in in OCS or CCS? No?

"I watched an ambush the other night. Good unit, good leaders, conducting a good ambush. But you know *what*? They'd been doing the same thing in the same way in the same place for fucking *years*." With this he spared a glare for Kuralski and the staff. "Why have we had our soldiers doing the same fucking thing in the same fucking place in the same fucking way for *years*? Why *didn't* we give them different problems, in different places, with different circumstances? *Why,* you assholes? Why?"

It had taken Carrera thirty-six hours of brooding to become as angry as he was. He'd nurtured the anger, cultivated it, so that he could release it on his subordinates. Once released, though, it ebbed quickly enough.

"Now listen," he said, more calmly. "I'm going to explain something.

"Battle drills—preset solutions, well rehearsed, for common battlefield circumstances—are an interesting subject. Likewise for Standard Operating Procedures, individual tasks done to perfection, crew drills, and formations. There are some very good armies that depend on them. The Federated States and Volgan Republic do; and maybe the Foreign Military Training Group is where we were contaminated from. There are also some very good armies that loathe them, the Sachsen and Zionis, for example.

"Generally speaking, I *don't* like them. There are a number of reasons for that. Listen, *carefully.*"

The assembled leaders did listen carefully. They also relaxed to a degree; when Carrera went into teaching mode, they knew, he was unlikely to shoot someone on the spot. They knew he was going into teaching mode when he pulled some index cards out of his right breast pocket. *When did Carrera need prompt cards to chew someone's ass?*

"Number one, remember that drills, if they're going to be reliable, must be conditioned into troops, almost as if the troops were Pavlov's dogs. So if you can't really condition something well enough to rely on it, *don't* make a drill of it.

"Two, conditioning takes a lot of time, time you probably won't have. So even if something can, in theory, be conditioned, if you don't have the time to condition it, don't waste what time you have on the impossible.

"Three, drills—like everything else—take place under certain conditions. If those conditions are subject to radical differences such that no amount of practical drilling can condition them all, do not train as a drill something that will only be true infrequently.

"Four, military units suffer losses. They are almost

never at full strength. If a drill requires a particular level of manpower or equipment, and you can reasonably predict that that particular level of strength will rarely be met, I would suggest you don't bother.

"Three and four are related in a way. We use *crew* drill for the tank and Ocelot crews, don't we? One thing about the inside of a turret; it doesn't change. The crewmen have seats they stay in. The gun doesn't move relative to the crew. The internal communications gear typically works. And the crew of an armored vehicle generally lives or dies together, no attrition that matters in the short term. So a drill for a crew like that makes sense. The same holds true for much that the mortars and artillery do. Their positions may change from place to place, but the important thing, the gun, is always the same. The positions they build to protect the gun and themselves are always the same, too. The casualties they take, mostly to other mortars and artillery, or air, tend to be either catastrophic or insignificant—the crew lives or dies together."

Carrera became reflective. "Actually towed artillery is a funny case. They don't usually come under small arms fire. Mines are only rarely a problem for them. For the most part they lose men to aerial attack and counterbattery fire from enemy artillery. That fire either is close enough to emulsify the crew, or it's far enough away, when it explodes, to do only limited damage to the crew, or it is so far away it is irrelevant to the crew. In cases one and three, that the artillery crew was drilled numb doesn't hurt matters. It can still either do the job or it is dead. In the middle case, because gun crews are much larger than the bare minimum needed to load and fire the gun, and because artillery crew drill is so simple that everyone can be, and in a good crew is, trained to do all the jobs, even with some losses the gun can still fill the important jobs with adequately trained troops and function at a reduced rate of fire.

"However, compare the problem at the crew level to a platoon of mortars, tanks or tracks, or a battery of guns. They always have to adjust: to terrain, to the enemy situation, to their own strength. The variables for infantry are infinite, a few drills won't do and the number that might do is impossible. So, before you decide to train something as a drill, ask yourself also whether the conditions—to include your own strength—are likely to be the same in war. I'll give you a hint; a line remains a line, even when you erase some portion of it. If you plan on doing a drill or formation with any unit above the crew level, you had best consider making it some variable on a line . . . wedges and echelons count as lines. Only that kind of formation or drill is sustainable after losses.

"In a similar vein: formations. If you've ever seen a platoon, normally of four vehicles, trying to bound forward by sections of two vehicles, when the platoon is down to only three vehicles, you'll know what I mean. It just doesn't work the same way. You end up with either an inadequate covering force—one vehicle—or the covering force is two vehicles and the single track sent ahead to bound feels alone and abandoned and advances most reluctantly. So under normal combat conditions the bounding drill has less benefit than you expect and need and all the time spent on drilling such movement tends to be wasted. On the other hand, a company bounding forward by alternating its platoons can work because even if a bounding platoon has taken some losses, it is still capable of covering its own front and has enough sub units left to give each other moral support to go forward. That, by the way, is the single most important reason legion tank platoons have six tanks instead of the usual four other armies have; so they can take losses and still have two sections capable of forming some variant on a line to cover themselves while they move forward by bounds."

Carrera flipped one of his prompt cards over. "Back to the main subject: Fifth, time to execute the drill in battle is another consideration. Some things don't have to be conditioned to be done. Even in battle there is often time to give more than one-word drill commands. So ask yourselves, before deciding to do something as a drill, if there would normally be time to give orders to have your troops act more appropriately than a drill would allow.

"Sixth, is the drill a matter of life and death for an individual, victory or defeat for a higher unit? I don't mean simply that under some rare circumstances a well-executed drill might be life or death for us or the enemy. I mean is a precise response virtually always that important. Reaction to a near ambush is that kind of circumstance. So is using a bangalore torpedo to breach an obstacle, especially when attacking a position held by an enemy with a very responsive artillery support network . . . if surprise fails you and you must clear a path quickly. In those circumstances a simple, on line rush, drilled in advance, may be your best bet.

"At a lower level, the individual level, there are also a few tasks like that. The whole field of combat demolitions is dangerous enough to justify drilling troops to do it perfectly every time. The time to put on a gas mask is about that critical, too. Although, if you want to see an interesting show, sometime have your troops come under a chemical attack when they are advancing at a crawl under fire, with inadequate cover and concealment. Our boys are already well drilled on immediate action for a chemical attack. I'd give odds that most of them stand up in direct fire to put on their masks. Hmmm. Maybe that's not such a good drill after all. See my point?"

Whether they really saw it or not, the officers and centurions nodded vigorously.

"Seven, 'only the very simple can work in war.' Clausewitz, as I'm sure you recognize. Complex drills simply won't work. Something will fail if a drill is too complex.

"Eighth, your enemy will adapt to your drills very quickly.

"Ninth and last, and why I'm not a drill enthusiast, is this: There is a mindset, common in many armies, which has no understanding of war as the chaos it is. To these people, everything is controllable, everything is predictable. They will forget that war is about prevailing against an armed enemy, who does not think about himself as a target set up to give you the best possible chance of success, but instead will do everything he can to thwart and destroy you. In peacetime maneuvers, these people and their units often do well, even better than those who see war more clearly. They then stretch the idea of drill beyond the legitimate limits it has, and try to make everything a drill, everything precise. Skills and purely measurable factors assume an unmerited importance. Leaders and troops are not trained to *think*. Their *moral* faculties are not developed.

"Let me give you an example from Old Earth history. After the First World War there, the victorious French Army developed some very standardized drills for higher formations. The German Army examined these division level drills in wargames on maps and came to the conclusion that they were, most of the time, more effective than the more chaotic approach the Germans had favored. Nonetheless, the Germans didn't adopt the French methods. The French continued to drill; the Germans continued to treat war as uncontrollable chaos and trained their army accordingly. France fell in *six weeks* in 1940. So much for the efficacy of drill."

Carrera's voice grew hard again, where it had softened as he lectured. "Here are my orders. To the staff and especially the operations and training staff: I want you to redivide up the training areas, and especially the live-fire training areas, such that no unit ever has to train the same problem on the same spot of ground within a year. Dan, I also want you to monitor that no unit *does* train the same problem in the same way on the same spot within a year. I want you to relook the non-crew drills we may already have instituted and get rid of any that do not meet the nine points of guidance I just gave you."

Carrera glanced around for his Inspector General. "You," he pointed, "are to change your orientation partly away from administrative inspections and more toward inspection of training, in accordance with my guidance.

"Remember this, IG: There are five functions to training; only five things we can expect out of training. One: *Skill training,* the individual, leader, and collective tasks that soldiers and units should be able to perform. Two: *Conditioning* of individual nonconscious characteristics, attitudes and the physical body. Three: *Development* of conscious characteristics, judgment, determination, dedication, and so forth. Four: *Testing* of doctrine and equipment. Five: *Selection* of leaders, of people for special or advanced training, of people to keep and of people to eliminate from the legion.

"IG, there are no other reasons to train; everything we do in training must advance these causes.

"To the rest of you: if I discover you have not listened carefully, if I discover that you are not developing the mental and moral faculties of your units and your men, if I discover that you *ever* let training become routine, standardized and, in a phrase, mentally dulling, I will not only fire you, I will set you to turning large rocks into small ones, until you are old and gray."

"That's all."

INTERLUDE

13 July, 2078, Clichy-sous-Bois, France, European Union

The Moslems had not, as many feared and others hoped for, ever become a majority within the European Union. For one thing, the United States and Australia, along with the Republic of Western Canada, had, after a time (and only for a time), refused to take more than a pittance in culturally Christian but politically social-democrat European immigrants. Moreover, the EU itself began to institute border and emigration controls that even Stalin and Castro would have approved of. For another, the unsustainable social democratic state had not, in fact, been sustained. When elderly German or French citizens went hungry, the Moslems were bound to be starved.

This, of course, resulted in violence. But the Euros, always with that mix of bloodthirsty fanaticism lurking beneath the soft exterior, had traditions for dealing with inassimilable foreigners who caused trouble.

✧ ✧ ✧

The Army and Foreign Legion trucks and buses, bearing two battalions of paras, three of infantry, one of engineers, and a *lot* of building material, showed up before dawn. In an operation well planned and well rehearsed, the Moslem ghetto of Clichy-sous-Bois was surrounded, and the beginnings of a barbed wire fence put up, before the sun was much above the horizon.

The welfare state required lots of young people and lots of taxes to support it. Unfortunately, both the ethos of the welfare state—which could have been called "Maximum License"—and the taxes, which made raising a large family highly problematic, ensured that there could never be enough babies born to keep up that tax base.

There was a solution, of course: major immigration of young workers from elsewhere. This was a solution not without its problems, however. Those problems eventually became highly pressing, as when a group of Moslem "youths" burned down a few government buildings in Paris on Bastille Day.

And then someone remembered that foreign workers did not necessarily have to be *free* to be useful.

"Live with the new reality, Imam," said the legionnaire officer to the senior cleric in the *banlieue*. "Your people will be fed, *if* they work. But you have abused our hospitality too much for us to allow you the freedom of our country any longer."

Nearby, more Army and Legion trucks and buses, joined now by police vehicles, dropped off Moslems by the hundreds who had been seized in the great sweep up.

"We will riot," answered the imam, huffily. "We will—"

The legionnaire cut him off. "You will maintain control or we will cut off your water, your heat, your food. There will be no riots."

"The conscience of the world—"

"Means nothing. You forgot, I think, that when we banned speech that might offend you and yours, we also took upon ourselves the power to ban any speech we desired to ban. Every silver lining has its cloud, Imam."

CHAPTER FOUR

War is pusillanimously carried on in
this degenerate age; quarter is given;
towns are taken and people spared;
even in a storm, a woman can hardly
hope for the benefit of a rape.
—Philip Dormer Stanhope,
Fourth Earl of Chesterfield

**Officers' and Centurions' Club, Camp Balboa,
Ninewa, Sumer, 4/Intercalary/466 AC**

Carrera had extended his leave to spend local Christmas
with his family. And he'd felt like a rat, too, camp-
sick the whole time for his army and guilty that all
those deployed couldn't be home with *their* families.

Patricio Carrera, *Dux*, in Latin, or *Duque*, in Spanish, commander of the deployed portion of the *Legion
del Cid*, drummed his fingers with irritation while
watching the projection screen set up in the main
room of the club.

"What are you going to do if you win, Adnan?"
Carrera asked of the Sumeri, Adnan Sada, seated to
his right.

"To answer that question, Patricio, you have to answer the question of why the people would have voted for me."

"Because here, in Ninewa and over in Pumbadeta provinces we've got relative peace?"

Sada laughed, slightly and cynically. "That's a part of it, too, of course. But the real reason, only somewhat related to that, is that I am not a nut, either tribalist, sectarian, fascist or leftist, that I am not really a democrat, and that I am ruthless enough to hold things together. If they vote for me, they're voting to hold the country together, whatever it takes. They're also voting to get rid of this experiment in parliamentary democracy which scares the living shit out of most of them."

"You mean they *want* to have 'one man, one vote, once'?"

"Pretty much," Sada agreed, then amended, "or rather, they *don't* want there to be a chance for the rise of the sort of lunatics democracy tends to throw up in this kind of society. They also want their traditions and their tribes respected. They want someone able to keep the Farsi at bay; yes, even the ones who share sect with the Farsi would prefer being a majority in a non-sectarian Sumer to being an Arab minority in a non-Arab state."

"Are you planning on de-socializing?"

"There's no way to," Sada answered, definitively, "not entirely. It's the curse of a single-resource economy. When someone tells me how to divide up the oil without just pouring money into corrupt hands . . ."

Sada's face suddenly looked grim as his voice acquired a hint of despair.

"Most Arabs, you know, think Allah gave us the

oil as a special gift because he loves us. I suspect he gave it to us as a trap because he hates us."

Carrera looked down, thinking, *Balboa, too, is something of a single resource country, the Transitway. The other major income producer, the legion, is not, strictly speaking, a part of the economy. How would Balboa divide the Transitway? When they've tried it just meant huge bribes for private profit.*

Sada continued, "I *am* of a mind to de-socialize most of those things the previous government took control of: agriculture, construction, liquor distilling. Who knows, maybe I'll be able to buy a decent local beer and whiskey someday, rather than having to rely on the legion's unofficial imports."

Sada was not one of those Moslems who took the proscription against alcohol too very seriously.

"In any case," Sada finished, "I will deliberately wreck this doomed-to-fail, absolutely impossible experiment in parliamentarianism and work to create what can work, a federation of the tribes with a national army. And, after all, what the hell difference what kind of government we have provided it doesn't try to govern *much*? I will *never* be able to eradicate corruption so I'll just have to work with it, even to regularize it."

That sparked a thought for Carrera. *When the day comes, as it will, when the government of Balboa has to go, how will Parilla and I organize the country? Around the provinces that, outside of* Valle de la Luna, *don't mean much? Around the tercios of the legions? It's something to think on. Of course, first we'll have to fight the Taurans who are only in Balboa to ensure we can't get rid of the government.*

Carrera's thoughts were interrupted by a loud cheer and some warbling from the female serving staff at the club, which included several dozen Sumeri hookers, war widows mostly, that the legion had taken under its wing. He looked up and saw that the main screen showed election returns from Pumbadeta and its environs; a sweep for Sada.

"*They* appreciate that, as far as they can tell, I saved them from *you*," Sada commented, with a grin.

It was true enough. Without Sada's personal example and intervention Carrera *had* been determined to kill every Pumbadetan male capable of sprouting a beard. And they'd known it.

Nice to see they pay their debts, Carrera thought.

There was another cheer, and more female warbling, as the results for Ninewa were shown on the screen. It was rather more subdued, though. There had never been any doubt of how the base province for Sada's own force, now a near mirror image of Carrera's, would vote.

"Babel is the real question," Sada observed. "It's going to be close."

The officers and senior noncoms—centurions, sergeants-major, signifers, tribunes, and legates—couldn't have been more interested in watching the election results on the main room's four-meter projection screen than they would have been if the election had been held in their base country of Balboa. After all, it was *their* man, *their* ally, Adnan Sada, running for the highest office in the Republic of Sumer.

Surrounded by the others, Carrera's and Sada's fingers continued to drum. Watching the numbers shift was as nerve-wracking as any battle.

No, thought Carrera. *It's* more *nerve-wracking than a battle. For in battle I have control, a control I know how to use to good effect. Here, with this election, I have little.* Unconsciously, he stopped the drumming with his right hand, moving the thumbnail to his teeth to nibble.

Sitting to Carrera's left, Sergeant Major McNamara noticed the nervous biting and, thinking to kill two birds with one stone, poured a fresh drink into the crystal glass on the armrest between them. The whiskey made tinkling sounds as it splashed over the ice.

Thank God, John McNamara thought, *that he's cut down on the drinking since seven years ago.*

Still unconsciously, Carrera stopped his nail gnawing to pick up the glass. Unseen by Carrera, Sergeant Major McNamara smiled slightly at the Sumeri, Qabaash, seated behind Sada. Qabaash rarely smiled outside of battle. He did offer his glass behind Carrera's back to McNamara for a refill.

"Heretic," Carrera whispered when he turned and saw the drink in Qabaash's hand.

"It's not what you *Nazrani* would call a mortal sin, *sayidi,*" Qabaash answered. "Besides, Allah is the all merciful, the all-forgiving, despite what some Salafi assholes would have you believe. And He knows I need the bloody drink now, if ever I did."

Carrera nodded, then replaced his own drink on the armrest. Re-fixing his attention on the screen he went back to his gnawing. This time McNamara gave off an "ahem" to remind his chief of the proper decorum.

"Well, dammit," Carrera answered, "this election decides the war. If we win it, we'll have won. If Sada loses . . ."

"Civil war," Qabaash supplied. "There is no one else to hold the country together, just a bunch of corrupt tribal and sectarian idiots who'll pull us apart. And no, I don't mean random terrorism; I mean civil *war.*"

Carrera and McNamara tactfully refrained from mentioning that civil war in Sumer was potentially just another employment opportunity for the *Legion del Cid.* Besides, they really did want to win the war in Sumer. It wasn't as if there would be a lack of other employment opportunities, after all, not in the long run.

"*Il hamdu l'illah!*" exclaimed Qabaash. To God be the praise.

Carrera looked back at the screen. The precincts for Babel had begun to report in. The few initial reports quickly became a cascade. Mentally echoing Qabaash, he thought, *Thank you, God or Allah, or whatever name You prefer to go by.*

Turning to Sada, Carrera offered his hand. "Congratulations, Mr. President."

The hookers' warbling grew to a torrent of sound to compete with the thunder of slapped backs and smashed crystal.

Executive Mansion, Hamilton, FD, Federated States of Columbia, 12/1/467 AC

James K. Malcolm should have been president. Everything he'd ever done in his life, from serving in the armed forces, to taking initially unpopular antiwar and progressive stands, to his series of marriages to increasingly wealthy and connected women, to being photographed windsurfing off the coast of Botulph;

everything had been geared to one sole end, that he should rest his feet on the presidential desk and guide the country to his version of a progressive future.

But it had not yet come. He'd had his chance and blown it almost three and a half decades before he'd made his runs. Twice he'd tried. The second time he'd even failed of nomination, despite his latest wife's money and even a substantial portion of his own. He'd been offered the vice-presidential slot and turned it down, instead taking the job of secretary of war, an infinitely more important job than vice-president as long as the country was at war. He had one more chance at the office of president, and SecWar seemed the best place to spend his time before he took that chance.

And to do that, I need to be remembered as the man who ended the war in Sumer. Moreover, I need the extreme Progressives to see me as the man who surrendered. I also need to be seen as the man who disengaged favorably by the Independents. And I need to do that without at the same time looking *like I surrendered to the Federalists.*

I also need to be the one who oversees final victory in Pashtia. For that is what will be remembered in eight years.

After having been announced via intercom by the receptionist, Malcolm politely knocked at the door to the president's office, then waited patiently to be asked in. When he entered he affected not to notice that the president was rearranging his trousers even as a female intern was reapplying her lipstick.

After a second's more fussing with his belt line the president stood and advanced, offering his hand. The intern slipped out a side door.

"Good of you to come by, James," President Karl Schumann said as the two shook hands by the desk. "Please have a seat." Schumann indicated a couch on the other side of the Trapezoid, as the presidential office was known.

After Malcolm had seated himself, and Schumann had taken a chair opposite, the president asked, "What are we going to do about Sumer and Pashtia?"

"As far as Sumer goes, Karl, we can do pretty much as we like. Their election two weeks ago of a man who has expressly vowed to get rid of the parliamentary constitution we gave them fairly well absolves us of any further obligations there. On the other hand, I am reliably informed that that man, Adnan Sada, *is* very capable and *very* ruthless and quite possibly doesn't need any more support from us. Win-win, and we can start pulling out in a couple of months."

"All to the good," Schumann agreed. "What about Pashtia?"

"That one we must fight out," Malcolm said. "It's the only campaign in the war that has strong bipartisan support. Moreover, the last administration, mostly by virtue of invading Sumer and sucking up jihadi money and fighters that would otherwise have gone to Pashtia, made Pashtia look like it was won already."

"And wasn't it?"

"No, Karl," Malcolm said. "With Sumer lost to them, the *Ikhwan* know they must fight it out in Pashtia or give up all claim to legitimacy. Moreover, the money and fighters that used to go to Sumer will now go there. Worse, they have developed other sources of funding. Worst of all, the programs the last administration tried to use to interfere with that funding we caused to be destroyed to discredit the Federalists in order to regain power. We can hardly use those programs ourselves."

Schumann chuckled. "Are you really a man of principle, James? Is that even possible? Never mind; the same media who undermined the last president to get us back into power will completely ignore anything we do that helps us stay in power."

"I'm not so sure of that, Karl."

"Never mind that, either, James. *I* am sure. The press has a price though."

Malcolm cocked his head, inquisitively.

"The mercenary group from Balboa must go. The editor of the *First Landing Times* was explicit about that."

"Oh, Mr. President, they're *going*."

Camp Balboa, Ninewa, 25/1/467 AC

Carrera had known what was coming, at least in rough outline. This explained why he had had VIP quarters assigned to Virgil Rivers and a dusty tent with an unmattressed cot to the assistant deputy undersecretary of war, the disgustingly fat Kenneth O'Meara-Temeroso. Rivers, being a gentleman, had, of course, protested. Carrera had answered, "It's the quarters you're assigned or the guard house for both of you." Rivers had then immediately walked in the direction of the guard house before being escorted back to his quarters.

"He'll get even for that, Pat," Rivers said, later that evening, over drinks in Carrera's adobe brick bungalow. The quarters were fairly cool in themselves, made more so by a small and straining window air conditioner and several overhead fans. Rivers was a little surprised to see that his own, temporary, VIP quarters were considerably more ornate and comfortable than Carrera's permanent hooch. He didn't know that the VIP quarters were actually the ones Carrera had shared with Lourdes.

Carrera shrugged. "What's he going to do that he isn't going to do anyway? Don't sweat it, Virg; I'm just getting my digs in first. He *is* here to fire us, right?"

Rivers just nodded, half saddened and half embarrassed.

"Oh . . . cheer up, for Christ's sake. It isn't like there's much to do here anymore. Sada—he's the Sumeri we've been working with since shortly after the beginning—anyway, Sada wants to hire one reinforced cohort of about two thousand men as a backup reaction force. I'll give him a cut rate, something I would never do for your SecWar. That will help pay the bills. And then I think there may be some private contracts here and there from people who need a little muscle. Have to see how that rolls out, though. In any case, we have enough to get by on until the FS realizes it *needs* us again."

"That won't be long," Rivers said. "One of the big advantages you've got is your troops are well trained and well equipped, but they're not spoiled. You can get by in a logistically austere environment better than FS troops can. I give it eighteen months and we'll be begging to hire you."

Carrera agreed, "Yes, we need about a third to a half the transport an FS division does. So, again yes, we're better suited to a place— Pashtia, say—without good road, rail or ports. As for Pashtia, do you really think it will take eighteen months?"

"Maybe not," Rivers conceded.

Carrera checked his watch. "Virg, I'm accompanying a Cazador maniple on a raid tomorrow morning at o-dark thirty. It's more of a training opportunity than a serious problem but I really need to hit the rack now. A driver will be parked outside all night. I won't offer you the full hospitality of the camp but I will point out that the O' and C' Club has several dozen women available for hire."

Rivers held his hands up in mock terror, then said, "Tempting, but no thanks."

"Up to you. We should be done by noon or so. I'll see you and his lowliness tomorrow about fourteen thirty; will that suit?"

"Just fine."

The next morning O'Meara-Temeroso awoke and discovered he had not, after all, slept alone. Filthy, and having no clue about communal washing facilities, he scratched at his obscenely obese and smelly flesh in rage and misery until Rivers found him and drove him to his own quarters and the blessed shower.

Seeing the comfort which with Rivers had spent the night enraged O'Meara-Temeroso even more. After that, the bureaucrat was not only frantically scratching; he was spitting with fury. Rivers made no comment, but merely pointed to the shower and handed the assistant deputy undersecretary of war a bar of harsh but fast-acting flea soap. To add injury to deliberate insult, the soap burned like the devil, especially around the more tender spots.

Thus, when Rivers and O'Meara-Temeroso arrived at the camp and legion headquarters, and were escorted to Carrera's office, the undersecretary was almost apoplectic with anger, rage and hate. Carrera could see a vein throbbing in his head.

The undersecretary proceeded to spit out, "You're fired, you fascist mercenary bastard. Do you hear me? EFF-EYE-ARR-EEE-DEE. FIRED! When your contract runs out in three months there will be no more, d'ya hear me? No more! Moreover, we're going to pay whatever is due you directly to your sponsoring government. You can go to them to beg for scraps from the table."

Click.

Carrera smiled serenely. He admonished, "Please, Mr. Undersecretary; control yourself. Three months, you say? That's no problem. Since you have just announced a material breach of our contract this legion will be gone from Sumer in two weeks. Oh, we'll have to turn over some of our equipment and supplies to the Sumeris; that or burn them. Never fear though. We'll keep track and when you come looking to hire us again everything you've cost us will be added to our fee, with interest from today. Hope you appreciate having to send an additional FS division over here in a hurry even though your administration promised to draw down the war."

The serene smile became positively radiant.

"Good day to you, sir. You can thank General Rivers that I haven't had you shot. But before you leave answer one question; is your name O'Meara-Temeroso because your mother wasn't quite sure who your father was and just decided to split the difference?"

Xamar, 9/2/467 AC

The tough part had been coming up with a single sailor from the Yamatan ship, *Tojo Hidecki Maru*, willing to beg for his life. Twenty-one of the twenty-two captives had simply glared at their captors, returning curses and spit for kicks and blows. Courage was perhaps the most notable trait for the Yamatans. With no other audience to their bravery, they endured for the sake of their ancestors.

One had been younger and weaker. After beating him mercilessly, tearing out his finger- and toenails, crushing his testicles, and applying flame to the soles of his feet, that Yamatan had been turned into a weeping, pleading caricature of a man. He begged for the camera now.

In mid-plea a single shot rang out. In the camera's view the sailor's head exploded in gory technicolor. The body flopped bonelessly to the tiled floor and twitched. The firer raised his rifle over his head and shouted, *"Allahu Akbar!"*

The camera shifted angle to the leader of a Xamari pirate band. The chief's head and face were covered. He spoke no Japanese and so made his announcement in English.

"You were warned. That was one. We hold another twenty-one of your sailors. Meet our just demands or those will also be killed at a rate of one per day, beginning tomorrow at sunrise. The rate—either of payment or of execution—will not change. If you pay us our just demand of twenty-two million FSD by this evening, the remaining twenty-one will be released unharmed. If you do not pay before twenty days have

passed, it will cost you the same amount but all you
will receive is the last man and the bodies of the
other twenty-one. The choice is yours."

Within a few hours copies of the tape were on their
way to Yamato . . . and *al Iskandaria* news.

MV *Uhuru Mercy*, off the Xamar Coast, 12/2/467 AC

To the four hundred and seventy-four crew of the
Mercy there was no choice. Rather, the choices were
either continuing on, canceling their mission to the
small and impoverished Uhuran state of Mpende, asking
one of the world's navies to grant an escort, or hiring armed guards themselves. Abjuring violence, they
chose, not without a certain nobility, to remain true
to their principles and continue on, without escort or
guards, and even with the warning that piracy along
the Xamar coast was growing completely out of hand.

There was no large cross—hateful symbol to the
pirates—to mark the ship. Neither was there a large
red star. The cross would have been little more than
an aiming point but the star would have declared the
ship quite off limits.

The Xamari pirates came at night, a night virtually
without moonlight. The engines of their three small
craft were muffled. They had arms in their hands.

Their boats, too, had been muffled, with rubber
inner tube bumpers around the prow to absorb the
shock and sound of coming close alongside a target
ship. The boats' captains eased back on the throttles as
they came alongside, matching speed with the *Mercy*.

At each boat's prow a man stood with a grapnel and

rope. These they swung to a blur before launching them upward. Two of the three took hold immediately. The third took two tries before it found purchase.

As fast as the grapples were set, other men, one per rope, scampered upward bearing rope ladders on their backs. A single good climber, armed but otherwise unencumbered, followed the ladder bearers and stood guard while the ladders were affixed.

It all went very smoothly after that. A dozen men climbed up one rope ladder, fifteen up a second, nineteen up the third. Once assembled on the deck their leader, a son of Abdulahi by a not very important wife, gave his last minute instructions.

"Go forth from top to bottom. Capture all and assemble them here. Kill only when you can't help it or when the infidels disobey. Rape none of them; there will be a fair division of spoils later. Report to me here when you have found the ship's safe. Destroy none of the medical equipment or supplies; they can be sold. Now go forward and do your duty by your clan and your faith."

UEPF *Spirit of Peace*, 13/2/467 AC (Old Earth Year 2521)

Going after the filthy capitalists, down below, was one thing. After all, how much sympathy could one summon for a class always eager to underbid each other for the rope that would be used to hang them all? But going after nongovernmental organizations, the shaft of Robinson's spear; that was something else again.

"It's pretty depressing," observed *Peace's* captain, Marguerite Wallenstein. "Bad enough that the local office of Amnesty, Interplanetary was defanged. What do we do when one part of our overall program attacks another?"

Robinson nodded his head glumly at the tall blonde. Though Wallenstein was approximately a century and a half old, antiagathic treatments kept her looking, and acting—in bed at least—like a twenty-five year old. Overall, Robinson much preferred her to the other crew with which he made do from time to time.

"Depressing is hardly strong enough," he said with disgust.

The news was all over television, down below. Likewise, the local net was eaten up with it; a hospital ship captured, its safe robbed, a dozen of its crew butchered for the cameras. Even now the broadcasts showed a long line of impressed civilians in the former capital of Xamar unloading everything from crates of morphine and antibiotics to X-ray machines to cots.

Worse, the captors had announced that unless ransom was paid the crew would be auctioned off as slaves. Since the going ransom was what had become the standard of late, a million FSD a head, no one who was willing to pay was also in a financial position to. No more was Robinson, even had he been inclined.

On the other hand, the new progressive administration in the Federated States, which *did* have the wherewithal to pay, simply could not for political reasons.

Wallenstein rested her chin on slender, graceful hands. "The cheapest way to get them back, you know, would be to send someone to bid on them ourselves. They couldn't go for more than twenty or thirty thousand FSD each, not at open auction."

Robinson smiled. "Aren't you clever, Marguerite? But that's still more than we can lightly pay. This fleet operates on a shoestring, as you know as well as anyone."

"Not us . . . but what if we drop a hint in a friendly ear?"

"Whose ear? The World League couldn't even pay that; it might mean they'd no longer be able to have servants to fill the water carafes at their meetings. The Taurans aren't interested since the crew is Columbian. And the progressives in the FSC would be turned out of office if they paid or even if they bid."

Wallenstein began to smirk, then snicker, and finally to chuckle.

"What's so funny?" asked Robinson.

"Well . . . I was just imagining the World League killing two birds with one stone. They bid on the captives but then keep them as slaves to fill the water carafes at the meetings."

Though Wallenstein was joking, Robinson considered it seriously for half a minute. Sighing, he answered, "Nah . . . they'd need to keep them either at the headquarters in First Landing or at the other one in Helvetia. Slavery's illegal both places."

"I was only *joking*," Wallenstein insisted.

"In any case, the problem appears insoluble without intervention. No, not the problem with these captives. They really matter for little, whatever happens to them. But we must damage Terra Novan commerce even while the Kosmo movement damages the social cohesion of its nations. Make me an appointment with Mustafa, would you Marguerite? And have my shuttle prepared to bring me to Atlantis Base for that appointment."

Parade Field, *Isla Real*, Balboa, 13/2/467

It had actually taken closer to three weeks, rather than the two Carrera had said it would, to pull the deployed legion out of Sumer. At that, they'd left a bit under twenty percent of its strength—one reinforced cohort—behind to serve as a palace-guard-of-last-resort for Sada as he assumed the extraordinarily dangerous job of President of the Republic.

Even then, it wasn't precisely a moneymaking arrangement for Carrera. Sada and Sumer just couldn't afford to pay what the FSC had paid. Instead, they paid only the operational costs. Fortunately for all concerned, these were low now since the serious fighting had ended.

"Adnan," Carrera had told Sada, "look at it this way; it isn't a gift. I'm not losing any money on the deal. Besides, you're our ally. We have few enough in the world that we're not about to let one go under. Besides, I just *hate* to lose."

Less that not-quite-twenty-percent, the rest of the legionaries were back in Balboa in time to celebrate the sixth anniversary of their baptism of fire back at Multichucha Ridge in Sumer. That celebration had begun with a parade. The parade was now ending.

"Pass in review," ordered the legionary adjutant.

Immediately the drums picked up a marching beat, followed by the pipes playing "The Muckin' o' Geordies' Byre." The order was repeated and modified by the cohort and maniple commanders.

"Maniple . . . forward . . . mark time . . . right wheel . . . mark time . . . forward . . . MARCH," carried down the serried ranks.

Cruz stood in the first rank of his maniple, fourth from the right, next to Arredondo. His eyes scanned the reviewing stands for signs of his wife and children but, with the stands packed to capacity and then some with well-wishers and close family come to give the returned legion a good homecoming reception, there was no way to pick out one small cinnamon woman and two still smaller children from the mass. *No matter; I'll find them when the parade's dismissed.*

Cruz heard the maniple commander call out, "Maniple . . . right wheel . . . MARCH."

He stepped off as did the rest of the unit, but adopted a half step to keep the front rank relatively dressed. The half step continued until the wheel was complete. At that point, all moved out with a full step down the field. At the right edge, as the troops faced, there was a shiny coffee can lid nailed to the ground. Here the commander ordered, "Left wheel . . . MARCH." Another thirty meters on there was another shiny lid. Here the unit wheeled left yet again. At that point they were very close to the pipes and drums. Whatever randomness was in their step, and the legions didn't practice parading all that much so there was some, was beaten out of them by the heavily pounding drums. As the maniple approached the band and reviewing stands, and the music and the "ooohs" and "ahhhhs" from the crowd grew, the legionaries threw their shoulders back and walked even more proudly erect. Cocks of the walk, indeed.

Instead of eagles, maniples carried small upraised palms atop their guidons. Cruz saw the palm rise on the commander's preparatory command, "EYES . . ." The entire maniple gripped the slings of their rifles with their left hands, freeing their rights. When they saw the palm and pole drop parallel to the ground on the order, "RIGHT," they turned their heads toward the stand and brought their right hands up to salute.

On the stand, Parilla and Carrera—Carrera to the left—returned the salutes and held them until the guidon had passed. Once the two leaders had dropped their own salutes, the maniple commander ordered, "READY . . . FRONT." Immediately, salutes dropped, right hands returned to rifle slings, left arms lowered to the sides to swing normally and eyes returned to the front. From that point, it was only a question of marching off, and meeting the families. There was no need to turn in individual weapons; in the legions, soldiers were trusted to keep their weapons at home or in the barracks. This was so despite a few suicides and a couple of unfortunate incidents where a legionary had come home to find out his wife had not been all that lonely in his absence.

Cruz's mind was just beginning to dwell upon unpleasant possibilities when he felt a light and gentle tap on his shoulder. He turned around and . . .
Holy shit!
Cara was there. So were the children. So were two women he didn't recognize. The two unknown women, however, were with a couple of men he *did* recognize.
"*Señores!*" he said, bracing to attention and saluting.
Both Carrera and Parilla returned the salute; then Carrera reached over and took Cruz's rifle from his shoulder.
Smiling, Carrera said, "See to your family, Centurion.

I think *Duque* Parilla and I are competent to watch your rifle for you for a while. I'll have my driver drop it by your quarters this evening."

Later—*much* later—in bed, Cruz asked Cara, "Where did you meet Parilla and Carrera?"

Cara snuggled into his shoulder and answered, "Actually I'd never met them before today. But the day you went off to the war the first time, when I saw you off at the airport, Lourdes Carrera—well, actually her name was Nuñez-Cordoba back then— and Mrs. Parilla were nearby when I started to cry. They came over to comfort me and we all ended up crying together. They saw me and the kids outside the reviewing stand and invited us up. That's where I met the *duques*."

"Oh."

The couple lay silently for a long time, neither sleeping but both enjoying the warm feeling of being together again; that, and the afterglow from making love. Admittedly, this separation had been much shorter than most. Still, Cruz had been away at the war for two and a half of the last six years and had spent more than half the remainder training in the field. More than three quarters separation in the first six years of marriage would have done—indeed, had done—for many marriages. That theirs had lasted so well so far was mostly attributable to Caridad. Even so . . .

"Ricardo?"

"Si, mi amor."

"When this enlistment is up . . ." She hesitated, nervously, before continuing, "when this enlistment is up, could you consider getting out?"

"I'll have to think about it, *corazon*. I'm forty percent of the way to earliest retirement. That would be
a lot of money to throw away."

"You can't spend it when you're dead, Ricardo."
Count on a woman to come up with a reasonable
answer. *Dammit.*

Puerto Lindo, Balboa, 14/2/467 AC

Carrera could be pretty damned unreasonable. He had
given Fosa, *Dos Lindas'* skipper and commander of
the *classis*, eighty-seven days, from commissioning to
first sailing. This would probably have been impossible
except that Fosa had begun training nearly four months
prior to commissioning and for certain elements, pilots
and maintenance crews, three months before that.

It would be another three months, too, before the
ship was expected to be fully operational. Oh, yes, each
of the parts worked. The pilots could take off and land
from the short, narrow and pitching deck. The aircraft
maintenance personnel were fully capable of keeping
the planes serviceable. The deck crews could recover the
planes and strike them below; or refuel them and rearm
them on deck. The navigators could navigate; the cooks
could cook; the black gang could oversee and keep up
the reactor and the generators. Intel was getting fairly
deft at incepting radio and cell phone transmissions,
along with the more routine intelligence gathering skills.
The demi-battalion of Cazadors was perhaps the most
ready of the ship's divisions, as there was really nothing
important aboard ship that changed things when they
got to the land: load helicopters, fly, dismount; then
spot, capture or kill; then reload and go home.

Simulators and training exercises aboard ship helped, of course. And there was one simulator for every third aircraft except the remotely piloted ones. For those, their normal control stations with a simulator program loaded were sufficient. Moreover, all the simulators were linked onto the ship's main computer so that entire exercises could be run without ever leaving port.

The Cazadors could not be fully linked into that simulation system, though the leaders could, after a fashion. Instead, every fourth or fifth night for the last month, they'd launched from the stationary ship via helicopter to raid some or another spot ashore. Most of the rest of the time, when not spent planning a raid, the Cazadors trained on the limited training facilities of the *Academia Militar* Sargento Juan Malvegui; there or at Fort Tecumseh, on the other side of the Transitway to the east.

Underway replenishment, or UNREP, had not been practiced. The nearest the *Dos Lindas'* skipper could come was to force resupply through the means that would be available at sea; via air and from ship to ship. This was a substantially different undertaking, though, in the calm waters of *Puerto Lindo*, than it would have been in a Force Twelve hurricane. (Actually, *nobody* tried doing UNREP in Force Twelve. Fosa intended to give it a shot, though.)

In any case, none of it could yet be said to work together properly, under exactly realistic conditions. They'd not yet really tried.

Tonight, with almost no moonlight and bay lit only by the lights of town, the shipyard, and the military academy, that would change.

It began to change as soon as *Dos Lindas'* skipper,

Roderigo Fosa, turned to his executive officer and ordered, "Take her out, Tribune."

High Admiral's Quarters, Atlantis Base, 19/2/467 AC

In the end, Mustafa had refused to travel unless the UEPF sent a shuttle for him. Even a private charter was impossible, especially so as—whatever their other failings, national security-wise, were concerned—the FSC's Progressive administration was even more fanatically dedicated to getting *him* than even the Federalists had been. Mustafa didn't know that the Progressives were so determined to get him precisely so they could have an excuse to call off the war. There had been days when, had he known this, he might just have turned himself in, if only in order to take pressure off of his movement to allow it to rebuild from the twin disasters of Pashtia in 460, Sumer beginning in 461, and continuing on to the current day.

The shuttle, a pumpkin-seed shape, had come almost silently in the night, to a spot Mustafa had picked that would be safe from prying eyes. There he had boarded through the lit rectangle of the hatch, been strapped in by the crew chief—an act Mustafa felt deep down to be highly impious—and then been flown at a very high speed to the UEPF's base colony on the island of Atlantis, in the middle of the *Mar Furioso*. A darkened limousine bought by the UEPF from Sachsen had picked him up at the landing field and whisked him briskly to the high admiral's quarters.

Most Salafis, most Arabs or Moslems of whatever sect, would have spent anywhere from hours to days in small talk, beating around the bush, before getting to the point. Mustafa was not like that. Perhaps it was his nature, perhaps merely because he was not a well man and felt he might have little enough time left. Whatever the case; when Robinson went directly to the point Mustafa picked right up without further waste of time.

"You've got to stop this decentralized mayhem, to assert real control over your movement, and to begin to seriously plan, not just leave everything up to the will of your god," Robinson began, after the usual, but curt, greetings.

"I know," Mustafa said, and then lit a cigarette.

"You've got to begin a campaign of finan—what did you say?"

"I said that I know. The *Nazrani* have taught me; Allah helps those who also help themselves. Faith is still key, of course. Yet the Maker of Universes would not have allowed us to fall as low as we have, despite our perfect faith, unless He also wanted us to think, work and plan for our own good, and His."

"Oh . . ." Robinson was momentarily nonplussed. "Well in that case, we can begin to plan and fight a war, together."

"Before that, infidel, tell me why. Why are you willing to help us?" Mustafa raised his hands as if fending off a blow . . . or a lie.

"And do not speak falsely. I know you have no love for us. Not only do you not share our religion you do not share *any* religion."

Robinson poured himself a drink. *And why not? If the Salafi can smoke, a custom I abhor, I can drink.* And, indeed, the Salafi said not a word. That, too, suggested a very changed outlook.

"I don't really care who wins," the high admiral admitted. "Or if anyone does, provided that the Federated States and the civilization they share with the Taurans . . . oh, and Yamato, too, of course . . . provided they all lose. If the cosmopolitan progressives win this planet they will turn it into something that is not dangerous to my home, Earth. If you win you will turn it into something that would not have been dangerous to my world even a thousand years ago. Either is acceptable to me and I see no reason why it would matter if both of you got half a world. I care only that those who could be a threat to my world never become one."

Mustafa, lips pursed, rocked his head from side to side for a minute, thinking about that. "Are you so sure my people could never become a threat?"

"Yes, I am that sure. To be a threat you must travel space. To travel space you must progress technologically. And that kind of progress is everything your movement abhors. That much, at least, you share with the Kosmos. At least your side is honest about it."

Robinson hesitated briefly before adding, "And . . . frankly, the Kosmos have little long-term chance of global success, not here. They only succeeded on Earth because immigration patterns to Terra Nova pulled away more and more of the traditional, religious and nationalist sorts, leaving the Earth behind for my ancestors. There is no new world such people can leave for from here."

Mustafa nodded. That wasn't important. "And you wish to help, more than you helped with the attacks that began this war?"

"I will help more, much more. Still no nukes, though."

Mustafa shrugged an indifference he did not truly feel. *Nuclear weapons . . . what a dream to have them and use them on the* Nazrani *and the atheists.*

"Details?"

"First, I need your support in taking over the direction of the pirates operating off the coast of Xamar and the Straits of Nicobar. They can—"

"Xamar I already control," Mustafa interjected. "The Nicobars listen to no one. I've tried."

"Then the question is whether they should be attacked and brought to heel or if they can be induced by incentives."

"What sort of incentives? And how do you provide incentives to ten thousand men, every one of whom considers himself a chief answerable to no one?"

"By helping one chieftain to become paramount, to rise above all others."

Isla Santa Josefina, Balboa, 20/2/467 AC

Montoya loved flying. He'd hardly imagined, as not much more than a boy standing in a legion enlistment line, the power and the freedom and the sheer joy of *flight*. Though he'd known then that the legion had, or at least intended to have, aircraft, he'd *never* imagined himself actually conning one. What was he? Just a poor farm boy from the interior. Who was he to think he'd someday be a pilot?

But the *Legion del Cid* was an equal opportunity employer, he'd found. It was also a miserly employer of human talent. While he'd not shown any remarkable leadership ability at Cazador School, he had shown toughness, determination, and at least a modicum of brains. He could be taught. Moreover, when he'd been talked into volunteering for some hit missions by Cruz, he'd shown considerable personal courage and determination. There were places in the legion for people like that. In Montoya's case, that place had eventually come to be in a cockpit. And he just loved it.

What he hated, though, were the carrier takeoffs and the landings. Those scared him silly. Every time.

No, not landings on the ground, even on pretty rough ground; he'd had lots of experience in those, flying a Cricket. His plane could take it, no problem. On the other hand, landing or taking off from a pitching, weaving, postage-stamp-on-the-ocean? Trying to catch the arrestor cables? Reversing thrust at the last minute so he didn't overshoot and end up crushed or drowned—most likely, both—under the prow? Trying to time his take off so that he hit the leading edge of the flight deck on an upswing? (The deck crew was becoming a big help there, though, he had to admit; especially as they gained experience.) That sinking feeling as the plane dropped almost like a rock as he left the flight deck behind? Gag . . . shiver . . . barf.

He shivered again, half at the memory of the last takeoff when his landing gear had plowed furrows in the ocean before pulling up and half at foreboding over the next landing.

It got progressively worse, too. It seemed like the skipper was actually *looking* for rough seas and bad weather to launch in. They'd lost one pilot already, and cracked up both that plane and a Yakamov-72 helicopter. At least the Yakamov crew had gotten out.

From this and other evils, deliver me, O Lord.

In some ways, Montoya wished he'd been picked to

fly a Cricket, as he used to, rather than a Turbo-Finch Avenger, usually called a Finch. With the *Dos Lindas* facing into the wind, and even a mild headwind, the Crickets took off practically straight up. And for landing, their stall speed wasn't much above the carrier's cruise speed. Piece o' cake.

On the other hand, Crickets don't generally fight. I'd prefer to fight, even if getting to and from the fight soils my flight suit. And speaking of which . . .

The island—the *Isla Santa Josefina*—loomed out of the gloomy dusk ahead. Montoya adjusted his throttle to pick up speed, veered a little left, then right, and mentally reviewed his firing run. Trees began near the water's edge. A slight pull back on his stick, then an equally slight push forward, lifted the Finch and set it on a heading and altitude that would allow its fixed landing gear to *just* skim over the trees.

The central hill dominating the *Isla Santa Josefina* lay ahead. Again Montoya eased back on the stick, causing the plane to just miss the jungle below. He felt a pressure in the seat of his trousers. As soon as the plane cleared the summit, Montoya pushed forward to drop the nose, causing his stomach to lurch.

There's the target.

Ahead, in Montoya's view, three old, rusty armored vehicles sat in the open. As he aimed the plane by feel, his thumb flipped off the safety cover on the firing button over his stick and began to press. With each press of the thumb two rockets, one from under each wing, lanced out. As soon as he had bracketed the target Montoya pulled the stick to the right. The nimble Finch acted like the crop-duster it was and turned away athletically.

Damned good thing, too, thought Montoya. Looking to the left he saw the next bird in the training attack was firing almost before he had cleared away.

The *Isla Santa Josefina* had been purchased by the legion as a range. No one actually lived there for the excellent reason that the Federated States had used it as a chemical warfare testing ground during the Great Global War and never spent a drachma or expended an ounce of sweat cleaning it up afterward. It had come to the legion pretty cheaply.

The legion hadn't spent much on it either. It had decontaminated a small landing area for boats and a couple of observation posts. Nearer the center of the island a few target spots in the impact area had been cleared. Cleared paths connected the landing, the OPs and the target spots. The rest was not only presumed to be at least somewhat chemically toxic, and much of that contamination being with very persistent nerve and blister agents, but had had an absolutely amazing amount of ordnance dumped on it over the last several years from the main island, the *Isla Real*, as well as three much smaller islands purchased to serve as firing positions for mortars and artillery. The new ordnance, too, had the effect of breaking open some of the three thousand dud chemical warheads believed to be still on *Santa Josefina*, either at the surface or just below it.

Even the few people, forward observers for the artillery the most part, that went there, went with full chemical protection—suits, rubber booties, gloves and masks.

✧   ✧   ✧

The *Dos Lindas* couldn't see either island, not even from its own island on the starboard center of the flight deck. It could, however, see the mass confusion on the flight deck as the crew attempted to crowd seventeen Cricket Bs and five of the Yakamovs in position to load troops and take off. It really shouldn't be as hard as they were making it look.

No matter, thought Fosa. *Practice makes perfect and they'll practice until they puke and drop.*

Though said to be "slightly modified" the B models were actually fairly substantial modifications of the basic Cricket. The cabin had been lengthened and widened to allow four (or if they were feeling *really* friendly, five) passengers. The wingspan had also been increased by about thirty centimeters a side. The single engine in the nose was taken out and replaced by two slightly smaller and individually less powerful ones on the wings. Also, and this was important given the mission, the two smaller engines were slightly *quieter,* together, than the original single was, alone. In the nose had been placed a fairly sophisticated thermal imager *cum* ground sensor for recon and for limited visibility landings. In addition, to either side of the engines were hardpoints, four in total, for rocket and machine gun pods. Underneath was a single hardpoint to which could be attached a light homing torpedo, just in case one of the Yakamov ASW helicopters happened to find a submarine where no submarine ought be.

Fosa and the commander of the Cazadors, Tribune Cherensa, had arranged for an opposing force at one of the training areas on the *Isla Real.* That was where the Crickets and Yakamovs were heading, once this batch of Cazadors was boarded. Twenty B models and five Yakamovs weren't quite enough to move the entire demi-battalion in one lift. A further three platoons and the unit's four Ferret light armored vehicles still waited below, assembled on the hangar deck.

The skipper looked out from the open bridge at the lead Cricket. He recognized Cherensa standing beside the plane. Cherensa saluted, which salute Fosa returned. Then the Cazador boarded his Cricket.

Picking up a radio microphone that looked more like an old-fashioned telephone receiver, Fosa gave Cherensa and the deck crew the time-honored command, "Land the landing force."

High Admiral's Quarters, Atlantis Base, 20/2/467 AC

It was really all very sickening to Mustafa, though he tried to hide it.

But the more Robinson explained, the more the Salafi realized how badly he had screwed up the war, to date, and how much had to be done to redeem it.

Robinson tried to be gentle with the Salafi, downplaying mistakes as much as possible while still making the point.

"You saw only Pashtia, the Federated States and the Tauran Union, Mustafa," the high admiral had said. "You assumed that, because the attacks originated in Pashtia that the FSC would only attack Pashtia. You assumed that all the mujahadin would come to Pashtia to fight. You thought that, because it was a place where there were no railroads, hardly any roads, no ports, no navigable rivers, and few good airfields, the FSC would not be able to support any very large army there. You were correct in this, of course. You thought that you could meet what they could support there on fairly equal terms. This, too, would have been correct had they elected to meet you there only. You forgot that they were able to attack somewhere else, somewhere closer to your holiest city, somewhere that would attract the *mujahadin* away from Pashtia, where they might have fought on more even terms, to Sumer, where the Feds held all the cards."

Mustafa could only accept it for it was nothing but the truth. He knew now that there had been other mistakes in plenty.

"I never even considered it as a possibility that Kashmir would turn against us, or even play a neutral part," he admitted. "I thought the Federated States would grow sick of the killing after they'd lost a couple of hundred soldiers. I counted on Allah doing too much, forgetting that he cuts the coat to fit the man, or that he might demand more of us than that we fight and be willing to die. The *Nazrani* have taught me though, and taught me well."

"You know I do not believe in your god, Mustafa. But, accepting for the moment his existence, let me tell you something a wise man of Old Earth once said. 'God is not willing to do everything and thus take away from us our free will and that share of the glory that belongs to us.' Within that man's mental framework, he was right, and you would be well advised to follow his teachings.

"It is a truth of war," Robinson continued, "that groups in conflict tend to come to resemble each other. This is true tactically, technologically, and morally. You have learned from the FSC not to trust everything to God. What do you suppose they've learned from you? How have they become like you?"

Mustafa thought upon this for a long time before answering. When he did answer, he said, "They have learned to use terror, as well. In fact, they have learned to do it better than we do. We've knocked one country out of their unholy coalition, Castille. They've knocked out at least four from what should have been ours, Sumer, Pashtia, Kashmir by threatening genocide and Fezzan by threatening to extinguish its leader and his family."

"Those, yes," the high admiral agreed. "Other places, too. More than that, faced with a non-state adversary like yourselves, they have also learned to use and develop non-state allies."

"Those stinking Latin mercenaries."

"Well . . . following the same man who wrote about God and free will, they're not technically mercenaries. But, yes . . ."

"I think," said Mustafa, finally, on this, the last day of his conference with Robinson, "I think that we are agreed on all the important things."

"Yes," said Robinson, then recapitulated, "You will, with my help, gain complete control of your movement. This will leave you potentially more vulnerable to attack but will also make your own attacks make sense in the larger plan for the first time. Serious attacks on the FSC will end, though planning will continue. Within the FSC, you will build a group of supporters for when the time comes to renew attacks there."

"Agreed."

"You will make peace with the Royal Family in

Yithrab. Active operations there will end so that you can continue to draw financing."

That was tougher. Mustafa *loathed* the Yithrabi government and longed to see it gone, but . . . "Agreed."

"To increase financing, I will take operational control of the pirates along the Xamar coast. Using the intelligence assets available to my fleet, I will guide Abdulahi to seize those ships most likely to yield good return and to intimidate the shipping companies into paying protection. When and if the time seems suitable, I will send a totally inadequate number of UE Marines to 'control' the coast and suppress piracy. They will, of course, fail to do so, but will help secure Abdulahi's position as paramount chieftain." *Especially will they be inadequate and fail because half my Marines have been sent back to Earth.*

"Agreed."

"Within one month, you will identify to me one lesser pirate emir in Nicobar. We will both then throw our efforts behind him to make him the paramount chieftain of the Nicobars. Then we will do with them as we intend to do along the Xamar coast."

"This will be tougher, you know?"

"It might be *impossible*," Robinson agreed, "but we must try."

"Yes. We must also try to get rid of those mercenaries."

"This is especially true," Robinson added, "since they have begun to develop a fleet which just may be aimed at the Xamari and Nicobars. For now, though, they appear to be unemployed and out of the war."

The high admiral continued, "Within Pashtia the first prong of our strategy will be to ensure control of the opium crop and that there will be a crop. This not only helps finance your movement; the crop ultimately helps to undermine the FSC. The second prong will be to go after the Pashtian collaborators who assist the FSC's coalition and terrorize them into supporting you while at the same time engaging and driving away the FSC's lesser and unwilling allies like Tuscany and Gaul. The third will be to drive out of the war the FSC's willing allies, Anglia and Secordia, by engaging their forces and driving their casualties up to politically unacceptable levels."

Mustafa, who had better intelligence on the Anglians and Secordians than Robinson did, commented, "Their troops always seem willing enough to fight."

"No matter, their politicians and most of their people really want out. Kill enough and they will leave. Moreover, while random terror has not worked with the FSC or Anglia, it has worked with Castille, appears to be working in Gaul and may well work to drive Sachsen out of the war."

"I agree about the others, but with the Anglians there is a problem even if it did work," the Salafi objected. "Without the Anglians and the Secordians, the Federated States might just rehire the mercenaries and they have proved *much* more effective."

Robinson shook his head. "Not for four years, at least, and possibly not for eight or more. As long as the Progressives are in power, the mercenaries are not likely to be hired." Robinson believed he had this on the very best authority. That said; the Khans were not nearly as certain.

The high admiral continued, "After the Anglians and Secordians are gone, and Pashtia has seen the last of the other allies in the coalition, you will begin actively seeking fights with the FSC troops."

"There is something else you can help with," Mustafa said.

Robinson gave the Salafi a quizzical look.

"They rule the air. They can find us from the air. They attack us from—"

"I can't do anything to interfere with that."

"I'm not asking you to. But you can balance things out. From space, surely, you can also tell us where *they* are, no?"

The high admiral went silent for a moment, scrunching his eyes in thought.

After several long moments he answered, "I can get you something to allow you to see our view from over Terra Nova, a direct feed from the fleet's sensors. What you do with that would be up to you."

"That would be sufficient."

"Maybe not quite sufficient," Robinson countered. "If you started sending real-time intelligence to your guerillas, it would be traced to the Peace Fleet. Let me see what I can do about providing you some limited secure communications."

Village of Jameer, Pashtia, 5/3/467 AC,

Noorzad had understood immediately what Mustafa's message meant when he had received it, two days prior. During the Volgan imperial incursion, while Mustafa had been off collecting money and volunteers and living the good life in Kashmir, Noorzad had been at the bleeding edge, putting the theory of resistance warfare to the practical test. He had learned much in that time.

"And about bloody time, too," Noorzad said, to no one in particular.

Still, Malakzay, trudging along nearby, had heard. "What was that?"

"About bloody time," the one-eyed bandit chieftain repeated. "About bloody time Mustafa began to direct and control the jihad. About bloody time we got assigned some missions with a point greater than, 'survive and fight.' About bloody time every little band of mujahadin was not in the war alone. And about bloody time we had a concerted plan to take care of the collaborators."

"I've heard of no plan," Malakzay objected.

"It's suggested by the message Mustafa sent; that, and by this mission and by the device the messenger brought."

Malakzay thought upon that. He had to admit that if anyone was likely to be able to tie disparate bits of information together to make a coherent whole, Noorzad was that man.

"Any word from reconnaissance?" Malakzay asked.

"Yes, the village appears effectively disarmed."

The Taurans had an interesting approach to individually owned firearms; they banned them. No one had a right to arms except governments; that was the almost universal Tauran view. Still, they were reasonable. They banned the weapons and then paid for a buyback program. Since the buyback program paid slightly more than replacement cost (and normal Volgan firearms were frightfully cheap), there was no real bar to the local Pashtians selling their, generally poorly maintained, rifles to the Taurans operating in the south of the country and then buying newer ones.

The downside, though, was that once the Taurans had banned rifles and bought them "all" back, they presumed that anyone with a rifle was breaking the law and attempted to arrest them. These arrests usually fell out in one of two ways. If the potential arrestee was a *mujahad*, there would be a firefight which the Taurans were usually barred by their national governments from engaging in. If the arrestee was a simple otherwise harmless civilian, he would submit to arrest and the confiscation of the firearm. Since, however, the civilians did *not* want to give up their arms, they hid them. Sometimes they hid them too well.

The guerilla band entered the village in the dead of night, silent as a plague. In two- to three-man teams, they kicked in the doors and burst into each house on a prearranged signal, a shrill blast of a whistle. Men and women, boys and girls, were herded out into the dusty central square at bayonet point. The women were only just given the chance to cover themselves with whatever was to hand. Stumbling in the darkness, men cursed and the women and children either wept or stood in shocked silence as the mood took them.

Only one of the villagers had had his rifle near to hand. That one was shot as soon as he appeared.

Noorzad left them alone, but guarded, as the bulk of his band went through the village with a fine tooth comb looking for anything that might be of use. They found little; a couple of donkeys to add to the train, some food, a little ammunition. They also found some kerosene and wood.

The guerilla leader left the villagers alone, that is, until the sun had arisen. He wanted them to see clearly what was about to transpire.

"Who is the headman of this village?" he demanded, his one eye glaring in the sun.

Hesitantly, an older man, his beard long and half-gray, raised a hand.

"Where is your family?"

Several other hands were raised, two of them from women with small children clustered around. At a nod from the chief, a half dozen guerillas prodded the rest of the populace away from the headman's family until they stood alone in a distinct cluster.

At another nod, four guerillas seized the village head and dragged him to a wall. He was certain he was going to be shot and begged for the intervention of Allah. He would have been happier had his God intervened and caused the guerillas to shoot him.

First they beat the headman, but only enough to break his will so he would not resist. Still, the guerilla's hardened fists and booted feet bruised him, broke small bones, cut the skin over his skull.

When they were sure enough he would not resist even what was coming, one of them raised the headman's left arm to the wall. A second took a long iron spike with a broad head and held it, point first, to the villager's wrist. A third drove the spike through the wrist and into the wall.

The headman screamed like a lost soul when the cold iron tip drove through the nexus of nerves in his wrist. Unimaginable agony shot through that entire side of his body. The second nail elicited even greater screams.

Unmanned, ashamed, the village headman hung his head and wept.

Then, with the headman quietly weeping and his people in shock, Noorzad began to speak.

"You call yourselves Moslems. Yet I see a school built by the infidels to educate your youth away from the faith of your fathers. You call yourselves Moslem, yet I see that rather than trusting to Allah you have let the infidels dig a well for you." He glanced at the small clinic. "I see you have more faith in infidel medicine than in your God."

"You may keep none of this. Before we take them from you though, see what the price is that your headman will pay for his impiety.

"Bring out the headman's women."

Roughly, the guerillas parted the mothers from their children and forced them to the center of the group. Then they uncovered and took those of the girls who looked to be past the age of nine, forcing these too, into the circle. The first two of the brothers to object, one eleven and one thirteen, were beaten, stunned, dragged to the wall and—shrieking in agony—nailed up beside their father. The others stayed quiet or, like the women, wept as the mood and their age took them.

There were about one hundred guerillas and seven women and girls. The rape went on for a very long time, guerillas taking turns guarding and violating. When they were done, and even had seconds, the guerillas forced the men and boys of the village old enough to sprout a beard to likewise violate the headman's females. By the time they were done, even the youngest girl, a nine-year-old, had ceased to weep.

The nine-year-old didn't weep either, when two of Noorzad's band began to beat her with iron bars, smashing the little bones and pulping her skin, finally spilling out her brain in a shower of splintered bone and blood. She did scream, though. After all, they'd started at her feet.

When they were done with the nine-year-old, the other women were likewise beaten to death. In the end there were just seven piles of blood and bone and ragged scraps of skin.

After that, Noorzad had the villagers tear down their school and their clinic. He also made them pile the firewood at the feet of the headman and his two nailed-up sons.

Then he poured a measure of kerosene and lit the wood. The screams of personal agony which had lessened under the shock of watching their mothers and sisters, wives and daughters, raped and bludgeoned began anew and rose to a crescendo as the flames ate away skin and set subcutaneous fat alight.

As the chief and his sons burned down to greasy ash, Noorzad went around the circle of villagers, choosing from each family group one son to be trained as a fighter and to serve as a hostage. Lastly, he blew up the well.

Noorzad's parting words were, "Now you see the price of cooperating with the infidel. Now you see the price of forsaking your faith. Do not forget. Also do not forget that there are those among you who are also with *us.*"

With that, Noorzad's band trekked into the night.

INTERLUDE

14 August 2080, *Yasukuni-Jinja*, Tokyo, Japan

At night, the scene would have been lit well enough to read a book by the garish neon of the city. In the day things were better. One might even imagine oneself back in a purer, truer time. One could, that is, if not for the large groups of immigrants, many of them recent and few of them much assimilated, who came to the shrine to, in all too many cases, gawk and sneer.

The immigrants were not the only ones capable of sneering. Watanabe Ishihara, for example, sneered at two groups in alternation. The first was Chinese, immigrants from the mainland. The second was Korean, and conversed in Korean, by the simple and elegant *torii*, or Shinto gate, that led to the shrine.

His companion, Shintaro Soichi, caught the sneers and corrected, "Despise the Chinese if you want, Ish. After all, they despise us as much as we despise them, and perhaps more. But the Koreans are a different story. There are almost twenty-two thousand of them here, *our* illustrious fallen *eirei*, our heroic spirits, as much as *theirs*. They have an arguable right to be here. Maybe they have an *in*arguable right to be here."

Watanabe looked down, shamefacedly. Of course Soichi was right. It was just that, "I resent that we have lost, that we are dying out, that everything for which our ancestors strove will belong to those who come to replace us. But, the Koreans, at least, are welcome. Mostly."

"*And* the Taiwanese?"

"Oh, all *right*. Them, too."

Like the rest of the industrialized world, and, to a lesser degree, even much of the non-industrialized world, Japan had seen a precipitous drop in population coupled with a frightening increase in the age of that population and a terrifying decrease in the percentage of that population still working.

Things were never as bad as the doom mongers had predicted, of course. Things never *could* become as bad as they predicted. Even so, they were bad enough. What helped Japan out more than anything was that their old folks were, generally speaking, willing to work until they were carried feet first out of their offices and factories.

This, however, only delayed the inevitable. There came a time when, despite the best will in the world, the older ones simply couldn't work anymore and had to be supported. And with so few young being born, the burden became too great. Japan, like Europe, had had no choice but to permit large-scale immigration. Too, like Europe, Japan couldn't assimilate them.

❖　　　❖　　　❖

"We must take it all with us, when we leave," Soichi said, his gaze sweeping across the expanse of the shrine. "There will be none left behind to pray to the spirits of our *eirei*."

"In principle, I agree," Watanabe shrugged. "But can we fit five thousand colonists? Ten thousand? Maybe twenty thousand, for all this weight of wood and stone and bronze."

"We must take . . ."

"All," Watanabe supplied. "I suppose you're right there, too. And the *sakura*?"

"Cuttings, and perhaps a few trees. And then there are the living national treasures . . ."

"A fair sampling will come," Watanabe said, "As will a prospective Son of Heaven."

"Who?" Soichi asked,

"Higashikuni . . ."

"Oh, damn. Not *that* branch."

"Best I could do. Besides, what difference that his multi-great grandfather was screwing some French whore?"

CHAPTER FIVE

Show me just what Muhammad brought
that was new and there you will find
things only evil and inhuman, such as
his command to spread by the sword
the faith he preached.
— Emperor Manual II Palaiologos

Village of Jameer, Pashtia, 6/3/467 AC

The bodies, or what was left of the bodies, were still
there when the Tauran, specifically the Tuscan, column
arrived, about midday. Flies clustered on those of the
women and girls in thick, black, buzzing clouds. Even
the nine-year-old, legs splayed, appeared to have grown
pubes, so thick were the blood-lapping flies.

Tuscan Brigadier General Claudio Marciano stepped
from his vehicle, took one look, and promptly threw up.

"Animals," he muttered as he wiped traces of
vomit from his lips and face. "Only animals could
do something like this."

Marciano's aide-de-camp, *Capitano* Stefano del
Collea, didn't answer. Instead, standing next to the
vehicle, he simply went pale and shook with hate.

181

The two were mountain troopers, *Ligurini*, members of an elite corps. They were the best infantry Tuscany on Terra Nova produced and some of the best in the world. Other mountain troopers from Marciano's command, the *Brigada Julio Caesare*, worked their way cautiously through the town.

There was no firing as the *Ligurini* swept through, only sullen glares from the villagers. *You promised what you could not deliver. You failed us.* So the villagers' eyes seemed to accuse.

"What the *fuck* can we do, Stefano? With three battalions of infantry here in our sector I don't have enough to put even half a squad in every little village. I don't have enough even to put in a single man."

"We could go hunting," del Collea suggested. "We're better men than they are. They may know *these* mountains but we know *mountains.*"

"It's the only way," Marciano agreed, "The only way and I am forbidden to do it." The general smashed a fist into his palm in sheer frustration. "Forbidden to so much as fire a shot except in point self-defense. 'No offensive operations,' the government says, Stefano. 'Don't risk casualties.' Tell me, Stefano, what the *fuck* is the purpose of even having soldiers if it isn't to risk casualties?"

The captain just shrugged. He was as helplessly frustrated in this as his commander.

Marciano took off his green, feathered hat and wiped his brow. *This was just a demonstration of frightfulness. But the word will get out. By this time tomorrow, day after at the latest, every school and clinic we've built, every well my sappers have dug, will be torn down or filled in. No one will risk this*

*kind of obscenity just to have a nicer building to be
sick in or a western style school desk. All the good
we've thought we'd accomplished will be undone.*

"If I could transfer my commission," del Collea
said, "I'd join the FS Army. They, at least, are allowed
to fight."

"If I could transfer my commission," Marciano
rejoined, "I might join the Balboan mercenaries and
take the entire brigade with me. They go out of their
way to fight."

"They do have mountain troops, you know, General."

"I know . . . but they're not *our* mountain troops.
I would miss the Ligurini, Stefano."

To that the captain had nothing to add. He left his
general to his own thoughts for some minutes. When
Marciano spoke again it was to say, "Fuck 'em."

"General?"

"Fuck the politicians. Tell the commander of the
company— Romano, isn't it?—to follow those sons of
bitches and kill them."

The device Noorzad carried, the same one brought
by the messenger from Mustafa, beeped low. He
answered it.

"Noorzad? Mustafa. Some friends inform me that
there is a company of infantry on your tail."

The device was surprisingly static-free. Though
unmarked, Noorzad was pretty certain it had come
from off world; that, or was an offworld technology
perhaps manufactured on Terra Nova.

"I can handle a company of infantry," the guerilla
chief said.

"Yes, I am sure you can. But you cannot handle

the battalion that will descend from the air if you are found, or the air strikes that will come. They are already gathering."

Unseen by Mustafa, Noorzad shrugged. "I understand. I will split my men up, ditch most of the weapons. We can take shelter in the villages nearby."

"You are not concerned they will turn you in?" Mustafa asked.

"After what we did in Jameer? No; word will have spread like the lightning. They'll be too afraid to go against us."

Escuela de Montañeros Bernardo O'Higgins, Boquerón, Balboa, 8/3/467 AC

Jesus, this shit terrifies me.

Ricardo Cruz had his left hand jammed into the crevice of an otherwise nearly sheer rock wall. The hand was formed into a fist, effectively locking him to that wall. His other hand searched for further purchase higher up while his booted feet rested precariously on a couple of finger-widths of ledge. A rope was coiled around his torso.

Cruz's job was to get the bloody rope up the cliff, attach a snaplink to whatever could be found, and create a belay system so that the rest of the men could follow safely. On the way up Cruz mentally recited the very unofficial and much frowned upon version of the Cazador Creed.

Considering how fucking stupid I am . . .

Aha! There was a little outcropping of rock. He grabbed tight hold of it and began working his left leg to another little spit of a ledge.

Appreciating the fact that nobody lives forever . . .

The ledge and the outcropping held. Heart pounding, Cruz unballed his left fist, removed it from the crevice and began feeling up and along the wall for another place to anchor his hand before he risked moving his lower foot.

Zealously will I . . .

Cruz's foot slipped.

There were actually four legions now, since the last, but probably not final, reorganization. The field legions were numbered I through IV; plus the air *ala* and the naval *classis*, which retained their tercio numbers, and the training and base legion, which was not yet numbered at all. At the moment, two of those legions, I and II, were at or just over full strength. The other two were at roughly seventy percent, for III, and forty percent, for IV.

Under the reorganization, which had been implicit from the start, the *Legion del Cid* would operate on a four-year cycle. While one legion was fighting or ready to go, another was at full strength and training to fight, while a third was building up to full strength and training at lower level unit and individual tasks. A fourth was, practically speaking, broken up with its personnel either in school or supporting school. Since this was the year the married soldiers could actually be home nearly every night, sometimes Carrera referred to the fourth, or school, year as the legion's "Reproduction Enhancement and Divorce Reduction Program."

Legio IV was currently in school, hence the forty percent strength. It would be replaced by *Legio* I after the terms of service of that legion's one-term volunteers ran out. Arguably, during the school year, a legion was not really a legion at all, since it consisted only of cadre and those were mostly in school or supporting the training legion or other units. But, since the school year legion had an Eagle, had a chain of command, had equipment and *would* be filled to strength at some point, it was still considered a legion.

What was not generally considered, outside of by Carrera and his staff, was that, since there was a reserve clause in the enlistment contract, every legion could be brought up to strength in a matter of days. This presupposed that the troops would come back voluntarily as Carrera had no legal way of making them return.

I think that's a safe bet though, Carrera thought. *And besides, their business and student loans all go into default if they fail to answer the summons.*

Legio III's cadre had completed their refresher training the previous year and was in the process of building up to one hundred and five percent strength. *Legio* II was at roughly one hundred and five percent strength, and was working up to divisional operations.

Legio I, recently returned from Sumer, still had seven months left on the enlistment contracts of the sixty percent of its strength that were one-term volunteers. Rather than waste the time, or let the men go slowly crazy from boredom, Carrera had them training. To be more specific, he had them training to return to the war, but in Pashtia.

As a young officer in the Federated States Army, Carrera—then under the name Hennessey—had acquired a fine loathing for general officers. Oh, yes; he'd known a few he thought were better and more useful than sandbags. He'd even known a few he genuinely admired. But those few had been few indeed.

One of the distinguishing marks of worthwhileness, a *sine qua non* of good generalship, in Carrera's view, was that the general ought not let *himself* become a hindrance to training. Since people became, frankly, freaky when a general—or a senior legate or a *dux*—showed up with all his entourage and all his pomp and circumstance, Carrera thought a general could assist training best by, in most cases, seeing while not being seen. Thus, while Cruz inched up the wall, Carrera and Soult hid in a sheltered draw and watched through binoculars. They'd parked their vehicle two miles distant and walked in guided by map and compass. Carrera loathed being dependent on the global locating system.

Soult, a senior warrant officer now, as was Mitchell, had stayed on. Most of Carrera's original group, those still alive, had.

"You're pretty confident, aren't you, Boss?"

"Confident about what?"

"That we're going to be rehired by the FS. I mean, why else go through the expense of training at this . . . intensity?"

Carrera adjusted the focus on his binos to key in on a youngish trooper scaling a wall. He spoke as he turned the adjusting wheel.

"I *am* somewhat confident, yes, Jamey. But I'd have the troops training like madmen anyway just because I think it's the right thing to do, that it's . . . *immoral* for soldiers not to spend every possible minute and every dollar, every drop of gas, and every round of ammunition you can spare on it.

"What's more . . . ah, fuck."

Soult looked into his binoculars until he saw what had caused his chief's outburst. When he did see it—a climber who'd slipped until he hung by his fingertips from a small rocky outcropping—he repeated, "Fuck."

. . . try to fuck every female I can talk into a horizontal . . . FUCK!

Cruz felt his lower foot slip vertically. That put excess demands on the other one, which likewise lost its hold on the rock ledge. His left hand hadn't quite found purchase. In much less time than it takes to tell about it he found himself hanging by the fingertips of one hand, and not even all of those. His body slammed the cliff face, almost causing him to lose his death grip on the outcropping. Moreover, while his helmet protected the bulk of his head, in slipping he had managed to scrape the left side of his jaw along the rough rock wall. He felt hot blood drip down his neck.

His first instinct was, frankly, akin to panic. It lasted milliseconds before training and experience took over. *I've been scared witless before and overcome it. I can again.*

As Aristotle had said, "We become brave by performing brave acts." This Cruz had done often enough to deserve the title of "Brave."

The first thing Cruz's questing fingers found was a tiny little spur of rock. It would never do to support his entire weight but, gripped by two fingers and a thumb, it was just enough to take some weight off of the over-strained fingers of the other hand. His heart began to slow, if only slightly. *Okay . . . so I have at least two or three more minutes of life. My fingers will hold that long. A lot can be done in two or three minutes.*

Next, his foot found the previous ledge it had occupied. He was unwilling to take quite the same perch he had had previously. He spent some of his one hundred and twenty to one hundred and eighty seconds feeling around for the best position he could find. When he found it he tested it, spending a few more precious seconds. He then allowed his foot and leg to take some weight from his whitened, tired fingers.

At last, breathing a little more easily, Cruz found a spot for his other foot and began to rest his fingers in turn.

"I recognize the face, boss, but who is that kid?"

"I think it's a centurion, junior grade named Cruz," Carrera answered. "Volunteer for the original legion. Decorated twice . . . mmm, maybe three times; not sure. Two kids. Wife's name is . . ." and here Carrera had to struggle to remember, ". . . mmm . . . Cara or . . . no; *Caridad*, I think. Good kid. Going places if he stays with us."

Unseen by Carrera, Soult smiled. *Gotta admire the boss's memory.*

"You actually *know* his wife? I mean, we've got fifteen hundred officers, twenty-five hundred optios and centurions, maybe a thousand warrants and you know his *wife*?"

"Long story," Carrera answered.

Soult shrugged, then asked, "Hey, boss; does it

bother you when . . . you know . . . when you have to meet the wife and kids, or the parents, of somebody who got killed?"

Carrera was a long time answering. "Jamey, it bothers the hell out of me. But you know what keeps me going?"

"Revenge?"

"When we first started, sure, that was all I had. But the fact is, I keep going now for two other reasons. One is that we have to win this war for the sake of our civilization, for our kids and grandkids."

"And the other?"

Carrera sighed. "The other is that I love this shit; that I'm addicted to it."

Cruz didn't have time to think any deep thoughts until he reached the top of the cliff and secured and lowered the rope. After that, he thought, *Maybe Cara was right. Maybe I should give this shit up.*

If only I didn't love it so.

UEPF Spirit of Peace, 10/3/467 AC

I love it when a plan comes together, thought High Admiral Robinson, as he watched a distant image of Xamari pirates in half a dozen boats swarm, engage and board a Balboan registry freighter.

It hadn't been all that easy for Robinson, setting things up as he had. It had helped, though, that nearly half of Terra Nova's global shipping was registered with the Republic of Balboa and most of the rest was with an otherwise insignificant country in Uhuru. The Balboan government needed merely to be reminded of the World

League's discountenancing of privately armed merchant vessels and that, with a large, uncontrolled and potential hostile army inside its borders the government needed whatever friends it could get . . . *or should we arrange to pull out the TU troops that are there to safeguard you, Señor Presidente?*

Robertsonia, the other large flag of convenience registry on Terra Nova had needed a bribe that was so low it was pitiful. The Tauran Union had, of course, begun to enforce the World League's edicts. The rest of down below, except for the Zhong, didn't much matter. And to the Zhong, every non-Zhong ship seized by the pirates was all to the good.

While the currently in-power Progressive Party in the FSC also frowned on armed merchant ships, it had a large and powerful surface navy, more powerful in fact than all the other navies combined, to protect its own shipping. A task force of this had been sent off to suppress the piratical scourge along the Xamar coast. It was signally failing to do so. In part this was because Robinson was passing to Abdulahi which ships could be attacked without risking engagement with the FSN; in part because the FSN's Rules of Engagement, or ROE, forbade taking any seriously deterrent action even if they happened to be in a position to engage. The Progressive Party's domestic "mandate" was not so strong that it could afford to alienate any of it constituencies, progressive, pacifist, racial, environmental, or other.

Neither the World League nor the other—marginally— significant naval powers on the planet were taking any significant action to suppress the pirates.

Even better, Mustafa's man among the Nicobars is gradually bringing the other pirates under his control.

Nicobar Straits, 11/3/467 AC

A thick haze floated over the water, reducing visibility to no more than two hundred meters in the *daytime*. At night, a sailor could, sometimes, see the end of his nose. The haze was not from the weather. Rather, it was mostly smoke from grass and brush fires that raged uncontrolled upwind of the Straits.

On any given clear day the Straits would have a steady hum as more than one hundred and fifty ships made passage through it. When the haze closed down like this, though, all the ships stopped engines and dropped anchors. Even the risk of pirate attack was better than risking a wreck.

Parameswara, chieftain of his own band of pirates smiled in the silence. Tonight was not a night for piracy. The ships were safe for the nonce from him and his men.

I have a better fish to catch tonight, he thought

One remarkable feature of Nicobar piracy was not that it was entirely Islamic, but that it was *not* entirely Islamic. Indeed, there were Hindu pirates, Sikh pirates, animist pirates, Buddhist pirates . . . even "Christian" pirates. There were Chinese pirates and Tamil pirates. There were white, black, brown, and yellow pirates. In all, there were—and not counting mere part-timers—some thirty-three *large* bands of pirates, plus substantial numbers of small time free-lancers, not more than half of either Moslem.

They all hated each other; that was key.

It had taken some time, and considerable intelligence support from Robinson, before Mustafa had determined the solution to his problem. It was really elegant in its conceptual simplicity. Mustafa would help and direct one not terribly large or powerful Moslem group, under the leadership of a fat, middle-aged Malay cutthroat named Parameswara, to take over, one by one, all the non-Moslem pirates. That band would then be large to take on the largest of the Moslem bands. That united band would then be large enough to have little difficulty taking over the rest of the Moslem bands. At that point, there would be enough Moslems under cohesive leadership to exterminate the previously allied non-Moslem pirates.

That was one elegant concept. More elegant still, so much so that Mustafa nearly shivered when he thought upon it, was that the ultimate targets of the pirates, *his* ultimate target, the shippers of the industrialized world, would pay to have Parameswara do this.

In the short term, the Malay would do precisely as he said, suppress piracy. The shippers, like all their ilk, rarely thought in the long term. Short-term returns were what kept them in their cushy jobs. Short-term returns were what got them golden parachute packages. Indeed, that much at least Terra Nova's capitalists shared with its progressives. There was little practical difference between a progressive, or an outright socialist, promising to rape an economy for short-term gain to buy votes from the masses and a capitalist raping a company for short-term gains to buy votes from the stockholders.

So, at least, Mustafa thought of it. And, in principle, giving money to Parameswara to protect their ships from pirates was not substantially different from paying it to Abdulahi, as an increasing number of shippers were, to keep his merry boys from seizing their ships.

The part Mustafa had the greatest difficulty in

understanding was the failure of the shippers to arrange for their own ships' protection. *Is it that we are charging one drachma less than it would cost the shippers to hire mercenaries for protection? Are they really that short-sighted? They must be.*

One form of aid Mustafa had given Parameswara was a company of his own mujahadin. That company had also brought with it modern weapons ranging from rifles to heavy machine guns and rocket grenade launchers, or RGLs, sufficient to arm ten times Parameswara's band. In addition, they had brought money, a doctor, night vision equipment and radios.

Mostly, they brought expertise. The war to gain control of the pirate factions of the Nicobar Straits would be fought mostly on land.

The engine was killed even as the boat's pilot turned the wheel hard a port, toward the coast. Landfall was a subdued scraping of muck along the lead vessel's bottom, followed by a shuddering stop. There was no sound except the lapping of small waves on the hull of the boat, the sound of feet scraping along a dirty wooden deck and the quiet splashing of men easing themselves over the side to the waist-deep, murky and polluted water.

Mustafa's man—called, simply, *al Naquib*—sniffed at the unpleasant smell composed of mixed smoke, salt sea, rotting jungle vegetation, and pollution. It was so unlike his native desert that inside he cringed.

Still, the mission was important and if al Naquib had to put up with a few esoteric smells to complete it, then so be it. He, too, eased himself over the side and into the foul water. Parameswara followed.

"Place not far," the Malay bandit advised. He spoke a sort of pidgin Arabic that served as a lingua franca along the Straits.

"I hope not," al Naquib answered. "My men are not used to the jungle. *I* am not used to it either."

"Not far," the Malay repeated, then left to take the lead to guide the mujahadin toward their target.

The village sat on a low promontory above a slow flowing, greenish river. Culturally and ethnically the place was Chinese, part of the diaspora on Old Earth that had been replicated by forcible immigration to the New. The ethnicity could be seen in the architecture, smelled in the aroma of cooking, and heard in the sing-song speech of early-rising women. Boats were tied up to the riverbank, below the village. Most were unpowered. One, however, sitting low and lean and rakish, had a powerful outboard mounted to the stern. This was the boat the men of the village used for their piratical forays.

Parameswara eyed the boat hungrily. It would make a fine addition to his small fleet. *Only let the Yithrabi, al Naquib, do his job as Mustafa promised me he would.*

In the dank, green jungle surrounding the village, al Naquib was doing just that, positioning the men of his company by squads. The early morning calls of birds covered the sound of his movements, and it did those of his men and Parameswara's, and the few words he spoke. Even without the birds, it is doubtful they would have been heard over the chatter of the village's women.

Yuan Lin was the village chief's senior wife. This didn't protect her from having to rise early, just like any of the other women, to clean and to cook. At most, her position allowed her to drop some of the more onerous duties on the younger women.

She was doing just that, slapping into submission the chief's newest concubine, a fifteen-year-old Cochinese girl seized from a refugee barge, when armed men began emerging from the steamy jungle surrounding the village. Lin opened her mouth to call out a warning. She stopped and closed it again when she saw just how *many* fighters were swarming the place and how quickly they were doing it.

Wide-eyed, Lin stood with a basket of laundry on one hip, her free hand still raised to strike the Cochinese, when a man materialized in front of her and made pushing motions with the rifle held crossways in front of him. She used her free hand to grab the Cochinese by the ear and pulled her in the direction—the center of the village—where the armed man had indicated he wanted them to go.

The thing that was surprising, perhaps, was that Lin was neither terribly upset nor terribly afraid. She had herself been seized in a raid when she was even younger than the Cochinese. As she'd discovered then, she was a woman, she was not a threat or competitor, and she had value. She might be raped but she'd been through all that before and survived well enough. Nothing worse was likely to happen to her now. As a matter of fact, Lin didn't even necessarily object to being raped as long as she wasn't going to be permanently damaged by the experience.

Al Naquib and Parameswara stood in the village center, watching as the people—men and boys, women and girls—were herded, cattle-like, inward.

"Fine," al Naquib said, "you have control of the village. Who do you want killed?"

"Maybe . . . nobody," Parameswara answered. "Dead, they no use . . . me . . . anybody. I see how it fall out."

Mustafa's man merely shrugged, *Up to you.*

Parameswara nodded and walked out into the center of the square.

"I'm glad you were all so eager to talk to me," he began with a smile, eliciting a nervous chuckle from the villagers. "And I hope you don't mind that I invited a few close friends along." Parameswara's hand swept around, taking in the more than two hundred that accompanied him.

That earned another mass chuckle, a bit more sincere than the first. After all, why not? He hadn't killed anyone yet and it never hurt to laugh at someone else's jokes. Even Chang Tsai, the chief of the village, joined in the laugh. He, most especially, feared being dead soon. What better reason to try to ingratiate himself with Parameswara?

The Malay chief had a gift for oratory. He spoke of the rising sun and the setting sun. He talked of the low tide always returning as a new high. He talked of the Prophet and he spoke of the Buddha. He waxed eloquent over the future and the past.

What he means is, we join him or he kills every man, woman and child in the village, thought Chang Tsai. *It would be better to join.*

Kamakura, Yamato, 15/3/467 AC

Yamato had this much difference with the Salafis; whereas the Salafis emigrated to Terra Nova to recreate the seventh century of Old Earth, Yamato had preferred recreating the latter third of the nineteenth and earlier third of the twentieth, with a *profound* nod of respect to the thirteenth through seventeenth. About the entire Pearl-Harbor-to-the-deck-of-the-USS *Missouri* fiasco, back on Old Earth, they preferred to forget (though the rebuilt *Yasukuni-Jinja* had some hundreds of thousands of mementos). They were none too interested in delving too deeply into the mistakes of the Great Global War, either.

That meant, in practice, that the Imperial Court still had tremendous power within the country, though the power was almost always expressed subtly. Indeed, it was usually expressed so subtly that no one could really be certain what the emperor actually meant, most of the time. Some of this was, of course, in the way questions to the Throne were phrased.

"His Highness said *what*?" asked Mr. Yamagata of his colleague, Mr. Saito. Each was a representative of a major shipping company. Yamagata's brought in oil; Saito's exported finished goods.

"I mentioned to His Highness," answered Saito, "that ships bringing oil to our land endured many dangers. He answered, 'Sometimes we must endure the unendurable.'"

Yamagata took off his bottle-thick glasses and cleaned them with his tie.

"That is a remarkably forthright answer from Him," he observed. "It seems clear enough, then, as clear as it ever is, that the Imperial Navy is not going to help us. What do we do then?"

"I came to the same conclusion. As to what we must do, I asked the emperor, 'Shall not the sons of

the Son of Heaven resist tyranny and robbery?' He
answered with the questions, 'Does not the law forbid
private persons from bearing arms? Has the land not
seen untold misery from uncontrolled violence?'"

"Shit!" exclaimed Yamagata.

"Shit," echoed Saito more softly. "It was a curious
audience. Before I left, His Imperial Highness said,
'Sometimes, we must allow ourselves—like Miyamoto
Musashi—to be tossed about by the waves of the sea.'"

Yamagata's left eyebrow lifted, subtly. "Wave tossed?
Ronin?"

Ronin meant, in Japanese, "wave man," as a mas-
terless samurai was said to be tossed through life
on the waves. Many ronin, throughout the history
of Japanese culture (which history and culture were
largely carried over to Yamato on Terra Nova), became
mercenaries. Miyamoto Musashi—old Japan's "sword
saint"—had been ronin.

Saito shrugged. "That much of His Highness' words
I did *not* comprehend."

"Perhaps I do," answered Yamagata.

BdL Dos Lindas, Mar Furioso, 3/22/467 AC

The seas were calm and the waves were light, the
ship barely taking notice of them.

Montoya took his meal standing in the crowded
wardroom. There were seats, a few of them, available, but he'd discovered he really enjoyed watching
the maintenance crews in the hangar deck at work.
There was a euphony to it, a symmetry. Of course,
the irregular pounding from the engine repair shop
next to the wardroom was anything but euphonious.

Working in harmony together or not, the crew was frazzled; there was no better word. Montoya had flown three training missions yesterday and two already today. This was bad enough on him; on the ordnance, fuel, maintenance and deck crews it was simply exhausting. And that bastard Fosa showed no indication so far that he intended to let up for an instant.

Is he going to push us until half of us are dead? Already, half a dozen pilots and twice that in deck crew had perished under the relentless drilling.

From the speakers Montoya heard played six notes of Wagner's "Ride of the Valkyries," then, "Battle stations; battle stations. Pilots . . ."

Seems he is.

Montoya's plate was dropped and he was out the door before the speaker had a chance to finish, ". . . man your aircraft. RPV pilots to your stations. Cazadors to the assembly area on the hangar deck."

A few weeks ago there'd have been a mad dash for the hatch and a human traffic jam both there and at the ladders leading topside. The sailors and pilots moved just as briskly now, but they'd learned the techniques of transforming themselves from a mob to a mass. Montoya waited his turn at the hatch, then again at the ladder, before easing himself into the only kind of river that flowed uphill.

Topside, Montoya saw what he'd expected to see. Three Crickets were parked in a shallow upside-down V just forward of the carrier's Island. Well behind those were half a dozen Turbo-Finch Avengers in two Vs. On the port side the men of the alert company of the

Cazador demi-cohort struggled to organize themselves before boarding the eight Yakamov helicopters lined up along the angled deck.

At the top of the ladder Montoya turned half right, which is to say toward the stern and the Finches, and began to trot to where a staff officer of the air group was sorting pilots to planes.

"Montoya!" the staff weenie shouted to be heard over the growing roar of engines and the loudspeakers on the island playing "Ride of the Valkyries." "Number four spot. Your load is rocket and gun pods. Tribune Castillo is Air Mission Commander. Orders will be radioed just prior to take off. Go, son!"

The crew chief for the plane gave Montoya a leg up onto the wing. Standing, he threw one foot over onto the aircraft's seat, then pulled in the other. To save half a second he'd developed the technique of simply tossing his legs out from under and letting his ass slam into the seat. As his ass hit, his hands were reaching for the helmet. Only when it was on, and a commo check made, did he begin to strap himself in.

The radio crackled. "Boys, this is Castillo. Target is a small boat about seventy-five miles from here on a heading of Three One Two, I say again, Three One Two. Just FYI, the skipper informed me that the target boat is small, fast and under radio control so it is going to be a bitch to put down. There'll be a control boat about two miles to the north of the target. DON'T go after the control. It's painted white while the target is sea green so even you blind bastards ought to be able to stay away from it. Now let's wait for the Crickets to get out of the way and we'll take off in standard order, One through Six."

"Any questions?"

FSS *Ironsides*, Xamar Coast, 32/3/467 AC

"Any questions?" asked the admiral commanding the *Ironside*'s Carrier Battle Group after he explained the rules of engagement for the carrier and her escorts. Had a kinder fate intervened the steel-gray old sea dog just might have become the chief of naval operations for the FS Navy. As it was, the Progressive administration was nearly certain to last past the admiral's mandatory retirement date. And the Progs would never let him or anyone like him become CNO. The same was true of the Army, FSAF and FSMC. The most aggressive, most traditional, most militaristic and least progressive senior officers had already been given the word: "There will be no place for you in the future and the sooner you retire the better for everyone."

"Just one, sir," said *Ironside*'s captain, a former shoo-in for admiral himself, now doomed, it seemed, to be cast aside. "What's the fucking point of our being here?"

"Why, to suppress piracy, Captain," the admiral rejoined. "Didn't you listen to me when I explained the rules of engagement? They're clear as thin mud."

"On, not nearly that clear, surely, Admiral. Rule One: 'Guaranteeing free travel by merchant shipping is the number one priority' makes sense enough. But then we run into Rule Two: 'All human life is to be treated as sacred.' I think that must include pirate life as well, no? Rule Three: 'Ships and boats will not be stopped on the high seas without a warrant emanating from probable cause as determined by a federal judge.' There's going to be time to get a warrant? I don't think so. And then there's Rule Seventeen: 'Ships and boats not in the act of attacking merchant shipping will not be attacked.' Does that mean that once a pirate's made a successful attack and is on the way back we cannot engage? I think it does. And Rule Fourteen? 'All hostage situations will immediately be referred to the National Command Authority for determination of appropriate action.'

The captain crumpled up his paper copy of the ROE and dropped it disdainfully to the deck. "It's a waste of time, Admiral. We could deploy the entire fleet here and under these pussy rules it *still* wouldn't stop the piracy."

UEPF Spirit of Peace, 1/4/467 AC

Always good to see my prime enemy wasting its time, mused High Admiral Robinson, watching on his screen as a group of Xamaris returned from a raided ship.

The FSN wasn't interfering, so the Xamaris must have grabbed some of the passengers or crew. The ROE for the battle group, a copy of which Robinson had received almost before the admiral commanding, made any quick reaction, or any action that might be proactive, essentially impossible. These he had passed on to Abdulahi, together with some pointed suggestions on just how to use the ROE to advantage.

Not only is the bastard using them to his advantage, but in the face of TN's only real naval power's helpless flailing about, its inability to control what amounts to seagoing camel drivers, more major shippers are buying

*protection from Abdulahi. So, of course, the incidence
of piracy is down; the FSN can hardly explain that it's
down because they failed; the Progressive administration gets to trumpet its "success" . . . and much of
that protection money still goes to support Mustafa.*

*Things are going well in Nicobar, too, if not so
spectacularly. Mustafa's boys down there are expanding
nicely; seven bands, it is, fallen under Parameswara's
control. Of course, supporting Parameswara is a net
money drain on Mustafa, for now, and not a small
one. But he'll make all that up and more once the
Nicobars can get in on the racket in style.*

Nicobar Straits, 7/4/467 AC

It had all been going far too well, Parameswara knew.
Something had to go wrong eventually.

"Eventually" came in the form of another group of
Malay pirates heading out just as Parameswara's group
was moving in. The outgoing pirates spotted one of
Parameswara's launches looking alone and vulnerable
and motored over to seize it. By the time they realized that that launch was not alone it was too late;
the seizure turned into a fight that quickly escalated
into a general melee at sea.

Parameswara's boys won that fight handily. When
they were finished, and it only took a matter of minutes, three of their foes' boats were burning on the
haze-covered water. The boats themselves were draped
with hacked and shot bodies, the blood that collected
in the scuppers beginning to steam from the heat.

It's a terrible waste of good seacraft, Parameswara
mourned.

Worse, though, was that the fight, while desperate in places, had overall gone too easily and ended too quickly. Their blood up, Parameswara's men hastily forced a landing and began an assault into the village from which their fellow Malay pirates had come. There, the massacre became general with the assaulting pirates shooting or hacking down old men, women, children and even the dogs and pigs of the place.

It was only with the greatest difficulty, and only after the huts were already burning, that the pirate chieftain and al Naquib were able to bring the men to order. By that time, there was nothing left but fifty or so women and children, most of them already raped at least once, remaining. The survivors wept, some of them. Others stood in shock. Parameswara was shocked himself.

"It was so damned unnecessary," he cursed at no one in particular.

"I'm not so sure," said al Naquib, who was rapidly picking up the local lingo. "We had already, maybe, made as much peaceful progress as we could. Didn't you pick your early conquests based on how likely they would be to fold *without* having to fight or massacre? Didn't you push the ones most likely to resist to the back of the list? Was not this group one you thought might put up a fight anyway?"

Parameswara shrugged. It was true but . . .

"Well, they did. And they've paid for it. Now there are just about enough survivors to spread the word: If you resist the great new pirate king, Parameswara, all you will earn is death. So let's let these go with nothing but the clothes on their backs, their eyes to weep with and their tongues to spread the word."

❖   ❖   ❖

Within a fortnight, the first chief of the still independent pirate bands along either side of the Nicobar Straits arrived at Parameswara's newly fortified coastal town to offer his allegiance to the new paramount chief.

First Landing, Hudson, FSC, 16/4/467 AC

Matthias Esterhazy had no real idea why Mr. Saito and Mr. Yamagata had asked to see him. Their credentials suggested only that they were deeply involved, and very prominent, in Yamato's considerable shipping industry. He considered it most likely that they were interested in doing business with either Chatham, Hennessey and Schmied, Patricio's family firm and no inconsiderable shippers themselves, or its Balboan subsidiary, Alexander Steamship Company.

He'd done business with the Yamatans before, especially when he'd worked for SachsenBank. Thus he was unsurprised that the two businessmen, and a third who'd accompanied them, beat around the bush with meaningless pleasantries for more than an hour.

Actually, the third man—they'd introduced him only as "Captain Kurita"—said absolutely nothing. *He's the interesting one,* Esterhazy thought. Old, clearly he was very old, Kurita sat serene and upright. However silent Kurita may have been, and however ancient, Esterhazy saw keen intelligence in his eyes and thought he detected a wry amusement in his face.

He'd almost stopped listening to Saito and Yamagata until he heard, "And in the long run, it's just unsupportable, the price they demand to allow our ships passage."

They'd worked their way from "Nice weather you're

having here" to "Help" and Esterhazy hadn't even been aware of the transition. He looked at Kurita's face again. Yes, there was definitely amusement there. Perhaps he'd seen Taurans and Columbians trying to communicate with Yamatans before.

Kurita turned that gnarled, ancient face toward Esterhazy and spoke his first words since introductions. "Danegeld, Tribune Esterhazy. They don't want to pay Danegeld."

Matthias's head flew back in surprise. That the Yamatan had used the expression "Danegeld" was one thing. He could well have— indeed probably had—been at least partially educated in Anglia or the FSC. But that he knew Esterhazy's legionary rank was simply shocking.

"I have kept up my contacts with Imperial Naval Intelligence, Tribune," Kurita explained, "even though the men who run it are the grandsons and even great-grandsons of the men I served with in the Great Global War. They told me who you were."

Mentally, Esterhazy made a note to inform Carrera that Yamatan Naval Intelligence kept a file on the legion. He also did some quick calculations. Kurita had to be over ninety years old. He didn't look it.

"The Great Global War?" Esterhazy questioned.

"Yes . . . at the end I was captain, Battlecruiser *Oishi*."

Subtracting 410 AC from 467 AC, and adding in a reasonable time to progress in rank, Matthias came up with the astonishing figure of at least ninety-seven years for Kurita. *Wow; and he doesn't look a day over eighty.*

Kurita went silent and serene again, while Saito

picked up. "As the good captain, says, Mr. Esterhazy, we do not want to pay Danegeld. It never ends and, if history is any guide, the price always goes up past the point one can afford to pay. For that matter, how much longer until the pirates themselves go into the shipping business and drive us completely out? Whatever your principal might charge us to end this problem, it will certainly be less than what the pirates will cost us in the long term."

"My principal, as you call him, Mr. Saito, is not really in the naval business—"

"Yes, he is," answered Kurita, "now or soon."

"And you have no idea what he charges—"

"Yes, we do."

Once again, Esterhazy turned his gaze back onto Kurita. *Maybe you do. And, one supposes, you also know about his little fleet.*

"It's likely to cost on the order of five billion FSD a year, sirs. It could be twice that, even three times."

"We know," said Saito. "And what will it be over fifty years if the problem does not end now? And what is the price when the price becomes so high we are economically strangled? We are an island country that *depends* on imports and exports. Mr.—Tribune Esterhazy, without freedom of the seas, we *starve.*"

"Moreover," interjected Kurita, "Mr. Saito and Mr. Yamagata are not alone in this. All seventeen major and minor Zaibatsu in Yamato, plus one which is in bankruptcy for the moment, wish to offer their support. In addition, His Majesty's Navy is willing to provide a certain amount of under the table support, to clandestinely curtail operations and overstate expenditures to provide aid beyond the merely monetary."

"You understand I must speak to my principal before I can commit."

"We understand," answered Kurita, and for the first time Esterhazy realized that it was he, not the businessmen, who was senior. "And we have one additional condition."

"And that would be?"

Kurita's serene look became for a moment predatory. *Decades* fell away. "They have robbed and murdered my countrymen. *I* will accompany your flotilla. *I* will see these bandits destroyed."

BdL *Dos Lindas*, Isla Real, 27/4/467 AC,

"I'm amazed at how well you've done," Carrera said admiringly to Fosa, as the two stood on the open, upper bridge, high above the flight deck. Below, two crewmen refueled a Cricket as a small team of four rearmed a Finch, easing rockets into the nineteen-round outboard pods and winding .41 caliber ammunition into the inward ones. The .41 ammunition was the same as used in the legion's new standard heavy machine gun as well as in the long-range sniper system. In this case, it was being cranked into pods that held .41 caliber, electrically driven, tri-barrels. These same guns were mounted in various spots on the carriers and her escorts. The rockets were standard Volgan 57mm folding fin types, a mix of high explosive, incendiary and flechette.

Fosa shrugged. "The foreigners helped a lot. A decent budget helped more. We could use another month but . . ."

"You sail in nine days," Carrera said simply. "You will sail in company with one frigate, two corvettes, two patrol torpedo fasts, a minesweeper, an ammunition ship, and two other supply ships. Someday, I may actually have a submarine or two for you. You will also have one former passenger liner, the *Wappen von Bremen*, which will have aboard her *full* recreation facilities. In addition, you will have certain ships put under operational control from time to time, upon which you may put armed men, and which I encourage you to use as bait. If I ever decide to finish up a Suvarov-class cruiser, you'll get that, too.

"You may assume," Carrera continued, "that all ports will be officially closed to you. That said, certain concerns in Yamato have volunteered to resupply your resupply ships, but only at some considerable distance from Xamar. They don't want to appear to be involved.

"From this bay you will make transit, then proceed to the Xamar coast. There you will take all actions consistent with suppressing piracy along that coast. Your rules of engagement are *suppress piracy*. You may, insofar as I am concerned, legally and morally consider yourself in a time and space warp that has put your and your group on Old Earth in its eighteenth century. Destroy them without pity or mercy."

"About fucking time, sir," smiled Fosa, wickedly.

"And you are going to pick up an observer, a passenger, named Kurita. From what I've been told you two will get along famously."

SS Estrella de Castilla, 1/5/467 AC

The ship was drifting, so much was obvious. It did not answer hails. The crew didn't come on deck to wave at the helicopter as it buzzed.

Going lower, low enough to actually look into the ports for the ship's bridge, the helicopter from the *Ironsides* saw nothing. It turned toward the portside, scooted around the ship's superstructure and swept the rear decks. Nothing. Then it made a radio call.

The second chopper was different and came from a different ship, the troop carrier FSS *Tiburon Bay*. The chopper carried thirteen tightly crammed FS Marines in full battle gear. The leader of the Marines, a second lieutenant due within the month for promotion to first lieutenant, had no idea what to expect. He was pretty sure though, that ships that floated without crew represented potential problems.

The remainder of the Marine infantry platoon flew behind in echelon left. The last three would circle until the first chopper's passengers could secure a landing spot.

The lieutenant, DeSmedt was his name, looked out at the deck of the ship as the choppers made one circling recon pass. If someone were going to shoot, better they should shoot now before the helicopter put itself in a vulnerable position, stationary, on the deck, or hovering, just above it. Door gunners from all four birds kept careful watch just in case.

DeSmedt saw that the deck was uneven, with pipes showing, hawsers unstowed and a liberal layer of junk scattered about. As the lead chopper passed the stern, he saw the ship's name: *Estrella de Castilla.* Still, there was no fire. He tapped the pilot and made a downward motion with his thumb.

The lead pilot guided his aircraft down in an easy descending arc. When he was over a part of the deck that seemed to have slightly less junk about than the others, he pulled the bird up to a low, ground-effect hover. Rotor wash kicked trash around even so; it could become a danger if they kept this altitude and position. The pilot signaled Lieutenant DeSmedt to *unass*.

DeSmedt tossed his rucksack and then jumped from a dozen feet over the deck. The jump was a little awkward; he lost his balance and fell, slamming his helmeted head on a hatchway.

Thank God for aramid fiber, he thought. *Then, too, if I didn't have a thick skull would I ever have become a Marine?*

By twos the rest of the Marines followed their lieutenant down until all thirteen men were aboard the derelict and watching for trouble. The chopper pulled up and away, allowing the flying junk, such as had not blown to sea, to settle back on to the deck.

DeSmedt gave the order to the squad leader, "Sergeant, have Charlie Team clear this junk off and fuck environmental regulations. When the platoon sergeant and the rest land, tell them I want them to start clearing the ship from the top down. The rest of you," he pointed at a vertical hatchway into the superstructure, "standard drill; thata way."

Whether the power was off and the batteries dead, the men didn't know. Nor were they going to even *think* about flicking a light switch on a ship that might have been "wired for sound." Instead, they relied on the flashlights affixed to their rifles' barrels and whatever light made its way in from the scarce portholes.

It didn't matter anyway; they could find their way to what they were looking for by smells alone. Those—the smell of rotting meat (and meat rotted fast in these climes), the coppery-iron stink of gallons of blood, the stench of shit . . . worst of all, the pervading odor of fear and terror—were sufficient guides.

Hearts were pounding so hard the men might have thought they would burst through their chests as the lead team of two men reached what had to be the hatch from which emanated all the stench. Whatever it was, and all the Marines had a strong feeling they already knew, it was going to be bad.

DeSmedt was right behind the first two Marines. Before he could see what the flashlights at their muzzles found, he felt them stiffen.

"Jesus Christ, El Tee," one of the men exclaimed.

The lieutenant pushed passed the men. Inside was an abattoir, he could see, even from the little illuminated by the flashlight. He turned his own rifle against the wall and saw a man, what had been a man, already green tinged and beginning to blacken. The corpse's face was set in a rictus grin, below which, on his throat, was another, newer, grin, red-tinged and gaping. DeSmedt moved his rifle's aim along the wall and saw next a body with a similar dual grin. That one, though, had both eyes gouged out. Next a man hung by the neck from a pipe in the ceiling. His trousers were down around his ankles. When DeSmedt saw that this one had been castrated and his penis likewise removed he couldn't hold his bile any longer.

The pungent smell of vomit was added to the stench of death.

Still, DeSmedt was a Marine. Once he'd evacuated his stomach, and despite his dry heaves, he continued to sweep the room. Along one wall he found no bodies. Instead, there was a message painted. He was pretty sure it was painted in the crew's blood.

The message read, "Thus to the infidel who fails to pay the *jiylah*."

"It's in English, El Tee," murmured one of the two lead Marines. "Why would they put it in English?"

"Because they had a pretty good idea who was coming and wanted us to get the word out."

"What word, sir?"

"*Jizyah*'s a tax, or maybe sometimes a toll, the Moslems levy on non-Moslems. I'd guess that some people . . . some shippers . . . are paying it and the pirates want everyone to."

BdL *Dos Lindas*, Marguerita Locks, 1/5/467 AC,

The carrier almost filled the lock chamber. They'd had to remove the lighting on one side of the locks to allow space for the angled flight deck. The ship was held fast in position by extremely heavy locomotives called "burros," as water poured out of the lock to drop the inside level to match that of the sea. The burros would actually pull the carrier out of the locks before it could proceed under its own power.

All but a few of the carrier's aircraft sat topside for the transit. Those that were down below, in the hangar deck, were in for routine maintenance.

The escorts had already formed at *Puerto Lindo* and would meet the *Dos Lindas* a few miles out to sea.

Fosa fumed, and it wasn't because of anything having to do with the locks, the aircraft, the escorts, or his Yamatan supernumery, Commodore (by courtesy bumped up for the duration) Kurita. It had nothing to do with the speed of transit and it had nothing to do with the efficiency of the entire operation. Fosa's mood wasn't based on leaving behind his home, nor even his wife and children.

No; what had him ready to shit nails was that for the duration of his ship's transit *someone else*—a Transitway pilot—was commanding *his* ship.

"Roderigo-san," Kurita said, with that same serene smile he almost always showed, "if it makes you feel any better, when I was a real captain I'd have given anything to have taken *my* ship, Battlecruiser *Oishi*, though the Transitway, even if I had to put her under someone else's command."

"Huh? Why is that?"

The serene smile, as it sometimes did, turned feral. "Because that would have meant my country won the war."

Fosa immediately recalled that there were worse things, *much* worse things, than having to let some stranger con one's ship. "It was pretty bad losing, wasn't it?"

Kurita's smile went from feral to serene to nonexistent. "It was worse than bad. We couldn't surrender; we didn't even know *how* to surrender, really. We were staking everything on being able to make the Federated States pay an unacceptable price in blood so that they would give up before we did. Then they nuked us and for a brief period of time we thought they would not have to pay that price and so we considered surrender. But then the UEPF nuked them and we *knew* they could not bomb us into surrender and would have to invade."

Kurita shook his head, very sadly.

"We were wrong. Unable to convince us one way, they took a different, and far more brutal, way. They imposed a total blockade and, just as with cities under siege, they refused to let anyone escape. They came in with defoliants and attacked the rice crops. They bombed and burned any food stockpiles they could identify. They attacked the roads and rails so that what food there was could not be moved to the cities."

Kurita shuddered, as he said, "Over twenty million people, almost all civilians, and mostly the very old and very young, either starved to death or died of starvation-related causes. *Then* we surrendered."

"God, you must hate them," Fosa said. "The FSC, I mean."

The serene smile returned. Kurita shook his old and dignified head. "No . . . no, I actually don't. We'd have done no less. And they tried to give us an easy out by using the atomic bombs. What a bargain it would have been if we had been able to surrender after only losing a couple of hundred thousand instead of twenty million.

"No, Roderigo-san; if I hate someone over it, I hate those who prevented the FSC from following through and making us surrender when it was possible and cheap. I hate the UEPF."

INTERLUDE

19 April, 2085, Boston, Massachusetts, United States of America

Students are young. Thus, they are subject to the fads and fashions of the young. Perhaps more importantly, they are fickle and generally contrary. If the older generation is traditionalist, patriotic, religious, the students will be antipatriotic, nontraditionalist, and irreligious. If on the other hand . . .

There was snow on the ground. Not that this was particularly unusual in Boston in April. But for there to be so *much* snow on the ground? The students were pretty sure—indeed the consensus of the world's scientific community was—that it was the dread phenomenon of global cooling, caused by failure to create more heavy industry in the Third World, in accordance with the mandates of the Kyoto IV Treaty.

Nonetheless, that phenomenon of global cooling was *not* what had the students out in their thousands in protest. Rather, it was the restrictions on free speech explicit in the latest UN Treaty on the subject.

And so, to show their defiance, as university students are wont to do, some thousands of them crossed over Harvard Bridge on their way to Beacon Hill, bearing banners stating such seditious and antiprogressive sentiments as, "Congress shall make no law . . . abridging the Freedom of Speech" and "The Declaration of Independence was Hate Speech." Tsk.

The protestors' intentions were to cross all three-hundred and sixty four point four *smoots* (and an ear) of the bridge, then proceed up Massachusetts Avenue to Commonwealth Avenue. From there, they were to march by the site of the Boston Massacre, then go to the Common where they would present their grievances.

Students in Massachusetts came from all over, even the dreaded red states of the deep South. The governor, however, was a home girl. As such, she, too, was progressive. And the plain and open expression of all those unenlightened banners was anathema to her. Fortuitously, however, she was the commander of the Massachusetts National Guard.

"The adjutant general says his birds are ready to lift now, Governor," announced an aide. "Flight time about twenty minutes."

"Tell him to hold," the governor ordered. "We don't want to miss anyone."

There had been a *lot* of research into nonlethal weapons, over the years. There had been developed rays that caused the skin to suddenly feel painfully hot. Similarly there was ultrasound that stunned and disoriented. Some caused an unbearable itching and still others created nausea. All of those, however, tended to disperse crowds, rather than drop them in their tracks for convenient collection. So there was gas . . .

The choppers came in low, skimming the town-houses of the Back Bay. Dropping to treetop level they skipped over the Public Gardens. At Charles Street they began loosing a gas, invisible, tasteless, odorless. Wherever they crossed protestors dropped in their tracks.

Watching the scene from her office, the governor misrecited:

"By the rude bridge that ached the flood,
Their unprogressive flag unfurled,
Here once the protesting students stood,
And got gassed and shipped to another world."

"Where do we send them, Governor?" the aide asked.

"First to jail, then to court and then to Southern Columbia," she answered. "It looks like that's going to be our dumping ground for unenlightened malcontents."

CHAPTER SIX

These, I take it, were the characteristic acts
of a man whose affections are set on warfare.
When it is open to him to enjoy peace with
honour, no shame, no injury attached, still
he prefers war; when he may live at home
at ease, he insists on toil, if only it may end
in fighting; when it is given to him to keep
his riches without risk, he would rather lessen
his fortune by the pastime of battle. To put it
briefly, war was his mistress; just as another
man will spend his fortune on a favourite,
or to gratify some pleasure, so he chose to
squander his substance on soldiering.

—Xenophon, on the Spartan,
Clearchus, *The Anabasis*

Quarters #2, *Isla Real*, 2/5/467 AC

The nightmares had started coming again, since Carrera
had returned from Sumer. They'd been bad—horrifying, really—before he'd begun to gather the means
of revenge. Then they'd tapered off, even becoming
somewhat rare. Whether this was because he was

actually *doing* something to destroy those who had murdered his wife and children or because he was typically so exhausted at the end of the day that he had not even the energy left to dream, he had no clue.

Then the fighting had begun and the nightmares had gone almost completely. Again, he could not say whether they had stopped because he was advancing the cause of vengeance—he didn't delude himself that he was really in search of justice—or because of exhaustion, of for some other reason or reasons.

He never told anyone, not even his closest friends and *especially* not Lourdes, his second wife, but he was a superstitious sort and a part of him really felt the dreams came from the shade of Linda, reminding him not to let the murderers of her children get away.

Whatever the case, since returning with his troops from Sumer the nightmares had begun coming again with increasing violence and frequency. They were repetitive, as well. Tonight's was one of the worst; the one where he had just met Linda for the very first time and she burst into flames before his eyes. He awakened from that one screaming, as he always had. Lourdes held him tightly until he calmed down.

It was perhaps one reason that he loved Lourdes as much as he did. She should have been jealous that her husband was still in love with Linda. She probably *was* jealous that he was still in love with Linda. After all, what woman likes being in second place? But she understood that the world was imperfect and was thankful for what she did have.

Besides, she took care of him. He needed her, even if he was gone most of the time. He needed her, even though he was more at home in the field with the legion. He needed her, even though she could never completely replace Linda.

Perhaps he loved her most because she loved him as much as, perhaps more than, Linda had. And he felt terrible, terrible guilt that he couldn't, not quite, fully reciprocate.

He spent virtually all early mornings out with one or another maniple, joining that ever-so-lucky tribune at daily physical training. That meant he would be able to see every maniple commander at PT about once every two years.

More often than not he would go directly from PT to his office, shower, grab a quick bite at the Headquarters mess, and then either go look at training or attend one of the meetings that he did his damnedest to limit. This morning, given the performance of the previous night, he thought he probably ought to have breakfast with Lourdes. The eldest boy—little Hamilcar was four years old now and in prekindergarten—would be at school. The younger, still just a baby, would likely be asleep.

As he drove himself to his quarters, he thought, *I wonder if it's even a good idea for me to join them at PT. How much stupidity do these kids go through on the off chance I might show up? Maybe it would be better if I do what I do in the field; watch but almost never let them know I'm watching. Something to consider, anyway. And, then, too, what the hell is the point of watching something once every two years? I don't know that there is any. Do I get a picture, or just a false picture?*

As Carrera turned his sedan into the parking lot for Quarters #2, he sighed to himself. *This garrison crap is a new playing field and I probably still have things to figure out. I wish . . .*

He didn't finish the thought. Had he, it would have been, *I wish I could go back to the war.*

Carrera eased the car under the columned carport to the right side of the white-painted quarters. Once underneath, he stopped the car with a gentle touch on the brakes, turned it off, and exited. Hearing the door close, *Jinfeng*, the trixie, stuck her brightly feathered head out from a bush and screeched a welcome.

It was eighteen steps along the side and front of the wraparound porch—like the porte cochere, also columned—to the centrally located front door. He'd not had the legion skimp on anybody's family quarters, and his was nearly eleven thousand square feet on three floors. He didn't need it. Lourdes didn't need or want it and slightly resented having to have domestic help to keep the place up. But there were social obligations that went with command and some of those social obligations involved *space*. A full half of the first floor was a ballroom and industrial kitchen. Even *that* was only just big enough to accommodate the occasional dinners he threw for senior legates, their sergeants-major, and their wives.

The household kitchen was much smaller and cozier. He found Lourdes there, hunched over a computer, ordering supplies from the main commissary. Although legion pay was generous by local standards, it didn't necessarily permit two cars, or even one, per family. He'd made arrangements for a local company to provide a delivery service. For some it was a necessity. For others, like Lourdes, it was a damned nice-to-have convenience.

Carrera's steps were catlike, virtually silent. It wasn't anything he tried to do; in fact, he'd tried to cure himself of it since it tended to give people unpleasant shocks when he materialized behind him. Lourdes didn't know he was even standing behind her until she felt his hands cup her breasts. She immediately inhaled sharply and leaned her head back against his waist, near his groin.

"Coffee, breakfast, or me?" she asked.

"You."

"Good, because coffee would make a real mess on the bed."

She knew he wouldn't be long. Even on those rare mornings when he came home after physical training he was invariably out the door by 08:15. That left her perhaps half an hour to enjoy the post-coital nearness of her man. Over the last two years, ever since she'd turned up pregnant in Sumer with their second child and he'd put his foot down and insisted she go home where she and the children would be safe, opportunities to be together had been all too infrequent.

Infrequent! She mentally snorted. *A couple of weeks twice a year. No, less than that; one year he didn't come home for eight months. Then there was this last Christmas.*

And now? Now he's home for a while. Maybe it will be a long while. But it won't—she felt a tear begin to form; she stifled a sniffle—*it won't be forever.*

The thing is, and the tear rolled across the bridge of her nose and then down the cheek on the other side, *that he leaves me because he has to avenge* her. *He still loves* her. *More than he does me? I don't know . . .*

probably. He must because he leaves me even though that will never bring her and her children back.

Then, too, why do I love him. Because the little DNA analyzer in behind my nose tells me he's a good genetic match? Probably . . . somewhat. Because he's rich and powerful? No, he wasn't either of those things when we met. Because he's good looking? He isn't all that good looking.

No, it isn't any of those things, or not them entirely, anyway. I think it's . . . because he has honor. Honor? What a rare concept now. Who can even agree on what it means anymore? It's not what it once was, in the olden days back on Earth or the early days here, when it was all appearance only. A man was honorable if he had high repute, never mind if he deserved it or not. A woman could screw half the world but, so long as no one ever found out, she was honorable.

No, Patricio has honor inside. He doesn't care what the world thinks of him. He knows what's right. He knows that it's not right to turn the other cheek to a movement of homicidal maniacs, and he does what he can to fight it.

Mendoza residence, Avenida Central, *Ciudad Balboa*, 2/5/467 AC

Marqueli's little hands shook as she opened the envelope from the legion's higher education board. What it would do to Jorge if his thesis proposal were not accepted . . . she didn't know and was afraid even to think about it.

They must *accept. They* must. *What Jorge wants to do, it's important. Carrera sees that. And even*

though Jorge's blind, he sees more clearly than any-
one with sight.

She inhaled, exhaled, and then forced herself to
open the envelope.

The contents were printed on very nice paper;
she could feel it in her fingertips. Still not daring to
unfold the letter, she wondered, *Do they waste good*
paper on rejections?

With trembling finger she began to unfold. As
soon as her eyes reached the line, "We are pleased
to inform you . . ." she shouted, "Jorge!"

She hadn't needed to shout. Since losing his eyesight Jorge had, like many of the sightless, developed
remarkably keen hearing. Still, half the joy of the
thing was listening to Marqueli's little feet dancing
around their small, legion-provided, apartment in the
city. They'd been assigned those quarters when Jorge
had entered the BA program for disabled legionary
veterans. They would remain in it as part of the new
program. The building was both near the University
of Balboa and more than large enough to accommodate the eighteen disabled Ph.D. candidates, six per
year at a standard three years per course of study.
At seven floors with four apartments for each of the
top six floors, it could have held twenty-four families.

The apartments weren't huge, each having a small
kitchen, combination living and dining room, two
decently sized bedrooms and a small office. Each also
had a balcony looking towards the campus. There
was an elevator that ran from the parking lot, which
was in a stilted area beneath the building, to the top
floor. They were furnished, if sparsely, and, all in all,

could have been called "comfortable." Since all but
one of the candidates was anything from disabled
to severely disabled, the building was modified for
handicap accessibility. The bottom floor was devoted
to an academic advisor, on one side, and a "club" on
the other.

For the most part the first six doctoral candidates
selected had been free to choose their own subjects.
That is to say, those selected were those who wished
to study and write on something Carrera wanted written. One candidate would write on "Combat Ecology,"
which had absolutely nothing to do with the natural
environment but would deal instead with the way
social factors, technology, doctrine and tactics fed
upon each other and caused each other to develop,
often in odd ways. Other candidates wanted to explore
subjects like "Command in War," "Technology in War,"
"Organizing for War," and "Supplying War." (That last
candidate was a former supply clerk who'd lost both
legs in Sumer to an improvised explosive device.)
Jorge's proposal, "History and Moral Philosophy," had
also been accepted.

Jorge sat on the legion-provided sofa in the living room. He'd been at his desk, braille-reading a
text on Old Earth's ancient Rome, when he'd heard
Marqueli's shout.

He couldn't see to read the damned letter, of
course; Marqueli had had to read it to him. (Well,
that was her *job*. The legion also hired the spouses at
a small stipend of one hundred and ten FSD a month
to be "assistants" to their husbands. It helped defray
the greater expense of living in the city and without
making the relatively simple finance and accounting

system of the *Legion del Cid* any more complex than
necessary. The one candidate who was unmarried was
also given a girl-hire. They would soon be sleeping
together.) Still, Jorge Mendoza sat with the letter
held lightly but firmly in his hands. The letter made
the dream real.

Now I can do some good. Now I can be heard,
he thought.

Isla Real, First Tercio Centurions' Family Quarters, 3/5/467 AC

"Can you hear me, Ricardo?" Cara asked in a furious
voice. "I am proud of you, yes. I love you, yes. But
I cannot—do you hear me? CANNOT!—stand this
anymore! You were almost killed two months ago.
How many more times were you almost killed that I
never found out about? Do you have any idea what
it's like for a woman to lie awake at night worrying
that her husband—the man she loves most in the
world—might be lying dead in a ditch? Or captured
and butchered—yes, I've seen the films on the TV—by
some ragheaded maniacs? Or blown to bits by some
coward's bomb with never even a body to bury?"

She buried her face in her hands and began to cry.
That was, for Cruz, worse than the anger. The anger
he could fight against. Against the grief and the hurt
he felt helpless.

"But, Cara," Cruz answered, despairingly, "I don't
know how to *do* anything else. And I'm good at this.
Then, too . . . I don't know if I'd like doing anything
else."

"You have veterans' benefits. I checked; they're

matched to your rank. As a centurion, junior grade you could go back to school full time and earn a degree, then maybe teach . . . or be an engineer . . . or a doctor . . . or a lawyer."

Cruz shivered. "I *hate* lawyers. My father would disown me if I became one. And I can't stand snivelers. How can someone be a doctor when he can't stand people who whine about being sick? Other than our own kids, I don't really like kids. So how could I teach? And engineering doesn't really interest me. What's the challenge in working with unthinking, inert material when I've grown used to building with the hardest material of all to build with, men?"

"If you loved me, you would think of something you could do," she insisted, through tears.

"If you loved me, you wouldn't ask me to give up a job I love for one I would hate," he countered.

To that objection Cara had the definitive answer. She ran off to the bedroom in tears, slamming and locking the door behind her.

Each tercio's caserne had a club for officers and another for centurions. These were mostly frequented by the junior officers, lowest grade tribunes and signifers, and the centurions and optios. There were larger and considerably more ornate clubs for seniors at the main cantonment area on the north side of the island, overlooking the bay.

The theory behind the club was, at one level, organizational and, at another, moral. Carrera believed that men could best identify with and care about all the members of groups of between about one and two hundred. Anything smaller was too likely to be demoralized by losses; anything larger was too big for every man to know every other, care about those others, and value the good opinions of those others.

He further believed that men could normally feel that way about two groups at a time. These groups were, presumptively, the maniple—most armies said "company"—to which the soldier belonged and, for leaders, the leadership corps to which they belonged. For example, within a tercio of four cohorts, there were approximately one hundred and sixty officers and warrant officers. They represented a primary group that had a potentially serious emotional hold on each of them. Thus, there was an "O" Club to each tercio caserne. There were also about two hundred centurions and optios, so they too belonged to a primary group in addition to their maniple and, thus, had their own club. There were also, within each cohort, something over two hundred noncoms, corporals and sergeants. Though this was a bit large, there was a noncom club for each of the four cohorts in a tercio. Soldiers had a club within their barracks for the roughly two hundred men of their maniple.

Guests from outside the applicable unit or corps were, by and large, not welcome except by special invitation. Girls were always welcome, of course.

Some armies looked at the clubs as businesses, to be kept if profitable or at least self-sustaining and to be discarded if they failed to support themselves. Carrera considered them to be, in the broadest sense, training opportunities, to be supported whether they made a profit or not.

As a practical matter, legionary clubs typically broke even. If they found themselves with an embarrassing profit they threw large parties. If they found themselves operating at a loss the price of drinks went up until the loss was made good or the club manager had the money squeezed from him ("squeezed" being something of a euphemism).

Arredondo found Cruz sitting at the bar squeezing a lemon into a rum and cola.

"I didn't think you drank, normally, Ricardo." *First names only in the club.* "Hell, you usually give away the little rum bottles in the combat rations."

"Normally, I don't, Scarface." *Or nicknames, where appropriate.* Arredondo had a broad scar running from one side of his jaw up to past his hairline, a gift of some long-deceased Sumeri rebel. Since the scar was honorably earned, Arredondo rather liked the nickname.

"And, besides, the ration rum's pretty vile. This"—his finger indicated his drink—"is the good stuff."

Legionary combat ration rum was 180-proof suicide-in-a-little-bottle that was only palatable if cut—much cut—with something. On the plus side, one could theoretically pour it into raw sewage, mix it up, wait a few minutes, and then drink with reasonable confidence that all one was drinking was shit, not the various bugs that usually went with it. Best of all, it made legionary rations *very* popular with FSC forces, such that a six-for-one trading ratio was standard fair market value whenever the two forces worked in close proximity.

The ration rum was vile, true enough, but Esterhazy had seen to the creation of a not unimpressive microbrewery to produce *Cervesa del Cid* on the island. Arredondo signaled the bartender for a beer. While waiting for his drink, Cruz's boss rubbed the scar on his cheek. He looked at Cruz's face, then at the rum and coke. Adding one somber face to one rum and coke he came up with the perfect question: "You have a problem, Ricardo?"

"Bad one," Cruz answered, succinctly "Cara wants me to leave the legion. I don't want to. But if I don't, I think she may leave *me*."

"Ooo, that sucks."

"No shit."

"How are you leaning?" Arredondo asked as the bartender set a frosty mug down in front of him.

"I'm not," Cruz shrugged. "I have no clue what to do. If I leave the legion, I'm going to be miserable. If Cara leaves me, I'm going to be miserable."

"Switch over to one of the reserve cohorts of the tercio?" Arredondo asked, helpfully. Each tercio had several reserve cohorts, composed of discharged regulars and volunteers who joined expressly for the reserves. The reserves only served one three-day weekend a month, plus a month a year, for which they were paid at standard rates and were entitled to a reduced scale of benefits. They were obligated to come when called but, so far, there had been no call up.

"I considered it, Scarface, but it wouldn't really be the same. I'd feel second-rate. I'd see the regulars often enough to realize what I was missing, too."

Arredondo absentmindedly bit at the right quadrant of his upper lip. "What's her problem?" he asked.

Cruz shook his head. "I . . . think . . . yes, I *think*, that it's a mix of things. Mostly, though, it's that I'm gone a lot and she doesn't want me to get my ass shot off."

"Well, you can understand—"

"I *do* understand. That doesn't make it any easier."

"Could you buy her off if you took some other kind of duty? Like . . . mmm . . . maybe took over a slot as a combat instructor or basic training platoon centurion? I think I could arrange that."

Cruz had considered it, but, "I don't think so. That would still keep me gone much of the time and there would still be the chance that I might get sent back to the war."

Arredondo tilted his head to one side. "It would be more than a chance, Ricardo," he admitted. "We've got a little break going now while the Tercio Don John takes up the fight at sea, but that can't last. We'll be back at the war within a couple of years, I figure."

Nodding, Cruz agreed, "So does Cara. I think that's part of her reasoning, if *reasoning* is the right word to use when discussing a woman's thoughts. Right now, while the ground forces are not in the war, I can leave with a good conscience. If we were still engaged, our boys still under fire, I probably couldn't . . . wouldn't anyway. She knows that."

"'Women are stupid but clever and bear considerable watching,'" Scarface deliberately misquoted. "Did you tell her you're probably moving up to take over the platoon? That it would mean a promotion and a not-exactly contemptible pay raise?"

"I mentioned it. She wasn't impressed. Hell, Scarface, if it were about money then she'd have to admit I make more here than I am likely to on the outside, even with reserve pay tacked on to whatever I might make as a civvie."

Cruz sighed deeply. "It really comes down to the fact that she wants me home and she doesn't want me hurt or killed. And I don't know how to argue against that. She wants me *out*."

Ciudad Balboa, Presidential Palace, 5/5/467 AC

Presidente de la Republica Rocaberti had problems.

The Republic of Balboa had a Gross Domestic Product, exclusive of the LdC and its various enterprises, on the order of just over twelve billion FSD a year. Of that, the government managed to squeeze out about a tenth. Thus, the loss of income from legionary contributions, amounting to roughly one hundred and sixty million a year, *hurt*. Not only had services had to be curtailed, but—far, far worse, from the point of view of those families that actually ran the country— the rake-off potential had virtually disappeared. Those chief families were not happy about it, either.

That was one reason why the government had acquiesced in the legion's creation of half a dozen military schools. It had not only reduced expenditures, it had also left more to disappear down the rat hole of familial corruption.

The legion had done other things, too, that reduced government expenditures and made more available for graft, even as it made the graft more obvious. The reserve formations did a great deal of what was sometimes called, "civic action," building clinics and schools, road improvement, opening factories, and such. Admittedly, the factories just flat refused to hire anyone who was not either a reservist, a discharged regular, or the spouse of a slain or disabled legionary (indeed, that requirement was the biggest single limitation of legionary economic expansion within the country), but there had been quite a bit of trickle down. The Civil Force, Balboa's police force *cum* armed force, was also given full post-service employment rights as a matter of courtesy and good public relations.

Of course, the downside was that the legion was buying affection at a greater rate than the government could hope to. Then again, the Balboans were a realistic people. They knew their government was unutterably corrupt from the word go. They basically *had* no affection for it. It had been put in power by foreign, gringo, arms. It was maintained now by foreign, Tauran Union, arms. It was simply despised.

And now there are rumors that Parilla is going to retire from the legion and enter politics, thought the president. *That's intolerable. Not only is Parilla a frightfully honest man, but he's a peasant, a stinking* campesino. *He has no connection to the old families. Worse, he's approximately as ruthless as his pet gringo, Carrera.* A Presidente Parilla *means many true gentlemen in prison or in exile, including, most likely* me. *If he applies legionary rules retroactively, it might mean many true gentlemen put against a wall and shot.*

President Rocaberti shivered at that thought. The legion, back when there was only one, and that one at one third strength only, had had not the slightest qualm about shooting his nephew; shooting him like a dog without the slightest regard for the man's clan or its position. How much more ruthless would they be with four regular legions, the equivalent of as many in reserve, and owning the government?

Shoot me? Rocaberti thought, fingering his neck. *No, I'll be lucky if they don't* hang *me, along with every adult member of my clan that ever took an illicit dime. They've got to be stopped.*

He said it aloud. "They've got to be stopped."

"*Quoi?*" asked the Gallic commander, General Janier, of the Tauran Union brigade stationed in the Transitway area.

Janier was a tall, elegantly slender, but sadly toad-faced officer who understood Spanish perfectly well but refused to lower himself to speak it. His country's contribution consisted basically of himself and his headquarters, plus a commando battalion. The line combat battalions were provided by other, lesser, TU members, in rotation. This had become a national pattern for the Gauls, to provide low risk headquarters troops and commanders, plus a small elite force, but leave the bulk of combat capability for others. To give them their due, they were good at that sort of thing; despite having one of the least competitive economies in the TU, they still managed to take a central position in that organization and run the thing to suit the Gallic Republic to a tee.

The Taurans had been brought in to "secure the Transitway" once the terrorist threat had grown out of hand as a result of the LdC's participation in the war. That had been merely an excuse, though. They were really there to secure the government—internationalist, emotionally detached from its country's and people's welfare, and therefore corrupt, pro-TU and pro-UEPF—from the legions. Any securing of the Transitway from terrorist attack was merely incidental.

Janier repeated, "*Quoi?*"

Sighing with frustration, Rocaberti explained the problem to Janier, in French. He ended by pointing out, "And outside of your brigade we have nothing. Our police and militarized police are underarmed and unreliable. The people despise us. Even the FSC, which has fallen desperately *out* of love with the legions, still could probably not intervene against them here."

The Gaul smiled with satisfaction. It was good to have one's protectorates actually need protecting.

The ambassador to the Republic from the UEPF added, "Don't count on us. We are still stymied from direct action by the FSC. If there is any one issue the bulk of the people there agree on, it is that the UEPF is the enemy. Even their progressive politicians can't openly disagree with that, not if they want to keep their jobs."

Janier's smile grew broader still. Yes, it was very good to be needed so desperately. But, one had to be realistic.

"There is no practical way, at this time, for the TU to do more than safeguard the Transitway and your government. I have four battalions, one of those mechanized but one also a very lightly equipped commando battalion. Usually, too, I have another infantry battalion undergoing jungle training here. We could fly in a couple more on fairly short notice, maybe even three to five more battalions *if*, and only if, we planned it well in advance, had control of the airfields and the skies, and if we impressed civilian air carriers. If your 'legions' decided to hit us first, or to mobilize their reserves and hit us first, we wouldn't have a prayer."

"Allies?" Rocaberti asked.

"The Zhong have forty or fifty thousand illegal immigrants here, plus about as many legal ones," Janier answered. "They could perhaps be induced to intervene to protect what they consider to be their people. But such intervention would be—" He looked at his dumpy adjutant, a Gallic major who appeared even more toadlike than Janier.

"Major Malcoeur, what *could* the Zhong bring to the field?"

The major was widely believed, within his own army, to have no real talent but licking the boss's ass. This was unfair. Though he was quite a talented asslick, he was, at least, very thorough in his official duties. "With warning—a lot of warning, *mon General*—they could fly in a brigade or move a division by sea. These are not mutually exclusive. If we provided sea and air lift they could probably double or even triple that. They have a large army, over one hundred divisions, but little in the way of strategic transport."

"We have a . . . close . . . yes, a close connection with the Zhong Guo," said the ambassador from the UEPF. He, too, spoke French. "I will make inquiries."

"Not yet, Mr. Ambassador," answered Janier. "Before we bring them in too closely, I need to find a way to crush these 'legions' with or without the Zhong. That I do not have yet."

Isla Real, Quarters #1, 7/5/467 AC

Carrera had stuck himself with having a ballroom in his house. Parilla's burden included keeping a very secure conference room in the basement of his. On the plus side, it also served as a place where he could have a drink without being nagged by a loving wife who worried endlessly over his health.

"This is screwing me; you realize that, right?"

Parilla blew air through his lips. "Yes, I know. And if I don't retire and become president of the country what happens? We've gone just about as far as we can go with this, as things are. In fact, we've gone as far as I ever wanted to go. My country has an army again, even if that army is not under the government of the country and even if a substantial proportion of it is expatriate."

A secure conference room didn't at all rule out comfortable leather chairs. Parilla rested his head on the back of his. "But what I didn't realize was that there are ends beyond ends . . . unintended consequences. What I didn't realize was that we would automatically be put in opposition to the government here such that one of us must go. I certainly didn't foresee TU troops here in my country. God knows, I didn't foresee fighting a war *here*."

Carrera grimaced and shrugged, then shifted his rear forward to rest his own head on the back of his seat. He admitted, "Neither, I suppose, did I. I just focused on destroying those who murdered my family; something—you might note—I have so far failed to do . . . or even to get appreciably closer to doing. Sometimes I despair of it."

He was silent for a few moments. Then he asked, "Okay, so let's suppose you resign and run for president. We have over forty thousand 'election workers' in the form of the reserves. We have a *lot* of sympathy and affection from the people. If you retire and run, you will probably win. *Then* what?"

"Then I invite the Tauran Union to leave, with our thanks and gratitude."

"Won't work," Carrera objected. "They are here at the

invitation of the government, yes, but they also have a mandate from the World League to, 'secure the Balboa Transitway for the common benefit of mankind.' That means they have a mandate they can present to their own people as a legitimate reason to stay no matter what any given chief of state here might say. Moreover, since you— that is to say, we—represent 'the forces of fascism and reaction,' you and we are inherently illegitimate in their eyes. The short version of which is—"

"The short version of which is, they are not going to leave peaceably," Parilla interjected. "Yes, you're probably right. Fight them?"

Carrera's face screwed up in distaste. "Given a choice, I'd rather not. We are not friends but we do have a lot of the same enemies, even if the Taurans' heads are stuck so far up their asses that they can't see it. Besides, probably we wouldn't end up fighting them only."

"You say you would rather not. That isn't really the question. *Can* we fight them and win?"

"Sure," Carrera admitted. "We can fight and defeat them here in Balboa, especially if we get in the first hits and without warning. *That*, however, means only a limited defeat for the Taurans—no, let's be accurate here, for the Frogs who run the TU like they owned it—and much motivation to get even, even if they won't admit that that's their motivation. In a long war, they outclass us in almost every way."

"In what ways do they not outclass us?" Parilla asked. Carrera was as much his superior in military matters as Parilla was Carrera's better in affairs political.

Carrera didn't even have to think about it. "Easier to answer it what areas they do: industry, population, wealth, size of armed forces, technology, diplomatic clout, naval power. Add to that that our own government is on their side. Our advantages at the moment are better-trained and -led troops with adequate if not superior equipment. Oh, and superior ruthlessness. Even then, though, the best half of our troops, the regular legions, are stuck here on the *Isla Real* with only the reservists on the mainland. The TU has enough naval and air power, easily, to prevent us from deploying regulars to the mainland in a crisis."

"That's half the reason we built the military schools, isn't it?" Parilla asked, rhetorically. Carrera simply nodded.

"Do things change if *we* are the government?" he asked.

"Yes. Then we can redeploy the regular legions to the mainland. Then we can expand the reserves to a serious militia system along the lines of Helvetia's and Zion's. Then we can build defenses, expand our industry, and hit them economically by denying them access to the Transitway."

"So you agree then, that I must become president."

"I always agreed, Raul. It's just that it's screwing me by making me take on your duties here and my own overseas once we are rehired."

"Will we be?"

"Oh, yes. We'll be rehired, probably within six months, to save the *Tauran Union's* collective ass in Pashtia."

Indicus Koh Mountains, Central Pashtia, 9/5/467 AC

The winding mountain pass was sheer-sided, and strewn with rocks on both sides. Behind the rocks, and dug in where there was enough soil for that, Noorzad's band awaited the arrival of the point of the enemy column at the marker, a scraggly tree, which would signal the beginning of the ambush.

At the other end of this road was a Tauran Union base camp. Cutting the road would not cause them to starve. It would, on the other hand, make life difficult as supplies would have to be flown in by helicopter.

Life was good for Noorzad and his band. Still, while his men enjoyed the benefits of battlefield success, honor, respect, trophies and—best of all—female slaves, he was quite indifferent to the material rewards. Oh, yes, he made use of the slave girls. That was under the advice of the Prophet (PBUH) and, so, was not only not a vice, it was a positive religious virtue. And religious virtue *mattered* to Noorzad. The only thing that mattered more was the triumph of his religion, submission to the will of Allah across this globe.

He knew his followers were not so pure of heart as he was himself. Some were here for revenge, after losing family. Others were in it for the money or the excitement. Some wanted to wipe out the shame caused by so many centuries of defeat of the sons of the Prophet by the bastard children of Christ. Some were in it for the robbery and rapine. Most were a mix.

Of all his band, only he was in the war purely for the advancement of his faith. Oh, yes, he liked the action, just as he liked the use of the women his men captured. But he would have done it without the women and, if he'd had a talent for anything but action, he could have done it from behind a desk.

Fortunately, he didn't have to do anything for which he lacked talent. All he had to do was fight. As he was about to do, as a matter of fact, with the Tauran Union column moving through the pass below.

The first sign of the ambush, to the Tauran troops in the truck column, was a large explosion at the point that blew a goodly boulder right through the cab of a truck, turning the driver and the column commander into so much strawberry-colored paste. The two soldiers who had been in the bed of the lead truck disappeared in the smoke and dust from the blast. Alive or dead; none could say.

Not that anyone cared to say. The explosion was the signal for riflemen, machine gunners and RGL gunners lining both sides of the pass to open up. Trucks exploded in living technicolor as machine guns set white-skinned soldiers to dancing the ballet. Many ran in panic, with no obvious regard for direction. Others froze in shock where they were, oblivious to what cover there might have been. Some tried to return fire but, with the leaden hail coming from both sides and above, the only cover available either left one open to fire from the other side of the pass or put one in a position—under a truck, typically—where no return fire was practical.

Noorzad didn't laugh at the plight of the Taurans; killing the infidel was too serious a business to laugh over until the job was done. These, at least the ones in the backs of the trucks, were Royal Haarlem Marines, so he thought. *They* weren't panicking, though under the circumstances their resistance was marginal. Little by little it was beaten down.

When he was satisfied that resistance was completely

crushed, Noorzad gave the order to sweep into the kill zone. The sweep was not a precision movement. By ones and twos his men arose from their rocks and walked carefully downhill into the kill zone, rifles at the ready. Noorzad followed at a distance; for this he didn't need to lead from in front. Scattered shots ahead told him that his men were finding wounded.

He watched calmly as one of his men put the muzzle of his rifle to the head of a prone Tauran. The enemy soldier simply closed his eyes; not even having the will anymore to try to resist.

And that is why Taurus is doomed; their people no longer have the will to resist, but only to close their eyes to the reality around them. I wish the FSC were as accommodating.

Noorzad walked the line of trucks, many of them aflame. From somewhere—perhaps one of the trucks had contained personnel files—papers billowed in the smoky wind. Around him his men were stripping bodies of weapons, money, watches and boots. Still other parties ransacked the trucks for useable supplies. Much could not be used, of course, and would be burned or detonated in place. Still, there was much valuable loot.

He gave a few curt orders to his men, reminding them of their priorities. Then Noorzad spotted the prisoners. He was surprised, really; he hadn't expected any.

Private Verdonk was *not* a Marine. To understand that is to understand what followed. The Marines *believed* in something, even if it was only a faith in the Korps Mariniers, Haarlem's Brigade Princess

Irene. Verdonk had never believed in anything. He'd known few people in his life, and none of those at all well, who really believed in anything. Believing in things—in people, in religions, in one's country and one's culture—this had fallen out of favor in Haarlem. Instead, from kindergarten to old age, one was expected to believe in everything. The problem with that was that faith in everything meant no special faith in anything; to love all mankind was to *love* none of it.

Love? What did Verdonk know of love beyond some hasty thrusting on a moldy mattress with some girl who meant even less to him than she did to herself? His people? How can you love a people that have given up on themselves? His country? What was a country within the Tauran Union except a lower mechanism for collecting taxes and redistributing income, for obeying and enforcing the *diktats* of the bureaucrats? His culture? His people had given up on that when they'd given up on themselves.

It was fair to say that, inside Verdonk, feeling was a vacuum awaiting fulfillment. He'd joined the army in search of that, joined it and discovered that the army was no better than the people from which it sprang.

And I didn't have the courage to join the Marines. But then, few do.

Noorzad looked over the baker's dozen prisoners his men had taken. Seven, he saw, were female. One was quite attractive; the others acceptable. They would become slaves. In fact, they already were.

The men were of more interest to Noorzad. Whether women submitted to the Faith or not was more or less irrelevant, so long as they submitted to the rules.

A whip was a good enough tool for that. And Mary the Copt had made a perfectly acceptable slave for the Prophet, peace be upon him.

But the men? He'd been toying with the idea, of late, of seeing if any of the prisoners could be converted to the true faith instead of being killed. He'd never before tried but had heard rumors that others had had success with the attempt. It was also said that the fundamental emptiness of Tauran lives made such people truer converts, once they had had the chance to experience the richness and fullness of being in submission to the will of Allah. He thought it worth a try.

After all, they can always be killed later if it doesn't work.

He spoke a few words to his followers. The women were separated and hustled away. Then he spoke to the men, even as the cries and screams elicited by the mass rape of the women began. That the Haarlemers almost always spoke English rather well helped.

"Are any among you here Christians or Jews?" he asked.

All the Haarlemers were afraid to answer affirmatively. There were no Jews and, as a matter of faith, no real Christians among them anyway. Some might have answered that they were, since they went to services on rare occasion. But they were too afraid of being killed as infidels.

"I see," said Noorzad softly. He'd expected them to be either too faithless or too afraid to announce a faith if they had one. That was part of his plan. More loudly, he announced, "Then you are all either pagans or atheists and must be killed." He began to turn away.

"Wait!" pleaded Verdonk.

That, too, was part of Noorzad's plan.

HQ, Legion del Cid, Isla Real, 18/5/467 AC

"Gentlemen, I need a plan," Carrera announced at a special meeting called with certain key staff officers.

This was no big deal; his staff was used to it. They knew, too, that whatever he wanted they could almost certainly deliver on. After all, they'd never failed him yet. His next words, however, were a bit out of the ordinary.

"Rather," he continued, "I need a transformation plan, one that converts the legions as they are into a corps. I need to be able to do that without irreparably breaking the system that we have. I further need to be able to transport that corps to the southern border of Pashtia with full supplies for six months' intensive operations. After that takes place—in fact I need it before the deployment takes place— we need to be able to fight our way from Mazari Omar to Chabolo. Following that, we will need a plan to redeploy most of that corps, leaving a standard legion behind for interdiction and counter-insurgency."

Now *that* was ambitious. The staff sat silent until Dan Kuralski whispered, "Holy shit."

Kuralski looked up, asking, more loudly, "Do you have any idea what you're asking, Pat? To transform from legions to a full corps, to get those to an inland railhead . . . We'll screw everything up, organizationally. Do you have a contract for this?"

"Not yet. But my family senator tells me that Hamilton, FD, is getting into a panic. The Taurans are crumbling in Pashtia. The Progressive Party administration can't commit more FSC troops without crumbling, too. That leaves us. Harriet is pushing—and, yes, it is costing us, costing me, to have her push—for them to rehire us for Pashtia. By the time they do that the country will be half lost. I could be convinced otherwise but for now I think nothing less than a corps can fight its way to Chabolo and retrieve the effort there. Do you think we could get by with less?"

Kuralski didn't answer that question. Instead he started thinking aloud on what a corps might look like.

"We could take three legions. Then we strip off the mechanized cohorts and the Cazador cohorts—maybe minus one maniple each— to create a brigade of each. For headquarters and support for those brigades we can raid the schoolhouse for cadre, the head of the Armor School and Cazador School and their staffs becoming brigade headquarters. Maybe we should do the same with the air *alae* from those legions. That leaves the infantry legions with four infantry cohorts, a heavy maniple and a Cazador maniple, the combat support and artillery cohorts, and the service support and headquarters cohorts. Maybe, too, we strip off one maniple of heavy artillery each to form a corps artillery, the Artillery School providing headquarters, as well. We could do something similar with the other combat support branches like engineers, air defense and MPs. We can probably curtail courses for the D echelon legionary cadre to fill in gaps. God, though, that leaves little enough here."

"I know," Carrera agreed. "Assume we'll actually call up some of the reserves for the first time. Assume that we'll leave D echelon to fill up to replace the corps later on. Beyond that, you're chief of staff. So go staff it, Chief. I want to see a preliminary OPLAN within . . . oh, two weeks."

Barco del Legion Dos Lindas, Xamar, 26/5/467 AC

"I once wanted to see this sight so badly," said Kurita, looking out at the steaming Uhuru coast from the bridge of the *Dos Lindas*. "Back during the war we tried so hard to get this far. And then the FS Navy caught us in the open, far from land-based air support. And they butchered us. My ship escaped, barely, along with half a dozen destroyers and two light cruisers. The rest went down."

Fosa contemplated how that must have felt, saw in his mind's eyes his own fleet going down in smoke and flame, sailors trapped below decks slowly drowning, some struggling in the oil-covered water as the flames licked along the surface to drive them below to death. He shivered, though if Kurita saw it, he affected not to notice.

Instead, Kurita asked, "What's next, Captain-san?"

INTERLUDE

5 January, 2091, *Finca* Carrera, Guayabal, Panama

Belisario Carrera shook with rage. "This land has been in my family for nearly five *hundred* years. What the fuck do you mean that the UN is taking half of it?"

The uniformed policemen, local boys all, escorting the executive assistant to the deputy special representative for the secretary general to the Republic of Panama, looked down at the ground, ashamed and disgusted. They understood that attachment to the land. But what choice had they? They had their own wives and children to think about.

"There is no call for profanity, Mr. Carrera," said the sweating, suit-clad bureaucrat, stiffly. His accent was strange to Belisario, his Spanish clipped and harsh. "No call at all. Your democratically elected government has agreed to allow the United Nations to assist it in better apportioning your nation's wealth for the betterment of mankind. That your ancestors stole this land for themselves does not mean, sir, that you own it. It is part of the common heritage of the Family of Man."

Belisario's thirteen-year-old daughter, Mitzilla, chose

250

that moment to come out of the house to stand beside her father. "Get off our land, you bastard," she said.

The bureaucrat looked down at Mitzi's face and then continued on. When his eyes reached her chest they opened wide with surprise and desire. He tore them away, most reluctantly, and returned his attention to her father. He said, "Perhaps, for a suitable consideration, something can be worked out, Mr. Carrera."

Belisario said nothing. But he looked at the UN representative in a way that said, without words, *You are a dead man.*

It was a UN court that sat in judgment over Belisario. A national court simply could not be trusted to give a proper judgment. In neither case, though, would the sentence have been death.

"Belisario Carrera," said the judge, "you have been found guilty of the premeditated murder of Robert Nyere. We have no death penalty, as we have grown above such barbarisms. If we did, I would certainly have no choice but to sentence you to hang by the neck until you are dead. I would enjoy passing such sentence, Mr. Carrera, as the man you murdered, a flawless and faultless gem of mankind, was my nephew. As is, I sentence you to transportation for life to the colony of Balboa, on the Planet Terra Nova. May the planet kill you in a way I am forbidden from doing.

"Bailiff, take him away."

15 April, 2099, Long Island, New York

It wasn't bad enough that Detective Juan Alvarez, as a city employee, had to pay tax to the city of New

York, along with the State of New York, and the United States. No, no; that wasn't nearly bad enough. *Now* he had to pay as well, after filling out a half inch thick stack of virtually incomprehensible forms, to Earth's United Nations.

Actually, it was worse than that. The UN didn't collect a single tax. This would have been too simple and employed far too few bureaucrats. Instead, Alvarez had to pay to the General Assembly Fund, the Peacekeeping Fund, the Food and Agricultural Organization Fund, the Arts and Humanities Fund, the Reparations to the OAU for the Loss of Human Capital Fund . . .

"For Christ's sake," Alvarez blurted out, putting his head down and running thick fingers through thinning hair, "*my* family were goddamned serfs to the Spanish. Most of my wife's were serfs to the English. Why the hell are *we* paying the descendants of people who made money selling slaves for having sold those slaves?"

There was no answer, of course, or none that would satisfy. The real, and unsatisfactory, answer was that money was collected to go to the Organization of African Unity, in order to employ bureaucrats who knew nothing and did nothing, and pad the accounts of the chiefs of state of the countries that made up the OAU and those of their families.

With a sigh, Alvarez wrote out a check and attached it to the Human Capital Fund return, then added those to the pile. The next form was the tax return for the Repatriation Fund for non-Islamic citizens of the Zionist Entity. This, however, was an optional tax, mostly paid by Islamics across the world: Alvarez crinkled up the form and tossed it into the wastebasket.

UN direct taxation was not something federally

mandated, nor even approved. Instead, over the last fifteen years, a growing number of states of the United States had adopted UN taxation within their state tax codes. They received a percentage back, much as private corporations and companies did with the sales tax, for what they collected on behalf of the UN. There was talk of an amendment to the Constitution. Certainly the Supreme Court had been no help since it had unilaterally decided it was subject to the laws and rulings of various international tribunals.

"I could move down south," Alvarez said aloud. "They don't collect for the UN, yet. But . . ." He shook his head, no. The language of the American Deep South was now mostly Spanish, and Alvarez didn't speak Spanish. Not much work for a police detective in North Carolina who couldn't speak Spanish, less still in Texas.

"Besides, they're a mess down there; Mexico in Confederate gray. I couldn't afford the bribes to get on a police force even if I did speak Spanish. No wonder great-great-grandpappy wet his ankles in the Rio Grande. No wonder . . ."

Alvarez felt one of those rare epiphanous moments that happen, sometimes, when two or three different little reminders hit all at once. *The Jews are leaving Israel en masse for Terra Nova, and the more that leave, the more want to. When the going got tough in Mexico, not that it was ever likely to have been too easy, Great-Grandpappy lit out for greener pastures. And there's not too much fucking bureaucracy on the New World.*

"Honey?" he called out to his wife. "I just had an idea. . . ."

CHAPTER SEVEN

Set a thief to catch a thief.
—Gallic Proverb

Set a lawless non-governmental organization to
destroy a lawless non-governmental organization.
—Patricio Carrera

UEPF *Spirit of Peace*, 27/5/467 AC

"Computer, center on target and enhance scale."

At Robinson's command the image on his Kurosawa
screen shifted, then changed, going from the western
half of the continent of Uhuru and the eastern half
of the Sea of Sind to a narrow view of the Xamar
coast and, finally, to the little flotilla comprising the
Dos Lindas task force. It was in real time; he could
actually see the aircraft taking off and landing.

"From here we could toss a rock down and destroy
their flagship, but . . ."

"But," Wallenstein interjected, "the FSC has made
clear that any direct military action on the part of the
UEPF on any target down below will be an instant
casus belli. No matter the party in power, none have

ever wavered from it. They'd be hounded from office if they did."

Robinson sneered, not at Wallenstein but at the memory of his predecessor, the high admiral who had scorched two of the Federated States' cities.

"I wonder if he knew the trouble he would cause us."

Wallenstein shook her blonde head. "I doubt it. It's easy to forget how quickly an uncivilized and uncontrolled people can advance if they have good reason to."

"Which reason my predecessor certainly gave them. And all for nothing since they won that war anyway. The only difference was that there were twenty or thirty million fewer Yamatans to see the end. Oh, well, spilled milk and all. Besides, he paid with his life, after a fashion."

Robinson turned his attention back to the Kurosawa. "I can't attack them directly. I *can*, however, make sure they not able to attack anyone else."

Wallenstein made a quizzical sound.

"It's simple, Marguerite. That contemptible little fleet can only affect the sea it occupies and about three or four hundred kilometers around it. Even that three or four hundred, though, is constrained by the speed of their aircraft and the chance of being in the right place at the right time. *We* get to choose whether those times and places will be right."

Robinson's voice changed to the neutral, uninflected tone used for talking to machines. "Computer, connect me with Abdulahi."

To the high admiral's mild surprise, the answer came almost immediately. A melodious voice said, "Yes, High Admiral; Abdulahi here."

There's a shock; one of those down below actually listening to instructions.

Whatever his thoughts, Robinson confined his words to business. "Friend, that new threat I told you of has taken up station off your coastline."

"I see that, High Admiral," the Xamari answered. Robinson had transferred to him, as he had to Mustafa, the means of tapping directly into UEPF surveillance and sensing systems. "We can easily avoid them."

"Excellent, Abdulahi."

BdL *Dos Lindas*, Xamar Coast, 4/6/467 AC

"This is superb, Commodore," Fosa complimented Kurita on the sushi the Yamatan had prepared from fish he'd caught himself the night before.

Kurita smiled slightly, and nodded, acknowledging the compliment.

Fosa looked around at the Yamatan's quarters. In warship terms they were the height of luxury, measuring all of about three hundred and twenty square feet. Even Fosa's own were not quite so large. They were furnished well, as warships measured such things. Kurita had hung on one wall a portrait of the emperor he had served ably and bravely in the Great Global War. That emperor had long since joined his divine ancestors. His memory retained Kurita's loyalty, even so.

It wasn't the size or the luxury, nor even the portrait of the emperor and what it said of Kurita, the samurai, that impressed Fosa. It was the unbelievable cleanliness of the quarters.

He'd asked of his senior naval centurion how the place had gotten so completely sanitized. The centurion had shrugged, "Got no clue, Cap'n. He never asked us for anything but a mop and bucket, sponges and some rags. Oh, and liquid cleaner."

Fosa was left with the only possible solution; that Kurita, at nearly a century old, had gotten down on his ancient hands and knees and *made* quarters fit for his emperor's portrait. That was rather humbling.

"I saved it from my battlecruiser," Kurita had said in explanation. "When we had to . . . surrender"—and the word came out only with painful difficulty—"I took it last, as I was leaving. Every day I apologize to it that I and my comrades failed in our duty. Perhaps someday the emperor shall forgive us."

Which helped convince Fosa, not that he needed much convincing, that the Yamatans were not just odd, but *admirably* odd.

"How goes the hunt?" Kurita asked.

"Not well," the captain said. "Admittedly we've only been on station two weeks but . . ."

"But given the frequency of reported piratical attacks near this section of the coast a week should have seen at least two," the commodore supplied.

Fosa nodded. "Yes, but there's been nothing. Attacks north of us, yes. Attacks south of us, yes. Nothing here."

The Yamatan quoted, "All warfare is based on deception. Therefore, when capable, feign incapacity; when active, inactivity. When near, make it appear that you are far away; when far away, that you are near. Offer the enemy a bait to lure him, feign disorder and strike him. When he concentrates, prepare against him."

"Musashi?" the Balboan asked. "*The Book of Five Rings?*"

Kurita shook his grey head. "Sun Tzu."

"Do you think someone is reporting on our positions and dispositions, Commodore?"

"Unquestionably," Kurita answered. "The only real question is who."

"Not the Federated States Navy," Fosa said. "Even if the legion is in bad grace with their government their armed forces are still strong friends."

"I agree," the Yamatan said. "That leaves the Tauran Union, the Volgans, the Zhong, and the UEPF. In any case, it hardly matters *who*, for our purposes. What matters is the fact that that someone, to all appearances, *is* reporting on us."

"I wonder if the FSN can shed any light," the Yamatan wondered. "After all, they're rather . . . oh . . . *capable.*"

FSS *Ironsides*, Xamar Coast, 6/6/467

The twin-engined Cricket B came down at an angle that made the deck crew blanch. It didn't roll but hit, bounced once and then again, then came to an almost unbelievable stop.

"It ain't natural," pronounced one of the deck crew. His purple overalls marked him as a "grape," or fuel handler.

An officer from the bridge crew was on hand, detailed to escort Fosa and his small party down to the captain's port cabin. The party didn't include Kurita.

"I do not hate them, Captain-san," the Yamatan had explained, "but it would be . . . awkward, even so. My family was in Motonari, you see." Motonari was one of the two cities in Yamato atomic bombed by the FSC.

Being led through the carrier's innards was a less intimidating exercise for Fosa than had been the approach that showed how completely it dwarfed his own command. *One hundred thousand tons and more. God, what a ship.*

The passageways seemed more to a human scale to Fosa, and then he came to the hangar deck.

I could almost fit Dos Lindas *down in it,* he thought in awe and wonder. He did some measurement by eye. *No, I could fit* Dos Lindas *into it, if we ripped off both flight decks.* Then he consoled himself with the thought, *It's not the size of the ship in the fight; it's the size of the fight in the ship. That, and the rules of engagement.*

The rest of the journey afoot was uneventful, but informative. Twice Fosa stopped to ask his escort officer questions about the ship's operation. Both times he made a mental note to at least consider changing SOP on the *Dos Lindas.*

The captain met him warmly by his port cabin's hatch. Leading him into the quarters, somewhat larger than Fosa's and Kurita's combined, the *Ironside*'s captain made the introductions, the important one of which was to the admiral.

Fosa was surprised to see a bottle of rum sitting on the captain's table. "I thought all FSS ships were dry," he said.

The admiral shrugged. "Yes and no. The chaplain is allowed sacramental alcohol, and the ship's medical staff keeps medicinal brandy. In our case, the chaplain believes in having sacramental bourbon and scotch, rum and cognac, along with the wine. That particular bottle was being held as medicinal rum until it could be properly blessed."

"I see. How . . ." Fosa wanted to say "morally ingenious" but didn't know how far his welcome stayed. He let it go.

"We *can* be morally ingenious," the admiral said.

Lunch and small talk followed. It was a decent meal, but no better than what was served aboard *Dos Lindas*, and perhaps not as good. Fosa made a point of inviting both the captain and the admiral, as well as the other two officers present, signals and operations, to come aboard his own ship at their earliest convenience.

"Regretfully, Legate Fosa, we cannot," the admiral answered for all. "If we did, it would be lending official FSC sanction to what we suspect—to be honest, what we *hope*—is your mission and your rules of engagement. That, our government and the . . . people . . . in charge would never tolerate."

"I understand," Fosa agreed. "Perhaps in some future time, some happier time for your service."

Ironside's skipper said, "The admiral meant what he said, Legate. We sincerely hope you will be able to do what we are expressly forbidden from doing, which is to say, we hope you can do even the slightest good." The captain pushed a folder over to Fosa. "Take a look at that."

Fosa opened the file and saw that it contained a couple of dozen eight-by-ten glossies and a couple of printed sheets of paper. When he looked carefully at the first photo he said, "My God . . ."

The admiral answered, "Our God had nothing to do with it."

The photos were of the massacre, the butchery, of the crew of the *Estrella de Castilla*.

Fosa shuffled through the photos as quickly as he could. When he came to the first printed sheet he began to read. Halfway through the rules of engagement he exclaimed, "How in the hell can they expect you to do anything under this nonsense?"

"They don't expect us to *do* anything, Legate," The admiral explained. "They expect us to make the *appearance* of doing something. Don't you have progressives at home? Appearances matter a lot more to them than actually *doing* anything."

Fosa took from his white uniform blouse a folded piece of paper of his own. "My commander gave me full latitude to write my own ROE. This is ours."

The admiral scanned quickly, then passed the paper on to his subordinate.

"Admirably direct," was the admiral's sole comment.

"Admirably traditional," said the signals chief when the paper reached him.

"Legate," the captain asked, "what does your fleet consist of?"

Fosa laid out the composition of the fleet, omitting only the precise nature of the recreation ship, dubbed "Fosa's Floating Fornication Frigate" by all the crews of his task force. As he spoke, the ops officer began jotting onto a notepad.

"So you have no long-range strategic recon," observed the ops officer for the carrier battle group. "We can make up that lack."

"It would help," Fosa agreed. "But . . . *can* you?"

"Officially no," the admiral said. "Unofficially, I think we can provide that and quite a bit more. But it will all have to be under the table."

"Under the table would be fine. But I think I am

under a looking glass. *Someone* is telling the Xamaris where my ships and planes are at any given time. Nothing else can explain how they've been so successful at avoiding us. It can't be all bad luck."

"It isn't. I can't tell you *how* I know; but I can tell you that I *do* know that the UEPF is sending data to someone inside Xamar. And it's not their ambassador because they, like everyone else, pulled their embassy out of Xamar years ago, when the place collapsed."

"The UEPF! Damn. Then I haven't a prayer of doing any good."

"Oh, I wouldn't say that," the ops officer disagreed. "Tell me; can you put those two patrol boats of yours back aboard their tender . . . mmmm, maybe preferably just before a serious storm?"

"Sure," Fosa shrugged. "But why?"

"Because if you can re-embark them aboard your ship, and get your ship close to the *Ironsides*, you can conceivably unload them and hide them under our flight deck. The UEPF may lose track of them, for a while, at least."

"Okay," Fosa said, "I can see that working once. But after that?"

"After that, something else." It was the ops officer's turn to shrug. "Give us a little time."

"All warfare is based on deception," Fosa said and laughed at himself slightly.

"Clausewitz?" asked the admiral.

"No, sir, Sun Tzu. My . . . well, you might call him my supercargo, Commodore Kurita, quoted it to me just days ago."

"Tadeo Kurita?" the admiral asked.

"Yes, sir, that's him."

The admiral whistled. "He's still alive? Tough old bird. My father told me about Kurita, about him leading what was left of Yamato's Second Fleet in breaking free and running for home after they lost at the Battle of Kuantan. The old man said he'd never seen such seamanship or such guts."

"I think that would pretty much describe Commodore Kurita, Admiral."

Kamakura, Yamato, 8/6/467 AC

An airship passed by gracefully overhead, bearing tourists who wanted to view the sacred cherry orchards from the vantage point of the sky. The cherry trees, or *sakura*, were in bloom, though a few petals were beginning to fall.

"Kurita advises patience," said Saito to Yamagata, as they sat below, under the cherry trees. "He says the pirates are being very coy and making good use of the considerable aid they receive from on high. He further advises that the *ronin* fleet will, in his opinion, produce good results with time."

Yamagata said nothing for a while, his attention seemingly fixed on a cherry blossom making its leap into immortality. It fluttered and spun to the ground, joining there the very few which had chosen to die young, in the full bloom of glorious youth.

During the migration from the home islands of Old Earth, it had been impossible to carry fully grown trees. Instead, the settlers had taken along saplings, a few, seeds and some cuttings, which they had carefully nursed into growth. Even then, many—most—had not survived. These trees were descendants of those who had and were, like the Yamatans themselves, of remarkably hardy and tough stock. Raising the trees had been as high a priority as the growing of food, for without these reminders of both the beauty of life, as well as its ephemeral nature, the settlers had feared losing some part of their essence.

With a sigh, Yamagata said, "The patience of the program's backers is not unlimited. We must have results, and soon. We lost another ship's crew yesterday. The Federated States Navy stood by and allowed it to happen because the pirates threatened to kill the crew if they were interfered with."

"His Majesty still will not allow our fleet to intervene," Saito said.

Yamagata grunted. "It is the curse of those who allow others to be their primary line of defense. It is the curse of being insufficiently self-reliant."

"It is the curse of losing a war," Saito corrected. "Still, let us trust Kurita's judgment. It is not *his* fault we lost, last time. He will not permit us to lose again."

Yamagata sighed. "I am still not sure it was wise to tell Kurita about our *special* source of information. We haven't even told our own defense forces or the FSC."

Saito clapped his colleague on the shoulder. "Do not fear, friend. He will not divulge anything that cannot be disguised as coming from somewhere else."

BdL *Dos Lindas*, Xamar Coast, 9/6/467 AC

A kimono-wearing and tabi- and tatami-shod Kurita stared down at the display showing the deployment of the ships of the task force around the carrier. His normal serene smile was missing, which caused Fosa to infer that something with his deployment was drastically wrong. He asked as much.

Kurita answered. "Yes, I am concerned, Captain-san. No matter that the *Ironsides* Task Force may warn you of the approach of danger. I assure you that before they can act, they will have to get permission from the FSN or even the Executive Mansion in Hamilton. By the time they are allowed to, it will probably be too late."

"You are thinking of Farsian submarines, Commodore?" Fosa asked.

The Yamatan nodded, then said, "I would not expect them soon, certainly not until we begin to show some success. But I *would* expect them. It is better to be ready, always. And we must also consider the possibility of suicidal dive bombers."

Fosa had considered that threat when outfitting the ship. Indeed, the mix of air defense guns and missiles aboard the *Dos Lindas* was very powerful for that reason; that, and the possibility of suicidal boats. The task force had more light cannon and heavy machine gun power than the entire *Ironsides* Battle Group.

His own experience of naval warfare was . . . well, actually it wasn't. The Commodore, on the other hand, had more real experience than the entire crew of the *Ironsides* and all its escorts, *combined.* He'd listen to Kurita's advice, he decided.

"Order the escorts to increase dispersion from the carrier to twelve miles," Fosa told the radio watch.

Kurita's serene smile returned.

"How goes it with shipping aboard the patrol boats?" he asked.

"They're already on the deck of the transport," Fosa answered.

"It's going to be a big surprise, you know, when the Xamaris attempt to take another boat under the nose of the FSN and discover that there's someone else there not so constrained by progressive rules of engagement." Kurita gave a slight chuckle then glanced over at the meteorology chart.

"Yes, Commodore, the storm is coming along nicely. By this time tomorrow we will be fighting it. The cargo ship carrying the patrol boats, the BdL *Harpy Eagle,* will broadcast that it is in trouble, but we shall have our own troubles. The mighty FSS *Ironsides* will ride to the rescue. When the storm clears, the *Harpy* will be nicely alongside the *Ironsides* with the boats hauled up and undercover of the flight deck. And then we wait, but not for long."

"Indeed, hopefully not for long, Captain-san. My . . . principals are growing anxious for some indicator of success."

The next day's morning sky was red and angry. By noon it had turned black and forbidding. By nightfall the smaller ships of the flotilla were fighting for their lives amidst thirty and forty foot waves that threatened to swamp them with each buffeting. Partly from the wind and waves, and partly to avoid ramming each other in the murk, the ships scattered.

Almost, *almost,* the *Harpy* was not pretending when it made the call to *Ironsides* that she was in trouble. By the time the FSN carrier arrived the *Harpy*'s hull and decks were groaning under the strain, half the crew puking down below decks and most of the rest puking above.

Ironsides took a position into the wind from the

smaller cargo ship, placing it in the lee and protecting it to some extent from the buffeting. *Harpy*'s captain went below to bid farewell to the crews of the patrol boats. He knew it might be a last farewell.

Chief Warrant Officer Pedraz, commanding the *Santissima Trinidad*, looked out at the white-tipped, green-hued hell separating the two ships and thought, not for the first time, *Mama never told me there'd be days like these.*

If he hadn't been so brown Pedraz would have been white. Even as it was, he had turned relatively pale with fear. His kind of boat was never intended to sail in this kind of weather. And then . . . but he really didn't want to think about the risks of getting away from the *Harpy* and close to the *Ironsides*. Most especially did he not want to think about hooking up to and being hauled up by the huge supercarrier.

The *Harpy*'s captain walked up and placed a hand on Pedraz's broad shoulder. "Are you ready, Chief?"

Exhaling, Pedraz nodded that he was.

"No time like the present then. Take advantage of the protection *Ironsides* is offering while we can."

Gulping, Pedraz nodded and shouted for the deck crew to raise and lower the *Trinidad* over the side. As the lines began to tighten, Pedraz scrambled aboard.

The warrant and the captain had gone over this at length. If there were no crew aboard, it would be long minutes before the *Trinidad* could get away from the potentially crushing hull of the *Harpy*. If the crew was aboard and something went wrong with the lowering, they might all be killed. Since mission had priority . . .

The wind dropped off radically as soon as the boat was sheltered in the *Harpy's* lee. Still, *Harpy* rocked abruptly, causing *Trinidad's* crew, more than once, to have to use long poles to dampen the inevitable thumping against the side of the hull. This problem actually got worse as the patrol boat moved closer to the sea's surface and the swings widened.

When he felt the water take control of his boat's hull, Pedraz looked up to signal the boatswain to cut the *Trinidad* loose.

No luck; the spray was so thick neither could see the other. Worse, radio was right out lest the traffic be intercepted by those watching from above. *Fuck!*

Up above, on deck aboard the *Harpy*, the boatswain cursed as he realized he'd lost sight of the *Trinidad*, even though it was scant yards below. The lines that led down to the boat went alternately tight and slack with the rocking of the larger ship.

In the water . . . but just *that,* thought the boatswain. That would have been fine except that the rocking of the ship wasn't a steady side-to-side motion. Instead, the ship was more or less corkscrewing, with a port lean and bow high followed by a starboard lean and bow low.

Okay . . . this is manageable. He ordered the men manning the davits to let the boat down another five feet. After that, while the lines still went almost tight in a not fully predictable sequence, there was enough slack for the boatswain to risk cutting the *Trinidad* loose.

Mission had priority. Without worrying about whether the *Trinidad* was safely on its way the boatswain led his small crew to the next set of davits to raise and lower over the side the other boat, the BdL *San Agustin*.

It was a few moments before Pedraz realized the ship had cut him loose. He had just enough time to silently thank the boatswain before ordering crew to action stations. The motors started without trouble, thankfully, but the sharp waves—exacerbated by the nearness of the *Harpy*—dropped the troughs below the props at odd intervals. The meant the boat could only pull away from the rocking and veering— hence dangerous—ship in spurts as the props bit.

The driving got better but the waves got worse as the boat moved farther from the ship. Once it was completely out of the ship's lee the waves became an awesome rollercoaster that made the ship's previous, nausea-inducing buffeting seem like love taps in comparison.

Gunning the engines to top a white-foamed crest, Pedraz thought, *Show me a sailor who's not afraid of the sea and I'll show you an informal burial at sea waiting to happen.*

The *Trinidad*'s bow cleared the crest and hung suspended over the water. With resistance lessened and the engine at full throttle, the boat lurched forward until reaching the tipping point and . . .

"Yeehawww!" Pedraz exulted, now that he was free of the fear of being crushed by the *Harpy*. The bow plunged down like a rollercoaster car on steroids, the rollercoaster having plainly been designed by a lunatic on LSD.

The waves were steep and the troughs were deep, but the wavelength was long and the angle at least survivable. The boat continued its plunge for the bottom, the crew hanging on for dear life.

A seeming wall of water arose before Pedraz's eyes. He knew it was probably half illusion—a result of the *Trinidad*'s angle as it rode down the wave. Even so, his heart skipped a beat. He cut back on the throttle lest the boat's bow go straight into the water below.

Then he gunned it again as the boat reached the base of the trough and began the long climb up and over the next wave. No problem; Pedraz had the storm's measure and timing now, and his crew had faith in their little boat's skipper. With a lighter heart, he forced his way closer to the dimly sensed *presence*—given the thick, blinding spray one could hardly see it as more than a dim presence—of the *Ironsides*.

FSS *Ironsides*, 14/6/467 AC

Pedraz had to admit it, the FSN squids had made himself and the other seventeen men of the crew pretty damned comfortable over the last several days. He'd missed his rum ration, of course, and the food wasn't really as close to home cooking as was served aboard legionary ships and boats. Still, the quarters were comparatively spacious and the mattress, oh, *much* better.

The break was over. A remotely piloted vehicle from one of the frigates escorting the *Ironsides* had spotted what appeared to a medium sized group of Xamari pirates collecting and boarding three smallish boats for an excursion.

Pedraz had watched in real time in CIC as the pirates gathered.

"Do they always act like that?" he'd asked of a Spanish speaking sailor manning a visual screen.

"Generally, yeah, Chief. They dance around, shooting their rifles into the air to psyche themselves up. Then they get all the old men, women and kids cheering. Then they board and launch. By the time we are allowed to do anything it's always too late. See, we can't do a damned thing until they've actually committed piracy on the high seas. By then . . . by the time we can act; they'll have grabbed the crew as hostages and we're stymied."

After watching the pirates' boats for a while, Pedraz commented, "Slower than shit, aren't they?"

"Yeah," the other sailor agreed. "And that's how you're going to get them, this once anyway."

Pedraz went back to watching the slow progress of the pirates' vessels. He estimated them as doing no better than ten knots. A few quick mental calculations told him they needed to get at least eight miles offshore for him to have a decent chance of both intercepting them before they reached the boat and not warning them in time for them to turn around.

After what seemed to Pedraz to be a very long time watching, *Ironsides'* operations officer spoke up, in English. "Tell Mr. Pedraz to man his boat and to have the *Agustin's* crew man as well. We'll lower them to the water and then signal when it's time to leave."

Xamar, Abdulahi's Headquarters, 14/6/467 AC

The pirate chief's smile grew into a chuckle as he watched three of his boats closing on the lone freighter. He watched on a laptop's screen, the laptop hooked into the receiver provided to him by those space-faring infidels overhead.

Such a useful toy it was, that receiver. It was not only capable of giving him the locations of any naval vessels that might interfere with his operations, it gave him the precise locations of potential targets and identified—though this was trickier—ships belonging to companies that were already paying the *jizyah*. It would never do to seize those who paid to avoid attack unless, of course, those payments were late.

Abdulahi panned back, to embrace a broader ocean area. At this scale he could make out the two infidel carrier groups, which he thought of as "the greater and the lesser infidels," both the distinctive flat tops and their smaller escorts. He could close the view in, also, to watch the take offs and landings of their aircraft. That, however, usually cut off the view of the escorts unless they happened to be very close to the carriers.

Recentering the cursor on the waters between the target freighter and where his own boats had to be, Abdulahi clicked to lower the scale to where he could just make out his vessels. The two carrier groups disappeared off to the sides of the screen.

One might have thought that the pirate lord would have paid more attention to the threat to his operations, rather than the targets. But there was emotional satisfaction in watching the targets taken. The threat? Well, he knew the rules of engagement as well as the captains and crews of the warships did. The FSN wasn't *allowed* to be a threat until it was too late and the others, the infidel mercenaries, were not nearly as capable and were, moreover, being watched by the space-faring infidels who would warn him if the mercenaries got into a position to interfere.

UEPF *Spirit of Peace*, 14/6/467 AC

While Abdulahi concentrated on the target, Wallenstein— from Robinson's desk—focused on the threat. She, unlike the Xamari, was not restricted to a laptop screen. Instead, she had the latest in Terra Novan video technology, and something every bit as good as anything produced at home, the high admiral's two-and-a-half meter Kurosawa. With that, and the processing power inherent in the ship's computer, she was able to track both war fleets as well as the pirates and their targets. Symbols stood in for full views of the ships.

That is to say, she was able to track everything but didn't see the need. Once she'd identified that the mercenary fleet was in no position to interfere with the pirates with their own ships, she focused in on the carrier to ensure it wasn't launching aircraft at the pirates. That kept her rapt attention. The only thing that had bothered her was the disappearance of the two patrol boats from the ocean surface. This had not troubled her long, however, for she had found them sitting under tarps atop the ship the screen identified as the *Harpy Eagle*.

BdL *Harpy Eagle*, 14/6/467 AC

The boatswain spared a glance overhead, silently praying that his camouflage job would do.

The hardest part had been assembling the frames in the midst of the storm, with the wind roaring and the waves sometimes washing over the deck. It had actually been fairly easy to construct the frames out of cheap lumber down in the cargo hold. Taking them apart and stowing them in an open space within the deck level of the superstructure hadn't been hard. But getting the frames out and built when no man could hear a word, or sometimes even see another for all the spray in the air? The boatswain rather hoped they'd not have to try this trick again and certainly not in a storm like the last one.

Safe enough bet, though, he thought. *Like most tricks, it's unlikely to work more than once.*

Still silently, the boatswain said a small prayer for the success of the *Trinidad* and the *Agustin.*

BdL Santissima Trinidad, 14/6/467 AC

The sea state, so long after the storm, was low and the bow rode high, skipping over the waves, propelled by twin screws driven by sixty-two hundred horsepower. Pedraz stood at the helm, giving light taps to the wheel to cut expertly across the waves. His body bounced in time with the beating of the hull.

Up front, on the 40mm, stood Seamen Clavell and Guptillo. The pair wore legion standard (plus) body armor and helmets, though Clavell's helmet covered a set of headphones that were hooked into the boat's intercom. The "plus" came in the form of a silk and liquid metal apron that extended over the crotch, and liquid metal greaves covering chins and knees. There wasn't a hell of a lot of cover on a patrol boat.

A few paces behind the gun crouched two more of the crew, likewise accoutered. One of these carried a clip of five 40mm shells and was close to the forty. The other had the same but was closer to the magazine well from which more shells would be passed upward.

Pedraz looked to port where Seaman Leonardo Panfillo clutched the spade grips of a .41 caliber heavy machine gun. The shiny brass belt draped down before disappearing into a gray-painted ammunition can. Pedraz looked for signs of worry in Panfillo's face. There weren't any—and perhaps this made perfect sense after having braved the hair-raising transfer during the storm—but only a look of grim determination.

Satisfied with Panfillo, the skipper glanced to starboard where Esteban Santiona manned the .41 on that side. He was heavyset, was Santiona, but the weight helped him control the vicious vibration of the HMG. *Something*, at least, made the sailor such a bloody good gunner; in informal competition with the gunners of the other boats in the tercio Santiona had, frankly, kicked the rest of the patrol boat maniple's posteriors.

"Esteban," Pedraz shouted over the roar of the engines and the pounding of the water. "Leave a couple of the bastards for the rest to practice on, got it?"

"*Si, mi* skipper," the rotund gunner answered without looking up.

The *Ironsides* and Pedraz had worked out a simple method by which the supercarrier could vector in the patrol boat to the targets without being too obvious about it. The method was that the *Trinidad* and its sister ship were assigned a flight number, Blue Jay Four Three. The *Ironsides'* radio room broadcast vectors under that flight number. Pedraz heard and adjusted his course while *Agustin's* skipper merely followed Pedraz. The carrier couched the directions in terms of naval aviation but had schooled Pedraz to ignore the parts irrelevant to him. They'd also told him not to acknowledge the directions. For further deception, *Ironsides* had put up an aircraft that would follow those directions.

One never could tell who might be listening.

UEPF Spirit of Peace, 14/6/467 AC

The computer on Robinson's desk spoke. "Captain Wallenstein, I have discovered an anomaly."

"Go," ordered the captain, simply.

"There are two small surface craft in the area of focused observation that should not be there. Moreover, when the largest of the vessels in the area broadcasts certain directions, an aircraft responds by taking those directions, but so do the surface craft."

Crap! "Show me."

The Kurosawa immediately panned in to show the *Trinidad* and the *Agustin* skimming the waves, leaving broad V-shaped wakes behind them. Resolution was just fine enough for Wallenstein to make out darkened blobs on deck that had to be men.

She hit an intercom button. "Admiral? Marguerite. Come back to your quarters *immediately*."

Abdulahi could read a chart as well as the next pirate. When Robinson called to warn him of the position, direction and speed of the patrol boats bearing down on his men he knew immediately that they were on an intercept course. He tried frantically to call the leader of the band on the radio but, maintenance being what it was among the Xamari . . . •

It took longer than a radio would have, had it been

working, to get through via cell phone. It was pretty amusing, really, that Xamar couldn't have police, fire or medical services, that courts were right out, and that transportation was catch as catch can. Even so, somehow they managed to keep cell phone service up and running. Some called it "connectedness."

What a silly word, Abdulahi thought, while waiting for his son to answer the phone. *It's touted as the route to civilizing the more barbaric parts of Terra Nova, whatever "civilizing" may mean. In practice, it means that a slave dealer in Pashtia can know whether the price for fourteen-year-old female virgins or fat little boys is higher in Kashmir or among the brothels of Taurus. It means the drug smuggler can easily learn both where he might obtain the best price for his merchandise and where the risk of arrest is least. It means money laundered from crime and corruption. It means corruption extending its influence to yet new places from its more familiar paths.*

"Connectedness" means that, when you mix a gallon of cat piss with a gallon of goat's milk, the mix tastes a lot more of the former than of the latter.

When we in Xamar were still a real country then being connected to the rest of the globe would probably have been a good thing, for us and for everyone else. As is? It makes everything worse. I couldn't be the pirate I am, nor what used to be my country the mess that it is, without our "connectedness." And I'm not sure it wasn't our "connectedness" to the rest of the globe that ruined us.

"Lungile" he was called by his Bantu-speaking concubine mother, herself taken as a girl in a slave raid by Abdulahi. "The good one," it meant, and to his mother he had indeed been a good son. As son of Abdulahi, Lungile was the leader of the three pirate vessels. Nineteen years old and closing to action, Lungile didn't hear the ringing at first over the straining, gasping sounds of his boat's overused and undermaintained diesels. On approximately the fourteenth ring he noticed it and answered, "Yes, Father?"

"My son, it's a trap. How far are you from the target?"

"Perhaps forty minutes, Father." The boy's voice sounded calm enough. "What is it this time? More of their silly sound machines? We can face those. What to fear from a demon's wail?"

"Ai, forty *minutes*? Then it is too late for you to take hostages. And it may be too late also for you to turn around and make it back to shore. Lungile, my son, it is not the sound machines. There are two small warships almost upon you. Our friends say they are fast, partly armored and well armed with cannon and machine guns. They say the boats are from the infidel mercenaries."

It was still an even and calm voice that answered, "Then we will run, Father, and if we cannot escape we will sell our lives as dearly as possible."

The boy's mother had never been a favorite, but Abdulahi had always had a soft spot in his heart for the boy, himself. So brave and forthright he was, so full of fire was his heart. *I will miss this boy. I will . . .*

"My son . . ." and the father's voice choked with emotion and pain, ". . . if you must die then, yes, die like men."

"*Il hamdu l'illah*, Father; we shall if we must."

❖   ❖   ❖

In CIC, aboard the *Ironsides*, a sailor huddled over a screen and watching a real time image from a military satellite. He whispered a curse and announced, "They're turning for home."

The captain looked at the ops board and answered, "They're probably too slow to escape but they might get in close enough to swim for it."

"Wouldn't matter, Cap'n," his ops officer said. "If those legion boys catch 'em in the water they'll kill 'em anyway."

"War crime?"

"No, sir. In this one type of case the international law enforcement model makes perfect sense. It really is a law enforcement problem and the law says, 'kill 'em,' Skipper. Fleeing Felon Rule, it's called."

The captain nodded. "Call the *Trinidad*. Give them the code word for we've been made and give them the pirate's new course."

"A stern chase is a long chase," Lungile whispered to himself. "But when one boat is four times faster it isn't long *enough*."

His own boat had begun life as a sport fisher, back when Xamar had actually had tourism. As such, it had a flying bridge and a climbable mast above it. Lungile stood atop that mast, gripping the ladder with one hand and surplus Volgan binoculars with the other. Through the binoculars, pressed tight to his eyes, Lungile searched for his pursuers. He'd caught glimpses of them, each one closer, when waves happened to have lifted both boats simultaneously. The mercenaries boats looked . . . Lungile searched for the right word . . .

"Like sharks," he decided, "like predators."

Lungile turned away from his pursuers toward the distant beckoning coast and safety. There was no real chance of making it unless he could somehow drive off both of the enemy craft. But to fight them . . .

"Hard left," he shouted to the helmsman.

Lower, with no flying bridge, Pedraz saw the smoke from the badly maintained diesels before ever he saw the smoke's source.

"XO, take the wheel," he ordered, backing off and pulling out a set of binocular that hung hard by.

Immediately his assistant, Cristobal Francaís, answered, "Aye, aye, skipper." Francaís was huge, towering above his captain. His long arms reached out as he right-stepped to take the wheel seamlessly.

Pedraz raised the binos to his eyes, swept the horizon until catching sight of the smoke, and looked down from that. The smoke grew thicker but the boat was not visible. He waited, keeping the glasses fixed at the lowest part of the column of smoke . . . he waited . . . he waited . . . he . . .

"They've decided to risk a fight," he announced. "Radio! Get on the horn to *Agustin* and *Dos Lindas*. Tell them the pirates are ready and waiting, arms in their hands. *Agustin* is to stand off at .41 caliber range and engage the two to starboard. We will take on the port pirate ourselves before going to join *Agustin*."

"XO?"

"Aye, Skipper."

"I want to go straight in to about six hundred meters then cut sharp a-port."

"Roger, skipper."

Pedraz flicked a switch on the headphones he wore, in common with the 40mm crew, uncomfortably under his helmet. "Main gun?"

"Aye, Skipper," Clavell answered.

"You may open fire on your own hook when the target is visible and in effective range. Forward port and starboard Heavy Machine Guns?"

"Port here, Chief," answered Panfillo.

"Esteban here, skipper."

"I don't expect you to actually hit anything until we're within two thousand, so hold your fire until then."

"Aye, aye, skipper."

"Aye."

The rocket grenade launchers were the older version. They could reach out to eleven hundred meters—the rocket motor would drive them that far—but the integral fuse self-detonated them at just over nine hundred. They could hit a target the size of a tank at three hundred, but would generally miss at four. A larger target, something like the eighty-two-foot length of a patrol boat like the *Trinidad* or *Agustin*, they could, at least *conceivably*, hit at something like six hundred.

It didn't really matter that the RGLs weren't very likely to hit. They were the best the pirates had and so they *had* to try.

Lungile pushed and cuffed his RGL gunners, four of them to the forward deck where the backblast wouldn't endanger the ship or the other crewmen, the other two to the rear. He ordered the two to the stern to load fragmentation rounds. These were forty-millimeter, rather than seventy, and might, he thought, extend the practical range of the shells as the fragments reached forward in a cone after the shells exploded. Other crew, armed with rifles and light machine guns, he put to lining the gunwales on the side he was presenting to the enemy.

They'll never close to where we have a decent chance of a hit, thought Lungile. *Best to try for the longer shots, then. At the speed they look like they're making, that would be . . . mmm . . . maybe two minutes. We'll wait . . .*

Then Lungile saw the flashing flame and the puffs of smoke from the forward deck of the infidel boat.

The 40mm, L56 gun was not so much a lightweight as a miniature heavyweight. In the other version, the longer and higher velocity version purchased for the *Dos Lindas*, it fired up to four hundred and fifty, eight-hundred-and-seventy gram shells per minute from a one-hundred-and-one-round magazine. On the patrol boats the legion had mounted the lighter weight, simpler, slower firing, and frankly obsolescent, land version. This had only a forty-three round magazine but, on the plus side, the weight and recoil were not enough to capsize the boat. The crews thought this was a pretty good tradeoff.

Guptillo's job wasn't to keep the magazine filled under full rate of fire; that was impossible. Rather, he and the other feeders were tasked to reload the fixed magazine after it went dry. This took considerably longer than emptying the thing did.

It could have, perhaps even should have, been a much more sophisticated system than it was. Ideally, given the rise and fall of the bow, the gun would have had an integral laser range finder and pseudo-stabilization system that allowed it to fire only when the elevation matched the sight. It didn't have anything like that. Instead, it had Clavell and the finest fire control computer in the known galaxy, the human brain.

The problem with using the brain as one's fire control computer, however, is that it is an absolute *bitch* to program.

With the first salvo of infidel shells, Lungile knew he had a chance, if not a great one. He thought he saw four short-falling shells impact and explode on the ocean's surface. At least one shell, he knew for a fact, overshot the boat. He knew it because it went right through one of the crew standing above the open-backed wheelhouse, waving his rifle around and shouting imprecations at the enemy. Apparently the pirate's body didn't create enough resistance to detonate the shell. This helped, though the body practically exploded anyway, showering the crew with blood, bone and meat, and sending one other pirate down with a chunk of rib buried in his throat.

And still the enemy boat was too far away to engage.

"Wait for the order, you bastards," Lungile shouted at his gunners.

"Clavell, you bastard, you missed!" Pedraz shouted into the intercom.

"Sorry, Skipper. But hey, I bracketed it. Did you see that fucker go poof?"

Pedraz simply grunted, then said, "Hold fire until we're closer; twelve hundred meters should do."

"Aye, Skipper."

"And Santiona and Panfillo, you're going to have the same problem Clavell did, the rise and fall of the bow. Hold fire till we get to eight hundred."

Lungile's eyeball was no better calibrated than Clavell's. His weapons were considerably less sophisticated. Yet, as his mother was fond of saying, "The lion runs for a meal; the antelope for his life."

He couldn't run, of course, the pitiful ancient engines of his craft would get him nowhere when pursued by such swift opponents. Unlike the antelope, however, *he* had fangs.

"Fire!"

Pedraz saw the flash of flame and the balls of smoke erupt from the pirate ship at the same time Clavell opened fire again with the 40mm.

The forty is high velocity, but not that *high. I wonder . . .* FUCK!

"Incoming!" Pedraz screamed, loud enough to be heard over the engines even down in the galley, just as half a dozen much larger balls of flame and smoke appeared in the air between his boat and his chosen target.

Santiona, like the other side machine gunners, scrunched down over his .41 to take any fragments on his helmet and the shoulder-reinforced *lorica* body armor. This left his legs open and unprotected but for the greaves. The greaves, moreover, didn't quite cover his bulky legs. That, of course, was where he was hit.

He felt a sort of plucking in three or four places on his legs and thought little of it until he looked down and saw his uniform rapidly reddening. Santiona felt suddenly nauseated. Then the burning began, a result of the hot bits of metal lodged in his flesh.

Shouting, "Medic!" the wounded gunner released the spade grips and sat heavily to the deck, his hands pressing to staunch the flow of blood. As soon as his rear hit he remembered his duty and also shouted, "Replacement gunner!"

The medic hustled up from a spot at the rear of the deck from which he could normally keep his eyes on all the crew in action. He stopped at the hatchway just long enough to shout down to the engine room, "Replacement gunner on Number Two!" before dashing over to render aid to Santiona.

Lungile felt a momentary rush of joy mixed with relief when he saw the half dozen RGL warheads self-detonate and then one of his enemies fall to the deck. That rush was shortlived, as the apparently wounded man was replaced almost immediately and someone else— a medic, Lungile assumed—began tending the man on deck before dragging him off.

Another reason for the short duration of the pirate's joy was that the enemy boat veered sharply to Lungile's right, slowed to about twenty knots and opened fire again. This time, at that slow speed— still twice that of his own bucket—and with the range closed and the bow no longer doing the samba with the sea, the 40mm proved deadly. Another five-round burst lanced out. This time, three of the five shells found the bow of his boat. It half disintegrated in fire and metal shards mixed with smoldering wood splinters. A dozen men screamed in pain as splinter and shard found them.

One of the shells hit very near the waterline, near enough to it, in fact, to blast a hole large enough to let the sea come pouring in. The bow lowered and the boat slowed with the increased resistance. As it lowered, still more water gushed in.

Clavell switched his fire to single shot, traversing left to right and then back again, raking the gunwales. By this time he knew that his shipmate was hit. Clavell was in no mood for the niceties. His shells smashed in the wooden bulwark, knocking pirates down like ninepins. Especially did he concentrate on those who seemed most willing to fire; for them he would sometimes donate a second shell.

After about thirty rounds of 40mm, two .41 caliber heavy machine guns, one amidships and the other near the stern, kicked in. At that point Clavell felt free to concentrate on the stern and the engine compartment. Four shots and the thing was not only dead in the water and sinking, the parts still above water were beginning to burn. Pirates, such as still could, began dropping their weapons and jumping overboard. Many of those who could not rise to jump began to pray and scream as water rose or fire spread around them.

"Cease fire! Cease fire!" Pedraz ordered. "Cris, hard a starboard. Let's go help *Agustin*."

Lungile trod water fifty or sixty meters away from the ruin of his boat. His heart seethed with hate for the enemies that had killed his men, robbed him of his first command, and caused him to fail his father.

"I'll make you pay, infidel filth. I swear I will."

That would have to wait, however, for Lungile's

next incarnation. Since the Salafis did not believe in reincarnation, it might have to wait forever. Lungile, struggling in the water, looked over to see an impossibly large shark's fin towering above the surface and veering towards him.

So much for oaths, the Xamari thought, sadly and hopelessly.

The shark slowly cruising a few feet below the water, and not very far from Lungile's scissoring legs, didn't really care about revenge or reincarnation. It did care about lunch and it did care about the invigorating aroma of blood in the water. Mostly it cared that lunch was, apparently, served.

I love *Uhuran food*, thought the carcharodon megalodon, as it slid over onto its side to take Lungile at the waist, slicing him crudely in two and filling the water with the scent of very fresh blood.

INTERLUDE

6 June, 2100, Clichy-sous-Bois, France

The immigrants had served their purpose. They had bought time for the populations to be *regularized*. They could go now. According to the papers, they should have gone ten years prior.

Spain and Italy were Islamic now, except for the Vatican in the latter. And the Vatican's independence was merely formal. The imposition of *sharia* law had allowed the central and important European powers, the core of the EU, to cast those southern Latin states out. Both sides were happy enough with that, though the dethroned pope, residing in a dank dungeon beneath Saint Peter's while awaiting his ritual burning at the stake, was *not*.

Give the people in charge their due, though; this was not to be a racist pogrom. Former Moslems who had cast off their worn shackles and joined the secular humanist majority of Europe were welcome to stay. It was only these, these wretches still resident in the cramped and filthy *banlieues* of France, or the slums of England and Germany, who had to go.

Moslem Spain and Italy would not take any. They were poor enough and growing poorer still by the day. There was no room within either of them, or both together, for the forty or fifty million disenfranchised Moslems of the central powers. Switzerland, perhaps the premier military power of the Continent, had said, *"Nein,"* and massed its troops on the borders.

That left only one outlet . . .

While French troops went to England, mostly via Calais, for the great clearing out, and English Guards regiments landed at Bremen before marching to surround the Moslem quarters of Berlin and Stuttgart and Frankfurt; German troops, a full corps of them, had rolled to Paris on a mission that the EU called, "Human Hygiene." It was believed that the troops—German, French, or British—would be as harsh as necessary only if they did not share a language with the bulk of the people they were to uproot. The Scandinavians and the Benelux had likewise exchanged troops for the same reasons.

Gendarmes waved—well, not *all* the French were *always* sorry to see the Germans roll into Paris, after all—as the grenadiers and pioneers of Second Panzer Division relieved them of responsibility for securing that portion of the electrified wire perimeter. While grenadiers climbed ladders, and others stood by their armored vehicles, the pioneers cut a portion of the wire fence for the rest to pour through.

From loudspeakers mounted atop heavy vehicles came the command, *"Kanacken . . . RAUS."*

CHAPTER EIGHT

And all the time—such is the tragi-comedy of
our situation—we continue to clamour for those
very qualities we are rendering impossible. You
can hardly open a periodical without coming
across the statement that what our civilization
needs is more "drive," or dynamism, or self-
sacrifice, or "creativity." In a sort of ghastly
simplicity we remove the organ and demand
the function. We make men without chests
and expect of them virtue and enterprise.
We laugh at honour and are shocked to find
traitors in our midst. We castrate and bid the
geldings be fruitful.

—C.S. Lewis, *The Abolition of Man*

Xamar, 27/6/457 AC

Abdulahi was stuck in three ways. All three were
exquisitely painful. In the first place, he found himself
forced to pay compensation to the families of the men
he had lost at sea a couple of weeks prior. In some
cases this included coming up with new dowries for
old wives, always an expensive proposition. Secondly,

he had to deal with Lungile's bereaved mother. This was particularly bad as she had no other children. The *reason*, however, that she had no other children was that after the first she had become unpleasantly and unattractively fat. Abdulahi had never been able to bring himself to touch her again, given that he had younger and slimmer wives, concubines and slave girls to spend his time on. But now, in good conscience, he had to give her some of his . . . attention. Worst of all was that he had neither the means of retaliating against those who had so unrighteously slaughtered his men and his son, then stood by smiling as sharks took care of the survivors, nor could he even go to the world press for justice. If he did, the news that it was possible for pirates to be made to suffer so severely would have most of his followers back to farming and hauling fishing nets in no time.

He'd expected the infidel mercenaries to broadcast the news of their success. It was quite a surprise that they had not. Perhaps those for whom they worked had vetoed passing on the news. Or perhaps the mercenaries had some reasons of their own for keeping quiet. It was something to think upon.

Mustafa had promised him that it had been a fluke, that the mercenaries couldn't repeat their trick. Abdulahi had his doubts. Already he could think of a couple of ways, a couple of different tricks, that his enemies could use against him. He'd had rumors from ports and ships up and down the coast of helicopters flying in heavily armed, uniformed men to stand guard on certain ships. He'd placed those ships off limits to his followers, of course. But what of the armed men he didn't know about? What of the loss in revenues from ships he could no longer attack safely?

Dear God, what if the shipping companies paying the jizyah decided to pay the mercenaries for protection instead? Will I have to cut my tolls? Can I afford to cut my tolls? Will some successor rear his head if I do, and if I have to reduce the stipends to my followers?

Abdulahi shivered at the thought. In the hard world in which he had grown up and lived, the rule of the wolf held sway. If he lost his power, he would also lose his life.

I must go to Mustafa, Abdulahi thought. *He has the ships and the trained men to handle this problem.*

The Base, Kashmir Tribal Trust Territories, 29/6/467 AC

"*Can* we take out this enemy?" Mustafa asked of his assistant, Abdul Aziz.

"From what I've been able to gather, Prince, it will be very difficult. They have a good group of escorts and an absolutely amazing array of machine guns and antiaircraft cannon—missiles, as well—to guard their major ship. Moreover, the pattern of their attack on Abdulahi's men suggests that the Federated States Navy is committed to assisting them, even if under the table, so to speak."

"Perhaps a submarine from heretic Farsia?" Mustafa suggested.

Abdul Aziz shook his head. "Too noisy. Even if the mercenaries lack sophisticated antisubmarine warfare capability, the FSN is the *definition* of sophisticated.

For that matter, the mercenaries may not lack the capability. We simply don't know."

"Hopeless, then?"

Abdul Aziz shook his head. "No, Prince, not hopeless. But . . . very difficult. At the very least, taking out their aircraft carrier will be very, very difficult. I do have an idea."

"Let me hear it then."

"We would need to expend a reasonably fast freighter and probably its crew."

Mustafa shrugged. Ships and mujahadin were replaceable, hence expendable. He had twenty-seven ships and nearly a thousand seamen, all dedicated to the cause.

"We would need to load the ship with explosive—I am not sure of the best mix—and ram the carrier."

"I don't have anything that fast," Mustafa answered.

"I know, Prince. We would also have to attack the carrier's propellers. I found a short bit on the Global-Net that said the carrier has AZIPOD drive. This is very good but also, I think, more vulnerable if we can detonate a ton or two of explosive near the carrier's stern. If we can, we can jam, or perhaps even totally destroy, the drives. This would leave it vulnerable to ramming. Still, Prince, this is only an idea . . . almost off the top of my head. I need to plan more, much more. But before I can plan, I need to know if you are willing to expend a freighter, several smaller fast boats, and perhaps ten or twenty million FSD for torpedoes and missiles . . . and for something else, too."

"Define 'something else'," Mustafa said.

"It occurred to me, Prince, that one way to get a ship close to the enemy carrier would be to pay them for protection as some other shippers are doing. Our ship could be 'running from' Abdulahi's men toward the protection of the carrier. Or, at the very least, pretending to keep close under protection of the infidel ship. The small fast boat could be lowered over the side when they got sufficiently close. Torpedoes and missiles could be fired to add to the confusion. This is all very rough, of course."

Finished, Aziz bowed his head, awaiting Mustafa's decision. The chief thought hard for some time, in silence. He smoked two cigarettes, sipped absently at his coffee. In the end he decided.

"Make your plan carefully, Abdul Aziz."

El Hipodromo, Ciudad Balboa, 29/6/467 AC

Parilla had retired the week before. There'd been a parade, Carrera serving as Commander of Troops for the event to honor his friend. Speeches had been made, and more than a few tears shed. Lourdes and Mrs. Parilla had cried. Indeed, Raul Parilla, himself, had had to wipe a few unfeigned tears away at leaving the finest military force *he'd* ever been part of, and the only one with which he had shed his blood.

His final comment had been, "If I didn't feel I had to do this, both for the legion and for Balboa, you would have had to carry me off this island feet first."

Running a presidential campaign from the island seemed like a bad idea from any number of perspectives. On the other hand, Parilla's old home in *Ciudad Balboa* was too dangerous a place for him to stay anymore. After all, the government still hated his guts. The Tauran Union's pet creature the Cosmopolitan Criminal

Court—in effect a Tauran court, masquerading as a world court, for the prosecution of non-Taurans—still had a warrant out for his arrest. There were Tauran Union troops along the Transitway to execute that warrant, too, if he ever grew sloppy.

Carrera had turned the original "home" of the legion, the *Casa* Linda, over to Parilla and his wife, rent-free. It had stood empty for the last several years, ever since the legion's headquarters had moved out to the *Isla Real*. It, and Parilla, would be the better for it being occupied again. From there, and with a couple of maniples of legionaries around it for security's sake, Parilla would run his campaign for president of the country.

The city's racetrack was one of only two places in the country that would really do for Parilla to announce his candidacy. Capable of seating upwards of fifty thousand, or perhaps even sixty in a pinch, the hippodrome was surrounded by open fields and parks, as well as a broad series of parking lots.

The other potential spot, the *Furiocentro* convention center, was not as scenic and was also in an area a bit too built up for safety. After all, that CCC warrant was still hanging around out there. The real advantage of the *Furiocentro*, that it was easily reachable by public transportation, could not outweigh that disadvantage.

There was no sense in running for president once the country was already plunged into a civil war. One way to prevent civil war, or rather to prevent a skirmish with the Taurans that might degenerate into foreign invasion and perhaps then civil war, was to present a threat too great for the Taurans lightly to risk confronting it. That way came in the form of one hundred and sixty-four helicopters, a mix of IM-71s and heavy-lift IM-62s, carrying three full cohorts, two infantry and one Cazador, to the *Hipodromo*'s parking lots just at dawn. These landed and disgorged their roughly three thousand troops, then lifted off to various points around the country from which they would bring in about five thousand prominent supporters of the legions, and avowed Balboan nationalists, to help fill the racetrack's stands.

Some of the legion's naval assets, in particular the dozen large Volgan hovercraft used to transport recruits to the island for initial training and legionaries to the mainland for R and R and leave, were set to bringing in *campesinos* from outlying provinces. Still others would meet any of the several hundred buses chartered by the legion at various spots within the city and the Transitway Zone. Fixed-wing aircraft, as well, were sent to pick up supporters from outlying airfields.

Just to cover all bases, the legion had further paid to have on hand thirty-four hundred off-duty police to help with crowd control. It never hurts to have the cops on one's side.

By ten a.m. the troops and police had a cordon around the area, one tercio was formed up inside to parade, the stands were filled past capacity, and the television studios had their news and camera crews waiting for Parilla to emerge.

Carrera and McNamara sat in the private room in the hippodrome while Parilla went through his paces calmly.

"You're not the least bit nervous, are you, Raul?" Carrera marveled.

"Nervous about what?"

Parilla really didn't understand the question. There was a crowd; he was going to speak to it. He'd done it a thousand times before. Hell, he'd been dictator in all but name before. What was to worry about making a speech?

Carrera smiled and shook his head. Some people had the political bug and the talent to pull it off. He didn't. Though he liked to teach, he hated making speeches and rarely finished one, on the few occasions he had, when he didn't feel like a fool. Even when he had to talk to troops—and those were the only crowds he was remotely comfortable with—he kept his words short and to the point, the better to get off stage as quickly as possible.

Then Parilla understood. "God doesn't give everything to one man, my friend. You're a soldier, unquestionably the finest I've ever known. I'm not half the soldier you are and I never could have been. But politics? *That* I can do."

I'm glad one of us can, Raul, Carrera thought.

Turning to McNamara, Carrera said, "Sergeant Major, let's take our place outside so the future president of the republic can make a proper grand entrance."

Meanwhile, the opening show was beginning.

She was as black and as glowing as high quality anthracite. Her color was made the more remarkably and beautifully striking by the large red blossom she wore in her wavy, midnight hair and the long dress that matched the flower. With huge brown eyes, high cheekbones, a body to die for and a smile that made one think of Heaven; she was Miss Balboa, 466. Today was the day she repaid the legion for funding her win of the national crown and her almost successful attempt at the Miss Terra Nova title.

Artemisia Jimenez, legionary Legate Xavier Jimenez's niece, was going to repay her debt by her presence, her speech and her singing, today. She would add her support later on and throughout the campaign. Her voice, clear and sweet, had been her talent for the beauty pageants.

Professor's Ruiz propaganda department had come up with the song. It was not new, by any means, but had, like many others in the legionary repertoire, been scavenged from the history of Old Earth. In its translated form it was called "Mañana Sera Mejor," *Tomorrow will be better.*

The band played a medley of legionary tunes as Artemisia mounted the dais. The selections included small excerpts from *Juventud Adelante* and *Canto al Aquila*, the "Hymno Nacional" and "El Valle de las Lunas." The tune from "Mañana Sera Mejor" was interwoven with the others to accustom the audience to it and, with the program sheets that had also been passed out, make it easier for them to follow along and join in.

Artemisia gracefully removed the light shawl she wore and draped it over a microphone stand after she removed the microphone. As she did she saw two uniformed men emerge from a side door onto the dais. Her breath caught in her throat.

The crowd hushed; even at a distance her flesh exuded an aura of untouchable, ultimate femininity that one could only admire, desire, or aspire to.

Stealing sidelong glances in the general direction

of the men in uniform, Artemisia began to speak an introduction for Raul Parilla that either came from the heart or was a first-class imitation. She could have been reading the menu from any given restaurant and the people listening would have been as rapt.

"That fucking bastard," President Rocaberti fumed at his short, pudgy nephew. "That miserable fucking peasant piece of low class shit. The filthy swine."

The president's nephew, Arnulfo, another Rocaberti and cousin of that same Manuel Rocaberti who had been shot for cowardice in Sumer six years before, answered, "Sex sells, Uncle. And Artemisia Jimenez is about as sexy as it gets. Clever of them to use her. Cleverer of them to have supported her ambitions early on. Why didn't *we* think of that, Uncle?"

"We didn't think of it, Arnulfo, because politics in this country had always been the province of the good families, of those with the dignity of position and wealth. Who ever thought we'd actually have to *fight* an election rather than simply coming up with an agreement among those who mattered as to which clan would have the honors this time around?"

"Parilla and his pet gringo thought so," Arnulfo answered. "Maybe it wasn't such a good idea to have brought in the Taurans, after all. I doubt that either of them, Parilla or Carrera—"

"And that's another damned thing," the president interrupted. "What goddamned business is it of this fucking imported maniac how we run our country? He's not even a citizen."

Arnulfo shrugged. At heart he was an honest and fair-minded sort, or as honest and fair-minded as someone raised to care for family above all could hope to be. "His blood's buried here, whatever could be found of it. He's remarried back into us. All his friends are here. Nearly everything he owns, and apparently he owns a *lot*, Uncle, is here. As I was about to say, when you brought in the Taurans, you threatened all that."

"Spilled milk," the president retorted. "And you don't know that we wouldn't have had to face an election, anyway, a *real* election. Parilla has wanted to be president for decades and was only kept from the office by the machinations of Piña. Besides, all the money they have gained using *our* citizens as cannon fodder is rightfully ours."

"They seem to have redistributed quite a bit of that money, Uncle, a lot more than we would have in their shoes. Have you any idea how much they've plowed back in to the Republic? It's in the billions; schools, clinics, factories, banks, parks, job training. The list goes on. They even put some into producing a real competitor for Miss Terra Nova, and, let me tell you, *that* earned them a lot more in good will than they paid for it."

"And how many sons were lost in earning that money, would you tell me that?" the president asked huffily.

"It seems that a hundred-thousand-drachma death gratuity and lifetime pension and care for wives and parents, plus education for younger siblings and children, go a long way toward stifling resentment for lost sons, Uncle. Especially when our families are large, and jobs and farmland quite limited."

The president bit back an answer, then sighed. His face assumed a hopeless look. "You mean we are going to lose the election, don't you?"

"As things stand now, Uncle? Stinking. We haven't a prayer. We'll lose the presidency. We'll lose the legislature; both houses, mind you. And a few months after that we'll lose the Supreme Court. And right after that, you can be sure the investigations will start."

"Investigations?"

Arnulfo pointed at the television against one wall. "Listen for yourself, Uncle."

Parilla scowled and pointed directly into the battery of TV camera's facing the stand. "Tell us where, *Presidente* Rocaberti, tell us where. Where is the money from the cable television deal? Tell us *where*."

Led by legionaries scattered among them and dressed in mufti, the crowd chanted, "TELL US WHERRRE."

"How much was the bribe to your family that turned management of the Transitway over to the Zhong? *Presidente* Rocaberti, tell us how much."

"HOW MUUUCHCHCH?"

"Where are the donatives the boys of the *Legion del Cid* earned and turned over to the government, Mr. President?"

"WHERRRE?"

"How much have the Taurans paid you to let us become their colony?"

"HOW MUUUCHCHCH?"

Parilla stopped speaking briefly, to allow the crowd to compose itself. After all, this was a speech to announce candidacy, not an incitement to riot.

He smiled broadly, then joked, "For the answers to these and a hundred other questions on how the old families have robbed the Republic and the people, stay tuned for election night results, my friends, because today, now, this minute, I, Raul Parilla, am announcing my candidacy for the office of *Presidente de le Republica*. And I promise you that when I am elected we **SHALL HAVE ANSWERS**. I promise you, as well, a better, a more honest, tomorrow. So help me God."

That was the cue for both the band and Artemisia. After a drum roll, and the playing of the first bars, she began to sing,

> "*El sol del verano*
> *Es renacido*
> *Libre es el bosque*
> *Por mi . . .*
> "*O' Patria, Patria, enseña nos;*
> *Tus hijos esperan por ti.*
> *El dia viene quando se levantas*
> *Mañana sera mejor!*"

The president's hand lanced to the remote, to cut off the images shown on the screen as the camera panned along the galleries. They were all singing, all fifty thousand plus of them.

His nephew stopped him. "No, Uncle, we need to see this."

> "*O Patria, Patria, enseña nos;*
> *Tus hijos esperan por ti.*"

"We're screwed," he said.

"We're screwed without some desperate measures," Arnulfo agreed. He didn't add, but thought, *Though sometimes desperate measures might include just coming clean and giving back some of what we've stolen.*

> *"Mañana sera,*
> *Mañana sera,*
> *Mañana sera mejor!"*

Panshir Base, Pashtia, 32/6/467 AC,

Every day got a little worse. What had begun with directed terrorism and the distant siege of ambush of roads and blowing of bridges had grown to the point that most of the Tauran Union troops were confined to their bases, under frequent if not quite constant mortar and rocket attack. The Anglians and Secordians fought to keep the roads open, to rebuild the bridges, even to combat the terrorism on behalf of the TU troops that were forbidden by their governments from actively seeking battle.

In the larger sense, though, those English-speaking men and women were fighting to let the Progressive administration in Hamilton keep its promise not to commit further Federated States troops to the war, but to rely on their "allies." In the largest sense, they were all fighting to prevent what their governments considered the ultimate disaster.

That ultimate disaster? It was not that the Salafis should regain control of Pashtia, nor even that they might use it for further attacks. No; the TU leadership—though many around the globe considered that expression to the ultimate oxymoron—lived in desperate fear that the fickle populace of the Federated States might once again elect an administration that quite simply considered the TU, indeed the rest of the world, to be largely voiceless and irrelevant.

"And even *that's* not enough to get the bastards

to let us *fight*," fumed Claudio Marciano, as a large caliber mortar round detonated inside his camp, a few hundred meters to the east of his sandbagged command post. Following on the heels of the explosion he heard the cry "Medic!" and the scream of an ambulance siren.

"'Fighting never settled anything,' *Generale*," quoted Stefano del Collea, his eyes turned Heavenward in mock piety.

"Tell it to the city fathers of Carthage," Marciano retorted. "You know what bugs me about it, Stefano?"

"No, sir. I mean, other than the unnerving blasts, the wounded troopers, the sheer frustration of being here and not allowed to do our fucking jobs, sir, what could possibly be troublesome?"

Barely, Marciano restrained the urge to slap his cynical aide with his helmet. Instead, he said, "What bothers me is that they're able to keep this up at all. I mean, without the roads—which our masters made us give away—we can still get enough to eat. Our enemies are not only apparently eating; they've got the logistic wherewithal to bring in shells by the ton-load."

Del Collea sighed. "I know, sir."

About five thousand meters to the southwest, in a small village the Tauran command had made into a no-fire zone, Noorzad looked on approvingly as one of his newer recruits, Ashraf al Islamiya, strained to carry forty kilograms worth of heavy mortar shells to the guns. He ported them—two at a time, one over each shoulder—from a small cave in which they had been painstakingly secreted over the last several months, to the firing position in the town square. There, two 120mm mortars chunked out their twenty-kilogram cargos toward the infidel base.

Noorzad had chosen this firing position precisely because it was an absolute no-fire zone, a place where all fire, even in self-defense, was forbidden to the Taurans. Had some other village in range been a no-fire zone he'd have used that. If there had been no no-fire zones, he'd have forced all the villagers to squat around the mortars anyway. That, he had learned, would stop the Taurans from shooting back no matter *what* he did.

Still, the patent idiocy of the Taurans was not Noorzad's reason for approval. Rather, it was the spirited way in which Ashraf put his whole body and will into carrying the shells. It showed Noorzad the power and the truth of Islam. It reinforced in a most satisfying way that of which he was convinced anyway; that his way of life, his religion, and *his* truth—which was the eternal truth—would triumph.

With a grunt, Ashraf flipped one shell off his shoulder to be caught by an assistant gunner. The assistant likewise grunted as he took the shell, but paused to pat Ashraf lightly on the arm and smile encouragement. Then the assistant turned, took the shell in both hands, and eased the finned base of the thing into the mortar tube. He released it to slide down, ducking while covering his ears with his hands.

When he turned back to Ashraf, he saw that the new man was shaken with the muzzle blast. The assistant tapped him, still lightly, on the face and twisted to show him how to deal with the blast while carrying a shell. This involved hunching one shoulder and pressing the ear on that side into it, while reaching across the head with the free arm to place a hand over the other ear.

The assistant took the next shell from Ashraf, who trotted back to the mouth of the small storage cave to get more. As Ashraf took the next pair he realized that he felt . . . *What an odd sensation. I am . . . more than pleased . . . perhaps, even, I'm a bit happy. Why? Well . . . that someone had cared enough to show me even this one tiny thread of the ropes that went into serving a mortar. Whatever I was told about the Salafis was a lie; once you are one of them you* are *one of them.*

He could not remember a time in the army of Haarlem when any of his then comrades had really cared much.

The shells were expended and the mortar crew breaking their gun down to hide it in the cave from which it had been drawn. They would camouflage it just before splitting up and pulling out. Ashraf, once known as Verdonk, helped with the disassembly, insofar as he could. Mostly, he was in the way of an otherwise expert crew.

"Ashraf," Noorzad called out in the English he shared with ex-Haarlemer. "Stop for a few minutes and come over here." He then said much the same thing in Pashtun, "Send the new one over."

The assistant gestured with his hands and his face, *Go to the leader. We'll make do without your help for a bit.* He was careful not to add, by voice, gesture or expression, *Besides, you're just in the way.*

What the hell; the ex-infidel kid is trying.

Ashraf turned and walked to Noorzad, who gestured for him to sit.

Feeling distinctly uneasy—after all, it was not so long ago he'd been given the choice of accepting Islam or having his throat cut— Ashraf sat.

"You're learning your duties well, Ashraf," the guerilla chief said. "All your fellow mujahadin say so."

The former Haarlemer breathed a small sigh of relief. Apparently this little meeting was *not* to announce that leaving his throat unslashed had been a fixable mistake.

"Thank you, Noorzad. I've tried."

"Yes, yes," Noorzad agreed. "You've tried very hard and succeeded rather well. Soon you will be a fine crewman for the mortars. It's not enough though."

Ashraf almost felt the bite of a razor's keen blade drawing across his throat. He stiffened. "Not enough?"

Noorzad effected not to notice the nervousness in Ashraf's body's stiffening and in the convert's wavering voice.

"We are simple fighting men. To fight we can teach you. But the reason why we fight, the advancement of God's way? This we are not really quite up to."

"No?" The Haarlemer had never met such a bunch of religious fanatics in his life. He'd never even imagined such. *They* weren't up to his religious instruction?

"No," Noorzad said. "I am sending you and your other Haarlemer reverts"—"reverts" because one did not convert to the natural faith of Islam; one reverted to it—"on to a madrassa, a school, in Kashmir. It is safe there and there you will receive more and better instruction in the faith."

Ashraf felt a small surge of relief. They weren't going to cut his throat. And he was going to get out of action for a while. It would feel odd though, leaving the first home in which he'd felt comfortable, in years.

Hovercraft pads, Main Cantonment, *Isla Real*, 2/7/467 AC,

In contrast to Cara's happy smile, Cruz's face was a stone mask, a study in "Man, hiding his misery." While Cara played with the kids, he just looked longingly in the general direction of his tercio's camp, a few miles up the coast.

Their household goods were long since packed up; the three bedroom bungalow they'd shared turned back over to LHD, the Legionary Housing Directorate. They had a place waiting in the city now, while Cruz attended university. He'd met the new neighbors and found he had nothing in common with any of them. Maybe his classmates at the university would be better.

Maybe, but I doubt it.

Somewhere in his personal bag Cruz had the orders assigning him to Seventh Cohort (Reserve) of the First *Tercio* (*Principio Eugenio*). At least he'd be able to soldier one long weekend a month and a month over the summer. The three month's pay he'd earn would come in handy, too, since a legionary veteran's student stipend, even for a centurion, was something less than generous for a married man with two children. Really, it wouldn't be enough to live on, but for the guaranteed loans. And those came with strings.

Cara never thought about that. She was happy enough that her man would be home and out of danger. She never seemed to have considered how miserable he was going to be without that danger, and always stuck at home.

Cruz heard a growing whine and looked out to sea. Yes, there it was; the huge, Volgan-built hovercraft that would take them from the island to the landing point in the City. From there they'd take a taxi to their new apartment, their new "home."

Home? Cruz thought. *What is home? It's not just the place you live; it's not just the place your woman is. I think . . . maybe . . . it's the place you're happiest. And I'm leaving home.*

Hamilton, FD, FSC, 2/7/467 AC

Dating from early in the history of the colonization of Terra Nova, the Federated States' Executive Mansion looked less a home and more a fortress. Within it, in an office marked by golds and greens and tasteful old woods, the president of the FSC conferred with his secretary of war.

"Cut the bullshit, James," said the president of the FSC to his secretary of war. "The war in Pashtia is *not* going swimmingly. Our 'allies' are not doing their part, despite what you promised me, they promised you, and I promised the people who elected me and the newspapers and television stations that supported me. Right now, the Office of Strategic Intelligence is convinced that Pashtia will fall about two months before mid-term elections. *That*, my advisors assure me, will cost us both the House and the Senate. Losing those will stymie the social programs we counted on getting passed to be reelected. All of which means that, unless the Pashtian situation is turned around, we'll all be looking for jobs after that election."

"But Mr. President—" Malcolm began.

"Can it, James. No bullshit. We're in trouble and no two ways about it. Now how are you going to fix this and save our skins? And, please, spare me the nonsense about massive formation of TU troops to turn the tide. They're not coming, not today, not tomorrow, not *ever*. And if they did come they still wouldn't *fight*."

Malcolm hung his head. He'd been so sure that troops would be forthcoming. He'd been convinced that with the right platitudes, the proper kowtowing to the Tauran Union, the World League, the humanitarian activist NGOs and the world press, he could persuade the Tauros to really commit to the war. He'd been absolutely certain that the Gauls and the Sachsens would really help if only they were approached the right way. He'd been equally certain he had that way.

Bah! I couldn't even talk them into providing what they promised, *let alone more. I couldn't talk them into allowing what little they have sent to actually go out of their bases and* fight.

This was too uncomfortable a train of thought. Malcolm quickly added the mental amendment, *If only the previous administration hadn't so thoroughly poisoned the waters.*

He never considered that maybe the water was poisoned to begin with.

First Landing, Federated States of Columbia, 2/7/467 AC

Although a local virus had the effect of substantially reducing the harmful effects of some of the things found in tobacco, it had done nothing to make its nicotine less of a poison in sufficient dosage. Indeed, in the form of nicotine sulfate, it was one of the better insecticides and lethal to humans in dosages of as little as fifty or sixty milligrams. It was even more useful since it was readily absorbed through the skin.

Khalid could have purchased simple cigarettes or cigars to prepare his mixture. There was, however, a simpler way, taught to him by his Volgan instructors. This was to purchase a commercial insecticide and distill out the impurities, leaving fairly pure nicotine sulfate. This he had done, achieving a highly concentrated and extremely deadly form of the stuff, with only enough liquid to make it free flowing.

In his hotel room he attached a baby's snot sucker to some clear, flexible tubing cut to the length of an umbrella. With the squeeze bottle at the end of the snot sucker, he vacuumed an appreciable quantity of the nicotine sulfate solution into the tube. This he plugged with a small cork, very tightly. The entire assembly he then taped to the cane of the umbrella, making a small slash in the material to allow the corked tube to protrude through slightly.

The umbrella stood by the hotel room door. Meanwhile, Khalid, his hair lightened and green contacts covering his own brown eyes, studied the picture in the folder he'd been given. The picture was of one Ishmael ibn Mohamed ibn Salah, min Sa'ana, a very minor scion of Mustafa's clan, currently attending school in First Landing. The boy was only twenty and lacked both the finely developed paranoia of the older members of his clan, as well as their money to hire guards and drivers.

Boy, thought Khalid. *Boy, I don't know why you have to die. Nor do I care. But enjoy the morning, even so. You will not see the sunset.*

With that, Khalid closed the file and stood, walking to his bag to place the file within it. He closed and locked the bag. With that he left, taking the umbrella with him and placing a "Do Not Disturb" sign on the room's door.

Outside the hotel, Khalid hailed a taxi which brought him to the corner nearest Ishmael's small, student apartment. He waited a short time, then saw the boy leave, smoking a cigarette.

Which is why I chose this method. It will take a while for them to notice the outrageous amount of nicotine in your system. With doctors in the Federated States as they are now, they may not even care to look. After all, you are one of those utter unmentionables, those vile untouchables. You smoke, boy, and it's going to be the death of you.

The boy, Ishmael, disappeared into a nearby subway entrance. Khalid followed him down, neither so closely as to be obvious nor so far behind that he couldn't run to catch the train should his target enter one.

There was no train. There was, however, a fair crowd. Using the crowd as cover, Khalid moved to within two feet of Ishmael. Then he settled down to wait for a train.

Unfortunately, the next train entered the subway on the other side. Khalid really wanted not just the noise—in case the nicotine caused the boy to cry out—he also wanted everyone's attention focused on the train's arrival, and movement to begin in the crowd, to cover his own withdrawal.

As expected, the next train arrived on his side, with a tremendous rattle. Nearly everyone but Khalid turned their attention to the train, and about half-

lurched forward half a step, as if to gain an advantage
for boarding.

Khalid was prepared to make a similar half-lurch, if
his target did. This proved unnecessary. He pointed the
tip of his umbrella at the boy's calf. At the same time,
he reached the other hand over and gave a squeeze
to the snot sucker. As little sound as the popping cork
made, there was no chance of it being heard over
the sound of the train. The nicotine sulfate sprayed
out, soaking the target's cloth-covered calf. Khalid
immediately turned away, and walked into the mass
of humanity gathering by the edge of the platform.

When Khalid turned and looked through the window
of the subway car, there was a small crowd gathering
around a prostrate, quivering form.

St. Ekaterina Caserne, *Fuerte* Cameron, Balboa, 4/7/467 AC

The stiffly marching Volgans sang in voices designed
to knock birds dead at a mile.

> *"Pust' yarost' blagorodnaya*
> *Vskipaet, kak volna*
> *Idyot voyna narodnaya,*
> *Svyaschennaya voyna!"*

"Catchy," Carrera complimented. "What's it mean?"

Samsonov, the Volgan colonel of paratroopers Kuralski had contacted and hired—along with the bulk
of his regiment—some years back, puzzled over the
translation for a moment before answering, "Comes
from Great Global War . . . but maybe older than

that. Not sure. Means . . . mmm . . . something like, 'Let waves of righteous fury . . . Swell up as never before . . . And spur us to the victory of . . . Our sacred people's war.' You like?"

"It's excellent. Can you have one of your men make a translation and send it on to Professor Ruiz. Maybe send him a small chorus to demonstrate, too."

Samsonov, old, stout and blond where he wasn't balding, answered, "Easy . . . not those men singing now, though." He gestured at the company marching by. "Those men aren't bad but . . . regimental chorus much better."

"As you prefer."

The Volgans, roughly thirteen hundred of them, weren't on the legion's official strength. Rather, they were employees of General Abogado's Foreign Military Training Group, a subsidiary of Chatham, Hennessey and Schmied, that had provided training expertise to the legion since the beginning. Most of FMTG now was, in fact, Volgan since the Balboans and other Latins were long since capable of conducting Initial Entry Training and most specialty training, along with the Cazador School and other leadership courses. With the bulk of the aircraft being Volgan and a fair number of the ships of the *classis* likewise, those departments were staffed almost entirely with Samsonov's countrymen, as well. Even for the aircraft bought from the FSC, the instructors were a mix of qualified Volgans and Balboans.

Samsonov's regiment, and it was a reinforced Volgan parachute regiment in organization, provided both the Controller-Evaluators and the opposing forces at the legion's *Centro de Entrenamiento para el Ejercito Expedicionario*, or CENTIPEDE. The CENTIPEDE had served to put the finishing touches on cohorts just before they deployed to the war. Even without a contract, for the nonce, training continued. Being elite soldiers from an army with an impressive tradition, this suited the Volgans just fine. It suited them even better that they weren't in Volga, anymore.

It was possible that there was a more anti-Tsarist-Marxism leaning group in the world than Samsonov's paratroopers; indeed someone had once suggested as much. No one had ever proven it, though. Samsonov's men loathed Marxism as only those who'd lived under it could. They likewise didn't much care for the corrupt rump of the Volgan Empire that still lived.

One reason they were pretty content to be in Balboa was that they earned standard legionary wages—for the enlisted men about fifteen times more than Volga paid its army—and lived and ate, oh, *much* better.

Many had married into the locals and some had even transferred over to the legion. In turn, there were now to be found the odd Garcia and Gomez, seconded from their home tercios and standing among the Gureviches and Gregoriis of Samsonov's regiment. In time, Carrera expected something like complete assimilation. The notion that FMTG was anything but an arm of the legion was rather fictive, anyway.

"These dirty rotten Fascist pigs
We'll shoot between the eyes.
The garbage of humanity
Is headed for demise."

"What's the title?" Carrera asked.
This time the translation came more easily. "We call it . . . 'Holy War' or . . . maybe better, 'Sacred War.'"

"Oh, *yeah*." Carrera smiled. "I want that in the Legion's song books."

By the time the marching company of Volgans had passed out of earshot, Samsonov was leading Carrera into the regimental headquarters. They passed by banners more or less dripping with battle honors from the Great Global War, the Volga-Pashtia War, and everything in between. Carrera stopped to finger the streamers, respectfully.

"An honorable regiment," he whispered.

Samsonov answered the whisper. "Was my father's regiment . . . uncle's before him. Eventually . . . fell to me but in worst of times. When your man, Kuralski, found us we were reduced to raising corn and pigs to eat. That would be fine for some nonentity motorized rifle regiment but we . . . *paratroopers*. Even at that, government going to close us out. They begrudged us . . . cost of our uniforms . . . and of heating oil for winter."

The Volgan colonel spat.

Reluctantly, Carrera released the battle streamers. "How many of your men are veterans of the war in Pashtia?" he asked.

"About three in ten, or perhaps bit more," the Volgan answered. "Why?"

"I'm not just operating off faith, here," Carrera said, "I am reasonably certain that we'll be rehired soon to go to Pashtia. It's a different environment from Sumer, one my men aren't used to. We're capable of doing the mountain training and such ourselves—"

"And better than we could," Samsonov interjected.

"—but I don't know how the Pashtun act and think and neither do my men."

"We can help there. Quite lot; truth. But have you considered Pashtun? They're . . . first class . . . mercenaries and, if well treated, loyal to salt."

Carrera nodded. "I've got someone over there looking to do just that. But it's hard, he told me, to sort out the worthwhile ones from the infiltrators. Actually, he said it's impossible and I told him to forget it and concentrate on buying up land and pack animals, while collecting intelligence."

Samsonov rubbed his nose. "I can help with that. Some tribes trustworthy; some not. And I know Mullah, Nami Hassim, who is very learned, very scholarly, and—fortunately—utterly corrupt athiest"

"Can you send a recruiting team over to help my man?"

"Sure . . . what else you want?"

"I want you to restructure to prepare us for Pashtia. Abogado knows."

War Department, Hamilton, FD, 7/7/467 AC

Kenneth O'Meara-Temeroso squirmed in his chair in Malcolm's plush office. He couldn't, he just *couldn't*, do what the secretary was demanding of him. Besides, it was Malcolm who had sent him to Sumer expressly to fire, hurt, and humiliate Carrera. How could he go back and beg for help now?

"It won't even work," O'Meara-Temeroso objected. "It's a waste of time. That bastard will never forgive us for trying to stiff him. And he won't take the pain he caused us by pulling out so abruptly as sufficient payback, either."

Malcolm smiled warmly. His tan seemed particularly

orange today, to match. "I don't care if you have to suck his dick. I want troops for Pashtia and I want them *fast*."

Whatever his failings, and they were many, ranging from obesity to a remarkable arrogance coupled with stupidity, O'Meara-Temeroso was still, at least arguably, a man. This was too much. "*You* suck his dick. I'm resigning."

And with that he stood, abruptly turned, and walked out.

One worthless, arrogant bureaucrat gone, mused Malcolm. *Hmmm; who might this Carrera person listen to? Hmmm . . .*

"Suzy," Malcolm said pleasantly into the intercom, "get me General Rivers, would you?"

"I remember his last words on the subject very distinctly, Mr. Secretary. He said, 'We'll keep track and when you come looking to hire us again everything you've cost us will be added to our fee, with interest from today.' Are you prepared to pay that, Mr. Secretary? The bill is going to be enormous. And since we tried to send funds Carrera considered due to his organization to another, the national government of Balboa, he's not going to give us credit."

"What do you think he'll charge us?"

"As much as he can squeeze. In fact, as much as he thinks it takes to hurt us. We pissed him off pretty badly and he is not the . . . forgiving type."

"But he needs money," Malcolm objected. "He doesn't have a national tax base to pay for his war machine."

"Someone—we think the Yamatans—are funneling a

great deal of money to him right now. And he already had quite a lot. I don't think he's hurting."

Malcolm sighed, bleakly. It was so . . . frankly inconceivable, that a mere mercenary should be so difficult. *Ah, well. Needs must. . . .*

"General Rivers, I want you to go see him and see what he'll take. Don't commit us to anything yet. See what he might take that isn't in the form of dollars. The president doesn't want to go to Congress over this. Maybe we have something he wants . . . weapons . . . gold . . . I dunno. But the president wants him and what the President wants—"

"I'll leave day after tomorrow, Mr. Secretary. But I can't promise anything."

Motor Yacht *Suzy Q*, Xamar Coast, 9/7/467 AC

The storm trick wouldn't work more than once. At least, it wouldn't work twice in a row. The *classis* needed something else, rather, several somethings else.

The *Suzy Q* was one of those things. Oh, she was a real yacht, all right, one hundred and ten feet worth of outrageous luxury. Even the girls aboard were luxury models, hookers taken from the *Wappen von Bremen* and paid a hefty bonus for sunning themselves topless on the forward deck. Everyone had been surprised that so many of the girls had volunteered when asked. Six had been needed, thirty-two had volunteered, and that was even before the danger bonus was mentioned. Who knew; perhaps they had begun to think of themselves as *legionettes*.

Whatever the motivation, they did a very impressive job, sunning and stretching, nonchalantly showing off their assets to the fishing boats they passed. The *classis* assumed, not unreasonably, that at least *some* of those boats reporting directly to Pirates-R-Us.

In anticipation of that, the boat was not quite so yachtlike under the surface. Both sides and the stern had been heavily reinforced with resinated aramid-fiber armor plates. Three .41 caliber machine guns were positioned on each side to fire outward, as was a seventh to fire astern. The machine guns had been modified with a special jacket for water cooling. They could fire for half an hour or more before the barrels overheated. As a matter of fact, the half hour was about as much as the testing committee had cared to check. No one really knew how long they could fire without a let up. Besides the .41s, under the forward deck a single front-shielded 20mm was poised to be raised by hydraulics. An additional seven Cazadors and an equal number of sailors posed as crew in civilian dress, over and above the hidden seventeen slotted to man the machine guns and 20mm.

The Cazadors didn't get the girls' danger bonus, though they drew normal combat pay.

Centurion Rodriguez, admiring the girls from the wheelhouse, thought, *Screw the bonus; watching the girls is bonus enough.* Standing next to him the *Suzy Q's* skipper, Warrant Officer Chu, had much the same thought.

Both were making plans for their next scheduled visit to the *von Bremen.*

"Sweet duty," mused Rodriguez.

"That it is," agreed Chu. He pointed at the boat's radar screen. "But it's about to get a lot less sweet."

"*Suzy Q* this is *Ironsides;* company coming."

Chu picked up the microphone and answered, "We see 'em coming, *Ironsides*. No problem, just the one boat."

"Shall I have the girls start their routine?" asked Rodriguez.

Chu noted the distance on the screen by eye. He shook his head slightly. "No . . . wait a bit. They won't be here for half an hour. But why don't you have the *Santissima Trinidad* close it up some?"

The pirate vessel was crammed to the gills with mujahadin. At least, they liked to style themselves as holy warriors; it gave them a warm and fuzzy feeling to be doing the work of God while filling their pockets.

"And aren't *those* some bits of divine workmanship?" asked the boat's chief rhetorically, looking over the exceptionally well-breasted and tanned girls standing by the target's bow and gesturing frantically. "And won't they bring a good price at market?"

He'd asked rhetorically but his assistant had been listening even so. "The boat itself will bring a better one," he said, "and anyone who can afford that boat and those girls will probably bring a better ransom still."

"Oh, look," tsked the pirate chief. "We've frightened them; they're running below. Well, that won't matter. Cheat of us our gaze now, we'll enjoy your bodies all the more later."

The chief turned to his assistant. "Fire a shot across their bow and tell them to kill engines and prepare to be boarded."

Women end up whoring for any of a huge number of reasons. Some, albeit few, actually like the work.

Others have no other skills. Some are lazy, and those often do very poorly even at hooking, while others just want to raise a lot of money in a hurry and then retire back home where no one knows what they've been and done.

Jaquelina Gonzalez's reasons were none of those. At the age of fourteen, she'd had the poor judgment to get involved in one of Colombia Latina's innumerable guerilla wars. Worse, she'd chosen the wrong—the losing—side. Undocumented, fleeing for her life, with no assets but those God had given her and no skills that anyone wanted, she'd found herself drifting into whoredom as a better alternative to starvation. Unofficially, she was the leader of the girls on the *Suzy Q*, and one of the senior hookers on the *Wappen von Bremen*, as the girls counted such things.

For the life of her, she could not have answered why she'd volunteered for this job. Maybe it was merely to get away from the *von Bremen* for a while. Maybe it was something else.

Whatever her reasons, Jaquelina had serious doubts about her wisdom once the pirate vessel got close enough for her to see the men waving their rifles and machetes. Rape? Well, she'd been raped before and survived it. Torture? Yes, she made the mistake of being captured once and so she knew about torture. Come to think of it, though she really didn't like to think of it, the two—rape and torture—had gone together.

"Come on, ladies," she ordered, "time for us to go below."

She waited at the hatch, shoving the other girls ahead of her, before she, too, went below to the armored compartment built especially to house them.

Just before descending, Jaquelina heard a familiar blast from forward of the ship.

The pirate chief saw a portion of the forward deck begin to rise and was very quick to add up two plus two and come up with "Holy fucking shit; it's a trap." When a three-meter-long section of the port side of the boat swung out he directed an RGL gunner to fire, "For the love of Allah and the hope of seeing your family again!"

The RGL flew true and a gaping wound appeared in the target's side. Dimly, through the smoke from the blast, the pirates could see what had to be a machine gun and perhaps a body slumped over it. Two more shells flew in short order toward the rising 20mm, missing it but hitting the shield and sending the men waiting to man it sprawling. The Xamaris had little time for congratulations as two more openings appeared, even as a much larger gun continued to rise on the deck.

The 20mm sat unaimed and unmanned until a couple of Cazadors could be rousted from below. When they arrived, the larger gun began to toss out its shells, knocking down the Xamari pirates in groups.

"Close and board!" screamed the pirate chief. "It's our only chance!"

Two of the girls with her screamed when the boat was rocked by the blast. Barely, Jaquelina restrained herself from pasting them. *Didn't they know what they volunteered for? Then again, did I?*

She felt a bit better once the other guns opened up. But then she realized there was no fire coming from amidships, the same direction as had come the blast. Jaquelina, too, could add two plus two and come up with "Holy shit."

"Oh, fuck," she whispered, then asked, "Who'll come with me?"

The fire was terrible. The pirate boat had no armor, and its wood was little more than tissue paper to the heavy guns engaging it. The infidels' main gun, on deck, simply tore the wheelhouse and most of its occupants to bits.

The chief of the boat, miraculously unhit so far, lay on his belly amidst a layer of spilled blood, torn flesh and bits of shattered bone. One arm upraised and his hand grasping the wheel, he steered through a hole made by the enemy and he steered directly for the target ship. Already, the larger gun was over-shooting. He suspected he was under its arc of fire. Already the boat had closed to the point that the two remaining heavy machine guns could only fire at its stern corners. There was a chance if, and only if, the pirates could get close enough to board. And that seemed at least *possible*.

Only one girl was willing to go on with Jaquelina, her friend and lover, Marta. Marta was an enormous amazon of a woman, dwarfing Jaquelina in every dimension. Nervous—well, *terrified*, to be honest—the amazon followed the little hooker out of their armored shelter and down the smoky central corridor of the ship until they reached amidships. There, they turned to the direction from which had come the earlier blast.

Marta shrieked when she saw one crewman, sans

head, lying on the blood-soaked deck. The other gunner was slumped over his gun, burned and barely breathing.

"Shut up, Marta," Jaquelina ordered as she went to the slumped and hurt gunner. "This one's still alive."

Together, the two eased the hurt Cazador to the bloody deck. The boy's face was a mess, which caused Jaquie to *tsk* and Marta to shudder.

"He'll live, I think, though he won't be very pretty," Jaquie announced.

Marta didn't reply directly, pointing instead out the hole in the hull and saying, "Maybe he'll live. *We* won't."

Jaquie's eyes followed Marta's pointing finger. There, a scant fifty meters away, the chewed-up bow of their attackers plowed a shallow furrow in the sea.

"Fuck!"

Jaquelina tore her gaze from the enemy vessel and let it come to rest upon the gun. *Looks like . . . mmm . . . a scaled-down version of the FS Model Fifty heavy machine gun. Well . . . I know how to use one of those, courtesy of the Arenista National Liberation Front. That jacket around the barrel looks funny but . . . oh, it's for water cooling. Those can fire a llllooonnnggg time without overheating.*

She knelt down behind the gun. *Ammunition's already fed. Looks like . . . mmm . . . three hundred rounds; two boxes.*

"Honey, we're in business," she said to Marta. "Go grab a couple more cans of ammunition."

Jaquie's right hand lowered to the wheel on the gun's traversing and elevating mechanism and began to twist it counterclockwise to raise the line of fire. Her left hand took hold of the left spade grip. She rested that thumb on the gun's butterfly trigger. Scrunching herself as low as possible, so as not to be seen by the pirates massing on their ship's bow in preparation for a boarding, Jaquie shifted her right hand to the traversing wheel and moved the gun's traverse to the right side of the mass of pirate humanity.

"Now we wait until they line themselves up," she muttered. "Come to Mama, babies."

Centurion Rodriguez and Warrant Chu were more or less pinned in the wheelhouse. While Chu tried to steer the boat aport to gain a little distance from the pirates, Rodriguez attempted to poke his head around the fortified wheelhouse corner to return fire on them.

"Fucking bastards!" Rodriguez cried out, jerking his head back and rolling in pain on the deck while clawing wooden splinters from his face and one bloody eye.

Jaquie had blood in her eye as the pirate ship closed to within fifteen meters. She made a quick, fine adjustment to the traversing wheel and used her thumb to depress the gun's trigger. The pounding of the heavy machine gun's blast in the close confines of its cabin was painful to her ears. Even so, she kept up the fire with her left hand while twisting the traversing wheel with her right. In her line of sight she saw pirates bowled down, spraying blood. As often as not, the heavy bullets punched right through two and even three and four men before continuing on. She heard their cries of victory turn to despair and the sound raised a wicked grin on her face.

The gun gave a clang and the grin turned to a grimace of pain. A return shot, aimed or just lucky, had hit it causing the bullet to carom off the side plate to bury itself in her right side, just below the ribs. Even so, she never let up with her left thumb nor stopped traversing with her right hand.

Note to self: Next time I really need to ask for body armor.

Chu let go the wheel to pull Rodriguez back behind fuller cover. The blood flowed too thickly for the sailor to see the damage. He pulled a water bottle from a holder above deck and poured its contents over the centurion's eye.

This is probably a mistake, he thought, as he reached to remove a thin spike of wood from the white of the eye. Rodriguez screamed, once, as the splinter was removed. Blood flowed even more freely afterwards. Still, the pain became more or less manageable.

"Thanks, Chu," he whispered. "See to the defense . . . I'll be all right."

Blast the pirates into eternity Jaquelina could do, wounded or not. What she could not do was stop the progress of their boat. It continued on, closer and closer, until it rammed the side of the *Suzy Q,* staving it in and causing water to pour through the rupture.

"Marta!" she screamed, "See to the wounded boy and let's get the fuck out of here!"

Jaquelina stood up and backed away from the gun. Blood suddenly began to rush from her wounded side. "*Mierde,*" she muttered, and promptly fainted.

The bilge pumps kicked in automatically, relieving Chu of the burden of flipping a switch while trying to lead his own crew and the Cazadors. Whatever or whoever it was who'd taken over the central .41 on that side might have knocked the pirates' dicks loose, but just couldn't stop the boat or kill them all.

Well before he'd been enticed into becoming a squid, Chu had been a pretty fair riflemen with the Fourth Tercio. He picked up Rodriguez's bayoneted rifle and, screaming something unintelligible even to himself, launched himself bodily to the spot where his hull was breached and the pirates oozing over the side.

He was joined at the boarding point by *Legionario* Tomás Guillermo, the latter likewise charging forward with bayonet point to the front. The prow of the pirate vessel was on a rough plane with the side of the *Suzy Q.* They met, Chu and Guillermo on the one side, half a dozen half-panicked pirates on the other. The pirates towered over the little legionaries but, since both the legionaries had body armor— better still, training—the first two Xamaris met went down with screams made gurgling by the blood filling their lungs.

"Get the fuck away from my fucking ship you scum-sucking bastards!" Chu cried.

By the time Marta got on deck, Jaquelina carried under one arm and the burnt legionary slung over her shoulder, the other hookers had also emerged. Marta set Jaquie down gently and just as carefully laid the legionary alongside her.

"Does anybody know first aid?" Marta asked.

"Sure," answered one of the girls brightly. "I know just what to do; I've watched the legionaries." She then proceeded to fill her not unimpressive lungs with air and screamed "Medddiiiccc!"

❖   ❖   ❖

With their own boat sinking under them, the legionaries had little choice but to swarm the other. Leaving
their machine guns and grabbing rifles, they followed
Chu and Guillermo in a surge over the gunwales. The
pirates had little chance of stopping that charge. While
the bodies and not-quite-yet bodies were being rolled
over the side to the gathering sharks, the legionaries
collected their wounded and dead and carried them
across. A half dozen pirates they saved for questioning. Besides, Fosa had said he thought it would be
good for morale for the rest of the fleet to see some
of their enemies hang.

UEPF *Spirit of Peace*, 9/7/467 AC

"We'll call that one a draw," High Admiral Robinson
decided, looking at a high resolution recording of the
Suzy Q's fight with the Xamaris.

Wallenstein shook her head. "No . . . I don't think
so. Sure, the pirates managed to sink the mercenaries'
yacht, and sure the mercenaries only got a crappy, slow,
tramp fishing boat in return. But all the pirates died, if
you count the ones the mercenaries hung off the flight
deck of their aircraft carrier and those they fed to the
sharks. Those pirates won't be going home and people
in Xamar are eventually going to wonder what horror it
is out at sea that eats their sons and doesn't even spit
out the bones. No, Admiral, sorry, but it was a loss."

Robinson, being a Class One, hated being corrected
by lesser castes. Even so, he was willing to admit
Wallenstein was right to the extent that he changed
the subject slightly.

"I understand that the FSC is considering rehiring those mercenaries for employment in Pashtia."

"For a very impressive amount of money," Wallenstein agreed. "How do we use that?"

She already had a number of ideas of how to put the deployment out of country of the legions to good use but, since she wanted Class One status more than she wanted life, she thought it best to let the high admiral recoup from being corrected.

"They're going to have to send sixty-five or seventy percent of their force over if they're going to do any good," Robinson said. "The Taurans are collapsing in Pashtia. That will put the Tauran forces in Balboa on a rough par with the legions, not counting the mercenaries' reserves. It might be enough for the Taurans to interfere with the election there. Our ambassador says that this Parilla bastard is certain to win any open and fair election."

"What do you have in mind?" Wallenstein asked.

"Well . . . suppose we have the World League and the Tauran Union insist on sending observers to oversee the election. Perhaps we can have that idiot ex-president from the FSC go, too. You know the one, Wozniak. No matter how the elections go, they can insist there was voter intimidation, ballot-box fraud, the usual. Then the government of Balboa can refuse to step down. The Tauran troops can protect that government as long as they match the rump of the Legion in power."

"What about the FSC?"

"About one quarter of the FSC is Progressive, which is to say, Taurophile and United Earthophile, at heart. That's probably enough to stymie any FS support for mercenaries that even the more fascistic among them consider to be distasteful. So it would be just the Taurans against the Balboans."

Wallenstein considered that. "I don't think the Taurans are enough."

With that, Robinson agreed. "They're not; no tolerance for heavy casualties. The Taurans and the Zhong together might be enough though."

Robinson had no clue he was almost echoing Gallic General Janier. Still, the objective reality of the matter was available to both men. Why should they not draw similar conclusions?

"They might," Wallenstein conceded. "I wonder though, if we're not actually creating exactly the threat we fear."

And that was as far as she was willing to go. She did, after all, want Class One status.

INTERLUDE

SUPREME COURT OF THE UNITED STATES
CORDER, GOVERNOR, UTAH *v.* SIMPSON, COM-
MISSIONER, INTERNAL REVENUE SERVICE
CERTIORARI TO THE TAX COURT OF THE
UNITED STATES

Argued October 13, 2104—Decided March 1, 2105

The overwhelming weight of international opinion that fair and just taxation of the richest portion of humanity for the benefit of the poorest and most exploited is not controlling here, but provides respected and significant confirmation for the Court's holding that the Fairness in Taxation Act of 2101 is both constitutional and binding upon those states which have, so far, failed to implement its provisions. See, *e.g., Tomlins, supra,* at 831–832, and n. 30. The United States is the only country in the world that continues to deny to its superior organization, the United Nations, its fair and just due in fiscal and tax matters. It does not lessen fidelity to the Constitution or pride in its origins to acknowledge that the concept of national— still less so, state—sovereignty has grown dated, and no longer meets the aspirations of a kinder and more enlightened world. Express affirmation of certain fundamental rights by other nations and peoples underscores the centrality of those same rights within our own heritage of freedom. Correspondingly, their entitlement to support and development lays a duty upon the so-far privileged portion of humanity to pay. The duty to pay implies, indeed, requires, the right to tax.

CHAPTER NINE

So where are those villainous louts,
those mercenaries?
—Mohammad Saeed al Sahaf
(aka "Baghdad Bob")
Old Earth year 2003

Isla Real, 10/7/467 AC,

The airplane, a legionary Cricket but fitted out with
VIP seats, landed in the typical Balboan swelter. Its
landing roll was a bit under eleven meters. As soon
as the door opened Rivers felt a wilting blast of wet
heat. Carrera's AdC, a junior tribune named Miranda,
met Rivers at the airfield with apologies from Carrera
for not being there personally. The tribune took Rivers'
single bag.

"The *Duque* is in the field with a cohort at the
moment, sir," Miranda explained. "He'll be along within
the hour and hopes you will understand."

Rivers grunted a noncommittal response, while
thinking, *He's got to know why I came. Is this his way
of saying, "Stuff it; I won't work for the FSC while
the Progressives are in charge?" I wonder.*

Miranda showed Rivers to a gleaming staff car, a Yamatan job, and then held the door for the general to enter. He then took over the front passenger seat and directed the driver to proceed.

You've got to be impressed, thought Rivers as the staff car took him on the short ride from *Punta Cocoli* airfield to legion headquarters. *Seven years ago a single brigade without a home; now it's grown to a fair-sized corps with a damned nice home.*

On the way in, Rivers had counted the ships anchored in the bay from his aircraft porthole. Now, on the ground, Rivers took the trouble to count filled and empty aircraft parking spots as the car eased along the road. What he counted impressed him still more. *Over five hundred aircraft. Christ, he's outwinged PanColumbian Airlines and half the Tauran Union. Of course, most of his aircraft are smaller.*

And the troops looked fit, well fed and disciplined, he thought, too, as the car passed a company-sized unit. The troops wore helmets and body armor, but had a spring in their step that told of a light and comfortable panoply. *I like that camouflage pattern.*

The pattern was a pixilated tiger stripe material Carrera had had made up by a company in the FSC that specialized in such things. The material was printed, and the uniforms cut and sewn, by a factory in the City he and Parilla had set up to provide employment to war widows, reservists and their wives, and disabled legionary vets. Those folks put a *lot* of care into the uniforms they made. They made other clothing, too, which sold rather well in the Republic and had even begun to acquire a small overseas market.

The staff car stopped at an intersection as a column

of nineteen Volgan-built tanks rolled across, each preceded by a walking ground guide. *And they're pretty professional in other respects, too. Well I suppose I should have expected that.*

The car turned left at Miranda's direction and entered into a long, tree-lined thoroughfare before ending at a ring road surrounding an amazingly green parade field with a large, white-painted headquarters building on the other side of the field. It navigated around the parade field, pulled up to the columned front of the building and then stopped. Miranda got out, opened the door for Rivers, and led him between the columns and into the building.

The door opened into a broad interior vestibule, reaching up three floors to a battle-scene mural painted on the ceiling. On the upper floors it was surrounded by a marble rail. The bottom floor, the *planta baja*, was of a locally cut and polished, golden oak-colored granite. Upon the floor stood a slightly larger-than-life-sized marble statue of a fully equipped legionary holding a bayoneted bronze rifle in "charge bayonets" pose. The walls were mostly bare, though portraits of uniformed men with decorations for valor about their necks hung in places. Officers, a few, plus centurions, noncoms and enlisted men, all in undress khakis, bustled from room to room, across the vestibule and through the corridors. The whole place had an air of elegant efficiency.

If he can afford to build this, Rivers thought, *he's not hurting for money. Oh, Lordy, is this going to sting.*

Miranda beckoned Rivers on, through a door, up two flights of steps, down a quiet corridor and, finally, into Carrera's office. Rivers noticed the secretary was male and uniformed as well. He also noticed the boy was missing an arm.

Waste not, want not.

"The *Duque* said to make you comfortable, sir. Is there anything I can order for you? Coffee? A beer? Whiskey or mixed drink from the mess in the basement, if you like."

"Coffee would be fine . . . ah . . . Tribune. Just fine, thank you. Cream and sugar."

"Very good, sir."

Miranda turned and left as Rivers sat on one of the chairs. In a few minutes, the one-armed boy brought in a tray holding a cup of steaming hot coffee. He set it down and left without a word.

The rear wall of the office was mostly a very large window, Rivers noticed. He walked over to it and looked out on the scene of cows and the solar chimney that ran up the island's central massif. The cloud formed and continuously renewed above the chimney was . . . *rather soothing to watch,* Rivers decided. He was still watching when he sensed a sudden stiffening that seemed to take in the entire building. A few minutes later Carrera entered the office.

"Sent you back to try to rehire us for Pashtia, didn't they?" were the first words out of the *Duque*'s mouth. "Good to see you, Virg," were the second set, uttered as Carrera stuck out a hand in friendship.

Rivers shook his head, then Carrera's hand. "How do you do that?"

"Do what?"

"Predict things like that."

Carrera shrugged, then answered, "I keep up with the news. I also spy on the Army."

Yes, and you have enough friends in the Army—Marines, too, now, for that matter—to keep pretty up to date, too, don't you? Rivers thought.

"I meant what I said back in Sumer," Carrera continued. "The Progressives pissed me off royally. They're going to have to pay through the nose to get back in my good graces and get my troops into the war."

"I think they know that, Pat. That piece of filth undersecretary, O'Meara-Temeroso has been . . . let's say, offered up as a sacrifice."

"Was he? Good. Do they? Do they know how much?"

Carrera went to his desk, bent to a drawer and pulled out a file. From this he took a small spreadsheet and passed it over.

"That's what I need to reestablish something like control over the important parts of Pashtia, if I begin moving in three months. I'll only begin moving in three months if the FS hires me now."

He pulled out another sheet. "This is what it will cost *next* month." Another. "And the month after." Another. "And the month after that."

He pulled a fifth sheet out and handed it to Rivers. "And *that's* the penalty for trying to stiff me in Sumer."

"Jesus, Pat," Rivers said, more than half in shock. "We can't pay that. Congress would freak out."

Carrera smiled. "Oh, yes, you can. It will cost you a third of your gold reserves and that's the form I want it in. For that, you don't need congressional approval. The president owns it."

Rivers went from half shocked to fully so. Gold was . . . special. To give away a *third* of it . . . ? *Sure, that asshole, Malcolm, mentioned gold, but I don't think he was serious.*

"For that you get a small corps with the equivalent of twenty-six FSA combat battalions, with adequate combat support, service support and aviation, for a year," Carrera continued, "of which I guarantee two hundred and fifty days' of active campaigning. After that, if things work out, I can cut back both the scale and the intensity to the point that you won't have to pay all that much more than what it cost to keep a full legion in Sumer. Tell that orange-faced, windsurfing gigolo, Malcolm, that he can take it or pound sand. It makes no difference to me. Tell him I'll also have a list of various war materials the FSC *will* let me buy and intelligence and support they *will* provide or it's no deal.

"In addition, there is the matter of support to my naval forces. . . ."

Hamilton, FD, 12/7/467 AC

"Where the hell does this arrogant son of a bitch think he comes from?" asked Malcolm in a fine rhetorical rage. "Who the fuck does he think he is? Doesn't he know who the fuck I *am*?"

He thinks he's the only one who can save your bacon and the only one who both can and will provide troops willing to fight. He thinks that he has you over a barrel, thought Rivers, back in the SecWar's office. *And he's right, too.*

Rivers felt guilty—he *really* did—at the Progressive SecWar's discomfiture. He should be, he knew, more apolitical, even totally apolitical. *Oh, well, tough shit; I despise the Progressives and I do enjoy watching the SecWar impotently rage.*

In a repeat of Carrera's performance back on the *Isla Real*, Rivers took a sheet from a folder and passed it over. "This is what it will cost if we don't hire him now. And this," he continued, passing over another sheet, "is how much it will go up in two months. He didn't say so, Mr. Secretary, but I think that if the situation gets worse any faster than he has anticipated, these prices will go up even more."

Panshir Base, Pashtia, 14/7/467 AC

In the military of most of the world, Class One supply—the most absolutely important class of supply—was food. And it was beginning to run short.

Marciano and his aide, del Collea, stood outside the command bunker watching a heavy lift Taurocopter Civet stagger in under max load. This was no mean accomplishment with food, the chopper's main cargo, as food tended to cube out a carrier—to fill up its interior space—long before weighting it out. In this case, the Civet had another load slung underneath. Moreover, though it was not normal procedure, the Civet also carried a ton and a half of fuel.

Jets circled overhead. This was a futile attempt at intimidation of the guerillas who had Marciano's Tuscan *Ligurini* Brigade besieged. The pilots of the jet were under strict orders not to bomb lest civilians be hurt. Deep down, Marciano was beginning to wonder if the political masters in the Tauran Union to which his own country's politicians kowtowed weren't really more concerned that the Tauran forces not harm any of the guerillas. Certainly, the effect of not aggressively engaging the guerillas had been civilian deaths an order of magnitude greater than his forces would have inflicted if they'd gone hog-wild.

The chopper began a slow turn to the right, aligning itself with the short airfield. This was not, strictly speaking, necessary as the helicopter could simply hover in. That, however, burned fuel and fuel was becoming scarce, hence the mixed load.

Del Collea, younger and with better eyesight, saw the missiles first.

"Shit," he said, *sotto voce*.

"What?" Then Marciano saw them, too.

Two were fired. Only one hit. That one was enough. It impacted on the tail boom, severing the connection of tail rotor and transmission. The tail rotor stopped spinning vertically which caused to Civet to immediately begin a horizontal spin. The pilot apparently tried to fight it but ended by losing all control over the helicopter. Quite possibly vertigo caused him to lose all control over himself, as well. Marciano and del Collea couldn't see that, though. They could, and did, see the helicopter go into a graceless, wavering, spiraling descent that ended in a very impressive— there *was* that cargo of fuel— fireball.

"Going to be short rations for a bit longer," del Collea muttered.

Kashmir, 15/7/467 AC

Ashraf had imagined a long and dangerous trek to get from his guerilla company's area of operations to the school he was to attend. In fact, he'd lain awake for most of two nights, worrying about ambush, air attack, long marches and sleeping rough.

As it happened, Noorzad had simply given Ashraf's escort some money, and the two, plus some other ex-Haarlemers, had hopped a bus, gone to the Pashtian capital, Chabolo, and caught a flight to Kashmir's capital. From there, it was a simple taxi ride—oh, yes, with the usual forceful haggling—to the school. The school operated openly, making no pretense of hiding what it was.

After turning over his charges, Ashraf's escort had departed, leaving behind only some words of encouragement. Ashraf had been taken under the wing of his advisor, Majdy.

Majdy was, like Ashraf, Haarlem-born. They were about of an age. Indeed, most of the school's student body was in their early twenties. Moreover, most of the student body were "reverts," Taurans or Columbians who had accepted Islam, and in particular the Salafi version of Islam, and then joined the jihad. If they shared any language it was typically English. Arabic, so that they could learn to read the Koran in its original sacred language, was a major part of the school's curriculum.

Until that time though, the students and their advisors—and there was an advisor for every student—would communicate in the common tongue or in their native language. Majdy, of course, also spoke Dutch.

"Did they feed you on the flight?" Majdy asked politely.

Ashraf grimaced. That was answer enough.

"Come then, brother," Majdy said. "You must be hungry. There's no sense in going any further while your mind is on food."

With that, the advisor led off out of the dim reception

area, through a green and white tiled garden courtyard, and toward a single story building from which came the enticing smell of food, well prepared.

Executive Mansion, Hamilton, FD, 17/7/467

The president was shocked. "He wants two thousand tons of gold? Two-fucking-*thousand*?"

Malcolm sighed. "He wanted two thousand, seven hundred, but has agreed to settle for two thousand plus the difference in FSD. Oh, and he wants the right to buy some things directly through our channels: radios, night vision equipment, some ordnance. Plus intelligence support."

"What? Not tanks and up-to-date aircraft?"

Again, Malcolm sighed. "When he insisted on the right to buy items that's what I thought he wanted. I offered, as a bargaining chip. But, no, the fucker's very happy with his mix of major equipment now. He only wants the radios for commonality and interoperability, and the ordnance and night vision because ours is incrementally better than what he can buy elsewhere."

The president scowled as if to say, *If you had delivered the Taurans as you promised . . .*

"Why gold?"

"It seems he's begun raising revenue by selling rights to the stuff to the rest of the world's very wealthy and very nervous. Based on what he's sold, against what we believe he's bought, he is overselling by quite a bit. I'm told that won't matter, as long as the price remains fairly stable and there's no run on his assets. I've got to warn you, Mr. President, that this much gold, if he uses it all to back his certificates, will make him completely independent and fully capable of waging war, or doing anything else he likes, completely on his own."

"How much of this is because we tried to cheat him?" the president asked.

"Maybe fifteen percent. It was a mistake, but with the press howling for blood it was perhaps an unavoidable mistake."

Malcolm's face grew thoughtful. "You know, Mr. President, we could hire a lot more troops from Latin Columbia and even western Taurus for this much money."

The president shrugged. "What would they do then? Insist on not being used for combat? Insist on being deployed someplace we don't need them? No non-Islamic government can stand the prospect of casualties anymore. They can't even stand the prospect of enemy casualties. And noncombatants? No, it's your fucking mercenaries or nobody."

Malcolm refrained from answering, *Unfortunately, they're not* my *mercenaries.*

Isla Real, Quarters #1, 19/7/467 AC

With Parilla retired and him and his wife now living in the Casa Linda for the duration of the presidential campaign, Carrera had had a choice: leave the larger Quarters One unoccupied, which struck him as wasteful, move an underling into larger quarters than he had himself, which struck him as preposterous, turn Quarters One into a Bachelor Officers' Quarters, which struck him as altogether too noisy, or move in himself. He'd chosen the latter, and turned his old Quarters

Two over to his favorite legion commander, Jimenez. It had been a toss up between Jimenez and Kuralski. The latter, however, had few social obligations while Jimenez had many.

One really pleasant side effect of having Jimenez for a neighbor was that the stunning Artemisia Jimenez, Xavier's niece, spent a fair amount of time—all the time she wasn't actively campaigning for Parilla—at Number Two, serving as her bachelor uncle's social host.

For his part, Jimenez was lost in the place. He had no family or, rather, his legion, the fourth, was his family. Still the mansion didn't go completely to waste as a very large number of junior officers tended to come by quite regularly whenever Artemisia was in residence.

"And so I ended up with a BOQ next door anyway," Carrera muttered, watching a half dozen of the horny bastards mowing Jimenez's yard while his niece looked on approvingly.

"What was that, Pat?"

"Nothing," Carrera answered Esterhazy. "Just thinking out loud. So what do you think about the gold?"

"Oh, wow!" Esterhazy answered, enthusiastically. "It's . . . well . . . Do you realize what this means, Pat?"

"Yeah, I do," Carrera answered. "You have enough gold for your precious metal certificate scheme even without invading the legion's existing assets."

Esterhazy rolled his eyes. "Not just that, Pat. You're going to have enough gold to set up *your own currency*. You can pay your men with your own drachma, pay your bills with your own drachma, buy equipment, bribe, build—whatever the fuck you want to do—in honest-to-God, hard, backed *currency*. By the way, how much of the two thousand tons will we have to play with?"

"Not all," Carrera answered. "The FSD we're promised won't pay for the full campaign, though it will pay for most of it. We'll need to sell some gold."

"No!" Esterhazy objected. "Sell none of it, except as PMCs. I'm serious about that currency. We can get something designed and a print plant running in a few months."

"Fine. Go back to the FS—or do you think we should go through Taurus or Yamato?—to get it set up."

Esterhazy thought on that for a bit before answering, "I wouldn't trust the Taurans and the FSC's currency technology is . . . substandard, at best. Yamato, then, I think."

"Good. I agree. Denominations?"

"Mmm . . . I think we ought to keep with the drachma-equivalence everyone is used to; peg the value of the Legionary drachma to the Federated States drachma, at least initially."

Carrera thought about that for a moment "I suppose we can always drop equivalency if the FSD starts to drop or increase substantially."

"Whatever's more convenient or profitable," Esterhazy agreed. He was about to say something else when he suddenly stopped and began to laugh.

"What's so funny?" Carrera asked, with irritation.

Esterhazy immediately stopped laughing and explained. "Pat, it just hit me. With this, the *Legion del Cid* becomes sovereign, as much as any state on Terra Nova. You have your own army. You control your own territory, this island. You have a diplomatic branch, me. Now you're going to be coining your own money. I don't know that there are many, or any, attributes of sovereignty left. Nukes?"

Carrera didn't even *think* about answering that one honestly. Instead he said, "Well . . . now I have the money to add nuclear power to one of the Suvarov-class cruisers and refit it to support the *classis*."

Mendoza Apartment, *Ciudad* Balboa, 21/7/467 AC

Jorge didn't have an answer. He was beginning to wonder if there *was* an answer. And if there was no answer to the question, then his entire project was false, a fraud.

The question? Simply put, it might be called, "My family or my country?"

"It's a basic question, 'Queli," Mendoza said aloud as he paced in a area in the living room that Marqueli ensured was always kept clear of obstruction for just that purpose. "And one that if I cannot answer it makes my whole thesis nonsense. I am insisting, just like that old book the *Duque* had translated, that morality must be rooted in the survival instinct or it's just a meaningless platitude. But I keep running into the problem that the survival instinct relates to either the self or to one's personal gene pool and has nothing to do with any artificial construct such as a country or a civilization. Those things only have moral meaning when they enhance the chances of the survival of oneself or one's genes. And both can require the sacrifice of either the self or the gene pool, so where does that leave me?"

"Sit, Jorge," his tiny wife ordered. Obediently, he paced to the couch and plopped himself down.

She patted him on the thigh affectionately, then stood and went to the bookcase. From this, she drew a book of Old Earth poetry that Carrera had had translated and published. She opened it and scanned the index, then broke the book open to a particular page. From that page she read:

"For Romans, in Rome's quarrels,
        spared neither land nor gold,
Nor son nor wife, nor limb nor life,
        in the brave days of old."

"Sure," Jorge answered. "But *so?*"

"Those lines were about old Rome's best and bravest days. The lines that follow talk about the days that came, when people watched out for their own and to hell with their country. I am sure they thought . . . or felt, in any event . . . that they were doing right to care for their own, directly. But I want you to imagine, Husband, the descendants of those old Romans, in the days of the Gothic sack. Imagine their sons slaughtered, their wives and daughters enslaved, raped and led off in chains, all the treasure hoarded by their ancestors stolen. Do you not think those later Romans, at that terrible moment, wouldn't have given anything they had if they could only undo the work of their ancestors who put family over country?"

"Perhaps they would have," Jorge conceded. "But it was too late, it is always too late, by the time people realize. And even so, that doesn't invalidate the objection to my thesis."

"Yes, Husband, it does. By your own words, isn't it ultimate survival we're talking about?"

"Yessss," he answered, warily.

"Fine. What does being in a state of nature, without civilization or *patria*, do to that?"

"It makes it 'nasty, brutal and short,'" Jorge answered, slightly misquoting Hobbes.

"Exactly," Marqueli agreed. And why should she not have recognized it? She'd basically taken Jorge's degree along with him. "And society—*patria*—enables us to make life something else, something less 'nasty, brutal and short.' In enhances the possibility, for nothing is a certainty, Jorge, that our gene pool will survive, does it not?"

"Sure." Jorge shrugged. "But the optimum is to have someone else sacrifice for the common good while preserving one's own gene pool."

"And then what happens?"

"Oh," he said, suddenly brightening.

"That's right," she said. "Then it becomes obvious, then common, then everyone guards their own and everyone ultimately loses."

"But couldn't one watch out for one's own and hide it?"

"Has that ever happened, Jorge? I mean in the long run? Doesn't it always come out, even if never openly admitted to? Doesn't it always begin with just one or two or a few . . . mmm . . . what was that term Professor Franco used?"

"Amoral familists," Jorge supplied.

"Right. 'Amoral familists.' They begin to look out for themselves and their own, alone, and it spreads like a wildfire. And soon enough—eventually, at any rate—they lose exactly what they were trying to save."

"All right then; I can see that," Jorge conceded. "That doesn't matter though as it will happen anyway. People *are* shortsighted. They *will* preserve their own."

"Then that kind of person has to be cut out from

society before they have a chance to spread their infection," Marqueli said.

Hajar, Yithrab, 28/7/467 AC

"It's like a plague has descended upon our clan," said the family's chief, Bakr ibn Mohamed ibn Salah, min Sa'ana. "Mahrous in Anglia, Hassan in Gaul, little Ishmael in First Landing, Mohammed Khalifa, here in Hajar, Cousin Rashid to a knife from some woman he was in *bed* with . . . nineteen others . . . even that thoroughly misnamed little apostate houri in Helvetia, Adara, had her throat cut on the street."

"Well, as for Adara," said the brother, Yeslam, "*that* job we should have done ourselves."

"Of course," agreed Bakr. "But the point is, we *didn't*. And someone did. The pattern is too obvious to ignore, someone is trying to make our family *extinct*."

"And they don't care how many others they kill to do it, either," added Abdullah, also a brother and one of only two of the clan to graduate from a Tauran or Columbian law school, the other being the late Adara. "How many killed along with Mahrous? More than twenty, wasn't it? So there's no protection in more guards, or in hiding behind innocents . . . not that we're not innocent . . . of course."

"Of course," agreed Bakr, very drily. "Of *course*." Bakr's eyes went up, scanning the ceiling as if expecting a bomb to burst through at any moment. "And you are right, 'of course.' Normal, even abnormal, security measures are fine for normal, or only somewhat abnormal, threats. But this threat—and despite the fact that every murder has been different, I am convinced there is a single agency behind it—this threat will escalate to any conceivable means to make us extinct. He must hate us a great deal."

"Mustafa!" both Abdullah and Yeslam said together. "Who does not hate us after what Mustafa has done?"

"Mustafa is a hero!" insisted Khadijah, stepmother of Mustafa and prouder of him, by far, than she was of her own children. "He fights for the Faith! He does his duty by Allah and the people!" She left out, *unlike you sots who work, when you work, for mere money*!

"Silence, woman," Bakr commanded. "We allowed you here as proxy for Mustafa. But let me tell you, were he here, himself, I would cut him down like a dog and offer his head and his balls to whoever is trying to extinguish us in the hope they'd *stop*."

All went silent then, even Khadijah who was known to be something of a shrew.

"We should have more expert assistance with this problem," said Abdullah.

"My eldest boy has a son with the army," offered Bakr. "Perhaps we should invite him. Yes, let us invite him. But let us also begin to set up a secure base, here, and call the clan home from their travels."

"It would cost much gold," observed Yeslam.

Bakr nodded, but said, "Much good the gold of this world will do us if we're killed."

First Landing Harbor, FSC, 35/7/467 AC

The deal had been complex in certain particulars. Malcolm, knowing how annoyed Carrera was with him, didn't fully trust him to go through on the deal once the gold was delivered. Carrera, for his part, absolutely didn't trust Malcolm to deliver the gold once his own troops were committed. It had led to a week-long impasse until Virgil Rivers had suggested a compromise.

"Send it in a carrier," he'd suggested. "Send the carrier with a full battalion of Marines to guard it. Carrera has enough firepower to make sure the carrier can't run off with the gold. The carrier, along with the Marines, has enough firepower to make sure that Carrera can't take the gold and then refuse to deploy. Given that his troops will be expecting to fight, he'll fight."

That had seemed fairly reasonable to both sides, though it had taken another week to hammer out a schedule to transfer the yellow bricks. In that week the nuclear aircraft carrier, FSS *Sarah Jay*, and its escorts had sailed to First Landing, where the bulk of the FSC's gold was stored, from its base in the state of Dominion.

The gold arrived at portside in something over five hundred trucks escorted by a full motorized infantry brigade. There were possibly even more members of the press there at the dock than there were Soldiers, Sailors and Marines, combined. Along with the press had come a small brigade of protestors. What the protestors wanted was anyone's guess, based on the signs they carried. Perhaps it was fairest to say that what they really wanted was publicity. Since the press was there . . . .

BdL Wappen von Bremen, 1/8/467 AC

There was no press in attendance. Neither Jaquie nor Marta had anyone they wanted to impress back home. Indeed, both had, for very different reasons, excellent cause not to want anyone at all to know where they were or what they were doing.

Fosa had helicoptered over, along with Rodriguez's platoon of Cazadors and most of Chu's boat crew. Some of the men still sported bandages and casts. Jaquie looked for the machine gunner whose face had been burned but didn't see him. Presumably he'd been evacuated for the superior medical care available back home, ashore.

The captain of the *von Bremen* had had cleared a large open area on the ship's mess deck. Into it had filed the two honorees, the four other girls who'd volunteered to sail aboard the sadly sunken *Suzy Q*, most of the rest of the hookers, some of the sailors and Cazadors whose turn it was for R&R aboard Fosa's Fornication Frigate, plus Fosa himself and Rodriguez's and Chu's boys. There was room, if barely.

"Attention to orders," ordered the captain of the *von Bremen*, once everyone was assembled.

The sailors and Cazadors present stiffened to attention. The girls really didn't know what to do, but took their cue from the military men and stood a little straighter. All talk ceased.

Fosa walked forward to where Jaquie and Marta stood, flanked by Chu and Rodriguez. "Publish the orders," Fosa ordered.

Von Bremen's captain read off, "Award is made of the *Cruz de Coraje*, in Steel, to civilian auxiliaries Jaquelina Gonzalez"—Fosa hung a ribboned cross around Jaquie's neck—"and Marta Bugatti"— he stepped right and did the same with Marta—"for gallantry in action in support of Legion objectives, aboard the auxiliary motor vessel, *Suzy Q*, on the 9th day of September, 467, off the coast of Xamar. On that day, aboard that vessel, the awardees, noticing that a critical weapon station had been knocked out, of their own accord, and having no

duty to do so, moved to restore it to action, manning
it until forced to abandon it by the sinking of the ship.
In the course of their action, one auxiliary, Jaquelina
Gonzalez, suffered grievous bodily wounds but continued
to fire until forced away by rising water, while the other,
Marta Bugatti, saved both Gonzalez and . . ."

"I didn't do anything," Marta whispered to Fosa.

"You did enough," he answered. "Now shut up."

". . . Cazador Barros, by that point incapacitated
by wounds, from drowning—"

"But I . . ."

"Shut up," repeated Fosa. He glanced over at Jaquie
and saw she was crying.

"Are you all right, Miss Gonzalez?" he asked.

She just nodded her head, sniffling.

Later, Fosa, Rodriguez and Chu sat with the two
girls at a table in an isolated part of the mess deck.
Fosa pulled two envelopes from his uniform jacket
and placed one in front of each girl. Jaquie was still
sniffling and paid no attention.

Marta took hers and opened it. Her eyes flew wide
and she said, "This is a mistake. Our bonus for going
on that boat was already paid and is in our accounts.
This is—"

"It's a gift," Rodriguez said. "We took up a collection
among my boys and Chu's. Quite a few of the others
in the maniples, boats and ships chipped in, too. The
skipper, here, matched half of what we raised from
his discretionary funds."

"Besides," added Chu, "we know that Jaquelina wasn't
able to work for the last few weeks. And that you lost
time nursing her. Think of it, too, as recompense."

"But . . ."

"Shut up, Marta," Fosa said.

"Yes, sir."

"I made a call back home, to Carrera," Fosa continued. "He said he's got another yacht—this one purpose built—headed our way to replace the *Suzy Q*. He also agreed that I can form a permanent unit of women to serve as bait and to otherwise help out. It will have room for two corporals. You don't have to give us an answer right away, but if you two want in . . ."

Isla Real, 11/8/467 AC

The *Sarah Jay* stood in the harbor, surrounded by her escorts. From time to time, an elevator arose onto the flight deck bearing a small chest full of gold. On deck, the container was met by a mixed group of FSN and legionary officers. These jointly opened the chests. The contents were then weighed and inventoried before the chests were resealed with legion-marked seals. The pile stayed under the watchful eyes of both sides as it was loaded aboard one of the *Sarah*'s helicopters. Once loaded, one officer from each service boarded the chopper and accompanied it to a portion of the airstrip that was under guard so tight ants crept between them nervously and on tiptoes.

From the strip, a chest or two at a time, the gold was taken to an old Federated States Army coastal artillery bunker. It was the most secure thing available.

"Screw that," Carrera muttered, watching the gold being trundled off. "We need something a lot more secure." *For this, and for the nukes, too.*

"Sir?" Sergeant Major McNamara asked.

"It's just not enough, Top," he answered. "We need something like the Federated States Reserve Bank in First Landing."

"Dunno, sir," McNamara answered. "I t'ink wit' maybe t'ree or four divisions worth of troops we got plenty o' security as is."

"Not that many for much longer, Top. Maybe the equivalent of one left after we deploy."

"And t'at's anot'er t'ing," Mac scowled. "It ain't right, you taking off and leavin' me behind."

Carrera nodded, then sighed. "Tell me how many other people I can trust absolutely, Top. Parilla gone to politics. Kuralski back in Volga and he's going to link up with us just before we go into Pashtia. Kennison? Gone. Some of the rest of our original group gone and the rest in critical positions. Most of the first rate Balboans commanding cohorts, tercios and legions. Who have I got left I can trust absolutely, would you tell me that?"

"Miss Lourdes?" McNamara offered. "Oh . . . you meant people you can trust t'at can watch out for t'e legion *and* Lourdes, didn't you? You one son of a bitch, you know t'at, boss?"

Carrera nodded. He didn't add, *And this promises to be one miserable hard fight and I don't want to lose you, too, old timer. I've lost too much already.*

McNamara sighed. "Well, t'en, if I can go to t'e fucking war at least I can kick some hiney to get t'e boys out on time."

And with that Mac turned away and began to stride toward what was called "the Green Ramp"—though it wasn't a ramp at all—where a maniple of troops from Third Cohort, Second Tercio was preparing to

board an aircraft heading for Thermopolis, just south
of Pashtia.

Presidential Palace, *Ciudad* Balboa, 14/8/467 AC

The meeting was conducted in French as Janier still
didn't deign to speak Spanish. In a way, it was comforting to President Rocaberti that the Gauls were
so firmly arrogant. It boded well for the prospects
of himself and his clan that the new masters he was
trying to bring in would be likely to prove much more
amenable, and give little more than lip service to
concepts popular among the world's progressive circles.

The problem with the FSC, the president thought,
*is that they really believe their own propaganda. They
not only believe it, they honestly expect people to fall
in with their program. The Frogs are more practical.
Indeed, while claiming to be in the forefront of cosmopolitan progressivism one can't help but note that they
gave up their colonies in Uhuru only in name, and
still retain control and economic dominance. Moreover,
their servants, the presidents and prime ministers in
those colonies, manage to do quite well, graft wise.
There's no reason the Gauls won't continue that fine
tradition here, once they're in charge.*

Even the fact that Janier sat at the presidential desk
didn't upset Rocaberti, though his nephew Arnulfo
was plainly annoyed by it. It just went to prove that
the Gauls could be counted on to rule.

Malcoeur conducted the briefing for the very small
number of people allowed to attend. These consisted of the president, his nephew, one of his two
vice-presidents, the ambassador from the TU, the

ambassador from United Earth, the minister of police, and Janier and Malcoeur themselves.

"What the general has in mind," Malcoeur was saying, "is that we shall bring in election monitors from all over that part of the world sympathetic to our aims—our Uhuran colo . . . I mean, allies, the Tauran Union, United Earth, some of the more progressive-minded politicians and ex-politicians from the FSC, and perhaps a few of the more pliable nongovernmental organizations as well."

Janier nodded and said, "I think we can count on these people to reject even the possibility that a party of militaristic fascist beasts could actually be elected, so they'll instinctively insist the election was tampered with, fixed. We can even arrange a few incidents to take place under the eyes of the monitors and the press, if necessary."

"That would be my department," said the minister of police.

"Even so," agreed Janier, casually stubbing out an awful-smelling cigarette. "It is extremely important that the Tauran Union appear neutral, if the rest of the plan is to work. Is it not possible, Mr. President, for your party to add to the turmoil?"

"Surely, *mon General.*"

Malcoeur waited until his chief seemed satisfied with that answer before continuing, "With the support of an international community outraged at the fraud and violence in the elections, the president will be in a good position to refuse to abide by the results. At that point, the mercenaries are placed in the unenviable position of acquiescing or starting a war. We believe, if the scale of the current deployment is as large as it seems, that they will feel they're in a very poor position to commence a war. Acquiescence, therefore, seems assured."

The minister of police *harrumphed* and said, "If you're wrong about that, Major Malcoeur, I feel I ought to tell you that my police are heavily infiltrated with ex-legionaries. I can only rely on a few of my units and all of those are in the city. The countryside, to include my own police, is heavily in favor of Parilla."

"The general understands that," Malcoeur reassured the policeman. "Those units of yours which are reliable will be critical to the eventual arrest of the mercenary leadership to break the impasse. We will, of course, back you up in that. And as for the countryside, does it really matter? The Transitway and the two terminal cities do not depend on the countryside nearly so much as the countryside depends on them. With those remaining under our control, the countryside will feel the pain."

"Which is all well and good," the policeman agreed, "except for one thing. Those mercenaries going to Pashtia are not going to stay there. They will return."

Before Malcoeur could answer, Janier said, "I'm counting on it, Mr. Minister."

Wappen von Bremen, 15/8/467 AC

Girls will sleep with girls. Oftentimes, even most often, sex has nothing to do with it. Instead, they seek only the comfort of a warm body nearby.

For Marta and Jaquie, however, it *was* about sex, at least in good part. After years of sex with altogether too many men, it wouldn't be too far off to state that neither of the girls cared for men anymore as sexual partners. That didn't eliminate the desire for sex, of course, and like many prostitutes they'd turned to women or, more specifically, turned toward each other.

In the warm aftermath, still entwined in each others' arms, Marta suddenly burst out with, "I think we should do it."

Jaquie smiled and answered, "In case you weren't paying attention, love, I think we just did."

"I meant—"

"Shush. I know what you meant. I talked to Rodriguez about it . . . well, indirectly I talked to him about it. There's one big problem. If the legion caught us in bed together while we were members they'd put us both against a wall and shoot us."

"They'd *what?* Just for making love? That's insane! Or is it because we're both girls?"

"No . . . the way Rodriguez explained it, it not only isn't insane it's the only sane policy. If we're having sex then there's a dangerously good chance we're in love . . . or will be. If we're in love with each other, personally, there's an also dangerously good chance either one of us would put the welfare of the other ahead of the legion's or the mission's. Rodriguez said he'd never heard of a regulation against girls being with girls or boys being with boys, but there's an expansive rule against mutiny, and we'd fall under it."

"I wouldn't want to give you up," Marta sighed.

"Well, I've been thinking about it, too. Four years and the legion would pay for us to go to school. We could learn business . . . or nursing . . . pretty much anything. We'd never have to sell our asses again. We could be together, free and clear."

Jaquie and Marta both went quiet at that, lying on

their backs and thinking hard. After what seemed a long time, Marta rolled over and put her face between Jaquelina's breasts, careful not to press too hard where Jaquie had been wounded. As she slipped one hand down between Jaquie's legs, Marta said, "If we're going to have to stop this, for a while, let's enjoy what we can, now."

Kirov Tank Factory, Saint Nicholasberg, Volgan Republic, 16/8/467 AC

Khudenko and Kuralski clashed glasses full of vodka. *"Vashe Zdorovie,"* the Volgan said. *Your health.*

The glasses were considerably larger than the usual fifty-milliliter jobs. Indeed, it took Kuralski several gulps to empty his, though Khudenko managed with two. Practice tells.

"So your boss got the contract he wanted, did he?" Khudenko asked.

Kuralski grinned. "He did. He always knew he would. It goes well with you, Victor? With the plant?"

The Volgan put down his glass and extended his hand, palm down and fingers slightly spread. These he wriggled. *So, so.*

In explanation, he said, "We've never managed to acquire a second customer as good as the legion, though we've made some sales to the oil wogs and a few in Uhuru, Colombia del Norte, and western Taurania. Right now we're operating at less than full capacity though, and it hurts."

Dan Kuralski reached into his coat pocket and withdrew a list he'd prepared in Cyrillic. "I think this can keep you fully employed for a while longer."

Khudenko scanned down the list quickly. "We can provide about half the armor from on-hand stocks," he said. "The rest will take . . . say . . . five weeks. Is that soon enough?"

"It is if you can get it to the railhead at Thermopolis within three weeks after that."

"This, I think, we can do. But I'll need to hire a lot of guards for the trains. I think I can get a regiment from the army for not too much."

"We've already got a Volgan regiment for that. Don't sweat it."

Khudenko nodded. He knew about Samsonov's group and its relationship with the legion. "We don't make the rest of what's on this list. You know that, right?"

"We don't want you to produce the other material, of course, but to acquire and ship forward," Kuralski answered. "I'm here for the next two months to assist in that."

"There will be many bribes needed. *Large* bribes. A third of the rolling stock in this country is in private, and generally criminal, hands."

Kuralski shrugged. "Whatever the market will bear. Money's not really an issue. There's something else we need, too. We'd like you to set up at Thermopolis a forward maintenance depot from your workers here to match the one you've set up in Balboa. We'll provide a rather generous bonus to them, if that helps. And Samsonov's boys will be staying on to guard."

Khudenko rubbed one hand across his face. He removed that hand and began to tap on the table, thinking hard.

"There's no way to both produce the tanks *and* provide the depot. Unless . . . is it acceptable for us not to be ready until a week or so after the last equipment or supply train reaches the railhead?"

"Mmm . . . sure; that will work," Kuralski answered. "We shouldn't have lost much or need much higher level maintenance until then, anyway."

Isla Real, Quarters #1, 18/7/467 AC

The phone rang. Lourdes answered it, then called out, "Patricio, it's Adnan on the phone for you. The secure line."

Carrera patted her posterior lightly and took the phone. "Carrera."

"Pat, you bastard, what do you think you're doing?" Sada shouted.

"Huh?"

"You're going to war in Pashtia and you forgot about me," the Sumeri chided. "And I thought we were friends."

"What are you talking about, Adnan?"

"You're going to war again," Sada explained, "and you haven't asked me for help? What kind of friend is that? What kind of friend leaves a friend owing a debt and doesn't let him try to pay it back. Harrumph!"

"Ohhh. Well . . . I thought you had enough problems at home."

"My biggest problem, friend, is that you've got Qabaash hiding his head in shame and throwing things at walls because you're leaving him out of this. Look, this is the deal and I won't take no for an answer. Over the next week Qabaash and one light infantry brigade— the *Salah al Din*—from the Sumeri Presidential Guard are going to fly to Thermopolis, along with the cohort from the legion I have here. Don't worry about the expense; I'll cover it. The oil market's been very good to me."

"That's a good brigade," Carrera conceded, "and I'd appreciate having my cohort back, but, again, can you afford to lose it?"

He heard Sada sigh into the phone on his end before he explained, "Barely, but yes. Right now, Pashtia has problems because the lunatic Salafis lost here. If they win in Pashtia, they'll come back here stronger than ever."

"Adnan, if—no when—they lose in Pashtia, they'll come back to Sumer anyway."

"Yes, that's true, my friend. But if they lose in Pashtia, they'll come back here much weaker than they will if they win. So not another word. Qabaash and company are coming."

Carrera, unseen by Sada, nodded his head. *There is faithfulness. There is honor. Thank God for you, Adnan.*

"I'll be expecting them, friend," Carrera said. He saw Lourdes mouthing "Ruqaya?" and asked, "Is your wife there? Lourdes wants to chat."

EXCURSUS

From: *Legion del Cid: to Build an Army* (reprinted here with permission of the Army War College, Army of the Federated States of Columbia, Slaughter Ravine, Plains, FSC)

The insurgency in Sumer, of course, continues today, albeit at a very low level. It is unlikely to completely disappear anytime soon.

With the gradual drawdown of the insurgency in Sumer, and the building up of the Sumeri security forces to the point where they were able to defend law and order and maintain control of the country without resort to wide-scale terror and massacre, it proved possible to reduce the commitment of coalition forces to the security mission. By 466, for example, the Federated States Army and Marine Corps were able to drop their troop commitment to two divisions, then one, plus equipment parks for three more. Since casualties had dropped to near nothing, this was a military commitment the Progressive administration in Hamilton could continue. Moreover, Sumeri contributions to the maintenance of these divisions, once the oil began steadily flowing again, made them little more expensive than they would have been had they been stationed in the Federated States. They were much cheaper to maintain in Sumer than in Taurus.

The war however, was far from over. Sumer had been only one campaign among many: Pashtia, Eastern Magsaysay, Kush and Amazigh also were active at some level. For that matter, the insurgency existed across the entire globe and was fought, in one form or another, wherever it could be identified and targeted.

The major advantage of fighting the largest of the campaigns in Sumer had been that, being so centrally located, it had served as a magnet for insurgent volunteers and monetary donations from all over the Salafic and Islamic world. Much of the success the Federated States and its coalition had met with elsewhere could be directly attributed to the pull of the Sumeri insurgency on the Salafi mind.

With their infrastructure within Sumer largely destroyed, these volunteers, and the charitable and religious front organizations that directed them on behalf of the overall movement, began to reorient themselves in the only place where they still had a chance of striking back to any effect: Pashtia.

Pashtia had seemed to the uneducated to be quite safe and secure in the antiradical fold. What these missed was that it was in large part thanks to the insurgency in Sumer itself that Pashtia had achieved as much stability and progress as it had. Certainly it was not the number of troops committed there that brought about relative peace. Pashtia could not even support, due to lack of road, rail, and navigable river, any substantial number of first quality coalition troops. The infrastructure of Pashtia had not much improved over that found by the Volgan Empire during their abortive ten-year campaign there. If the Volgans had found themselves logistically limited to a corps of about one hundred thousand soldiers, the Coalition was unable to field more than half that number, which half required even more in the way of logistic support than the previous Volgan total.

The insurgents, on the other hand, needed little but willingness to fight and the most basic of supply. Uniforms were a detriment. Food and fuel were purchased or taken from the economy. Weapons were light and largely individual. A single column of five donkeys and a driver, moving at night and feeding off the local vegetation, was able to provide ammunition for an insurgent company sufficient for a month's operations.

Thousands of guerilla volunteers, the younger brothers of those who had once gone to Sumer, began to flood Pashtia by the middle of 467. These came in in one of four ways. From the east they came through Farsia, itself something of a model for theocratic dictatorship and always eager to confront the Federated States and its allies or to help those eager to fight them. From the north, Kashmir—populous and somewhat radicalized, and never really exercising control of its common border with Pashtia—saw thousands of young men flock to the cause. In the south, the ongoing war between the Volgan Republic and its own Islamic radicals turned the entire area for hundreds of miles to either side of the border into, from the radicals' point of view, one big war zone. From the Volgan and FSC points of view, there were two which should have been one but which could not, for political reasons, be joined.

Of course no small numbers simply bought tickets, boarded aircraft, landed in Pashtia's capital, Chobolo, and disappeared into the countryside.

It is estimated that some ten thousand guerillas entered Pashtia between mid-467 and mid-468, adding to the thousands already there. To have confronted and neutralized these required, by normal doctrine, some one hundred thousand coalition troops. These were available. The logistic infrastructure, however, simply wasn't there. Arguably, after the long, drawn out and bloody campaign in Sumer, neither was the will.

Money, however, was not a problem.

The legion began investigating Pashtia in either late 466 or early 467, the record is unclear. It is clear that no later than mid-467, a recruiting campaign had begun in Pashtia to attract and raise one cohort of mixed foot and mounted scouts plus some other auxiliaries from among the Pashtun, notably those Pashtun whose tribes had formerly sided with the Volgan Empire and then switched allegiance to the FSC-propped national government. These were brought to Sumer, trained, and equipped and to some extent integrated with the existing Balboan-Sumeri forces in the provinces of Ninewa and Pumbadeta, Sumer, before being redeployed to Thermopolis.

PART II

CHAPTER TEN

We eat and then we shit. Do we eat in vain?
> —The Great Helmsman,
> on guerilla warfare

We kill you. Then we slaughter your sons to half-extinguish your line and sell your wives and daughters to dishonor the other half, sparing and taking only the youngest, converting them, and using them against your cause. Have we killed you in vain?
> —Patricio Carrera,
> on counter-guerilla warfare

Thermopolis, 13/9/467 AC

In the setting sun, as far as the eye could see, military encampments stretched out. To the north, northeast, and northwest were three large camps holding one legion each. These were minus most of their armor, four-fifths of their Cazadors, all their aviation but for a half dozen each Crickets and medium lift helicopters for command, control and medevac, and some of their engineers and artillery. Near the airfield to the south of the town were three camps, one for the Cazador tercio, one for the *Salah al Din* brigade of Sada's Sumeri Presidential Guard, and—to either side of the strip—one large one for the three cohorts of aviation formed into a single, large *ala.*

On that strip, and nearby it on helicopter pads, troops boarded aircraft. Qabaash's brigade filed quietly aboard sixty-seven IM-71 medium lift and a dozen IM-62 heavy lift helicopters. Theirs was, in many ways, the toughest mission, involving, as it did, the deepest insertion to block the *Ikhwan* from either reinforcing the operational area or escaping from it.

The seven provinces that comprised the legion's initial objective for pacification were infested with insurgents. They could be expected to run as soon as the battle turned against them. This was no cowardice but merest good sense. When they ran, as Carrera was certain they eventually would, Qabaash's battalions would have to stop them and, moreover, they would have to stop them largely on their own, without artillery support, and with only limited support from the air.

Of course, there were other passes. Qabaash couldn't hope to cover every little goat and camel trail. But with every easy pass over the mountains blocked, the Sumeris could at least ensure that little in the way of vehicles, heavy weapons, or ammunition, got away.

The *Salah al Din* was taking with it enough supplies for thirty days of existence, assuming they cut wood for fuel to cook their meals, and about three of full up combat. Emergency resupply was possible, but not something Qabaash counted on or Carrera felt he could promise. There was too much for the helicopters to do.

For the other places, the footpaths and goat trails, there were the Cazadors. These were going in via a mix of helicopters and Crickets, depending on the landing site chosen. While the choppers carrying the Sumeris would race almost directly for their objectives, the Cazador carriers would touch down anything from three to nine times each to confuse the enemy as to where they had actually dropped troops, or even if they had dropped troops at all. Most would continue to touch down even after leaving behind their passengers to add to the confusion. At some of the passes, and with the prevailing winds, Crickets could practically hover over a spot.

While the Sumeris, with three dozen heavy and twenty-seven light mortars among them, and being deployed in larger units, would be able to hold on on their own for some time, the Cazadors were not intended to fight much, if at all. Instead, they would call in aircraft or, as the rest of the force advanced, artillery on any enemy groups they saw trying to cross the mountains to the north.

Each Cazador team had, in addition, two sniper rifles—one in .34 caliber for long-range shots and one in .51 caliber subsonic for closer-in work—to engage individuals and small groups. Still, the Cazador teams' primary weapon was the radio.

The enemy had some radios. They had a great many satellite and cell phones. For those, Carrera had a special trick.

Miguel Lanza was getting a bit long in the tooth to be flying attack missions. Still, commanding the entire deployed portion of the *ala,* over four hundred aircraft, he felt the urge, the need, to lead from in front. He'd never gotten the hang of helicopters, though he'd tried. The g's inherent in flying the CAS, or close air support, mission were getting to be a bit much for him. By he could, by God, still fly a transport converted to a bomber with the best of them.

If Lanza had assembled all of his medium transports, he could have lifted a grand total of perhaps three hundred, two-thousand pound bombs. This would have been enough to scour mostly free of human life perhaps ten or fifteen square kilometers. That was a drop in the bucket for an objective area of this size, perhaps a tenth of a percent. Oh, yes, they could have extinguished a guerilla company or two, maybe even three. That would not have much mattered.

Instead, Lanza's transports were going to drop some very special bombs, one or two over each of the several hundred spots that the Federated States' Office of Strategic Intelligence had indicated held a body of guerillas of platoon size of better.

A red warning light flashed on the instrument panel of Lanza's cockpit. He spoke into his throat mike, "Stand by to roll in three minutes."

The crew chief answered back, "Roger, three minutes."

Lanza's aircraft was flying at very near its maximum altitude of ninety-two hundred meters. Given the power of the weapon they carried, this seemed hardly enough to Lanza. As soon as he felt the plane lurch as the bomb fell away, he accelerated to his maximum flight speed of four hundred and seventy kilometers per hour and hauled ass to get as far away from the bomb as mechanically and aerodynamically possible. Lanza had absolutely no desire to lose every bit of avionics in his bird to an overpowering flash of electromagnetic pulse.

✧   ✧   ✧

The bomb was contained within what appeared to a standard two hundred and fifty-kilogram casing. That appearance was deceiving; the casing was made of a nonmagnetic material, epoxy resin in this case. Inside, moreover, instead of the usual explosive component, the bomb contained a much smaller amount of explosive, a capacitor, three reels to release long wire antennae, a stator coil and a number of other things the precise nature of which was classified at a fairly high level.

Along with those other things, and this was not classified, was a global locating system guidance package that would guide the bomb in on a set of coordinates punched in from the cockpit. This particular set of coordinates happened to correspond to the headquarters of Noorzad's group of guerillas, now grown to the size of a small battalion.

The bomb knew none of this, of course. It "knew" that its capacitor was suddenly powered up and cut free of the power source from which it had been drawing. At the same time, it "knew" where it was. Shortly thereafter it "knew" it was falling even as it "knew" where it was going and how to navigate to that point. Almost the last thing the bomb "knew" was that it had reached a preset distance over the target. At that point the three thin wire antennae deployed. Shortly after that, the bomb reached the point of optimum detonation. After that, it didn't "know" anything.

"Look, I am telling you, I *know* they're on the move—"

Noorzad was speaking into his cell phone, talking with Mustafa's functionary, Abdul Aziz, back in Kashmir, when there was a significant explosion several hundred meters overhead.

It was far enough overhead, however, that it struck Noorzad as more on the order of a large mortar shell than the dreaded aerial bombs the FSC dropped with such terrible accuracy. And yet he was, so Noorzad knew, most unlikely to be within range of any of the infidels' mortars.

He decided it was harmless and returned to his conversation.

"As I was saying Abdul . . . Abdul?"

Noorzad pulled the cell away from his ear and looked at it. It didn't seem any different, except that it had gone dark. He shook it a few times, then tapped it with his finger. Nothing.

"Give me your phone, Malakzay," he ordered.

Malakzay took his own phone out of a pouch on his ammunition belt and pushed the button to turn it on.

"Nothing, Noorzad. It's dead. I checked it just this morning but—"

"Shit."

Noorzad noticed another explosion, also seemingly small, a kilometer to the east where lay one of his companies. Farther away, other flashes briefly lit the night sky before disappearing. The guerilla chieftain had a sudden sense that those lights indicated that other lights, the lights of seeing and knowing, were going out.

A sudden thought occurred. "Malakzay, your phone was turned off?"

"Yes, Noorzad. You know what a pain in the ass it is to recharge the batteries."

"That means that whatever weapon the infidel is

using can attack our electronics even if they're shut off." He paused, thinking hard, before exclaiming, "Quick, get me half a dozen messengers, fast and smart men on fast horses."

It was commonly believed that Samsonov's boys had recruited one group of Pashtun for Carrera. At one level, this was true: there was a central department for the Pashtun Scouts (numbers of whom were not actually Pashtun). At another level, though, it was false. There were several more or less independent groups. One of these groups was composed of four hundred and eighty-seven honest-to-Allah horse cavalry, supplemented by a small group of twenty legionaries detached from various cohorts and tercios to direct and maintain communications with legionary headquarters.

These now splashed on horseback across the Jayhun River, which separated the city of Thermopolis from Pashtia proper. The river was low, this late in the season, but still as icy cold as if it were full of the annual snowmelt.

The cavalry carried rifles and machine guns, of course, and even had a section of light mortars. Still, there's nothing like cold steel between real men and every Pashtun on horseback also carried a lance and a sword. Tradition; *that* was the thing.

A very small detachment had crossed early, three days prior, at a ford nowhere near as good as this one. They'd crossed, ridden deep and then circled around. The mujahadin guards watching the ford had seen nothing amiss in twenty-one riders, looking for all the world like their comrades, coming up from behind. And then, from the distance of twenty yards,

the lances waved in greeting had lowered. Spurring
their horses, the scouts had charged, spearing the
guerillas like so many boar.

Those same forward scouts now stood in their stirrups, wearing genial smiles and waving *their* comrades
forward with the heads of their erstwhile enemies.

From the mass of horsemen winding their way
through the flood, two emerged and, forcing their
way up the riverbank, rode to join the Scouts as they
waved their lances and severed heads. Of these, one—
Rachman Salwan—was another Pashtun, though he
had some odd, non-Pashtun words in his vocabulary.
The other was one of the legionary officers, Tribune
II David Cano of the Fourth Tercio, on detached
duty to the Scouts for the campaign.

Cano had been hand-selected for the job—along with
nineteen others, officers, centurions, and noncoms—by
Carrera, Samsonov, and a Pashtun, *Subadar* Masood,
recommended by Samsonov and flown specially to the
island. Following selection, the twenty had been given
a crash course in Pashtun by some of the Volgans who
still had pretty fair fluency in the language and a few
Pashtun flown in for the exercise. Still, at best, so Cano
thought, he spoke a pidgin.

Despite the lack of real fluency, Cano had taken
so well to the Scouts, joining them at their meals,
discussing their lives and their problems, playing
some of their tribal games, that Rachman Salwan
had taken a liking to him and taken him under wing.
Being senior in the tribe among the young horsemen
who'd signed on with Samsonov's recruiter, Rachman
served—unofficially, since the cavalry scouts didn't
have a very formal chain of command outside of the

legionaries placed over them—as the senior noncom for the squadron.

"Praise them, *Sahib*," Rachman advised in a whisper, "but not too much. Tell them, '*Aafaran!*'"—bravo—"Tell them they were '*dzhangyaalay*'"—courageous—"But do not promise them any reward yet. The heads and the honor are enough for good Pashtun serving in the field."

Cano appreciated the advice; Rachman was more a friend or even a brother than a subordinate. He stood by his stirrups, waving a rifle and shouting to his men—*yes*, my *men*—of their valor and their skill.

The Base, Kashmir, Tribal Trust Territories, 14/9/467 AC

Nur al Deen scratched his head with puzzlement while Mustafa tapped his fingers with irritation. Both men watched underlings mark the large map of Pashtia that hung on one rocky wall deep in their underground complex near the Pashtian border. Each mark represented a group of mujahadin with which he had lost contact or with which his headquarters still had communications. There were many more of the former than of the latter. The rest? Were they dead? Hiding? Engaged? He didn't, couldn't, know.

"You know," he muttered, "I am really beginning to *hate* this group of infidels."

After tugging absentmindedly at his beard for a few minutes, and playing with his worry beads for a few more, Mustafa stood and returned to his quarters. Once there, he closed the door behind him, went to a small casket and removed from it the device given him by High Admiral Robinson for direct communication.

"Robinson here, Mustafa. I see the problem."

"Seeing does me little good," Mustafa snarled. "What is it? What can you do about it?"

"They're using EMP—electromagnetic pulse—bombs, frying the internal workings of your phones and radios," the high admiral answered. "I can't do anything about it. We have none aboard the fleet and the only things I do have that can generate electromagnetic pulse are nuclear weapons. As we've discussed, I can't use those. Given time and warning, which I didn't have"—*time to have a little chat with Intelligence, I think*—"we could have hardened your radios and phones against them. Even now I can send you some simple methods to protect what you have in the north of the country. But the southern part? No, too late. We could manufacture some EMP bombs ourselves and slip them to you, but not in time to do you any good. I *can* advise you of enemy movements from up here but—"

"But I have no way to get the information to my fighters on the ground," Mustafa finished. "They'll have to escape on their own."

"I fear that few of them will, Mustafa. The enemy has blocked all the major passes and most, I think, of the minor ones."

"Then we are helpless."

Cruz Apartment, *Ciudad* Balboa, 14/9/467 AC,

Cara sighed helplessly. Ricardo had his eyes on the television screen, a bottle of rum in one hand, a glass of some local cola in the other. Nothing she'd been able to do had pulled his attention from either rum or television since the legion had commenced operations in Pashtia. Sometimes, she thought she saw him rub at his eyes. Tears? She didn't know and really didn't want to find out.

God, what have I done to him? she wondered. *He doesn't eat. He isn't studying. He won't pay any attention to me or the children. I thought he would learn to be happy . . . happier, here with us. Why aren't we enough for him?*

Was I just selfish, demanding he get out of the legion? I don't know. I do know that if he'd stayed in he'd probably be over there now and it would be me watching the television for any sign of him and worrying myself sick. So what did I do? I substituted his misery for mine. Maybe that wasn't fair.

But he's my man, not the legion's. I own him. My rights are superior to theirs.

Again she sighed. *But are they superior to his?*

Sanda, Pashtia, 15/9/467 AC

The town ahead wasn't much, perhaps two hundred houses, a mosque and a few stores. Even so, it promised resupply and some refuge from the eyes in the sky.

The plane, blotted out by the sun, wasn't even a dot to Noorzad when it began its dive. His first warning was when a horse screamed—always more horrible than the scream of a man—as large-caliber bullets pierced its torso, flinging it in blood to the ground.

The column, which had been trudging wearily to the mountains to the north, and safety, suddenly erupted in bedlam. Men shouted; animals squealed. Then came the sound of the enemy's machine guns— a *brrrrp* of explosions so close together they sounded like cloth ripping—and the whine of its engines as it pulled up and around for another pass.

Soon, much sooner than could be accounted for by a single plane, a salvo of rockets erupted overhead in the glare of the sun. Flechettes, they had to have been, as pockets of men, horses, mules and donkeys were scythed down along the line of march. Some of the horses were felled with as many as a dozen of the finned nails entering their bodies and then tumbling to slice out inch-wide routes through their flesh. Men, small targets as they were, might take half as many. To the targets it made little difference.

Many of the riflemen and machine gunners returned fire as Noorzad had trained them to. Unfortunately, he had trained them to engage helicopters and relatively high performance jets. These new infidel planes made a hash of their training as they fired and turned without ever entering the curtain of fire thrown up by those on the ground.

Should I have stayed and fought where I was? Noorzad wondered amidst the confusion. He shook his head. *No, that would have just gotten my entire group isolated, surrounded, and destroyed. It is more important to preserve a seed, a kernel, from which more mujahadin can grow.*

Noorzad lifted his eyes heavenward and saw both of the enemy aircraft twisting in the sky. He thought, but could not be sure, that they had their canopies pointing downward. The aircraft separated, one moving to the north of Noorzad's band, the other to the east. He thought the one that flew to the north was farther out than the eastern one.

This, too, was different from what he was used to.

Normally he'd have expected the aircraft to make a pass or two, drop some bombs, fire some rockets, and then move on. To have the infernal machines . . . linger . . . well, that was disturbing.

As he'd thought, the eastern plane was closer. It came in, low and menacing. It fired its machine guns in bursts, veering slightly southward with each ripped-cloth roar.

"Cut the lead! Cut the lead!" Noorzad tried to shout over the din. No matter; his men, such as were firing, were too intent on their hoped-for target, or seeking cover from its guns, to listen.

In the confusion, Noorzad lost track for a moment of the plane that had gone to the north. Suddenly remembering, he turned his eyes in that direction and saw that that enemy bird, too, was diving in. He saw a glint of dull light; from the undercarriage, so he thought.

The thought brought absolute terror. Noorzad had seen silvery canisters under aircraft before.

"Naaapaaalm!"

Some of his followers heard his shout, saw the aircraft bearing in, and followed Noorzad in running out of its line of flight. Even the heavy bullets of the other plane held small terror in comparison to being burned alive. Still, many did not hear or, if hearing, did not understand. These kept their positions and either hid or fired as the mood and their degree of manhood took them.

Noorzad looked behind himself as he ran. He'd guessed right, he saw, and took no satisfaction in it. From underneath the second aircraft, the one from the north, two cylinders tumbled end over end until reaching the ground. There they broke apart, spilling their incendiary contents along two parallel straight lines with almost no dispersion. The burning stuff moved like a mini-tsunami, passing around the boulders and covering such of his men who'd remained behind in fire. Their common howl of utter agony sounded even over the roar of flame, engine and machine gun.

We've got to split up, Noorzad thought, breathlessly. *Together we're simply too inviting a target.*

Noorzad took a hiding position between two boulders and pulled out his map. Yes, there were enough small towns like Sanda that he could hope to hide the bulk of his force while he escaped with the small, hard core that had been with him for years.

Mazari Omar, Pashtia, 16/9/467 AC

Press conferences with the legion were rare, very rare.

Still not rare enough to suit me, thought Carrera. *Even so, I suppose I owe it to the legionaries left behind, and the families of those who are here, to let them know what's happening.*

The limited number of pressies, deliberately limited, actually, was clustered around Carrera in a town square in front of a mosque that was little more than rubble.

The whole town was considerably the worse for wear, Carrera saw. With the awful task of blocking escapes, driving the enemy from a roughly triangular area two hundred miles wide and one hundred and fifty deep, and searching out the thousands of little towns and villages, and likely cave complexes, his forty-eight maniples of infantry, fifteen of Cazadors, and dozen of mechanized troops were, to say the least, stretched.

Still, the town had blocked the only possible supply route from Thermopolis and so the problem of the town had had to be solved. He'd solved it by flattening the town in substantial part. Not for him the risking of his own troops to limit collateral damage and loss of civilian life. He didn't have enough troops for that and the collateral damage meant almost nothing to him.

"They know we're coming," he'd said. "It's up to them to get out of *our* way, not up to us to tiptoe around them."

Not that he'd blasted the town indiscriminately, far from it. Rather, with his one hundred and eight long-range, Volgan-designed and built 152mm howitzers, his thirty-six *Tsunami* multiple rocket-launchers, hundreds of sorties by Turbo-Finches and Nabakovs in the bomber role, and, over the last twenty-four hours, his thirty-six heavy mortars, he'd pounded every known and likely enemy hiding position with considerable precision, aided by real time reconnaissance from both his own air assets and the FSC's.

Since the enemy insisted on trying to hide among civilians, however, his precision had meant more civilian casualties rather than fewer.

"Tough shit," he said to a reporter who asked about civilian casualties. "If they want to save civilians, let them not hide behind the women's skirts. I'm certainly not going to pander to their deliberate violations of the laws of war."

One might have thought that the global press would have intervened and interfered. They said not a word. They'd learned, over the years, the legion had no compunction about killing members of the media they considered to be in the enemy camp. There was not, in fact, a member of the FSC's or Tauran Union's press within thirty miles of Mazari Omar. And of the members of, say, the Islamic world's press, particularly al Iskandaria . . .

"That's them over there, gentlemen," Carrera told the remaining assembled members of the Fourth Estate, all carefully vetted members of the Balboan and other Northern Colombian media. "Yes, those dozen swinging from the lampposts. We caught them with enemy propaganda in their video recorders. They were then duly turned over to our Pashtian allies who tried them and hanged them as enemy combatants found not wearing uniforms. The chief mullah for my Pashtun, Mullah Hassim, approved the sentences completely."

Not all the buildings of Mazari Omar had been damaged. Most were, in fact, still standing and even in reasonable repair. Of these, many were requisitioned by the legion. In the case of public buildings there would be no recompense, though the few owners of private real estate that the legion needed were compensated with cash on the spot.

In one such, an apartment building of three floors that had the distinct advantage of having a very open ground floor, the MI, or military intelligence, maniple had set up shop.

Larry Triste was not in command of the MI maniple; that was far too low a posting for the Intelligence Officer for the entire deployed corps. Still, the MI maniple worked for him; its commander, a Tribune III, took his orders from him. Sometimes, that same tribune muttered, "I'm not in command. I'm just the XO for Legate Triste."

That wasn't quite fair but it was at least understandable. And Triste really did try to keep his hands off the day to day running of the maniple. Still, when he asked . . .

"Goddammit, where did that fucking guerilla battalion *go* that the air engaged by Sanda yesterday?"

. . . people hopped to find the answer.

"Sir," answered a junior warrant, "If you'll look over here"—the warrant pointed at a map hanging on one wall—"we've tracked that battalion for the last several days. Based on their normal daily progress, and accounting for slowing down as the hills begin their ascent to the mountains, they're somewhere between Sanda and this pass." The warrant's pointer touched lightly on a spot where the track ran through a ridge.

"They're not there, however, or at least not in the strength we've been tracking."

"Yeah, so? Where are they? What strength are they in?"

The pointer touched lightly on seventeen towns spaced about three miles apart within an oval on the map.

"We think they've split up. We think that one group, maybe the core of the battalion, took all or at least most of the horses and ran for it. That would explain why we can't find them where they ought to be. The others are likely in these towns."

Triste sat silently for a minute, gazing at the map and thinking on it. Finally, he nodded his head, once, decisively.

"I think you're right. Get me the ops shop."

17/9/467 AC, Sanda, Pashtia

They'd worked out the technique over the long campaign in Sumer. It was helicopter intensive, infantry intensive, and military intelligence, military police, civil affairs, and PSYOP intensive. Thus, the legion could not do it everywhere simultaneously.

The first the townspeople of the targeted area knew of it, it was announced by the drone of well over one hundred helicopters bringing in two heavily reinforced cohorts of infantry supported by dozens of highly visible attack aircraft flying escort. The townsfolk's initial instincts were to fight. Initial instinctive urges to fight often wither when faced by overwhelming force.

The helicopters landed in a swarm, like locusts, *everywhere*. The troops they carried disgorged with practiced, professional speed and ease, and then raced to surround every town in the target area, plus another eight outside of where they expected the enemy to be. Loudspeaker teams from a psychological operations maniple accompanied the infantry. These advised the townsfolk not to resist, but to stay inside until they were ordered out. A single battery of 160mm mortars, set up just outside the target area, began to register fire at points outside the towns to reinforce what the PSYOP people said.

When fire came from one town, the heavy mortars, the attack aircraft overhead, and a single maniple of infantry reinforced with fourteen Ocelot light armored vehicles attacked brutally, destroying the town along with most of its men. The PSYOP teams broadcast the result of that resistance and the attack, as a warning to others. Indeed, only women and children were spared, and that only where practical.

Sanda was picked as the first town to be cleared as being the most likely to contain terrorists. The townsfolk were ordered to line up and come forward in single file to a point west of the town. They were met by troops from the MI using dogs specially trained to smell women. When people wearing women's clothing that did not smell quite right passed the dogs, the canines alerted.

Three of Noorzad's band were caught that way and carted off for *rigorous* questioning.

Other dogs sniffed for explosive residue and weapons oil. Several more terrorists were captured. Another was shot down on the spot for being a potential suicide bomb. The legion preferred to use shotguns for this purpose as they had much better immediate knockdown and endangered bystanders less. People behind the victim suffered little beyond being splattered with blood and bits of flesh.

From the initial dog-sniffing station the townsfolk were sent through a medical station that not only administered inoculations but also drew blood for DNA samples. There, too, everyone was subjected to facial recognition imaging which went directly to military intelligence. The DNA results from the medical screening would arrive at the MI headquarters sometime in the next twenty-four hours.

Men were then separated from women. The men were kept under intensive guard and required, on pain of death, to be utterly silent. One shooting was sufficient to make the legion's determination in this regard very plain. The women and children, on the other hand, were left in groups and much more lightly guarded.

It was with the women that questioning began, the interrogators being among the relatively few—and absolutely critical—women in the *Legion del Cid.* "Who is your husband? Who is your father? How many brothers do you have? What are their names and ages? Where are they? Your sister is where? Married to whom? Look at this picture. Who is this man? Look at this one. Is that your father? Your brother? Look at this one. Is that your house? No? Who lives there?"

By day's end, the legion had a complete family tree for the town of Sanda, imperfect only insofar as someone had lied. It also had some leads and partial family trees for some of the neighboring towns.

And that was where the DNA came in. Noorzad had dispatched thirty-two of his men to Sanda after his column was attacked. Those men could threaten the townsfolk into lying for them. They could not fool the DNA analysis that identified them as genetic outsiders. Of that thirty-two, eight had already been captured or shot. The remaining twenty-four were ostentatiously separated out from the rest of the men and, again, sent for *rigorous* questioning.

At that point blankets, water, and food were passed out to the men.

Only then, when the rest of the men in the town saw that the most serious immediate threat to their families was identified and removed, were the men questioned, privately and individually. In particular, the MI folks were interested in who within the town could reasonably be said to be part of the infrastructure of the guerillas. Those that were so identified, in secret, were further questioned. Some were sent away for more serious inquisition. After questioning, the rest were taken, one at a time, to search out portions of the town and especially the houses the women had identified as their own.

At about that point certain discrepancies crept up. Those responsible, male or female, were taken away to be questioned, once again, *rigorously*. Most of the discrepancies were cleared up in fairly short order. A few more people were sent to trial as potential guerillas. All of those were sentenced to be shot. Most then decided that discretion was, after all, the better part of valor.

The quality of voluntary information delivered to the MI suddenly grew to amazing heights. Sentence was then suspended, and prisoners released, on the understanding that if there were ever again any reason to suspect those half-pardoned people of further guerilla activity that not only would they be killed, but the legion would send their own auxiliaries, Arabs or Pashtun, back with pictures and orders to kill every relation on whom they could get their hands.

A few of the captured guerillas were kept on hand for further questioning. The rest were given a very quick trial, made to dig their own graves, and then shot.

Then the group, less one platoon to watch the town, moved on to the next.

Kibla Pass, Pashtia, 19/9/467 AC

In anyone else's army Sergeant Quiroz probably would have been a commissioned officer. He had a university education, from the University of La Plata. His IQ was in the range of the low 120s. He had no criminal record and was, all around, a good soldier, respected by superiors, peers and subordinates alike. Hell, Quiroz had *been* an officer in the army of La Plata.

In the *Legion del Cid*? "No, not good enough. Especially are we suspicious of you having been an officer in an army we consider, at best, fourth-rate. Centurion track is the best we can offer, and you'll have to prove yourself as a noncom first."

Thus it was that Quiroz found himself leading a nineman squad of Cazadors, in a hide position overlooking a donkey track that led through a pass on its way over the mountains to the north. His nearest friendly neighbor was six miles to the east. And he didn't even have all his squad with him as five of the nine were sleeping in a hide some hundreds of meters away.

"Company, Sergeant," one of Quiroz's men announced. "Thirty men . . . no, thirty-one, on horseback with a donkey train. They look awfully tired. Might just be nomads."

Quiroz crawled up to the scout's position and gestured for his binoculars.

"No . . . not nomads. Nomads would have rifles but not machine guns. Those fuckers are heavily armed. Hmmm . . . more than we can take in a heads up fight."

The sergeant scuttled backwards, snakelike, and pulled a map from the cargo pocket on the leg of his trousers. He knew, generally, how far the advance of the *Legion* had gone and also knew that they were not yet in artillery range. Even the rocket launchers wouldn't reach so far from the very front. And those, being soft-skinned, were rarely right at the front.

"What's available for air?" he asked his radiotelephone operator, or RTO.

"Nothing, Sarge. I asked. Well, there are two Turbo-Finches heading this way but they're each carrying loads of scatterable mines for further up the pass. Not even any gun pods."

"Mines, huh? Tell them I *want* those aircraft." Quiroz glanced at his long-range sniper. "Salazar, what's the range?"

"About fifteen hundred meters," the sniper answered. "It's a pretty long shot. They'll start to run right after the first shot too, and then I'll never hit them."

"Can you make that shot?"

Salazar wet one finger and held it up in the breeze. "Possibly," he answered, reaching for the waterproof case to his rifle. "Just possibly. If I had a 'forty-one' I'd be a lot more confident."

"Get ready to try."

"Roger."

Quiroz looked at the last man in the group, a new private, and said, "Go back and wake the others. Bring them here, loaded for bear."

Hard, hard, Noorzad mourned, in thinking of the men he'd left behind. *Hard it is to break up this band I worked and fought so hard to build. Hard to lose the company of comrades until we meet in Paradise. Hard to hear the screams of the wounded and the dying. Hardest of all to think that the horrible things I've done might be for nothing.*

"No," he said aloud. "It can't be for nothing. Allah would never permit such a fate."

"Chief, we've got company," said, Malakzay, gesturing as he rode to Noorzad's left.

"Eh? Oh, shit, not again."

Noorzad looked over his shoulder and saw two of those damnable planes these infidels used. Even this small core of his band had been struck three times from the air in the last two days.

"They're just circling," he observed. "We probably don't look like much from above."

Malakzay looked around at the loose column and answered, "Maybe not, but from the ground we look a lot like what we are."

"They're coming low to look us over," Noorzad announced at the top of his voice. "Look *innocent*, boys."

The planes indeed came in low, not more than one hundred meters above the ground. At just about that distance from the tail of Noorzad's column they began emitting smoke as if from the mouth of a volcano. Noorzad's eyes caught numerous small objects— indeed, hundreds of them—erupting from squarish containers on the planes' undersides. The first of these hit ground yet, to Noorzad's surprise, did not explode. He was just digesting this bit of information when one of the cylinders in his view sent out what looked like six or seven almost invisibly thin wires with small weights on the end. One of his fighters reached for one of the wires.

"Sto—"

Boom.

Quiroz had watched with keen interest as the planes swept over the guerillas, dispensing their cargo. He didn't know too much of the technical details of the scatterable mines. From where he lay, though, it looked like the two Turbo-Finches had laid down a fairly thick pattern.

He saw in his binoculars as one of the guerillas

reached over to touch either one of the mines or one of the tripwires they emitted. He then saw a good sized puff of angry, black smoke appear as that guerilla was tossed backward. Best of all, he saw that the guerilla didn't arise and that no one went to his aid.

"Salazar, you can take your shot anytime now."

"Roger, Sarge," answered the sniper, easing himself into firing position behind his .34 caliber, scoped rifle.

"Shit, shit, shit! These bastards are as evil as the Blue Jinn!" Malakzay exclaimed, glancing down at the torn and faceless body lying on the ground.

"Blue Jinn, indeed," answered Noorzad. "but cursing them does no good. How do we—?"

The bullet's crack came as a surprise. Not far away from the two a single man was struck down with a small hole in his chest and a much larger one in his back. As he fell he hit a mine's tripwire very near to where the wire emerged from the mine. The mine promptly jumped up and blew up, scattering guts to the wind. Another guerilla, too near to the explosion, went down shrieking and clutching at his groin where a largish fragment had torn off his scrotum and testes.

Quiroz grunted with satisfaction as he saw the guerillas drop. "Good shot, Salazar."

The sniper didn't answer. Already he and his spotter were scanning for another target. Unfortunately, the guerilla band had gone to ground—albeit not without setting off another mine. Of good targets they saw none.

After visually sweeping the entire area, the sniper announced. "No good targets, Sarge."

. Quiroz muttered, "True, but only for some interpretations of 'good targets.' Buuut . . . kill the horses, Salazar. Radio; get on the horn and tell headquarters we've got a band pinned. Tell them we can't take them all and if they want prisoners they need to reinforce."

Quiroz stopped speaking for a moment, tapping his face with his fingers. His eyes settled on his assistant, *Cabo* Vega, then on the other sniper, Legionary Guzman.

"Vega," he said, "take charge here. I'm going to take Guzman forward and act as his spotter. We'll be"—Quiroz's finger pointed—"somewhere over by that boulder that looks like a tit. Keep on the horn nagging headquarters to get some infantry here."

As usual, Noorzad found the screaming of the horses somehow more disconcerting than the screaming of his own men. After all, was not the horse especially praised by Allah? And yet the Holy Koran held out no hope of Paradise for them, even should they be killed in God's cause.

The one good thing Noorzad could see was that the enemy fired infrequently, however well. *It must be only the one sniper,* he presumed. *Thank Allah for small favors.*

Then came the moment when two beings, a man and a donkey, screamed out almost simultaneously. That told him there was a second sniper team out there. Worse, perhaps, while he could make out both the shot and the sonic boom of the initial sniper butchering his men, this new source of fire made neither. *That, that possibility of being killed silently, was terrifying.*

"Malakzay?" Noorzad called out. "Are you still with me?"

"Yes, *Sahib*. Here I am."

A bullet snapped overhead. *A miss, thankfully*. Yet another struck a rock nearby but that one made no snap beyond the striking of the lead on the rock. The snipers had given up on surprise and, to an extent, even very careful shots. It was as if they were trying to hold the mujahadin in position for some greater menace. That was worrying, as well.

Noorzad hesitated. He *hated* giving the order. But . . . *crack!*

"Pass the word to stampede the horses straight up the eastern side of the trail, herding them north."

"But Noorzad . . ."

"Just *do* it!" he snapped.

It was only a couple of horses, at first, Quiroz saw. Quickly that brace became a herd and, moreover, a herd with some riders in it as a few of the enemy used the horses to try their own breakout attempt. The horses set off mine after mine. But what would fell a man immediately didn't necessarily do the same with animals five times bigger. It was a strange and horrible scene, the more horrible as more horses were swallowed up in the billows of evil, black smoke only to emerge moments later trailing dangling intestines and broken limbs.

"What the fuck have you stopped firing for, Guzman?"

The .51 sniper shook his sturdy brown head and answered, "It's just too . . . nasty . . . sorry, Sergeant." He settled back into the stock to resume firing.

"I think the way is clear, Noorzad," Malakzay announced. "The last couple of animals standing made it through."

The sun was setting to the west now. Soon it would be dark. Did the infidels have their cursed night vision equipment? Noorzad had to presume that they did. But . . . he knew from his experience with the Taurans that the things were limited. He thought he could escape under cover of night.

Crack!

Kibla Pass, Pashtia, 20/9/467 AC,

The sun was high overhead, casting a shadowless light down onto the gruesome scene. The Cazadors had come out, dressed in the pixilated tiger stripes they shared with most of the legion. Beside them, lined up on the road, were about one hundred tall, lean and fierce looking men mounted on hungry-looking horses. All stood well to the north of the minefield. It was long duration and was not supposed to self-detonate for another two weeks. Still, quality control at the factory being, at best, imperfect, it generally didn't pay to take chances.

"*Quien esta el jefe aqui?*" one of the ruffians asked.

Quiroz did a double take on seeing a mounted, bearded, dirty horseman who spoke such clear Spanish. He'd been advised over the radio of the Pashtun Scouts arrival, and so had held his fire. Still, the incongruous appearance of border bandit and good Spanish came as a shock.

He saluted the speaker and announced, "Sir, Sergeant Quiroz reports."

Cano returned the salute from horseback, then dismounted. "Tribune Cano, Sergeant, Fourth Infantry Tercio seconded to the Pashtun Mounted Scouts."

Cano took a moment to look around at the scattered bodies of men and horse. He put out his hand and said, "Damned fine job."

"Thank you, sir. We got maybe half of them. Maybe even two-thirds. The rest got away."

Cano heard the subtle rebuke. "We rode as fast as we could, Sergeant. But we got the word late and intercepted two small groups of guerillas on the way." Cano shrugged. *Fortunes of war.*

"What now, sir?" Quiroz asked.

"We're going to try to pursue up the mountains," Cano answered.

"Well . . . sir . . . make sure they don't do to you what we did to them."

"How could they, Sergeant? They are not men so good as yours, nor are my men so bad as them." Cano laughed, "And *they* don't have aircraft to drop mines on our heads."

INTERLUDE

4 September, 2105, Turtle Bay, New York,

In over a century and a half, no one had been able
to strip the UN bureaucracy of its perks. No matter
how constrained the budget, and in olden days it had
been sometimes very constrained indeed, free parking
was their charter-given right. Remuneration at the
highest level found anywhere on the planet their just
due. Generous educational benefits for their children
only fair. Fresh water poured by human servants an
utter necessity to the forwarding of their sacred work
on behalf of mankind.

One of those servants poured now for the three-
person hiring committee tasked with sorting out the
right kind of people from the mass of aspirants.

"Goldstein won't do," said one of the committee,
Guillaume Sand, placing the file aside.

"Of course not," agreed another, Ibrahim Lakhdar.
"Like we accept *Jews* anymore. They've served their
purpose."

"To be fair, Goldstein claims not to be a practicing
Jew," objected the third, Alan Menage.

"It's in the blood," Lakhdar sneered.

Menage shrugged. *No sense it getting Ibrahim all worked up over it. Besides, it isn't like I really care about the Jews.*

"Here's an interesting one," said Sand, opening a different application file and diverting the subject away from Lakhdar's distressingly *open* anti-Semitism. "Louis Arbeit. Harvard. Sorbonne. Early volunteer work with International Solidarity Movement. Parents are both Colleagues of Proven Worth. Mother: Christine Arbeit, D1 with the Human Rights Commission. An up and comer, I hear. Father: Bernard Chanet, Deputy Director for International Disarmament. His grandmother recently retired from the European Parliament."

Ibrahim took the file, impatiently, and began flipping pages. When he reached the background information page on the applicant's father, he signaled one of the water servants to bring a telephone. He spoke a number and, after a brief pause, a face appeared.

"Bernard? This is Ibrahim Lakhdar, with the hiring committee. Yes, yes . . . I am normally with Human Rights. I know your wife. I was looking over your son's application and I was wondering if you might not give a little boost to my nephew. He's a fine boy and he's interested in working disarmament . . ."

CHAPTER ELEVEN

(Light ye shall have on that lesson,
but little time to learn.)
—Kipling, "The Islanders"

Kibla Pass, Pashtia, 1/1/468 AC,

Carrera stood in the fierce, bitterly cold winds of the Pashtian highlands. Despite the heavy wools, silks, polypropylene, and windproof outer shell, he shivered as the wind whistled through the pass and around the rocks. The wind seemed to be saying, "Avenge us."

"I'm trying; God knows I'm trying," he whispered back.

Down below, on the plains around Mazari Omar, his men were still busily rooting out the insurgency. It was probably a fruitless task. No matter what damage to the guerillas he did, the Taurans were taking back over even as he cleared areas out. They were good soldiers, many of them; he'd particularly been impressed with the Tuscan *Ligurini* under Generale Marciano. (Under cover of the legion's combat operations, and in the absence of a treacherous press to report what he was doing, Marciano had pushed his own forces out to actively engage the guerillas. What would happen after the *Legion del Cid* left, Marciano didn't know.)

Ordinarily, using the kind of rules of engagement the Taurans had, it might take as much as fifteen years to destroy an insurgency, if, indeed, it could be destroyed at all. The Federated States' methods, having some of the stick to go along with the carrot, could do the job more quickly, if, again, it could be done at all. Carrera's methods used much less of the carrot, much more of the stick. It remained to be seen whether that would work any better. The Pashtian insurgency— ha! insurgency was practically a way of life for them!—had always been almost singularly tenacious.

It doesn't matter, Carrera thought. *I am not here, ultimately, to quell an insurgency, though I and my boys will give it our workmanlike best. Ultimately, I am here for the money that brings me closer to revenge and the revenge itself.*

"It's a cold dish," whispered the wind.

That's all right. I've never minded cold food. But . . .

"But what?" asked the frozen breeze.

"But I miss Lourdes, and I miss the children. And I think maybe I need a break."

That was particularly telling. Only this morning he'd chewed out his chief logistician over something that, in retrospect, was just not that important. The week prior the goddamned nightmares had come back with a vengeance. His drinking was up again; it had to be or he'd never get any sleep. Yet alcohol-induced sleep was not very restful. And then he'd seen off a couple of dozen of his killed and wounded at the airport at Mazari Omar and found himself starting to cry.

Bad sign, very bad sign. But what the hell can I do?

The Base, Kashmir Tribal Trust Territories, 2/1/468 AC

If ever a man looked downcast, and in need of rest, it was Noorzad. Oh, he'd made it out, along with a critical dozen of his key followers. The rest? Bombed, burnt, butchered. Even after escaping from the mines dropped by air, he'd found a new group of fast horse cavalry on his tail, relentlessly tracking him over the mountains. He'd had to sacrifice the last of his newer people to those cavalry to buy time for the rest to escape.

His one weary eye, the white patches on his skin that told of frostbite, and the general air of sheer exhaustion he exuded; all said he needed a break.

There was one good thing, one tiny bright spot, amidst the disaster. Coordination between the lesser, mercenary infidels and the greater infidels in the north of Pashtia had been poor. Noorzad had half expected to be met by yet another ambush as he and the pitiful remnants of his band emerged from the snows of the central mountain range. Instead, there'd been nothing except some sympathetic tribesmen who'd provided camouflage for the guerillas on their way to the nearest city.

Once there, things had improved considerably. Noorzad had acquired a new satellite phone and reported in to Mustafa, seeking guidance and orders. Those had been simple, both to receive and to follow.

"Come home."

Now he was "home." However exhausted Noorzad might have been, he still could hardly wait to rebuild his force and return.

"That will be a while," Mustafa advised as he

poured tea for the both of them with his own hand.
"Our . . . infrastructure was not well rooted in the
south of Pashtia. Our defenses were weak. And this
enemy is not as weak as the Taurans. Worse, though
he doesn't have the firepower of the greater enemy,
he makes up for that with a ruthlessness to match
our own."

"The men I left behind?" Noorzad queried.

"It was not your fault," Mustafa cut him off, insisting,
"You had no other choice. To stand and fight would
have meant being slaughtered. But . . ."

The lesser chief raised one eyebrow. "But?"

"As near as we can tell, they've cleaned out your
band completely. And no, we cannot take hostages to
trade because these infidels not only won't trade—that
much we learned when they were in Sumer— they've
already shot or hanged all their prisoners . . . unless
they've spared a few for questioning."

A look of mental agony flashed briefly across
Noorzad's face. If he had known, he would have
stood and fought rather than run. Not that he'd
cared about most of his men, especially the spoiled
Yithrabis. But he'd left *friends* behind.

Mustafa read the look well. "No," he said. "That
is, I think, part of their method. They shoot their
prisoners precisely to make us want to stand and fight.
They may someday sell our women and children as
slaves to the same purpose."

"What now?" Noorzad asked, willing away his feelings of personal failure.

"Now the winter is upon us. The passes are mostly
closed. South of the mountains the infidel is continuing to clear out our people and the filthy, decadent

Taurans are setting up shop again. In the spring, the mercenaries will surge over the mountains to reinforce the Federated States and Anglia. We cannot stop them, though we can bleed them."

"Cut their supply?"

"No . . . I think not," Mustafa answered. "The Federated States troops require more in supply per man, even for light infantry, than the Volgans did for their armored troops. They *must* have their comforts, at least when in base. The lesser infidels seem to require much less. They live . . . rough." There was a tone almost of admiration in Mustafa's voice. "I don't think we can appreciably interdict their supply lines."

Noorzad sighed sadly. "Then . . . my men go unavenged?"

"No," Mustafa smiled. "No; we have a plan and a means to hurt these infidels in return."

Xamar Coast, Motor Yacht *The Big ?*, 4/1/468 AC

The *Legion del Cid* tended to take a somewhat legalistic approach to counterinsurgency and piracy suppression. They could have simply started at one end of the Xamar coast and worked their way to the other, killing everything that lived and making the entire coast uninhabitable. But, much as they never sent someone for serious torture until a duly constituted court had pronounced sentence of death, so they would not destroy a village unless it could be directly linked to the support of piracy.

They had such a village now. Early this morning *The Big ?*, "?" for question, thus camoflaging the boat under the usual idiotic practice for naming yachts, while keeping the Q-ship inside joke, had passed close to some fishing boats to allow the crews to get a look at the awesome mammary display on the forward deck. Then the yacht had sailed directly southward, paralleling the coast and heading generally towards a village suspected of being a pirate haven. Overhead, silently, a small remotely piloted vehicle with a high resolution camera had caught good quality facial shots of the villagers as they'd cheered their own boat out to intercept the infidel yacht. Was this entrapment? Who cared? It wasn't as if the village wasn't predisposed to piracy. It wasn't as if they hadn't had a boat ready.

The *Suzy Q* had been little more than a field modification. *The Big ?* was almost purpose built from the keel up by a Sachsen shipbuilder with some long tradition of building clandestine surface raiders. She mounted hidden side-firing machine guns, as had her predecessor, three per side. However, the firing ports on *The Big ?* were centrally controlled, as were the guns themselves, from an armored fire control station just under the cockpit.

That fire control station also had command over the two main guns. Forward, there was, as with *Suzy Q,* a rising gun, hydraulically driven. There was also a stern gun mounted to fire through a port that opened under central control. Both were 40mm high-velocity pieces, firing from fifty-five round magazines. All the positions, along with the hull itself, were now fairly heavily armored.

More thought had been given to tactics now, too, given the sad end of *Suzy Q*. The side guns and the forward gun were not to be the primary engagement stations any longer. Instead, when under threat the boat would turn away from any attacker, allowing its rear 40mm to begin the engagement. That station, the entire stern, in fact, was extremely well armored. Indeed, under the smooth-appearing white hull was not only a three-centimeter belt of steel, outside of that steel a complicated matrix of boron carbide resin, ceramic, polyurethane, and tungsten proofed the hull against the largest weapons the pirates had shown so far, the shoulder-fired rocket grenade launcher.

Because of the weight of the stern armor belt, the engines had had to be placed somewhat forward of center. This gave the boat some peculiar handling characteristics, notably a comparatively tight turn radius and a comparatively quick recovery from a tight turn. The engines themselves, twin diesels with an aggregate horsepower of over eight thousand, were capable of pushing the boat at almost the speed of the *Santissima Trinidad.*

Moreover, except for an excess of fold-down bunks in the crew spaces, it looked like a yacht even to a suspicious boarding customs agent. Even the guns were not obvious from inside the yacht, being hidden behind what looked like storage spaces and under fixed bunks.

Though they were crew, as corporals Marta and Jaquelina had a stateroom of their own. Since Marta was a screamer this was less of an advantage than it might have been. In fact, the two slept together but *approximately* chaste. *"Approximately"* because while Marta was a screamer, Jaquie was not and Marta was a very giving girl.

"Kinda silly, isn't it?" Chu asked Rodriguez.

"Huh?"

"C'mon, Rod, you only have to look at them to

see they're in love. Everybody knows it and looks the other way."

"Oh . . ." Centurion Rodriguez sighed. "I told them to cool it before they ever signed on as regulars. I'm a little surprised they took my advice, really."

"Yeah."

Chu's eyes scanned the instruments. "*Classis* was right. We've got company coming."

Rodriguez nodded. "I'll go have the girls put on their act and get my boys standing by."

As the Cazador left the cockpit, Chu picked up the microphone for the encrypted radio. "*Dos Lindas*, this is *The Big ?* We have company coming and we are preparing to engage."

Combat Information Center, BdL *Dos Lindas*, 5/1/468 AC

Fosa saw that there was a new kill recorded for *The Big ?* on the operations board down in CIC. Below the Ops board, a chart showed the intercept course between the *Dos Lindas* and a helicopter chartered by Hartog Shipping, based in Haarlem.

Haarlem still did quite a bit of shipping around the globe. As such, her merchant fleet had suffered more than most from the pirates' depredations both along the Xamar Coast and through the Nicobar Straits. It wasn't really surprising then, that a mid-sized Haarlem company, Hartog, had contacted Nagy and asked about hiring protection from the *Legion del Cid*. Nagy had entered negotiations, in consultation with both Fosa and the Yamatan representative, Kurita, and hammered out a workable, and sufficiently profitable, deal.

As part of that deal, the Haarlemers had insisted on face-to-face contact with the commander of the flotilla. There had seemed no principled reason to refuse.

The Haarlem registry helicopter had come in with the morning sun. Undaunted by the machine guns ostentatiously trained on it, it had flown twice around the *Dos Lindas* before settling down to a marked spot on the rear deck. There it was met by a small party of escorts and brought down to CIC to meet the skipper.

Fosa shook hands; Kurita bowed slightly. The Haarlemers introduced themselves as Ms. Klasina Frank and her administrative assistant, Christian Verdonk. Frank seemed extremely pale and rather plump, quite in contrast to the very deeply tanned and athletic-looking Verdonk.

Both Haarlemers' faces were guardedly friendly as Fosa led them through a tour of the ship. He took them through the five decks of the ship's tower, then down to the deck encircling the hangar and finally down to the hangar deck itself where he'd assembled one company of Cazadors and a roughly equal number of ship and air crew. Frank and Verdonk walked the line, following Fosa. He didn't lead them down each rank.

Later, over a cordial but not overly friendly lunch in Fosa's quarters, which meal the visitors barely touched, the skipper explained, "We cannot guarantee you protection. You understand this? The most we can do is try, within reason, to conform our deployments to the passage of your company's ships, to come as quickly as possible, if we are in practical range, if one of your ships is attacked, and to station small parties of Cazadors on some of your ships as they make the passage. In theory, we are capable of conducting rescue operations, but as a practical matter, we've never really been able to rescue any crew once they were taken to shore. I doubt we ever shall be able to."

"Hartog Shipping understands this," Ms. Frank said, looking up from her uneaten rehydrated pork chops. Shrugging, she added, "We are not paying so much that we could ask for more. As long as you will be willing to go to the aid of ships as you are able, or let one shelter under your wings at need, this is enough."

Hajipur, Sind, 6/1/468 AC

Ownership of Hartog Shipping was an interesting subject. Indeed, it was so interesting that a not inconsiderable portion of the both Federated States intelligence and investigative assets, with a healthy assist from Yamatan Imperial Intelligence, had gone into trying to determine just who owned the company, and others like it. Between ships owned but leased elsewhere, and some of those passing through four or five or, in one case, even *nine* nominal leasers before being leased back, plus shadow corporations, secret stock ownership, and front organizations, it had never proven possible to determine ownership of the company to any degree of certainty. This was actually *normal*.

Mustafa didn't have that problem. He knew who owned Hartog. For all practical purposes, *he* did. At least he had a controlling interest.

For the most part, he exercised no control. Rather, he left it to the company management to keep the affair solvent. He had, however, intervened to the extent of having two of the company's lesser assets filled with thoroughly reliable, even fanatical, Salafi skippers and crew. He had also intervened to obtain the company's sailing schedule, then passed that on to Abdulahi in Xamar so that the latter could attack a few Hartog vessels. This was a necessary cover for what was to follow.

The chosen ship, the *Hendrik Hoogaboom*, was an older, dry-bulk cargo carrier of roughly sixty-eight hundred tons capacity. Measuring one hundred and two meters in length at the waterline, and just under eighteen in beam, she was of a perfect size for her chosen task. Indeed, she was not really very well suited anymore for her designed task, being more or less uneconomical to run. Neither Mustafa nor Hartog Shipping would much miss the *Hoogaboom* once she'd completed her mission.

On the bridge, standing besides the ship's captain and future martyr to the cause, Abdul Aziz sighed with satisfaction. The *Hoogaboom*'s rebuilt engines barely strained as the much modified ship left the tugs that had guided it out into the dredged channel that led to the sea.

"Three more stops," The captain said. "And then one more on the way to Paradise."

"I'll be leaving with the next stop, Captain," said Abdul Aziz. "I must report back to Mustafa."

The Base, Kashmir Tribal Territories, 18/1/468 AC

Three men, Mustafa, Nur al Deen, and Abdul Aziz, walked the trails within the fortress. There came from the north the steady crackle of small arms fire as the mujahadin practiced marksmanship. For the most part the practice was a wasted effort. Yet it had one great virtue. In any group there are always exceptions. The marksmanship training program, useless as it was to train any appreciable number of decent shots, was still absolutely critical to identifying the rare naturally superb shot for further, more useful, training. Federated States Army, Taurans, and even the legion had had occasional cause to curse those rare genuine marksmen the Salafis now fielded.

Along with the rifle and machine gun fire, the din was frequently punctuated with much larger blasts as others among the holy warriors were trained in the intricacies of combat demolitions, booby traps, and other improvised explosive devices.

Mortars, too, could be heard as their crews practiced this simplest of the artillery arts. These, though, fired from outside the perimeter of the fortress and directed their fires even farther away. It might have been more effective to fire from inside at targets outside. In the past, as a matter of fact, they had. Quality control at the factory, however, was never all that great and there had been a number of unfortunate accidents. Mortar firing was all done outside the perimeter, now.

After the cacophony of the ship fitting in Hajipur, Abdul Aziz barely noticed the blasts of mortars and demolitions. Mustafa and Nur al Deen were fairly used to them. None of the men so much as twitched, even at the largest of the explosions.

Abdul Aziz explained, "The greatest weakness to the plan, Sheik, is hitting the target's motive power before it notices the threat from the *Hoogaboom*. The enemy carrier is more than twice the speed of our

ship, and based on the tour given to our two undercover reverts, extraordinarily maneuverable."

"I do not see," Nur al Deen huffed, "why we need
to make this extraordinary expenditure to destroy
a single ship. A single cigarette boat with a ton of
explosives should be enough."

Mustafa laid a hand on Nur's shoulder. "It would
not be, my friend. We have reason to believe that
such a boat would be most unlikely to get anywhere
near the carrier unless covered by something like the
Hoogaboom. Even if it did, the great infidel in space,
High Admiral of Pigs Robinson, assures me that the
carrier is sufficiently well built and compartmentalized
that it would take as many as three such hits to put
it down. There is no chance, none, that we could get
three cigarette boats close enough."

"And," added Abdul Aziz, "With two thousand tons
of a mix of ammonium nitrate, hydrazine, and aluminum powder, the *Hoogaboom* need not get all that
close to destroy the ship, two hundred meters or so."

"I still think it's a waste," insisted Nur al Deen.

Mustafa stopped walking and turned. "My friend,
one thing I have learned since we began this. Defense
does not win. We must attack, and attack, and attack
again."

"Abdulahi is not enthused about the prospect of
martyrdom for more of his men," Nur al Deen said.

"This is true," Mustafa agreed. "But then he, too,
must learn that he must attack and hold nothing back.
He should study Parameswara."

"Parameswara isn't being asked for one hundred
and fifty suicide bombers," Nur al Deen answered.

BdL *Dos Lindas,* 19/1/468 AC

"Security and economy of force are principles of war, Captain-san," Kurita intoned. "Defense is not."

Fosa paced the rounds of his bridge nervously. Indeed, he grew more nervous the closer the *Dos Lindas* approached to shore and the possibility of land-based cruise missiles, torpedoes, or suicide boats. The FSN had been clear that an attack on the fleet was being prepared. Sadly, they could not provide the first clue as to its nature.

"I know that, Commodore. And I know we have to do this. Hell, it was my idea. But I still hate the idea of getting closer to a threat I don't know the nature of."

Resuming his pacing, Fosa took all of three steps before he stopped and turned. Facing the Yamatan over one shoulder he observed, "*You're* taking this all very calmly."

"I was captain, Battlecruiser *Oishi,*" was Kurita's only, and completely sufficient, response.

Fosa grunted while Kurita turned his attention back to the contemplation of the eternal beauty of the sea at moments before action.

It was several hours before sunrise. Only one of Terra Nova's three moons shone. In the relative darkness, the sea twinkled with thousands of stars. Kurita amused himself with the notion that the stars were his old shipmates, come to watch him in action before he joined them at the Yasukuni shrine that had been dismantled and sent spaceward from Old Earth so many centuries ago.

Above the winking sea, the *Dos Lindas* cruised

under half power toward the shore. The carrier was blacked out, with not even deck lights showing. Crewmen, who would normally be allowed to smoke on portions of the flight deck, were instead confined to air- and light-tight compartments before they could indulge their vile habit.

On deck every functioning Yakamov helicopter sat with engines idling. Forward of them were a baker's dozen of Cricket Bs, the upengined and expanded variant of the legion's standard recon aircraft. Between the Crickets and the choppers sat four Turbo-Finches with light ordnance loads of about one ton each. None of the aerial troop carriers had more than their crews aboard.

The Cazadors were going in under strength. One half of one of the eight line platoons was detached to *The Big ?*, though they'd be nearby at sea and could land by rubber boat if needed. Another two platoons were split up among various Yamatan and Haarlemer freighters. Still, with the headquarters and support troops that were going to land, there were just over two hundred Cazadors in the landing force. These waited below, in the hangar deck, playing cards, sleeping, or sneaking off for a quick cigarette as the mood took them.

UEPF *Spirit of Peace*, 19/1/468 AC

"Computer?"

"Yes, High Admiral?"

"Put me through to Abdulahi in Xamar."

The call went through almost instantaneously; Abdulahi had learned since he'd lost three ships to the infidels' ambushes not to let the high admiral's warnings pass.

"Yes, Admiral Robinson?"

"Your enemies are moving inshore, between the villages of Sanaag and Gedo. I can't tell which of them is the target. Possibly both are."

"The villages? What reason could they have for going after villagers?"

Unseen below, Robinson rolled his eyes. *Were these people incapable of understanding the nature of the war they were in or the nature of their enemies, the nature they themselves brought forth?*

Forcing disdain from his voice, Robinson answered, simply, "Terror."

That Abdulahi understood. "I'll have a column on the road within the hour, High Admiral. Thank you."

"I don't know that it will do you any good."

"Perhaps not, High Admiral, but I have to try."

Again, Robinson rolled his eyes. "You can reasonably expect them to cover the roads by air, Abdulahi."

"We have some antiaircraft weapons mounted on some of our vehicles."

"I doubt that light ones will be enough."

BdL *Dos Lindas*, 19/1/468 AC

The Cricket Bs, being the slowest, were the first aircraft to take off. With the carrier's nose into the wind, even fully laden with five Cazadors and a pilot, it was a strain to keep the things from taking off on their own. With Fosa's command, "Land the landing force," the deck crew removed chock blocks, the pilots gunned engines, and— *fwoosh*—the things were gone into the night in a couple of eyeblinks.

The Finches were next to depart. These had superb

short take off capabilities, but nothing like the miraculous abilities of the Crickets. They needed every inch of the flight deck they had to get airborne.

Rafael Montoya was lead bird for the Finches, this mission. As usual, he nearly wet himself as his plane reached the end of the flight deck and began to fall to the sea. As usual—now, at least—he maintained control of his bladder as he fought his plane back into the air.

"I have *got* to find another line of work," he muttered, once he was sure he was not going into the drink to be ground to pulp underneath his own ship.

Once clear of the ship, Montoya veered left and began a long spiraling climb to five thousand feet. There he loitered until the last of the Finches was airborne. Then, together, the group turned east. If everything worked out, they'd be past the coast and able to turn to make their initial attacks with the sun behind them.

The Yakamovs, with eighteen Cazadors loaded— actually, slightly *over*loaded—each, took off almost vertically even as the elevators began bringing up the last of the Crickets and Finches for the *other* part of the mission. Once airborne, the Yakamovs dropped down to skim-the-waves level. One never really knew what the wogs might have bought, in terms of warning radar and air defenses, from somebody or other.

UEPF Spirit of Peace, 19/1/468 AC

"They're bringing more aircraft up on deck," Wallenstein said, as she and the High Admiral watched the carrier's ops in high resolution real time. "That's . . . odd. We know they can launch everything more or less at once if they really want to. We've *seen* them do it."

Robinson worried a tooth with his tongue. There was absolutely no chance of a cavity in any of his teeth, of course; it was a nervous affectation.

"Maybe tougher to get everything on deck and launch it at night?" he mused. "I don't know. It is, as you say, 'odd,' Marguerite."

The couple went silent then and stayed silent, watching the launch of the last of the mercenaries' aircraft on the high admiral's big Kurosawa. Bored after a bit, Robinson directed Wallenstein to come over. He snapped his fingers lightly and pointed at the deck, indicating she should kneel down between his legs. She did, of course; sexual service from their inferiors was a given right of the higher castes. Wallenstein hardly objected; she still desperately wanted Robinson's support for a jump in caste. Refusing him, or even performing at less than her very best, would jeopardize that. She sucked expertly but only automatically. Her mind was still working on other things.

Suddenly, Wallenstein pulled her head off. Her face took on a horrified look. "High Admiral," she said, "I just had the most *appalling* thought. We've been assuming all along that the mercenaries are unaware, and the Federated States only dimly aware, that we might be helping the other side. What if they know? What if they're counting on it? What if they were counting on us warning Abdulahi?"

Combat Information Center, BdL *Dos Lindas*, 19/1/468 AC

Fosa and Kurita watched the large plasma screen—this one, too, was a Kurosawa—intently. The screen showed

numerous markers. Central was the carrier itself, shown
as a green triangle. Nearby were two smaller markers,
green squares, for the *Santissima Trinidad* and the *San
Agustin*. Ordinarily, there would have been corvettes
in place. Indeed, not long before they'd been there
on station around the carrier. Now, however, they
were needed elsewhere. The plasma screen showed
them—another two green squares—racing at thirty-
seven knots to a point that would place them within
range of a long arc of the main coastal road. They
were due to arrive within fourteen minutes; so said
the display. Wide circles around the corvettes' markers
indicated maximum range for their guns.

A last important green square, *The Big ?*, likewise
chugged toward the coast. It moved much more slowly,
however, at some twenty-four knots. That didn't matter;
it wasn't expected to be needed until later in the day.

Above the town of Gedo a blue circle was superim-
posed, Montoya's Finches circling like vultures. Another
blue marker, this one in a V, showed the remainder
of the carrier's Finches heading in. Further lines from
both markers went generally north, intersecting the
coastal road. Numbers above the lines indicated the
time required for each group to reach a point on the
coastal road from their present position. The lines
shifted as they were moved by the crew of CIC. The
times shifted as well.

Another blue V indicated the flight of Crickets and
Yakamovs. This group, too, had a line that ran to the
coastal highway. Like the Finches, the line and the
times shifted and changed.

From the town and running up the highway was a
series of eyes, outlined in black. These were the RPVs,

watching the highway. Beneath the eyes, shown in red, was a long dotted column. This was the enemy, the enemy they'd expected to come from the capital of Xamar once the pirates were apprised of the fleet's movements. It was to the center of mass of this that the lines pointed. It was time of flight to this that the numbers indicated. It was this that the corvettes' markers sought to capture within the wide circles that showed maximum range for their guns.

Although the other chart showed times of flight, ease of management required that a different screen show in one convenient place the times for interception from each force to the enemy column. For the aircraft, those times were based on what was possible within their minimum and maximum speed, along with the speed required to intercept simultaneously, with the speed of the truck convoy from the capital factored in. When all subunits on the chart showed a time between nine and eleven minutes, Fosa took the radio microphone and announced, "Black this is Black Six. Roland. I repeat, Roland." Fosa then turned the mike over to his operations officer who quickly and efficiently relayed the speeds and course the various elements were to assume. The entire thing could conceivably have been digitalized, but this just wasn't that kind of force. Besides, voice worked well enough.

Every marker on the plasma almost immediately changed course to intercept the column at precisely the point it was expected to be in ten minutes.

Montoya keyed his mike and announced, "In ten . . . heading: 262 . . . speed: 137 . . . on one from five . . . five . . . four . . . three . . . two . . . one." He then adjusted his throttle and eased his stick over to head toward the convoy. A glance to either side with his night vision goggles told him the others were following in a V behind.

A toss of the head backwards and the goggles flipped up, clearing his vision so that he could see his instruments. Everything appeared nominal, so he threw his head forward to bring the goggles back over his eyes. Then, followed by his wingmen, he dove for the dirt. He intended to come in low out of the rising sun.

"Fucking wogs are never going to know what hit 'em."

Abdulahi might have been willing to send lesser sons to sea, even to sacrifice a few here and there for the greater good of his line. For the core of his power base, the mobile column of over a thousand well armed and—by local standards—well trained cousins and nephews and family retainers, nothing and no one would do to lead except his number one son, and presumptive heir, also called Abdulahi.

Abdulahi the junior stood in the back of the second truck in the column, scanning ahead. *Darker than three feet up a well digger's ass at midnight,* Junior cursed. Even the one moon that had been showing had gone down. The sun was not yet up. The stars gave little light, even where they reflected off the sea beside the road. Only the headlights of the trucks provided illumination, and that only ahead and only when they actually worked. Many drove on one light, or even none.

Worse, perhaps, than the darkness was the noise. The trucks would have made a cacophony even had they been well maintained. They were not, however, well maintained. Added to the roar and backfiring of out-of-tune engines were the squeals of badly maintained brakes, the squeaks of abused shock absorbers, the whistles of leaking air tanks. In all, beyond the noise of the column Junior couldn't hear a blessed thing.

That didn't matter, as it turned out, as Montoya's flight was already lining up and the shells were already leaving the corvettes' guns by the time Robinson had alerted Abdulahi the senior to the threat.

The 76.2mm shell was no great shakes. Even coming it at a relatively high angle, its burst radius—more of an oval, actually—was no more than about fifteen by twenty-five meters. Moreover, because it was high velocity, the shells had to be of fairly high quality steel to withstand the stresses of firing. High quality steel produced many times fewer fragments than did simple, cheap iron.

On the other hand, the guns firing from the corvettes were capable of tossing out eighty shells each in forty seconds and, moreover, doing so with considerable accuracy. By the time the computer-controlled guns had emptied their magazines, a sixteen-hundred meter section of Xamar's coastal highway had been *deluged* with fire and flying chunks of glowing hot steel casing.

Combat Information Center, BdL *Dos Lindas*, 19/1/468 AC

"YeeHAW!" Kurita exulted, when the image from the nearest RPV showed the road begin to erupt. Immediately, everyone stopped what they were doing and simply stared at the normally ultradignified and reserved Yamatan.

"I've always liked Columbian films," the commodore said, stiffly, by way of explanation. It didn't really explain much.

Fosa suppressed a smile, then picked up the microphone. "Good shooting, corvettes," he said. "Reload and stand by to support the Cazadors."

"Already reloading, Legate," the first corvette answered. "Half full now," responded the second.

"Roger . . . break. Bluejay One: Finches, you may make your run."

Montoya's voice came from the speaker. "Wilco, Skipper." The other flight leader answered, "On station in three, Skipper."

Unbidden, the leader of the Cazadors—still aboard the Crickets and Yakamovs—broke in. "Leave some for us, ya greedy bastards."

Montoya had slowed slightly, to allow the other three birds in his flight to line up on him. Now, with the first rays of sun creeping over the horizon, the four Finches divided up their prey, then separated laterally themselves.

For himself Montoya picked a half dozen trucks, one of them already burning. As his thumb flicked off the red safety on his yoke, he sang out, *"Hojotoho! Hojotoho! Heiaha! Heiaha!* Hey, where the hell's a PSYOP chopper to play "Ride of the Valkyries" when you really need one?"

Veering left, Montoya's thumb pushed the firing button. Fifty-seven-millimeter rockets lanced out at a rate of six per second, preset. The rockets were almost evenly divided into high explosive, incendiary—the classic shake and bake—and flechette. Still veering,

Montoya switched to his second pod by twisting a dial with his free hand. Once again he thumbed the firing button. Downrange, Hell was materializing.

Junior couldn't believe his eyes. One minute he'd been riding forward in pre-triumph mode to punish the wicked infidel and earn the gratitude of his father and glory among his people. The next, his column was half turned into twisted wreckage, and the roar of engines was replaced with the screams of the dying. With the next, the darkness was illuminated by the combination of just-rising sun and just-spouting flame.

There was an explosion off to Junior's left. Seconds later virtually the entire complement of the rear of the truck in front of him fell down with a god-awful collective moan. The moan was soon replaced by the sound of a dozen men, weeping like brokenhearted girls, as their organs failed from flechette wounds and their life's blood gushed out to fill the bed of the truck and run out the back in a small wave.

Junior watched the blood well from the truck in stunned horror, oblivious even to the other explosions and bursts of some smoking *stuff* that billowed around him. Some of the smoking shit must have touched upon the contents of a ruptured fuel tank. The truck ahead suddenly burst into flame. The weeping changed to screaming.

It wasn't until one of the attacking aircraft passed by overhead and to the front that Junior awoke from his shock. It was the pilot passing by that did it, so close that Junior could see the whites of his eyes and the gleaming smile as he looked down to survey the damage.

In that moment Junior *hated* that pilot in a way he had never hated anyone before; fully, completely, with all his heart and soul. From that hate came the spur to action.

Bluejay Two came in from south of the column, three Finches in trail formation. The last two were separated by about three hundred meters each from the one ahead. The lead Finch's pilot selected the last third of the column to receive his attentions. Seeing what appeared to be two otherwise undamaged trucks unloading a couple score infantry, the pilot donated to them one of his rocket pods. He was rewarded with the blossoming of white phosphorus flowers and fertilizing of the ground with a mass of men tossed down and about by flechettes and high explosive. Another truck burst into flame.

The pilot pulled back on his stick, easing his dive and pulling up parallel to the ground and about fifty meters above it. Ordinarily, he'd have used his machine gun pods now. The execution paragraph of the order called for "maximum fright and terror, initially," however. Since terror and napalm were virtually synonymous . . .

Junior's attempts to bring some order out of the chaos ended when he saw two tumbling cylinders coasting through the air. The sudden burst of bright orange flame at the tail of his column was enough. Hate was not forgotten, exactly. It was just that *everything* was forgotten as Junior began to run away from the ruined column as fast as his legs would carry him. It was a good thing he did, too, as more orange-colored hell burst first around the middle of the column and next along the front.

Even while running he turned and saw the long flaming tongue lick along the column, engulfing men, turning them into writhing, shrieking human torches. The tongue seemed to cover the entire horizon. This was an optical illusion, induced by stark terror. In length, the tongue of fire was actually no more than two hundred meters.

Like their chief, the violence and sheer frightfulness of the naval artillery and aerial assault proved simply too much for the mass of the men. In their hundreds—hundreds still because, for all its frightfulness, aerial attack is rarely completely effective—they streamed to either side of the column, abandoning weapons, leaving comrades and relatives behind.

Once safely away from the epicenter of the infidel attack, Junior was able to throw himself to the ground and take stock of the situation. Around him streamed hundreds of his followers, leaderless and half bereft of weapons. To the west he could hear the slapping of waves against the rocks of the shore. To the east bursts of machine gun fire told him that the enemy were herding the rest of his people toward the water.

"Do they mean to murder us all?" he wondered aloud. Then he heard the whop-whop-whop of incoming helicopters and the high pitched whine of turbines.

"Move it. Move it, you bastards," screamed the senior centurion, First Centurion Saldañas, of the fleet's Cazador detachment. Saldañas had a brother who was a squid, but that brother, Tribune I Saldañas, was currently back in Balboa.

As a practical matter, nobody could hear the centurion

over the noise of the Yakamovs and Crickets. He was convinced, however, that the sheer vibrations of his voice were enough to add half a mile an hour to any group of infantry that ever lived. Most of the troops would have agreed with that assessment.

Two platoons of Cazadors, plus the maniple headquarters, had come in on a dozen Cricket Bs. The remainder, three platoons, the company headquarters, medics, mortars, and the demi-cohort headquarters landed via helicopter. The Crickets had all landed on a short stretch of road to the north of the column. The Yakamovs had touched down in a line parallel to the column and opposite it from the sea. Once the troops had debarked, the Yakamovs again lifted off and began to sweep to the east, away from the column.

It was often held, as a matter of the customary laws of war, that there was an absolute right to surrender and to have that surrender respected. This was sheer ignorance, however. In practice, there was no such right, for in practice there were always circumstances in which prisoners could not be taken. Let a heavy bomber circle an artillery battery with nothing but white flags showing. The bomber's choices were limited to bombing anyway, or not bombing and leaving the battery to resume operation of its guns as soon as the bomber departed. This was not a choice at all. *Bombs away!*

Let a descending parachutist drop his rifle and take out a white flag which he then waved vigorously. If he was descending to an area where he could be taken captive, all well and good. But what if the wind, a factor out of his control, carried him toward his own lines where he could not be made prisoner and where he would be rearmed? *Kill 'em quick, before they get away!*

Similarly, when terrified men attempted to surrender to circling aircraft . . .

Door gunners to either side searched out and shot down whatever Xamaris they found in the grass. Some of those Xamaris tried to surrender, of course, but aircraft don't typically take prisoners. These didn't either; given the enemy's treatment so far through the war of any aircrew that came into their hands there was no surprise in this . . . except perhaps to those Xamaris who thought it worth trying.

The infantry, on the other hand, typically could take prisoners. Spreading out in a long, uneven line, they swept toward the sea. Any Xamaris about whom there was any question of intent were shot down on the spot, or double tapped as the need arose. The rest were herded toward the ocean. For those who begged for their lives, and who appeared to have no weapons, the Cazadors extended fingers and bayonets seaward, instructing them that there their surrender would be accepted.

All the Xamaris clustered by the ocean shore, to include Junior, were certain they were going to be shot. They felt *immense* relief when they saw the Cazadors culling out groups of twelve or fifteen and taping their hands behind them but *not* shooting them.

In the end, three hundred and forty-nine prisoners were taken. Disarmed and searched, in some cases, strip searched, these were held under guard of a single platoon at the beach while the two corvettes and *The Big* ? came close inshore to receive prisoners. The rest of the Cazadors reboarded helicopters about noontime. They then went to teach the village of Gedo a very *sharp* lesson on the subject of supporting or encouraging piracy.

Gedo, Xamar, 19/1/468 AC

The village had not been close enough for the people to hear the gunfire and the explosions coming from the ambush of the column. Thus, it came as a complete surprise to them when suddenly a half dozen aircraft swooped in to rocket their small fishing fleet into so many disassociated splinters. Even as the Finches were destroying the place's livelihood, helicopters landed on the three landward sides and began disgorging heavily armed and armored men. Most of the men were dark, if not so dark as the villagers of Gedo. Mixed in among them were some light enough to have been Taurans, and others, very black and usually as tall and slender as the villagers themselves.

The villagers didn't even consider resistance. Most of the young men and most of the town's arms had disappeared at sea recently— no one knew why—and so there were few even to offer resistance. Loudspeakers directed them to move to the seashore and this they did.

Saldañas directed his men to separate out the women and children from the men. While this was going on, three Cricket Bs landed nearby on a short strip marked out on the sand. One of these disgorged some audio-visual equipment and what appeared to be a laptop computer, along with a couple of operators.

From the other two emerged six men in naval dress uniform, six folding metal chairs, six small field tables and one gavel.

At the Cazadors' gestured directions, the men of Gedo, such as remained, stood up and faced a camera held by one of the men from the first Cricket. This was connected to the laptop held by another. The camera swept along the row of faces. All the prisoners were then faced left for another sweep of the camera, and right for a final set of shots. The Cazadors then ordered them, still with hand gestures, to sit while keeping the same positions. Sitting down on the sand, with hands bound, was no mean achievement. Several fell over and had to be righted by the Cazadors.

The laptop operator pressed a button. The laptop whirred as it analyzed the faces just fed into it with the images recorded previously, as the village had cheered its young men to sea. Circles began to appear around faces as the computer matched distances between eyes and noses, lengths of noses, distance from nose to the corners of mouths, and each of about fifty different features that combine to make each face unique. When it had finished, and the words, *"análisis completo,"* appeared on screen, the laptop operators went down the line of men, separating out those who had not appeared previously, cheering on the pirates.

The rest were marched, one by one, before the four-member court. The defense, for one of the six naval officers landed by the second and third Crickets was indeed the counsel for the defense, had a very tough time of it. No one spoke the local language and Arabic, a form of which was widely understood here, was quite a bit different in Xamar than in Sumer.

Instead, a local was found who spoke English, as did most of the naval officers. Thus, charges were read off in Spanish, the defense counsel (not a lawyer, just a naval officer detailed for the purpose) translated those to English, and the Xamari translated that for the accused.

Typically, the trials went something like this:

Judge Puente-Pequeño: "You are accused of being an accessory before the fact to the act of piracy at sea. How do you plead?"

Defense Counsel, after translation: "Not guilty."

Judge: "Let the record show that the accused has entered a plea of Not Guilty. Prosecutor?"

Prosecutor, pointing to the laptop which showed the accused cheering the pirates: "That's him there."

Defense: *Eloquent shrug.*

Judge: "Has the accused anything to say in his own defense?"

Defense, after translation: "He has four wives and seventeen children to support, Your Honor. Besides, this is on land. Piracy law runs only at sea. Moreover, the defendant claims ignorance of the purpose of the column we engaged while it was moving here and of the boats that left and never returned."

Prosecutor, very wearily: "The former nation of Xamar has dissolved, Your Honor. It lacks sovereignty. It has become a ward of the World League, which also lacks sovereignty. Piracy law runs at sea because no one can hold sovereignty there. It also runs here, because no one *does* hold sovereignty here. As far back as the time of Julius Caesar, on Old Earth, it has been proper to try for crimes committed at sea people caught on land but otherwise under the sovereign protection of no one and acknowledging the sovereignty of nothing. As for the ignorance claim, Your Honor, frankly, in a area which has fallen under control of piracy, where national sovereignty is extinguished, where the Big Bad Motherfucker in Charge is the chief pirate, where the relief column is led by his son, and where everyone knows what the family business is, I think that the 'I didn't know' defense is fairly weak."

Judge, even more wearily than the counsel for the defense: "This is the thirty-seventh trial in which the defense has made the same lack of jurisdiction argument and the thirty-seventh—word for word— rebuttal by the prosecution. It is also the thirty-seventh attempt at claiming innocence through ignorance, likewise thirty-seven times rebutted. Gentlemen, cease. The court has already found it has jurisdiction, that the members of the column understood the business upon which they were engaged, and that this village understood the purpose of sending armed men to sea."

Judge, picking up gavel: "The accused is found guilty." *Tap*. "He will be shot following termination of these proceedings." *Tap*. "Next case."

Defense: "But Judge, what about the women and children? We're leaving them with nothing."

Judge: "We're leaving them—" the judge pausing briefly as a Cazador sergeant leading a squad shouted, "*A punta . . . Fuego!*" and a fusillade rang out "—with their eyes to weep with, and their tongues to spread the word. For our purposes, that's all they need. Next case." *Tap*.

INTERLUDE

18 November, 2105, Turtle Bay, New York,

The news had come in from Terra Nova and that news was *grim*: substantial parts of the new world torn apart in rebellion and the former secretary general's great-great-grandson, Kotek Annan, *butchered* by barbarians. Hardly an eye was dry, at UN Headquarters, with the thought of that brilliant boy done to death—without the slightest provocation; it could not be doubted—by regressives. The secretary general, Eduoard Simoua, was beside himself with grief.

Unfortunately, though Simoua wanted to make the gesture of sending yet another Annan to govern the new world, none were suitable. This was the judgment of the clan's patriarch, and to that judgment Simoua had to bow.

Briefly, Simoua thought about sending one of the retired officers from the various national armed forces that worked for the Department of Peacekeeping out to take charge. *But no, none of those with the requisite experience and ability is really to be trusted. Most certainly, are they not to be trusted unsupervised.*

Well, in a sense it's a disarmament problem. Why don't we send off one of those people? They've all got the right attitude. And they can be relied upon. But who, specifically?

"Bernard Chanet is here to see you Mr. Secretary."

"Send him right in, Irene," said Simoua, rising from his seat warmly to greet his proposed new governor for the world of Terra Nova.

Warm and fulsome greeting or not, Chanet seemed, at best, disinterested. Rather, his interest was made manifest when he asked, "What's in it for me and mine?"

Oh, so that's how it's going to be, thought Simoua, with a mental shrug. *No problem.*

"What do you want?"

Oh, so they want a patsy that desperately, do they? thought Chanet. *Things there are worse than I thought. My price just went up.*

"Amnesty?"

"Amnesty for what? What have you done?" Simoua asked.

"No, no," Chanet said, explaining, "I want you to have my son put in charge of Amnesty, Interplanetary."

"But they're . . ."

Chanet's uplifted eyebrow stopped Simoua before he could say "independent." Not that the organization was a wholly owned or wholly funded subsidiary of the United Nations, but since the UN was *much* better funded now, what with direct levies of tax coming from the citizen of the United States . . .

"We have . . . *influence*," Simoua conceded. "This could be arranged . . ."

"For life," Chanet amended. "With right to select his successor."

"That's impossible! Why, in the last thirty years since I took over as secretary general, we've only made appointments like that twice. And both of those were special cases."

"More special than a war being waged against our control of those portions of Terra Nova that aren't under the governance of major powers here?" Chanet asked.

"Perhaps not," Simoua conceded. "Note, though, that the major powers here do not govern Terra Nova; they dump there."

Chanet nodded his head at the correction, then went silent, leaving the secretary general to think.

If there were some clamor to take this job, Simoua thought, *I'd tell this arrogant upstart to stick it. Sadly, the line for the posting isn't even one deep, outside of the fascist ex-officers in the Peacekeeping Department. It will be expensive though. Why, I'll have to bribe all nine members of the Interplanetary Executive Committee, including the Treasurer. Doable? Yes.*

"Fine," Simoua told Chanet. "You leave in four weeks as a special representative of the secretary general with plenipotentiary powers. Your specific instructions will follow, along with the forces we will allocate to you. And your son has the chair of Amnesty. Later, we can meld the chair and the secretary generalship. As for making those permanent, let's let him keep them for so long that no one remembers when it was even possible for someone else to have them. Legalities can follow the custom, once established."

CHAPTER TWELVE

Katana wa samurai no tamashii.
(The sword is the soul of the samurai.)
—Ancient Yamatan Saying

Bimali, Xamar, 24/1/468 AC

No operation is perfect. Several score men from the butchered column made it back to Abdulahi with wild tales of frightful airplanes and equally frightful infantry swooping in to massacre his followers. None could say what had happened to their chief's heir and the uncertainty was an ulcer eating at the old pirate's innards.

Uncertainty ended shortly thereafter as a single Cricket landed at Bimali's dirt airstrip. From it emerged three armed Cazadors and a legionary naval officer in dress whites. The naval officer was the same one, Tribune Puente-Pequeño, who had served as judge at Gedo.

"Bring your chief, Abdulahi, here," was all the naval officer said.

It was several hours before Abdulahi made an appearance. By that time, the Cazadors had set up a tarp and prepared tea. The naval officer and Abdulahi sat under the tarp and sipped tea for some time before the pirate chief spoke.

"What happened to my son?" he asked.

"Abdulahi, the junior? We have him."

"I want him back."

"Your son was captured while leading an armed band en route to prevent a legitimate action against piracy," the naval officer said. "As such, he is an accessory after the fact to piracy. Thus, he has been sentenced to death, along with all his men. They are being held pending review of the sentences. After review of the sentences, they will be hanged and their bodies dumped at sea."

"You can't do that!?" Abdulahi insisted.

"Why not?" the naval officer answered. "Who's to prevent it?"

Abdulahi's mouth opened to answer, but no words came out. In fact, there was nothing to prevent it. The enemy fleet, what he knew of it, was no great shakes as fleets went. But it was still infinitely superior to anything *he* had. The World League? No, there was nothing there. They couldn't even prevent his former country from dissolving into anarchy; they surely couldn't do anything now. The United Earth Peace Fleet? No, the Pig in Space, Robinson, had made it clear he could not intervene directly. Indeed, without the advice of the High Infidel, his main striking force would never have been destroyed. Yes, he'd have lost a village and the way in which he'd lost it would have terrified his followers. But he'd lost that anyway and his followers had been terrorized anyway.

"What do you want?" Abdulahi asked hopelessly.

"That's simple. You must cease all piratical activity

against shipping under our protection and return all hostages held. Your son will not be executed, though he will be held for some years, if you comply. Otherwise, he will hang, along with a number of his men, the very next time there is an attack at sea. More will hang with each further attack. When we run out, we'll grab more. After all, you're all guilty; we can take anyone we want. We also want your means of communication with the UEPF. We will know if you retain the means, I assure you."

And what good did the supposed "intelligence" I got from space do for me? Nothing. I can give that up. But end our attacks at sea . . . ?

"I cannot control my followers," Abdulahi answered. "If I once could have, that ability was lost to me when you destroyed my column. There will be more attacks," he mourned, "and then you will hang my most beloved son." His chin sank on his chest. Barely, the heartbroken old man restrained his tears.

"I think," Puente-Pequeño countered, "that after the example we just set in your town of Gedo you will have less problem controlling your people than you suspect. Besides, we didn't say you must stop all piracy, only that you must never again touch a ship under our protection. Some shipping we want you to attack."

"Eh?" The pirate's chin lifted and his eyes lost a part of their mournful look.

Smiling the naval officer said, "There are certain shippers who have paid you not to attack their shipping, is this not so?"

Warily the pirate chief nodded.

"Good. Who are they?"

Abdulahi rattled off the names. Mentally, the naval

officer checked off all those known to have been buying off the pirates, plus some others who had been unknown. There was only one missing.

"You forgot Red Star Line," the officer said.

"Oh, yes. Sorry. It's just that they've been paying us so long . . ."

"No matter. We want you to attack them, all those who paid you off, until such time as we say 'halt.' As you attack them, we shall make them pay a great deal for protection, all they should have paid us this last year plus interest and penalties. By the time they have broken, you should have enough of a ground force built up that you can maintain control in the future. Moreover, we will send some first rate infantry to protect you and your family, and to help you keep control, while you rebuild."

Abdulahi looked wonderingly. He had thought himself powerful and ruthless. He had followed Mustafa because he thought he had found one even more powerful and ruthless than he was. But these mercenaries? They were beyond anything he or even Mustafa had contemplated. And their power, though small in the big scheme of things, was magnified by their callousness, lack of pity, mercilessness, cruelty and heartlessness to terrifying heights.

Perhaps the deal is not such a bad one.

Commodore's Quarters, BdL *Dos Lindas*, 25/1/468 AC

One of Kurita's ancestors, back on Old Earth in the early twenty-first century, had had an interesting theory. Possessed of an ancient sword, a family heirloom dating back to before the *Sengoku Jidai*, the Period of the Country at War, that ancestor had observed that the sword was old and "tired," as the Japanese said. It had seen too much use, had been polished too many times. It was thin and most of the high carbon layer had gone from it.

"All weapons are living beings," had said this ancestor, "This is merest revealed truth. They have souls. Is my family's sword less alive because it has lost weight? I think not. I think that all it ever was is still contained within that weary core of metal. And yet, does it not look sad?"

The ancestor had mused upon this, neither resting nor eating nor drinking, for three days. At last, with his mind free of normal mortal limits, he had had an insight. "We live as well. And we do not become different, or lose our souls, by changing our kimonos. Perhaps this sword merely wants a change of clothing."

Kurita's ancestor had spent two years searching out the right swordsmith for the work he had in mind. In Japan's revival of its ancient art, many swordsmiths had appeared. Few were of sufficient artistry for his family sword, however. Of those few, none initially would undertake the job. Screams of "Heresy! Blasphemy!" arose wherever he'd tried.

At last he had found one, a smith willing to try new things or—in this case—old things in a new way.

For two more years this smith studied the Kurita family heirloom. Looking at the temper line, the little dots of pearlite and martinsite, he saw back to the technique used by the earlier smith, saw the painting on of the clay wash, saw the precise glow of the charcoal in the brazier.

The smith took a *gunto* sword, a relic of Old Earth's Second World War, and experimentally attempted what Kurita's ancestor had wanted with it. He was disappointed to find that this really told him nothing, that the solid make up of the new sword did not replicate the problems of recladding a properly layered sword. Moreover, he found he had wasted much of the rare and expensive *tama-hagane*, the traditional steel produced from iron rich sands in the last remaining *tatara* smelter in Japan, in Shimane Prefecture.

Next the smith had experimented on a worn out *tanto,* or dagger, though not one as old as the Kurita sword. This *tanto,* unlike the *Gunto* sword, had been made in the traditional manner. The result *worked,* for certain values of work. Still the smith was not satisfied.

Armed with the insights gained from working on the *tanto,* the smith then obtained a sword forged in the seventeenth century and falsely labeled as the work of the great smith, Kunihiro. The forgery had been well made—how else could it even hope to pass itself off as the great master's work?—and much was learned from resheathing this.

At length, the smith felt ready. He took several pounds of *tama-hagane* and from it forged a four thousand layer, high carbon skin, or *kawegane*. Using the old Kurita sword for the base, he forged around it this new skin, welding the two together with heat and the strokes of his hammer. Did he hear the sword scream under the pounding. *No matter; I scream in the dentist's chair, too.* Then he tempered it in such a way as to recreate a temper line, or *hamon,* essentially indistinguishable from the original.

Last of all, the smith added every distinguishing

mark found on the sword prior to recladding it. A warrior is, after all, entitled to the honor of his scars.

Fosa and Kurita sat opposite each other, cross-legged on a rice straw mat on the floor of the commodore's quarters. The sword lay between them on a silk scarf. Though it glowed from the daylight streaming in through the portholes, to Fosa is seemed to glow with an inner light as well.

"It's . . . beautiful," said a stunned Fosa, stunned because the commodore had never before shown him the sword. He did not wear it aboard ship.

"It's unique," Kurita corrected. "The smith who did this was hounded from the art for tampering with tradition. Eventually, he borrowed the sword and killed himself with it; so say the family legends. My father gave it to my care when I took over command of the Battlecruiser *Oishi*. I have no heir, and all my nephews are swine. I imagine I will send it to the restored *Yasukuni* when I feel my time is upon me. After all, though the shrine boasts nine and ninety rocks from my people's battlefields now, it has never had a rock from a naval battlefield. It does have that one forty-six centimeter shell but that was never fired, of course. A sword, however, should do well enough."

"You should wear it," Fosa said. "Here on the ship. I think the men would approve." *Hah, they'll think it's great.*

"Perhaps I should."

"You still have people who make such weapons in Yamato, do you not, Commodore?"

"Yes. It has experienced something a rebirth of late."

Again Fosa looked at the sword, admiringly. "Is there one you might recommend?"

"I shall enquire," answered the commodore. "They live, you know? Swords, ships, rifles, too. All the weapons of man have their own souls, their own spirits. Thus the wise men of Yamato teach. And I have always felt it was true."

The sun had gone down and the quarters were empty except for Kurita and the sword. The sword was still out, though now illuminated only by the candles the commodore had lit.

Is the sword my agent, the old man wondered, *or am I its? It's a good question. Am I the Zaibatsu's agent to the legion . . . or have I become the legion's agent to the Zaibatsu? I do not know. I do, however, know that the mission here for which the legion contracted is about over. Yet I have told my principals none of this. Why should this be?*

The commodore cleared his mind and concentrated on the dim glow of the sword before him. After a long time he looked up, with a smile.

Ah . . . now I understand. It is because after all these years away from the sea and my calling, I am again at war and happy. And the legion has made it so.

The next morning Kurita awoke, as always, very early. He dressed himself, as always, but added a sash. He prepared and encoded one message. Then he prepared another in plain text. Through the sash he stuck his family heirloom, taking a moment to look in the mirror to ensure it was adjusted to the perfect angle.

Kurita's first stop was at the door to Fosa's quarters. He knocked and, when Fosa answered, passed over the plain text note and said, "Encode this and send it to the highest placed intelligence officer in your organization, Captain-san." Then he left a stunned looking Fosa and walked to the radio room to send the encoded message to Messers Saito and Yamagata.

Most of the crew members barely noticed the sword. Perhaps it was just that, for the first time, Kurita seemed fully dressed. Of those who did actually notice it, the uniform sentiment was something like *cooolll*.

When the message was received, in distant Yamato, and had been decoded and presented to the Zaibatsu representatives, a very confused Yamagata read it off for Saito.

"I want a sword made, or bought, if one be found suitable." said the message, "Make it a katana. It should be made by a master smith, and in the old Bizen style. Full furnishings should be provided, with a blue lacquer scabbard and blue-wrapped *tsuka*. Inscribe on the blade . . ."

Casa Linda, Balboa, 26/1/468 AC

Balboa had seen its share of rule-by-lunatic before. All things considered, rule-by-kleptocrat was to be preferred. Parilla's presidential campaign faced that, fear of political lunacy, as its greatest handicap.

"It's not a completely groundless fear, Raul," Professor Ruiz advised. "Yes, we can and we have put a lot of emphasis into the public works the legion has sponsored. Yes, we can show a lot of pretty girls to catch attention. Artemisia Jimenez, in particular, seems to be an attention grabber." Both Parilla and Ruiz unconsciously sighed, *Ah, Artemisia . . . what a delight!* "Still, you can talk the good fight, talk national rebirth, talk anticorruption. But the longer the campaign goes on, the more people are exposed to counterpropaganda, the more a lot of people become afraid of you, afraid of the Legion, and afraid of what you might do with both the presidency and the military power. Most of them are middle class, but some are poor."

Parilla shook his head, uncomprehending. "But we've done so much for the poor."

Ruiz's mouth formed a moue. "Ah . . . no. You've made a minority of the poor fairly middle class by bringing them into the *Legion del Cid*. You've also left a much larger number behind. You've actually *given* very little and most of the benefits are either general, clinics and such, or indirect. Some of the support we had may have slipped away because you've never once mentioned creating a social democratic welfare state here."

"Social democracy? Patricio controls the money and *that* he will never go for. I start talking welfare state and I'll lose *his* support. Come to think of it, I start talking social democracy and I probably wouldn't vote for myself. How bad are the numbers?"

"It isn't that they're *bad*, exactly," Ruiz answered. "Just that they're down from where they were and where they should be. I don't like the trend. I also don't like the effect of the advertising campaign the other side is using. They're getting a lot of mileage out of comparing you to Piña. And then there is the number of people put to death by the legion, starting with Rocaberti back during the initial campaign in Sumer and continuing through today. Forget the number of Sumeris we've strung up; how many legionaries have been executed for one or another crime?"

"Maybe a hundred," Parilla admitted. "Or a bit less. But most of those were for crimes that would warrant death even outside the military."

"Not here they wouldn't," Ruiz corrected. "And the idea of applying the death penalty here, if the government changes, has a lot of people scared. Piña had people killed; you and Patricio have had people killed. Some don't see fine distinctions like the fact that he killed political opponents and you've shot or hanged traitors, deserters, rapists, and murderers."

Parilla bridled. "Now *that* is unfair."

"Politics is supposed to be *fair*?" Ruiz asked, rhetorically.

"Point taken."

"Another thing," Ruiz added. "The advertising the other side is using is sophisticated and, because there is so much of it, expensive. I think they're getting a fair amount of financial backing from the Taurans. Our ruling classes have two distinguishing features. One is that they're corrupt. The other is that they're *cheap*; cheeseparers, at *best*. They'd never spend this kind of money on their own, though they'd be perfectly happy to let someone else do it on their behalf."

"Yeah, I know them," Parilla agreed. "What are the numbers looking like?"

Ruiz was actually an art—or, at least, cinema—professor. He'd run the legion's propaganda program since inception. As such—with politics being as much about propaganda as about reality, and perhaps more—he'd been tapped for the political campaign. Starting with no real background in the subject he'd surrounded himself with other professors from the university who did have such a background. The numbers came from them.

"We're expecting a relatively high turnout, on the order of eighty percent."

"That *is* high," Parilla agreed. "We haven't seen a turnout like that since the vote on the Transitway Treaty with the Federated States."

"Yes. Of those, right now we can count on maybe fifty-five percent, including absentee ballots, voting our way. That's down about nine percent from where we thought we were when this started. Another drop like that and we're toast."

Parilla bit at his lower lip. "Worse, if the current party can show that kind of support no amount of bribery will keep them from outlawing the legion, here."

"High stakes, indeed," Ruiz agreed. "So what's left? Social democracy is out. More sensitive military laws and regulations are probably out."

"I've got to discuss that with Patricio."

Firebase Pedro de Lisaldo, Pashtia, 28/1/468 AC

His aide had brought three messages to Carrera while he visited the firebase before going out on a patrol with one of the platoons that shared it with the artillery. One was from Fernandez. It had been hand-carried in coded form, translated back at headquarters in Mazari Omar, then brought forward. The second was from Parilla. It, too, had gone through encode and decode. The last was from Lourdes. Carrera read the last first, smiling halfway through then laughing outright when Lourdes passed on some of the news of their son's latest antics.

So I caught Hamilcar carting off one very unwilling kitten in his arms. As soon as he saw me he just opened his arms and let it drop to the floor. Then he put his head down like a man on his way to the firing squad and walked back to bed without a word. You should have seen it . . .

He *could* just see it, actually. Carrera folded the letter and tucked it into the pocket closest to his heart. He'd answer in a few days when he got back from visiting the troops.

The next read was Parilla's.

. . . And so Professor Ruiz tells me that, against our expectations, we might lose. I know I don't have to tell you how bad that could be. Would it be bad enough? Would it be worth establishing a legion-supported welfare state? And if we did, how would we ever escape it?

One thing that did occur to me that we could do, Patricio, is to announce we're expanding the reserves and dropping—better we should say "modifying," I suppose—the entrance standards enough to let come in maybe half the people who want in. Maybe we can open up some more to women. What those would do to the quality of the force

> *I cannot say. Yet I do wonder if quantity*
> *does not have a quality all its own . . .*

"I'll consider it, Raul," was all Carrera said, and that only to the air.

Lourdes' letter was important to his mental well being. Parilla's to his political future. Fernandez's, though, was important to everything. He never sent a message that wasn't absolutely critical. Carrera began to read.

Oh, God, thought Carrera, *if Fernandez's supposition is right, then the stakes just went through the roof.*

He looked back to the report, hand carried by trusted messenger to this remote firebase in the Pashtian foothills.

He read:

> *Patricio,*
>   *The events in Xamar make it clear, as clear as anything can be clear, that the UEPF has completely sided with the enemy, which we suspected, and is actively aiding him, which we did not know but feared. Looking backwards in time, I cannot say how long this has been going on. I can, however, state that it has been going on for a long time and may, indeed, have begun before your family was destroyed. It may have been part of that destruction. I am reasonably certain it was part of the murder of my daughter.*
>
> *Consider the following:*
> *1. We have acquired testimony, partial intercepts of communications, and a device by*

*which communication took place between
the pirates of Xamar and the UEPF.*

2. *We have partial intercepts of communications between your enemies in Pashtia
and Kashmir and the UEPF.*

3. *We have recorded conversations, obtained
by bugging the current president's office,
in which the ambassador from the UE
has participated in planning to split the
country, or outlaw the legion, or both.*

4. *We have acquired a new intelligence
source . . .*

Carrera read that intelligence source and could
only say, "Holy shit."

He then continued and didn't stop reading until he'd
digested the message completely. It wasn't exactly a
shocking surprise, except for the new source of intelligence. He'd known that the UEPF had been at least
unsympathetic. But outright enmity? Helping the enemy
kill innocent women and children without overwhelming
good cause? What could be their motivator? Then again,
did it even matter what their motivation was? Didn't
the facts of the matter say all that needed to be said?

*So I'm not just going to war with the TU someday,
I am going to have to deal with the UEPF as well.
And I don't know how I can even touch them . . . oh,
yes I do. God, that would suck. But would it work?*

Carrera closed his eyes and summoned up a mental image of the *Mar Furioso*, to include the Island
of Atlantis. After long minutes of contemplation he
answered himself, *Yes, it would probably work.*

That, however, is for the further future. In between

I have to deal with the Taurans and probably the Zhong. That's already being worked back home. So besides tonight's patrol, what do I have to worry about except the UEPF?

UEPF *Spirit of Peace*, 12 January, 2522

Robinson had begun to worry as soon as the robo-drone from Earth had come in with the monthly dispatches and he'd been given the set marked "Eyes Only: High Admiral." Earth rarely communicated anything to the fleet beyond the merest routine, what parts would not be available and would have to be procured locally, what money would not be forthcoming, what art would be sent for auction, how many slaves would be on the next boat out and their quality. Slaves from Old Earth were always a dicey commodity. They had to be physically attractive, but also both ignorant and stupid lest they give away more of the conditions on Old Earth than the Consensus wanted known.

In any case, that sort of message was all routine. This—with its "Eyes Only" qualifier—just had to be bad news. He took the dispatches and, Wallenstein in tow, went to his cabin to read them.

"Shit. It's worse than I imagined," Robinson muttered, after scanning the first few lines of what appeared to be the only non-routine message among the group.

"What is, Martin?"

Robinson handed over the dispatch but explained verbally anyway. "The Inspector General is coming to pay us a call."

Wallenstein's eyes flew wide. "The Marchioness of Amnesty is coming *here?*" *Hmmm, another supporter for my bid to enter Class One? Possibly. Have to find out her tastes. I'm sure Robinson wouldn't mind sharing me for a worthy cause. And she's by no means an unattractive woman.* "Any hint of why?"

"None. It's got to be bad, though. A visit from the IG is always bad." Robinson's face grew contemplative. After a bit, he continued, "Fortunately, she likes girls as well as boys. I want you and . . . let me think . . . the Marchioness is also a Domme, so . . . yes, you and Khan and Khan's husband, to be her escort party."

"How long do we have to prepare?"

"Two months."

"No problem then. I can set up a dungeon and order appropriate costumes from Atlantis Base in that time."

"Good girl, Marguerite. I knew I could count on you."

"Hmmm. Should I order up a slave or two from below in case the IG wants to actually damage a playmate?"

"Excellent thinking, Captain. Better make it one of each."

Santissima Trinidad, 5/2/468 AC

"It's been sixteen fucking days, Skipper," said Francais in a tone of unutterable boredom. Even the speed of the ship, a modest and fuel saving eight knots, was dull.

"I can count, XO," answered Pedraz.

"Business" had dropped off radically since the coastal raid on the village of Gedo. Pedraz didn't know why, but suspected it had something to do with the prisoners the classis had taken.

Is Fosa capable of saying, "We'll hang them if you give us a scintilla of trouble?" Pedraz wondered. *Oh, yes. And would Carrera—God bless his black heart—back him up in that? Puhleeze.*

All of which suggests there won't be a lot more business hereabouts. Which means we're stuck here on a tiny movable island for the foreseeable and indefinite future. Fuck. Well, fortunately the legion has no rules against drinking and the beer locker is full.

From Santiona on the rear deck came the cry, "I've got one!"

And the fishing's not bad either. On the other hand . . .

Santiona's rod was bent so far that . . . well . . . honestly Pedraz couldn't remember seeing a stout sport fishing rod *ever* bent so far. *Good thing I insist on the men tying themselves in with safety lines.* Idly, Pedraz wondered what it might be. Then he saw the fin.

And then he saw more of the fin. And still more. And more still. And . . .

"Oh, fuck. It's a MEG!"

The aliens—the "Noahs"—who had seeded the planet of Terra Nova with Old Earth life forms some time between five hundred thousand and five million years prior had been thorough; you had to give them that.

The Noahs had brought over some of everything, so far as the colonists could tell. There were sabertooths and mammoth, orcas and phororhacos. They'd also managed a very impressive array of sea life.

"Meg, MEG, *MEEEGGG!*"
"Fuckfuckfuck. XO, gun it!"
"For where, Skipper?"
"Who the fuck *cares?* Just *move!*"
Until he turned, Francais hadn't see the shark's fin,

now standing over two meters above the water and plowing a furrow in the waves. When he did see it, about three hundred meters abaft the boat, his jaw dropped and his hand automatically pushed the throttle full forward. The previously purring engines roared to life as the boat's nose rose measurably. At the same time, Santiona and most of the rest of the crew were thrown to the deck.

Santiona began sliding off. Desperately, one-handed, he clawed at the plywood of the deck, shrieking the whole time, "Meg, Meg, Meggg!" As his head went past the deck's edge, he felt the safety line about his waist suddenly begin to tighten.

It did not tighten enough to stop him, however, before he'd gone over the stern bodily. Coming to a sudden and painful stop, Santiona hung there, chest down and feet in the water, while that huge fin got closer. He couldn't take his eyes off the thing, but stared at its approach as if possessed. All the while he screamed, "Meg, Meg, Meggg!"

The head lifted above water. A flash of sunlight told that the shark was hooked. It never occurred to Santiona to drop the rod; oh, *no*. He held on to that as tightly as the rope constricted his waist. In seconds, the fish was close enough for him to see its saucer-sized eyes and the glittering rows of jagged ivory in its mouth. The scientists insisted that the *carcharodon megalodon* transplanted to Terra Nova never went over forty-two feet. Nonetheless, ever after, Santiona would *insist* that they grew to one hundred and twenty. That size could grow to two hundred if he'd had a few.

That future "ever after" would have to wait as the fish gained on the boat.

✧   ✧   ✧

The shark was actually a tad under thirty-six feet, by no means an unusually large specimen of its type. Its brain was no better than the species norm, either. It had smelled the hooked fish, all rotten and wonderful, and just naturally taken the offering.

It had been about ready to say, "Foul and slimy with just a hint of risqué decomposition; my compliments to the chef," when the hook bit.

Ouch . . . now that's hardly sporting.

"No!" Pedraz shrieked at a sailor uncovering a heavy machine gun mounted port side, aft. "Don't shoot at it; you might piss it off. Get over here and help me with Santiona."

The skipper was hauling on the rope. Sadly, he was getting nowhere with Santiona's considerable mass on the other end. The fish was still gaining slightly. For his part, Santiona just kept screaming, "Meg! Meg! Meggg!" while bouncing—thump-thump-thump— off the stern and keeping a death grip on the rod. "Meg! Meg! Meggg!"

Another sailor, and then a fourth, scuttled along the deck to take hold of the line. With four strong men pulling, even Santiona's bulk began to rise.

"Meg! Meg! Meggg!"

The fish was confused. The thing ahead of him, trying to run away, really didn't look like the baleen whales that made up much of its diet. It didn't smell quite right either. Only the spurt of urine rushing into the water from the thing dangling off the back really reminded it of its normal prey.

And those cheap bastards are trying to haul it in.
Well, we'll just see about that. The fish sped up.

"Christ! The fucking thing is speeding up!"
"Meg! Meg! Meeeggg!"
"XO?!"
"I'm giving it all she's got, skipper."
"C'mon, you lazy bastards; PULL!"

So close . . . sooo close . . . one more effort . . .
but . . . no . . . tiring . . . life's just so unfair. Sigh.

Pedraz breathed a sigh of relief as he saw the space
between boat and shark widen. After a time the fin
turned away. Then it disappeared. Santiona's cry had
grown softer, "meg . . . meg . . . meg." The rest of
the crew alternately swore or just stood or sat, drained.

"Doc?" Pedraz called.

"Here . . . skipper," gasped one of the line haulers,
lying on his back nearby.

"Huh? Oh . . . didn't know you were so close.
Doc . . . go break out a bottle of medicinal rum." He
looked over at Santiona—"meg . . . meg . . . meg"—
and thought, "No . . . make it *two* bottles. Prescribe
to the crew as you think they need it."

"Aye, aye, Skipper."

Rising unsteadily to his feet, Pedraz staggered to
the cockpit. "And you were bitching that you were
bored?" he said to Francais.

"Well . . . Skipper. It's not like we have any *girls*
aboard."

From the stern continued the chant, "meg . . .
meg . . . meg . . ."

❖   ❖   ❖

Quarters #1, *Isla Real*, Balboa, 7/2/468 AC

"Miss Lourdes," for McNamara had never quite gotten over calling her "Miss Lourdes," even when she'd become "Señora Carrera," "for t'e love of God, please tell t'e boss to call me forward. I just can' fockin' stand it no more. And I ain't got so many years left to me that I can afford to be here when t'e fightin's t'ere."

Rank and position are curious things. In any given military organization there are usually five or six people that run it. Sometimes it's the commander. Sometimes—and usually unfortunately, if so—it's the commander's wife. Sometimes, at the company or maniple level, it can be one lone sergeant, and not necessarily a senior one, in the training NCO slot.

In the case of the *Legion* one of the true movers and shakers was *the* Sergeant Major, John McNamara. Part of this was that he had Carrera's ear. Much of it, though, was what the man was, himself.

Lourdes sighed. Patricio had asked her to be a shoulder for the sergeant major to cry on if—*no, Patricio had said "when"*—being left behind got to be too much for him. He must have told Xavier, too, for it was Jimenez who'd asked Lourdes to ask McNamara for lunch. He'd come, of course, and sounded like he'd been happy to. But he'd come with his craggy black face a mask of utter misery.

"What's the problem, John?" she asked. She avoided answering the question because one of the other things Pat had told her was, "I need him to stay here, to watch over the legion's base and over you and the kids, too. I need him to keep watch out for Parilla. I need him *here*."

It was McNamara's turn to sigh. *Yes, sure as shit the boss told Lourdes already that I can't come and play.*

"It everyt'ing, Miss Lourdes. Jimenez don' need me here; *his* legion, t'e Fourth, and his sergeant major can do just fine wit'out me. T'e Training Legion don' need me eit'er, with Martinez running t'ings. So I end up helpin' Parilla with t'e presidential campaign and . . . well . . . it just ain't me. It's dirty shit, nasty, no place for a soldier to be.

"And besides all t'at, Miss Lourdes, since t'e kids grew up and t'e wife passed on I've had nobody to fight wit'. I'm *bored*."

"I don't think I can help, John. Patricio never has anyone do anything without a good reason. If he wants you, myself and Xavier here, it's for a purpose. I don't think we can buck him in this."

Artemisia Jimenez had only just caught sight of McNamara's vehicle as it pulled into Quarters Number One's driveway. She was too late to actually *say* anything to the sergeant major. Still, she raced to put on gardening clothes and posted herself nearby so that when he emerged . . .

"Why hello, Sergeant Major," she purred, looking up as he neared his auto. "If I'd known it was you visiting Lourdes, I'd have popped over."

Most women simply stood. Artemisia was fundamentally incapable of simply standing. Instead, like a fast action movie of a flowering plant, she *blossomed* onto her feet.

McNamara was not made of stone. Watching the sheer *presence* of Artemisia Jimenez blooming so closely would have taken the breath from any man. It did with him, as well. It did so, so completely, in fact, that McNamara simply bid her a nervous good day, got in his auto, and drove away.

If I were not more than twice her age, if I were not so old and seamed and gangly and outright ugly, Mac thought, *I would never have left there.*

"Shit," Artemisia said aloud, watching the car drive off. "What did I do wrong? Damn, and he's so *perfect.*"

Quarters #2, *Isla Real,* 7/2/468 AC

Artemisia thought her uncle was possibly the second-most manly man she had ever seen. The first was . . .

"Uncle Xavier, could we ask Sergeant Major McNamara over to dinner? I saw him visiting Lourdes Carrera today and he looked extremely sad and lonely."

Jimenez was no fool. His niece's tastes in men had proven decidedly odd over the years. And she'd never shown the slightest interest in any of the young men who sniffed about the balconies so regularly. Jimenez folded his daily paper and put it aside.

After a sigh he said, "Arti, Mac's a fine man, but he's old enough to be your father . . . maybe your grandfather, if he was precocious."

Am I that obvious? Or am I only that obvious to my older male relations?

"I don't care, Uncle. Ever since I saw him at the hippodrome, I've been fascinated."

"He's not rich, Arti, though I have no doubt that Patricio would fix that if he ever saw a reason to, or Mac asked. And he *is* old, nearly sixty. There's no guarantee he could ever father children on you."

Artemisia sniffed, pointedly. "Trust me, Uncle; women can tell. He could still father a score of children. Give him ten women and he could father two hundred. Uncle, the sergeant major is a *man*."

Jimenez smiled at his niece. "Well . . . yes, I suppose he is. But what makes you think he might be, or even could be, interested in you?"

Artemisia didn't have to blossom for her uncle. A simple tilt of the head and half pirouette sufficed.

"Well," the legate conceded, pulling on one ear ruefully. "I suppose he could be at that."

Jimenez's eyes narrowed with suspicion. "Young lady, you go hurting McNamara's feelings and you will find you are not too old, not too high and mighty, to find your old uncle pulling you over his knee and paddling you so that you cannot sit for a month."

Horrified, the niece shook her head. "*Hurt* him, Uncle? No . . . oh, nonono. I'm serious about this one. I intend to make him the happiest man in the world. Don't you see? He just . . . *smells* right. He's the right one. I swear; I'll never hurt him."

Still looking suspicious, Jimenez had to concede that Arti seemed sincere enough. "Very well then. You can hunt him, my little Diana. Though I foresee much wailing and gnashing of teeth from the Bachelor Officers' Quarters."

"Will you help, Xavier?"

"Brazen hussy. What is it with you and older men?"

"They're real men, Uncle Xavier, not boys. Besides,

I was in love with you when I was a little girl and I guess that just typecast me for impossibly old men."

Slightly embarrassed, Jimenez thought about that, his head bobbing from side to side. At length, he had to agree. God knows, *he'd* been not nearly as much of a man at age twenty-five.

"Well . . . I suppose that my own sergeant major could use a little more advice . . . and perhaps I could, as well. And then there's the whole . . . well, never mind. I suppose I have been underutilizing this most impressive training asset. Niece, please invite Sergeant Major McNamara, Sergeant Major Escobedo and his wife, and Legate Guttierez and his wife to dinner, next . . . mmm . . . let's say next Friday. Mess dress? Yes, that will give us an opportunity to show off your not unimpressive . . . assets and give you a chance to see just how impressive Sergeant Major Mac can be in full regalia."

With a yelp of joy—with her uncle on her side, poor McNamara didn't stand a chance—Artemisia launched herself to wrap her arms around Xavier and squeeze him tight enough to collapse lungs. After a moment she backed up and looked at him seriously.

"Xavier," she said. "If you had not been my uncle, I would have gone after *you*."

INTERLUDE

7/6/47 AC (Old Earth year 2106), Terra Nova, Balboa Colony

The shuttles came down in broad daylight, the better to intimidate the population.

Belisario Carrera, watching from a jungle-shrouded perch overlooking the *ciudad*, counted them as they descended. Multiplying by twenty-four, he came up with a number of new opponents that set his teeth to grinding and his stomach to churning.

Still, there's no way to tell from here, Belisario thought, *how many are actually aboard, what their equipment is like, or what kind of soldiers they are. Hmmm . . .*

"Pedro?" Belisario called, summoning a short, stocky and dark, loincloth-clad fighter.

"*Si, jefe?*" Pedro asked when he had crawled up to his leader's observation post. He massaged a sore shoulder as he lay upon the ground, gift of a captured UN rifle with altogether too much kick.

"I want you to . . ." Belisario began and then stopped. Pedro was a *cholo,* an indian, but he was also very nearly the brightest of Belisario's followers. He was among the bravest. If Belisario asked Pedro to go into town and spy, Pedro would certainly do it. But the risk?.

I must risk it. I must risk him.

"Pedro," Belisario continued, "I need to know what we're facing. Can you go into town and look around for me?"

The *cholo* didn't say much, ever. He didn't now, either, but just nodded and began to slither backwards.

Belisario returned his attention to the town below and the parade of descending shuttles. *So even here I cannot escape Earth and its corruption. Ah, well, at least here I can fight and have a chance. But I do wish that before I left I'd killed more slowly that UN bastard who wanted to trade me my own land for my daughter.*

The *ciudad* wasn't really much of a *ciudad*. Even Pedro, *cholo* or not, knew that. Only the stone church had any real presence, at least since Belisario and his men had attacked and burned to the ground the local UN offices. It wasn't difficult for Pedro to keep a smile off his face as he passed the ruined UN compound. After all, there was a substantial group of uniformed men busily working to rebuild it.

Looking carefully at the soldiers, Pedro engraved on his mind the image his eyes saw. *Big, strong, tough looking. Red cloths wound around their heads. Cloths look pretty neat. Might get one. Keep rifles close by or slung across backs. Hotter than shit and they still haven't taken off shirts. I smell trouble.*

Pedro had his basic letters and numbers. He counted, in all, about one hundred and fifty before moving on.

I thought other fucking UN bastards looked tough, he thought, a few hundred more yards down the street. He, like the civilians of the town, rapidly got out of the way of another group of soldiers, marching silently in three files and about fifty ranks, separated into five groups. *They short shits, like me. Eyes different, though. Skin lighter. But little fuckers look* mean. *And them big fucking curved knives they carrying? Scary.*

After three hundred of the toughest looking men he had ever seen, Pedro breathed a small sigh of relief as he got close enough to see the next group, just emerging from the shuttles.

Hah, that more like it. Them look like Botswanan fellahs we kick shit out of while back. Smell worse, though. Jesus, nobody tell dirty fuckers "Cleanliness next to Godliness?" I mean, I know water tight on fucking transport ships but . . . ewwww. It ain't like you sweat any in deep freeze. Them nasty fucks musta been stinky when board ship.

Then Pedro smelled something he had only ever smelt once before in his life. That time had been at Tocumen Airport, in Panama, on old Earth, as he had been about to board the aircraft that would take him to the United States to be shuttled up to the *Amerigo Vespucci.* He didn't know what caused it. At first he thought it might be the helicopters roaring by overhead.

But, no . . . them too far away . . . downwind, too.

A horn sounding behind him half scared Pedro out of his coppery skin. He turned quickly, and found himself staring into eyes that just emerged above a long, green painted, solid-looking slope. He looked above the eyes, looked further up to what appeared to be a pipe sticking out of a half a trash can stuck on front of the universe's biggest frying pan. Up; a machine gun mounted atop a flat roof, with a soldier nonchalantly resting one hand on the gun, while waving with the other for Pedro to clear away.

Oh, shit; they got tanks.

CHAPTER THIRTEEN

We could wait no more
In the burning sands
on the ride to Agadir.
Like the dogs of war
For the future of this land
on the ride to Agadir . . .
—Mike Batt, "Ride to Agadir"

Firebase Pedro de Lisaldo, Pashtia, 28/2/468 AC

"*Sayidi*, it's not like they don't know we're coming for them," said Qabaash, in the confines of the conference room tent near the main command post for the legion's expeditionary force. "And, to a considerable degree of certainty, when. We can choose the exact time and the place and even the manner, but we cannot choose the fact or the season. The Kibla Pass must be cleared; they know this. They will be waiting and they will be prepared."

"'Prepared' is possibly an understatement, boss," added Triste. "Even if what the FS Army has caught moving into the area represents ninety percent of everything that was sent up there by the *Ikhwan*, and

467

it doesn't, that other theoretical ten percent is going to be a bitch, taken head on."

"What are we facing?" Carrera asked.

"A reinforced brigade," Triste answered. "I can't tell you exactly *how* reinforced they might be. Assume more than their fair share of heavy mortars, possibly even a few tanks, *lots* of RGLs . . . fair amount of antiaircraft, guns and shoulder-fired guided missiles, both. That's all pretty concentrated on the best landing zones, too. Some of the guns are reported to be in caves that cover the LZs and which are a just plain bitch to see until it's too late.

"Assume mines and booby traps and *major* improvised explosive devices. Assume the sides and underbeds of the road through the pass are wired for sound"—milspeak for wired to explode—"and that most of the LZs will be mined and covered by direct and indirect fire."

Miguel Lanza, head of the air *ala*, usually kept fairly quiet at these little brainstorming sessions. Today was different.

"*Jefe,* there are half a dozen LZs within six or eight miles of the summit of the pass in which I could set down Qabaash's entire brigade in no more than three or four lifts. Every one of them is entirely unsuitable; I'd lose nearly every bird I tried to set down."

"Fine. What's *not* unsuitable?" Carrera asked.

Qabaash raised an eyebrow at Triste, who proceeded to produce a photo and a large-scale map and hand them over to Carrera. "This one might work, boss."

Carrera's face looked highly dubious. The photo showed a somewhat narrow ledge—no more than fifty meters in width—hunched against a series of cliffs with serrations in them. On the side away from the cliffs was a sheer drop.

"What's this good for? Maybe five or six birds landing at a time. It would take forever to get Qabaash's brigade on the ground."

"I think more like four birds at a time, *jefe*," Lanza corrected. "And the cross winds coming around that rock outcropping will be very difficult. But no; it won't take forever. Assume we'll have to underload the helicopters some because of the thin air. Okay, so it takes damned near everything I have to get all of the *Salah al Din* brigade into the air at once. Call it one hundred and twenty choppers, anyway. At four per lift, or one per lift for the IM-62s, it will take just over an hour to get everyone in and out."

"But I can be moving on the pass on foot as soon as I have two companies landed," interjected Qabaash. "That's less than ten minutes . . ."

"Closer to five," Lanza corrected.

"Better still, closer to five minutes after the first chopper touches down and I am already on my way to the pass."

"And then what, Qabaash?" Carrera asked, frowning. "You've got two companies heading into a meatgrinder with at least a battalion dug in *strongly*." He looked over the map and photo again. "And you've got two, count 'em, *two* crappy trails from the landing zone to the objective."

"That's only if they all go towards the real landing zone," Lanza said. "I can buzz and false insert at every other good and even remotely possible LZ in the area. They'll never hear or see enough to know which is the real landing. I might lose a couple but . . . really . . . they don't have to commit to a landing, just to buzz the spot. The artillery can prep—"

"Not much artillery," interrupted Harrington, the logistician. "If you're moving all of Qabaash's boys at once there'll be nothing left to airlift guns and shells into range. Only the multiple rocket launchers can range to the summit of the pass from where we can resupply by truck."

"Okay," Lanza conceded. "Have a little faith. With the MRLs, the Finches, aerially dropped guided bombs from the Nabakovs, and gunship support we can still put on a good show of prepping enough landing zones that they won't know where we're coming from. That means Qabaash will face at most—"

"A company," Qabaash finished. "And the day two companies of *Salah al Din* can't handle a company of *Ikhwan* irregulars will be a cold, happy and batless day in Hell." He sounded very pleased at the prospect of demonstrating this point in the near future.

Carrera held up his hand for silence. Immediately the others shut up.

"We'll do it. As Qabaash and Lanza say. Terry?"

"Here, boss," piped in Terry Johnson, for the nonce commanding the *Tercio de Cazadores*. His new rifle project was progressing under his assistant, another Volgan enticed away from the *Rodina*.

"I want you to start inserting teams all over the area within the next couple of days. In particular, get a platoon—a company if you think it needful and possible—into the area of the LZ . . . mmm, what should we call that LZ?"

"Let's call it 'Landing Zone Agadir,' Patricio," Qabaash

supplied. "It was a small but lovely fight back on Old Earth, long ago."

"Agadir, then. Dan?"

"Yes, Pat?"

"Work up the orders for review within two days."

Compared to most modern command posts, headquarters for the legion was really rather sedate. True, underlings scurried about. Maps were updated. Occasionally one might hear a voice or two raised in argument. For the most part, though, it was calm and quiet. And so it should have been. There was little reason for frenzy in a force that placed a premium on individual initiative at lower levels and which rarely tried to manage a battle in too exquisite a detail outside of artillery preparations.

(On the other hand, if one really *wanted* to see frenzy, one could always go down to a cohort command post.)

Instead, the CP for the legion was a place for the housing and support of the commander and the staff, a place for planning future operations, and a meeting place for those times when face to face orders to groups of men had to be given. Ordinarily, there really wasn't any reason for frenzy.

Instructing his driver to get a meal and some sleep, Carrera entered the main tent, ordering, "At ease," before anyone had a chance to disrupt work by calling, "Attention." Stopping by the operations and intelligence maps, he took in an overview—updated about three hours previously—of the current operation. There were no surprises, he noted, with satisfaction.

He then grabbed a sandwich from a tray thoughtfully left there by the HQ mess platoon, before retiring to his own, attached, tent to catch up on correspondence.

On the top of the pile of printed off sheets was a missive from Parilla.

> *Patricio:*
>
> *That you are willing to fund a major expansion of the reserve components helps us. I am awaiting the right time to make the announcement. Fernandez suggests forcing an "incident" with the Tauran Union troops here so that we can appeal to patriotism rather than simply looking like we're trying to buy votes. I like the idea in principle, but am concerned that forcing a small fight with the TU might turn into a large fight that we are not ready for. Especially are we not ready while you have eighty-five percent of the force—to include a hefty chunk of the training base returned to their parent tercios—over in Pashtia. Moreover, while you are over there, with your base areas surrounded by Tauran troops, you might be vulnerable. So I think I will not follow Fernandez's advice, at least for a while. Have you any ideas on how best to precede the announcement? One thought I had was not to make it at all, but to start major public works of a defensive nature, hiring fifty or sixty thousand of the unemployed, and making those defensive works plainly and obviously oriented against the Taurans. That might get us the patriotic response, coupled with self interest, and is also do something we ought to be doing anyway . . .*

"Note to self," Carrera muttered. "Have Sitnikov brief Parilla on plans for fortifications on the *Isla Real* and along both sides of the Rio Gatun. Also, check on progress in designing the expansion."

He tapped the side of his nose several times, thinking. "Hmmm . . . I hate to lose Kuralski but I think maybe I need to send him back to Volga for a bit."

> *. . . providing you and Fernandez are right— and, no, I don't disagree—about war with the Tauran Union and possibly the Zhong being inevitable.*
>
> *It is strange to think of us being on our own against the second- and third-ranked powers of this world. Always before we lived under the shadow, but also the covering umbrella, of the Federated States. We never had to worry about defense against anyone but them; and defense against them, as you helped prove almost twenty years ago, was impossible . . .*

"It was impossible then, Raul. Now? Now, if the entire force were home? I think the FSC would probably get sick of the bloodletting before they conquered Balboa again." *And what would I do in such a case? That's a no-brainer; my loyalty is to my legion.*

Carrera continued with the letter:

> *There are moments when I seriously doubt the wisdom of the course we have undertaken, moments when I doubt it is worth it for me to become president. But then I*

think of the legion, of what we could do for Balboa if we could spread the wealth around without it automatically gravitating to the pockets of the idle, corrupt and useless rich.

In any case, enough of an old man's idle prattle for now. Your time is valuable and, so the newscasts and the intelligence reports say, well spent. Give my warmest regards to the officers, centurions, warrants and men of the legion. I miss you all very much and look forward to your speedy and safe return home.

"Fine old man," said Carrera, putting the missive aside and picking up the next, from Fernandez.

Duque:
The only good news I have to report is that our friends above are due to receive a visitor that has to be most unwelcome. Apparently the UEPF, too, has an Inspector General and apparently like any IG, theirs is a pain in the ass.

Yes, this comes from our very special intelligence source. How long this source can last is anyone's guess, however. Sometimes I think that the best use of this asset is not in the detailed intelligence we receive, but in what it tells us about the mindset of the UE and the UEPF.

Patricio, they are not only more corrupt than we have imagined; they are more corrupt than we could imagine. For one thing, two slaves—and we didn't even know they kept slaves on their base on Atlantis Island—are going to be taken up to space shortly for the sexual amusement of their IG. The slaves are not necessarily expected to survive the experience. How do people like this get control of an entire world? How do we prevent them from gaining another?

"I'm working on it, Fern."

I think we are now in a position to begin to fulfill the other half of our contract with the Yamatans and move the classis *to the Nicobar Straits. There are NO indicators that the Xamari pirates are anything but cowed for the moment, and even for the foreseeable future.*

The rest of Fernandez's message was routine. Carrera finished reading it quickly and put it into the "save" pile. His AdC would see to it that the message joined several hundred others in a secure file with a self destruct mechanism integral to it.

The next report was from *Obras Zorilleras*—or OZ, though it had passed through Fernandez's office before being sent onward and bore his initials. It concerned several of the projects Carrera had been briefed on over a year ago.

Progress has been mixed, Duque. *The auxiliary propelled stealthy glider, which we are calling the "Condor," exists in prototype and has been tested using ground based radar. The reduction in signature is between two and three orders of magnitude. We are planning a test using the FSC's airborne warning radar. This, however, requires three things: that we know the flight schedule of the drug interdiction patrols they run off our coasts, that we manage to get one of our people aboard their AWR flights, and that we have the prototype in position . . .*

Carrera read a handscrawled note in Fernandez's writing on the margins of the page. "I'm working on it."

On the other hand, the submarine—the Megalodon—has been nothing but problems. We've had to redesign the thing twice, and scrap half a dozen proposals for the power plant. The acrylic casting apparatus from Anglia is still on order. Undersea gliding has proven to be somewhat problematic, once we did the rest of the math, and unless slightly aided by the propeller it makes more noise than simply using the propeller on its own. That said, in combination the two are quieter than either is alone.

Right now, it is a thin teardrop-shaped outer hull, a much thicker and cylindrical inner pressure hull, which will be powered either by molten carbonate or solid oxide fuel cell. These are both expensive but almost within the budget you gave us. (Can we have more money?)

*While we have dropped the idea of using
a facetted fairing for the outer, non-pressure,
hull, the better to reduce flow noise, we
have modified the principle by connected
the inner and outer hulls with conoidal
projections which will do much the same
thing. By this we mean that, once active
sonar has reached and passed the thin,
outer, streamlined hull, the conoidal connections will further scatter it and absorb
it. This is only effective for active sonar, of
course . . .*

"Yeah . . . right . . . "of *course*" . . . what the fuck
do *I* know about this shit?"

*. . . and active sonar is the least likely to be
used. Still, the inner and outer hulls needed
to be connected somehow and this way
gives us something out of the arrangement.*

*The test ballast tanks for the Megalodon
are prepared in prototype, since we were
able to obtain the necessary acrylic casting
machines (which are much smaller) and
other materials needed for them. This is a
new concept, and not one that everyone is
in favor of. Still, they have the potential to
be remarkably silent as compared to any
other system in existence.*

*Basically, they take advantage of the
very low boiling temperature of ammonia.
The ammonia is kept inside of flexible tubing made of fluorocarbon elastomer with*

a sputtered layer of aluminum (750 Angstroms) followed by silicon monoxide (500 Angstroms) with an aerogel insulation layer. We are working on a different system, one using carbon dioxide rather than ammonia. This has issues.

"Pity I never studied any of the hard sciences but chemistry. This is all Greek to me. Still, OZ has produced before. They probably will again."

Carrera skipped ahead to the line, *We believe we can have a working submarine within fifteen months, and produce two every three months thereafter. Greater funding would increase this.*

"Something to think about, anyway. But let's see some progress before we commit, shall we?"

We have a fixed prototype of the Self-Propelled Laser Aid Defense (SPLAD) and are working on motorizing it.

Work on the Self-Propelled, Anti-tank, Heavy Armor (SPATHA) has gone well. Design of the modification of the Volgan T-27 to a turretless antitank vehicle is complete and the Kirov factory has produced the first three prototype vehicles. We have been successful in boring out the tubes from 152mm guns to 165mm, as well as in reducing the length of the tubes. Mechanisms to handle the reduced recoil from the shorter, lower velocity tube are designed. Kirov has subcontracted for three full, reduced recoil 165mm guns to

mount in the prototypes' fighting compart-
ments. They have also arranged to have the
requisite machinery built and forwarded
to us. Test firing of the High Explosive
Plastic shell against standard tanks with
pigs strapped in place of the human crew
has shown catastrophic kills to the crew
can be achieved by the HEP shell. (FYI,
one test pig was impaled to its seat by
the coaxial machine gun being torn from
its mount and driven backwards. Most of
the others suffered broken necks along with
other injuries.) Kirov has further produced
a composite armor design which can be
mounted to the front of the SPATHA and
which is demonstrated to be good against
the best Tauran cannon for at least one
shot in any given area.

A spinoff of this is in the realm of fortifi-
cations. When we looked at the design of the
composite, and realized that the hexagonal
plates within it, if scaled up, would serve
equally well against aerially dropped deep
penetrating bombs . . .

"Well that's an interesting concept. Note to self:
Advise OZ and Sitnikov to get together, too."

Speaking of air, we have been approached
by an Anglian company that has a very
interesting design for a series of lighter-than-
air ships. We think you should consider it,
or at least consider the smallest version that

is intended for long term aerial surveillance. Their proposal is attached.

"Hmmm. Maybe."

Moreover, they have one mid-sized version built, capable of medium airlift or surveillance—if outfitted—that they are willing to provide, with flight crew, for testing in Pashtia. They say they will only charge for operational costs. The chief advantage to their system is that it is not actually lighter than air, but only almost as light as air. It is aerodynamically shaped, more or less like a pumpkin seed, and gets some lift from that. The shape is such that it does not need nearly so elaborate a ground setup to operate. Thus, it would be the first airship capable of tactical and strategic lift to undeveloped theaters of war.

"All right, then. Note to self: Have OZ set this up."

We have closed down the program on the terminally guided, reduced bore artillery shells, as Volga already has such a shell and is willing to sell. Their shell, which is 122mm with a sabot to fill the bore of a 180mm gun, seems adequate for the purpose you gave us.

Lastly, for purposes of this report, the Suvarov-class heavy cruiser has been reequipped with new 152mm, long range

*guns, the pebble bed modular reactor is
installed and has passed initial testing, and
the refit is other wise 90% plus, complete.
Crew have been assigned but are still in
billets at Puerto Lindo pending completion
of the refit.*

XXXX

Report ends.

XXXX

"Well, that's not bad. Let's see what Lourdes has
to say." For a moment Carrera felt an almost overwhelming surge of sheer horniness.

Most of Lourdes' letter was expressly designed
to increase that level of horniness. In self-defense,
Carrera skimmed over much of that. Then something
caught his eye.

*It was as expert a roping job as I have
ever seen, Patricio, and I grew up on a
cattle farm. Artemisia Jimenez culled your
Sergeant Major from the herd, lassoed him,
trussed him, and branded him hers with a
dexterity I can only admire. And all in less
than two weeks. The wedding is tentatively
set for the week after the current contract
in Pashtia is up and you, and the bulk of
the legions, have returned.*

*And, yes, my love, I know what you are
going to say, that he's more than twice her
age, that he's a simple soldier and she's a
sophisticated very near winner for Miss
Terra Nova. I've spoken to her, personally*

and privately, and when she says she's in love, and moreover in love for the first and only time in her life, I believe her. Please trust me in this.

Besides that this is good for John, I must tell you it is good for me, too, as he's stopped whining about joining you in Pashtia and settled down to doing good work, the kind of good work he is better at than anyone, right here.

"Wow. The beauty queen and the old centurion? Wow. Note to self: appropriate wedding gift. Money? Possibly. House? Maybe. All expense paid honeymoon for a bare minimum."

They've asked me to set up the wedding and be the chief bridesmaid and I think John would like you to be best man. Xavier is, of course, going to give away the bride. I've been making one of the nicer upstairs rooms available to them so that Xavier can pretend not to notice that she's acting like a cat in heat and Mac's acting like a teenager.

Speaking of which, beloved, I will be wearing a mattress on my back when I meet you at the airstrip, just as you said. But you had best make sure you're the first one off the plane.

"Gotta love that girl . . ."

Kibla Pass, Pashtia, 14/3/468 AC

Gotta love it when a plan comes together, Carrera thought as he watched the huge flight of helicopters pass overhead carrying Qabaash's brigade north to seize the summit of the pass. Qabaash had begged for the chance to go in first and, after a phone call from Sada, insisting that he needed the good press back in Sumer, Carrera had agreed. Besides, he'd seen the *Salah al Din* brigade in action both here in Pashtia and in Sumer. They were . . .

Well, Hell. They're good soldiers under a first rate commander. I don't have anybody any better for this than Qabaash. Oh, sure . . . maybe Jimenez, back in Balboa. But he is *back in Balboa while Qabaash* is *here.*

Atop the mountain range the enemy awaited; intel from both the FSA and the legion's own sources confirmed that. The air had been pounding their positions for two hours and would continue to do so for the just over an hour's flight to Qabaash's landing zone.

The pickup zone, here well below the mountains, was already hot enough to have to cut the helicopters' combat load. There would be no sling-loads underneath, either. Not that it would have helped all that much if the ambient temperature south of the mountain range had been less; the air above was thin enough that the choppers had to fly with reduced load anyway, despite the cold helping with the air density.

Strictly speaking, Qabaash's brigade was not going to be the first in. The Cazadors had claimed that honor as much as two weeks ago for some units, back when snows were still falling. Indeed, it was under the cover of the snows that they'd been able to come in by Cricket, chopper and even parachute, without being seen. It had been under the snow's cover that they'd been able to build hide positions undetectable to the enemy.

Still, the *Salah al Din* Brigade and their fire-eating commander were the first going in with the intention of finding a fight. They'd land and secure the landing zone—that narrow ledge lodged between cliffs—then fight their way overland to the summit of the pass. After that, it was intended that they spread out, north and south, to the military crests on either side. Even if they didn't take them, they'd attract enough attention in the south to make the climb up easier for Carrera's main column. In the north, if all else failed, they'd still be able to get a good jump off position for the rest to continue the attack.

Distantly, Carrera heard the roars of massed diesels, hundreds of them. That would be the mechanized tercio moving up to their assault positions. *Damned shame about what the treads are going to do to the highway. Still, that's why God made sappers. We'll lay a better road down after we pass than this place has ever seen before.*

Carrera waved—futilely, as the IM-71s lacked windows in the passenger compartment—at the departing Arabs from *Salah al Din.* "Good luck, boys, and good hunting."

As the last navigation light from the helicopters was killed by pilots interested in survival, Carrera got in his vehicle and instructed his driver to take him to headquarters.

It was an odd thing, really, the drive back. They passed column after column of infantry moving up on foot. That wasn't the odd thing; that was simply part of the scheme of maneuver. No, what was odd was that the columns all stopped to cheer him as they passed each other. He waved back, of course, and held out his hand to shake whatever hands he could, but uncertainly and even with a touch of embarrassment.

Why should they cheer me? The bloody Sumeris did, too. Makes no sense. I am nobody but a nasty bastard out for revenge and using them to get it.

The driver provided half the answer. "The boys sure seem ready for another fight, sir."

The other half, or perhaps it was more than half, is that soldiers love a commander who leads them to victory. It has ever been thus, and that, at *least* that, Carrera had done. He felt his mind and spirit click into full battle mode.

They'd go in underloaded and would need another piece of land considerably larger and flatter than their chosen landing zone for their supplies.

There was a platoon of Cazadors, minus one squad keeping eyes on the objective, ringing that landing zone. Qabaash, wearing his night vision goggles, was the first to spot their infrared strobe. He flipped the goggles up, waited a moment for his eyes to become accustomed to the gloom, then looked generally in the same place, scanning for any visible indicator of enemy fire.

No flashes. Qabaash breathed a sigh of relief. *Good, it was only the strobes and not machine guns.*

He tapped the pilot and pointed. The pilot gave one thumb up where Qabaash could see it. What did he care if the signal meant something rather different in Sumer than in Balboa?

Qabaash felt the helicopter start to heel over, then begin its spiraling descent. The other three birds in the lift followed. Qabaash keyed the radio and spoke the signal to the waiting Cazadors. Suddenly, lights began flashing on all over the drop zone, marking safe spots for individual helicopters to land.

The landing zone was barely big enough for four helicopters at a time. This lift of four carried Qabaash, a small portion of his command post, and part of one infantry company. The next lift in would bring in the remainder of that company.

As soon as the chopper touched down, the clam-shell door in the rear opened to disgorge the troops. Qabaash, sitting at the front of the passenger compartment was the last out. He threw himself to the ground along with his men while waiting for the choppers to lift off. It was easy enough to walk into a spinning tail rotor in the daytime. At night it was hard not to.

With a rush of air and a roar of engines the IM-71s lifted off.

Under two minutes until the next comes in.

Qabaash looked around with his goggles over his face. He couldn't hear a bloody thing for all the air-craft buzzing around. There wasn't a *lot* of light but what there *was* the goggles magnified more than ten thousand times. Though the picture was grainy, it was still clear enough to see squads of his men racing to the assembly area nearest the worse of the two trails out from the LZ. It would be a special beneficence of Allah if no one shot anyone on the same side.

"Light of the world, Maker of the Universes, let it be so," Qabaash whispered.

The CP was supposed to set up under a rock

overhang to the west, between the trails. Grabbing the two radiomen who had accompanied him, Qabaash headed that way. Once there, he met his forward air controller and his operations officer, his fire support officer and his "intelligence puke." They had been scattered among the other three birds. By the time the command group had assembled, the second flight of helicopters was just touching down. For a few minutes vocal communication was impossible without shouting.

Twenty-four lifts of four IM-71s each would be just enough to bring in the combat, combat support, and command and control elements of three Sumeri battalions. After that, the heavier lift IM-62s, supplemented by airdrops, would bring in the rest of the men and the truly weighty stuff, along with the supplies required for several days' combat and several weeks' sustenance.

But I'm not waiting for anything, Qabaash thought. *"Boot, don't spatter," as that Old Earth general is reputed to have said. One company at the pass in one hour will be better than three battalions in three hours. And moreover, we can have two companies at the pass in an hour, since Carrera—Allah bless his infidel heart—approved landing one company right in the pass once we had their attention firmly fixed on us attacking from the east.*

Ah, Patricio, how does one not admire a commander with the balls for that? How does one not love the man who saved his country? Infidel or not, we shall not fail you.

With a rare smile, Qabaash headed himself and his men to the flashes and the sounds of aerial bombs exploding in and around the pass.

❖   ❖   ❖

The shout rang through caves and along little rock gullies and draws, "To arms! To arms! The crusaders come!"

Allah is there no end to these infidels? Noorzad mentally muttered.

After the losses of the previous year, and after escaping with only a small cadre, Noorzad's group had been built up again into something the size of a large company or small battalion. There had not been enough time to train them. Especially had there not been enough time to train junior leaders. And as for the theory of guerilla warfare? No, the men were very nearly clueless except for Noorzad and his closest dozen followers. It hadn't helped matters any that of the nearly two hundred and fifty new men given unto his care back at the base, just over half were oil Arabs from the Yithrab peninsula.

Spoiled rotten little huddlers at apron strings, was Noorzad's learned judgment.

Nonetheless, semi-trained or not, spoiled and pampered children or not, Noorzad's crew were still among the best available to Mustafa. Thus, they'd been dispatched to the Kibla Pass to reinforce the fifteen hundred or so mujahadin already there. They'd come with only their small arms, some RGLs and a few light mortars purchased from Zhong Guo.

Little enough to work with. And Nur al Deen expects us to fight to the death for this? With these men and these arms? Mustafa understands better. No . . . I will do what any smart guerilla does. I will buy a little time, spill a little blood, make the enemy spend money. And then I will leave, splitting up my men

*into smaller groups to escape through the mountains
as best they may and rally in Kashmir. And if they
have to leave heavier weapons—mortars, machine guns
and RGLs—behind? Well, so what?*

The call to arms rang through caves and along little
rock gullies and draws. It was picked up and repeated
from man to man, bringing such of the mujahadin who
were not already manning the trenches and the bunkers
out of their early spring shelters and into the open.

This suited the Turbo-Finch pilots just fine as they
swooped down from the skies to lace the rocks with
machine gun and rocket fire and lay napalm and
white phosphorus along any obvious or even likely
defensive positions. There was return fire, enough to
bring down one Finch and send another staggering
home with smoke pouring out from under the wing.

Noorzad grunted in satisfaction at that. *Cost them
some time. Cost them some blood. Cost them some
money. And when it comes time to run I'll leave the
Arabs behind to cover the withdrawal of the rest.
And good riddance.*

Well-trained troops initiate an ambush with their
greatest casualty producing weapon.

Idiots do so by shouting *"Allahu Akbar!"*

Up near the point, Qabaash heard the shout, as
did the squad ahead of him, and flopped behind a
boulder moments before the rocks began to ring and
the air to crack with the sound of incoming bullets.
He put one arm on his fire support officer's shoulder,
squeezed once and said, "Mortars. On those idiots
ahead. No more than thirty rounds with two white
phosphorus to mark the end. Now."

They shame me by being from the same culture,
Qabaash thought. *They humiliate me that we share a
religion. Well, we'll soon fix that.*

By this time most of the *Salah al Din* was landed
and the 120mm mortars, at least, were set up and
ready to fire. Ammunition was still, and would be
for some hours, rather limited. No matter; Qabaash
just wanted to stun them a little. For the rest . . .

"And pass the word: Fix bayonets."

Muamar al Rashid ibn Rashid had heard the shout
and, like his comrades, popped his head over the lip
of the trench to his front and let off a burst. It was
a thirty-round burst and of that thirty rounds two
went in the general direction of the enemy and the
rest went well off into space. No matter. Muamar's
job was to be there and to pull the trigger. Whether
anything hit or not was the will of Allah.

And it certainly is exciting, thought the young
Yithrabi. *Just like I imagined. Mother and Father will
be so proud. I wonder what that sound—*

Kaboom. Boomoomoom. Kaboom.

Qabaash carefully counted the number of mortar
rounds that came in. After reaching "Twenty-seven," he
stood in plain sight of all his men. Unusually enough
for an Arab leader, he carried a rifle, though in his
case he'd selected a Draco sniper rifle. Affixed to the
end of that rifle was a bayonet.

A couple of bullets sang by. *If they weren't aimed,
I'd be worried.*

"Sons of Sumer!" He cried out loudly enough for
even the tail of the column to hear. He lifted his rifle

one-handed above his head for all to see. "Grandsons of the great Sargon! For the honor of our brigade! For the glory of our country! To the exaltation of our God!" Qabaash's eye caught the two white bursts of white phosphorus that he'd asked for. "Chaaarrrggge!"

None of the broadcasts on al Iskandaria News Network had seen fit to mention what it was like to receive fire. Some of the old timers could have told Muamar, but they were few and the new recruits many. That lesson had had to be skipped.

The shells had come in, exploding with a fearful crash and—far, far worse—making Muamar's innards ripple in a way that was as near to being raped as the boy could imagine. He heard a scream and turned to see a friend clutch at his face with blood pouring out through his fingers. Instantly Muamar felt the need to throw up. Then he heard a shout coming from the enemy side. When he looked he saw a tight knot of men coming toward him led by a laughing and screaming *jinn* in battle dress and carrying a long rifle. The Yithrabi shat himself and collapsed down to the bottom of his trench.

There is a difference between what is called "marching fire" and the "spray and pray" technique used by almost all Salafist forces. The Salafis pointed and shot, expecting that Allah would grace their piety by providing hits they had not really earned by dint of serious training. The marching fire used by the point company of the *Salah al Din* was also merely pointed, though it was *well* pointed. But Qabaash's crew knew they wouldn't get any hits or, at least, that they were most unlikely to. Instead, marching fire put a lot of bullets in the right general area to frighten the enemy down into his holes so that one could advance quickly and more-or-less safely.

As a practical matter, "spray and pray" fails because it has no end game. "Marching fire's" end game is to close with the bayonet, the rifle butt and the hand grenade. One works to advance the tactical objective; the other does not.

Qabaash had quickly sprinted ahead of the lead squad, then slowed to a jog. Though he carried a sniper rifle—a good commander is entitled to his little eccentricities—he held it low, rather than to his shoulder, and pumped out a single round every fourth step. The first squad took their cue from their brigade commander—that, and the way they had been trained to execute marching fire in the past—and likewise sprinted to catch up to him, then slowed to a jog. In their case, they fired short bursts rather than single rounds and fired them every other step, using the interval to bring their rifles back more or less on target. The remaining two squads of the lead platoon did likewise until there was a fairly thick—thick in battle terms—line of men screaming and cursing and putting out roughly ten thousand rounds a minute into an area not more than one hundred meters by two and with ricochets off the ground thrown in to increase the effect.

A few of the people in the trench tried to surrender. The Sumeris weren't really interested. By the conduct of the great Salafi conspiracy across Terra Nova and especially within Sumer, these men had put themselves beyond the pale. By joining that conspiracy they had assumed personal responsibility for all the crimes committed in its name.

The short version of which is that most of those who probably wanted to surrender were simply shot down. The Sumeri troops had learned the laws of war from the *Legion*.

Qabaash dropped back as his troops swept across and over the trench. He looked behind him to see the remainder of the lead company racing up. Hearing a piteous, mewling sound he looked down and saw one of the Salafis cowering and shivering in the trench. A strong odor of human shit arose from the Salafi. Obviously he had no fight left in him. Just as obviously he had not made manifest his desire to surrender. As such . . .

"God is great," whispered Qabaash as he placed the muzzle of his Draco against the back of Muamar's head and pulled the trigger.

The commander of the lead company, *Naquib* al Husseini, trotted up to stand beside Qabaash. Al Husseini looked down at the exploded skull of the Salafi in the trench and grimaced, then shrugged.

"*Amid,* you should not do that. Your job is not to lead charges but to direct them," the *naquib* chided.

"Time and place for everything," Qabaash answered, adding his own shrug. "I don't think there will be much more resistance. Push your men *hard* for the pass, Husseini."

"*Aywa, Amid.*" Yes, Brigadier.

In the west the sun was setting on a day of disaster. It was said that the infidel had already pushed fifty kilometers to the north from his starting line in southern Pashtia. The summit was lost, of course. Noorzad had seen that happen himself, escaping with about half his followers—and almost none of them the dirty Yithrabi city boys he so generally despised.

The enemy had used none of their "EE-EM-PEE" bombs on his communications. No matter; by this time Noorzad's cadre knew to keep spare phones and radios in metal boxes called "Faraday cages" to protect them from the effects of the bombs. The enemy had had an equally dirty trick, though. Somehow they'd managed to dial *every* telephone number for every cell and satellite phone the mujahadin had set to detonate explosive devices along the highway. They'd done something similar with wide-spectrum radio. Between these, the infidel had detonated virtually every explosive device. Noorzad suspected they'd flown a plane up the road at high altitude to do this.

Bastards. Sons of whores. Is there no end to their iniquity?

There were about one thousand mujahadin caught between the enemy's point of advance in the south and the summit he had already seized. If they were smart they'd give up the defense of the pass as a bad job and simply fade into the surrounding mountains. Some would be that smart, Noorzad suspected. Others would not. Such was life. Of those who tried to escape, some would fall to the sniper teams the infidel scattered about so liberally. Others would not. That, too, was life.

The cave in which Noorzad and the remaining six-score of his followers sheltered was dark and dank and, overall, miserable. It did have some virtues, though. While expanded inside, it was a naturally occurring cave with only a crawlspace for an entrance. Thus, there never had been the usual crowd of trucks and workers outside it to tell the spying eyes overhead that it was there. The best proof that the enemy didn't know about it was that they were all still alive. Almost as important, the cave contained food. This, the men would need for their upcoming trek down the mountains and back to the Base. The cave also had money and that, too, would be needed.

"And so, what now, Noorzad?" asked Malakzay.

"And now we split up and return to the Base," answered the chieftain. "There we rebuild and then we do it all again . . . and again . . . and again until the last of our lands are freed of the invader's polluting footsteps. They will grow sick of it before we do because, after all, we have no place else to go and they *do*."

25/3/468 AC, The Base, Kashmir

"Try to understand, Mustafa, there was no place Abdulahi could run to and they had his chief son and heir," said Nur al Deen. "He *had* to give in to them. And, at least, he had the good grace to send us a message detailing all he has been forced into and what the enemy has not thought to force him into. He also promises to return to the fold as soon as possible."

"Did he tell them about our little project for the enemy fleet?" asked Mustafa.

"He insists he has not, but has begged us to delay our strike until he can identify the ships his people—especially his son—are being held on and to avoid those ships or ship if at all possible."

"Easy enough to promise," Mustafa sneered. "When the time comes we will act as we must."

The *Ikhwan* chief turned his attention to Abdul Aziz. "How goes that program?"

"Everything is ready and the ship sails for the Xamar Coast even as we speak, O Prince. But . . ."

"Yes?"

"The infidels' foul work off Xamar is basically done; Abdulahi's message tells us as much. Will they stay there? I think not. I think they must head for the Nicobar Straits and very soon."

Mustafa stroked his own beard in contemplation for some moments. "Do you think they will leave before we can strike?"

"Not before we *can*, Mustafa, but perhaps before we should. That accursed aircraft carrier will be more vulnerable in or near the Straits than it would be off Xamar, being confined at the one but with the entire Sea of Sind to run through at the other."

More beard stroking ensued, followed by extensive moustache tugging, and even some hair twirling.

"You are risking losing the assets we gained along the Nicobar Straits," Mustafa objected, still tugging at his beard.

Abdul Aziz's head rocked from side to side. "We are also risking them if we take this one shot at the infidel fleet and miss."

"He speaks truth, Mustafa," said Nur al Deen. He'd come around. "We will only have the one chance."

"Let it be so, then," agreed the Prince of the *Ikhwan*. "I shall inform Parameswara and al Naquib of what we need."

INTERLUDE

7/6/47 AC (Old Earth year 2106), Terra Nova, Balboa Colony

"Tanks? Are you sure, Pedro? Tanks?"

"*Jefe,*" Pedro answered, half offended, "you know something big as a house that still moves and has a gun even bigger 'roun' than my dick; you let me know."

"Shit. Tanks." Belisario paused, then said, "Sorry, Pedro. It isn't that I didn't believe you. It's that I didn't *want* to believe you. Shit. How the hell do we fight tanks?"

Pedro shrugged and answered, "We no fight, *jefe*. We stay the fuck away. They only three of them, anyway. Or maybe four; Pedro not sure."

Belisario shook his head. "Easy to say, Pedro. It's not that easy to do. I don't know much about tanks but I do know that they can go a lot of places you wouldn't expect. They can also move faster in anything but the thickest jungle than we can on horseback. And, then, where the tanks really *can't* go the helicopters we both saw *can*."

"They got airplanes, too, *jefe*."

21/7/47 AC, Terra Nova, Balboa Colony

Belisario never heard them coming. He had no *clue* as to how they found his band through the thick jungle canopy overhead. One second he was riding his horse, half asleep and letting the animal pick its way along the jungle trail. The next, the world seemed engulfed in explosions as salvo after salvo of rockets came in on his narrow little column.

As quickly as the attack had come it passed, leaving only the screams of the wounded men and horses.

"How the fuck do I fight that?" Belisario cursed aloud.

CHAPTER FOURTEEN

Your opponent can't talk when he has
your fist in his mouth.
—President William Jefferson Clinton

UEPF Spirit of Peace, 35/3/468 AC

Transfer between ships was always a pain for someone.
Given the nature of the cargo, it was critically important
that whoever it was a pain for, it not present the slightest
difficulty or discomfort for the hereditary marchioness
of Amnesty, Lucretia Arbeit. One of the crew of the
shuttle already had a bright red welt rising on her face
from the Marchioness's leather riding crop. Arbeit was
an absolute stickler for protocol and the unfortunate
Class IV had regrettably failed to go belly down in full
proskynesis as Arbeit passed through the shuttle's portal.

There were two ways to make transfers when two
spinning ships were involved. One was very difficult,
involving lining the ships up stern to stern, killing
rotation in both, docking and then recommencing
spin, with one spinning opposite to its usual direction.

That was almost never done. Instead, shuttles were
used, the receiving ship taking control of the shuttle

and matching its spin to that of the ship. This was the method used to bring Arbeit aboard the *Spirit of Peace*.

The hangar deck could only accommodate a few dozen in the reception party. They, excepting only High Admiral Robinson, executed full proskynesis as the Inspector General emerged from the shuttle. Proskynesis was for lowers; among Class Ones a broad equality reigned. He and the imperious marchioness settled for shaking hands as the crew ungracefully arose from their supine positions of homage.

"Lucretia, how truly delightful to see you once again," Robinson said with no obvious insincerity. Then again, Old Earth's elites learned to mask their feelings quite young.

"Martin, dear boy, you cannot imagine what a simply ghastly trip this has been and how pleased I am to see you at the end of it."

Robinson smiled warmly. "May I present my staff and crew?"

"Please."

Turning, Robinson introduced Wallenstein first. She bowed, saying, "At your service, madam." Then, as she lifted her head, she also licked her lips slightly just in case the IG had any doubts as to how completely at her service Wallenstein intended to be.

"Charmed, Captain," Arbeit answered with a nod and a subtle swipe of her tongue across her own lower lip.

"My ship's sociologist, Lieutenant Commander Kahn."

Kahn the wife practically quivered in anticipation of the pleasurable beatings she expected the IG to administer. "I'm sooo thrilled to meet you, Admiral," she gushed.

"My operations officer . . ."

✧   ✧   ✧

Later Robinson said, "What I don't understand is why you are *here*, Lucretia. The IG practically never visits the fleet here. It's been over a century."

"Yes, I know, Martin," Arbeit agreed in the intimacy of the guest VIP suite. "The Consensus sent me. They've heard things are going badly here. Things are not going so well at home, either. We might need you to bring the fleet back."

"The reverted areas?" Robinson asked.

"Yes . . . but not the way you might expect, Martin. There was a raid on Buenas Aires from some barbarians in the Pampas reversion. The city was taken and sacked. For three days it was sacked."

"My Annan!" Robinson exclaimed. "Buenas Aires? That's—"

"Inconceivable?" Arbeit supplied. "Impossible? Nonetheless, our last outpost in southern South America is gone. We've had to pull out of everything south of Montevideo."

"But . . . well . . . Lucretia you can't take any of the fleet away. You just *can't*. Let me explain."

Robinson proceeded to lay out the situation on Terra Nova and the long-term threat it presented to the ruling caste on Old Earth.

"I had no idea things here were so dangerous for us," Arbeit said.

"Some of my staff think I'm being optimistic in believing we even have a chance to eliminate the Terra Novan threat, long term," the high admiral answered glumly.

"Be that as it may, I may still have to take some of the fleet back home with me. What good does it do to eliminate a threat here and lose our home and position there? And even if I decide I can't do that,

I'm going to need some excellent reasons for not doing so when I report to the Consensus."

"I can understand that," Robinson agreed. "I'll even escort you down below, myself, so you can see."

"Will you escort me through my little games, too, Martin?" Arbeit asked with a smile.

"Sorry, Lucretia, but they're not to my taste. Wallenstein will take care of that."

"Your lovely ship's captain? What is she, a Class Two? She looks like fun."

"Oh, she's great fun for a lower," Robinson agreed. "Just don't damage her. I need her too much for that."

"Don't worry, Martin," Arbeit assured. "I *never* damage a playmate over Class Four. Now if you have some slaves you don't need . . ."

"Already taken care of, Lucretia. Though they haven't yet been told they're lost souls."

"Not a problem, Martin. I *love* explaining to lowers that their future has become grim."

BdL *Dos Lindas*, Sea of Sind, 1/4/468 AC

Xamar was lost to view behind them. The weather above and around the ship was foul, winds howling through the wires of the ship's island and white-capped waves pounding the hull. Only a few crew stood watch above and those took care always to have a hand grasped to something, lest a freak wave wash them over the side. The aircraft were struck below. Rather, they were struck below and more or less compressed to one end of the hangar deck; the space thus freed being filled with several hundred of the crew, all that could be spared from necessary duties.

The forward elevator was lowered almost flush to provide a speaking platform. On it, where they could be seen by that portion of the crew assembled, stood Kurita, Fosa, and a few of the staff, each man, like the assembled crew, unconsciously swaying with the roll of the ship. There was a large wooden box to one side, marked as being an engine for one of the Crickets. There was nothing unusual in there being a major assembly for one of the aircraft sitting on the elevator that joined the flight and the hangar decks.

The ship's senior centurion, Sergeant Major Ramirez (for—except for the *position* of captain and honorary rank of commodore—the legion's classis maintained the same rank structure as the ground and air components), stood in front of the Cricket engine crate. Above the crate and the deck, above the captain, commodore, sergeant major and staff, an aramid fiber tarp stretched taut over the elevator to keep out the wind and keep off the rain. Rain still dripped in places, causing the men standing on the elevator to adjust their positions to keep dry. Ramirez barely kept a smile off his face, for he was the only one on the ship besides the mail clerk who was in on Kurita's little scheme.

For his part, Fosa's own face bore something of a clueless expression. Kurita had asked for permission to address the crew and, while the captain had had no objections, he also had no idea of why the Yamatan would wish to. Congratulations from the Zaibatsu that had hired them?

Why bother? We've got what we need with the expansion of the contract to the Nicobar Straits. Decidedly odd.

At a nod from Kurita, Ramirez walked from in front

of the crate to the edge of the elevator. He called the crew to attention, then turned and reported to the commodore, "Sir, ship's company present or accounted for."

Kurita returned the salute. Ramirez dropped his own and walked back to his post by the crate. Stepping forward, Kurita began to speak, his left hand resting lightly on the *tsuka* of the sword thrust through the sash about his waist.

"Somewhere in Uhuru," Kurita began, "a child sleeps tonight with a full belly. A year ago the odds were good that that child went to bed hungry to the point of pain and with no guarantee of awakening the next morning. That belly is tonight full—the child can be sure of waking up tomorrow—for one reason; that commerce again flows uninterrupted. Commerce flows to and from Uhuru for one reason; that you have destroyed those who would prey upon it, interrupt it and destroy it.

"This day we sail to another theater, to continue the good work we have left completed behind us. For know this, my comrades of the *classis*; there are children in Sind who will go hungry tonight for the inability of their parents to send the product of their hands overseas to purchase food. There are children who will go hungry because the oil that powers the farm machinery that helps grow their food is also cut off or bought too dear.

"*You* have done this, my friends. You will do this. Both things, what you have done and what you will do, you have done under the command of Roderigo Fosa."

Kurita went silent for a moment as Ramirez quietly lifted the top from the engine crate and removed from inside a long, silk-wrapped package. This he handed to Kurita.

Taking the package firmly in the center with his right hand, Kurita used his left to remove the wrapping. Silk cord and silken wrap fell away to reveal a sword, its scabbard gracefully curving from the tip to where it met the handguard, or *tsuba*. A low gasp came from Fosa, the staff and the crew, minus Ramirez and the mail clerk, both of whom smirked broadly.

"*Capitán* Fosa, front and center," Kurita ordered.

Gulping, Fosa moved to stand in front of the Yamatan. Kurita drew the sword. Its gleaming surface shone in the lights of the hangar deck, drawing Fosa's eyes down. He saw inscribed in miniature upon the blade a gold-filled eagle, a tiger, and a shark. Guessing what was to come, Fosa's eyes began to mist.

"Your organization grants broad rights to its units to establish their own traditions. Captain-San. You—though I think you did not realize it at the time—established one such when you granted me permission to wear my family sword here aboard your ship."

"This sword is newly made. Well, all traditions must begin somewhere. New or not, it was made by a master smith, working in the old ways. That is, he worked in the old ways except to memorialize upon the blade the forces you have commanded in the service of the commerce that binds man and feeds his children. Thus you see the eagle, for the air wing of this vessel, the tiger, for the Cazadores who dominate the land, and the shark for the ship and fleet."

Kurita expertly returned the point of the sword to its scabbard and deftly slammed it home. Taking Fosa's left hand with his own, he turned it palm up and placed the new katana into it. Fosa's hand closed automatically.

Leaning forward, Kurita whispered, "The sword is the soul of the samurai. Draw your new sword, Captain Fosa."

Stepping back, Kurita drew his own and raised it high overhead, his left arm likewise rising. Fosa, still in shock, mimicked the action.

"Banzai!" the Yamatan shouted, his cry ringing through the hangar deck.

Behind him, Ramirez also shouted, "Banzai!" throwing his own hands up.

"Banzai!" Kurita again shouted, this time extracting a weak, "Banzai," from the crew.

"Banzai!"

A little louder, the crew answered, "Banzai."

"Banzai!"

Still louder, "Banzai!"

Ramirez piped in, in his sergeant major's bellow, "Banzai, motherfuckers!"

"Banzai!"

"BANZAI!"

"BANZAI!"

Thus did the *classis* and Tercio Don John acquire a new tradition. *Banzai, motherfuckers*.

University of Balboa, *Ciudad* Balboa, 15/4/468 AC

The plaza rang with shouts. *"Viva Parilla! Viva la Republica! Viva los Legiones!"*

Part of the crowd, Jorge and Marqueli joined in the shouts. It was, after all, their legion, too, just as Parilla was their candidate.

There'd been some question about whether they'd attend the rally. The streets weren't precisely safe for the politically involved of late. Of course the incumbent government condemned the violence, even while President Rocaberti plotted it with his political cronies and the Gaul general, Janier, even while they drummed up radical students (not to say that Parilla wasn't himself radical, after a fashion), and hired thugs with Tauran Union money.

It was to be noted, though it almost never was by Terra Nova's Kosmo press, that the government, the Tauran Union, and the World League only condemned the violence that occurred when the reservists in the legions were out in enough force to pound silly the students, the thugs, and the dregs hired by Rocaberti and Janier. When the thugs had the numbers—and they needed a lot of numbers to outnumber trained men, even reservists—there was nary a word.

This rally the dregs weren't supposed to have the numbers, what with two entire reserve infantry maniples—four hundred men, almost unarmed, but mean and very, very willing—standing by, mixed in with the crowd. Still things sometimes go wrong, intelligence fails, threats arise suddenly and . . .

"Oh, crap, Jorge; it's starting."

From where the couple stood, on some broad steps leading down from street level to the flat, Marqueli saw a crowd of not too well organized, rather scruffy looking types (though there were also a couple of hundred better dressed males of college age and demeanor) entering the plaza from two sides.

Cruz had the nearly fifty men of his reserve platoon around him, none of them uniformed except for the uniformly grim looks on their faces. Half the men had wives with them, as did Cruz. All of them had small clubs, truncheons, concealed under their working shirts and guayaberas.

"Second Platoon, Third Maniple! To me!" shouted Cruz. Instantly the men shuffled the women to form a cluster behind Cruz and formed themselves in a thick line between the women and the swarming thugs and students. Cruz pushed Cara to join the rest of the women.

"Stay with them, *miel*," he said. "They won't get through us."

Parilla's followers at the edge where the thugs swarmed went under more or less quickly, though the *legionistas* took a few, or rather more than a few, down with them as they fell to the ground, bloodied and broken.

Cruz's eyes swept over the crowd, following the progress of the thugs and opposition students. Some of his men turned to look at him. *What do we do, Centurion?* In answer he just spat at the ground and removed a small club from under his shirt, holding the club up to advise his men to do the same.

The mass of the people at the rally, caught by surprise, ran away from the swarm. Like water they parted and passed around the solid seeming mass of reserve legionaries. Some drew their own clubs, brass knuckles and a couple of knives and fell in with Cruz's men. Some fell in with the double line brandishing only their fists and the sneers on their faces. Still others, from well behind the skirmish line, ran over to join. In moments Cruz found himself commanding the equivalent of a full maniple, over two hundred men.

"I'm Centurion Ricardo Cruz," he shouted to be

heard over the panicked sounds of the fighting and the crowd. "Hold your position until I give the word."

He was pleased to see the newcomers turn and nod. Most of them were also soldiers, he suspected. He took a moment to look behind him. Cara nodded. *I trust you to defend me, my husband.*

"There are some soldiers forming a line, Jorge," Marqueli said.

"Lead me to them," he answered with grim determination.

"Don't be ridiculous—"

"Woman, obey your husband. *Lead* me to them. For this I don't need to see. I just need to be able to hit."

Marqueli started to object, then stopped herself with her mouth still open. *He's still a man, still a legionary, eyes and legs or not. I can't take that away from him.*

With a deep sigh she took his arm and said, "This way. You fool."

"Warrant Officer Mendoza reporting for duty," Jorge said to Cruz as Marqueli stepped back out of the way.

"Cruz. Centurion. But . . ."

"I can still fight," Mendoza answered, his chin lifting proudly, before Cruz could finish the objections.

"All right," Cruz agreed. He'd rather have a blind legionary with him than any other dozen sighted men. "Stand by me. And Miss . . ."

"I'm his wife," Marqueli answered.

"If you would stand with mine and the other women then, Mrs. Mendoza."

Reluctantly, fearfully, Marqueli turned away even as Cruz turned his attention back to the thronging political thugs. Her head kept twisting back to look at Jorge even as her unsteady feet carried her to where the other women waited.

There really wasn't a set of commands to govern this situation, so Cruz made it up as he went. "Look at me, you assholes!" he shouted, pointing at Mendoza once he had the men's attention. "This man is one of ours. Blind, and not afraid to fight. Blind, and still able to see that it's better to fight than to run. Now . . . maniple . . . *attención*. Dress right . . . DRESS. Prepare to engage in melee . . . move."

The stiffening of the skirmish line to attention likewise caused the mixed group of students and hired street rumblers to stiffen and stop for a moment. Cruz took advantage of their loss of momentum by ordering, "Charrrge!"

Instantly his little command lunged forward, leaving Mendoza behind. Not to worry, though, as within seconds the sound erupted of breaking bones and teeth, ripping flesh, and the screams of the beaten. Mendoza, with his keen hearing, followed that. He could have followed it easily enough with normal hearing.

He heard someone very close shout, "Death to the fascists!"

That's identification enough. Jorge's fist lanced out precisely at the origin of the sound, catching a student in the face and sending him to the concrete of the plaza. Jorge's keen ears picked up the sound of his foe landing. He grunted with satisfaction and advanced . . . right into the flailing fist of another hireling. Mendoza blinked, was struck and then dropped like a sack. He never heard Marqueli's scream.

❖   ❖   ❖

Cruz had to admit it; he was having the time of his life. Why, there were no end of targets, no end to the opportunity to work off his frustrations. He was squatting over one victim, a student he thought, alternately throwing lefts and rights—his club was lost somewhere behind him—at the young man's rapidly disintegrating face—and laughing maniacally the whole time.

"Motherfucker!" *Wham.* "Piece of privileged shit!" *Kapow.* "Pampered momma's boy!" *Crunch.*

Teary-eyed, Marqueli knelt with her husband's head on her lap, cradling his head and sobbing his name repeatedly. Frantically, one hand tried to wipe away the blood that poured from a gash on his head. She nearly burst from inside with relief when she saw his eyes flutter open.

It took him a few moments for his head to clear. When it had he looked up directly into her face.

"I thought you were beautiful when I first saw you singing in the choir in church back home," he said, groggily. "You've improved."

The Tauran Kosmos were out on the streets of Balboa in force and with all their normal self-righteousness intact. Was there a street brawl in the course of the campaign? (And there were many.) Rest assured, the progressive, TU-supported incumbent regime partisans were the innocent bystanders in every case. Such, at least, was what was reported in the cosmopolitan progressive press. Moreover, no less a personage than the former president of the Federated States of

Columbia, Johnny Prince Wozniak, was on hand to give his stamp of accuracy and approval to every claim of the press that tended to put Parilla's followers in a bad light or elevate the standing of the incumbent faction. Wozniak had never met a corrupt politician, dictator, or terrorist faction from the undeveloped parts of Terra Nova that he hadn't instantly loved.

No one on the planet really understood Wozniak's thought processes. Many, indeed, denied he was even capable of thinking. Whatever the case, incapable of higher thought or not, he was all too capable of speaking. Which he did. At every possible opportunity. Moreover, he was terribly bitter that he'd been rejected by the people of the FSC after a mere one term. If he could support cosmopolitan progressivism, support terrorism, support totalitarianism and kleptocracy, while at the same time undermining the long term interests of the Federated States, so much the better.

A *very* embittered man, was our Johnny Prince Wozniak.

"I loathe that man," commented Parilla, at seeing one of Wozniak's more inane pronouncements carried on the airwaves.

"He gave us back the Transitway," Ruiz objected.

"Yes, he did," Parilla agreed, "And thereby deprived us of the pride we would have had if we had fought to get it. And thereby led directly to the dictatorship of Piña. Which thereby led to the invasion. Which led to the destruction of the only force in the country with the prestige to, at least potentially, fight the corruption of the Rocabertis and their ilk.

"Ah, never mind," Parilla continued. "There's nothing

to be done about the do-gooding weasel, except to note that the harm he does all over the planet is in exact but inverse proportion to the good he claims he's doing."

Ruiz shrugged. "I think Patricio loathes the man even more than you do."

"It's possible. When our comrade, Carrera, hates someone he doesn't do it halfway. Never mind; no one is persuaded by Wozniak except those convinced in advance."

"That's really not true, Raul. In this country, the man enjoys considerable status. Some people really are being converted by him."

"Enough to matter to the election?" Parilla asked. "Enough to overcome the good will Patricio is buying us through public works and expanding the force?"

"Part way, at least."

"*Chingada.*"

"Fernandez isn't worried at all, you know."

"I know, and I don't understand it," Parilla answered.

"He says our models are all wrong, that our analysts are contaminated by patterns of voting in the Federated States and Tauran Union. He says that people there will vote to preserve the welfare states they have. He insists that people here will not vote to create a welfare state where we don't have one. He says that they're not weak and spoiled like the Taurans and the Columbians."

"Is he right?"

"God, Raul, I don't know. I *do* know that he has his own sources."

Parilla contemplated that for a moment. *Yes, he has his own sources and they are generally good ones. I wonder . . . Nah.*

"Has the government budged any on the question of voting on the Isla?" he asked.

"No," Ruiz answered. "They insist that any vote taken there by any but the few civilian residents would be inherently suspect. All our men, those who are citizens, must return to their normal home to vote."

"Which breaks up our unit cohesion for the one legion we have left here," Parilla observed. "And deprives us of perhaps twenty-five thousand votes from those deployed to Pashtia and at sea."

"Is there any chance of Patricio returning the bulk of the force prior to the election?" Ruiz asked.

"Essentially none. He's just about to fan out from the temporary base he established at the north end of the Kibla Pass and he'll need every man he has in order to establish control over the area. And he's already short because of the Cazadors he sent to Xamar to guard the pirate chief."

"In some ways, he's really an idiot, you know, Raul? The job he does there won't make a lot of difference if we lose our base here."

Fire Support and Logistics Base Belisario Carrera, Pashtia, 18/4/468 AC

The base was north of the line where mountain turned to relatively flat desert. The ambient temperature was a *lot* higher. And there wasn't a really good source of water, though the engineers were drilling.

Least of my problems, thought Patricio Carrera.

He was short Cazadors and he was short Pashtun Scouts. They were the most useful troops he had for keeping open the Kibla through which virtually all his supplies must pass. Thus, that's where roughly two-thirds of them were, hunting down the remnants of the *Ikhwan* forces that had escaped the slaughter in the mountains. He was especially short Cazadors, what with having sent two maniples of them to watch over Abdulahi in Xamar as he rebuilt his local force.

Of course, they're not only watching over and out for the bandit, they're also watching him to make sure he keeps his end of the bargain.

He could have made good some of that lack by stripping off the individual cohorts' scout platoons, Cazadors in all but name. Somehow, he didn't think that would work to anyone's benefit. He'd have had to also strip off some of the combat support maniples' headquarters as well, that, or overtask the Cazador maniples' headquarters he already had. And besides, what would the cohorts do for recon then? It would be an organizational nightmare.

Note to self: Check on progress with the Ph.D. candidate who's writing up "Organization and Task Organization for War." Soonest.

Carrera had one thing to help make up for the loss of Cazadors and Scouts, as well as the lack of aircraft for the main effort with the number that were supporting the lighter forces in the mountains around the Kibla. The Anglian-built lighter-than-air recon platform had arrived the week prior and was already sending back useful intelligence. For now, it was only useful for spotting. Even so, Lanza's crew was thinking on ways to rig up bomb racks and even downward firing gun pods so that it could act itself on the intelligence acquired without having to wait for airmobile or air forces to bring in combat power.

But I'll have to buy it and crew it myself to do that; the Anglian company is firm that their crew is not allowed to take part in offensive combat missions. In any case, while the recon the LTA ship provides is good, it is awfully weather dependant around these mountains. I'm not convinced this is a good buy for the legion.

That said, if the limeys' semi-autonomous small LTA jobs can be made to work, I can mount cameras in them capable of tracking the ins and outs of every stinking village in our area and I can do it for a fraction of what it costs the FSC to put a satellite up.

Carrera let out a small sigh. *If, if, if.* "If ifs and buts were candied nuts . . ."

This FSLB was temporary, though the gringos had given some hints they might want to take it over. And why not? Since the legion had come they'd put in an all weather airstrip, excavated a foss and with the spoil built an earthen wall to keep off sniper fire, and mined the living shit out of the one place from which an enemy might look down on the camp, with *every* mine well booby-trapped. And hadn't *that* pissed off the Kosmos?

Carrera smiled at the memory of outraged progressive sensibilities. *It wasn't like I made a secret of it. Rather, I had the troops march the villagers closest to the mined area and then witness while goats were driven in. None of the goats survived more than a few steps past the marking wire. Perhaps a few less kids will be tempted to cross the areas concerned after the demonstrations.*

It was a matter of some small debate whether the

Kosmos were more angered that they were held in such scant regard or by the sheer fact of the mines, themselves.

Fuck 'em. As if I care. As if anyone who matters really cares what the progressives think. As if they're capable of any higher purpose than constraining the overly enlightened and the weak to leave them even more vulnerable to the strong and the ruthless. Cultural Human Immuno-deficiency Virus; that's all they are. And to think, my parents tried to raise me to be one of them. Blech.

The mines themselves were quite sophisticated, each being on an integral timer. Within a month after the legion made its planned departure ninety-eight plus percent of them would make a joyful sound unto the Lord on their own. The rest—the defectives—would experience battery failure within a few days of that.

This area wasn't important anyway, not to the *legion*. They were here only for a short time before moving on. While here, they intended only to weaken the insurgency before moving to the border to establish a series of bases from which they could block infiltration of *Ikhwan* fighters and their supplies. It was up to the FSC, Secordia and Anglia to destroy the insurgency once it had been weakened and once the one legion that would remain for the next contractual period had established an effective block of the infiltration routes from Kashmir.

In the long run, though, who knows if that matters? Half the infiltrators come in on perfectly open passenger flights. Half the supplies they use are sold to them by the locals. And that's not even counting the food. I wonder why the FSC can't bring themselves to use food as a weapon? The Tauran influence over the Anglians and Secordians and their influence on the FSC? Silly; but they'll never win until they're willing to control the food.

Speaking of food . . .

Carrera caught sight of a maniple of infantry, with a train of two dozen mules in tow. They were apparently waiting for the word to move out and were otherwise just sitting around. He walked over briskly, took the report of the tribune commanding the maniple, then proceeded with a barrage of questions.

"How long have your men been waiting here in the sun? . . . Why did you bring them out early?" Voice rising, "What do you mean your medics haven't shown up yet? Didn't you coordinate with the cohort medical platoon? How long have you known they would be late? Why did you bring your men out into the hot sun if you knew you wouldn't be leaving for two hours? . . . Come with me . . . Break down that mule's pack. . . . Can't you see it's overloaded, you dumb ass?"

By the time he was finished with the tribune, that worthy had been turned to a quivering mass of protoplasm and Carrera felt ashamed for going too far in chastising a subordinate.

He walked off in vast inner turmoil himself. *And I'm doing it more and more often. What the hell is wrong with me? Where's the patience of which I was once so proud? Where's the humanity? Christ! I never lose my temper.*

All of which could be summed up in the word, "Fuck."

Santissima Trinidad, 20/4/468 AC

The boat advanced at the speed of the *classis,* a stately and sedate twelve knots. The speed was set by that of the slowest vessel in the flotilla, the steamer, BdL *Harpy Eagle,* which served as safe berth for the patrol boats. At that speed, the bow needn't lift nor the engines strain. The forward gun was manned, as was the con, radar and sonar. Most of the crew were unemployed for the moment, even so, and hung out on the rear deck behind the con, drinking some of their ration beer and eating lunch from paper plates.

"Watsa matter, Santiona, tired of fishing?" Pedraz asked.

"Fuck that shit," the heavyset sailor answered. "I'll never toss a hook in the water again as long as I live. If I ever fish again, it'll be with hand grenades or big nets."

"Pity," said Pedraz. "I'll bet that meg is still following us hoping for a chance at your plump ass again."

Santiona suddenly looked to the stern, fearfully. "You don't really think so, do you, Chief?"

"Nah," Pedraz answered, lightly. "You're fated to die at the hands of a jealous husband, young seaman."

"All things considered," Santiona answered, "I'd rather not. But that still beats being eaten by a fish."

"I think they're dying out," Francais said, from behind the wheel. "Fish that size, it's *got* to be hard to keep fed. Especially with the loss of whales and such over the last couple of hundred years. It would need a lot of space to hunt in. That would make it hard to find mates."

"Good riddance," answered Santiona. "When the

last one is dead and washed ashore I'll be all that much happier."

"Oh, I dunno,' answered Francais. "They're magnificent, for all they're dangerous. Be kind of sad when there're no more."

"Hah!" Santiona snorted in reply. "You haven't been looking into the maw of one with no more than ten feet between you and its teeth. You haven't smelt its breath."

"Oh, *puhleeze*! Besides, they don't breathe."

"As a matter of fact," Santiona continued, unfazed, "I've decided I hate all fish. So when I take my discharge, after this tour, I'm gonna use my vet's benefits to get a fishing boat. Then I can kill the slimy scaled bastards wholesale."

Guptillo snorted. "Not me. When this is over I'm heading to dry land and, God willing and the river don't rise, I'll never get my feet wet again."

"Farmer?" asked Pedraz. "My people were farmers. Hard work and you're an awful soft city boy."

"Used to be soft, Chief. Hard to stay that way on a patrol boat."

"True enough," Pedraz agreed. "It's still awful hard work."

"No matter, I didn't want to be a farmer. I was thinking about the university and maybe taking up agronomy."

"That would be easier," Pedraz nodded. "Pay better, too."

"And no one will be shooting at you," Clavell added.

"That *would* be a plus," said Guptillo.

"Ah, you're all pussies," said Francais. "Me; I'm sticking with the *classis* until the day I die."

The Big ?, 21/4/468 AC

The yacht was almost fifty nautical miles ahead of the
flotilla. Their cover had pretty much been blown off the
coast of Xamar, but there was good reason to expect
with a name change and a new paint job that they'd
be clandestine enough in the Nicobar Straits. The
new name, even now being painted in two alphabets
on the stern, was *Qamra*, Arabic for "moon." Almost,
almost, Marta had suggested calling it the *Queer*, but
since the crew had been so understanding of her and
Jaqueline's love affair—at least to the point of ignoring
it— she thought better of rubbing it in their faces.

MV *Hoogaboom*, Kolon Thoṭa, Anula, 24/4/468 AC

Kolon Thota was about as neutral a port as one could
find in this war. Oh yes, the island of Anula had its share
of civil strife and civil war, but neither Moslems—nor
the Salafi fanatics among them—nor Christians were
implicated. There were, of course, a fair number of
Moslems on the island. Enough of them were Salafi, too.
But the decision had been made early on by Mustafa to
keep the island as neutral territory, a safe harbor and
entranceway for the *Ikhwan*'s operatives into the rest
of the world. The port was modern, fully equipped,
and well staffed by skilled shipwrights and chandlers.

It was, thus, a perfect spot for the *Hoogaboom* to
have made its final preparations for the attack on the
Dos Lindas. It was also a perfect spot for Abdul Aziz to
intercept the ship with his hand-carried change of orders.

The captain looked terribly . . . disappointed. Abdul
Aziz could well understand that. When one works

oneself into a mind set to commit martyrdom for the cause, any delay is hardly to be tolerated. For one thing, delay brings with it the doubt that one will have the courage to endure the imminence of death—even with the certain promise of Paradise.

"But there's nothing for it, Captain," Abdul said, sympathetically. "The enemy fleet has moved. There is no real chance of catching them at sea. Moreover, at the Straits of Nicobar our chance of catching them as we have planned is even greater than it would have been off the Xamar coast."

"Success or failure is in the hands of Allah," the captain intoned.

"That's true, of course, Captain," Abdul agreed. "Yet the mullahs are gradually coming around to the idea that Allah cares about how hard we try, and the cleverness we bring to the fight. Mustafa and Nur al Deen are convinced of it."

"Seems impious to me," the captain said. "Still, orders are orders and the Koran enjoins obedience. We shall wait."

After a moment's reflection the captain asked, "Would you care to inspect the ship?"

"Please. Mustafa expressly ordered me to see that you lack for nothing. Indeed, I've brought half a dozen Tauran slave girls for the enjoyment of your crew."

The captain thought on that for a moment. "We appreciate the slave girls, of course, but . . . should we keep them until the day? Sell them off just before? Kill them?"

"Anything but selling them beforehand, Captain, would be fine."

Matera, south of the Nicobar Straits, 25/4/468 AC

Parameswara and al Naquib rested on a fallen log under a deep, dark jungle canopy. Both men were soaked with sweat. For all that, they weren't so wet as the gangs of loincloth-clad slaves struggling under the lashes wielded by al Naquib's company of *Ikhwan*. A road paralleled the route of the column, about five kilometers to the east.

The slaves' burdens were conexes, or things that looked remarkably like conexes, painted in a mottled pattern and rolling on smooth, even logs cut down from the jungle. Moving the logs left behind as the conexes progressed was nearly all the rest the slaves got from their back- and heart-breaking labor of pulling on the ropes that moved the metal boxes forward.

"How much further?" the pirate king asked.

Al Naquib pulled out a small device, not much larger than a cell phone, and consulted it. "About three hundred kilometers, by the global locating system," the *Ikhwan* answered. "Call it forty or fifty days . . . *if* the slaves last through it."

"Do you think I should go ahead and move out to arrange relief crews?" the pirate king asked.

Al Naquib thought upon that. After a few moments reflection, he answered, "That, yes. But not only for us. The people coming from the north, on the other side of the Straits, will need help as much as we will. But I am also concerned that you not leave a power vacuum behind you."

I love this Arab, Parameswara rejoiced. *He understands my problems without my so much as voicing a complaint.*

Puerto Lindo, Balboa, 26/4/468 AC

Two Suvarov-class cruisers had been subjected to a
greater or lesser degree of refit. Neither had been
given a new name yet but had to make do with their
old Volgan ones. They'd be christened with legionary
names later on.

Of the two, one was complete only to the extent
of having serviceable guns and being generally livable.
Like the second light aircraft carrier, this one would
go to the *Isla Real* and serve as a stationary training
vessel. The other was intended to join the classis as
a warship.

"Doesn't lack for much, does she?" Sitnikov asked
of the chief of the port's shipfitters.

"Well, she really isn't fit to stand in line of battle
alone, if that's what you mean, Legate," the shipfitter answered. "Her guns are fine though, along with
her armor and her new AZIPODs. Radar's okay, of
course, and being old Volgan it's actually better than
newer stuff if she's looking out for stealthy aircraft.
The sonar's the pits, though."

"Got to compromise somewhere," the Volgan
answered. "And she's not sailing without a good escort
with better sonar. How about the other three ships?"

"How about the concrete emplacements for them
on the island?" retorted the fitter.

Sitnikov put out a hand, palm down with fingers
spread, and wriggled it. "Carrera sent me an odd idea
that he wants me to think about before we commit to
a design for the coastal artillery. I'm thinking about
it, too."

"I don't suppose . . ."

Sitnikov considered for a moment before answering, "No; I really can't discuss it. I can say that it won't matter to the ships' turrets; that it won't change what you have to do."

"Fair enough. Well, when you say the concrete pads are ready we can tow the ships to the island. I've got crew ready to remove the turrets and a ship with a crane rigged to lift them off and transfer them to land."

"That's all we need of you. The legion will see to the rest."

University Hospital, University of Balboa, 28/4/468 AC

The doctor looked utterly befuddled. He closed the file on his desk and said, "Jorge, I haven't a clue why you can see again. Your records indicate there was never any physical reason for your blindness. If there was no physical reason, then the blow you took in the brawl two weeks ago can't have been the cure, or at least not the physical cure. Your records indicate that your eyes were always able to see but that your mind refused to process the information. Maybe that fist coming at you was threat enough to overcome whatever reason your mind had for blocking off your sight."

"But I never saw the fist coming, Doctor," Mendoza answered. "It wasn't until Marqueli brought me around that I could see." Mendoza didn't remember that he'd blinked.

The doctor removed his own glasses and began cleaning them with a corner of his guayabera. He shook his head with frustration.

"I can't explain it, Jorge. I can only observe and

report. If you would like, I can make you an appointment with a head doctor."

"No . . . no, thank you. I've had my share of those."

"Is this going to cost you any of your disability benefit?" the doctor asked.

Marqueli answered, "We've told the legionary disability office. They checked and said Jorge was already maxed out with the loss of his legs. He won't lose anything just for getting his sight back. They even said that he's still entitled to a paid helper—presumptively a wife and therefore me—with vision or not."

"That's generous," the doctor admitted. "But he was taking a doctorate. Will that . . ."

"No, doctor," Mendoza said. "That's a totally separate program. Though I admit . . ." He glanced over at his wife.

"Yes?" she asked.

"I'm going to miss you reading to me."

She smiled, warmly, and reaching over to pat her husband's hand. "I still will if you like. On the other hand, you can read to yourself a lot quicker than I can read to you. I'll bet you, husband mine, that you make much faster progress this way than the old way."

"That's a thought, isn't it?"

In another ward, one at the opposite end of the hospital and behind doors continuously guarded, Khalid looked into a mirror at his new face and wondered, *What, if anything, is left of me?*

Khalid had done his last hit, involving ricin and a pressurized gas projector, on the streets of Hajar, Yithrab. Unfortunately, he'd been made. Only a fast journey to a prearranged spot in the desert, and a last minute Cricket flight from the air arm of Sumeri Intelligence, had gotten him out of the country. His old face was known now and he could never have continued to work as long as he'd kept it.

It was amazing what could be done, though, with some small shifts in the corners of his eyes, a widening of the nose, pulling back of his ears, shaving down of the cheekbones, the addition of a spurious scar, and a change in the shape of his mouth.

The only problem is, it doesn't feel like me *anymore. I almost wish—*

Whatever thought Khalid had been about to complete, it was lost to the interruption of seeing a small, dark, and rather feral looking man appear in the mirror behind him.

"Legate Fernandez," Khalid said, before turning around.

Fernandez said nothing at first, but just peered intently, trying to match Khalid's new face to his old. Finally, satisfied, the intel chief shook his head and said, "Not a chance you will be identified short of a DNA screening. Very good.

"You know you've been detached from Sumeri Intelligence to work for me for the next two years, correct?"

"Yes, Legate, I understand that," Khalid said. "What I don't know is why."

Fernandez smiled and answered, "Given your work history, *that* is a fairly stupid question, no?"

Khalid's smile, strange in this new face, grew to match Fernandez's.

From under his left arm Fernandez drew a thick, bound, and sealed portfolio. This he opened and

withdrew what looked to Khalid like a score or so
of folders.

"These are, for the most part, your targets," Fernandez said, passing them, and the portfolio, over to
Khalid. "One is travel documents, another rules of
engagement. Still a third has financial information.
Specifically, that folder contains a list of smallish
bank accounts that will hold, in the aggregate, enough
money for several years' independent operations plus
operational expenses. The accounts match the travel
and identity documents. We'll fill them in the order
given and at the times given.

"Your rules of engagement for these will be different from what you have become used to in the
past," Fernandez explained. "All of these men are
either major reporters, producers, or editors for the
media in the Tauran Union and the Federated States;
or they are, broadly speaking, politicians; or they are
academics; or they are entertainers. There is a certain
amount of overlap in those last three. All have given
considerable vocal and literary moral support to the
enemy. Some may have given more concrete support
to the enemy; intelligence, financing, and the like.
All have also attacked both the *Legion del Cid* or
President Sada at one time or another. You are not,
however, to kill them right off."

Khalid looked interested but at the same time
confused.

Fernandez let the obvious confusion pass for the
moment. "As I suggested, when you leave here, you
will be on your own until your target list has been
serviced or otherwise rendered ineffective. It will be
rare if we, or Sumeri intelligence, ever contact you,

though you will be required to contact us upon successfully servicing a target. We have, you see, learned much from the enemy.

"Whenever one of those editors, reporters, academics, entertainers, or politicians says or permits *something* to be said against the enemy, or against Islam, or against Salafism, then you may kill them. Given who they are, that something is certain to be very mild. You will leave a copy of whatever it was they said, or wrote, or permitted to be published by the body or near enough to the body that it will be found. You may have to interpret this guidance very liberally. For example, if one of them puts out something in favor of women's rights, or gay rights, that would be considered sufficient to make them active targets. If one of them makes a speech that is not recorded, you may have to write a slogan condemning the speech."

Khalid's confusion grew. "I don't understand this . . ."

It was Fernandez's turn to smile. "We've thought about this for a long time. Our reasoning is . . . complex.

"They will have a choice or, rather, some sets of choices. In one set, they can continue to present only negative views of us, and the war, and thus lose credibility with some of their audience. Or they can be 'objective' and die, with the *Ikhwan* taking the blame. In either case, their voices will be silenced or, at worst, made ineffective. Eventually, we expect, many will realize they are being killed for expressing their views and simply shut up."

"Many of them really are too stupid to get that message, I think," Khalid said. "Moreover, most of their target audience is too stupid to understand and accept that the press, the academics and the progressives are simply putting out blatant propaganda on behalf of the enemy. They are all progressives and Kosmos, are they not, these pols, reporters, editors and professors? The target audience cannot even accept that they are held in as much contempt as they are by the people you want me to kill. In any case, under the rule you have given me, some of them *will* simply stop giving off any message that is remotely critical of the enemy and most of their audience will not even notice."

"We understand this," Fernandez agreed. "That is the other set of choices. For those who will not get the message we will want you to have evidence that the people you killed *were* assassinated. We can show that evidence, without turning it over, of course, to certain persons among the classes of targets in order to spread the word in an unprovable way. Imagine, if you will, Khalid, that you kill . . ." Fernandez took the folders and rifled through them until he came upon one in particular. "This woman, say."

Fernandez opened the folder to show Khalid a picture of a woman, taken from her own GlobalNet site. She was well dressed in a cream colored suit, and, if a bit overweight, all in all, was by no means unattractive.

"This is Sarita Iapes. She is not only highly critical of the war effort but of the legion and President Sada in particular. She's been a nexus for anti-war effort reporting for years. So, say, someday you wait in ambush in an automobile and simply run her over, a routine hit and run. But you have a camera going so that you can give us a picture of her in the moment before you kill her. We show that picture to, again, say, David Prefer, one of her reporters, and explain to the wretch that she *was* killed, and, approximately, why."

"Understand, Legate," Khalid said, shaking his head doubtfully, "I merely want to understand the mission perfectly so that I can execute it perfectly. Okay, so you do that. All it does it shut them up. It does not make them report on us favorably."

"We don't need favorable reporting," Fernandez explained. "That would be overreach. The danger with these people is that they are not a neutral asset. They're with the enemy, even if they don't know it. It would be too much to expect them to change one-hundred-and-eighty degrees. It is sufficient that they merely stop harming us and helping the other side; no need to help us and harm the other side. Indeed, if they did that, they'd be in as much danger from the *Ikhwan* as they are from us and they likely *know* it. In that case, they'd probably take their chances and continue to support the *Ikhwan*."

"So . . . we are going for the minimal but achievable goal?" Khalid asked.

"Yes. Moreover, if two years goes by without ever a negative comment from one of them on either us or the enemy, then you may assume they have taken the hint and shut up. In that case, put them on the inactive target list."

"Cle-ver," Khalid said.

"If you are captured, of course . . ."

Khalid snorted. "*Allahu Akbar!* Long live the Salafi jihad."

"Quite. The Kosmos down there will insist on superior treatment for you as long as you can credibly claim to be on the side of the *Ikhwan*. Just remember, Khalid, they must be made to feel the hard hand of the war they support."

INTERLUDE

**25/7/47 AC, UN Compound, *Ciudad* Balboa,
Balboa Colony, Terra Nova**

"These bandits must be made to feel the hard hand
of the war they have brought upon themselves,"
insisted Bernard Chanet, with the pounding of his
fist upon his desk.

Major Dhan Singh Pandey, seconded to the UN
Peacekeeping Force for Terra Nova (UNPFTN), from
the Army of India's 11th Gurkha Rifles, said nothing.
His colleague and discreet lover, Amita Kaur Bhago,
32nd Battalion (Pioneer), the Sikh Regiment, scowled
and unconsciously reached for the *kirpan,* or sword,
she wore at her side.

She was not so even-tempered as Pandey. And the
sneering look this UN swine had given the work *her*
troops had put into rebuilding the compound already
had her tomcat-ready for a fight. Pandey reached out
with his own hand to place it atop her lighter one.
"Not yet, lioness," he whispered.

"I don't like this greasy bastard," she whispered back.
"What does such as *he* know of the hard hand of war?"

"We'll discuss it later. Now take your hand *off* of your *kirpan*."

Chanet noticed the byplay, though he couldn't hear what was said. Especially did he notice Amita looking him over as someone the world would be a better place without. He'd noticed, too, what a damnably handsome woman she was. But seeing the white knuckled hand gripping the hilt of the long dagger she wore killed any lust before it could quite form.

Chanet had shuttled in earlier in the day from the main base at Atlantis, bringing with him the deputy special representative for the secretary general, Tariq Lakhdar, age twenty-four. It was Lakhdar who would see to the local efforts, under Chanet's overall direction. And why not? Chanet had owed a favor to Lakhdar's uncle, after all.

"I don't like the look of the other greasy bastard, either," whispered Amita.

"*Later.*"

The small assembly held the leadership for the entire peacekeeping force for Balboa. Besides Chanet and Lakhdar, the civilian leaders, and Pandey and Bhago, from the Army of India, there were four captains from the Organization of African Unity, one German, seconded from 5th Panzer Division, a Belgian Commando, a Ukrainian aviator major, and David Duff-McQueeg, a British Royal Marine, in overall command.

Amita liked none of them, finding the Africans undisciplined, the German arrogant, the Belgian grotesquely beery, the Ukrainian incomprehensible, and Duff-McQueeg, who . . . "Stupid, rude, limey bastard. No wonder they couldn't hold on to India. I never really understood the American Revolution, or our own resistance, until I met that piece of shit."

"Amita, *later!*"

Duff-McQueeg stood up and announced, "We've driven off the main guerilla band. But we'll never get full control until we can cut off their food. The first thing we're going to do is to establish ration controls, *tight* ration controls, here in the city. That means no, you bloody Sikhs will *not* be giving out food at the temple I am sure you intend to establish . . ."

CHAPTER FIFTEEN

> They imagine they're the wave of the
> future, but it's only sewage flowing
> downhill.
>
> —Lois McMaster Bujold,
> *Shards of Honor*

Building 59, Fort Muddville, Balboa, 29/4/468 AC

"Magnificent, *mon General*," Malcoeur toadied. He
was not talking about architecture.

"*Quoi?*" Janier asked, in a tone that meant, *shut
up, fool.*

General Janier never really thought the old headquarters for the FS Army in Balboa was quite grand enough
for his own, indisputable, magnificence. Oh, yes, the
arched gate underneath his office was all well enough,
even if not quite the triumphal arch the general would
have preferred. And the building was solid; you have to
give the Columbian pigs that. But it was such a utilitarian
structure, no marble, few mirrors . . . no quarters for a
mistress. How could a people even think of themselves
as civilized who could build a headquarters for a senior
general and *not* provide quarters for his mistress?

"Ah, well," said Janier aloud, "we'll soon have that fixed."

"Sir?" asked Malcoeur, cupping one hand to his ear to ward off the sound of hammers and saws coming from the just down the hall where Janier had evicted much of his staff to create an apartment.

"Nothing for your ears, Malcoeur, you rotund little swine," Janier sneered. He pointed at the aide with his marshal's stick with its thirty-two gold and silk embroidered eagles and ordered, "Bring me my topper." The top of the baton was engraved, "*Terror Belli, Decus Pacis.*"

While the toady scurried off to Janier's desk to fetch the general's headgear, Janier admired himself in the mirror. It was understandable; he *did* cut quite a fine figure in the blue velvet and gold-embroidered informal dress uniform of a marshal of Napoleonic France. Hundreds of golden oak leaves covered the facings, the collar, the shoulders, and ran down each sleeve.

Janier fingered one of the eight gold buttons on the coat, adjusting it minutely. He then tugged and twisted at the stiff, high collar. It was beastly uncomfortable. By the time Janier was satisfied with the collar Malcoeur, the "rotund little swine," had returned with the headdress.

It would be unseemly for the general to bow his noble head to a fat little wretch like Major Malcoeur. Instead, as Janier admired himself in the mirror, the major pulled up a chair, stood upon it, and gently lowered a replica of the golden laurel wreath worn by Janier's hero, Napoleon I, for his coronation.

The drone of saw and *wham-wham-wham* of hammer were distant in the conference room at the other

end of the long, white stuccoed and red tiled building. Indeed, so distant were the sounds that President
Rocaberti was hardly aware of them. What with the
election coming up, the numbers, country-wide, still
running against him, and the near certainty of criminal
charges if he lost; well, one could understand why the
president wasn't aware of much.

Thus, Rocaberti barely noticed when all the Gaulic
officers and functionaries present stood to attention
around the conference table and the chairs lining the
walls. Only he, his nephew, his minister of police, and
the ambassador from United Earth remained seated.
They remained that way, that is, until Rocaberti caught
sight of Janier, his porcine little aide standing behind,
glaring down at him from his nearly two meters of
imperious height. The aide made little gestures with
his hand, *Arise*.

*Does he have any idea how ridiculous he looks in
that outfit?* Rocaberti wondered. *Why is he glaring at
me? Does he expect me, the chief executive of a sovereign nation, to rise for him? The Frog bastard; he does.*

Rocaberti, never among the staunchest of men, stood,
along with the other Balboans who had accompanied
him. Only the UE ambassador remained seated and to
that worthy Janier gave a respectful nod before seating himself.

"Report," Janier ordered.

The operations officer answered, "Preparation for
flying in three more infantry battalions two days
before the election are complete, *mon General*. An
additional battalion of light armor has loaded ship and
will arrive at about the same time as the light infantry.
The government has already approved."

"What of the TU?" Janier asked.

"Why would we inform them? They'll be presented with a *fait accompli* once it's *accompli*."

On cue, the public affairs officer added, "*Mon General*, the news in both the TU and the FSC runs at ninety-seven percent that this election is in the process of being stolen by the mercenaries. Public opinion polls are in line with this."

"We have completed occupation of the former FSA facilities," said Janier's S-4, or logistics officer. "There will be adequate living space for all our troops, once they arrive."

"Very good," the general said somberly. "Where did the locals who bought the housing go?"

"Who cares?"

"Indeed," Janier agreed.

"We *have* to care," Rocaberti interjected. "Those people were among our prime supporters."

Janier shrugged. The opinion of this future colonial subject could not possibly be important. Nonetheless, for the benefit of his own people, he spoke, and naturally in French. "Gentlemen, the Balboans who support the current administration have served their purpose, though that administration will remain valuable as a convenient cover for our rule. Have we not maintained virtually all of our old empire in Colombia del Norte, Uhuru and Urania in just this way?

"For our part, we will simply be here, in force—real or potential— greater than the local mercenaries would willingly wish to face. When the election procedure is shown to be compromised, as President Wozniak will attest to, the government will refuse to abide by it.

We shall offer it our full support, of course . . . all in the interests of democracy—" every Gaulic officer present broke out in unfeigned and unforced laughter "—of course. We shall move our battalions, of which there shall be eight, to defend what can be defended, Balboa City and the Transitway area."

The ambassador of *La Republique de la Gaulle* said, "I am sure we can count on the Federated States' Department of State intervening on our behalf to threaten the mercenaries with severe sanctions should they initiate fighting."

"As I had supposed," Janier said.

"There is one major problem," Rocaberti insisted. "Within *Ciudad* Balboa there are some thousands of mercenary reservists. They may fight no matter what."

Janier sneered. As if some raggle taggle undeveloped world part-timers could pose any serious problem for the professionals of his force. *Absurd. Laughable. Impossible.*

War Department, Hamilton, FD, Federated States of Columbia, 2/5/468 AC

Rivers sighed and said, "This word you keep using, Secretary Malcolm? I don't think it means what you think it means. It might be 'impossible' for Pat Hennessey"—for Rivers still thought of Carrera as Hennessey—"to go to war with the Tauran Union. He'll do it anyway. He'll hit them wherever he can, as hard as he can, in as terrible and terrifying way as he can, and nothing we can do, short of nukes, will stop him. Nukes might not either."

Rivers neglected to mention that the intelligence

people had been hearing rumors that Hennessey was, himself, a nuclear power. So far the rumors had been fairly well squashed, mostly because if *he* had them they could only have come from one place, Sumer. And if they'd come from Sumer that meant that everything the Progressive Party had said about the lack of cause for war with Sumer back in 461 was a lie. That, of course, would never do.

"Even now," Rivers continued, "the *Legion del Cid* is redeploying two full legions plus support, nearly thirty thousand men, from northern back into southern Pashtia. They could have been moved simply because the large contract is about up. But Hennessey doesn't appear to be in any hurry to move them out of Pashtia, despite what it must be costing him extra to support them in country."

"But what can he do? It's absurd!" Malcolm shouted.

So hard to maintain calm with this man, River thought. "If fighting breaks out in Balboa, Hennessey will attack the Frogs there, in Pashtia, and everywhere else he can get at them. The battalion the Frogs keep in pristine comfort and safety in the southern part of Pashtia? He'll attack and extinguish it. If other Taurans interfere, he'll destroy them, too. If *we* interfere, he may not be able to destroy us, but he will fight us. And, Mr. Secretary, he has a more powerful force in the country than we do."

"But . . . but he *can't*," SecWar insisted. "He's one of *us*."

Like you, with your love affair with the Gauls, are one of us? You really don't see it, do you?

Rivers clasped his hands behind him and walked to the window. From this he stared out for long minutes, silently, while Malcolm seethed behind him. *How to explain this?*

Turning around, gesturing frantically with one hand, Virgil Rivers began, "In the first place, he's not one of *us*. You may think, because he actually was raised to be a Kosmo, a cosmopolitan progressive, that he's one of *you*. But that would be false, too, Mr. Secretary.

"Oh, he never learned love of country as a boy; that's true. Instead, he was taught that all distinctions between men are arbitrary. He told me this himself, once. He was deep in his cups at the time.

"He told me, 'They tried to convince me, when I was young, that the only possible nonarbitrary grouping was the family of man. Why they never realized that that was as arbitrary a group as any other, I don't know. How does it make sense not to hate people because they look a little different but love them because they look a little the same? Either is mere appearance.'

"Mr. Secretary, he also said, 'The only truly non-arbitrary group is the group one chooses for himself. I chose the Army.'

"But, Mr. Secretary, even the Army was never so kind, so loving, or so warm and comfortable as the force he has built for himself. He is *not*, sir, not in any meaning-ful way, a citizen of the Federated States or a soldier of the Federated States Army. He's a true Kosmo, perhaps the ultimate manifestation of Kosmoism. He's loyal to his own group . . . and nothing *but*.

"So, yes, sir. He *would* fight even us. Maybe there's some lingering affection; maybe he'd prefer not to. But he still would."

Malcolm's eyes grew wide with sudden understand-ing. "Fuck."

Kibla Pass, Pashtia, 5/5/468 AC,

"Up the fucking hill, soldier-boy," said the youngish centurion as he smacked a dawdling legionary across the buttocks with the stick that was his sole badge of rank.

Several things are required to make an army so that it can displace quickly. It must have limited baggage, not merely for ease of transport but for ease of breaking down and loading. It must have transport, of course, but not more than it can keep moving. It must have a staff capable of planning the movement with considerable efficiency but allowing for the inevitable screw ups. It must have soldiers willing and able to march hard. It needs officers and noncoms, pitiless in their drive to obey their orders and meet their march objectives. It needs a mindset, as an army, that inclines it to rapid movement.

Above all, perhaps, it must have a commander willing to give the order, "Move it, you fucks." As Carrera stood on a rocky outcropping overlooking the metalled road through the pass, he whispered just that: "Move it, you fucks."

There were still bandits in the hills. Aircraft circled overhead to watch for them, out to a distance of seven kilometers—mortar range—from the main column. Pashtun scouts and Cazadors, with dog teams, likewise secured the long, winding triple *eel* of men, machine and animals from interference. Even Carrera let himself be surrounded by half a dozen bodyguards; sharp men, well armed and armored and each one a match for him in size and color.

It was hardly secure, though, not against an enemy

who *would* die, eagerly, if he could just take one infidel with him. If the Legion hadn't caught so many of the *Ikhwan's* fighters and annihilated them or driven them far away, the passage over the mountains would have taken a lot longer.

One had to wonder, as some of the legionaries wondered, just how long Carrera had been planning the upcoming confrontation with the troops of the Tauran Union in Pashtia.

I've been considering it for the last five years, Carrera thought, to no one in particular.

Below, in tactical road march order, with trucks and other vehicles in between, the men sang. Carrera heard them singing a new song, "Rio Gamboa," which was mostly about getting back home:

> . . .*Centurio viejo, aun en la marcha.*
> *No tiene compassion. No tiene humanidad.*
> *No tiene miedo del enemigo.*
> *Y sigue Carrera a la battalle,*
> *Como siguemos. Porque siguemos?*
> *Porque somos el Legion, somos en la*
>   *marcha. . .*

"Pretty downbeat," Carrera muttered to himself, listening to the dreary but moving tune. "Well, that's fitting. It isn't, after all, like we're going to fight anybody but men who should be our *friends*, most of them."

> *Y somos cansado de la guerra sucia,*
> *Y de la batalle . . .*

"I'm sick of it, too, sons. I'm sick of it, too."

Tenemos esposas, tenemos niños,
Todos queridos . . .

"I know, boys, I know," the legate whispered. "And I can't tell you when you can go home either, nor even what kind of home you'll find when you get there. I can only tell you that I'm trying to make it a home worth living in."

Still the song went on. Mentally, Carrera translated:
Our legs are aching
And our backs are in pain
Over the mountains we sweat and strain.
Ruck up, boys.
Weapons off safe.
We're heading off again to earn our pay.
But old Centurion, he keeps on marchin'.
He fears for nothin', not even dyin' . . .

And that, Carrera thought, *is a pretty good summary of the centurionate. In a force approaching fifty thousand, itself already pretty elite, only about twenty-five hundred made the cut to centurion. They were awesome men when we started all this . . . and they've grown.*

This portion of the column passed by, struggling and straining, sweating and cursing, up the steep and winding pass. Some of the men recognized Carrera and waved. A grizzled centurion saluted, informally, with his stick. The waving became general and was accompanied by a different song:

Adelante, hijos del Legion.
Adelante, legionarios gloriosos.
Conquiste cada obstaculo . . .

Carrera stiffened to attention, and saluted in return. He watched the column crest a rise and then turn around a bend. When the last man had gone from view he looked again at where they'd come from and saw a tank, a Jaguar II, being winched, literally, up the pass.

Gonna have to buy a shitload of new power packs and even new armor after this one's done, he thought. *These things just aren't made to—*

The thought was cut off as a metal cable, seemingly strong but apparently defective, snapped, approximately between the winch and the tank. Both ends went flying at extraordinarily high speed. One was harmless. The other hit a walking legionary in the legs just above his knees. The cable cut through as if the legs weren't even there. The legionary tumbled, end over end, in a spray of blood. It was too quick for him even to feel pain, yet. That, however, would come.

Freed at one corner, the tank lurched back unevenly. The weight now was too much for the single cable remaining. It, too, snapped. In this case, since everyone but the one unfortunate man caught in the legs had fallen belly to the dirt, that cable passed overhead harmlessly. The tank, itself, began sliding back, while men behind frantically tried to get out of the way.

With considerable presence of mind, under the circumstances, the driver applied brakes to one side only. This caused the tank to veer and slam into a rock wall at which point it stopped. Before the shaken driver could emerge, a medic was attending to the now legless trooper, while a maintenance team by the winches began pulling two more cables from the back of a truck.

"Dustoff's already on the way, sir," one of Carrera's radio carriers announced.

Poor bastard, Carrera thought, with that part of himself he allowed to actually feel. *Neither you nor I wanted you to go home like that.*

Cruz Residence, *Ciudad* Balboa, 5/5/468 AC

He's been this way for the last three and a half weeks, thought Cara, unhappily, as she did the evening dishes by hand.

Her husband, with a smile on his bruised and battered face, sat on the living room floor playing with the children. He seemed content with the world, as he had most definitely *not* been content since he'd left the regulars.

And I know why he's this way, too. He got to fight. He got to be a man among men. He was able to test himself and rise above the normal human plane . . . if only for a few minutes. Oh, Ricardo, what have I done to you?

Putting the last of the plates on a rack to drip dry, Cara went and sat on the couch overlooking the rest of her family. She sat there, in inner turmoil, for about a quarter of an hour before saying, "Children, go out and play until it's dark. I need to talk to your father."

Cruz looked at her curiously until the kids were out the door and she began to speak.

Cara wasted no time. "I'm sorry, Ricardo. I didn't know what I was doing when I made you leave the regulars. I didn't understand how much you need it. So . . . if you want to go back, I won't interfere and I'll do my best to put up with the separation and the fear."

"What brings this on?" Cruz asked, raising one very suspicious eyebrow.

Cara sighed. "I'd hoped I could be enough for you. But you were miserable. And then I saw you fight, and you were happy, and you've been happy for weeks. But how long can that last, Ricardo? You need the fight, the struggle. You need it in your memory; you need it in your present; and you need the anticipation of it in your future. I see that now. I should have seen it then. I should have known it since we first met and you saved me from those *rabiblanco* assholes. You were meant to be a soldier first and a husband second. The man I *love* is meant to be a soldier first and a husband second. And . . . I'm going to have to learn to live with that."

"Can you learn to live with that?" Cruz asked.

"I don't know. I can try."

"Fair enough," her husband answered. Then he went silent for a while, apparently thinking. "You know," he said, "I've fought with and shed blood with the men of my reserve cohort, too, now. There's a good chance that fighting will break out here, come the next election. They'll need me then, if it happens. There aren't that many senior centurions in the reserves. How about if I stay with them, in the seventh cohort of the tercio, until this term of school is over? That will be after the election and we'll know what the future holds a little more clearly. If it looks best to go back, I'll go back. If it looks like it's best to stay with the seventh cohort, I can do that instead."

"It's only a reprieve for me," Cara pointed out. "One way or the other you're going where the fighting is going to be."

"Yes . . . but I promise to try really hard not to get killed."

Matera, south of the Nicobar Straits, 7/5/468 AC

Pour encourager les autres, thought al Naquib. He spoke excellent French, after all.

The spark for the thought were the dozen slaves, now made redundant by the arrival of the first of the relief parties provided by Parameswara. The slaves had spent the previous evening digging their own graves under the watch of al Naquib's troops. Now they knelt by those graves. Their hands were tied behind them. Most of the slaves wept. A couple pleaded weakly. The rest remained in a sort of catatonia induced by their coming obliteration. The slaves had been chosen for their weakness.

"The rest will work that much harder, afterwards," al Naquib had explained to his men. "We've already lost nearly a dozen. These are the ones next mostly likely to die. Best we get some use from them first."

Behind each slave stood one of the *Ikhwan,* one hand holding a slave by the hair and the other clasping cruel knives poised at the victims' throats.

Al Naquib raised a hand and then lowered it, quickly. The knives were drawn across emaciated flesh. Blood from a dozen living fountains spurted forth to the jungle floor in an audible gush. The weeping stopped immediately.

"For the rest of you," al Naquib announced to the other slaves standing by to witness the executions, "let this be your warning: the weak and the slackers will be put to death with no more mercy than I would show a scorpion or an *antania*. Pull your lines as if your lives depended upon it. They do."

Academia Militar Sargento Juan Malvegui, Puerto Lindo, Balboa, 9/5/468 AC

A long line of twenty tanks stood outside the physical training shed *cum* classroom. Inside, a Volgan instructor droned on in marginal Spanish about the capabilities and limitations of the Jaguar II tank and the Ocelot light armored vehicle Behind and slightly to the right of the Volgan was a table. Upon that table a black cloth covered an object.

Like many another fifteen-year-old in the wide shed that served as classroom and physical training pit, Cadet Sergeant Julio Acosta paid little attention. For one thing, the information was already in his cadet handbook. For another, the Volgan instructor would surely put him to sleep in no time if he actually tried to listen. The walls were decorated with cadets who'd been caught nodding off. Their feet were against the walls, about four feet in the air, and their hands widely spaced on the sawdust of the pit. From experience Acosta knew, and hated, the modified push-up position used by the academy cadre.

Instead, while pretending to take notes, Acosta wrote a letter home. He wrote:

"Dear Family,
    In the first place let me apologize for not having written in over a month. But, as I told you the last time I wrote, we are given little free time. Monday through

Thursday we cram five days of academics into four. Friday and Saturday we train as soldiers. Sunday is parade, church, and inspections in the morning; getting ready for the next week in the afternoon and evening. I couldn't write now except that I am in a class that I really don't need to pay attention to.

Thank my sister, Betania, for the cookies she sent. My whole platoon enjoyed them. (And no, sister, I didn't want to share them, but we are not allowed to keep any kind of food in the barracks.)

To little Eduardo; you tell me you want to be a soldier. I must tell you back, it is hard, little brother, very hard. Never enough sleep, running, marching, harassment all the time. If you are still interested when you turn fourteen in three years, we will talk about it again. In the interim, just keep your grades up in school and obey our parents. That is the best preparation you can do.

Mother and Father, I will be home the week before Christmas until three days after the Intercalary.

Not everyone will be returning to the Academy. Of the eighteen hundred who started here with me, six hundred are already gone. Some of the others remaining will be invited to leave. Do not fear that I will be one of those. My grades are high and my evaluations for leadership also

good enough to be retained. I would not
fail you, you can be sure."

Acosta stopped writing as the Russian instructor
was replaced with a Balboan one, a rather short type.
As usual the cadets began to chatter quietly among
themselves the moment one class ended. The new
speaker was a *Cristobalense*, Julio thought. For one
thing, he was black. For another, the cuff band on
his sleeve said "Barbarossa" which the cadet knew
was the local tercio. A silvery cross hung by a ribbon
around the instructor's neck.

For a few moments the new man just stood on the
podium, looking out over the cadets. Then, turning
to the boys with their feet upon the walls, he said,
"Take fockin' seats, *chicos*."

Gradually, the talk died down as the diminutive
black instructor continued to glare out over the crowd.
As the last whisper died away, the instructor began
to speak.

He said, in a hypnotically melodious voice with the
accent of the islands of the Shimmering Sea, "Close you
eyes, my children. Close you eyes and come with me.

"You in a tank; a big fockin' Jaguar. You out in
de desert. De sand be blowin', de rain fallin'. Cuz,
yes, my children, even do it never rain in de legion,
even out in de desert it rain *on* de Legion. You be
wet and chilled to de bone. You eyes be full of dust
and grit. It be darker dan t'ree foot up a welldigger's
ass . . . at midnight. You can'd see notin'. De end of
you gun barrel is a misty haze."

Eyes closed, Acosta *could* see it.

"You try to wipe de sand out of de eyes, but as

fast as you wipe you eyes dey fills up again with dat goddamn' sand. So you closes you hatch and you tries to look t'ru de tank sight. You can'd see notin'. Den you looks again. 'Wat de fock be dat?' you asks.

"It a tank, out dere in de desert, you tinks, but you looks again. Oh, shit! No it be t'ree tanks, no six . . . no eleven . . . no, over *twenty* fockin' raghead tanks and dey all be comin' to kill you little Balboan ass! 'What I goan do?' you asks. 'What de fock I goan do?'

The *Cristobalense* let the question hang, briefly.

"Open you eyes, children, open dem up and I tells you what you goan do. You goan reach deep inside youself, to where all you little fears and nightmares be. You goan think about callin de white Christ to save you ass. And you calls but you gets de busy signal. So dere you be, one little Balboan boy feelin' all alone in de desert wit' twenty tanks coming to kill you and no God to help.

"And you looks over at de gunner, you eyes wide like saucers in you head, and you asks him, 'What kind of load we be carryin, gunner?'

"And de gunner, he answers, 'Eight ronds HE, t'irty two ronds anti-tank.' And den you knows what you do?"

All the cadets looked up at the instructor with considerable interest. No, they didn't know what to do. And the instructor's face lit up with something that looked like religious devotion. Lifting his arms to the sky as if in prayer, the instructor said, in a voice that thundered across the shed:

"I tell you what you goan do. You goan call on de great Voodoo God: SABOT!" The instructor reached out and deftly pulled the black cloth away to reveal a small glass tray and a brightly polished round of tank ammunition, a sabot round, long alloy penetrating rod surrounded by a plastic sabot, or shoe. When fired, the rod would discard the sabot, cutting down wind resistance greatly, but more importantly putting all its kinetic energy against the very small portion of the target's armor struck by the point of the rod. Penetration of the armor, and death of the crew—a hideous, flesh melting, burning death—usually followed.

To this sabot round, however, anthropomorphic features had been added by a crude hand. The instructor lit a cigar and placed it on the tray in front of the round, pretending to make a small obeisance to it. "Say it wit' me now boys. Sabot!"

And the cadets answered "SABOT!"

"Sabot!"

"SABOT!"

"But de Voodoo God, he no hear you. And den you knows you needs anudder voice to pray wit' you. So you calls on you gunner to pray, too. You says 'Gunner—'"

"GUNNER!" the boys answered.

"Sabot!"

"SABOT!"

"Tank!"

"TANK!"

"Pray wit' me, boys! Gunner, sabot, tank!"

"GUNNER, SABOT, TANK!"

"Gunner, sabot, tank!"

"GUNNER, SABOT, TANK!"

"Louder so de great Voodoo God hear you!"

"GUNNER, SABOT, TANK! GUNNER, SABOT, TANK! GUNNER, SABOT, TANK!"

As the cadets turned the "prayer" into a chant the instructor stuck his right arm straight out, fist clenched, as if it were the barrel of a tank's main gun, and rotated his upper body like a turret. Between each rendition of the chant he pulled his fist straight back to his shoulder as if it were a recoiling tank cannon. The cadets joined him, sticking their own arms out, rotating them, then pulling them back for recoil, all the time laughing their heads off.

Soon, some of the boys thought, or perhaps merely felt, that a recoil should be accompanied by an explosion. The chant gradually changed to "GUNNER, SABOT, TANK, BOOM!"

"GUNNER, SABOT, TANK, BOOM! GUNNER, SABOT, TANK, BOOM! GUNNER, SABOT, TANK, BOOM!"

The instructor let the chant go on for some minutes before raising his arms to quiet the cadets again. When he was satisfied that he had whipped the boys into enough of a chanting and laughing frenzy to carry them through the unavoidably boring mechanical training to follow, he lowered his arms and said "De great god Sabot be pleased by you devotion. Five minute break. Den fall in on de tanks outside."

On his break Julio took the time to finish his letter:

> "But, as hard as this is sometimes, it can also
> be a lot of fun—and very funny, too—but
> I'd still rather be home.
>
> Love,
> Julio"

Casa Linda, Balboa, 1/6/468 AC

One of the peculiarities of Balboan democracy was
that elections were set for the most densely miserable part of the wet season. Whether or not it really
had been the theory behind this date that fewer of
the wretchedly poor would vote if the price for voting were to be standing in a long line in the middle
of a deluge, that was clearly the effect. It was, even
so, hard to credit Balboa's moneyed class with that
kind of foresight.

"And it's going to hurt us," Parilla said, staring out
into the downpour from the covered back terrace of
the *casa*, the one that looked north towards the *Isla
Real*. The sun was up, but only just, to his right as
he faced. Soon enough the entire country would be
a dutch oven, with a combination of about one hundred percent humidity and over one hundred degrees,
Fahrenheit, of temperature.

Ruiz sipped at his coffee and shrugged. "It will
and it won't. Sure, some of the very poor who might
otherwise vote will stay home. But the legionaries
could care less about a little rain or heat or sun. And
they'll all vote. And if one in a hundred of them votes
for someone besides you I'd be very, very surprised."

"A wash then, you think?" Parilla asked.

"About that."

Indistinct in the thickened air, a helicopter—Parilla
recognized the sound of a *Legion* IM-62—churned its
way eastward toward *Ciudad* Cervantes, carrying several
hundred legionaries to their home town to vote. On
the return trip the chopper would take a like number
of already-voted reservists, with their arms, to guard

the island. Still other reservists had assembled at the polls before sunrise, leaving their arms nearby and under guard. These would later march to the borders of the Tauran controlled areas around the Transitway and the pro-Rocaberti enclaves of *Ciudad* Balboa.

Whether they would be needed remained to be seen. Observation posts in the towns by the Vera Cruz training area, overlooking the old FSAF base at *Bruja* Point, reported a Tauran Union aircraft landing every forty minutes, not counting combat aircraft. Some carried troops; some carried supplies. One and all, though, they suggested that neither the Tauran Union nor the corrupt government it backed by backing Gaul was going to acquiesce lightly in any election that turned over control to Parilla and his mercenaries.

Both Parilla and Ruiz looked skyward at the sound of what had to have been a very large jet making a leisurely turn to the west. "What's Patricio doing about this over in Pashtia?" Ruiz asked.

"He's kept one legion to interdict the border, just as our contract calls for," Parilla answered. "The other two, while on their way home, he's maneuvered into position to crush the Tauran Union forces in Pashtia. The Taurans appear to know it, too."

"They've got to be shitting bricks," Ruiz chuckled. "He's holding their people there hostage for the good behavior of their people here."

Parilla smiled, saying, "Well, Patricio learned about taking hostages from the main enemy. And we've all seen how the TU reacts when someone is holding Tauran's hostage. The only problem is that the FSC can see what we're doing and is really pissed about it."

Ruiz disagreed. "I don't think they're pissed so

much as they're worried. A war here shuts down the Transitway. That hurts them nearly as much as it hurts us. After all, about seventy percent of the cargo passing through here either starts in the FSC, ends there, or both. And then if fighting breaks out here, they have to know Patricio will hit the enemy wherever he finds him and in the most destructive way he can. That would make a shambles of an already pretty shaky alliance in Pashtia. And then . . ."

"Yes?" Parilla prompted.

"Well, emotionally the FSC doesn't really give a shit about us. If anything, the ruling Progressive Party resents us because Wozniak lost his presidency, at least in part, over the Transitway. And their current government just adores the Taurans, and especially the bloody perfidious Gauls. Even though we're much, much more valuable to them, I don't think that emotionally they can do anything *but* take the Frogs' side of things."

"Idiots to go with their hearts rather than their heads," Parilla said.

"Idiots to set their hearts on the Taurans," Ruiz amended.

Panshir Base, Pashtia, 1/6/468 AC

The shell holes were long since filled in. The troops were well fed and had even been able to put on a little fat. All the ruined tents had been replaced. Even so, the *Ligurini* Brigade of Claudio Marciano was digging in frantically, entrenching, filling sandbags, breaking down ammunition.

They had reason to. Lightly armed as they were, they didn't stand a chance if the legion surrounding them should attack. That it should have come to this, and so quickly . . .

Seating in a canvas folding camp chair, deep in his bunker, Marciano sighed even more deeply. "I don't know what the idiot Gauls' game is, Patricio. They're playing their cards awfully close to their chests this time."

Carrera looked up at the roof of the bunker. *Pretty solid. Won't stop a 160mm though.* He looked at Marciano's altogether Roman face and asked, "What are your government's instructions if it comes to a fight between us and the Frogs? I mean . . . if you can tell me, that is."

"I can't tell you, exactly, Patricio, buuut, if you think about it . . ."

There are no Tuscan troops in Balboa, Carrera thought. *So fighting there need not spread here as far as they're concerned. But, as far as I'm concerned an attack there by the Frogs means general war and I won't be held back from destroying their forces here.*

"I'm going after them here, Claudio. If it's war then it's war to the knife and the knife to the hilt . . . wher*ev*er they may be. I'd leave your boys out of it, if I could, but I can't leave a strong enough force to guard you here. I'll have to destroy you so that I can redeploy that legion to take on Haarlem, Sachsen, Anglia, Secordia and the rest." He actually had a hard time accepting that "the rest" might include the FSC troops in country.

"And we have mutual defense treaties with them," Marciano said. "Mine is an honorable country, even if not all our allies are honorable."

Carrera thought, "And Romans in Rome's quarrels . . . spared neither land nor gold . . . nor son nor wife nor limb nor life . . . in the brave days of old." And Claudio, here, is a true Roman. I wouldn't insult him or his men by suggesting surrender.

"You've got good troops here, Claudio, but . . . you know it won't take a full legion more than a few hours to overrun this base. Please, tell your government that. Explain to them that the stakes are much higher than the Frogs are suggesting."

"I have. They find it hard to believe."

War Department, Hamilton, FD, FSC, 1/6/468 AC

It hurt, deep inside, for Malcolm to admit it. "Okay, Rivers, I'm convinced. I'm a believer. If we don't intervene to keep fighting from breaking out in Balboa then Pashtia is lost." *And with it, my chance to become president.* "I've got a meeting set up with the president and the secretary of state. I will do what I can to convince them."

"Convince them of what?" Rivers asked.

"Of the danger," Malcolm answered. "Of the need for mediation. Of the need to throw our weight *against* whoever fires the first shot."

"Then you had best hurry, Mr. Secretary," Rivers said. "The Frogs"—*Oh, how I love saying "Frogs" to this puke who so loves the Frogs*—"are flying in major numbers of troops and the legion's regulars and reservists are falling in on assembly areas on both sides and both ends of the Transitway area. The news is full of enough accusations of violence, corruption and fraud in the election process that either side can claim to have 'won.' If nothing changes, I predict a blood bath starting by midnight."

The Trapezoid, Executive Mansion, Hamilton, FD, Federated States of Columbia, 1/6/468 AC

"Then why not just threaten the stinking mercenaries if trouble breaks out?" thundered the secretary of state, Mary Darkling, a woman short, shrill, and seriously overweight. "We all *know* they're trying to steal the election down there. Wozniak is convinced of it. The global press insists upon it. Our allies, the Gauls, are certain of it. By taking the side of the mercenaries against our *real* allies we're undercutting the tradition and understanding of *decades.* It's absurd!"

Malcolm shook his head. Inside he felt precisely what Darkling openly insisted upon . . . but, "I'm with you in this, morally, Mary. But the practicalities are such that we just *can't* let this thing spiral out of control. I adore Gaul as much as you do. I want to help them, to induce them to help us. I want to try to overcome the suspicion and hostility that built up under the previous administration. But . . . *we're dealing with a maniac here!* The leader of the mercenaries is not susceptible to reason. He won't even take bribes at this point. I believe that, were he capable, he'd destroy the entire planet before backing down an inch. He's got an army and he's *going* to have a country . . . or he's going to fight to take one."

Darkling shot an accusatory glare at the president. *It's* your *fault for keeping us in that utterly illegal war in Pashtia.*

President Schumann understood the glare. He smiled and said, "The one thing keeping us from losing the center again and being run out of office, Mary, my dear, is that we promised to win in Pashtia. For that, for reasons largely logistic, we need the mercenaries. For reasons entirely political, we need them to bleed rather than ourselves. When I asked you for a diplomatic solution to Pashtia you gave me a blank stare. I'm a Progressive, Mary; I'm not an idiot. We *must* win in Pashtia or we must *lose* here."

Turning to Malcolm, Schumann said, "We need to force a delay until Pashtia is won and we can dispense with the mercenaries. So . . . I want you ready a major expeditionary force to Balboa. Sail them, post haste." He shifted his attention to Darkling and said, "Here's what I want you to tell our ambassador . . ."

Embassy of the Federated States, *Ciudad Balboa*, 1/6/468 AC

Had it not been for the position of the legion within Balboa, Ambassador Thomas Wallis would have been most unlikely ever to see the lofty rank he held. Medium height, medium build, nonpatrician, he had none of the connections within the Federated States' diplomatic service that were normally an absolute requirement for admission to the inner circle.

He had had one greatly redeeming feature, as far as the previous, Federalist, administration had been concerned. Wallis had spent many years in the armed forces before retiring and entering the diplomatic corps. He was, thus, a natural for dealing with that part of Balboa most of interest to the Federated States, the legion. He considered it only a matter of time, though, before the Progressives booted him. *The fact that I'm ex-military is enough to make me suspect to the Progs.*

Interesting, thought the ambassador, *that Muñoz-Infantes is sitting on the Balboan side of the conference table. Very interesting. I wonder what's going on there.* Wallis looked at Janier. *The Frog looks ready to shit himself.*

Is that Castilian bastard trying to tell me something? wondered Janier, for the nonce without his imperial marshal's uniform or laurel wreath.

How far is the Castilian willing to go to support us? wondered Parilla.

"Gentlemen," began the ambassador, softly and genially. With the utterance of the word he was immediately greeted by a storm of swears and accusation from both sides of the conference table. Conspicuously, Muñoz-Infantes kept quiet.

Soft and genial won't cut it, I see.

Wallis injected steel into his voice. "GENTLE-MEN! Be quiet!"

Those present shut up, not always with good grace. Wallis continued, "I am advised by the president, speaking through the secretary of state, to inform you that two carrier battle groups are en route here. Moreover, two reinforced regiments of Federated States Marines are, even as we speak, boarding ship to come here. One division of paratroopers is likewise being readied. Their orders are—consistent with Federated States policy with regard to the Transitway, and also consistent with our treaties—to engage whichever side shall first initiate hostilities in or around the Transitway area."

The ambassador raised his nose at an underling. Immediately, a map of the Transitway appeared on a wall-mounted plasma screen. On it could be seen two bright red lines, delineating boundaries. They corresponded closely enough to the old Federated States boundaries, with the exception that they also ran though *Ciudad* Balboa, chopping off the Old Cuirass district, wherein lay the presidential palace, from the rest of the city.

Understanding the implications, both Rocaberti's party and Parilla's once again burst into open argument. Janier's group of diplomats and officers, however, remained silent. The boundaries drawn would, for the time being, suit.

"Gentlemen, quiet!" the ambassador repeated. "These are not subject to argument. This *is* where you will maintain your forces and your political control until some more amicable settlement can be reached."

Infuriated, Rocaberti shouted, "Your own ex-president has said those bastards stole the election!"

"He never met a governmental thief he didn't love," retorted Parilla.

"None of that *matters*," insisted the ambassador. "What matters is that this is what we, the Federated States, have commanded. Gentlemen, in this 'our voice is *imperial*.' What matters is that two carrier battle groups and two regiments of Marines are on their way here to enforce our commands, and a division of paratroopers stands ready to reinforce them."

"But you *can't* split the City like this," Rocaberti pleaded. "It's . . . obscene."

The ambassador sighed. "Mr. President you are missing the point. That point is that hostilities must not break out. The boundary as drawn separates out the Tauran Union forces from what we believe to be over twenty thousand Balboan reserve legionaries.

Crossing over it will cause those legionaries to fight"—
Goddamn right, thought Parilla. *And it's closer to
thirty-five thousand.*—"and *causing* that will be taken
as initiation of hostilities."

"But you're putting them in control of three-quarters
of the population!"

"More like seven-eighths. President Rocaberti. Let
there be no bullshit between us," the ambassador continued. "There is good reason to believe that that is close
to the true percentage of the areas where a majority of
the voting populace went for Legate Parilla. Yes, quite
despite ex-President Wozniak's claims. Be grateful, Mr.
President, that we have left you with a safe enclave
where *President Parilla* cannot prosecute you."

Nicobar Straits, 2/6/468 AC

There is no safe harbor except in silence, thought
al Naquib, watching out over the polluted waters of
the straits and coughing from the smoky haze that
dominated it. *There is no safe harbor when the enemy
can listen in on every word spoken on a phone or a
radio, not when our ranks contain informers and spies.*

*The down side of silence, though, is coordination.
Everything*, everything, *depends on getting the word
at the proper time from a ship's captain I have never
laid eyes on nor even spoken to. And to add to the
uncertainty, half my force is on this side of the Straits,
half on the other.*

*Worries, worries . . . my life is worries. What if
my boats are spotted? What if the conexes with the
missiles are spotted? What if the* Hoogaboom *has a
delay. What if; what if, what if?*

Al Naquib pulled out a compass and oriented himself toward Makkah al Jedidah. Prostrating himself, he prayed, *I have done what I can, Lord, all that is in my power to do. It is in Your hands now. My men will do their duty. They are among the best of the faithful. My machines have been cared for, as the new learning says they must be. So, Beneficent One, I ask . . . I plead . . . I beg for Your favor tomorrow as my men go into battle. And, Lord, even if you withhold your favor from our undertaking, I ask that you see to the souls of my men who serve you.*

INTERLUDE

1/8/48 AC, *Ciudad* Balboa, Balboa Colony, Terra Nova

Warrant Officer Bourguet, seated in a metal folding chair, smiled down at the half-starved, eleven-year-old girl kneeling between his legs. She had tears in her eyes. Bourguet neither knew nor cared whether they were caused by shame or by the little brown wretch choking on his penis. The tears, themselves, pleased him almost as much as the girl's mouth.

There had been a short period of time when the hungry girls had stopped coming to the camp to provide service for food. After a little inquiry, Bourguet had discovered that the bloody Belgian commandos down the road had begun to offer more, to drive up the price. *Neo-colonialist bastards.*

The solution to the shortage was elegant in its simplicity. Bourguet had simply dispatched two soldiers to lie in wait for one of the colonial girls to approach the Belgian camp. When, the next morning, a small group of different girls had found a head and a pair of hands mounted on a stick beside the trail, they'd immediately turned around and gone to the OAU camp in search of something to eat.

Bourguet laughed aloud. Then he twisted the girl's hair in his fingers, pulled her head away and slapped her face to make sure she was paying attention.

"You," he said. "All fours. Like dog."

5/10/48 AC, Desperation Bay, Lansing Colony, Southern Columbia, Terra Nova

News traveled slowly on the new world. Rather, true news traveled slowly.

"But you can get the UN's lies right away," said Ollie Rogers to his assembled family and a few guests, over dinner.

Ollie now had five wives. One had died but three more, along with another seven children, five of them from those three wives, had come his way from the survivors of the wintry disaster that gave the bay its name. Of his thirty-one living children, natural and adopted, three had children of their own. Ollie considered it a mark of God's special favor that he had been so blessed with offspring. Though it wasn't as if he would not have been elected as leader of the colony even if he'd been a bachelor.

One of the guests, Benjamin Putnam, asked, "What do you believe, Ollie? Do you think it's true about the UN troops using or raping little girls up in Balboa?"

That rumor—really that set of rumors, for there were several variants—had become quite widely told over the last few months. The least of the variants told of pre-pubescent prostitutes being dismembered and their bodies put on display near one of the UN's bases, to drive their trade to where the money was less.

Rogers arose from the table and walked to the cabin's sole window, a wavy glass that the colony was just beginning to produce. Looking outside he saw a small cemetery, with a tree growing in the middle of it. They'd named the tree "the tranzitree," and the white wooden crosses around its base reminded Rogers that the tranzitree's fruit, with its bright green exterior and poisonous red interior, killed.

"Ben," Rogers answered slowly and deliberately, "we've both heard a lot of propaganda in our lives. That one has the ring of truth to me."

"Disgraceful," judged Gertie. She'd grown rather plump the last couple of decades but her husband still found her among the best of all women.

"Disgraceful, it may be," agreed Rogers. "But what can we do about it?"

"We can help them; the people the UN is trying to suppress, I mean," said Ollie's oldest son, also called "Oliver" or just "Junior."

"You have children of your own to watch out for," the patriarch reminded.

"We don't," said three of the boys, simultaneously.

Sheriff Juan Alvarez's son, too, spoke up, "And neither do I." Before the lawman could object, his son added, "And if we don't stop the UN up there, how long before they come here? Father, Mr. Oliver, you both left the homes you had because of them. Where do you—where do we—go . . . if they come here, too?"

"You'll need better arms than we can provide," Rogers said. He didn't say it like he thought it would be impossible to get those arms. "We have, after all, found quite a bit of gold here."

CHAPTER SIXTEEN

The winds of Paradise are blowing. Where
are you who hanker after Paradise?
　　—Motto of the *Ikhwan*

As a soldier I will fulfill my duties brilliantly.
I die with a smile on my face with the deep
belief that to meet my end on the *kamikaze*
battleship Yamato is the ultimate honor.
　　—Chief Petty Officer Yoshiaki
　　　Ogasawara Mikoto
　　　KIA 7 April, 1945 (Old Earth Year)

BdL *Dos Lindas*, Nicobar Straits, 3/6/468 AC

Except for having gone to a much heightened state of
alert, and maintaining a lookout for Gallic vessels of
war, the election had not much affected the carrier or
her escorts. They, like the single legion now deployed
on the border between Pashtia and Kashmir, had a
contract to fulfill. Now, without the specter of a major
war with Taurus in the offing, the *classis* was able,
once again, to concentrate solely on pirate hunting.

Which was . . . disappointing. Since the flotilla had

arrived on station, piracy in the Straits had dropped to, essentially, nothing.

"It's almost as if someone's *told* them to lay off," Fosa said, looking inquiringly at Kurita standing on the bridge overlooking the calm waters.

"Someone has," Kurita answered cryptically. "We don't know why. It could be as simple as the hope that if there's no piracy for a while the Zaibatsu will curtail your contract and send you home. It could be just fear—well founded fear, too, I might add—of what the *classis* will do if there *are* any incidents. It could be . . ." Kurita's eyes looked skyward.

Fosa's eyes, too, traveled upward. *Fucking Earth-pigs.*

UEPF Spirit of Peace, 3/6/468 AC

High Admiral Robinson (Wallenstein understood perfectly that UE senior officials were always "High" in order to make clear to the rest of humanity that *they* were *low*) and Captain Wallenstein sat comfortably in the silverwood paneled ship's conference room, along with a few others who were in on enough of the secret to trust. None, of course, barring only Wallenstein, knew everything. Ordinarily, Robinson might have enjoyed the show in the privacy of his own quarters, watching it on the big, crystal-clear Kurosawa. Still, in odd little ways the staff had helped quite a bit and were entitled to their reward.

On the wall past the end of the conference table— the table, like the paneling, brought up from below—a vision screen showed a small flotilla moving majestically through some jungle-lined straits. It was the dry season in that part of the world below, Robinson knew. Even if he had not known, the fires raging uncontrolled that sent thick clouds of smoke across the straits, often blocking the view, would have told him.

Peace was not only too far up to see in this much detail with its own sensors and camera; it was also in the wrong orbit. Instead, the real-time images were being sent by a skimmer launched by the UEPF *Spirit of Brotherhood* a few hours before daylight had arisen on the straits.

MV *Hendrik Hoogaboom*, Nicobar Straits, 3/6/468 AC

The captain of the *Hoogaboom* looked behind him, watching the last sunrise he would ever see in this life. The sun's light shone red, a result of filtering through and bending around the smoke that dominated the straits. In his hand the captain held a picture. It was a family picture, with the females' faces exposed. As such, it was not to be shared. The picture showed the faces of his wife, his two daughters and his three sons.

The captain knew that, by dint of his coming sacrifice, they'd be taken care of, in this life as well as the next. Whatever else might be said of the *Ikhwan*, it had to be admitted that it took very good care of its martyrs' dependants, lest the supply of martyrs dry up. One of the things that had hurt the movement, indeed, perhaps that infidel action that had hurt the most, was the sequestration, impoundment, and outright confiscation of funds for just that sort of reward. Living single men were cheap. Weapons and ammunition, even explosives, were cheap. To support the families of the fallen was *expensive*.

Thank Allah, thought the captain, *that the infidel press tipped the movement off to what their governments were doing when they went after the money. What would we ever do without the* First Landing Times? *I could never take the action I am about to if I could not be sure my family would be cared for. Thank You, too, Beneficent One, for the money given in humanitarian aid that frees up money for the fight and to care for the families of those fallen in Your cause.*

The captain looked at the covered switch on his control panel, next to the ship's wheel. It led down to the roughly two thousand tons of ammonium nitrate-fuel oil, hydrazine and aluminum powder mix in the bunkered hold. A second switch in the *Hoogaboom's* informal CIC likewise led to the explosive. The captain's executive, a Kashmiri fanatic named Ishmael, controlled that for the time being; later they would switch. Lastly, below the water line and out of the line of direct fire, was a pressure detonator. If every man on the ship were to be killed or incapacitated, as long as the *Hoogaboom* was well aimed enough to manage to hit the target or to ground near it, the ship would explode.

The captain looked at the chart of the Nicobar Straits that lay on his plotting table. It showed the positions of the major enemy vessel, and of the two torpedoes, the six cruise missiles, and the dozen fast speedboats that rocked hidden in the jungle inlets to either side of the straits. It also showed his own ship, moving, as was the enemy, to intersection with those speedboats.

Turning again and taking a last deliberate look at the sunrise, the captain told his radio man, "Per our *contract*"—which raised a slight giggle from the radio operator—"inform the infidels that we are making our passage and should pass them by within two hours. *Don't* call them 'infidels' when you do."

BdL *Dos Lindas*, 3/6/468 AC

Ash floated on the breeze, some of it still smoldering. Because of that, Fosa had ordered that all refueling and rearming operations take place below, on the hangar deck. There were some obvious downsides to this; for one thing, the ship reeked. But it was just unwise to take the risk of a deck fire from a stray spark.

Fortunately, the Finches had very long legs and tremendous endurance. It was not difficult to keep two aloft continuously, along with another brace of Cricket Bs. The Crickets kept fairly close to the ship, patrolling the edge of the water where it met jungle.

Annoyingly, one of the Crickets hadn't called in in a while and failed to respond to any radio calls to it. Fosa had already given the order to send out another to replace it.

The Finches he had farther out, in case a merchant ship under contract for protection should be attacked. Indeed, each Finch aloft was paired with a corvette, operating at a distance of about twenty-five miles southeast or northwest of the main *classis*. Even farther away, to the southeast, the *Qamra*, formerly *The Big ?*, churned along in leisurely fashion, trolling for pirates. Unfortunately, the best bait, the girls, had to be kept below for the most part. *Nobody* was going to be nude sunbathing on the deck with all the smoke and ash on the breeze. It would have been inherently suspicious had anyone tried.

Sealed out by thick, shatterproof glass or not, the reek of smoke still penetrated the bridge. It had to; the *Dos Lindas* was not a spaceship; it drew its air from its surroundings. Fosa was on the bridge, as was Kurita. Both scanned the waters, such as were visible, for threats or targets. There were none, just the enveloping smoke with occasional clear patches.

Unaccountably, and unknowingly imitating the captain of the *Hoogaboom*, Kurita pulled out a wallet from which he drew a plastic encased black and white photograph. Fosa stepped over to look. He saw a much—a *very* much—younger Kurita, in dark naval uniform, surrounded by kimono-clad wife and children. The children were beautiful but Fosa was struck mostly by the wife. He knew the story, of course; Kurita had long before explained that his family had been caught in the nuclear bombing of Yamato by the Federated States near the end of the Great Global War.

Your life must have been hard without her, my friend, Fosa thought. *Like our Patricio, losing a woman like that is like having your soul torn out.*

As if reading Fosa's thought, Kurita said, "Yes . . . it was . . . difficult."

"Well," the captain of *Dos Lindas* answered, "perhaps you shall reincarnate together, someday."

Kurita rarely laughed, but at that comment he began first to snicker, then to giggle, then finally was overtaken with belly-ripping hilarity. When he recovered, and that took a while, he explained, "Oh, no, my dear friend. She waits for me in Heaven. You see, when the Federated States decided to drop a nuke, they chose a *Christian* city. We are *Catholic.*"

Which goes to show that I will never *understand*

Yamato. How does a Catholic believe ships and swords are alive?

This understanding had not been helped by the late night haiku duel he had engaged in with the commodore the evening before over *sake*. The subject had been the great Kosmo crisis du jour, planetary warming. And beforehand, Kurita had warned, after explaining the rules, "Never bring a knife to a gunfight unless you bring a gun, too. Never bring a sonnet to a haiku fight."

Kurita, as the host, had begun:

> "Useful idiots
> Without original thought
> Believe in the faith."

Fosa though about that one for a moment, before submitting:

> "Government money
> Given for the right viewpoint
> Keeps Kosmos happy."

It was a weak addendum, so Kurita, always gracious, held himself in check:

> "Climate change requires
> Solar output be ignored
> Or lose nice funding."

Fosa nodded at that one, sipped at his *sake* contemplatively, then answered:

> "Great fireball in sky,
> How to explain you away
> When moons' icecaps melt?"

"Oh, very *good*, Fosa-san," Kurita applauded. "You're getting the hang of this." He then declaimed:

> "Wondrous hockey stick
> Replaces Christ's wooden cross
> Comes from white noise."

White? White? Fosa wondered. *How to play on that? Ah, sheep are white.*

> "Climate change white sheep
> Hate being out of the flock
> Lest they be shorn . . . baaaa"

"Bah! Bah, indeed," Kurita exhulted.

> "Great Climate Change!
> For heretics, deniers,
> Jail cells are waiting."

Fosa answered:

> "Even Progressives
> In Fed'rated States Senate
> Say, 'Piss on Kosmos!'"

From Kurita:

> "Climate change loonies
> Shriek, 'Heresy! Blasphemy!'
> Whenever questioned."

Fosa expanded:

> "Gathering firewood
> To burn up the deniers.
> We've seen this before."

After he stopped laughing, Kurita gave:

"Virgin SUV
Cast into the volcano
As the faithful dance."

At that point, Fosa gave up. The image of ten thousand grass-skirt clad Kosmos, deep in religious ecstasy,
sacrificing an innocent automobile to the dark earth
gods was too much. No doubt much of his mirth was
found in the *sake*, not the poetry. Even so, Fosa was
rolling on the floor laughing when, to cap his victory,
Kurita gave his last recital:

"High Kosmo leeches
Attend luxury conference
Always fly first class."

Fosa's reminiscences were interrupted by the sudden arrival of a Cricket on the flight deck. With a
plane needing as short a landing run as the Cricket,
and landing into the wind, to boot, all arrivals tended
to be very sudden.

No sooner had it landed, and the pilot killed the
engine, then that pilot was out the door and *racing*
across the flight deck to the tower. He disappeared
from view, only to emerge on the bridge moments
later.

"My fucking radio went down, Skipper," Montoya
announced, even before formally reporting. "I'd have
come back right away but there was something odd,
a boat, I saw hidden in the jungle."

"Odd?" Fosa asked.

"Three ways, Skipper. One was that it was pretty
well hidden. Another was that it looked fast, what I

could make out of it. The last was that there were armed men aboard, and they *didn't* shoot at me."

Kurita's finger beat Fosa's to the alarm: *Battle stations, this is no drill.*

Lovely word, 'karma,' al Naquib thought. *Pity we don't have quite the equivalent in Islam. But it was karma, or Allah's will, that the infidel aircraft spotted us. Maybe I should have ordered that aircraft engaged. Maybe I did right in not ordering it engaged. I'll never know in this life. What I do know is we must attack now, even though the enemy is not in the optimal position for our ambush.*

One hundred meters up a half choked inlet, al Naquib's boat wound its way through the maze of fallen logs and sand bars. To either side, he heard the distance-dissipated roar of large marine engines coming to life and doing likewise. He could not hear the motors of the half dozen boats on the other side of the Straits. Yet his chief assistant had told him they were likewise on the move.

Unseen and unheard by al Naquib, crews for the cruise missiles and torpedoes were frantically unmasking, activating their guidance systems, and preparing to fire. Hopefully they would launch in good time.

UEPF Spirit of Peace, 3/6/468 AC

"They're launching aircraft!" Robinson shouted. "Why the fuck are they launching aircraft?"

It was true. It was *more* than true. Robinson had watched this ship, off and on, for months and he'd never before seen such a frantic attempt to get as many aircraft into the air, as quickly, as he was witnessing now. As soon as a plane came up the elevator, a deck crew was manhandling it into position and sending it off. Pilots were lined up waiting for any bird to fly. Once, when an engine refused to start, the deck crew had unceremoniously dragged the protesting pilot out and pushed the thing over the side. Pilots, themselves, were boarding with small arms, an indicator that the planes were being thrown up either unarmed or so lightly armed that even a rifle could make a difference.

Robinson relaxed slightly when he saw the two trails of underwater torpedoes streaking from under the jungle layer that had hidden them. His spirits revived considerably with the appearance of a larger number of cruise missiles coming from the same jungle.

Abdul Aziz had, early on, thought that torpedoes and cruise missiles might be a useful adjunct to the *Hoogaboom* and its mission. Further reflection, however, had convinced him that the risk of detection, if placed aboard ship, was too great. This had not meant the idea was without merit, only that it needed further refinement.

Large torpedoes were out for a number of reasons; chief among these was that "large" equaled both "noticeable" and "too heavy and bulky to transport and set up in the jungle along the straits." There were, however, much smaller torpedoes available, from various Volgan crime syndicates, and for surprisingly little money. These torpedoes were not suitable for sinking a major warship, of course, but that wasn't their purpose. Rather, they were designed to home on engine noise to kill submarines. What would kill a submarine, Abdul thought, was likely to severely damage an AZIPOD.

This both torpedoes were trying to do, streaking under the water straight for the AZIPODs mounted at *Dos Lindas'* stern.

BdL *Dos Lindas*, 3/6/468 AC

"Fish in the water! Fish in the water! Fuck! Fish in the water!"

Fosa heard the sonar man's announcement and dread filled his heart. Looking at the screen and seeing the torpedoes aligning themselves for a run at the propellers, he was about to give the command to kill power when radar screamed, "Moonbats! Moonbats! Moonbats! Cruise missiles incoming . . . Raid count: three . . . no, four . . . ah, shit! Six! Skipper, Moonbats six, all quarters."

"Surface Action, Port and Starboard," Fosa ordered. "Weapons free."

There was a whining overhead and a sudden *CRACK* as the laser mounted above the tower engaged one of the cruise missiles. Two more, much more muted, *CRACK*s sounded as the fore and aft lasers likewise engaged. In the distance, and it was not nearly enough distance, two explosions that had to be in the half ton of TNT range, told that the lasers had scored, if imperfectly. There were still four cruise missiles incoming and the smoke, apparently, made engagement more than a little problematic.

Again, the defensive lasers fired. Again, only two hit, creating huge angry clouds of hot gas and flying metal. But there had been six missiles. There were still two . . . and there was no more time.

UEPF Spirit of Peace, 3/6/468 AC

"Fuck!" Robinson cursed as first two, then two more, of the *Ikhwan's* cruise missiles were destroyed. And then he saw a sight to gratify his heart as a massive explosion erupted on the ship's side, and another self detonated, so he thought, just above the tower atop the carrier. Within moments the ship's rear elevator, likewise, burst forth in smoke and fire. Atop the column of flame, Robinson thought he saw a helicopter being blasted upward.

"Take that, fuckers!"

PTF Santissima Trinidad, 3/6/468 AC

The air was still heavily weighted with smoke from the shoreline fires. Pedraz scanned through it, as best he could, with the binoculars he carried as a matter of habit now. Sweeping his vision along the shoreline, Pedraz whispered, "*Nada*. Just fucking *nada*."

Even though the PTF was a few miles away from the *Dos Lindas*, the battle stations klaxon sounded clearly across the water. Then came the message from CIC to all escorts to expect attack by surface boats, probably suicide boats, and to close in on the flagship. Pedraz pulled on a set of headphones and then reached for the klaxon.

Before Pedraz could give the signal for battle stations a half dozen speedboats swarmed out from the banks of the strait. Clavell and Guptillo, manning the forward forty, engaged even without orders. Their first several shots missed, but then they were rewarded by a major blast as one of the speedboats simply disintegrated when a shell found what must have been a huge charge of explosive.

Cheering was cut short as, just off the port side, a flaming streak shot past, followed by another to starboard. The machine gunners, moving as quickly as their legs would carry them from wherever the call to battle stations had found them, were mostly too late to bring fire on the cruise missiles. Only one gun actually engaged, and it missed.

No time for orders, Pedraz took the con, himself, elbowing Francais out of the way. Pushing the throttle to maximum, he twisted the wheel to point the boat away from the shore and towards the threatened carrier. Clavell and Guptillo swung the forty around to engage another of the small boats but the *Trinidad* turned faster than they could traverse the gun.

No matter, by the time the *Trinidad* was headed toward the carrier, the rear machine gun crews were fighting desperately, causing the speedboats to have to maneuver to avoid being hit.

Pedraz thought, *If nothing else, it buys time. Now if only—*

He saw a massive explosion between the *Trinidad* and the flagship. He was about to cheer when he saw another explosion, above the carrier, and then another near the stern. He wasn't sure it was the flagship being hit until he spotted the Yakamov helicopter being launched straight up, riding a column of fire and disintegrating as it flew.

"Oh, fuck."

In his headphones, Pedraz heard, "Skipper? Dorado. Sonar's got two fish in the water, running shallow."

Bridge, BdL *Dos Lindas*, 3/6/468 AC

The ship lurched, tossing to the deck everyone on the bridge not already seated and strapped in. None of the thick windows quite shattered, but every portside window cracked, along with most of those a-starboard. Even through the blurring of the cracks, even from flat on his ass, Fosa saw the abruptly launched Yakamov, streaking upward like a comet.

"Near miss . . . ah, Hell, call it a hit. Hit Alpha, island structure, zero-four level. Hit Bravo, hangar deck, starboard side aft. Fire on the hangar deck! Damage control parties away."

A smoke-choked and shock-strained voice from somewhere below came over the speaker. "There *are* no . . . damage control . . . parties near the . . . hit."

"My shshshiiippp!"

"Captain-san," Kurita said, groggily, "stay here and fight your ship. I will see to damage control." With that, the nonagenarian struggled to his feet and left, seeking the epicenter of the damage.

"Fight my ship . . . fight my ship . . . FIGHT MY FUCKING SHIP!"

In those few seconds, Fosa understood a part of what Kurita had been trying to tell him before, about ships having spirits and souls, about them being alive. At least he understood this much, that his ship was more valuable to him than his own life and must be preserved, at all costs consistent with its own honor.

Can something with honor be without a soul?

Hands gripping a plotting table, Fosa pulled himself to his feet. He heard machine gun and light cannon fire from all around as the gun crews finally got to their battle stations and began engaging the speedboats. Range was long but it couldn't hurt to try. He'd expended something over a million rounds of ammunition in training. If they couldn't get some stinking jury-rigged speedboats, no one could. He'd counted the number of explosions from cruise missiles. There had been six launches and six explosions. If the enemy had had more missiles, they'd have launched more, he thought. *What else threatens my ship?*

"Report!"

"That one above us took out the radar, Captain. Before that I had no hostile aircraft, Captain," Radar said.

"Ours are still trying to organize out of cluster fuck mode, sir," said the air boss.

Sonar announced, "Skipper, I've still got two fish in the water, one each, port and starboard. Counter-measures are not, I repeat not, effective. First impact expected in seven minutes."

Seven minutes . . . seven minutes . . . a whole lifetime can pass in seven minutes.

Fosa reached for the microphone. "Escorts, this is Fosa."

"*Trinidad*, here, sir" . . . "*Agustin*, sir."

"The flagship's been hit but I think we can save her," Fosa said. "What we can't do anything about from here are the torpedoes—you see them on sonar?"

"Aye" . . . "Aye."

Fosa gulped; this was a hard order to give. "I need you to try to bait the torpedoes away . . . and if that doesn't work . . ."

No arguments, no questions. "It's better they hit us than hit the *Dos Lindas*. Understood. This is *Agustin*, we'll try" . . . "*Trinidad*, Pedraz speaking. I'll give it a shot."

Unseen, Fosa nodded. "Good lads," he said into the microphone. Looking up at the operations board he ordered, "Warn the *Hoogaboom* off. Tell them we're under attack. And, air boss, get the planes onto those goddamned speedboats."

"*Hoogaboom* acknowledges, sir."

PTF Santissima Trinidad, 3/6/468 AC

"Nav, give me a plot for the torpedo on our side, an *intercept* plot."

"You're shitting me, right, Chief?"

"Just give me the fucking intercept, Dorado," Pedraz said to the navigator.

"Be a minute," Dorado answered.

"You've got fifteen seconds, Pedro, I want to pass about four hundred meters in front of the thing."

It didn't even take fifteen seconds. In half that time Dorado came back, answering, "Fuck . . . can't do it, Chief. We're not fast enough."

Pedraz picked up the radio microphone and, keying it, said, "*Dos Lindas*, this is *Trinidad*. No chance to intercept on our side. Sorry."

BdL Dos Lindas, 3/6/468 AC

"Captain, *Agustin* reports that they've caught the torpedo's attention and it's following them. They can stay ahead of it and lead it off. *Trinidad* says we're fucked. Impact, astern . . . two minutes."

"Hard a-port and then kill the AZIPODs."

The entire bridge crew turned and looked at Fosa as if he were mad.

"Hard a-port and then all, STOP, goddamit. Do it . . . then kill the fucking drives!"

The torpedo noted the instant drop off in screw noise. It might, had it been a less sophisticated torpedo, have then been fooled by the countermeasures the target deployed. It was, however, "competent" and, as such, had already eliminated the false noises from consideration. It had, further, tracked the speed of the carrier and was able, in general terms, to account for the continuing forward momentum of the target even if it lost its acoustic aiming point. A few degrees more steer and the torpedo continued on its merry way, aimed *almost* perfectly for the port side AZIPOD. Indeed, it would have been perfect, but that the ship was ever so slowly turning head on to the speeding torpedo.

For a nonagenarian, Kurita was fast on his feet. Perhaps it was that, unlike in most human beings, there was just no mechanism in him to give in to frailty or pain. Whichever the case, he was down on third deck, as close as he could get to the fire, within moments of leaving the bridge.

Many men, burned, broken, and bleeding, sat quietly against bulkheads or crawled from the consuming flames. Others, caught in the blaze, screamed like children. Of the former, Kurita thought, *Brave boys. I am so proud of you.* Of the latter, generously he thought, *In extremity even a samurai might scream. And death by fire is extreme.*

A fire-suited damage control party from another

section of the ship arrived, just as Kurita did, its centurion reporting to the Yamatan.

"There is not enough room for all your people here, Centurion," Kurita said. "Use half to fight the fire. Have the other half carry off the wounded to clear the way."

The smoke wasn't *bad*, yet, but it was bad enough. Coughing, Kurita grabbed a SCBA, a Self Contained Breathing Apparatus mask, from a dispenser and put it on. It would interfere with giving commands, but continued inhalation of the smoke was likely to make him far too *dead* to give commands.

The problem, though, is that it is hard to tell how much of this smoke is from fire and how much from the initial explosion. Are the fuel lines breached? We have power. Is the air circulation system feeding oxygen to the flames? Has the fire breached the hangar deck fire curtains to either side of the rear elevator?

The only way to determine the answers was to look. Kurita lightly felt the near surface of a hatch that led to a balcony overlooking the hangar deck. *Not too bad. I wish the design had included a window. I must advise this to Fosa-san as soon as possible.*

He opened the hatch and stuck his head out. His first thought was *Thank God the curtain was not breached.* Further inspection, however, showed that it *was* breached higher up. Thus, while no burning fuel was racing across the deck, hot smoke was oozing over and through the rent in the fire curtain's fabric. This was bad enough but what his eyes lit on next was actually enough to set his heart to racing.

Kurita lifted his mask and shouted, "Centurion, have your men stop work on the wounded! There is ordnance on the hangar deck and it MUST BE REMOVED!"

Then the deck lurched, knocking Kurita once again from his feet and slamming his head against a bulkhead. For a few moments he lost consciousness.

While the upward lurch of the deck threw Kurita from his feet, at the bridge the motion was much less. Fosa retained his footing, as did almost every man of the bridge crew. What he saw, though, when he looked at the engineering panel—a sudden Christmas tree of red and amber lights—made his heart sink.

Dead in the water. Shit . . . DEAD . . . in the water.

Fosa looked forward and saw that, *thank God for small blessings,* the *Dos Lindas* was at least not headed to land. It should, he crudely calculated, have lost all forward motion before there was a risk of grounding.

And when the corvettes get here, they can tow us a bit. Maybe it's not hopeless.

Fosa looked portward and saw a Finch diving on something he couldn't see for the flight deck. The Finch had all guns blazing. He saw it cease fire and pull up just before yet another massive explosion took place off the port side.

Indeed, maybe it's not hopeless.

MV *Hoogaboom,* 3/6/468 AC

Somewhere, deep in his heart, in a place he probably never would have admitted existed, the captain had hoped that the combination of torpedoes, suicide boats, and cruise missiles would destroy the enemy ship before he had to destroy himself and his own ship.

Yet reports broadcast from observers ashore were clear. The ship was aflame at one quarter, it had been hit at least twice, it was stopped dead in the water, drifting and powerless. But it was not sinking, nor even listing, and its combination of light cannon, lasers, machine guns and aircraft were making short work of the suicide boats that, again, deep at heart, the captain had half expected to hull the carrier.

One good bit of news, for certain values of good, was that the enemy ship was slowly turning to present its side to the *Hoogaboom.*

At least we will be certain to succeed, attacking at this angle with a helpless target. If self-immolation is difficult, and it is, the captain thought, *how much more difficult to do so without the certainty of success?*

"All ahead full," he ordered. "Auxiliary crews to the patrol boats. Lower the patrol boats as they're manned. And commend your souls to Allah."

As the captain gave the order, the Tauran slave girls, gifts of Abdul Aziz and Mustafa, began to scream and cry. *No sense in keeping their little hearts in fear,* the captain thought.

"Go below," he ordered to a seaman standing nearby. "Take a rifle. Kill the slaves."

PTF Santissima Trinidad, 3/6/468 AC

The forward forty-millimeter and three of the starboard side tri-barrel .41s spat death at a speedboat winding its way through the smoke in the air and the wreckage floating on the water. With all the surface turbulence— the result not just of natural waves but of the explosions that had churned the water—marksmanship left something to be desired. Even so, the men had adopted the simple expedient of beginning their fire low and letting the boat rock it upward.

The target boat was a flaming mess, with blood running out the gunnels. That was no reason to cease fire until the thing—

Kaboom.

A dark curtain of wind-borne smoke closed down around the *Trinidad* and the falling debris of its late target. Pedraz looked around for some recognizable landmark, without success. Then a sudden gust of wind tore apart the smoky curtain and he caught sight of the carrier.

Is there less fire and smoke now? Hard to tell. I can only hope . . .

But there is fire, and then there is "FIRE!" The side of the carrier, so much as was visible, erupted in blossoms of flame as the machine guns and light cannon, catching sudden sight of the *Trinidad* and not quite recognizing it, opened up.

"*KeerIST!*" Pedraz jammed the throttle forward and sprang back into the smoke. A quick glance behind him—very quick, under the circumstances—told him that the carrier's gun crews were following and walking—*sprinting*, really—their fire to where they thought the boat was heading. He jerked the wheel to change course.

"*Dos Lindas*, this is *Trinidad*. Have we *offended* you in some way?!?!?!"

BdL *Dos Lindas*, 3/6/468 AC

Kurita bent to one side and pulled his mask away to vomit. The blow to his head had given him a mild concussion and nausea had swiftly followed. He replaced the mask in time to see another group of damage control people, about a dozen of them, materialize on the hangar deck. Reseating the mask to get a breath of non-fatal air, he again pulled it away to shout down below, "Get the foam system into operation!"

The chief of that damage control party looked up at Kurita, recognizing him both by his short stature and his sword, and waved acknowledgment. He and his men split into two groups and immediately ran for the wound hoses at the forward corners of the hangar deck. These they took and began to drag to the stern. As they did so, men, individually and in small groups passed them by, carrying or dragging machine gun ammunition, rockets and bombs away from the fire.

Ideally, they'd simply have dumped the stuff over the side. Unfortunately, the hangar deck didn't really have a portal for that, a clear design flaw. Rather, it did have *one*, but that was very new and rather on fire at the moment.

"Drop it here. Drop. It. Here." The chief of the damage control party shouted to the ordnance carriers. They looked at him, not quite understanding, until he pointed at the nozzle of the foam hose he carried. Mental lights came on. They began making a pile, more or less carefully, of the ordnance they carried. As soon as there was enough of a pile the chief turned the hose on it and began to cover it with a thick layer of fireproof, and cooling, foam. More ordnance, and more foam, added to the pile.

Above, Kurita saw the foamed pile grow and began to breathe a sigh of relief. He never quite got the sigh out, however, as another wave of nausea overtook him, causing him, once again, to doff the mask, bend over, and hurl.

Sick at heart over the harm done to his ship and crew, Fosa peered desperately through the thick smoke of ship's fire, jungle fire, and explosion. Tracer still lanced out in mass, all around the boundaries of the ship, before they disappeared into the smoke.

Fosa heard the radio loudspeaker ask, "Have we *offended* you in some way?" He picked up the microphone and asked, 'What the fuck are you talking about, *Trinidad*?

"Your gunners are shooting at anything they spy," came the answer. "They engaged us . . . tried to anyway."

"Roger," Fosa answered. "I'll see to it." Before he could give an order he heard one of the bridge crew screaming into another microphone, one that serviced the ship's intercom, "You assholes nearly sunk one of ours. Identify your targets carefully. Dumb-asses."

Once again, smoke swirled around the tower, blocking Fosa's view. He said, "Order *Agustin* and *Trinidad* out past our cannon and machine gun range."

PTF Santissima Trinidad, 3/6/468 AC

For now, Pedraz was keeping *inside* the smoke. Later, when he was reasonably sure that he was out of range, or at least far enough away that the carrier wouldn't mistake his boat for a threat, he'd emerge into the open. For now, he and his men were on a definite post-adrenaline let down and would just as soon ride that out.

"Did we win, Chief?" Francais asked.

"Win? What's a win," Pedraz answered, sadly and quietly. "*Dos Lindas* is still there, after they threw everything they had at it. I guess that's a win. Though I don't know if she'll ever fight again."

"She will," Francais answered, as if sure. "As long as she floats and has a crew, she can be repaired."

Suddenly, without warning, the *Trinidad* emerged into the clear. Francais pointed and asked, "Skipper, what's *that* doing here?"

MV Hendrick Hoogaboom, 3/6/468 AC

The Tauran slave girls weren't crying or screaming anymore. Neither were there any klaxons or alarms. Instead, "All hands to battle stations," announced the captain, through the ship's intercom. Then he and his own bridge crew retired below to the armored CIC. From there, they'd direct the ship via video camera and remote control. There were redundant systems for both.

Down in CIC a mullah, one of the very few willing to die the same way they encouraged others to die, spoke into a microphone. His words were carried to small speakers all over the ship, and especially to the individual fighting compartments where the mujahadin waited by their machine guns to fight, if necessary, for the right to destroy the warship of the wicked.

"No doubt it is a clear honor," said the mullah, "a clear honor which Allah has bestowed on us. Honor on us; honor to us. He will give us blessing and great victory, now, and by the acts of the faithful inspired by us, in the future.

"Across this world, this is what everyone is hoping for. Thank Allah that the Federated States came out of their caves. Those who came and fell before us hit her the first. Now we shall hit her lackeys, those wicked and faithless ones, with the strong hands of true believers.

"By Allah, this is a great work. Allah prepares for you a great reward for· this work. By Allah, who there is no god besides, my brothers, we shall live in happiness, happiness such as we have never before experienced.

"Remember, the words of Mustafa, the great and pious. He said they made a coalition against us in the winter with the infidels. And they surrounded us as in the days of the prophet Muhammad. This is exactly like what has been happening recently, with the faithless and the apostates turning on the One True God. But the Prophet, peace be upon him, comforted his followers and said, 'This is going to turn and hit them back.' As we are hitting back, my brothers."

The mullah noticed the arrival of the captain and stopped speaking. "Would you like to address the crew?" he asked.

"No, holy man. My words are small things against the great words of Allah, and of his messengers, and of those who teach the faithful. Please, continue with this sermon."

· Nodding, the mullah went back to his microphone and continued, "And it is a mercy for us and a blessing upon us. It will bring people back. And Allah will pour upon us blessings untold. And the day will come when the symbols of Islam will rise up and it will be similar to the early· days of the Salafi, back on Old Earth. And victory shall be upon the sons of the Prophet . . ."

BdL *Dos Lindas*, 3/6/468 AC

"*Dos Lindas*, this is *Trinidad*. I've got a ship, a small-ish freighter, maybe five thousand tons, maybe six, heading towards you. Considering what we've just been through . . ."

Fosa picked up the microphone and asked, "Can you see the name?"

The speaker crackled back, "*Hendrick Hoogaboom*, it says."

"Didn't we warn her off?" Fosa asked aloud.

"We did, Skipper," answered a radio man. "About thirty seconds after the attack started."

Radar spoke up. "Captain, I wasn't paying close attention, but I don't recall them coming to a stop before we lost radar. I mean . . ."

"It would have taken a while for them to have come to a stop," Fosa finished. "I understand. But it wouldn't have taken this long."

It could just be a mistake . . . but what are the odds? What are the odds when you factor in the very complex ambush they set for us here? And then . . . oh shit, they never touched the pork.

Fosa's voice was just short of panic. "*Trinidad, Agustin*, STOP THAT SHIP!"

So far, so good, thought Kurita. Though the smoke was still atrocious and the heat almost unbearable, the fires were under control and there had been no more secondary explosions. He knew, from long years

at sea, that the ship was drifting without power. That
could be fixed and, so long as the carrier didn't sink,
would be, he was sure.

The damage control and firefighting efforts had
reach past the twenty-foot gaping hole in the hull
blasted by the cruise missile. Resting against this
while waiting for another bout of vomiting to claim
him, Kurita saw the outline of a freighter, bearing
down on the immobile *Dos Lindas*.

He heard the loudspeakers proclaim, in Fosa's voice,
"Surface action, Port. Surface action, Port. We're not
out of this yet, boys. On the port side is a ship . . .
I think it intends to ram us. Surface action, Port. All
guns: engage."

Kurita looked around, thinking, *Things are under
control here; nothing the centurions can't handle,
surely. Let's go see to the guns. They lost some crew
to the missile attack, I'm sure.*

PTF Santissima Trinidad, 3/6/468 AC

Clavell and Guptillo worked their gun furiously, sheltering behind the mantlet at the heavy return machine
gun fire from the ship. The *Trinidad*'s own machine
guns returned fire, of course, but seemed to be having absolutely *no* effect.

"Shit," cursed Clavell. He keyed his microphone and
told Pedraz, "Skipper, we're hitting the thing, easily,
and penetrating it, too. I can *see* the shells going off
inside. But they're having no effect that I can see."

Pedraz was about to respond when a sudden flurry
of fire burst from the *Dos Lindas*. He followed the
tracers to where they impacted on the bow of the

Hoogaboom. It was being chewed apart; that much was clear from the pieces of hull sloughing off under the fire. But beyond that? Nothing.

Machine gun fire raked out from the *Hoogaboom,* sweeping *Trinidad*'s deck. Most of the crew was under reasonable cover. Not so, the machine gunners, and notably Santiona who was the target. With a scream, he went down, minus his legs and with the stumps gushing blood.

Without being told to, the ship's corpsman raced out from under cover and began tourniqueting off the wounded Santiona's stumps.

Hmmm . . . even the forty isn't doing shit to the ship. Hmmm . . .

"Clavell, target that ship's machine gunners."

God, why the fuck didn't we mount torpedoes on this thing? We're a fucking Patrol Torpedo Fast and we don't have torpedoes? Shit.

MV Hendrick Hoogaboom, 3/6/468 AC

Deep in his steel cocoon, *Hoogaboom*'s captain thought, *Thank Allah they don't have torpedoes. If they did, we'd be lost. For that matter, thank you, Almighty, that none of their aircraft were carrying, or got off with, any large bombs.*

Overhead the captain heard what he thought must be aerial rockets smashing the upper deck. *No matter;* those *can't penetrate.* He looked at the screen tied in to the forward cameras. It was in this that the enemy ship was in view. There on the screen, the image amplified, a short man pointing with a sword directed the futile fire coming at *Hoogaboom*'s bow.

The captain laughed. *Maybe if you had a couple of days to chew through, it might do some good,* he thought. *But you have mere minutes.*

That worked, thought Pedraz, looking over the smoking holes in the enemy ship created by the forty, *but it didn't buy us much.*

Indeed, it had not bought anything but a reduction in fire from the freighter. It still closed on the helpless *Dos Lindas;* the distance now was just over one thousand meters.

Especially did it not buy us any time. Oh, God, for some time. With time even our forties could chew through. With time . . .

The patrol boats launched by the *Hoogaboom* went by the simple names of "Wahid" and "Ithnayn;" "One" and "Two." Why, after all, invest any emotion or any name into what amounted to throwaway weapons?

They'd held back, One and Two, after being launched. This was not out of any fear; the men aboard the boats had no expectation, nor perhaps even any desire, to live. But there were only the two. Ahead, they'd be vulnerable to the defensive armaments of the target. Astern, they could react to any threats that arose to their primary, and do so especially well against any threats to their primary's greatest point of vulnerability, its long, broad flanks.

Thus, when the captains of One and Two saw the tracers from *Trinidad,* they'd begun to move cautiously and carefully through the smoke to where they thought they would find the rear quarter of whatever was engaging the *Hoogaboom.* Side by side they moved until the bow gunner on One saw the infidel boat. He immediately engaged, followed by Two's bow gunner as soon as that boat had closed enough to make out a target.

Pedraz felt more than heard the incoming fire from his starboard aft quarter. Indeed, the first he actually heard was when the machine gunner on that point screamed at being chopped apart by the concentrated fire of first one, then two, then a half dozen enemy machine guns that came from astern.

Poor Marco, Pedraz thought as he applied throttle to get the hell away from the position in which he found himself. Unseen, Legionary Turco's body slid across the deck, leaving a broad swath of blood behind, before plunging over the stern. He'd never had a chance to strap himself in.

There wasn't a lot of advantage either way. All three patrol boats, *Trinidad*, One and Two, were sleek and fast and armed. *Trinidad* with her forty, was much more heavily armed. Sadly, though, the forty could not fire astern and *Trinidad* could not turn without presenting a vulnerable side to the pursuing craft.

"And that fucking freighter is closing on the *Dos Lindas*," Pedraz fumed. "Shit, shit, SHIT!"

A near burst of machine gun fire passed just to Pedraz's right, splintering the glass to his front. "Shit!" Pedraz repeated.

Nothing for it but to go for the glory, he thought.

"Cris," the skipper shouted to his XO, "get astern and be prepared to man Turco's gun. You'll know when."

"What are ya gonna *do*, Skipper?"

"*Diekplous*," Pedraz shouted, as Francais scurried astern. Then he said into his microphone, "Clavell, bring your gun to bear ninety degrees to port. Guys, we're gonna turn and go right in between them. Fire as you bear."

Both One's and Two's crews, and especially the gunners, laughed maniacally as they pursued the fleeing infidel boat. It had been all too rare, in this war, to see the enemy actually turn and run on the battlefield. Such moments were to be savored. Especially were they to be savored when the time available for such savoring was destined to be very short.

Sweating profusely, heart pounding fit to burst from his chest, Clavell huddled behind his gun shield, eye pressed firmly to his sight. Beside him, Guptillo held on for dear life against the turn he was pretty sure the skipper was about to make.

"If you ever made a good shot, Jose, make one now," Guptillo said.

Eye still to his sight, Clavell couldn't answer by nod. Instead, he stuck one thumb in the air.

Suddenly, the boat slowed and began to turn to port. Clavell cranked the gun down to compensate, never moving his eye from his sight. Sea passed in his view, then more sea, then more . . . then . . .

Kawhamkawhamkawhamkawhamkawham. Clavell depressed the trigger on the forty as the veer of the boat brought it into view and almost aligned. Downrange, his first shell missed, bursting in the water. His second missed as well. But he held true to his aim and trusted the movement of the ship to align the target perfectly. Shells three through five, rewarding his faith, found their target, smashing the front of Two like so much kindling. Enemy sailors, and pieces of sailors, went flying in all directions. Others aboard Two, those further astern, continued to fire after only a brief, shocked pause.

"And now we charge. *Banzai, motherfuckers!*" Pedraz shouted over the rising roar of the engines, the crash of the cannon, and the cloth-ripping hum of his machine guns.

The *Trinidad* spurted ahead, her machine gunners, plus Guptillo and Clavell, trading what amounted to mutual automatic broadsides with the *Ikhwan* fighters of One and those remaining aboard Two. Sailors on both sides went down, some suddenly and silently, others with curses and screams. The armor worn by Pedraz's crew helped, but at this range, perhaps one hundred meters, it didn't help *much*. And the greaves didn't cover the back of the sailors' legs at all.

Astern, Francais leapt to his feet, almost losing his footing to Turco's wet blood, and grabbed the spade grips of the .41-caliber tribarrel. From across the water, he and an *Ikhwan* gunner from Two stared at each other for what might have been the longest nanosecond in human history.

"Motherfucker!" Francais exclaimed as he deftly swung the tribarrel to bear on the machine gunner. Before the gun was on target, his finger was already depressing the trigger, causing the electrically driven barrels to spin and the gun to spit out its eighteen hundred rounds per minute. While the *mujahad*'s bullets went wide, Francais' swath of fire cut right across his target, from left hip to right ribs, slicing—though by no means neatly—the *Ikhwan* gunner in two, spilling his intestines to the deck.

Pedraz looked around his half ruined boat and his mostly ruined crew. Men shrieked in agony on the deck, with the boat's sole medic frantically going from one to the other, desperately trying to staunch the flow of blood here, relieve pain there.

Behind the *Trinidad*, One and Two lay smoking and dead in the water. Two was plainly sinking, though it was taking its time about it.

If I had more time . . .

Time was about up, however, and Pedraz knew what he had to do. "Clavell, cease fire," he said, gunning the engine and twisting the boat away. It made a tight turn, then headed off away from the *Hoogaboom* and slightly towards the carrier.

Picking up his microphone, Pedraz broadcast, "*Agustin,* this is *Trinidad*. Get the hell away from the freighter. Don't argue. Just do it."

BdL *Dos Lindas*, 3/6/468 AC

Kurita had stationed himself beside the one serviceable forty-millimeter gun on the carrier's stern port quarter. To either side of him, twenty-millimeter cannon and forty-one caliber machine guns churned futily at the oncoming scow. *And the forty does no good either. For that matter, the pounding isn't doing my head much good. No help for that, though.*

He watched a small and gallant patrol boat, the *Trinidad*, he thought, trading fire with, then turn and run right in between two patrol boats. *Glorious,* thought Kurita, *In the best naval tradition. Brave boys. Bravo. Banzai.*

Kurita watched as the PTF, smoking and clearly hurt, pulled away and began to retreat. *No shame in that, my friends,* he thought. *You must save whatever you can of this fleet. We here are, after all, just dead men now.*

No matter for me, of course. I've been dead since I failed my emperor. But it's a shame about the others.

Kurita watched a Finch swoop down to lay a barrage of rockets on the top of the freighter. They seemed to have no effect at all, except to cause a missile to be launched upward at the Finch. Then Kurita remembered something old and sacred. *I wonder if . . . but, no, there's no way to suggest it to you.*

Kurita looked out and saw a most remarkable thing. The small patrol boat he thought was the *Trinidad* turned and almost stopped, as about half a dozen men began to assemble on the rear deck.

"I . . . can't . . . go . . . into the water, skipper. With this blood . . . the sharks will come . . . for me. I can't."

"All right, Santiona," Pedraz agreed.

"You'll need a back up, Chief," Francais said. "And that's, rightfully, my place."

Pedraz had intended to make his last ride alone. It was frustrating and infuriating that more than half his never-sufficiently-to-be-damned, mutinous crew wouldn't go along.

"See, it's like this, Chief," Francais explained, with a casual shrug. "That ship is probably loaded with explosives. This wasn't a minor effort, here, after all, so I figure two, maybe three thousand tons. Nobody who gets off has much of a prayer of surviving that, if it goes off. So . . . all the same, I'd rather not jump ship. It wouldn't do any good anyway. Besides, like Santiona said, we put wounded into the water we'll have sharks all over everyone."

But still, Pedraz wanted to save *something*. He looked at the youngest crewman, and nearly the only one unhurt who could be spared. That youngest was a nice kid named Miguel Quijana. Quijana, like the others, wore helmet, body armor, and over that a life vest.

Pedraz grabbed the seaman by the shoulders and said, "Stay as much on the surface as possible. Watch carefully; when we hit you'll have a few moments between when the first wave of concussion passes under water and the debris starts falling. Remember, the concussion under water will be *worse*. Don't get under water until you can feel that wave of concussion pass. Then get under fast. Good luck, son."

With that, Pedraz turned the boy around to face the stern and, placing a boot on his rear end, shoved him off into the sea.

"For the rest of you, Battle Stations! *Banzai, motherfuckers!*"

Nobody left the boat, Kurita could see, except for one man deliberately booted off, probably by the captain. And then the boat began to move forward, picking up speed at an amazing rate.

Another man might not have understood. Yet Kurita understood perfectly and immediately. *Divine wind. Kamikaze.*

He tapped the leader of the forty-millimeter crew and said, "Go and warn the other gunners on this side, you and your crew. Get the hell behind cover. Now!"

Then, as soon as that crew had sped off, Kurita drew himself to attention, saluted the *Trinidad* with his sword, and began, softly and in an old man's reedy voice, to sing *Kimigayo*—

". . . Until pebbles
Turn into boulders
Covered with moss."

Fosa, too, saw *Trinidad*'s death ride, through the cracked windows of the bridge. He, like Kurita, stood to attention and saluted. Though he had his sword, the one that Kurita had given him, saluting with the hand just seemed more . . . *personal.*

Some members of the bridge crew, following their commander's gaze and understanding what the salute meant, likewise came to attention and rendered the hand salute. They and Fosa held those salutes all the way to when the *Trinidad* disappeared into the hull of the enemy freighter, and halfway through the incredible, barely sub-nuclear, explosion that followed.

UEPF Spirit of Peace, 3/6/468 AC

"They survived," Robinson said, later, in his quarters. "They couldn't have survived, but they did. The *Ikhwan* ship was *that* fucking close," he held out his hand with thumb and forefinger a bare inch apart, "*that* fucking close, and *still* that fucking ship survived. It isn't possible."

The high admiral of the United Earth Peace Fleet

nearly wept with the sheer frustration of it all. So upset was he that Wallenstein, without being ordered to, dropped to her knees and began to undo his belt. He pushed her away, roughly.

"No . . . not you tonight, Marguerite. Send me Khan, the wife. I want to *hurt* something."

INTERLUDE

2/1/49 AC, Atlantis Base, Terra Nova

A messenger was waiting when Bernard Chanet arrived at his office for the morning's work. Standing at attention, the messenger passed over a sealed letter from one of the outlying offices. Chanet was surprised at the origin of the missive; he had observers at several locations in Southern Columbia but was denied any control over the area.

Opening the letter, Chanet paced his office as he read:

> Your Excellency:
>
> I've had the most intriguing request and proposition that I thought I must present to you before going any further with it.
>
> A small group of the local regressives from North America, back home, approached me the other day and requested arms. I thought this especially odd in that they are already self sufficient for the primitive arms they tend to use. But, no, it wasn't flintlocks or

even percussion weapons they were looking
for. They wanted modern, military arms.

On the face of it, I'd have laughed them
out of my office. Yet the leader of the
group, who is also a political figure of some
local importance, had a most compelling
argument. He took out a pouch of gold,
weighing perhaps two and a half kilograms,
and proceeded to pour it out onto my desk.
He said to me, "One dozen modern rifles
and twelve-thousand rounds of ammunition
and it's yours. A thousand times that and
a thousand of these are yours."

I, of course, have no weaponry here
beyond the few carried by my security
staff. Yet it occurred to me that in your
position . . .

9/8/49 AC

Belisario had about given up hope. His band was down
to seventy-five men, perhaps less by sunrise, and he'd
found no solution to the problem. Even now his men
were scattered across two hundred square kilometers,
in little groups of five or ten, partly to ease foraging
and partly so as not to attract the attention of the
always-threatening UN air power. Of the modern
weapons he and his group had captured, few remained.
For those few there was no ammunition. Even Pedro
had wrapped and buried his prized heavy sniper rifle
for lack of anything to feed it with.

Hanging his head in despair, Belisario thought,
for perhaps the thousandth time, about just giving it

up and surrendering to the Gurkhas and Sikhs who hunted his men morn and night. They were good men, those. Better, by far, than the other troops the UN set loose to terrorize the population.

"Don't shoot, Dad," he heard and looked up. It was the voice of his daughter, Mitzi. She walked into the center of the camp, gripping an *escopeta* and accompanied by a young man.

A *gringo, by his looks*, Belisario thought. He saw half a dozen others, leading heavily laden mules. *Gringos, too, most likely*.

"Mom says 'hi,'" Mitzi said. "She told me to lead these men to you. Even loaned me her shotgun for safety and I *never* would have expected her to do *that*."

"Are you Belisario Carrera?" the young man with Mitzi asked.

"I am."

"Sir, I'm Juan Alvarez, Jr., from down in Southern Columbia, and, sir, I've brought some things I think you maybe need."

CHAPTER SEVENTEEN

The guerillas are the fish and the people are
the sea.
> —The Great Helmsman,
> on guerilla warfare

We fish with dynamite.
> —Patricio Carrera,
> on counter-guerilla warfare

Outside Panshir Base, Pashtia, 3/6/468

With the noonday sun high overhead, the valley was
bathed in stifling heat. Even high on the green hills
surrounding the Tuscan Ligurini base, it was oppressive. It was all the more oppressive for those troops
of the legion filling in fighting positions, mortar pits,
and ammunition dumps. These, stripped to the waist,
wielded their shovels with a will, however. When the
marks of preparations for the aborted attack on the
Ligurini were erased, they were going home.

With the election over, and with the FS-imposed
practical partition of Balboa, Carrera felt reasonably
comfortable standing down his troops, barring those

surrounding the local base for the Gallic Commandos. For the Gauls, he'd wait and see how well peace held out in Balboa. The rest would move on to Thermopolis, along with their equipment, and from there go home to Balboa via road, rail, sea and air. Even the ones surrounding the Gauls would eventually leave; they were just further behind in the order of movement.

Besides, it isn't like I'm not working on ways to hit them where it hurts even when I give up the ability to get at the Frogs and Tauros here.

Nor could anyone in the coalition really complain about the Gauls being confined to their little rathole. The legionaries surrounding them were also engaged in something the commandos had signally failed even to try to do (though to be fair this was not the result on any unwillingness on the commandos' part); hunting down and obliterating the insurgency in the area. In this, the legion was having some success.

Carrera drew a mental map of the country and the position of his troops within it. His mind clicked over each stage in the evacuation of two legions from Pashtia and he could find no flaw. *Gotta love a good staff,* he thought.

"Call from the staff, sir," said one of his guards, holding out a microphone. "Secure. Bad news, they say."

Of course, it's bad news, he thought. *Here I am enjoying a peaceful moment and pleased that I won't have to butcher ten thousand allied troops so, naturally, there is bad news. God, someday I hope to have a long talk with you about your sense of humor.*

He took the proffered radio microphone and announced, "Carrera."

The radio operator at the other end acknowledged

and said, "Wait one, sir, while we connect you to the *classis.*"

The classis? *My bad news is from the* classis? *This is going to be really bad.*

There was a series of beeps, and then a voice, distorted by the encryption devices and with odd, unrecognizable sounds in the background, said, "Fosa, here." The voice seemed to Carrera to contain an infinity of sadness and weariness.

"Carrera, here. What is it, Roderigo?"

"Patricio . . . I don't know how to tell you this, so I'll just lay it out for you. We got hit this morning, hit *hard.* I don't even have a final count of the dead and wounded, but both numbers are going to be high. I lost just about half my fixed-wing aircraft and two-thirds of the helicopters. I'm holed, though—thank God—it's not below the water line. Even so, I'm taking water at the stern and the hole is close enough to the water line that a big storm could put us down. One elevator is totally out. My drives are down . . . well, one is down. The other was blown clean off. My flight deck is warped, but not so badly we can't loft and recover aircraft. I've no radar. And I lost one of the escorts."

"Holy shit!" Carrera said, though he didn't key the microphone. *My brave sailors; where will I find your like again?* When he keyed it, he asked, "What happened, Rod?"

"It was an ambush in the Nicobar Straits. Somehow the wogs managed to assemble about a dozen speed boats, half a dozen cruise missiles, two torpedoes, and one big fucking suicide ship. We took one cruise missile hit, plus a near miss that did for the radar, a torpedo hit at the stern, and then the suicide ship . . . Pat, it must have been about a two-kiloton explosion . . . anyway, it went off about a klick away." Fosa hesitated and then added, "Well, it didn't actually *go* off. One of my escorts, the *Santissima Trinidad*, rammed it at full speed. *That* set it off. Pat, if they hadn't rammed it, we'd have been obliterated.

"Pat, I want authority to award gold crosses, four steps, to that crew, and three to its sister, the *Agustin*. Three and two just wouldn't be enough."

"Given," Carrera answered. "Is your ship recoverable? What about the wounded?"

There was doubt in Fosa's voice, mixed in with determination. "If I can get her to a port . . . maybe. But getting her back in order will be expensive. The wounded we're flying off with whatever I have that can carry a man or two."

"All right. I'll assume you're flying your hurt men to some safe port. As for the expense; *damn* the expense; a ship like *that* doesn't come along every day." *In fact, I haven't a clue where we could find another one. Rebuild the static training ship? Probably a lot more expensive. And besides, the ship that survived an attack like that has* mana. *It has* soul. *Men will adore her and fight all the better for her. Some other ship just wouldn't do as well.*

BdL *Dos Lindas*, 3/6/468 AC

"Captain, we've found something you ought to see."

Fosa nodded his head and said, "Pat, I've got to go. I'll report in around sunset. I might have a better idea of our chances then."

"Before you go, put me on the speaker," Carrera ordered.

Fosa looked over at the communications bench and gave the nod. A sailor flicked a switch. "Go ahead, Pat. Wherever the intercom still reaches, you'll be heard. Fosa, out."

From the speakers, echoing across the length and breadth of the carrier, came, "*Duque* Carrera to the officers, centurions and men of the *classis*, and of the tercios Jan Sobieski, and Vlad Tepes: Men, listen; don't stop working to save your ship, but listen. You've taken a hard hit . . ."

Fosa didn't really listen to Carrera's speech. It wasn't much more than the same generalities he'd been spreading, himself: *We've done well . . . they threw the worst they had at us and we took it and came back punching . . . we'll save the ship.* He just hoped it was all true.

At the base of the tower he turned around and looked out over the flight deck. Already crews with cutting torches were slicing away the warped sections and forcing some of the underdecking back into position. There was plywood and perforated steel planking, down below, that they could use to make some temporary patches, enough for the Crickets and maybe even a lightly loaded Finch.

From there, he descended down the double stairs to Deck 2. A balcony off that deck overlooked the hangar. He went to the balcony and looked down. The hangar was filled not only with burned and blasted airframes; it had become a morgue, as well. Even now, parties of crewman, some of them hurt themselves, brought in corpses and laid them out respectfully in rows. Some of his crew, Fosa saw, were curled up in fetal positions, their charred limbs eloquent testimony to the fire that had killed them.

You will not *throw up*, Fosa gave himself the order. Even so, he turned away.

The sailor who had summoned the captain from the bridge said, "This way, sir. By where we took the hit near the stern."

"Lead on."

The way led through the officers' quarters at the stern, past Fosa's and then Kurita's cabin.

What am I going to do without that old man to guide me? Fosa wondered. For, though he had put out the call to find the commodore, no one had as of yet seen a sign. The nearest thing to a report was the mutterings of a now legless and semi-comatose sailor in sickbay, a gunner on one of the port rear platforms. He'd said something about going "back for the commodore."

Fosa rested his hand lightly on the cabin's hatch, then continued on forward and past the filter room and the two rocket storage rooms.

"We found it out here, Skipper," the sailor guiding Fosa said as he pointed to the twisted scrap that had been a gun platform.

Fosa stepped gingerly out onto the ruin of the platform. It seemed solid enough. There was a ruined forty-millimeter gun there, as well. Fosa turned and . . .

"My God," he whispered.

There, against the hull, to all appearances a *part* of the hull now, was the outline of a small man. He might not have known who it was except for the ancient, once reforged *katana* that was apparently *welded* to the hull, and joined to the body's outline by the shadow of a thin arm.

Fosa crossed himself and said a small prayer for the soul of Tadeo Kurita, along with the wish that he now be reunited with his wife and children. *For, Lord, he was a good man, and a good sailor, and did his duty as he saw it . . . to the end.*

Fosa looked ahead to where the two corvettes were being rigged to tow the *Dos Lindas* to port. Astern, they'd managed to get the one remaining AZIPOD working, but it was non-steerable. The corvettes would pull the bow around to steer the ship, with the AZIPOD providing the bulk of the forward drive. He guessed he'd be able to make at least ten knots that way, maybe even twelve, which put the nearest useful and trustworthy port, in Sind, a good eight or ten days' sailing away.

"We're going to make it, Pat," Fosa told Carrera, later that night via secure radio. "We may be pumping like madmen all the way, and we're toast if were attacked at sea, or hit a really atrocious storm. But barring those, we'll make it."

"I've alerted Christian back in Balboa to push to make good your personnel losses," Carrera answered. "A freighter will be sailing in three days with replacements for your lost Crickets and Finches. It will be a month and a half before we can replace your Yakamovs. I've given orders that a cruiser be readied to sail ASAP. That, and that another escort be sent along. But, Rod, we don't have another Patrol Torpedo until we can have some built. Will a corvette do?"

"It will," the captain answered. "Pat, has the cruiser been rechristened yet?"

"No, why?"

"Because I'd like it to bear the name of *Tadeo Kurita*, if that works for you."

UEPF Spirit of Peace, 3/6/468 AC

In the limited confines of his quarters, Robinson paced furiously. *Nothing works;* he fumed, *nothing fucking works! It didn't even help to take a belt to Khan's ass because* she *likes it.*

Wallenstein sipped coffee shipped up from below. To all appearances, she was calm and composed. Inside, though, she was worried. *An unhappy high admiral is a high admiral who is less likely to get me a caste lift. This will not do. But . . . still, I have to tell him or he'll be even less likely to give me the boost I need.*

"Martin, we've got a decoded message we intercepted between the mercenary fleet and its commander. Not only is the ship not going to sink; it's going to be reinforced."

"With what?"

"A heavy cruiser. I believe it's the only heavy cruiser in commission in any wet navy down below. Good armor, ten six-inch automatic, long-range guns in five twin turrets. It's also nuclear powered, just like the carrier. I'm sorry, Martin, but the mercenary fleet is not only not substantially weakened, except in the very short term, it's growing. Worse, the Yamatan Zaibatsu appear to be so eager to get it back on station that they're paying two-thirds of the cost of restoring and refitting the carrier. I'm afraid that using piracy to both raise funds for the *Ikhwan* and to undercut the economy down below is . . ." Wallenstein hesitated.

"Doomed to abject failure?" Robinson supplied. "Tell me something I *don't* know."

BdL *Dos Lindas*, Hajipur, Sind, 15/6/468 AC

"I don' know, Skipper," the master of the shipfitting company said, shaking his head. The master was an old man. Underneath his turban, Fosa thought, the man's hair was likely as gray as his beard.

The *Dos Lindas* rode at dock, Cazadors guarding from the landward side while corvettes and the *Agustin* watched to seaward. Getting her here? Through one of the worst storms in the history of the Sea of Sind? With waves battering at the temporary patch welded over the spot where the *Ikhwan* cruise missile had struck home? That would take a volume. Suffice to say that there were a lot more *Cruces de Coraje* earned by the crew. Some heroism was never recorded. For that, for those unknowns washed over the side, Carrera had issued the first unit citation in the history of the *Legion del Cid*.

"I don' know," the master repeated, tapping the temporary patches on the flight deck with his cane as he and Fosa toured the ship with an eye to damages and estimates. "It gonna cost."

"That's not the point," Fosa said. "I don't care what it costs, as long as my fleet isn't being cheated. The point is, can you repair my ship?"

"We do flight deck, hull, hangar deck," the master shipfitter answered, with a shrug. "Those . . . easy. Cut sections from old ship up coast; drag down. Weld

into place. Paint. My people tell me can replace lost
AZIPOD, if you buy, and fix other. Have to wait for
dry-dock open up but . . . no sweat. Form and weld
on new gun tubs? Also, no sweat. Replace guns? You
get guns, we replace. Radar? You get radar; we replace.
Same, same; laser up top. Got nephew at SIT, Sind
Institute Technology. He good with shit like that. Him
got friends good, too."

"But?" Fosa asked.

"But got build new fucking elevator from scratch.
Hard. Tough. Expensive. Never do before."

"Hmmm. What if someone made an elevator and
shipped it here?" Fosa asked.

"Like other shit; you get elevator; we replace."

Kamakura, Yamato, 17/6/468 AC

"Kurita did request, in his last will and testament,
that we continue to support the *ronin* as much as
possible," Yamagata said.

"I know," Saito agreed, "and it's hardly that grand a
request. The problem is that nobody here has made or
designed an elevator for an aircraft carrier in decades.
Many decades. And the *ronin* need their elevator *now*.
Between design, tooling up, and actual production, we're
looking at half a year to a year."

"And no one makes elevators like this anymore, do
they?" Yamagata asked, rhetorically.

Saito shook his head in the negative. "The nearest
thing to what the *ronin* need—or, in any event, could
use—is a side-mounted elevator the Federated States
put on some of their amphibious carriers. The ship,
however, is not designed for that."

"Could it be modified?"

"I have sent a naval engineer to enquire. There is also one other possibility that gets them an elevator quickly and gives us time to have one custom designed and built."

Isla Real and Bay of Balboa, 20/6/468 AC

The waters quaked with the pounding of newly christened BdL *Tadeo Kurita* at gunnery practice a few miles away. From the bridge of the conning tower of the spare carrier, never given a name but referred to simply at BdEL1 (*Barco del Entrenamiento Legionario Numero Uno*, Legionary Training Ship Number One), the exec of the Tercio *Don John* could see the top of *Isla Santa Josefina*, the artillery impact island. The place was wreathed in smoke and flame, only the crest of the central massif visible, and that not all the time.

Overhead came a near continuous freight train rumble as *Tadeo Kurita* lobbed salvo after salvo toward the impact area island. If the *classis* exec cared to, he could have climbed topside and seen the cruiser as she fired. Even in daytime, the clouds above flickered with an orange glow with each broadside.

On the bridge, the exec studied diagrams of the ship. The schematics were old and the paper crisp and yellow with age. Worse, they were in Portuguese, which was more or less intelligible to Spanish speakers, but always a strain.

"Ah, well," muttered the exec. "Could have been worse. Could have been in something uncivilized . . . like *English*."

And with that, the exec set himself to solving the

problem of how to disassemble a major component of one ship, the elevator, get it loaded aboard another ship, somehow, and move it to a foreign harbor wherein sat a third ship, the *Dos Lindas*.

Fucking Fosa, thought the *classis* exec. *What kind of miracle worker does he think I am? Worse, how the fuck am I supposed to train replacement crew here with only one working elevator?*

The exec heard something very soft behind him. He turned and saw the Yamatan engineer, Keiji Higara, pensively tapping his lips while looking out across the bay at where a seaborne crane was in the process of removing turrets from one of those Suvarov-class cruisers not scheduled for refit.

"I am idiot," Keiji announced.

"Why's that, Hig?" the exec asked.

"I been worried . . . you know . . . getting this ship someplace where is crane powerful enough lift the elevator assembly out from hull. That was problem since docking facilities in *Ciudad* Balboa under . . . enemy control. Then, too, ship immobile. And whole time I been worrying . . . there was *that*." He pointed at the crane ship.

"You mean we can do it."

In answer, Higara snapped his fingers.

Quarters #2, *Isla Real*, 33/6/468 AC

"Look, it only makes sense, Patricio," Jimenez said, punctuating with a snap of his fingers. "I'm shipping over to Pashtia with the Fourth Legion in the not too distant future. So I'll have no use or need for this big old white elephant. Even when I come back, what do I need? A bedroom? An office? Someplace to eat?

Artemisia and Mac can give me all that, right here. *And* they'll have a place to stay suitable for their position."

Jimenez, Lourdes, and Carrera sat on the upper balcony, looking over the parade field. On the table between them was a bucket of ice and some scotch. The air was heavy, both with the natural humidity and the smoke of Xavier's and Carrera's cigars.

"Have you mentioned this to *them,* Xavier? Mac's a serious stickler for protocol and propriety," Carrera asked wearily, flicking an ash over the railing and onto the lawn. He'd just flown in that morning from Pashtia with the tail end of 1st and 2nd Legions and was clearly feeling the toll of both the long flight and the time zone change.

"No," Jimenez admitted. "Why should I? It's *your* house and *your* Legion; *you* get to decide."

It does make a certain sense, Carrera admitted to himself. *I get to billet my best friends and number one and two subordinates right next door where I can harass them mercilessly. Mac gets a house to go with the wife he's getting. Artemisia—God, she's achingly good to look at, isn't she?—gets the house she probably deserves. Probably? No probably about it. She makes my sergeant major happy and she deserves whatever I can give her.*

Jimenez continued, "Besides, Pat, Mac's living in the senior centurion's bachelor quarters. That's no place to raise a family and if you want your sergeant major happy you had better make his wife happy . . . and Arti wants a family. Soon. As soon as possible."

Jimenez smiled and then began to give off a most unmilitary giggle.

"What's so funny?"

With some difficulty, Xavier got control of himself and answered, "I was just thinking about how badly Arti wants to bear Mac's children. It isn't like they didn't start work on that *months* ago."

So much for Lourdes giving them the use of a room for privacy, Carrera thought, drily, looking over at his wife. She, too, was laughing, even while she tried hiding her face with her hand.

"Well, Patricio, I *tried,*" she said.

"What about when you get married?" Carrera asked.

Jimenez snorted. "What sane woman would marry me? Not an issue, Patricio; it's never going to happen. Besides, I'm married to the Fourth and that's bitch enough for me—no offense, Lourdes. No . . . I'll be just fine as a sometime guest here."

Carrera shrugged, thinking, *No, actually you won't be a sometime guest here, since we're going to be moving the legions to the mainland over the next year. So . . . I suppose . . . why not?*

"Yeah . . . okay," he conceded. "Mac and Arti can have Number Two. Now that she's about to be married at least the young signifers and tribunes will stop trying to serenade her under her window."

"Tell me about it," Jimenez said. "I mean, it wouldn't be so bad if they could *sing.*"

Isla Real, Quarters #1, 33/6/468 AC

Lourdes hummed the wedding march softly to herself as she crossed the hundred and twenty meters from her old home, Number Two, to Number One. Having Mac and Arti as next door neighbors was going to be great; she just knew it.

And, better still, when they thump the bed against the wall all night, I won't be able to hear it. Besides, it reminds me of what I am missing when Patricio is away.

Entering by the front door, Lourdes took one look at McNamara and Artemisia—coming down the stairs arm and arm, he looking guilty and she like the cat who fell into the vat of cream—and she started laughing again. She ran to the nearest room, her husband's library, to hide her discomposure. She closed the door behind her and covered her mouth again to try to stifle her laughter.

"What's so funny, Mama?" little Hamilcar asked, looking up from one of his father's books.

"I'll tell you when you're older," Lourdes answered. Curious, she walked over to the desk and picked up the book that her son had been reading. That he was reading was no surprise; the child had been literate for almost two years. The title, however, she found worrisome: *The Battle of Kuantan* by Tadeo Kurita.

Can it be genetic, somehow? she wondered, suddenly growing utterly serious and seriously worried. *Did my son inherit his father's taste for battle? God, please don't take my baby from me. He's not even five yet.*

After his mother had left, Hamilcar returned to his reading. Kurita's dry account of the exchange between his battlecruiser and the Federated States Navy's superdreadnought, *Andrew Jackson*, soon had the boy quivering with excitement and a wordless longing to *be* there, to trade shot for shot and blow for blow. Never mind that he was, half ways, from the Federated States, nor that his other half had had little involvement in the Great Global War. It was the battle, itself, that drew him. And, he already knew, it always would.

He knew, too, that he already understood things that were forever barred to most human beings, at any age. He understood, instinctively, without Kurita explaining it, what it meant to cross the *Jackson*'s T and why Kurita had accepted a couple of bad hits to get his own ship in position to do that. Hamilcar understood, without anyone explaining it, the logistic and time-space factors that had dictated why the Battle of Kuantan had happened where it had and when it had.

In short, Hamilcar Carrera-Nuñez already knew, at age four, that he had the *knack*.

He closed the book, sighing, and thought, *Mama and I need to have a long talk*.

4/7/468 AC, Main Parade Field, Isla Real

"I've seen you under fire, Sergeant Major, and I've never seen you look nervous like today."

"Sir . . . fuck you, sir," McNamara answered. "T'isn't every day a man gets married. And it's almost never a man marries a woman like Artemisia. If I'm nervous . . ."

"You have a right to be, Mac," Carrera answered, gently. "I just like pulling your leg and needling you. Because, you know, if I didn't know you were watching me, there's a half dozen times, over the years, that I'd have been gibbering. By God, I've a *right* to needle you. If only for the goddamned bed thumping that's kept me up every night but the last few."

To that McNamara had no answer, but only a sort of a question. "It worries me, sir, you know? I'm pushing sixty. She's less t'an half my age. I've got to, you know . . . get the gettin' while the gettin's good. T'e day's not long off . . ."

"My ass."

A white tent sat not far from where McNamara and Carrera traded jibes and worries. In the tent Lourdes and a bevy of bridesmaids fussed and fluttered around Artemisia Jimenez, fluffing, primping, and generally polishing. She looked amazing.

"Does my ass look fat in this, Lourdes?" Artemisia asked worriedly.

Lourdes looked. *I should have such an ass*, she thought. Then she looked again. "No, Arti, your rear end is not fat. But unless I'm much mistaken you've grown a cup size. How many months along are you?"

Artemisia smiled wickedly. "Six weeks. I *had* to, don't you see? He might have backed out."

"Does Mac know?"

"I was going to tell him tonight. Otherwise, he'll be so worried about me . . . hell, this is John McNamara we're talking about; he'd be so *embarrassed* at our being caught jumping the gun; he'd probably blow his lines. And those, he *must* get right."

"And besides," Lourdes said, drily "if he screws this up enough to delay the wedding, you'll need a new dress, won't you?"

Artemisia dimpled. "So you see my point in not upsetting him, right?"

"You've upset the signifers and some of the tribunes," Carrera said, pointing with his chin at two sets of bleachers filled to overflowing with sixty or more junior officers, all in dress whites and every man wearing a black armband.

"Young punks," McNamara said, when he saw.

"It's a compliment, Sergeant Major. Take it that way."

"I suppose so," he admitted, with bad grace. "T'ough if t'ey t'tought about it, t'ey'd realize t'eir lives are about to get a lot more pleasant when I have somet'ing to do besides ride *t'eir* asses."

"That's one way to look at it," Carrera agreed. "They really ought—" He hushed suddenly, even as the crowd did (for ringing the field there were *thousands* of legionaries, plus their families, who had come to watch).

Artemisia, escorted by her uncle, Xavier, brilliant in his dress whites, had emerged from the tent. Lourdes followed, as did another eleven women, about half and half Arti's close in-laws and the girls she had competed against for Miss Balboa. In the bleachers, sixty signifers and junior tribunes looked at the procession and suddenly had the same thought: *Well . . . there are some other opportunities out there.*

"You are *such* a lucky bastard, Top. I believe that's the only woman I've ever seen to match my Linda."

The band of the *Legion del Cid,* mercifully sans drums and bagpipes, picked up the wedding march.

Oh, God, I'm so nervous, thought Artemisia as she led her party forward along the carpets laid to protect her shoes and dress from the grass. *What if I'm not a good wife? What if he gets tired of me? What if . . . ?*

Stop being an idiot, Arti, you and he are perfect *together. It's going to be wonderful.*

But what if my tits sag after the baby comes?

Then you get pregnant again and reinflate them.

But what if he gets tired of my cooking?

Then you hire a cook. Lourdes already said that Patricio's gift to us is "impressive and of many parts." Besides, John's salary with the legion, plus his retired pay from the FS Army, is huge by Balboan standards. And I can work, too. And then, too, Uncle Xavier is going to contribute.

But what if—?

"I'm sooo glad t'at's over, sir," McNamara whispered.

Carrera answered, "Men don't enjoy the ceremony, generally, Top, but endure it because of the state it formalizes. By the way, did you know you're going to be a daddy?"

Mac sighed, embarrassed. "She hasn't told me, but, yeah . . . I kinda figured it out."

Smiling, Carrera chided, "Bad, wicked, naughty sergeant major. You should be ashamed. Oh . . . and Lourdes and I would like to stand as godparents, if that's okay with you and Arti."

"We'd be honored, sir."

"You got to be focking shittin' me, sir. I mean . . . well . . . we knew Miss Lourdes had set up the honeymoon but . . ."

Carrera just smiled as there, on the parade field, a smallish airship descended and lowered ropes to half a dozen waiting heavy-duty recovery trucks packed to the brim with sandbags. Chartering the thing had cost a not-inconsiderable fortune but for *his* sergeant major, no expense was too great.

"Shitting you about what, Top?" Carrera asked. "You and I are just simple soldiers. This kind of thing—an airship honeymoon to tour all of Colombia del Norte—seems too much to us. But *she* is . . . was Miss Balboa and she will, by God, have a honeymoon to set the continent wild."

McNamara scoffed. "T'at ain't it, you sneaky bastard. I know you. You ain't t'at nice. What you're doing is sending us on a whirlwind recruitin' tour, ain't you?"

Rather than deny it, exactly, Carrera answered, "Siegel's going with you as a sort of aide de camp. You and he and Arti are going to entertain every god-damned General Staff in Colombia Latina on your trip."

"T'at's nonsense, boss, no offense. T'ose arrogant assholes won't even talk to no noncom. Not even one wit' Miss Balboa on his arm."

"Who says you're a noncom?" Carrera asked. He pointed at Siegel, standing not far away. Siegel came running, bearing a carved silverwood box about two feet in length and perhaps four inches on a side. Wearing a huge smirk, he stopped, standing at attention and holding the box out. Carrera opened it and drew from it a baton, about eighteen inches in length and an inch in diameter. The baton was gold colored, as were all sergeants major's batons. This one, however, was encircled by harpy eagles spiraling down its length. They looked like, and were, solid gold. There was a jewelry store in *Ciudad* Balboa that *really* wanted to keep in the legion's good graces.

The crowd hushed. Rumors had suggested something like this. At the central reviewing stand Tom Christian announced, "Attention to orders."

"You see, Top," Carrera explained, "there *was* such

a thing as a praetorian prefect. Then, too, the origin of your rank, back on Old Earth, was 'Sergeant Major-*General*' . . ."

What was probably the most finely tuned, spotlessly clean armored vehicle not merely on this world, but on two worlds and in the history of two worlds, pulled up by the gazebo. The band picked up the Wedding March again while Mac and Artemisia, both still in white, walked to it. They were pelted by rice and chorley seed the entire way.

At the tank, McNamara put his hands on Arti's still-narrow waist and lifted her to a cushion thoughtfully placed behind the turret. He then scrambled up to stand atop the tank where he bent to lift his new wife to her feet. Gently—no mean feat given the nature of Volgan-built tanks—the armored vehicle trundled off to just underneath the airship. There, they dismounted in reverse order and began to ascend the gangway the airship had lowered. They stopped twice on the way up, Artemisia with tears in her eyes, to wave to the crowd.

Waving back, crying, Lourdes whispered to her husband, "Weddings do something to me. They make me horny. Take me home and fuck me. Now."

"Orders are orders," Carrera answered, reaching over gently to wipe away the tears flowing from Lourdes' huge brown eyes. "And those orders, my lovely wife, are always a joy to obey."

Isla Real, Quarters #1, 5/7/468 AC

Hamilcar had inherited the huge size of his mother's eyes, along with a blend of color from both parents. His were a brilliant green with the same dark circles

around the iris that gave his father's such a frighten-
ingly penetrating quality. He turned those big green
eyes up at his mother and said, "Mama, can I ask
you for something?"

Lourdes, puttering in the kitchen, stopped what
she was doing, looked down at her eldest and said,
"Yes, of course, baby. What is it?"

"When daddy goes back to the war . . . Mama, I
want to go with him."

Christ, no, not my baby, too.

"You're too small," she answered. "You're only
four. When you're a grown man of five we'll discuss
this again."

"Does that mean I can go when I'm five?"

"No, it means we'll discuss it. Then. Not before."

This was not an entirely satisfactory answer so Hamilcar upped the stakes. "Mama, if you don't tell me I can
go when I'm five . . . I'll go over your head." He heard
one or another of his daddy's soldiers use that expression. He was pretty sure he understood what it meant.

Lourdes *did* understand what it meant. He'd go to
his father to ask permission. *Which Patricio just might
give. And what objections will I have? I kept Hamilcar
in the war zone for almost two years when he was a
baby, just so I could be with my husband. I can't object
to him being there now that's he's past being a baby.*

"Do you want to break your mother's heart, Ham?"
she asked.

"No."

"Then please don't 'go over my head.' Wait until
you're five and we *will* discuss it."

Five is not so long a wait. "All right, Mama. But if
you don't let me go then, I will go over your head."

INTERLUDE

7/9/49 AC, Balboa Colony, Terra Nova

In the thick Balboan night, with monkeys and *antaniae* and even the occasional trixie filling the air with sound, with the steady drone of mosquitoes in their ears, the Gurkha Rifles and the Sikh Pioneers bivouacked close together and well away from the ad hoc OAU infantry battalion. Frankly, while the Gurkhas and Sikhs got along just fine, neither could stand the undisciplined rabble from the OAU. Less still could Majors Dhan Singh Pandey and Amita Kaur Bhago stand the . . .

"Overbred, cowardly, stuffed shirt, little boy bunging, limey bastard, Duff-McQueeg," as Amita usually phrased it.

"Please, Amita, be charitable," Dhan chided. "After all, we don't *know* he's a coward. Personally, I think he only stays with the OAU troops for the little boys they keep for him."

"We'll see about that when the fighting starts," she answered, automatically killing a mosquito that had landed on her wrist.

"I don't know fighting ever start," said Company

Sergeant Major Rambahadur Thapa, of Pandey's company. "We are end of supply trail, *sahib*. And jungle boys pretty good at keeping away."

That was true enough; Pandey's shrug admitted it. So far into the jungle and so far from any road was the task force that resupply depended on helicopters and shuttles. But the force was literally at the maximum distance the helicopters available could support. Another kilometer and the excess wear would begin to overwhelm the maintenance staff.

"We could drive twice as far or more without the OAU acting as a dead weight," Amita said. "Though in that case the task force commander would have no little boys. Worse, he'd be with us."

Dhan Singh Pandey opened his mouth to speak when the jungle erupted in heavy automatic fire coming from the direction of the OAU bivouac. He was about to call for his radio bearer when Amita held up her hand.

"I didn't hear anything," she said. "Sergeant Major?"

"Not me."

"Sir, call from the OAU," the radioman announced.

Pandey thought about that for half a second and said, "I'm sure you're mistaken, *Naik*."

Belisario hadn't rushed it. New weapons were fine. New weapons his men didn't know how to use were just expensive clubs. He'd spent a month just in training with the new rifles and machine guns and another two weeks in feeling out the enemy. In the process, he noticed something interesting. The Gurkhas would come running to help the Sikhs, and vice versa. But when he probed the OAU, or someone sniped at them, both Gurkhas and Sikhs indicated a profound disinterest.

This night, he'd decided to risk an attack. A *full* attack.

In the privacy of his tent Duff-McQueeg held a local boy, down on all fours, firmly by the hips while moving his own in a steady, rhythmic stroke. He was suddenly interrupted by the sound of heavy gunfire. He was tempted to ignore it, but then Warrant Officer Bourguet ripped open the tent flap and announced, breathlessly, "Sir . . . sir . . . the enemy . . ."

A large red stain suddenly blossomed on Bourguet's T-shirt, visible through his unbuttoned uniform jacket. Wordlessly, the warrant officer crumpled to the ground. His hands remained gripped to the material of the tent, which followed the heavyset warrant to the ground. Duff-McQueeg, and the boy, were trapped underneath. By the time Duff-McQueeg could extract himself from both the boy and the tent, he emerged to find a smoking muzzle pressed to the side of his head.

"*Señor Carrera, aqui!*"

"Bring him out, Pedro," Belisario said. He was almost embarrassed for the prisoner when he smelt the odor of shit. Then he realized the man had not shat himself and sympathy changed to disgust.

The tent material wriggled and distorted.

"Whoever you are, come out," Pedro ordered.

The boy emerged, pulling his threadbare trousers up.

"*Chico*," Belisario asked, "were you with this man by your own will?"

The boy spat at Duff-McQueeg and said, "They stole me from my village."

Belisario nodded grimly and said, to Pedro, "Get a rope."

The boy, with a look of utter hatred in his eyes asked, "Can I have a gun?"

CHAPTER EIGHTEEN

There is no love untouched by hate
No unity without discord
There is no courage without fear
There is no peace without a war
—Cruxshadows, "Eye of the Storm"

Runnistan, Pashtia, 8/7/468 AC

Rachman was terrified; Tribune David Cano could see it in his eyes. Yet the fierce Pashtun would rather die in horrible agony than ever admit to feeling the slightest fear.

And why the hell shouldn't he be terrified? Cano thought. *Poor bastard's never been up in a helicopter before. He's never even flown before. If I were him, I'd be shitting myself. What a great people these are. What a formidable people.*

It had been this way since he'd first been assigned to the Pashtun Scouts. *Everything* about them impressed Cano. Everything about them he liked. Were they rough men? Yes and so was he. Were they crude and uncultured, ignorant and savage?

Well, what was I but an ignorant ridge runner before

*the legion picked me up and sent me to school? My only
skill was riding a horse. But these people aren't stupid,
no more than I was. They're just uneducated . . . and
that can be fixed.*

Cano had the oddest feeling, in accompanying
Rachman and a hundred and nineteen of his fellow
tribesman going to their home villages on leave, that
he was going home as well. He'd fit in so well with
these men, enjoyed their company and their com-
radeship so much, that he just *knew* he was going to
belong, and perhaps better than he'd ever belonged
anywhere before.

He felt Rachman's fist pounding his shoulder and
looked over. The look of fear in Rachman's eyes had
disappeared as the Pashtun gestured enthusiastically
at what appeared to be a nothing-much village a few
thousand feet below.

"Home," Rachman announced over the *thrum* of the
Volgan-built IM-71. And again, with a mix of satisfaction and exuberance, "David, we are almost *home*."

BdL *Dos Lindas*, Hajipur, Sind, 8/7/468 AC

The moons Hecate and Eris were high, the former full
and the latter in three quarters. The bay of Hajipur
was bright under the light of the moons.

In the bay, surrounded by her escorts seaward
and her infantry force on the dock, with sailors and
Cazadors manning the guns, *Dos Lindas* sang with the
ring of the hammers and the rushing crackle of the
welding machines. She sang, too, with the sing-song
speech of the local shipfitters who still swarmed her
like industrious bees.

"She be good as new, soon, Skipper," said the master of the shipfitters. "Better den new."

Fosa knew it was true. Not only had the local boys, and a few girls, patched her up, they'd identified weaknesses and worn spots in the hull, seen a few places that wouldn't be the worse for a little extra bracing, and fixed all that as well. The laser topside, blown off by the near miss of a cruise missile, was replaced, as was every wrecked forty- and twenty-millimeter cannon, and .41 caliber machine gun. Even the lost crew, aviators and Cazadors were up to strength, though there had been an awful price to pay back home to make it so.

All that was needed now was the rear elevator. And that was coming soon, this very night, in fact.

We shall see home again, you and I, Fosa thought as he stroked a railing atop the tower rising high above the flight deck. *We could fight even as we are. Yes, we could not launch aircraft half so well, but we could still fight, we could still avenge our fallen comrades.*

But we'll have our elevator, my dear ship. Tonight it comes to us. And a new sister to fight at our side. And then we go back for revenge.

Fosa looked up at a bright flash at the entrance to the bay. A split second later came the report of a large caliber gun. This was followed, thirty seconds later, by another flash and another *boom*. Again: flash . . . *boom*. It went on through twenty-one blank shots, a custom that had followed man to the stars.

The speakers on the bridge barked, "*Barco del Legion Dos Lindas*, this is BdL *Tadeo Kurita*. We're escorting your elevator. And we've got ten six-inch guns. Let's get you up to one hundred percent. And *then*, let's go hunting."

Wilcox's Folly, FSC, 10/7/468 AC

Micah Fen was fat. That was the one thing *everyone* noticed about him. Indeed, it was the one thing impossible not to notice about him. At least, it was the one thing impossible not to notice until one came close. Within ten feet, perhaps even twenty-five if downwind, one was subjected to the foul odor of obesity necrosis that hung about him like a cloud of gnats about a dead dog's anus.

Khalid had spent a *lot* of time on the GlobalNet researching his targets. *And I never suspected how much the filthy swine would just plain* stink. *I wonder if his mind is half so rotten as his skin.*

For the first several months in the Federated States Khalid had done nothing but research and planning. He already had hit plans for most of his potential targets at obvious places, their homes, their offices, their lovers' homes. He still worked on those, but spent more time now looking for the excuse to execute the hit and leave the blame on the Salafis.

*I'd really never expected this one to come up within my hit parameters. Fen's been so consistent in his support of the Salafi Ikhwan, so thoroughly in their camp, I just never imagined he'd do something that would—*Il hamdu l'illah—*allow me to actually kill him.*

It would have been better, of course, if Fen had brought his busload of gays to a mosque rather than a Nazrani *church,* Khalid thought. *But that, I suppose, would have been asking for too much. After all, if nothing else, Fen can hardly have risked exposing the gays to the "righteous, Godly wrath" of the Salafis he wants them to support. So . . . a* Nazrani *church it had to be and a* Nazrani *church will have to do.*

Besides, Khalid thought, *even if imperfect it's still worthwhile even to just suggest to the gays here who support Fen that they're supporting a man who would turn them over to people who would crucify them.*

Khalid liked all the targets he'd been assigned, *qua* targets. Even so, it was especially pleasing, much more so than his usual hit, to be assigned to take out Fen. *Who, after all, encouraged the people who blew up my family, who murdered my mother, my brother, and my angel, my poor innocent little Hurriyah. Who better deserves to die?*

"You never really thought about it, did you?" Khalid asked. "You never realized that, if terrorism works, it can work on you and yours?"

Fen said nothing. He couldn't; his mouth was duct taped closed even as his wrists and ankles were duct taped to the heavy chair on which he sat. Nonetheless, his piggish eyes were full of pleading terror.

Only fitting.

"You really never had a second thought for your safety, did you?" Khalid asked. "However much you lambasted your country in film and print, however much you lied, however many people you caused to be killed by encouraging their murderers, you never thought that any of it could ever come back on *you*?"

"Sure, I understand," Khalid said, genially, removing a small roll of duct tape from a satchel and placing in on a table near Fen. "You're *Micah Fen*, star. Retribution is for little people. You only kept a bodyguard to keep away your adoring fans."

"It was easy, you know," Khalid continued, as he checked his digital camera once again. "Get on the GlobalNet, find your touring schedule, check for chartered flights, watch for the press throng, spot you, and then follow you to your hotel. You've got security at home, and you do travel with a bodyguard." Khalid's head inclined towards the cooling corpse of Fen's bodyguard, spreading crimson on the suite's thick carpet. "But outside of your cocoon, you were really very vulnerable."

"I put on a service staff uniform I took from a hotel storage closet and checked with room service to see which room had ordered the most grotesque quantity and quality of food. That had to be you. I came to this floor and bludgeoned a maid—she'll be fine; don't worry—then hid her in a closet and took her passkey.

"With the passkey, I just entered your suite and shot the bodyguard, twice in the chest and once in the head, with a silenced .45. By the time you woke up, you pustule, your mouth was gagged and your arm twisted behind your back. I doubt you would even have woken up if I hadn't dragged you to that chair you're taped to by your arm and shaggy hair. You would like to know why, wouldn't you?"

Glaring at Fen's piggish face, Khalid removed from his pocket a wallet containing a family photo. He opened this and showed it to his victim. "This little girl was my sister, Hurriyah. You praised and encouraged the men who murdered her. That was enough. I'd have sucked Fernandez's dick for the chance to kill you, but he—fine man—gave me the chance for free."

Fen shook his head emphatically. Khalid paid no attention. Instead, he put away the photo and wallet and drew from his pockets a clear plastic bag, a nail and a press release concerning Fen's pro-gay activity.

Khalid had scrawled a message in Arabic on the press release. He'd use his pistol to nail the press release to Fen's forehead after the fat fuck was dead.

With the camera, Khalid took a photo of his victim, bound and gagged. He then put the camera aside and pulled a couple of inches of the duct tape roll free.

"This is really going to *suck*," he said to Fen, happily. "It's going to suck for you, I mean. I, on the other hand, am going to *really* enjoy it. Take a deep breath, why don't you? No sense in making this too quick."

After placing the clear bag over Fen's head, which elicited a garbled set of pleas for pity and mercy, Khalid took the free two inches of tape and began to wind the sticky stuff around Fen's neck, sealing the bag. The rolls of fat about Fen's neck made it a tougher job than Khalid had anticipated, causing him to have to make three extra winds to ensure a good seal. Fortunately, he'd brought more than enough tape.

Khalid stepped back and picked up the camera. Already Fen had the bag billowing, as he tried to suck in oxygen to feed his almost incredible bulk. In a short time the actor-producer's head was whiplashing back and forth and side to side as he exhausted all the oxygen trapped in the bag and went into a full panic.

While snapping a picture of Fen's purpling face, Khalid was struck by a smell even worse than Fen's normal, unsavory aroma.

"Oh, you *shit* yourself, didn't you?" Khalid sneered. "What a *pig*! Aren't you *embarrassed*?"

In answer, Fen's head only whipped the more frantically as it fruitlessly sought escape from the bag that had cut off its air.

Runnistan, Pashtia, 10/7/468 AC

Nobody in the village fired his rifle into the air.
Instead, the men, Samsonov rifles and clones held
easily in their hands, clustered around Cano and
Rachman, forming a circle. The women of the place
stood behind their men, but that appeared more a
defensive arrangement than a mark of low status.
Oddly, the women were not veiled.

Among the villagers, Rachman and his men were
well known. All eyes were on the stranger, Cano.
From the encircling crowd one old man emerged and
walked toward the group.

"Father," Rachman said to the old man, "we have
returned in glory, all but for Filot who fell in battle
and was buried on the field. I have brought with us
our *hectontar*, that our people might rejoice to see
the leader of their sons and to see that that leader
is worthy. Father, David is one of *us*."

Cano followed the conversation, more or less. The
word *hectontar* was new to him, but he assumed it
was local dialect and thought no more of it. He was,
in any event, *much* more interested in the fact that
the villagers were not using their rifles as noisemakers;
in that, and in the unveiled women he saw behind
the men. He saw a pair of bright green eyes atop a
swaying, willowy shape, but lost them in the crowd.

"Since my son says you are worthy," said Rachman's
father, offering his hand in greeting, "I welcome you
to our village. Come; the day is warm. Let us sit and
talk in the cool of my courtyard."

While the rest of the group split up to follow their
own families home, Rachman and Cano followed

Rachman's father, Cano's eyes still searching for that willowy shape.

The courtyard was walled. Even so, the house was built on the side of a steep hill. From the courtyard's fountain, Cano could see out over wall to where a group of the village's young men were busily fighting over the corpse of a sheep, from horseback.

The game looked interesting, and even fun, though Cano had no idea of the rules. Based on the number of boys he saw being carried off the field, dripping blood, he wasn't entirely sure there *were* any rules.

Rachman's father saw Cano's interest and said, "It's for you, you know."

"Well, it *is* entertaining," Cano replied.

"No, not that," Rachman said. "The young men are trying to impress you with their skill and courage." Seeing Cano really didn't understand, Rachman huffed and added, "So you'll *hire* them on to join the scouts. We haven't had a good war that we had a chance of winning in . . . well, in a very long time."

"Ohhh." Cano shrugged. "I'm not sure how to even go about that. I don't know if the Legion is interested in expanding the Scouts, though they might be. No, they *should* be. I'll ask—"

He stopped suddenly as a willowy young woman, technically more of a girl, really, stooped gracefully to set a tray of assorted finger food—fruit, olives, Terra Novan olives with their wrinkled and gray skin, flat yellow chorley bread, honey, some other green and red sauces in bowls—between the three of them. She was unveiled and when she turned her head to smile and Cano saw her green eyes . . .

God in Heaven; she's beautiful, Cano thought. *Those eyes . . . that face . . . that shape . . .*

Rachman smiled, though his father laughed aloud. "This is my sister, Alena," Rachman explained. "She's fifteen."

Cano immediately looked crestfallen, which raised a laugh from both of the others. "Fifteen," Rachman said, "is *not* a problem."

Did Cano understand from that what he thought he did? He knew they'd never offer the girl—no, the *woman*; he'd seen that in her eyes and her smile—for anything dishonorable. It would be as a wife or nothing. But fifteen? He looked again.

The next time I see a fifteen-year-old that looks like that—even back home where the girls grow up fast—will be the first.

Cano shot an inquiring look at Rachman, then at the father. *Yes, they do mean it.*

He thought that, and then immediately looked even more crestfallen than he had before. "But I'm not a Moslem," Cano said. "And I can't give up the faith of my fathers."

All three of the Pashtun, father, son and sister, broke out in gales of laughter. Rachman eventually ended up on one side on the ground, shaking with mirth. The sister, Alena, sank to her knees and held her sides. Cano looked on, cluelessly. (*But doesn't Alena have a* wonderful *laugh?*)

Rachman's father recovered first. He picked up a wedge of chorley bread, dipped it into a bowl holding some sauce made from *holy shit* peppers, and said, just before popping the wedge into his mouth, "Son, take your war chief to see the *hieros*, why don't you?"

BdL *Qamra*, Hajipur, Sind, 10/7/468 AC

Though the sun had not yet set, Hecate shone indistinctly on the eastern horizon.

To the west, the fronts of the Hindu and Buddhist temples lining the waterfront were in shadow.

"They've got a god or goddess for everything, I think," Marta said to Jaquelina, the two sitting side by side on the forward deck, arms around each other's waists. Marta was relaxed enough but Jaquie seemed to her lover to be very stiff.

"Are you feeling all right, love," Marta asked.

Jaquie said nothing, but shook her head and leaned into Marta, tucking one shoulder under the larger woman's arm.

"Tell me," Marta commanded.

"It's nothing."

"*Tell* me."

Jaquie nestled closer in and admitted, "Honestly, I'm scared."

"Oh."

There wasn't a lot more to say. The carrier was still under repair. The other escorts were needed to secure it in a place that was something less than secure. Even so, the contract with the *Zaibatsu* required, at a minimum, that the *classis* maintain a presence in the Nicobar Straits. All that was available, or would be available before BdL *Tadeo Kurita* unloaded *Dos Lindas'* elevator, was *Qamra*.

Fosa had given the word the previous day. "Take *Qamra* out to the Straits and see if you can't take out one or two of the smaller pirate boats. We'll be along as soon as we've fitted the elevator. We'll *all* be along."

"We're going to be alone out there," Jaquelina continued, with a small shiver. "For a week or two. Maybe more. No backup. No help. Nobody scouting for us. No retreat if we get in trouble. Even the men are worried."

Marta leaned over to kiss the top of her lover's head, then reached out a hand to stroke hair and cheek. "You have too much imagination," she said. "We'll be fine. I won't let anything happen to you."

Jaquie backed off and looked intently into Marta's face. "I'm not worried about *me*, you idiot. I'm worried about *you*."

Runnistan, Pashtia, 10/7/468 AC

The *hieros* was carved into the mountain, about a half mile from Rachman's family's home. The trail seemed well-worn, to Cano, as if the people of the village followed it regularly to the rectangularly carved opening in the mountainside. He mentioned this to Rachman.

"We come here often, yes," the Pashtun said. "To commune with God . . . to dedicate the young men to His service . . . sometimes just to be away from people to think."

By the time they reached the carved opening, the sun was down. Rachman took a match from one of the two guards standing by the entrance. With it, he lit a small, oil-burning lamp. It cast a flickering light over what looked to Cano to be brick-sized, carved stones, framing a tunnel perhaps thirty inches wide. With the flame from the lamp Rachman lit a torch lying nearby.

"We took these when we left Old Earth," Rachman

explained, gesturing at the stones with the torch. "We had no money to pay for much extra baggage, not unless we were willing to sell off some of our patrimony, which we weren't. So say the legends, anyway. Each man and woman took one stone or one piece of something to rebuild this, here. Come, I'll show you."

The footing was even, if not quite smooth, and Cano, guided by Rachman's torch, felt his way along easily. Seventy-five yards or so into the mountainside the narrow tunnel opened up to . . .

At first, Rachman's torchlight reflected dimly from what Cano judged to be over one hundred dull mirrors. As the Pashtun circled around the room, lighting more lamps as he went, the things Cano took to be mirrors began to appear as round shields, plates, medallions, necklaces and . . .

"Holy shit."

"Very holy," Rachman agreed, "but not shit." He pointed with the torch toward a golden plate, perhaps fifteen inches across. "This is the image of our God."

"Where have I seen that face before?" Cano wondered aloud. "It was in an old book, at the legion's library . . . an old book from Old Earth . . . Al . . . Alex . . ."

"Iskander," Rachman supplied. "The avatar of our God. God made flesh. It is to Him that we pray. He will come to us again, so say the prophecies." There was no waver of doubt in Rachman's voice. His god *would* return.

"Ohhh." He thought for a moment about the implications. Then it hit him. "You are not Moslems?"

"We pretend, sometimes," Rachman said. "And give

little gifts to Mullah Hassim to make sure he doesn't raise an army against us. But, no, not Moslems. Which is why—" He raised one eyebrow, waiting to see if Cano could make the connection.

He could. "I would not have to convert to be a suitable match for your sister?"

Rachman was smiling broadly. "Correct, Hectontar Cano."

"She's only fifteen, and she doesn't even know me," Cano objected.

"She is already a woman, ready to bear you fine, strong sons and daughters. And you have two weeks to get to know each other," Rachman answered.

"I am a soldier and I might be killed at any time."

"She is the sister, daughter, granddaughter, great-great-great-great to infinity granddaughter of soldiers. She would understand."

"I don't even know if she likes me."

"I told her and my father about you months ago. They *both* like you. You don't already have a wife, do you?"

"No," Cano shook his head. "No wife. No girlfriend. I never had time to even look for either since I joined the legion."

"Well," Rachman said, "let's stop wasting time and get back to my father's home so you can get to know your future one."

In the flaring light of the torch and the lamps, all reflected by the gold and polished stone of the *hieros*, which Cano now understood to mean "shrine," or perhaps "temple," Cano said, "You are the strangest matchmaker I have ever heard of."

"No, no," Rachman disagreed. "You should see

my aunt. She has a better moustache than I do . . . though I think my beard is more manly . . . a little."

Outside, the guards began to laugh so loudly that Cano was sure it was true about the moustache and beard on Rachman's aunt.

"Alena can read, you know," Rachman said, as they made their way back to the entrance. "Father insisted upon it. Me, personally, I think it was a mistake. She's too smart as it is—"

"Way too smart," agreed one of the guards, just as the two emerged from the tunnel.

"Not bad girl," said the other, "just make you feel stupid." He shrugged. "Doesn't mean to."

"Good shot, too," said the first.

"Oh, yes, very good. Also good on horse. This important; means she can keep up with husband on campaign."

"Very important quality in wife," the first guard agreed. That guard put a hand on Cano's shoulder. "But better you than me, Hectontar. You see, she has the *sight*."

"The dowry for my sister will be immense," Rachman warned, changing the subject, and shooting a dirty look at the guards. "Immense! Not that anyone else is bidding, mind you," he admitted.

What the hell, Cano thought, *I make more in a month than these people do in a year. Hell, in three or four years. And I never spend it. It might be nice to have a wife to spend it on. To see those beautiful eyes light up . . .*

Cano gulped, nervously. "Rachman, you have to talk me through this. How do I propose?"

Nicobar Straits, BdL *Qamra*, 14/8/468 AC

It was a daunting enough proposition. Alone, untended, unsupported, Chu had to take his vessel into enemy waters and simply look for trouble or, failing that, wait for trouble to find him.

"Somehow, I don't think it'll be long," Chu said.

"What's that, Chu?" Centurion Rodriguez asked.

"Nothing . . . oh, just that I don't think it will be too long before trouble finds us, even with the girls below and undercover."

"You can count on it," Rodriguez agreed, staring into the smoke that still covered the waters of the Straits. "Sucks to be us."

"Tonight, you figure?" Chu asked.

"Or tomorrow, or the next night. Wish we had the rest of the *classis* with us."

"Yeah," Chu sighed. "Wish in one hand . . ."

BdL *Dos Lindas*, Hajipur, Sind, 15/8/468 AC

"Shit me a goddamned working elevator!" Fosa screamed at his chief engineer.

"It's not that simple, Captain," the engineer answered sheepishly. "Yes, we *thought* it would be that simple but we were wrong."

Fosa turned around and stared out of the bridge's wide, and new, windows, looking at the menacing shadow of the *Tadeo Kurita*. It wasn't particularly easy to calm himself down, but he did. He turned around again and asked, "All right; what's the problem?"

"It's the way this class, any class, really, of warships was built, way back when, Skipper. They can use the same diagrams. They can subcontract to the same subcontractors. But they're always a little different. In this particular case, we've got to modify the god-damned hangar deck and the elevator portal because it's *three* fucking millimeters too small. Or the elevator is three millimeters too big; take your pick."

"How long?"

The engineer looked at the master of the shipfitters.

"'nother week, Skipper. Maybe five day if go well."

"Fuck."

Runnistan, Pashtia, 16/8/468 AC

"Why were the young men using a sheep before?" Cano asked, as Rachman fitted him with padding and a helmet in preparation for his upcoming game of *buzkashi*. Rachman and the other players, standing nearby holding their horses, were already suited up.

"Oh, that was just practice. For serious games we use calf . . . soaked in cold water to toughen it up . . . and filled with sand."

"And the purpose of this is?" Cano asked.

"Show toughness and courage in front of soon-to-be wife," said one of the other players in Cano's team. Cano thought he was one of the two guards he'd met at the *hieros*, the one who'd said, "Better you than me."

"You must pay close attention, David," Rachman added, "to the young men on both sides who show real fighting heart. They're playing to impress you, after all. Well . . . that and to get rid of my sister."

Cano looked across the dusty playing field past the opposing team to where Alena sat, framed by a simple goal. She wore a long blue dress and, for the ceremony, she was veiled. Between them, in a small pit, was the corpse of the calf.

"We only play by these rules when it's part of a wedding," Rachman explained. "Otherwise, we fight to take the calf around a pole and bring it back within a circle we draw around the pit. For wedding, though, you must present calf, whatever's left of it . . . and of you . . . to new wife as trophy."

"How long do I have?" Cano asked.

Rachman shrugged, "Maybe couple days."

A couple of days? DAYS? "What if I lose?"

"Alena says you won't."

"And she has the sight, remember," added that same guard, pressing into Cano's hand a whip.

"What's this for?

"To hit people," Rachman explained patiently. "Well, you're not the type to let someone hit you without hitting back, are you, brother-in-law to be?"

The morning sun was rising, the horse was limping, and had he been afoot Cano would have been staggering, when the two reached the rectangular goal beyond which sat his bride.

The rest of his team, and even the other team, and especially the crowd, all cheered themselves hoarse as Cano undraped from across his saddle the remains of the calf. The sand was long gone, an entire leg was missing, and the thing was more than half in shreds. He tossed the calf, what there was of it, through the goal and dismounted.

Rachman was there to catch him and keep him from falling over. He was also there to help him walk through the goals to claim his woman. This was as well since the various whips and fists and flailing hooves of rearing horses had fairly well shut Cano's eyes. He'd never have made it to the goal without Rachman to lead his horse.

You know, Cano thought, *in a while, when it really starts to hurt, I'm going to regret this. But for now, before the serious pain begins, I've got to admit, that was* fun.

Alena's father walked onto the field, approached his daughter, and lifted her to her feet by her hand.

"Does anyone object that this proven man take this woman to wife?" the father shouted.

"NNNOOO!" roared the crowd.

The father led Alena to where Rachman and Cano stood. He took Cano's hand, eliciting a small yelp as the hand had been broken. Into it he placed Alena's smaller one. There was more ceremony, a feast, and a short trip to the *hieros* to come, but from that moment they were married.

It was a pity Cano couldn't see well enough to note the light in Alena's eyes.

She *had* the sight.

BdL *Qamra*, Nicobar Straits, 18/8/468 AC

It might as well have been night for the little bit the crew of the boat could see. Somewhere overhead the sun shone; they could see it there, a dim circle of something that was a little bit lighter than the smoke and ash that filled the air. Below, sonar listened attentively but fruitlessly. When the smoke was this thick, all traffic in the Straits simply stopped and dropped anchor. Then all passive sonar could hear was the sound of waves slapping the shore and the hulls of the becalmed shipping. And those sounds came from *everywhere*.

To Jaquie, the waves slapping the hull were not relaxing, as they might have been in a different place on a different kind of world. They were just a reminder that she and her shipmates were *blind*, blinder, in fact, than any bat.

So, while Marta dozed below, Jaquie walked the deck with a 9mm Pound submachine gun. *Nothing* was going to hurt her lover, not if she could help it. Nothing was—

What was that?

Liang Dao had had about enough. Did *he* care for the spread of Salafism? Not a chance; quite the opposite. Did *he* want to subordinate his people to some would-be sultan? No way. Did *he* want to get in, or take part in, a war with some people who had proven altogether too willing to take massive reprisals against anyone interfering with shipping?

Brother, my mother didn't give birth to any fools. I'm out of here.

So Liang Dao had done the only sensible thing when the other pirates had gotten together to attack the fleet patrolling the Nicobar Straits; he'd told his people to pack up and be ready to move at a moment's notice. They'd done it, too. They wanted no more to do with Salafism, or being on the blunt end of a reprisal, than Liang Dao did.

Not that Liang Dao or his people had any problem with piracy. They'd been pirates for millennia, and on two different planets.

But you've got to get away with it or it just doesn't pay. And those fucking round-eye bastard mercenaries won't let you get away with it. I shudder to think of what that fleet the Salafis failed to sink is going to do when it gets back.

Looking around his boat, a good-sized junk bearing nearly one hundred and fifty of Liang Dao's closest friend and relatives, he *did* shudder. He remembered seeing the *classis*—though he didn't know that was its name—pass by his coastal village months ago. The assembly had radiated menace. Had the Salafis succeeded in crushing it Liang Dao would have shed no tears. As was?

We've got to get the hell out of here. Unfortunately, we don't really have the funds to settle anyplace decent. Now if we could only pick off a small freighter or maybe some fat yacht . . .

Hey, what's that?

Jaquie crouched down and jacked the bolt on her Pound SMG. Something had nudged the side of *Qamra.* Driftwood? Maybe. Wreckage from the *classis*? Possibly.

Then again, maybe not, either.

Still keeping low, and keeping her back to the wheelhouse, Jackie moved toward the bow. At the edge of the wheelhouse, she peered into the smoke and thought she saw a man, possibly two of them, neither much more distinct than shadows, climbing aboard *Qamra.* She thought she saw a weapon in the hands of one of the boarders. As she raised her Pound to engage she heard another sound, coming from behind. She recognized the footsteps. If she hadn't, she'd probably not have turned and seen Marta, coming along the deck.

"Hon, dammit, what the hell—?"

A shout in a language, followed by the clear sound of a bolt being thrown home, propelled Jaquie instinctively to protect the one thing she cared about more than anything else in this world or the next. Pound forgotten, Jaquie launched herself at Marta to force her to the deck.

From up at the bow, someone fired a long burst.

Liang Dao was always nervous on a ship hijacking. You just never knew what might be waiting. And since those mercenaries had showed up, the risks had gone through the roof. Indeed, but for dire need he'd probably have left the yacht alone. And he could see the name of the thing, painted on the bow, in English and Arabic. You could bet some oil sheik would have armed guards.

Still, the wives and kids and cousins and aunts and uncles need to eat.

With a heart heavily thumping in his chest, Liang Dao jacked the bolt of his Samsonov and eased himself over the side and onto the boat. He landed, cat-footed, on the other vessel's deck and peered into the haze.

He saw something big, certainly a lot bigger than he was. The creature said something in a woman's voice but in a language he didn't under stand. He refrained from firing, because it was a woman, despite the huge size.

And then something jumped out from what he thought was the wheelhouse. By instinct, Liang Dao pointed and fired.

Marta's *lorica* had seemed heavier than normal when she put it on to go on deck to find Jaquie.

"That stupid bitch," she said aloud and angrily when she discovered Jaquie had doubled the plates in the front and back by using her own. She stormed out of the cabin and onto the deck to find and slap some sense into her lover.

After checking the stern, fruitlessly, she began to walk briskly toward the bow. She spotted Jaquie crouched by the front of the wheelhouse and asked, "Hon, dammit, what the hell—"

She didn't get another word out before Jaquie lunged at her. Toward the bow someone fired a long burst. Marta felt one bullet impact on her doubled chest protection, and heard two more whine overhead. Three others made a different sound. Jaqui's lunge struck her but the smaller girl impacted loosely, like a bag of skin and bones. It was still enough to knock her from her feet.

Marta felt Jaquie's body lying atop her, then smelt the iron-coppery blood her love spilt onto the deck in a torrent. Screaming, she grabbed the first weapon her hand came upon, Jaquie's already cocked Pound. Still lying on her back, head toward the stern, Marta pointed the thing toward her feet and the ship's bow, and pulled the trigger. She held that trigger pull until the bolt clicked back. She held it even after two splashes indicated she'd hit all the targets there were to hit.

The ship immediately broke into pandemonium, with klaxons ringing and the sound of booted feet running on deck. Up ahead, a single mount 40mm began to arise from the deck with a whine.

With the Pound empty, and the assailants gone, Marta bent over Jaquie's limp body, unwilling to believe what had just happened. Her fingers dabbed at the blood. "Please don't be dead . . . please?" Marta begged of the corpse. "You were the only good and decent and clean thing in my life. Please be okay?"

And then she raised her head to the sky and screamed an inarticulate shriek like a lost soul descending into Hades. A couple of crewmen or Cazadors, she neither knew nor cared which, bent to help her.

"Don't *touch* me!"

Leaving the body behind, Marta arose to her feet and walked up to the 40mm. By that time, two other crewmen were manning it. She tore them off and tossed them to the deck, taking the gunner's seat herself. She knew how to use the gun; she'd seen it done often enough.

A sudden gust of wind parted the smoke, revealing to Marta scores of people crowding a ramshackle junk. She didn't see them as people, however, neither the men nor the women . . . nor the children. Marta pressed a foot pedal to swing the gun around to aim at the other ship's bow. Her handles allowed her to bring the sights and barrel down.

In the wheelhouse, Chu asked, "Should we stop her?"

Rodriguez, who was one of those who had tried to lift Marta from the corpse, just shook his head, slowly.

From the junk, from the people upon it, there arose a great moan of despair as the 40mm began to fire, starting at the bow and sweeping down the length of the thing. Nor did Marta stop until the magazine ran dry.

She left no survivors.

Nicobar Straits, 34/8/468 AC

The *classis* proceeded in what amounted to an arrow shape: three corvettes in a V followed by one mine-sweeper, then the heavy cruiser, *Tadeo Kurita,* then by the *Dos Lindas.* Behind *Dos Lindas* came the rest, escorted by the single remaining patrol boat and *Qamra.*

Fosa wasn't overly worried about attacks on the support ships, not the way the *classis* was proceeding. He watched with a smile as a flight of Yakamovs took off, carrying a full load of Cazadors. Up ahead, *Kurita's* turrets, all that could be brought to bear, swiveled in their mounts to point generally to the west.

Yuan Lin had found a place for herself and her children. Rather, she had found a place for herself as one of Parameswara's concubines. The children were fed, clothed, and housed because the pirate chief liked his concubines happy.

Of course, happy doesn't mean I don't have to work, Lin thought, beating some dirty clothes against a rock in a stream a half mile from Parameswara's fortress. She was not alone. Thirty or more other women and girls, likewise engaged, were there with her in the clearing by the stream. *But it's not so bad a life,* Lin thought. *Para doesn't hurt me anymore than I like to be hurt. And the kids are doing well enough. And—*

She felt a sudden pressure in the air. It was like the prelude to of rain, really, except much more sudden. She looked up and saw the fortress suddenly bathed in smoke and fire. Then she heard the freight-train racket of flying shells, followed by the body- and soul-buffeting explosions from the fort.

The pounding went on for many minutes, the column of smoke rising to the sky. When it stopped, mere seconds after it stopped, she noticed small dots in the sky that she took for helicopters. They were descending.

Lin never heard the Turbo-Finch that dived down upon the group in the clearing. Before she could have, she and those with her were perforated by dozens of small finned nails called flechettes the plane had fired by rocket before the noise of its engines could reach ground.

UEPF Spirit of Peace, 34/8/468 AC

The ship was quiet, or as quiet as it ever was. There were still sounds from the vents refreshing the air. If one listened carefully, one could hear the crew going about the business of keeping the ship in space. High Admiral Martin Robinson was oblivious to all that, concentrating instead on the scene being played out below.

The big Kurosawa in Robinson's quarters showed it in all its gory detail. Starting in the southeast, and at this point about halfway through the Nicobar Straits, the "bloody, bastard, never-sufficiently-to-be-damned, mercenary swine" were doing their best to scour the Straits free of pirate life. Word was spreading faster than the fleet moved, however, so many of the little villages and towns were emptying themselves before the first shell came in or bomb dropped, before the first sound of a helicopter ferrying in troops reached them.

Even so, some of those troops were landing in the brush to either side of the straits. Robinson noted that the aerial attacks away from the coastlines, and the naval gunfire from the newly recommissioned heavy cruiser upon those refugees, tended to match where small teams of troops had been landed.

"It's not a total loss, Martin," Wallenstein comforted. "The people will be back, and back to their old occupation, in time. We can set things up again to support that useful pig, Mustafa."

Robinson said nothing, at first. Instead, he turned to manipulate his computer to have the Kurosawa zero in on the smoking ruins of Parameswara's fortress. A few hours ago there had been armed legionaries swarming the place. Now there was nothing but shot and hanged men, and women and children left with nothing but their eyes to weep with.

"I don't think so, Marguerite," Robinson said. "Not for one hundred local years. *That's* how badly those people are going to be terrorized."

"Well . . . the Tauran Union and the World League, down below, have issued very strongly worded condemnations," Wallenstein said. At that, even she had to laugh. "Condemnations. Like the mercenaries care about condemnations."

"They care as much as Mustafa does," Robinson said. "And why shouldn't they? They're Mustafa's children." *And, I suppose, mine.*

"I'm sorry, Martin," was all Wallenstein could say. "What now?"

"Now, I am afraid, I am going to have to do what perhaps I should have done years ago." Robinson hesitated before continuing; what he had in mind was a *serious* step. "I've contacted our people in Hangkuk. I'm going to purchase and, if necessary, deliver to Mustafa what he's been asking for all these years."

Wallenstein shook her head. "Oh, Martin, I can't tell you what a really bad idea that is."

"Would you rather see *our* world destroyed, Captain Wallenstein?"

The mention of her rank, and the implication of the caste that kept her there, shut Wallenstein up completely.

EXCURSUS

From: *Janus Small Arms Review,* Terra Nova Edition of 472 AC

The F-26 Rifle is a gas operated, electronically fired and controlled, magazine fed shoulder weapon of 6.5mm caliber. A joint development between Zion Military Industries (812 Ben Gurion Blvd, Nazareth, Zion, Terra Nova) and Balboa Armaments Corporation (57 Avenida Omar Torrijos-Herrera, Arraijan, Balboa, Terra Nova), a subdivision of the *Legion del Cid*, SA, the F-26 compares favorably with such weapons as the Volgan Abakanov, the Federated States of Columbia's M-42 Wakefield, the Sachsen STG-13, Gaul's Daudeteau-31, and the Zhong Type-57, with all of which it competes in the international arms market.

Specifications:

Caliber: 6.5mm × 31 SCC (Semi-Combustible Casing)

Weight: 4.1 Kg (Zion), 4.3 Kg (Balboa) w/o magazine or bayonet

Barrel Length: 533mm

Length Overall: 795mm (Zion's bullpup version), 1022mm (Balboa's conventionally shaped version)

Action: gas operated w/ piston, rotating bolt

Materials: The rifle makes extensive use of carbon fibers, plastics and glassy metal stampings. Unique among modern military firearms, the barrel is constructed of a relatively thin steel lining around which is wound carbon fiber (the barrels being produced under license from Thorsten Arms, a subdivision of Thorsten Prosthetics). This saves about 80% of the normal barrel weight. Moreover, given the high rate of fire, cooling becomes critical. The graphite barrel is superior to steel as a heat shedding medium, though there have been complaints from the field of it being too fragile for the uses to which it is sometimes put.

Max Effective Range: 850m

Rate of Fire: 3 round Burst: 1975 RPM. Full Automatic: 2 settings: 700 RPM and 1200 RPM. The weapon also has the capability of firing single rounds. The ROF is set by a side switch above and to the right of the trigger and controlled by an integral computer chip.

Sighting: All weather, day-night, medium range thermal imaging sight with integral laser range finder. The effective range of the sighting unit for target acquisition and range determination is 900 meters, day, and 250 meters, night, though this may be reduced by extreme dust, smoke or precipitation.

Command and Control: The rifle is the key component in "Soldier V," the joint Balboa-Zion project to create a fully digitalized ground combat soldier. As such, it contains its own global positioning system receiver with compass. The soldier's frequency hopping communication system is also partially contained within the rifle stock. Leaders can, by use of a heads-up display integral to the Mark V helmet, not only determine the relative locations of each of their soldiers or subordinate teams, but can also see graphic displays of their arcs of fire. This feature has substantially reduced both blue on blue fire and training accidents (except when the "moral training" magazine, q.v., is used).

International Sales:

Although acknowledged to be a superior battle implement, the F-26 and its cousins do only marginally well in international sales. This is for two reasons. The first is that the rifle is extremely expensive, at least twice the price of its next nearest competitor. The other is that both the *Legion del Cid* and Zion absolutely refuse to sell the rifle to Salafi and certain other states at any price, though the legion does issue it to its Islamic mercenary battalions, the Pashtun Scouts.

PART III

CHAPTER NINETEEN

La vengeance est un plat qui se mange froid.
—Pierre Ambroise Francois
Choderlos de La Clos

Camp San Lorenzo, Jalala Province, Pashtia, 12/6/469 AC

Fernandez shook his head ruefully and placed the report from Mahamda, his chief of interrogators, down on his disk. The intelligence coming from the *Mises* had dropped alarmingly. Mahamda's report was clear on why, too. He picked the report up again and reread the key paragraph.

"The Pashtun are simply too tough," Mahamda had written. *"They're not like the soft city boys from Sumer and Yithrab we were used to dealing with. Oh, yes, we can break them; but it takes three times longer. That's no different, in practice, from cutting my interrogation staff by a factor of three. And when they do break, the intelligence we gain is almost always old, too old to be useful tactically, though it usually retains its strategic value. Only when we have family members to threaten do they turn quickly. Nor will simply giving*

me more men do much better. This is delicate work, work that requires great talent and much training. Simply inflicting duress is rarely enough."

"And I don't have a solution to that," Fernandez muttered. "Patricio is still too delicate about threatening innocents; though he has made great strides. I wonder if we spoiled ourselves a little by going for the easy route and not developing enough tactical intelligence capability. Something to think on, anyway."

North of Jalala, Pashtia, 12/7/469

Alena sat up abruptly. She'd had another of her visions, this time in a dream. It hadn't been a particularly good one, nothing like when she had seen her husband presenting the calf's carcass to her on the playing field, nothing like the vision of their first night together (though the reality of that had far surpassed the dream). In fact, it had been downright horrible, all smoke and fire and screams and struggling, dying men.

She glanced at the horses, hobbled and guarded, a hundred meters away. *No . . . it wasn't them.*

Alena's eyes looked overhead. *No, no aircraft.*

Alena herself wasn't sure whether her visions came from somewhere else or if they were just the result of having a mind that could take and match a great many disparate bits of information and come up with probabilities from that, probabilities that that same mind imagined into visions. It didn't really matter which it was, she supposed, since the visions turned out to be right, more often than not. Best of all, unlike most men, her husband—she looked down warmly at the sleeping form beside her—*listened*. How could she not love a man who listened?

This vision was different from most. She sensed that the action she had seen was not to be immediate, nor close by.

What could have caused it? she wondered.

Her conscious mind was at least as good as her subconscious. She began to tally what she knew.

Point: the war is going fairly well, with new information coming in every day and deserters from the Ikhwan *giving themselves up regularly. This will make the other side desperate. Point: I have seen my husband's higher commander. He is a tired man, breaking down and unwilling to admit it to anyone. He is desperate, too. Point: the action has mostly moved to the border, but is stuck there because we can't cross to where the enemy shelters. Point: support for this war among those who fund it is waning. They, too, are desperate for it to end.*

She, too, shook her head. *No, those are not the keys. It was something else, but what?*

"David," she said, nudging the sleeping form beside her. "Husband, awaken. I have a prediction. Let me see the map."

With a grunt David sat up next to her. He'd learned, over the past two years of action, one hundred and fifty or more firefights, several awards and decorations and a promotion, and the past year with his wife, that when Alena wanted to see the map he'd be well advised to deliver. He reached into the saddle bags beside his sleeping roll and took the map and a blue-filtered flashlight out, unfolding the map in front of her and focusing the light for her to see by.

Alena's finger began tracing the map, stopping at points and gliding right over others.

Point: a platoon from the Cazador cohort was ambushed yesterday here. *Point: there was a report of donkeys being purchased by someone* here. *Point: there was a report of a delivery of explosives* here, *last month. Point . . . Point . . . Point . . . Point . . .*

Alena closed her eyes and began to rock back and forth. It was eerie, but Cano wasn't about to object. When she opened them she pointed to a spot on the map, a junction of backwoods trails, and said, "Bring your men *here*, before first light. Thirty to forty of the enemy, heavily armed, and leading a caravan. If you hurry . . ."

Some miles from where Alena studied her husband's map, Senior Centurion Ricardo Cruz shivered in the cold night air.

Despite almost ten years of the news networks' predictions about the "brutal Pashtian winter," it had so far failed to materialize anywhere below the high mountain passes. They were still waiting, expectantly, and devoted several hours a week to the subject.

On the other hand, while not exactly "brutal," the winter could be cold enough. Cruz thought it was "goddamned cold," for example. He thought so despite the roughly one thousand drachma worth of cold weather gear the legion was now able to provide each man deployed. *On the other hand, it could be worse. I remember that first winter, in the hills of Yezidistan . . . brrrr. Ah well, at least the wind blows from the other direction so we can get a little shelter from these rocks. Fortunately, too, it also keeps our scent out of the kill zone.*

This was Cruz's third year at war and ninth with the legion. In many ways it was the worst. He'd spent his second combat tour as an optio. Federated States Army troops would have called the position, "platoon sergeant." Now, even with his break from the regular forces, he was a full-fledged senior centurion leading a platoon of fifty-one men, including the attached forward observer team, Pashtun scout, and the platoon medic. If all went well, after this tour he'd go to the First Centurion's School, alleged to be a gentlemen's course—*And won't that be a fucking break?*—and take over as first shirt for an infantry maniple. The pay he'd receive in that position, nearly two thousand drachma monthly, would place him and his family easily in the top quarter of income in Balboa. Add in the very nice four-bedroom house the legion provided on either the *Isla Real* or one of the new casernes, the schools, beaches and other recreational facilities and it added up to . . .

It adds up to: I still miss Cara and the kids . . . and I need to get laid. Badly.

Just over two hundred of the Sumeri whores—war widows, mostly—that the legion had . . . acquired . . . had chosen to follow the eagles to Pashtia. These had been supplemented by several score more from the local community, generally slave girls purchased from the local dealers and given the choice of prostitution and care or freedom to go. Most stayed. Some of the girls had even managed to find husbands from among the men. This, however, was decidedly difficult in the close confines of the legion. Cruz didn't know of a single legionary who had taken a hooker to wife who had remained with the colors. It was just too awkward when every one of your comrades had had her at one

time or another. Whatever the justice of the matter—
and Cruz thought it was damned poor—people usually
just didn't think of hookers as really human outside
of fiction. Nor could a typical man stand to be in the
same room, sometimes the same universe, as someone
who'd had the woman he loved.

Sometimes, he had to admit, Cruz had been tempted.
The girls were segregated by the rank of the soldiers
they serviced. The group dedicated to the centurions
was, for lack of a better term, hot. They were also very
clean, as the legion's own medical staff checked them,
and the men, regularly. Moreover, careful, if confiden-
tial, record was kept of who'd screwed whom. While
venereal disease made its way in, occasionally, it was
damned rare.

Even so, when tempted Cruz had merely pulled
out his wallet, opened it to a picture of Cara and the
kids, and said, "Nope. Not worth it."

He pulled the wallet out now, looking at the picture
once again in the moonlight.

Cruz lay with a squad from his platoon in a rock-
strewn ambush position under the bright light of two
nearly full moons. His own optio remained back at the
objective rally point with the platoon's four donkeys,
the medic, the forward observers, and a few other
men. The rest of the platoon was out in three- and
four-man ambush positions around the central one.
Intel had confirmed that an enemy platoon of allegedly
about twenty-five men had departed a refugee camp in
Kashmir three days ago and was expected to use this
pass. Intel was right about such things perhaps one
time in five or six. That was often enough to justify
the effort. (Alena Cano's record was much better than

this, but who knew outside of her husband's group of cavalry?) Moreover, the ratio had been improving over the months as the legion discovered that the best way to ensure that the enemy did *not* come when and where expected was to land a helicopter anywhere within miles of the spot. Instead, the ambushers almost always trekked in on foot or, in the case of some of the Pashtun Scouts, on horseback, moving at night, with a few donkeys to help with the load.

A small bud in Cruz ear beeped low. "Cruz," he whispered.

"Centurion, this is Optio Garcia. The RPV reports thirty-two men entering the pass with fifteen donkeys. Heavily laden. Heavily armed. Light gunship"—a Cricket with a dual machine gun mounted to one side—"standing by. Two Turbo-Finches waiting at the strip. Reaction platoon waiting to reinforce, loaded on helicopters."

"Roger."

Cruz had had fourteen directional mines laid along a rough line of almost four hundred meters. He did some quick calculations. *Thirty-two men and fifteen donkeys . . . subtract four or five for point and rear guards . . . moving at night they'll close it up a bit . . . say, four or five meters per man, two staggered lines. They should fit inside the kill zone before we initiate. Of course, the point and rear guards will probably not be in the kill zone when we open up.*

Cold forgotten amidst the excitement of impending action, Cruz reached up and pulled the passive vision monocular down over his right eye. Then he tapped awake Majeed, his attached Pashtun scout. "Pretty soon. Make ready," he whispered.

Majeed sat up with a smile. With luck, there would be a bonus for this one. Majeed had his eye on a third wife. Legion scouts made a *lot* of money in comparison with the Pashtian norm. The multiple wives this allowed the scouts to support added much to their status and kept the recruiting lines for the few open positions somewhere between long and longer.

Carefully, the two Pashtun sniffed at the air. Nothing. They moved bare feet along the cold rock as they advanced into the pass, eyes scanning for any sign that the infidel awaited.

Brothers, Bashir and Salam had once thought to join the Scouts. Having been shamed by rejection, they'd vowed revenge for the insult and made their way north to the refugee camps that lay just far enough across the ill-defined border that there could be no doubt they were in the territory of Kashmir rather than that of Pashtia. There, the brothers had sought work and been hired to lead formed units and caravans of donkeys into Pashtia. The pay was not as good, not nearly as good, but at least they could strike back at those who had insulted them.

This was their third trip. They'd begun to consider the possibility of retiring after this one. While the pay was not so good as that given to the infidel legion's scouts, it was enough at least to pay for a wife each and a small plot of decent land. With that, they could grow enough of the poppy to eke out a decent living.

It was beginning to look like eking out a living would be better than continuing to lead convoys forward and dying in the process. Neither brother knew anyone who had managed to lead *four* convoys safely through.

Besides, they had already begun to loathe the Yithrabis, who looked down on them, criticizing everything from their illiteracy to their manner of dress.

Covering himself almost completely behind his rock, Cruz watched the two point men walk through. Even at a distance of one hundred and twenty-five meters, and in the fuzzy and grainy picture given by his monocular, they seemed fairly professional. He had to hope that one of the other point ambushes in the area ambush would get them. No sense in letting pros survive.

He shifted as quietly as he could to look to his left, the direction from which the sounds of donkeys came. *Yes . . . there they are.* Cruz saw thirteen or fourteen men, in a staggered double column, enter the kill zone. Behind those were the donkeys, tied together in strings of five or six with a man leading each string. Another group of thirteen or fourteen took up the tail of the caravan.

Shame about the donkeys.

He waited, his heart racing so fast he could not have marked the time by it even if he'd thought of it. Unconsciously, his hands reached for the two directional mine detonators he'd placed carefully against the rock to his front.

It took almost six minutes from the time the point of the main body entered the kill zone to when its tail did. All that time, Cruz's heart beat so heavily that he thought the enemy *must* hear it. Of course, they did not hear it. In fact, the only thing they did hear was . . .

Kakakakakaboomoomoomoomoom.

. . . as the directional mines went off. These Volgan-made munitions were flat cylinders with one point seven kilograms of explosive on one side and four hundred cylindrical bits of steel buried in a plastic matrix on the other. Most of the bits went high or low, of course, though even then some of the low ones would ricochet at man height across the kill zone. In all, tests had confirmed that at least a third, in this case about two thousand, bits of flying steel would cross at an acceptable graze to the ground. The mines were more directionally focused than the FSC-made versions and so had been laid at angles to sweep along rather than across the kill zone.

More than half the infiltrators were blown off their feet, screaming and spurting blood and bone. Immediately the men along the ambush line opened fire, while a machine gun to the right raked directly long the line of march. A few tried to return fire. They were shooting in the dark at barely seen muzzle flashes. Cruz's men, on the other hand, had F- and M-26s with integral thermal sights. They did *not* shoot blindly at muzzle flashes but instead were able to take careful aim at standing or kneeling men.

The fire went on for what seemed a very long time but was really no more than forty-five seconds. By the end of that time all of the obvious targets were down. Cruz thought he saw a few running pellmell across the rocks to his front.

Good. Right into Corporal Lopez's position.

A single white star parachute flare, hand held and fired, flew up with a bang and a whoosh to burst overhead. The squad leader of the squad Cruz had accompanied blew his whistle three times. Firing

ceased. Another whistle blast sent the men into the
kill zone. Most of them, as they crossed, carefully
shot each of the bodies laying there once again, in
the head, to make sure. A central team, two men,
looked around quickly and identified someone still
breathing who might be a leader. One of the team
rapped the supposed leader on the head with his
rifle stock and dragged him off. Another two-man
team went rifling packs and pockets for items of
intelligence. Some was kept, maps and notebooks,
typically, along with cell phones and the one radio
they found. The rest, along with weapons, were
dropped beside the intel team.

What was just business sense for the enemy infiltrators was a mercy to their donkeys. These were shot
quickly and even with regret. After all, the legion
could always use more strong and healthy beasts of
burden and, as anyone who dealt with them knew,
the Pashtian animals were the best.

Cruz had watched the squad go through its motions.
No sense in taking over from a perfectly competent
sergeant, after all. Nonetheless, while half the squad
provided far security to the kill zone and half assisted
the intel team in the search, he went out to look over
the intel gathered.

A map caught Cruz's eye. Picking it up and looking at it under the moonlight, Cruz spontaneously
whistled.

Bashir and Salam cowered behind a rock as the
infidel ambush went out into the kill zone. Bashir
began to raise his rifle to engage them, when Salam
slapped it down.

"Foolish Brother, do you think you can do any good?"

"What do we do then, O wise Brother?" Bashir asked quietly but sarcastically. "Do you think they don't have this place surrounded? We are not going to escape. Better to take one with us."

"God curse the day we ever left to join the *Ikhwan*," Salam said. "But, if we kill one of the infidels, they will certainly kill us. Then, if the tales are to be believed, they will take bits of our bodies and blood to identify our clan in the evil ways the infidels have. Then our clan will suffer. Do you want *that*?"

"No . . . no, not that," Bashir admitted, relaxing his grip on his rifle. "But what are we to do?"

"We escape," Salam counseled. "To Hell with the *Ikhwan*. Drop everything. We'll crawl out under cover of the night."

The Cricket's machine gunner saw the brothers through the thermal imager mounted over his gun. "I've got two in sight," he told the pilot, "but I don't think they're interested in fighting."

"Whereabouts?"

"Five-fifty to six-hundred meters southeast of the kill zone. They're crawling away. There's also a group of cavalry coming as fast as they can drive their horses. I recognize them. They're friendly."

"I see the cav," the pilot said. "I'm going to fly over low and direct them to the crawlers."

"Surrender now," Rachman called out in Pashtun once the airplane informed him by signal that the Scouts were close enough. "You are surrounded and there is an armed aircraft overhead that has you in its sights. Come out unarmed and with your hands up."

Unheard by any but themselves, Bashir and Salam breathed a deep sigh of relief that the infidels were interested in prisoners. They had reason to believe this was not always the case.

Cruz saluted Cano and reported, then added, "You missed all the fun."

Cano shrugged and pointed with his chin at Bashir and Salam, preceding the cavalry column with heads down and hands bound. "Not all," he disagreed.

Cano then turned and gave the woman riding beside him a mock dirty look. "Wicked wife! Incompetent. Call yourself a seeress. Hah! Thirty to forty heads you promised us, and on that promise I awakened my men for *this*? I should divorce you."

The woman just laughed, as did the Pashtun close enough to Cano to hear.

Even Cruz laughed at that. It was patently obvious, just from a glance, that this tribune would not leave the woman for anything.

"We've got a helicopter coming in for the prisoners, your two unwounded ones plus two we have that might or might not make it."

"Then Centurion Cruz," Cano said, "I present to you and your men two hale prisoners of war, compliments of this wicked woman whom I shall certainly beat mercilessly at some more convenient time."

The woman, Cruz noted, pulled a vicious looking dagger from her belt and began nonchalantly flashing the blade in the sun. Still, the whole time she smiled at her husband.

Camp San Lorenzo, Jalala Province, Pashtia, 14/7/469

There was a bit more rock and concrete in this camp than there had been in Camp Balboa back in Sumer. Moreover, while the "brutal Pashtian winter" wasn't all that bad it was somewhat uncomfortably cool in these hills at night and in the winter, even this far north. Thus, the spread of legionary barracks and offices, mess halls and warehouses were, in the main, wood-lined and heated. The wood had once been growing on the spot where the camp sat.

Standing in one such, with a small fire going in a sort of Franklin stove in one corner, a number of men—and one small boy—sat in comfortable chairs. All but the boy sipped something alcoholic, often enough scotch. A recently captured map was tacked to one wall. The map showed a valley dominated by a single, tall elevation in the center, with two streams that cut around the mountain, and long ridges to either side. Both mountain and ridges were heavily trenched and bunkered.

The legion hadn't needed the map to know this was *a* main enemy base; it was simply too obvious. What the map provided was considerable detail on the fortifications of that base as well as the suggestion that it was a regular meeting point for the elite of the enemy movement. Also, that is was *the* enemy base.

"The problem, Patricio," Fernandez said, pointing at the map that had been delivered by Cruz's maniple commander the day prior, "is that their base is in Kashmir and Kashmir has both a credible air force and nukes."

Carrera didn't·bother saying, *So do we . . . have nukes.* Fernandez was one of a very few who knew that the legion *did* have nukes. Moreover, the original three had been supplemented by another four that had needed reworking and recertification. And hadn't *that* been a bitch to arrange through some off-line Volgan contacts?

The problem was that Kashmir didn't *know* the legion had nukes and, so, might be inclined to discount the possibility and use their own. Nor would it have been altogether wise to have let them know.

"And even if they don't use the nukes, they have a real air force, a good one. You can't count on the Federated States to provide air cover for an attack into the territory of even a very nominal ally any more than you can count on them putting us under their own nuclear umbrella if we attack across the border."

"We can stymie their air force if we can helo in the air defense maniple," Jimenez suggested.

This was more likely than it had once seemed. A number of Volgan warships, laid up and rusting, had been stripped for their heavy, range-finding lasers. The lasers—power hogs, all—had then been mounted on three-hundred-and-sixty degree rotating carriages, with less powerful and power-consuming lasers mounted coaxially. The lesser lasers could send out low energy streams of light more or less continuously. When they got a bounce back from an aerial target they automatically fired the main laser, blinding or at least stunning the pilot. Since blind pilots cannot fly . . .

There was a treaty against this, against the use of lasers to blind. Carrera ignored that and, when questioned by the press during one of the very few press conferences he deigned to endure, had answered, "If we wanted to blind them so they would be blind, that would be illegal. In fact, we want to blind them so they crash their planes and *die*. This does not leave them blinded for later on in life and, so, is perfectly legal."

Even the Federated States hated that position, their pilots more so.

It was Greg Harrington's turn again to serve as the forward Ib, or logistics officer, of the deployed legion. He had more objections. "If that map and what's drawn on it is right—"

Lawrence Triste, also back from Balboa and serving as Ic, or Intelligence, interjected, "We snuck an RPV there last night. The map is correct. There are several thousand of them, well armed, with decent air defense, dug in like rats and surrounded by mines and wire."

"—well then," Harrington continued, "that's even worse. It will take hundreds of tons of artillery and heavy mortar ammunition to breach that place, maybe thousands—"

"Thousands," confirmed the artillery cohort commander. "Even though the base will be in range of our rockets without them crossing over or getting very far from a good road," he added.

"See? I can't move that much. I just *can't*. And you'll need infantry to clear the place, and to make sure there are no escapes. We don't have the lift, Pat."

Carrera turned furiously on his logistician. "You stupid fuck! I *pay* you to fucking solve problems, not to whine about what you can't do—" He stopped abruptly, shamefaced, and said, "I'm sorry . . . you didn't deserve that. I don't know what—" His voice trailed off.

Everyone went silent. Even Harrington wasn't angry, or more than a little hurt. Carrera, unlike the rest of them, had been at war for over eight years without more than an occasional break. The strain was telling . . . but none of them had the heart to tell him it was time for him to take a long rest.

The small boy in the company of men was Hamilcar, Carrera's first child with Lourdes. He was a good looking kid, and tall for his age. The stature, like the huge eyes, probably came from his mother. On Carrera's last visit home the boy had begged to come along and, since his mother had stayed in a combat zone with him as a baby, she had been in a very difficult position to refuse. Then, too, she was terribly worried about her Patricio and his health, both physical and mental. That last visit home had been . . . difficult.

Hamilcar was loathe to speak, surrounded, as he was, by half a dozen men that he had grown up admiring. But it seemed so obvious to him. He would have thought it would be obvious to his father, too.

Well, no one else was going to say anything. He'd have to. Clearing his throat he piped up in a little-boy voice, "Father, if you landed a cohort inside the enemy base, on that large hill in the center, it would draw them away from the outside. Wouldn't that help you?"

The room went quiet as every man turned to look at little Hamilcar in something between surprise and wonder.

"Acorn never falls far from the tree, does it?" Jimenez commented.

"Helps anyway," Harrington admitted grudgingly. "If we can crush their air defense so we even *can* land men on the hill. Plus . . . it's a damned steep hill . . . hard to actually land a chopper on. But it doesn't solve the other problems."

"Even those might not be insurmountable," Carrera said, calm again if infinitely weary. "The major problem is that if we hit it and don't get most of the leadership, then it's all a bloody damned waste."

Fernandez brightened. "I might have a solution to that, Patricio. Give me a couple of days."

Bashir had not seen his brother, Salam, since they'd surrendered. He'd been interrogated, of course, and warned that very severe consequences would follow if he didn't tell the absolute truth. It was also explained to him that Salam was being asked the same questions and that, if the stories didn't match perfectly, the severe consequences would be administered to both.

"Absolute truth from each of you is your only salvation," the interrogator had explained.

Bashir had only told one lie, that concerning the whereabouts and names of his family. Unfortunately, he and Salam had never been given the chance to work out anything between them. Bashir would remember the beating that followed for years. Even after he'd told the truth the beatings had continued until, apparently, Salam had likewise come clean. Or perhaps they'd continued just on general principle or to see if they'd come up with different answers. Bashir didn't know.

Their parents, plus their brothers and sisters were brought to the camp two days later, though they were apparently well treated. Neither attempted the slightest lie after that.

Fernandez spoke, through an interpreter, to Bashir first. The man looked pretty bad off, face bruised and eyes half-swollen shut. He walked like a much older, indeed a very old, man. That would pass, Fernandez knew. The guards were expert and had been under firm instructions to do no permanent damage.

He had the guard remove Bashir's manacles and offered the young man water and some food, legionary rations, in fact, which Bashir choked down, greedily. He especially liked the one-hundred-gram bar of honey-sweetened *halawa*, seven hundred calories of crushed sesame seed goodness in just over four ounces.

While he ate Fernandez made a show of looking over his file. "Ah . . . I see you tried to join us once."

"How did you—?"

"Your picture was taken when you were interviewed. We matched that to your picture taken when you were first brought here. The computers do that almost instantly. Hmmm . . . rejected, I see . . . well . . . no, not rejected. We placed you and your brother on the wait list. We'd likely have taken you in a couple of months."

"The recruiter didn't tell us that," Bashir answered. "He said if we could come up with a bribe he might get us a position in a couple of months."

Fernandez smiled evilly. Corruption was always a problem, though it was a problem the legion dealt with very severely. In reality there was only one punishment, death.

"Did he indeed? We'll see to that. I understand you tried to lie to us," Fernandez said.

"What fool would give you the names of their people?"

"Good point," Fernandez agreed. "We'll forgive you the lie though, of course, you and your brother are under sentence of death for aiding our enemies. Their guilt became yours when you agreed to help them."

"We've never been tried!" Bashir objected hotly.

"You will be . . . if necessary. Do you doubt the results of that trial?" Again Fernandez smiled, though not so evilly.

"No," Bashir said, with resignation.

"Still . . ." Fernandez hesitated, "you *did* cooperate fully once you realized you had to. And . . . then, too . . . what good is a boy who won't take a beating to protect his family?"

It was a slender reed, barely to be perceived. The Pashtun grabbed it anyway. "I could cooperate more."

"There would be great risks," Fernandez cautioned, "and not merely for yourself . . . great rewards, too, of course."

Later, after Bashir had been brought back to his cell to think a bit, Fernandez interviewed Cano and Alena, privately.

"Tribune," he said, "there is something very weird going on here. You were not supposed to be at that ambush. It was miles away from your patrolling area. Yet there you were. I checked back over the last couple of years. Your group of scouts is *always* nearby whenever trouble crops up and you are even remotely in range. You've got the highest kill rate of any group in the legion. Why?"

Cano just looked at Alena and said, "My wife's a witch."

Fernandez looked intently at the Pashtun girl.

"I'm not a witch, exactly," she said, looking up at the wood paneling of Fernandez's office. "At least I don't think I am. But I do pay attention . . ."

INTERLUDE

1 Easton Street, London, England, European Union, 11 January, 2126

In his plush office, all woods and wools and crystal, Louis Arbeit stretched like a satisfied cat after a kill.

The nature of the kill? Fifty-thousand small arms smuggled into various spots on Terra Nova in aid of the various insurgencies there. More on point; the payment received for them.

It was perfect, Arbeit self-congratulated. *Amnesty can go anywhere there; even the guerillas accepted us because we brought them arms. Oh, not directly, of course. That would have been too dangerous. Instead, we bought space from the Food and Agricultural Organization from what was set aside for them for cargo on the resupply, reinforcement and resettlement ships. And my father made sure that space was considered "hands off" by the crews. After all, it was only "food."*

The real food and the arms went to the colonies in Southern Columbia and Northern Uhuru. They paid us and then delivered the arms to the guerillas and the food to whoever needed it.

Arbeit sighed with contentment. *And at two-hundred grams of gold for an obsolescent rifle and one thousand rounds, we robbed those bastard guerillas, too.*

Looking up and out the window of his office, Arbeit thought, sadly, *A shame about the old man, though. I wonder if the guerillas would have assassinated him if they'd known how important he was to their supply of arms and munitions. Fortunately Mother is taking it well.*

He stood and began to pace about the spacious office. *The thing is, though; where should I best invest the money? Even after paying off my helpers, generously, I've still got four tons of gold just sitting in Switzerland.*

Maybe it's time to talk to SecGen Simoua about making my posting for life. A single ton of my gold should be enough to remind him of his promise to my father. Then again, the Swiss are said to have some new anti-agathics. New and pricey. *Since the old SecGen died, finally, I am reminded that I am mortal and need them. Perhaps Simoua would settle for half a ton.*

CHAPTER TWENTY

God helps a man as long as he helps
his brother.
> —Muhammad (PBUH)

Tariq Pass, Kashmir, 22/7/469 AC

This was not one of the big passes. Narrow and rugged,
untraversable by vehicles, it had three major advantages. It was located about where Bashir could have
gotten to if he had begun the trek back the night of
the ambush. It had a small, flat plain on the southern
side *just* large enough for a Cricket to land with two
men and take off again with its pilot aboard. Lastly, it
was not much used by anybody. Thus, it was unlikely
that the Cricket would be seen, still less reported.

The pilot brought the plane into the rough field
slowly, not much faster than a man could run, Bashir
thought. He was thankful beyond measure when the
thing touched down. His only previous flight had
been on the helicopter that took him into his brief
captivity. He'd hated that, but at least he hadn't had
to *see* the ground below him or the clouds around.
The Cricket gave no such mercy.

With hand gestures, the pilot directed Bashir to help him turn the plane around to face into the wind. They did this by the simple expedient of picking up the tail and shuffling sideways, pivoting the plane around the fixed landing gear. Then he'd clapped the Pashtun on the back and bid him on his way.

As Bashir caught his last ground-bound glimpse of the plane, before turning along the rock-strewn path, he saw the pilot pouring fuel into it from a twenty liter fuel can. When next he looked, the plane was already airborne.

Bashir didn't know why he had been selected. He was, and he knew it, the less intelligent of the two brothers. Moreover, the infidel, Fernandez, had made similar offers to both to which both had agreed.

What had decided Fernandez, though he never made this plain, was that Salam had seemed incrementally more likely to seek his own safety and abandon his relatives to their fate than Bashir had. The key to this was that that Bashir, unbeknownst to himself, had broken under beating much later than Salam, and then only after hearing his brother being pounded. "He's the better kid," Fernandez had told Carrera. "He cares more for his family."

Though he didn't know, Bashir suspected it might be something like that. Salam was a good brother . . . but you did have to watch him.

He'd been left off with very little: some food and water, the pack he'd been captured with, his rifle, a bandoleer of ammunition and a *very* small radio. The radio was underpowered, because of its size among other things. On the other hand, it would pick up broadcasts as would any other radio that looked like it; which is to say that looked like a cheap, yellow transistor radio made in Zhong Guo.

No matter about the range; a Cazador team was going to be inserted, at night, close enough to pick up any broadcast. That would not happen for another few days, giving Bashir time to get to his destination. He was instructed not to even try to broadcast for ten days, and then only to send one of two words, "yes" or "no" and, if "yes," a number, for the number of days until the event for which he was waiting was to take place. He was to avoid making other broadcasts entirely except under very narrowly constrained circumstances. Further, if captured and not accepted back into the *Ikhwan,* he was advised to make a place for his parents, brothers and sisters in Paradise.

Camp San Lorenzo, Jalala Province, Pashtia, 22/7/469 AC

"Snowbird One reports insertion is complete, Legate," one of the radiomen reported to Fernandez.

"So far, so good," he said. He turned his attention to a tall Pashtian girl sitting in the operations center, staring at a map. "Anything on your part, Mrs. Cano?"

Alena shook her head and answered, "No trouble, Legate, or none that I sense." She shrugged apologetically. "It's not something I can control," she explained. "Maybe something will come tonight."

Fernandez nodded. He didn't understand it, but he was too good an intelligence man not to note the more-than-coincidence. "Whatever you can determine," he said, "we'll appreciate."

Kashmir-Pashtian border, 27/7/469 AC

No one controlled the border. No one could even really define it.

It was a long trek and a rough one, running over foothills that would have been mountains anywhere else on the globe. The air was thin and, more than once, Bashir found himself short of breath. Nonetheless, he pushed on. Who knew? The foreign infidel maniac might go right ahead and hang his family from the multiple gallows Bashir had seen, just inside the walled compound in which he'd been questioned, if he was so much as a day late with his report.

Progress was slow up the mountain. Contraintuitively it was worse coming down. Not only was the way longer, but there was always the chance of falling and incapacitating himself. Somehow Bashir didn't think that evil bastard, Fernandez, would even wait for an excuse before fitting nooses and kicking boxes.

It was with a certain measure of relief, once he neared the base of the mountains somewhere along the ill-defined Pashtia-Kashmir border, that Bashir felt the rifle muzzle's cold touch behind his ear.

Bashir felt naked without his own rifle, as he was prodded and pushed along the well-worn, ancient caravan trail toward what his captors referred to as "the Base." They'd left him his pack, mostly out of laziness, he thought. No matter, the rifle would not save his family. What was in the pack might.

They'd searched the pack, of course; they weren't exactly *incompetent* and, what with the turns of fortune in the war to date, they had every reason to be paranoid. Bashir had a few rough moments when one of them shook his little yellow transistor radio a few times, hard, before laying it down with his other belongings. Fernandez had personally gone over his pack and with considerably more thoroughness. There was nothing inherently suspicious in it. As a matter of fact, there was a bullet hole in it of the right caliber, if anyone cared to take a micrometer to check, to indicate he'd been nearly killed by the infidels. Fernandez had seen to that, personally, too.

The caravan trail met a rough road. There the party waited until a four-wheel-drive vehicle, bearing three armed men, came along. One of the men in the vehicle, not the driver, had one eye badly afflicted with cataracts. Bashir was turned over to these, along with his rifle and his pack. He told the mounted group exactly what he'd told the previous captors. Bashir learned that the man with the cataracts was the leader and that his name was Moshref.

He told Moshref, when asked, "I was working for Mohammad Shah, leading groups into Pashtia to fight the infidels. We got ambushed." That was all true. The lies began shortly thereafter. "I was on point, with my brother," here Bashir shed a tear he didn't have to feign but had had to practice. "He was the older. He held off the infidels while I made my escape. I think he must be dead." Sniff. "You know how the infidels are able to see at night."

"The light of Allah guides our bullets, though," the driver said. "What are the crusaders' toys compared to that?"

The vehicle bounced along for what seemed many miles before crossing a narrow, rickety bridge and

entering a broad, steep-sided valley. Bashir thought
he saw bunkers, well hidden and in places connected
by trenches, along the crests of the surrounding ridge-
lines. In the center of the valley, dominating it, stood
a great massif. Streams churned and frothed to both
sides of the massif before joining and flowing out from
the valley. There were many women by the streams,
washing clothes by pounding them on rocks. Children,
hundreds of them, played near their mothers. It would
have all looked very normal but for the large number
of armed men training a bit farther out, and the air
defense guns on the high ground, pointing skyward.

"You understand, Brother, that we can't just take
you at your word," Moshref said. "The infidels are
clever, vicious and ruthless. Nor are all the faithful,
faithful in truth. We've caught infiltrators before."

Moshref's finger pointed to the right, indicating a
spot where a dozen large wooden crosses stood, a man
hanging on each, nailed through wrists and ankles.
All the men were dead, and even the freshest corpse
showed much flesh missing.

Children played around the feet of the crosses.

"We deal with them as Sura Five commands," the
cyclops said casually.

Since Bashir had very good reason to believe he was
the very first infiltrator to make it to the fortress, he
wondered if perhaps the dozen corpses were those of
truly innocent men. If so, it said nothing good about
the notions of justice held by Mustafa's followers in
the valley, nor about Mustafa, himself.

"I just came here to continue the fight," Bashir said.
"For the sake of my brother." *The best lies contain
truth,* Fernandez had advised him.

"Mustafa will probably want to talk to you himself."

It was several days before Mustafa made an appearance. Bashir didn't know if the leader had been there all that time or had just arrived.

"Tell me about it," Mustafa commanded Bashir. His assistant, and second in command, Nur al Deen, sat quietly to Mustafa's side, looking intently into Bashir's face.

The three sat on cushions on the floor of a room leading off from a deep, sloping tunnel carved into the rock. Bashir had the impression—he wasn't sure quite why—that the tunnel went much farther into the ground.

Bashir almost missed the question, looking about the room. The walls were bare and at least reasonably dry. The cushions rested on a rug, predominantly red, with blue, green, brown and black geometric decoration. The style was called "Baluch." The rug covered most of the floor, though a foot or two of bare rock were visible near where floor met wall. Other furniture was at a minimum, two crude and rough wooden chests, a small table, and a bookcase. There were more cushions piled in one corner but these would only be brought out if Mustafa had more guests. The guards, naturally, did not sit but stood with rifles in their hands.

"Tell me about it," Mustafa repeated.

"Ah. Excuse me, Sheik. I was just—"

"Never mind that. Tell me about it."

Bashir told his story.

"That entire party never arrived," Mustafa said, when Bashir had finished. "When another patrol went to investigate, it, too, disappeared. This was the work of the Blue Jinn."

Blue Jinn was a name the movement had given to Carrera. They had their reasons. Besides the eyes which were said to resemble those supernatural creatures, he seemed to them the embodiment of vicious malevolence, much as the Blue Jinn of legend.

"It was the grace of Allah and the courage of my brother that allowed me to bring word," Bashir supplied.

"Indeed. We will remember your gallant brother in our prayers. For the word and the warning you have brought us, you have our thanks. How may we repay you?"

Bashir shrugged. "To allow me to continue in service to the cause is repayment enough, Sheik. To allow me to repay the infidels for my brother . . ."

"So be it then," Mustafa agreed. "You will stay here and join our fighters for now. In time you may be sent back to continue the holy campaign to drive out the crusaders, and to gain your just revenge. For now . . . eat, rest, grow healthy, and train to serve the cause."

Mustafa turned his attention to the guards. "Assign him to the company of . . . Noorzad."

The guards led Bashir away. After he was gone Nur al Deen announced, in his Misrani accent, "He's lying."

"Why do you say so?" Mustafa queried.

"That's the problem; I don't *know* why. But he *is* lying. I sense the touch of the Blue Jinn or one of his evil minions upon him. He should be killed."

"And lose a likely gallant fighter for the cause? I think not. Besides, my friend, you forget." Mustafa's finger pointed towards the ceiling. "We have the greatest of plotters on our side. If this man is lying, or a spy, Allah will point him out to us before he can do more harm than He is willing to permit."

A religious argument was the most difficult to refute. Nur al Deen bowed his head slightly, in acquiescence.

Changing the subject, Mustafa asked, "How progress the arrangements for greeting our guest?"

"The new cave in which we will shelter his craft from observation"—now it was Nur's turn to point a finger skyward—"is almost complete. We're having to do it by hand as an explosion that size would be bound to attract unwanted attention from the infidel. Fortunately, we do not need to build an airfield."

"As I said, Nur. We have the greatest of plotters on our side."

Noorzad's company proved to be made up entirely of other Pashtun, Bashir discovered. Whether that was a cause for relief or not, let alone rejoicing, remained to be seen.

The commander, himself, was little cause for joy. Short, stout, ugly and taciturn, Noorzad had little to say to the newcomer. He looked Bashir up one side and down the other with a single cold, suspicious, blue eye. He asked a couple of questions, then announced, as if daring contradiction, "Marwat tribe."

The commander was frightening. Bashir bobbed his head in agreement. "Yes, sir, from around Daman. Speen-Gund. Begu Khel." Daman was a small settlement in north-central Pashtia. The later two terms were subdivisions of the Marwat tribe, Speen-Gund harking back to an acrimonious (and bloody) split within the Marwat on Old Earth. Seven centuries and a few thousand light years were *no* reason not to keep up a good feud.

Turning to one of his lieutenants, Noorzad commanded, "Get the names of his people. Send word to our people in Daman for anything that is known of this man. In the interim, he can dig. Take his rifle and give him a pick."

For the first time Bashir was glad that Fernandez had taken in his family. It was the custom of the legion to punish the families of their opposition. They also had a considerable ability to identify the proper family from what they called "DNA." Bashir didn't really understand that, though he believed it. It was said by his people that, even with a suicide bombing, if the infidels found so much as a scorched bit of bone or hair, or a drop of blood, they would visit vengeance on the family responsible.

Since his brother's body had been reported as found and immolated at the site of the ambush where they were captured, there would be nothing inherently suspicious about the disappearance of his parents and siblings. That was the infidel way. That it was also close to the time-honored tradition of his tribe and his larger people only gained respect for the infidels.

Bashir did not have to labor alone. With picks and shovels, litters and wheelbarrows, it seemed that Noorzad's entire company—of about ninety fighters, Bashir thought, though he could not count that high—was involved in the labor. "Labor" was an understatement.

The rock overhang underneath which they excavated pushed out perhaps four meters, or maybe even five, from the vertical. The men had chipped their way in about twice that, so that there was a cave of sorts fifteen meters deep and twenty five or thirty in breadth. Not that Bashir counted in meters.

"What is this for?" Bashir asked a squad mate, as he heaved the heavy pick up for another strike at the rock face.

"Not sure," the other answered, between pick-swinging grunts. "Some say there's a meeting scheduled between Mustafa and some of our key supporters around the world."

Bashir swung the pick, knocking away a not very satisfactory chunk of the gray rock. He lowered the pick, pausing briefly to rest on it. "Lot of work for a mere meeting."

The other just shrugged. "Speak of the devil," he announced, pointing his chin towards a nondescript, off-road vehicle leaving the fortress in a cloud of dust, "there goes Mustafa now."

"Tall bastard, isn't he?" Bashir commented. "Where's he going?"

"Who knows," said the other, wiping sweat from his brow with a filthy shirtsleeve. "He almost never spends two nights in the same place. The locals here are all supportive, all armed to the teeth, and each little family has its own fortress. The collaborators of the Kashmir government don't even *try* to come into this area anymore. Last few times they did, they got run off with a bloody nose."

Shit, Bashir thought. *I am supposed to pin a man down to being here on a precise day, at a particular time, and that same man makes it impossible to do so.*

And my family's life depends on my doing so. Shit.

✧   ✧   ✧

Bouncing along over what passed for a road in this part of the world, Mustafa thought, *Shit. Nothing seems to work out the way it should. When I launched the attack on the Federated States I knew they would come here and I expected to be able to bleed them white and drive them out in shame and disgrace, the same way we did the Volgans.*

Didn't happen.

Then I saw the hand of Allah in their invasion of Sumer. Surely, I had thought, that with the best army and the most militarized people in all the Ummah *the crusaders would meet their doom.*

Didn't happen.

Oh, it attracted the mujahadin in vast numbers, to be sure. And the crusader coalition killed them in vast numbers, too. It seemed so close. But with their allies and mercenaries they always had enough troops to meet any success we had while they built up a new government— whores that owe their souls to the infidels, the lot of them—capable of standing on its own. Meanwhile, we were barely able to hang on here.

I thought then that Allah had truly turned his face from us. Two campaigns; two victories for the enemy. That only shows how foolish I was, for God is the greatest plotter of them all. With the cost of their victory in Sumer, the FSC has lost almost all stomach for the fight. Even now, the bulk of their forces in Pashtia are the Tauros—more albatross than ally—and these mercenaries. These we can defeat. And so Allah shows his omnipotence and his wisdom while mocking our lack of faith. We lost here, to lose there, so we could win here and recreate a base for establishing His law in the world in a more perfect and secure fashion.

Curse me to Hell if I ever doubt the wisdom of God again.

Damn all shavetails.

Sergeant Sevilla, 3rd Cohort, 6th Cazador Tercio, *hated* having his signifer along on a mission. The kid—he was only nineteen—was just so damned ignorant. Oh, sure; he'd come up through the ranks just like all the others, proved himself in combat, gotten through Cazador School and SCS. And Sevilla had to admit, it was the right thing to do for him to have come with his most forward deployed squad, on his platoon's most dangerous mission. It showed the right kind of heart.

Unfortunately, this wasn't a *heart* mission; it was a head one. And the next new signifer Sevilla met who had his head in the right place would be the first. Oh, sure; if they lived they learned. And tribunes and legates, who really *were* important to the legion, had to come from somewhere. But the price in lives among the enlisted men, noncoms, and centurions was pretty damned high to produce those absolutely necessary higher officers.

Why, why, WHY did it have to be my platoon that got stuck with the new shavetail when we could have had a nice, wise, older centurion in charge? No heroics then; just do the mission and come home safe. The sergeant suppressed a sigh.

He didn't really have to suppress it. The squad, all eight including the signifer, was well below ground with a good camouflage job covering them above from prying eyes. Only one little opening had been left in the camouflage, natural vegetation supplemented with a burlap strip net, that covered the hide, and that was closeable.

Corporal Somoza lay at that opening, watching with a pair of nonreflecting binoculars toward the fortress to the south. Somoza's Hush Fifty-one sniper rifle, a .51 caliber subsonic with a silencer, rested against the earthen wall of the hide beside him. A Pashtun scout attached to the squad lay resting near the rifle.

Most of the problem was that from the hide you couldn't *see* much of the fortress, only some—not nearly all—of the bunkers and a few stretches of trench here and there. Somoza's perch was actually oriented on the most likely avenue of approach for a Salafi patrol, rather than the fortress.

The signifer wasn't happy with that. He wanted to be able to see and report *more.* Never mind that that wasn't the squad's mission, that they were only there to serve as a relay and retransmission station for someone below among the enemy. Sevilla didn't have a single clue as to how to identify the spy, except by a code word over the radio. He supposed that if someone were to show himself at the hide and managed to get the code word out before being killed then he'd likely be accepted as the spy for whose word the team waited. Then again, Sevilla was reasonably certain the spy would not know where to look for them; Fernandez was careful that way.

In the interim, all the Cazador squad could do was wait for the signal and hope they weren't spotted. That is, that's all they could do unless the signifer had a bright idea.

✧   ✧   ✧

Bashir was bone weary, every muscle in his torso aching, by the time he and his company were released to rest for the evening. Though he didn't have his rifle, they'd left him his pack. He unrolled the bedding, adjusting it to the firm ground, then took out the yellow radio before placing the now half-empty pack at one end of the bedroll for a pillow.

Lying down after placing the radio's earpiece in one ear, Bashir fiddled with the dial until he found an Islamic station broadcasting from the capital of Lahore, many hundreds of miles to the north.

The radio Fernandez had given him was much more sophisticated than it looked. Most of the short time he'd had available before he'd had to leave on the Cricket, Bashir had spent learning to use its features. One of these was an integral, and passive due to the nature of the system, global locating system positioner. By putting the dial at a given point, one where no station in range broadcast, Bashir was able to upload his current location to a small computer chip. By placing the dial at another, he was able to tap out his simple codes and phrases, which were also stored on the chip. A third notional frequency set the thing to "transmit." Flicking the on-off button halfway transmitted the contents of the chip in a burst and continued to do so every thirteen minutes for five bursts.

That duty done, and no one apparently the wiser, Bashir closed his eyes and went to sleep.

Sevilla shook the signifer awake. "Sir, we just got word from our infiltrator. I've got his location and he sends that the main target isn't there. He doesn't know when the target will return. There is a meeting scheduled for sometime in the near future. Corporal Somoza is already retransmitting the message."

Camp San Lorenzo, Jalala Province, Pashtia, 27/7/469 AC

"Dammit!"

"Be calm, Patricio," Fernandez advised. "Rome wasn't burnt in a day. Besides, we still haven't even figured out how to *do* the damned mission. Delays while we do figure it out don't hurt us."

Carrera slowly nodded his graying head. "I know. And I am still not convinced we *can* do it, even with the boy's suggestion."

"It *was* a hell of a good idea though, wasn't it?"

Again Carrera nodded, though this time with a slight smile at his son's precocious insight. Carrera found few reasons to smile anymore. "Clever boy, isn't he? I'm going to leave him with you when . . . if we actually go through with the attack."

"That would be fine," Fernandez agreed. "And yes, Patricio, he's a frightfully clever boy. Pity he didn't have a way to get forty IM-71s and eight IM-62s, of which no more than forty, total, will be functional on the day we move, to carry what we need."

That was a daunting problem. To take the fortress, even if the enemy could be enticed away from its rocky, bunkered and entrenched outside ring, required more than forty helicopters could lift. In the first place, to enable most of one cohort, minus its armor and softer vehicles, to survive attack until relieved required fifty sorties of IM-71s. Under the circumstances, it would be improvident to use any of the heavier lift IM-62s. Given that the cohort selected would go in with limited mortar ammunition meant that they would need continuous artillery support from outside. Even lifting one maniple of twelve 155mm guns with their required ammunition would take up all the IM-62s. But that wouldn't seal off the area from escape. It could be sealed off, at least to vehicle traffic, by using the 300mm multiple rocket launchers to drop mines at the fortress valley's two entrances. But those would have to move into position to range the fortress. This might well tip the enemy off.

It would also tip them off if the first two loads in—the Air *ala* was still configured to lift one infantry and the Cazador cohort in by helicopter in two lifts—were used to seal off the objective. Of course, the Cazadors, at least and in theory, could jump in. Carrera thought about the prospect of his men landing by parachute on either the rugged mountains around the fortress or the valley within it and shivered. In the former case, he would expect anything up to twenty percent broken legs and ankles before so much as a shot was fired. In the latter, his men would hang for long moments in the air while the defenders below shot them up like sitting ducks. *Gliders? Squad sized gliders? Maybe if I'd thought of it two years ago.*

And then there was the problem of intervention by the Kashmir Air Force, by no means a despicable one. Yes, they couldn't control the tribal lands along their border with Pashtia. That didn't mean they were willing to let anyone else do so. He could bring in the SPLAD, the Self-Propelled Laser Air Defense system, the Legion had had built. But that, too, meant weight and cube and less lift for the infantry. All that, taken together, meant the likelihood of intervention by a Kashmiri armored division before he could finish off the fortress and extract his men.

As far as sealing off the fortress from relief by Kashmir's also somewhat respectable ground forces . . . he could do it, for a while, by committing the legion's mechanized cohort. But a ground war between himself and Kashmir was something of a losing proposition. They already sided altogether too much with the Salafis. A direct strike would certainly push them over the edge from secret to open support.

Briefly, he thought about using one of his seven nuclear weapons. *But no, the downsides of that are just too great. Besides, I'd have to* know *it would get Mustafa and all his top lieutenants. They're just not that effective on a hardened, underground target.*

"Any change on the ground reported, independent of our infiltrator?"

"Not really, Patricio. They're still improving their positions, digging out caves and the like. That, and a lot of housework."

"Any good estimate on the number of women and children in their camps."

"Thousands," Fernandez answered, shaking his head. *Do they think the women and kids will be a shield? They're living in yesterday's war, if so.*

The Base, Kashmir Tribal Trust Territries, 27/7/469 AC

Khalifa, wife of Abdul Aziz, was as much a part of the movement as her husband, so she felt. She not only cooked and cleaned—for her husband, yes, but also as part of the communal kitchens for all the holy warriors of the base—but she raised the children who would go on to carry forth the movement, the boys, and to breed warriors, the girls. She had only had two, so far, but this was quite good considering her age, nineteen, and that she had only entered into marriage a bit over five years before.

She'd not met her husband before the marriage, of course; good girls rarely did. She had been pleased, though, at the choice her parents had made for her. Not only was Abdul Aziz good looking, to the extent her limited experience allowed her to tell good looking from bad, but he had a bright future. Everyone said so.

It was really only that bright future that had caused her family to go past first cousins to second, which Abdul Aziz was, in searching for a husband for their daughter. With no particular background in genetics, indeed without even the ability to read, Khalifa saw nothing wrong with either sort of match. It was not forbidden by the Holy Koran, of course, and was therefore permitted.

In any case, Abdul Aziz's tall and lanky frame was well matched to Khalifa's shorter and much more well rounded one. Though for all that, she was not a short woman at one meter, seventy. That height came from her pure *Bedu* ancestry. Along with it, she had inherited large, well shaped, not-quite-almond eyes, full lips and high cheekbones. Her husband, she knew, was as pleased with her appearance as she was with his. At least, in the five years they had been together his ardor had never flagged nor had it shown any signs that it ever would. This was a pleasure to the girl, and in more than her body.

Her two children were a boy, four, and a girl, two. She'd been disappointed in herself for failing to deliver a second boy. But her husband—wonderful man!—had shushed her apologies and told her, in all seriousness, that it was the women who would deliver this world to the sons of Allah. She should be proud, he'd said, as proud of her as he was. How could she not love such a man?

Khalifa knew a little, but only a little, of the outside. She knew she and her sisters were pitied by the women of the industrialized world who believed them to be little more than chattels. She could not for the life of her understand that. Oh, yes, there were men, even Salafi men, who abused their wives. But didn't those "modern" women understand that every Salafi girl had a father and brothers who loved them so long as they were worthy? A father and brothers, uncles and cousins, too, who would not only take a very dim view of their female relatives being abused but were very likely to abuse right back? Salafis who mistreated their wives tended to wind up dead. Fortunately, *her* parents had chosen well. *Her* husband cherished her.

It was with that thought; that, and the warm glow still remaining from the night before, reinforced by anticipation of the night to come, that Khalifa ground the beans for the morning's coffee happily and with a smile.

"Well, you check out," an unsmiling Noorzad announced to Bashir, alone, over the morning coffee. The rest of the company had already eaten and drunk and was back at work on the cavern.

"You are remembered both at the camp from which

the lost column set out and in your home area. But I have some very bad news . . ." The grizzled old fighter hesitated for a moment before continuing. "Your family has been taken by the infidels."

Bashir had to feign shock. He inhaled sharply, then allowed himself to exhale as his chin sank down upon his chest. "Have they been . . ."

"No," Noorzad answered. "No word of a trial. None of any murders, either. They're just being held, apparently for questioning."

"How . . . ?"

"The infidels have their ways," Noorzad answered. "They can find your whole life story and family tree from the smell of your camel's three-day-old fart, so say some. If they took your brother, or even the smallest part of his body, they can find out where he came from."

"The crusaders will know I am missing," Bashir wailed. That, too, had taken practice. "They'll torture my parents to tell them where I am."

"No matter," Noorzad answered with a shrug. "Your parents don't know. Nothing they can say can hurt the cause. Besides, the infidels rarely bother to torture, no matter what we might say to the contrary, unless they have some particular reason to justify the effort."

Bashir restrained himself from saying, *They'll beat the crap out of you for the slightest lie, or the merest failure to come clean, if they've got an interest.* After all, he wasn't supposed to personally know that.

But I really want to know, need to know, what the hell is supposed to fit into that huge cavern we're excavating. Unfortunately, I can't ask you about it, just like I can't ask you about . . . or maybe I can.

"Will Mustafa want to speak to me again do you think?"

Noorzad shook his head. "Not this week. Maybe next. He often commiserates with those who either have given, or may soon give, much for the struggle."

"Okay . . . well, if he won't need me any time soon, I'd just as soon join the rest of the company at work."

"Good lad," Noorzad answered with a personable and friendly slap to Bashir's shoulder.

Camp San Lorenzo, Jalala Province, Pashtia, 28/7/469 AC

No matter how closely or how much Carrera stared at the model of the Salafi base, he found no solution. *It's logistically impossible. Impossible!*

He tried picturing the attack under the most promising scenario developed to date. *The Cazadors jump in by NA-32s—damn the broken ankles—and get by with nothing but air for fire support until the artillery is in range and ready. The helicopters move in the whole artillery cohort, except for the rocket launchers, which can move themselves, then go back for an infantry cohort. By the time they come back with an infantry cohort the enemy is completely ready. Any guests they may have—and Mustafa—are long gone. So we keep shuttling in the troops until we can reduce the place, get in a war with Kashmir, and after we take it we pull out, fight a border war while the diplo-shits try to patch up a peace . . . and do it all over again in a year or two.*

Fuck! Fuck! FUCK! Maybe if I wasn't so fucking tired all the time . . .

All right . . . let's start at the beginning. What do I want for an end state? I want to kill or capture every Salafi in the area, and especially their leaders, destroy the base, and pull out before it becomes a Kashmir-Legion ground war. That means I need an infantry cohort in the center, two more plus the artillery to make a breach and peel the edges, and Cazadors and Pashtun scouts to seal it off.

Okay . . . the Pashtun Scouts could go in over a period of days by air. Some might even just cross the border on horseback. Let's see . . . eighteen Crickets of which fifteen work at any given time. Each carries three Pashtun. Do it over a period of days? No . . . not a chance. The longer they're out there the more certain it tips my hand, alerts the enemy and warns Kashmir. And they could be there for fucking weeks before we get word that the leadership will be there. Skip that idea.

Again he glared down at the terrain model, *willing* it to provide answers. Obstinately, the model refused.

Make a major effort to clear the area up to the border before we strike? That way we could march most of the way and cut the amount of lift needed. But . . . no . . . that will tip off the Salafis and Kashmir just as much as a bunch of my Pashtun wandering in their territory will. If only the base was in Farsia there'd be no problem; they're an open and avowed enemy and I can cross their border at will. If only Kashmir wasn't so completely in the Salafis' pockets while pretending to be a part of the alliance against the Salafis . . .

Wandering in their territory? In their pockets? Pretending? And . . . nukes. Carrera held the thought for a moment, searching for an answer that was almost at his fingertips. *My God, could it be that simple?*

His hand reached for the intercom. "Get me Subadar Masood and Tribune Cano from the Pashtun Scouts. And Jimenez . . . and Fernandez."

The Base, Kashmir Tribal Trust Territories, 29/7/469 AC

"But what the hell is this damned thing *for?*" Bashir asked plaintively of no one in particular. The work crew had hit a particularly tough section of rock. No one thought his question particularly out of place.

"You don't know?"

"No, I don't know," he answered, resting on the sledge hammer he'd been using to drive wedges into the stone. "And I don't suppose I need to. But this shit is *tough!*"

"Well," his comrade began, conspiratorially, "I heard that the chief of the Old Earth infidels is coming for a visit. All very hush-hush, mind you. This cave is to hide his shuttle—the little ship that usually carries him between the UE Peace Fleet and their base on Atlantis Island—from prying eyes." The comrade's eyes went up and he made a sign as if to ward off either the Old Earthers or the Columbian's spies in the sky.

"All this trouble for one Old Earth infidel? Makes no sense," was Bashir's judgment.

"Nor to me, Brother. Perhaps Mustafa thinks to wheedle some help. Allah knows, we could use it."

"Well, at least that explains why we have to dig this thing. But what's the hurry?"

"I heard from my cousin who works in headquarters that it's set for two weeks from today."

❖   ❖   ❖

"Two weeks? Two fucking more weeks in this hole!" muttered Sevilla. "Shit!"

"Never mind, Sergeant," the signifer said. "Just advise headquarters. Meanwhile, I'm going to take Somoza out tonight after the last of the moons goes down and have a look around."

"Bad, bad idea, sir."

INTERLUDE

United Earth Organization Resolution 5417 (proposed)

Resolution 5417 (2131)

Proposed before the Consensus on its 16728th meeting,

On 13 June, 2131

The Consensus (formerly known as the "Security Council"),

Maintaining the spirit implicit in the Noblemaire Principle for the remuneration and reward of its professional personnel,

Realizing that stability is no less important to peace, prosperity and freedom than is progress,

Recognizing that equality among persons is necessary to peace and progress,

Acknowledging the custom that has arisen of enfeoff-ment of certain offices and positions among the progressive class,

Reiterating in the strongest possible terms that progress is dependent upon the actions and authority of members of that class, supported by the peoples of Earth, as represented by this Consensus and the General Assembly,

Stressing that the Organization, and its affiliates and subsidiaries, must remain one "open to talents,"

Welcoming the support for this measure given by such organizations as Amnesty, Interplanetary, Doctors Across Worlds, the Interplanetary Association for Progressive News Reporting, Food is a Human Right, Inc., various transnational corporations, the European Union, the Organization of African Unity, The Chinese Hegemony, etc.,

Expressing its delight at the trust and confidence shown by the peoples of Earth and by their progressive representatives,

Determining that the peoples of Earth cry out with one voice for a class to lead them into a bright future,

1) *Confers* upon its own officers honorary titles in accordance with the schedule at table one, attached,

2) *Confers* upon the chief officers of those organizations listed in table two, attached, similar honors as shown in that table,

3) *Reiterates* that such honors shall be open to whosoever shall arise to such positions, in perpetuity,

4) *Directs* that the title of "Secretary General" shall be the highest such honor, and

5) *Declares* that such honors, that they may be open to the peoples of the Earth, shall be hereditary, also in perpetuity.

CHAPTER TWENTY-ONE

When you're wounded and left
on Afghanistan's plains
And the women come out
to cut up what remains . . .
—Kipling, "The Young British Soldier"

UEPF Spirit of Peace, 5/8/469 AC

It was only partly the playmates the fleet could make available to her in essentially unlimited numbers, and without any wagging tongues, that had kept Lucretia Arbeit, Marchioness of Amnesty and Inspector General of the UEPF, from going back home to Earth. Far more important was that this was *exciting*, as nothing on Old Earth could be exciting anymore, while still being safe. Oh, yes, the continuous pressure of the barbarians from the reverted areas could be exciting, but that was decidedly unsafe. (And even the gladiatorial combats that the Duke of the International Solidarity Movement staged, for special occasions, grew dull after a while.)

Arbeit, after all, was a Domme, not a sub. And the barbs back home had some odd and unpleasant ceremonies they were said to engage in whenever they got a representative from the Consensus in their hands.

No, no, she thought, sitting on a couch in High Admiral Martin Robinson's quarters. *Much better here. Much safer here.*

The ship wherein Arbeit sat orbited peacefully, from below looking like nothing more than a silvery crescent in the shadow cast by Terra Nova and the local sun. Inside it was not so peaceful, however.

"You're not seriously going to give those maniacs nukes, are you, Martin?"

Wallenstein, the speaker, was agitated and plainly upset. She'd gone along so far for the possibility of jumping a step in caste among the elite of Old Earth. She'd been willing to overlook a lot—even to *do* quite a lot, frankly—to advance that worthy goal. Turning nuclear weapons over to religious fanatics was pushing the boundary of cooperation and aid. Even the months that had passed since Robinson first broached the idea had not made it a bit more comfortable or acceptable.

"I don't see what has you upset, Marguerite," Robinson answered calmly, turning away from his computer monitor. "We've shunted the Salafis money, arranged for arms and explosives, used our contacts and supporters down below to serve as hostages to get more Salafis freed and to shunt them even more money. Nukes are just a matter of scale and degree."

"No they're *not* just a matter of scale or degree. Nukes kill whole cities!" she practically screamed. "Don't you realize the Feds down below will *fucking nuke us* to gas if one of their cities goes up in a mushroom cloud?"

That got Arbeit's attention.

Ignoring the sudden look of concern on Arbeit's face, Robinson shrugged. "I considered that, of course, my dear. But these will be Volgan, Hangkuk, and Kashmiri, hence not traceable to us. So . . . what difference?"

"Millions of dead people," she insisted. "*Millions!* Doesn't that mean anything to you?"

"If you will the end, Marguerite, you will the means. Would you rather millions of dead barbarians and lowers here or millions of dead elites back on Earth?" Now it was the high admiral's turn to become heated. "You've seen the projections yourself, Captain. In one hundred years the barbarians below will be beyond control. In one hundred years this fleet will have fallen apart around us. For the sake of the Holy Office of the secretary general don't you realize why I had to buy local nukes? *Ours* can't even be relied on anymore. Like this damned ship, like this damned fleet. It's all coming apart and *it isn't going to get any better. Ever!* We break the independent nations down there to our ways or they come out and break us.

"Just picture it, Marguerite: their soldiers marching through the Louvre, and our own proles pointing out the more valuable artworks for them. Our class reduced to servitude. Earth groaning once again under an unsustainable population and the *proles* put in charge."

"But *nukes?*"

The marchioness of Amnesty interrupted. "Marguerite, it has to be nukes. Martin is right; Mustafa and the Salafis are losing, slowly but surely. I've seen enough to know that. They need to hit back. We need them to hit back to break the will of the Federated States and its allies. Once that is done the local

World League can become a real government just like the UN did back home. Then the Columbians, the Anglians and even the stinking Balboans will slowly but surely be forced into the fold. With the World League running Terra Nova and ourselves running the World League their population can be cropped, their industry and scientific base can be crippled. Their foolish insistence on popular rule can be thwarted. Most importantly, they can be disarmed. It *has* to be nukes . . . the Salafi have no other hope . . . and we have no hope but them."

"That's one possibility, Lucretia," Robinson said. "It's also possible, and for us much better, that the Salafis should dominate the planet."

Arbeit shrugged. To her, it really didn't matter.

"When?" Wallenstein asked, weakly.

"A couple of weeks," Robinson answered. "The Salafis are making a place where we can shelter a shuttle for the delivery. Making it by *hand*, as a matter of fact, the yokels," Robinson sneered. "They'll all be better off once we're in charge. Only the Class Ones have the wisdom to run a world properly, let alone two of them."

Reminded, she began to ask, hesitantly, "Have you . . ."

"Have I put you up for Class One yet?"

"Yes, that."

"Of course. Speaking of which, Marguerite, I'll want you personally to see to my security down there." Robinson smiled and continued, "In the interim, I have other uses for you. Get your uniform off and get on all fours."

"And get your lovely head over here," Arbeit ordered, sliding her posterior toward the edge of her seat.

✧   ✧   ✧

Afterwards, Wallenstein lay on her side in the high admiral's bed, sandwiched between the two of them. She kept two knuckles in her mouth on which she bit down. Normally, Robinson was content to use her mouth or vagina. This time he'd wanted her ass and it had hurt. It still hurt.

It will all be worth it, she consoled herself, *when he and Lucretia sponsor me for Class One. Everything will be worth it then. All the perks . . . all the lower castes having to kowtow to me rather than me to the high caste. The best living arrangements. Servants. Proles to use as I've been used all my life. Respect.*

Arbeit slept silently. The high admiral snored. He'd fallen asleep as soon as he'd finished using her body, she thought, but the snore meant he was truly asleep. Still naked, she gently slithered out from between them and over to the computer the high admiral had inadvertently left running while he'd turned his attention to her.

Must see how their recommendation reads.

A captain had access to everything in his or her ship's computer files, ordinarily. She knew the admiral had sequestered some files concerning the operations to influence the planet below. Hopefully he would not have thought to sequester the report on her.

She typed carefully, quietly. There it was, in the recent files section, a report labeled "Wallenstein." She pulled up the file and began to read.

As an officer Marguerite Wallenstein is adequate, but no more than that, she read. Skipping ahead, feeling nauseated, she saw further, *While she has a obsession with reaching Class One status, nothing in her background and breeding suggests she would be*

*a suitable candidate. She has too many lower caste
and even prole attitudes to entrust any portion of the
direction of a world to her marginal capabilities. On
the plus side, she uses her mouth well and will gladly
and even eagerly do anything in bed her superiors
direct her to do. I earnestly recommend a tour as
military aide to a high ranking Class One, male or
female as the captain does not discriminate, followed
by retirement as soon as she becomes tiresome.*

The report was countersigned by the IG, Arbeit.

Feeling *wounded*, as near to raped as she ever had
in her life, Wallenstein returned to bed.

By the next morning Wallenstein had herself under
full control. She awakened before either of her partners
from the night before, then showered, dressed, and went
to her own cabin prior to ascending to the bridge. On the
bridge she took the morning report and gave a few orders
to the bridge crew. After that, she turned control over
to her executive officer and withdrew to her day cabin.

When Robinson showed up, she greeted him with
her usual sweet smile and said, "I have had a complete
sensor search done of the Salafi base area and there is
nothing unusual to report, Martin. I've also put your personal shuttle into maintenance to make sure it is ready."

This was all true. It was even the whole truth . . .
so far.

The Base, Kashmir Tribal Trust Territories, 6/8/469 AC

The truth was that the Salafis were fairly rotten soldiers, as the term "soldier" was understood over most

of the globe. Hopeless marksmen, most of them, their rifles were ordinarily little more than noisemakers. Hopeless, they were too, on the battle line. A culture that values family above all things in this life cannot produce military units where nonblood-related men must generally trust in, even love, one another enough to make them risk death for their comrades. And it took a very rare leader—Mohammad had been one such; to a lesser degree Sada, back in Sumer, was another—to get them to rise above that.

On the other hand, unlike any number of military skills and values, patrolling was something that did come more or less naturally to most of the Salafis. Oh, the softly raised city boys of Kashmir and Yithrab were fairly hopeless, at first (even *they* could be taught, eventually, though). But the desert *Bedu* and the hill runners of Pashtia? *They* grew up with the possibility of having their little encampments raided at any time for livestock and women. *They* grew up, from earliest boyhood, with the idea of walking around outside their camp's perimeter at night to catch any such raid, or scouts for a raid.

Those Salafis went out every night through gaps in the wire and mines around the camp to make sure there were no unfriendly strangers waiting in the darkness. Some of them even stayed out days at a time, carefully and nervously walking the hills and valleys around the base.

Perhaps they'd grown a little slack, what with all the months and years in the Base and never a sign of the enemy nearby. But a "little slack," for a *Bedu* or a Pashtun securing his immediate home, wasn't really all that slack. It might have been slack enough, for example, to miss a small hide, well camouflaged, on a hillside. To miss men entering and exiting that hide? To miss men exiting that hide *every night*?

Sevilla was both furious and frightened. The idiot signifer was out again, having taken three men with him this time. What the young fool expected to find out there was beyond the sergeant. Briefly, he considered sending a burst message to higher to get someone to order the signifer to stay put. This seemed disloyal, though, and the legion stressed loyalty to immediate higher authority.

The sergeant stiffened when he heard the rustle of rock below. Hands tightening on his rifle, a standard model, he flipped down his monocle and used the rifle to peer out from the hide. He relaxed again, as much as one could relax on a long range detached mission in enemy territory with an *idjit* for a leader, anyway, when he made out Somoza's familiar shape in the darkness.

Muttering a curse under his breath, Sevilla lifted the overhead net carefully and only enough to allow the patrol to reenter the hide. In a whisper the signifer passed on what they had found. This was, as the sergeant expected, precisely nothing.

I'm getting too old for this shit, thought the twenty-seven year old Sevilla. *Maybe it's time to go back to my home tercio, the Third Infantry. They might—probably would—stick me in the recon platoon and have me doing the same basic shit, but at least I wouldn't be out here eighty fucking miles from help. Besides, line cohort recon platoons are almost always led by centurions. Better, way better, than having my balls in a shavetail's hands.*

The overhead net rustled suddenly as something hit

it from above. Sevilla looked up for an instant, saw a glowing spark, and pulled his head down under his protecting hands while shouting, "Grenade!"

Grenades were fairly high tech items, pricey and of limited shelf life, to boot. There were some in the Base's deep bunkers, of course, even many. But they were rarely issued, the mujahadin preferring to make their own. One typical "grenade" consisted of a one pound block of TNT, dipped in glue and then rolled in small ball bearings, BBs, repeatedly until a decent amount of shrapnel had been built up. Into the fuse well of the TNT was placed a nonelectric blasting cap with a short bit of fuse, the fuse connected to a pull igniter, and the whole thing heavily duct taped to keep it both together and waterproof. Some of the grenades were fitted with a piece of rope tied around to allow a much longer toss. In a pinch, and much like an industrially made hand grenade, the thing could be turned into a booby trap or mine with minimal effort.

Of course, such an assembly was heavier than a grenade, a *lot* heavier. On the other hand, what with having many times the explosive and shrapnel it was just the thing for taking out a bunker or trench.

Or a hide.

The leader of the mujahadin patrol hadn't been certain, at first, that it even *was* enemy. After so long without a contact he'd begun to believe that the crusaders and their mercenaries had given up on the Base. Who could be out here, then? Probably it was only another patrol like his own. Or maybe some herders got lost. Or . . .

"No . . . it's the infidels," he whispered to his men once he caught sight of the distinctive silhouette of a Helvetian-style helmet. "Come. We'll follow."

They almost lost sight of the crusaders several times. The mujahadin were confused by the fact that the hide was nowhere one would reasonably expect an observation post to be, thus the route the infidels followed was nothing like the route they would have expected. They were persistent, however, and their persistence was rewarded when, unexpectedly, one of the enemy stood a little too high before crouching down to slither into the hillside.

The leader of the patrol had no idea how many men might have gone below. He only had five of his own with him. *Best to be safe then.*

Spreading his men out in a line above the hide, he took from a small bag slung around his neck one of the homemade grenades. He motioned two of his men to do likewise. Each unwound the roughly meter-long cord tied around their devices.

"All together now," the leader whispered. "Pull together, spin together, throw together. Ready . . . pull."

There was the small sound of three spring-driven firing pins being released and the only slightly louder pops of the pins hitting the primers. All three fuses caught immediately. The men whirled their charges by the cords and released them at about the same time. They sailed through the air silently to land either in or around the spot where the crusaders had been seen to enter the earth.

All three grenadiers hurled themselves to the ground and waited for the explosions. There was only one brief cry from the enemy before the bombs went off. The five men of the mujahadin patrol began to fire as soon as the last of the homemade grenades had exploded, then charged forward still spraying the ground to their front. There was no return fire.

UEPF Spirit of Peace, 6/8/469 AC

It was critical, Wallenstein knew, that she not only continue in obsequious pleasantness to the high admiral and the IG, but that she also continue to eagerly seek out opportunities to make her body available to them. This was no problem; she could feign passion while reading a book. She did so now, while plotting both revenge and her own advancement.

"Unh!" *I am senior in the fleet, after Robinson. Arbeit has civil rank but not line rank.* "Oh!" *If anything were to . . .* "Mmm." *happen to them . . .* "Ahhh." *command would devolve on me. Screw this . . .* "Ung" *I can think better with his cock in my mouth than with him lying on me.*

Impatiently, she pushed him off her and bent over to take him in her mouth. Her head motions were thoughtless, automatic, the result of many decades of practice.

He's got to be operating on sealed orders. The Consensus must have given them to him before we left Earth. They're probably locked in his computer in a way even I can't get to. But I have records enough of his orders to date to make a good case for thinking there were sealed orders and carrying through with them, even if there were not. Plus, Arbeit's going along with him makes my case even better.

Automatically, she pulled her mouth away to run

her tongue under the shaft a few times before she returned to her sucking-on-autopilot.

Besides, the Governing Council, even if they knew nothing of the state of Terra Nova today, would certainly approve of initiative shown in eliminating a threat. There's probably no better way, no better way left to me, to reach Class One than to eliminate such a threat.

Robinson began to moan and writhe under her ministrations. Now she did concentrate, moving her head and mouth briskly up and down to get the business over with. She still had much thinking to do, and could do without further distractions.

The Base, Kashmir Tribal Trust Terrortories, 7/8/469 AC

Bashir looked up from his digging, distracted by the apparition of five bound and bloodied men being led into camp by ropes tied around their necks. He recognized the uniforms, despite the blood, and had a sinking feeling that his sole contact with the foreign infidels had just been lost. With it, quite possibly, his family was also lost.

He managed to keep the despair from his face, to feign mere curiosity. When Noorzad invited all the men excavating to come and witness the punishment, he even managed to look cheerful as he walked over, still carrying a heavy sledge hammer in his hands.

A substantial crowd had gathered by the time Nur al Deen, Mustafa's lieutenant, emerged from a cave to stand on a rock overlooking the scene. He looked down upon the captives and spat, eloquently. Then he began to speak in Misrani-accented Arabic. The

Arabs among the crowd understood perfectly well. The Pashtun and Kashmiris were totally lost, most of them.

"He says their punishment is written in Sura Five of the Koran," one of the men standing near Bashir announced. "'Thus be it to all,' he says, 'who bring disorder to the world, who fight against the Prophet,' peace be upon him."

Bashir was no Islamic or Salafi scholar. He wondered, *What punishment is given in Sura Five?* Then he remembered the crosses.

Sevilla had picked up a little Arabic in Sumer, but this accent left him completely baffled. It didn't help any that he was suffering from a severe concussion, and that he had multiple bits of metal lodged in his flesh.

Through waves of concussion-induced nausea he looked around at the crowd. They looked dangerously cheerful, though not so cheerful as they became once the ugly old man in the turban standing atop the rock stopped speaking.

Rough hands grabbed Sevilla and the other four remaining and half-dragged and half-carried them to a flat spot by the base of the central massif. Others disappeared into caves, emerging in moments carrying large wooden beams and posts. Injured as he was, it took Sevilla long moments to identify the purpose of the wooden members. As soon as he did, he began to fight, to resist. It did no good, a few tugs on the rope about his neck caused it to choke off blood to his brain for a moment, taking consciousness with the fresh blood.

When he awakened it was to find himself tied hand and foot to a rough wooden cross. Looking left and right he saw that his comrades were likewise tied. He struggled weakly with the bindings and to no better result than to chafe his wrists and ankles.

Looking down across his chest, Sevilla saw someone take a sledge hammer from another. This one walked forward, accompanied by a man holding four silvery-gray, six-inch long spikes and a like number of wooden squares in his hands. The sergeant's struggles with his bindings grew frantic.

Both of the approaching men spat down on Sevilla's face before kneeling next to him. He felt a wooden square against the heel of his left hand. The square grew heavier as a fist holding a spike came to rest upon it. Frantically, he looked away as the hammer rose and fell and . . .

Oh . . . God . . . Blood ran from the sergeant's mouth where he bit halfway through his tongue. A few more agonizing blows finished driving the spike through wood and hand, affixing that arm firmly to the cross member of the crucifix.

Sevilla wished he could faint, but there was no such mercy. He was still conscious as his right arm was likewise pinioned. *Mustn't scream . . . mustn't cry out . . . don't give them the satisfaction. Oh, God, help me.*

He didn't scream, either, until the third spike was driven through his right heel. That's when the crowd began to laugh.

Bashir was sickened. *Thank Allah they didn't make me drive the spikes. This? This, was what I was serving?*

Guiltily, Bashir spared a glance at the five men hanging on the crosses. Their arms were raised above forty-five degrees when they hung limp. Obviously this impaired their breathing, for they forced themselves to put weight on their tortured heels every few minutes and gasped in air desperately when they did so.

They'd been up there for hours now, with no sign of an approaching, merciful death. Children clustered around the bases of the crosses, poking the men with sticks and throwing rocks, dirt and shit at them. Women stood a little farther off. They threw nothing, just stared and pointed and sometimes laughed when the crucified men wept, as they sometimes did.

"How long?" Bashir asked one of his comrades, pointing to the crosses with his chin.

"Two days," was the answer. "Minimum two days. I've seen them—one of them, anyway—last as long as five."

"We do this often?"

"No . . . not often," answered the other, digging in his ear, casually, for grit. "It's been months, actually. The last one was an infiltrator from the government in Peshtwa. He was young and strong like those. *That* was the one that lasted five days."

UEPF Spirit of Peace, 9/8/469 AC

In four days Wallenstein had come no nearer a solution to her problems than she had been when she'd found the high admiral's computer left on. She'd played the scenarios out in her mind many times. *One more time couldn't hurt,* she thought.

Option one: I inform those people down below that Robinson is delivering nukes to the Salafis. Result: whether they get the bombs or not the Federated States of Columbia probably launches an attack on this fleet which we could not survive.

She sighed, deeply, attracting the attention of her bridge crew. A casual glare put their attention back on their duties.

Option two: Arrest Robinson before he can deliver them and hold him on charges of delivering weapons technology to the Terra Novans. This is a clear violation of regulations and the Governing Council would uphold me.

Right. Sure they would, with Arbeit screaming "treason." Two chances of that, after humiliating two Class Ones: slim and none. Besides, the crew knows the game as well as I do. I couldn't count on their support. Worse, he really might be acting on sealed orders. I'd be arrested. Sent home, and find myself as guest of honor at one of the Duke of International Solidarity's gladiatorial combats, like as not.

No one paid any attention when she sighed once again.

Option three: Sabotage his shuttle. Forget it. I don't have a clue about making a bomb with what's aboard ship. The most I can do is not see if it hasn't been properly maintained. And, if he notices—and he's been very touchy about the entire subject since that fire that nearly killed him—the bastard will space me so fast . . .

And . . . that seems to be it. Stop him here; stop him en route; or stop him below. And none of those choices work. Fuck.

The Base, Kashmir Tribal Trust Territories, 11/8/469 AC

He was alone now, the pain almost entirely gone. With the pain had gone his strength, of course. Sergeant

Sevilla was barely able to stand to change the angle of his arms to allow himself to breathe.

The signifer had passed first, two days prior. Sevilla didn't know why. Perhaps it was the injuries he'd taken when captured. He forgave the boy his idiocies. What good could holding on to anger and hate do now?

The other three had all gone silent yesterday; their bodies hanging dark, cold and unmoving. Even the children seemed to have lost interest in them. There was little diversion, after all, in tormenting a corpse.

And I'm near enough to a corpse, Sevilla thought hazily. *Not much fun left in me for them, either.* Almost, he laughed at the thought.

He wondered sometimes if he wasn't already dead and had just gone to Hell. He saw things, things he knew weren't there. His mother came to him in those visions, weeping for her boy. He whispered to the vision, "Don't cry, *Mama,* it will all be over soon and I can join you." The visions didn't last. The feel of the rough wood on his back, the evening cold biting his exposed skin, the soreness where the nails had penetrated his flesh, spilling his blood and splitting his bone . . . all these told him he was still alive.

Unfortunately.

Tomorrow, I'll die, Sevilla thought, with utter certainty. Under the circumstances, he looked forward to it.

UEPF *Spirit of Peace,* 11/8/469 AC

Wallenstein and a collection of her officers stood at the broad, thick plexiglas window of the shuttle deck as Robinson and Arbeit boarded the admiral's gig. The lower classes of the deck crew were on their faces in full proskynesis before the marchioness of Amnesty. Robinson turned once, to wave jovially, then entered the hatch which closed behind them. The lowers arose and evacuated the deck.

The ship began to hum as air was pumped out of the bay. Wallenstein watched the pressure drop on the gauge intently, even as the balloon expanded. She hoped that the shuttle's seals would fail and the crew suffocate along with the high admiral. *No such luck . . . unfortunately.*

At her nod, the officer in charge pushed a button. This caused a hydraulic whine to begin as the bay doors began to open. They stopped with a *kachunking* sound.

"Son of a bitch," the OIC cursed. "You two," he pointed at two prole crewmen, "Get on the manual crank."

With straining and grunting effort, the proles forced the bay doors open by main force. The shuttle pilot applied the smallest amount of power to vertical lift, just enough to raise the admiral's gig a half meter off of the deck. Soundlessly, as far as the watchers could tell, it rotated until it was facing directly outboard. Gracefully, and still soundlessly, the shuttle moved forward until it was far enough past the ship for it to start main engines safely to descend to Atlantis Base.

Wallenstein's last thought as the shuttle departed was, *Crash, you bastards.* It was a hopeless prayer.

Atlantis Base, 11/8/469 AC

The small Class One terminal by the landing field was, Unni Wiglan thought, the epitome of good taste, well maintained. More a salon than a transportation facility, the walls were decorated with art from Old Earth, the floor—except where gold-flecked, polished marble showed through—covered with expensive local rugs from Yithrab, Kashmir, Farsia and Pashtia. Rather than even the superior, upholstered seating she was used to in the VIP sections of Tauran Airports invariably reserved for the very rich and officials of the Tauran Union and World League, plus some other select progressive organizations, the seating here was positively homelike, leather sofas and chairs with ottomans, fronted and flanked by coffee and end tables of rare silverwood.

Slightly smiling, blank-faced proles from Old Earth puttered about, sweeping and mopping, dusting and polishing. Unni gave them no thought; they were like the lower classes of the Tauran Union, there to serve and be cared for and not to be overtly noticed. The proles were as much furniture as anything else in the terminal.

The years had been kind to Wiglan. She'd kept her slim shape and, if she hadn't quite *won* the war against gravity, she seemed to have arranged an armistice. She kept her hair shorter now, off her shoulders as befit her age. The few gray streaks detracted not at all from her appearance.

Unni's heart fluttered with excitement. A portion of that was anticipation of the thorough fucking she expected to receive soon at the high admiral's command. After centuries of practice, he certainly had some technique. Then, too, she was going to be introduced to the marchioness of Amnesty, said to be a fine looking woman. Unni wriggled with anticipation.

More excitement, though, came from the sheer danger of the enterprise upon which she had, at Robinson's behest, embarked.

It had not been easy for Unni to overcome her personal revulsion with the Tauran Union's military. Moreover, she'd had little personal to trade beyond whatever prestige there might be in association with, and the occasional bedding of, a TU minister. Still, she'd been diligent in her high admiral's cause and he had funded her lavishly.

The results of that association, those beddings, and that funding waited outside in a Yamato-manufactured truck surrounded by tough looking, armed, UE Marines: from Hangkuk, four nuclear weapons, from Volga, another four, and from certain persons in Kashmir's nuclear program, four more.

A wall speaker chimed thrice and announced in a sexless voice, "Marchioness of Amnesty and High Admiral of United Earth Peace Fleet's launch arriving in five minutes."

Unni looked skyward, expectantly. She was surprised, therefore, when the Marine band outside began to play Earth's "Hymn to Peace" and she looked down to see the familiar pumpkin seed shaped launch with its blue- and white-enameled symbol of United Earth roll up almost silently to the terminal and stop.

The symbol split to reveal Robinson, in full regalia. He stepped down onto a small staircase that had thrust out simultaneously with the opening of the hatch. Three steps and the high admiral's feet were firmly planted on the purple carpet that was reserved for Earth's highest and noblest officials. The marchioness followed.

While Robinson strode the purple carpet, the truck pulled around to the far side and a crew of Marines in plain fatigues began to transfer its contents to the shuttle's hold. The other Marines, the armed ones in full dress uniform, marched smoothly at port arms to surround the small ship and line both sides of the purple carpet. They then faced outward on command.

Wiglan shivered to see the Marines march, their bodies stiff and their faces cold, hard and emotionless. How much more pleasant to be surrounded by the blankly smiling proles!

The high admiral entered, Arbeit on one arm, lighting the salon with his smile. "Unni, my very dearest," he said, enthusiastically, after introductions, "how can I, how can Earth and Civilization, ever repay you? You're a marvel!"

He swept her into his arms and whirled her in a complete circle before setting her on her feet again.

"It was only my duty," she answered demurely, once she had regained her balance. "Will you be here long?" she asked, her voice husky and full of hope.

"Sadly not, my dear. I'm off to meet Mustafa as soon as my shuttle is loaded."

Seeing the disappointment written plain across her face, Robinson amended, "But the marchioness and I will be back in two or three days. In the interim, make yourself at home in my quarters here on Atlantis Base. It's been too long and we have much catching up to do. For now though, Unni, I must leave and deliver our cargo to the forces for progress."

Camp San Lorenzo, Jalala Province, Pashtia, 11/8/469

The NA-21 lacked the range to make the flight from the *Isla Real*, back in Balboa, to Pashtia in one hop.

In fact, no less than three stops had been required to take on fuel and rest the crew. Flying a Nabakov, any Volgan aircraft, actually, was a comparative bitch. At each stop security men from Fernandez's department debarked and nonchalantly took positions around the aircraft, weapons hidden under clothing.

Now the plane came in blacked out, spitting flares and with its full anti-surface to air missile suite activated. It touched down on the hard-surfaced field, bounced twice and reversed thrust. The plane's nose began to point down and its tail to rise as it slowed.

Safe landing accomplished, the plane was met at one end of the airfield by vehicle-mounted military police who had absolutely no clue as to its contents. These formed a wide perimeter around the plane as it turned in place at one end of the runway. Turn completed, the MPs closed up and escorted it to a hangar, which they likewise surrounded. What went on after the hangar doors were closed they knew not.

Carrera watched the plane as it moved down the runway, turned, taxied and stopped. He'd been sweating this moment. A messenger reported to him and saluted. He returned the salute casually and took a piece of paper from the messenger's hand. The note read: "Targets at objective tonight and tomorrow."

Click.

INTERLUDE

30 April, 2155, Cygnus House, Chelsea, London, European Governing Region, Earth

The symbol of Amnesty, a lit candle with barbed wire wrapped around it, was emblazoned across the front of the mansion. The light of the candle was false but the barbed wire looked very real. *Only fitting,* thought Louis Arbeit, the *Marquis* of Amnesty, as his chauffeur opened the door to his limousine.

Once out of the limo, the marquis looked around with considerable satisfaction. It wasn't merely satisfaction at the quality of residence he'd acquired. No, the really thrilling part had been that his organization paid the entire bill, from mortgage to taxes to servants to gardeners to utilities to food. Add in the other perks that commonly went with being a senior part of Earth's new royalty and, well, it was worth much more than even the three quarters of a ton of gold he'd paid for it.

Life is good, the marquis thought, reaching for the handle of the ornate double door out front. *And with the newest antiagathics, it will be long, as well.*

"Daddy!" Arbeit's young daughter, Lucretia, screamed as he came through the double front door. The girl launched herself at her father, wrapping him in a tight hug. She then took his hand and led him out to a patio overlooking the garden.

"I supervised the cooks making dinner myself, Daddy," Lucretia announced, proudly. "Though I had to beat one for being naughty."

"Good girl, Lucretia," he father congratulated. "I hope you didn't damage her."

Lucretia hung her head slightly. "Not much, I didn't, Father. I will need a new riding crop, though," she added brightly.

"That's my girl."

CHAPTER TWENTY-TWO

And although it appears that the World has become effeminate and Heaven disarmed, yet this arises without doubt more from the baseness of men who have interpreted our Religion in accordance with Indolence and not in accordance with Virtu. For if they were to consider that it (our Religion) permits the exaltation and defense of the country, they would see that it desires that we love and honor her (our country), and that we prepare ourselves so that we can be able to defend her.

—Machiavelli, *The Discourses*, Book Two, Chapter II

The Base, Kashmir Tribal Trust Territories, 10/8/469 AC

As he usually did, Bashir lay down for the night with his yellow radio's earpiece in his ear. Also, as usual, he punched in the code, hoping against hope that tonight there'd be an answer. There had been none since those five poor devils had been taken and crucified.

The coded message he sent out was simple:

"tonight . . . tomorrow . . . tonight . . . tomorrow." He punched it in and pressed the key to transmit in a burst. *This message* must *get through or my family is dead*, he thought. Closing his eyes after the message went out Bashir was almost shocked to hear in the earpiece, "Message received. Thank you."

Camp San Lorenzo, Jalala Province, Pashtia, 11/8/469 AC

The chill early morning breeze raised dust across the regularly laid out encampment. By the airfield, in the tall, sandbagged control tower, Carrera scanned past the high earthen walls.

There were eyes on the camp. There were *always* eyes on the camp. You couldn't stop them from seeing. You couldn't stop their owners from reporting. The trick, then, was to make them think they saw something different, to make the unusual look normal and even the normal unusual.

The legion had since its arrival kept at least one cohort operating along the Kashmir-Pashtia border. That could remain there. Indeed, moving them without replacing them would have been inherently suspicious. Also, there were always at least four Pashtun Scout maniples and two to three Cazador maniples operating somewhere in the Balboan Zone of Responsibility, or BZOR. Few units operated without being in range of some kind of artillery or heavy mortar support.

Both Pashtun Scouts and Cazadors operated farther from camp than line infantry, and were much more likely to rely on air support than artillery or mortar fire if they found themselves in a jam.

Leaving one infantry cohort and the bulk of the service and support troops to guard the camp, Carrera had sent out one infantry cohort to replace the Cazadors and part of the Scouts. This was done slowly, over a period of days, so as to incite no comment. The infantry flew out with the morning supplies; the Scouts and Cazadors flew back, hidden in the IM-71s' closed, almost windowless, cargo bays.

At the camp's own airfield the Scouts had spent a mere day being partially briefed and fitted with civilian clothing suitable for travel. They were issued passports with visas. They'd then transshipped onward, some via the Legion's AN-21s and 23s for the major airport at Chobolo, the capital of Pashtia, still others on civilian buses to cross the border. Still others left openly on horseback. Clothing for the foot scouts had been easy, since the one-size-fits-almost-all robe was common dress where the Scouts were headed.

For the most part, for those who flew out, this was Sumer, where Sada's closest followers arranged further onward movement through Yithrab for some, directly to Peshtwa, Kashmir, for others.

The long-range patrol that had served as retrans for the legion's spy in the enemy base was not replaced. Instead, a very quiet remotely piloted vehicle took up station within range and circled expectantly.

Peshtwa International Airport, Kashmir, 11/8/469 AC

Subadar Masood spoke Urdu, the primary language of Kashmir, flawlessly and with a proper Peshtwa accent. He waited impatiently for a group of twenty-one of his scouts, all in civilian dress, to debark from the plane. With these, four legionary officers including Jimenez, and those men who had arrived previously, he would have a force of fifty-one men in the capital. This was just large enough to minimally man the vehicles he had purchased for cash over the preceding weeks, and also just few enough to excite no real comment in bustling Peshtwa.

Weapons, too, had been purchased. Masood smiled to think that he was buying from the very same men who made their livelihood selling to his enemies. Since *he* knew what he was about and the Salafis rarely did, he was confident, at least, of having obtained superior products.

Such purchases, on such a scale, would have excited comment almost anywhere else on Terra Nova: one man buying nearly six hundred rifles and machine guns, plus several tons of explosives and ammunition. In the decentralized ways of the Salafi movement, with no one really in charge (though Mustafa was still working on bringing some of the disparate submovements to heel) and its leaders more inspirational than operational, it was merely routine.

The only interest shown in the transactions by the government or any of its agents were requests for bribes, or *baksheesh*. Masood paid, of course; this was the price of doing business. He took some small satisfaction in haggling the bribes demanded down from the obscene—which *would* have excited interest, if paid—to the reasonable.

With weapons, ammunition and explosives excess to immediate needs all safely stowed in the cargo compartments of the buses, Masood directed the

drivers and co-drivers to mount up. Without fanfare
the column moved south to its rendezvous with the
rest of the maniples committed to the attack.

The Base, Kashmir Tribal Trust Territories, 11/8/469 AC

The admiral's launch from the *Spirit of Peace* didn't
need a landing strip, except as a convenience. The
price to be paid for not having one was expenditure
of fuel. Mustafa had promised fuel and Robinson had
believed him.

I was told this area was safe, Robinson thought
doubtfully, as he looked out the window to see a long
line of what looked like bomb craters. *Guess not.*

Robinson had been a bit skeptical when the Salafi
sheik had promised a cavern big enough to shelter his
launch. Looking out his portside window, however, he
had to admit that the excavation revealed as dozens of
men pulled aside its camouflaging curtain was indeed
impressive, easily as large as the VIP docking bay of
the *Spirit of Peace*.

The pilot hovered briefly until he was certain
that the concealing curtain was pulled far enough
away to permit his shuttle easy entrance. Then with
a few gentle adjustments of the horizontal thrusters
the launch began to slide left, into the cavern. The
Salafis replaced the curtain as efficiently as they had
removed it.

There was no Marine band for this landing, no
purple carpet and no salonlike terminal. The security
was just as tight, though, as on Atlantis Base, if not
so formal.

Mustafa was curt when Robinson stepped off the shuttle door with a burka-clad Arbeit. Robinson turned to help the marchioness to step down to the cave floor. "You have brought the weapons?" Mustafa asked.

"I have brought the weapons. The keys to activate them I retain," Robinson answered, tapping his forehead.

Mustafa smiled suddenly and brilliantly. "This is to be expected. We will emplace them where they will do the most good. You will detonate them. We will take the credit. The infidel will be destroyed."

Robinson refrained from pointing out that it would take more than a dozen wrecked cities to destroy the Federated States. Likewise he refrained from mentioning that the Federated States were very likely to launch a genocidal nuclear war against any place which so much as *might* harbor a Salafi if a dozen of its cities were nuked. Instead, Robinson intended to detonate only one of the bombs. This would leave the rest in place and hidden, in other words left as a threat, to force the Feds to pull back within their boundaries. *That* would leave the rest of Terra Nova to the either the *Ikhwan* or Tauran Union, the World League and their puppet master, himself.

Hoti, Kashmir, 11/8/469 AC

The town was one of the central points for the support of the insurgency in Pashtia, much as it had been during the earlier Volgan-Pashtian war. There were still refugees from that earlier war, hundreds of thousands of them, rotting in tent cities in the barren hills to the southwest. Hundreds of humanitarian workers made a fat enough living through dispensing the charity that kept those refugees rooted to the area.

To the northeast of the town was a fertile plain the produce of which, along with the retail arms trade and the fat pickings from foreign aid, made Hoti the pleasant and prosperous burg it was.

The town was also large enough, the dress similar enough, and the language common enough that something over four hundred and fifty newly arrived Pashtians made little impression on it or its people. There were always guerilla bands traipsing through Hoti or, at least, there had always been for the last thirty-three years.

The buses, four-wheel-drive sedans, and light trucks under Jimenez's and Masood's command, waited by the town's outskirts. By twenties and thirties the rest of the party, those who had openly entered Kashmir across the common border as "refugees," met the vehicles. There weapons and—for vehicle leaders, radios—were issued and, in some cases, mounted.

"I almost can't believe we're getting away with this shit," Jimenez told Masood.

"The ways of Allah are inscrutable," the *subadar* answered, with a sardonic smile. "His mercy is infinite. What's more, sir, we're nothing unusual, not even for size. We're not even forming up in any particularly remarkable way. The mujahadin have been doing this for over three decades, and almost without pause. I, myself, joined a guerilla column to fight the Volgans not two miles from here thirty years ago. Purely routine."

Jimenez commented, "But it still seems too easy."

"Wait until we reach the Salafi base, sir. We'll pay there for any ease we've had here. Then, too, this is the *last and only* time we'll ever get away with this."

"How are the vehicles holding up?" Jimenez asked.

"Not bad. We should lose no more than, say . . . a third of them. Yes, about a third, over the next portion of our journey. Less if Allah is especially merciful."

Jimenez consulted his watch. *"Fortes Fortuna adiuvat."*

"Yes, sir," Masood agreed. "She does. Great writer, Terence."

"You understand Latin?" The legate was flabbergasted. *"Latin?"*

"School in Anglia, sir. Every *proper* gentleman there studies Latin."

Jimenez couldn't help laughing with surprise. "Load 'em up, *Subadar*. 'Fortune favors the bold' *and* the timely. We have a group of cavalry to link up with."

Chabolo, Pashtia, 11/8/469 AC

A military headquarters in a theater of war is rarely precisely quiet. The Coalition headquarters here, in the capital of Pashtia, rocked with fury.

Virgil Rivers was as angry as the three stars on his collar allowed and encouraged him to be. "How dare that bastard? How *dare* he present me this . . . this . . . this fucking *ultimatum.*"

"It's not an ultimatum, Virg," John Ridenhour supplied calmly. Following his retirement from the FSA, he'd taken Carrera's shilling. "And please keep your voice down. It's an advisement. He has information that there will be a nuke or nukes at the Salafis' main base in Kashmir . . . today. He is acting on that. He is asking you to keep the Kashmir Air Force off his back while he does so. If you don't, and he and his force are destroyed, or the nuke gets away . . . on your head be it."

"John," Rivers answered, forcing himself to calm, "we both know that bastard and we both know it's an ultimatum . . . a fucking order. To *me*. Doesn't the son of a bitch know he *works* for me?"

Ridenhour gave a meaningful smile before answering, "The 'son of a bitch' works for nobody but himself. You know that. He did advise me to tell you that a similar message is going to President Baraka in Kashmir, but that it will be delayed a few hours until the attack is well underway. That message will say this attack is with FSC authorization and support. Baraka's no fool; if he doesn't get reports that you have scrambled your own fighters for air cover, he'll draw the obvious conclusion."

"Why couldn't Pat have come to me with this sooner?"

"So you could buck it to Hamilton? So the Foreign Affairs pussies in Hamilton could press for a 'diplomatic solution'? So the nuke or nukes could get away? Be serious, Virg, he's doing exactly the right thing."

"And another thing," Rivers continued, "how the hell does he *know* this? I've had not a word."

Ridenhour sighed. "Virgil . . . you boys give us a lot of technical intelligence. How often is it both right and *timely*, hmmm? The Legion gives *you* a great deal of intel from . . . other . . . sources. How often is it untimely or *wrong*?"

That was troubling. Indeed, everyone suspected the ways the legion obtained its information. No one on the same side, however, was willing to ask because no one *wanted* to know. The progressives never asked anymore because they were already certain that they did know.

"Why is it," Rivers asked, throwing his hands in the air, "that every time he does 'the right thing' it tends to be really fucking inconvenient for everyone around him?"

"It's more than a trick, I've discovered, Virgil," Ridenhour answered. "It's a genuine knack."

Camp San Lorenzo, Jalala Province, Pashtia, 11/8/469 AC

Not a man of the Cazadors thought they'd been pulled in early for a break. Excitement was in the air, along with deepest interest and a considerable flavoring of dread. That one side of the hangar had what looked to be six hundred main parachutes, harnesses and other air items but *no* reserve 'chutes added to the dread. More mysterious, and dreadful, another wall was lined with crates of foam padding, wooden sticks, and duct tape. The men talked and muttered among themselves, sitting on the cold floor of the hangar, until someone announced, "The *Duque*, commanding."

The nearly six hundred Cazadors assembled jumped to their feet and stood at attention as Carrera walked up to a low rostrum at one end of the hangar. A white sheet was hung behind him. "At ease," he called. "Seats."

Jesus, doesn't the boss look old and worn and thin? Man needs a break.

"Let's begin by asking a question," he began. "Does anyone here have a problem jumping at less than five hundred feet over ground without a reserve parachute? Come on now," Carrera insisted. "If you don't think you can or just don't want to try, stand up, report to Tribune Salinas of the Military Police there in the back. You'll be kept in isolation but no charges will be pressed. No hard feelings, either, at least from me. But if you can't do this we need to know *now*."

There was a stirring in the mass of troops. Most of them *didn't* want to jump that low. None of them were willing to admit as much. Carrera gave them a few minutes to settle down.

"All right then. I won't bother asking if you've got issues with doing an incursion into another country. It's a given that you don't or you wouldn't be here at all. Lights," he commanded.

Once the hangar had dimmed enough for a projector to work, Carrera called, "Map." Instantly, a large map of the Kashmir-Pashtia border region appeared behind him. All the men recognized it, despite the distortion caused by the slight waving of the sheet.

Carrera pulled a laser pointer from his pocket, flicked it on and laid a red point of light onto the Jalala area. "We are here." The red point shifted across the sheet until coming to rest on a fortress symbol on the other side of the border. "We are going there. Next map."

The previous, large-scale map disappeared to be replaced by one of the same scale but a smaller area, side by side with a small-scale map of the objective area.

"Your mission," Carrera continued, pointing at the objective map, "is to seal this off from escape. Before you do that, *just* before, other forces will infiltrate and attack the center of the Salafi fortress. Still another force, Pashtun cavalry that left some time ago, will seal the ends of the valley. Heavy infantry and artillery will move by helicopter to crack its shell and peel it. The mechanized cohort will cross the border here," again the point of light shifted to mark the major pass between Kashmir and Pashtia, "and take up a blocking position *here*," the light rested a bit farther north. "The Federated States Air Force will provide air cover at a distance. Our own Air *ala* will be in either the transport, the recon, or the close support mode.

"There's been no time to rehearse this, nor will there be except by back brief. For that matter, if we tried to rehearse it, it would just tip off the enemy. Nonetheless, we've been planning this operation for weeks. Your commanders have the plan. Cohort commander?"

"Sir!"

"Take charge of your men. And good luck to you all. Kick their asses."

Pickup Zone Papa Echo (Principio Eugenio), Pashtia, 11/8/469 AC

Every infantry cohort in the legion carried enough landing lights, sometimes called "beanbag lights," to set up a pickup zone for helicopter movement. These were color-coded, different colors marking different spots and different functions on the chosen field.

Cruz's platoon had drawn the duty of setting up the PZ. Pulled at the last possible minute from their patrolling, they'd filled the beanbags of the lights with dirt and rocks to keep the rotor wash from blowing them away. They'd then placed them on the ground in the proper positions. With the duty of setting up the PZ had come the duty of running it. This meant not only arranging the rest of the maniple for pickup, but taking charge of the dozen 160mm mortars that were to fly out ahead of the infantry to take up a firing position in range of the objective and a couple of miles across the border.

The mortars and their ammunition had been dragged up by their integral trucks, the trucks having to make two or three trips each for the full load of projectiles. The shells were palletized, piled in nets that would be slung by hooks underneath the helicopters. The guns would be manhandled inside by their crews. The trucks would remain behind on the PZ; there were no roads or even trafficable trails where the guns were heading.

Cruz removed his helmet and wiped a hand across his brow; helping the mortar maggots to move that ammunition from truck to pallet by hand had been a backbreaking task.

"What now, Centurion?" Optio Garcia asked.

"Now we wait for a bit."

Camp San Lorenzo, Jalala Province, Pashtia, 11/8/469 AC

Three of the deployed legion's twenty Turbo-Finches were down for maintenance, housed in hangars. Likewise was one of its four ANA-23 gunships. The remainder stood in their concrete floored and revetted, steel-covered bunkers. There were hinged steel walls in front of the bunkers, proof against heavy shrapnel and lowerable on their hinges to allow the aircraft to leave and enter. Only enough of the doors were lowered to allow ordnance crews, supplemented by nearly every clerk and cook in the camp, to trundle in, jack up, and load the bombs, rocket and machine gun pods, and napalm canisters required for the attack.

The gunships received a different load, mostly machine gun and cannon ammunition for their fixed, side-firing guns, plus a dozen each five hundred pound GLS-guided thermobaric bombs that would be dropped from altitude out the rear ramps to strike certain key targets.

While the ordnance crews strained and sweated, mechanics and avionics repairmen pored over the planes, checking status and making necessary repairs. There was to be no waiting for parts; Carrera had decreed they could strip the other, nonflyable aircraft down to the ground to make sure the minimum necessary were fit for flight and fit to fight.

Miguel Lanza, a legate III himself now, watched the progress intently from outside. *No sense in getting under the feet of men who sure as Hell know their business well by now,* he thought.

A voice came unexpectedly from behind. It was Carrera.

"Your boys going to be ready on time, Lanza?" he asked wearily.

Lanza nodded in the semi-darkness. "No problem."

"What are you planning to fly, Miguel?"

"Gunship," Lanza answered. "Lets me in on the action and gives me a copilot so I can control the operation. Also gives me the best commo and sensor suite of any plane we have. Besides, I'm really not up to CAS anymore." Lanza sighed at the injustice of aging.

"Good choice. Carry on."

Lanza watched Carrera amble away like a man ten years older than he was.

The Base, Kashmir Tribal Trust Territories, 11/8/469 AC

Oh, Annan, yes, thought Arbeit, *this is exciting.*

The bomb sat to one side of the deep cavern. Mustafa ran his hands over it lovingly. Lost in his visions of an entire infidel city turned to a smoking charnel house, he barely heard the words of the high admiral.

"Broadly speaking," Robinson said, "if you continue to carry on the way you are, you are going to lose. Moreover, you'll lose in the worst possible way from *both* our points of view." Unconsciously, the high admiral reached up to stroke his right breast pocket. *Yes, the detonation device is still there. The way Mustafa is looking at that bomb it's a damned good thing, too.*

He spoke in a dimly lit cavern attached to a deep tunnel by a narrow, roughly hewn rock side tunnel. This far below the ground no sound penetrated from above. The air was uncomfortably cool and, despite an attempt to pump in fresh air, rather stuffy.

Nur al Deen objected, "Every day new fighters, some in groups, come to join the struggle. Our strength is growing, not weakening. The enemy, the Great Demon called the Federated States, is weakening!"

"Not enough," Robinson countered. "Their use of mercenaries is not only keeping the financial costs of their war down, it is keeping the casualties down below critical mass as well. And there does not appear to be a practical limit to how many mercenaries they can field.

"Alternatively," he continued, "the mercenaries' unproven but obvious penchant for targeting families even in the Yithrabi Peninsula, Southern Uhuru, Taurus and the Federated States, itself, has slowly reduced your available recruiting pool to the ignorant children of your madrassas. Their murders of sympathetic media types hurt you as badly. *You are losing*.

"That is why I want you to use one of the weapons I have brought here on Balboa. That's the breeding and training ground for the legion. Rather, I want you to emplace one there, in order to threaten the legion out of any further cooperation with the FSC."

"And that's another thing," al Deen objected. "You have brought us twelve nuclear weapons. This is enough to do incredible damage to the FS, damage from which they will never recover."

Robinson scoffed. "On the contrary, they *will* recover. Look at Taurus and Yamato and the number of cities they saw erased during the Great Global War. You can't even tell anymore that the war happened. On the other hand, if you use these weapons more than once the FSC will *obliterate* you and your religion. You are the most urbanized population on this planet. The contents of just *one* of their nuclear missile-carrying submarines would be sufficient to kill one third of you outright, and leave another third to die slowly of starvation and disease. And they would probably not stop there. Don't you recall what they did in the GGW when we hit two of their cities to stop their use of nuclear weapons against Yamato? They imposed a blockade that killed a third of that country's people by slow starvation. They would hate you more and do more to you." Robinson left unsaid, *and they're quite likely to obliterate my fleet while they're at it, if I even suggested trying to prevent it.*

Mustafa stood back from the bomb, removing his caressing hands with regret, and paced the cavern for a few moments, head outthrust and hands clasped behind his back. "Sadly," he said, pointing at Robinson, "this infidel is right. But that doesn't mean he is completely right. The Blue Jinn and his people must pay."

"I want the control of three bombs."

"One," the high admiral answered.

"Three," Mustafa insisted. "One in the FS which will be used. One on Balboa which will be used. And one on Anglia with another in reserve."

Robinson considered this. *One used and one threatened knocks Balboa and the mercenaries out of the war. Two in Anglia, one used and one as a threat, probably prevents them from retaliating. That leaves eight for the FS, one used and seven threatened. Maybe . . .*

Robinson looked at Arbeit. Although only her eyes showed through the burka her head nodded deeply. "Done," he answered.

Hoti-Chobolo Highway, Kashmir, 12/8/469 AC

The road that had been smooth from Hoti turned into a kidney-pounding washboard five minutes after turning off toward the enemy base. Speed dropped, out of sheer necessity to maintain health, to under ten miles an hour.

The convoy traveled with lights on. Anything else would have been suspicious. Even so, a wary group of tribesmen did stop the lead vehicle carrying Jimenez and Masood.

"What you here for?" a rifle-bearing brigand demanded, once Masood had stopped and dismounted.

Bold bastard isn't he? Masood observed to himself. *Bet there are half a dozen machine guns covering us right now or he wouldn't be nearly so bold.*

"We come to join the great Prince Mustafa," *Subadar* Masood answered, which was, after a fashion, true enough.

The suspicious tribesman ignored the answer, or seemed to. Instead, he went to the vehicle and looked over the passengers. He reached in and pulled away the scarf Jimenez had pulled across his face. Jimenez's white eyes shone against his coal-black skin even in the darkness.

"What this one?"

"He's from among the faithful of Uhuru, come all this way to fight for Allah."

The tribesman asked a question of Jimenez, who stared pleadingly at Masood.

"He doesn't speak our language," the *subadar* said. "Do you, perchance, know any of the Arabic dialects of Southern Uhuru?"

Scowling, the tribesman answered, "Not even know where this *Uhuru* place is. How speak language?" he asked, rhetorically.

Masood shrugged.

"Mustafa great man," the tribesman announced. "Give my people many gifts. You give gifts?"

"As the Prophet, peace be upon him, said, 'Give gifts to each other and love each other and hatred will disappear.' We would be happy to share our blessings with our brothers," Masood answered.

"Prophet, PBUH, he say that?"

"Indeed he did. We are *brothers* in our faith, are we not?" the *subadar* asked.

"Not know nothing about no brothers. You give gifts?"

"Would money do?"

"Money do fine," the tribesman answered. "You give . . . one hundred rupees per man."

Two drachma, near enough, per man? About a thousand in all? Sounds very reasonable to me.

Masood reached into a pocket. "Can you accept FSD?"

"FSD good."

The Base, Kashmir Tribal Trust Territories, 12/8/469 AC

Robinson had slept in better places. Indeed it was hard to remember ever having slept in a worse.

Oh, the Salafis had *tried* to make him comfortable. They'd laid out for him and the marchioness a bedroll of stacked rugs and provided blankets. They'd even made provision of a slave girl—Volgan, Robinson thought—to warm the bed and entertain their guests.

She might have been more entertaining but for the whip marks Arbeit had added to her bare back; the girl already had a fair collection. Robinson had to turn off the light to keep the disturbing image of the girl's criss-crossed back out of his view.

The girl spoke no English. Neither did Robinson speak Arabic or Volgan. He'd had to make do with pointing and signs. She seemed to understand those well enough. In any case, she cooperated, albeit without any noticeable enthusiasm.

Which is perfect, thought the high admiral, drifting off to sleep with the detonation device clasped in his hand under his pillow. *The more of this world chained to these dolts the less of this world that will be a threat to* mine.

Bashir's sleeping arrangements were considerably less luxurious than the high admiral's. He made do as best he could against the cold and rocky ground with a couple of blankets and his pack for a pillow.

Having sent his message and—wonder of wonders—received an answer, Bashir was more than certain that an attack was imminent. This had its good sides and bad.

I've done my job; done everything they asked. My family should be safe now. But what about me? *When they attack they're going to see that their men have been crucified. They'll kill everything moving. Allah knows, I would. Shit.*

So how do I keep them from killing me, too?

He hadn't come up with an answer before sleep took him. As he nodded off, Bashir wondered if he'd see the next sunrise or if a bomb would kill him while he slept.

Camp San Lorenzo, Jalala Province, Pashtia, 12/8/469 AC

The eastern sky was just beginning to glow red when the first of the gunships began its roll down the runway. Heavily laden as they were, the birds needed nearly every foot of runway space before they achieved liftoff.

Once the first one, Miguel Lanza at the helm, was up and had gained some altitude, the next began its take-off run. A few minutes later, with the last of the gunships airborne and circling overhead, the first of the nine Turbo-Finches in this attack wave likewise rolled down the hardened strip. These took off in half-minute intervals and assembled at an altitude just below that of the gunships.

Even before the last of the Finches was airborne, Lanza looked out his cockpit window and saw Crickets lining up below, ready to join the others. Behind the Crickets came the heavier but much faster NA-21s and the Cazador-laden NA-23s.

Still in Lanza's view, the forty-one working helicopters of the *ala* lifted almost as one, then turned to the north. It was an awesome and thrilling sight.

This, Lanza thought, *this is why I joined.*

Carrera watched the aerial armada assemble overhead from the railed walkway that ran three hundred and sixty degrees around the airfield's control tower. A warmed-up Cricket stood idling near the base of the tower, its wings and fuselage bearing the legend "4-15." It had had installed a bank of radios and a map board. One pilot would fly its passengers, Carrera and two radio operators.

On the floor beneath the tower a temporary command post was set up. This would provide back-up control until another command post was set up near the objective. In the interim, Carrera was capable of running the entire thing in his head with only minimal assistance. Even bone weary, complex operations bothered him not a whit. It was creative thought that had become hard; that, and judgment. And he had Jimenez to help with judgment.

Looking to his right, Carrera saw that the heavily laden Cazadors were struggling into the Nabakovs' cargo bays, one man above pulling while two below pushed to get them up on the ramps.

There hadn't been time to get rough terrain jump suits for the Cazadors. Instead, they'd made their own, after a fashion, using duct tape to attach wooden leg braces and substantial foam padding. If they normally looked like waddling ducks before a jump, now they looked like children so insulated from winter cold they could barely move.

Even over the roar of engines, one could make out the singing as the men loaded aboard:

> *Thundering motors leave each man alone.*
> *He thinks one more time of his loved*
>   *ones back home.*
> *Then come mis compadres to spring on*
>   *command*
> *To jump and to die for our legion and*
>   *land.*
> *And from our airplanes, and from our*
>   *airplanes,*
> Compadre *there's no going back,*
> *Except in victory or fee-eet first.*
> *Now make ready to jump. Attack!*

The speaker radio in the control tower crackled. "Checkpoint Zulu Omega." That meant that Jimenez and the Scouts had sent the burst signal that they were at the bridge that served as the checkpoint for "two hours out." That was also where the cavalry would link up with them.

With a head motion to beckon his radio operators, Carrera left the control tower, passed quietly through the crowded command post below, and walked out to board the waiting Cricket.

Pickup Zone Papa Echo, Pashtia, 12/8/469 AC

"Incoming aircraft, Centurion!"

Hurriedly Cruz closed his wallet to put away the picture of his wife and children. *I've done this before; I can do it again.*

"Stand by your loads," he shouted to the mortar men who were already standing by. "Guide parties, assume guidance as soon as you have a bird."

Because they were under radio silence, the detailed operational control was a bit odd. There was a cross marked out off to one side of the PZ. The lead helicopter made for that, followed by another dozen in trail behind it. When the lead was about forty meters out it stopped and assumed a hover. The first of the guides stood up and pointed directly at himself and then at the helicopter pilot, who nodded his recognition. Then the guide made the hand and arm signal for "assuming guidance," two arms with flattened palms thrust straight up and parallel to each other, palms inward. He lowered his arms, turned, and began to run toward the first load. The helicopter followed slowly.

At that first load the guide turned and again made the "assuming guidance" signal. With more hand and arm signals he brought the IM-71 down to a soft landing. Immediately the clamshell door on the back opened up. A second helicopter was just setting down as this happened.

It was no easy matter for eight men to manhandle a 160mm mortar across rough ground and into the helicopter's cargo bay. Cruz had detached a couple of men from his platoon to assist with each. This was barely enough. Indeed, it might have proven impossible but for the fact that over the last ten years there had been plenty of opportunity to practice.

Once the heavy mortar and its eight crewmen, to which could be added one or two men from the mortar maniple headquarters, were aboard, the guide again took control of the helicopter, directing the pilot to shift left to where a large bundle of mortar ammunition awaited, the ammunition being bound up in a cargo net. As soon as the chopper was directly over the net, the guide thrust both arms directly out to his sides, parallel to the ground: "Hover."

Underneath, one of the two men who had assisted in loading the gun climbed atop the ammunition. In his hand he held a plastic handled screwdriver from which wire led downward. That wire was connected to another screwdriver, stuck into the ground a few feet away. Electricity arced from the hook underneath the helicopter to screwdriver. The wire carried the static charge to the ground, harmlessly. Then the legionary picked up a "donut roll"—a multi-layer thick circle of strap material, held together by a metal shackle—and attempted to slip it onto the hook. He missed. He tried and missed again. Cursing, on the third try he caught the shifting hook and pulled back on the donut roll to make sure it was firmly attached and the hook working properly. He jumped off of the ammunition and gave a thumbs-up to the guide.

The guide then whirled one arm over his head and

pointed into the direction of the wind. With a sound of straining engines, the helicopter lifted up, shuddered a bit at the load once the straps connecting the donut roll and the ammunition pallet lost their slack, then pulled the net off of the ground and began to move forward, gaining altitude and leaving a whirlwind of dust, rocks and vegetation behind.

The Base, Kashmir Tribal Trust Territories, 12/8/469 AC

Dust spurted from each of the wheels as the column moved up the winding pass. Some had broken down on the way and been abandoned, their passengers' cargo being stuffed into the other vehicles as time and space permitted. Cavalry rode to either side with Cano on the left and his brother-in-law, Rachman, leading the right. For this mission, both for her own safety and the intelligence insight she could provide, Alena was back at the Camp San Lorenzo.

Jimenez, riding in front with Masood, recognized from aerial photographs taken by the RPVs of the legion the steep sided pass that led into the enemy fortress.

The trucks and buses were adorned with white banners painted in black and green. "There is no God but God," said some. "Mohammad is the Prophet of God," proclaimed others. More than a few carried the message, "The sword is the key to Heaven and Hell." Still others proclaimed, "Death to the infidel."

"The horns, do you think?" asked Jimenez. "Really? Isn't that overkill?"

Masood shook his head in the negative. "If we

were what we proclaim ourselves to be, we would announce our presence among friends fearlessly. That means, yes, sir, the horns and the cavalry firing their rifles into the air."

Swallowing, Jimenez then said, "The horns then. Let them know we're coming so they won't guess who we are."

INTERLUDE

4 July, 2206, Cygnus House, Chelsea, London, European Governing Region, Earth

It had once been something of a day of mourning, in London, the anniversary of the Declaration that had utterly screwed up the proper ordering of the world. It was a happy day, now. And why not? The United States of America had ceased to be decades prior. It was now split among four governing regions, each with its own UE-appointed archduke to rule them. The world celebrated the Fourth of July now in memory of what *wasn't*.

Lucretia seemed to her father even more jubilant than the day called for.

Louis Arbeit, the marquis, had barely aged in all those years since he'd first assumed the mantle of leadership for Amnesty, Interplanetary. He'd spent those years well, moving the company from the relatively unremunerative harassment of unfriendly governments to more solid, sounder, and infinitely more profitable business arrangements. If there were political prisoners languishing in prisons and psychiatric facilities now, and there were, they were unenlightened, antiprogressive opponents of the UE. Amnesty had no interest in such.

One would hardly know that Lucretia was, herself, well along in years. She, too, had had the best antiagathics available. She could, and did, pass for twenty-two or -three, regularly. She bounced out to her father's favorite patio, bearing with her their morning coffee. The coffee came from the highlands of Panama where High Judge Nyere maintained extensive holdings farmed by the serfs that had been made of the locals. That land included what had once been the ranch of Belisario Carrera. It was worked by, among others, Belisario's collateral descendants, laboring under the lash.

"I made it especially for you, Father," Lucretia announced. They were still a very close family, even though Louis had stopped fucking his daughter decades ago.

He smiled, picked up and sipped at the coffee. *Ah, just right.*

Lucretia's lips smiled around her own cup. She, too, sipped, then said, "The world really is wonderful now, for people of our class, isn't it, Father?"

"Well . . . of course," Louis agreed.

"It's not so wonderful for people of my generation though," she said. "We have to wait and wait and . . ."

"We've had this conversation before, Lucretia. You'll just have to wait until . . ."

"No, I won't, Father," the daughter said. "I'm glad you like your coffee."

It was at about that time that the marquis of Amnesty noticed that his vision had become very narrow, and that his hand trembled as he lifted the cup back to his lips.

CHAPTER TWENTY-THREE

De l'audace, encore de l'audace,
toujours de l'audace.
> —Napoleon, quoting
> Georges Jacques Danton

Cricket 4-15, 12/8/469 AC

The scout plane carrying Carrera and his small party
flew alone. Above it, the thundering transports, gunships, and attack aircraft moved in formation. Below,
flights of helicopters, some the huge IM-62s, ferried
men, supplies and equipment forward.

Carrera's mind wandered a bit, as it sometimes
did these days. He thought of his original group and
where they were now. Most were still with the legions
in one capacity or another. Kennison had left when
his term was up and, sorry though he'd been to see
him go, Carrera had understood. Soult and Mitchell
were warrants now, teaching on the *Isla Real*. *Well,
they'd gotten a little too old and senior to carry my
radios but . . . I do miss not having those boys here
with me.* Daugher and Bowman had been killed, in
different actions. They'd died as they'd liked to live,

fighting to the end. Tom Christian had taken a second retirement and then immediately gone to work for the legions as a civilian. *Greedy bastard,* Carrera thought, smiling slightly. All the others were still on the job, most of them in uniform back on the *Isla Real.* Parilla was president of the rump of the Republic.

In the Cricket, Carrera used half his attention to keep a mental tally of where everyone *should* be, modified by the rarely broadcast code word for a delay or advance in the schedule.

Just shy of the Kashmiri border the Cricket dropped down behind some mountains and began to circle. A dozen helicopters passed, turned a few miles to the north, and began to set down their loads on a barren and fairly flat hilltop.

1st Maniple (Heavy Mortar), Artillery Cohort, in firing position. Check.

UEPF Spirit of Peace, 12/8/469 AC

Wallenstein sat her command chair on the ship's bridge fuming. It wasn't enough that she'd sold her soul to Robinson in exchange for a jump in caste. No, that price might have been worth it. But to be cheated out of her price? There was a reason that people used to say "Hell hath no fury . . ."

"Captain, we've got a lot of Novan air traffic near where the admiral set down," announced one of the lower caste sensor operators, turning away from his console to face his captain.

"Identification?" she asked.

The intelligence officer piped in half a second later. "Almost total radio silence, Captain. Based on flight paths I'm pretty sure they're coming from the mercenary base near Jalala, Pashtia. Their target looks to be the Salafi base in southern Kashmir."

Oh, my. Wallenstein was never so lovely as when her face lit with a smile. She looked particularly beautiful now. *Revenge will be sweet.*

"Ignore them," she commanded.

"But . . ."

"Ignore them!" she insisted.

"But shouldn't the high admiral be warned?"

"He knows," she lied, forcing her brain to think quickly. "This is just what he's been waiting for. Send to all ships of the Peace Fleet to cut off all communication except with this ship. Now."

The Base, Kashmir Tribal Trust Territories, 12/8/469 AC

If the sight of a large column of vehicles carrying armed men and blaring their horns was a shock to the leader of the guards at the pass, he failed to show it. He did raise an arm to halt the lead vehicle.

Masood had the right look and the right accent. Shorn of his uniform, he stood up in the lead vehicle, one hand resting lightly on a machine gun mounted to the roll bar. *"Allahu Akbar!"* He called to the sentry leader at the western entrance to the fortress valley. "We have come to join you in the fight against the infidel crusaders. Rejoice, brothers!"

The leader had had no word of any large group of reinforcements coming. On the other hand, they hadn't been told *not* to expect any. And, in the closed world of the Salafis and the Yithrabi culture from which they sprang, information was power. It was always hoarded, rarely fully revealed. There really wasn't anything inherently suspicious about a column of armed men who looked the part showing up and requesting to join the struggle. This one was a little large, to be sure, but hadn't Mustafa promised them all a growing force in their struggle against the infidel? Apparently he hadn't been lying.

The sentries waved the column through while the men riding the vehicles stood and cheered. To the flanks, cavalrymen fired standard Samsonovs into the air with the gleeful abandon of schoolboys. Soon enough, the entire camp was cheering while men and women emerged from caves and tents to add their voices and the rattle of their rifles to the air.

Jimenez, face nearly covered, looked out the side of the cross-country sedan as it made a turn into an open area at the base of the central massif. He noticed a large cave with a camouflage net over it. His eyes lit upon five rough crosses erected in the open area. Children played at the foot of the crosses. Men, or what was left of them, hung stiff and dead above the children, one of whom poked at a body with a stick. Still in their legionary battle dress trousers, but stripped of all other equipment and adornment, Jimenez recognized the remnants of the lost Cazador team.

You are going to pay for that . . . with usury.

And then he saw a head move.

Sergeant Sevilla heard the blaring of the column as though through a series of baffles. His grip of reality was quite poor by this point. He head was filled with rushing noises and his eyes went into and out of focus regularly. With a bit of the little strength remaining to him he forced his chin off of his chest and his head up enough to see.

More of the bastards come to gloat and jeer? May they burn in Hell.

Jimenez, riding in the back next to Masood, stood up and whispered, "One of our men, over there on those crosses . . . he's still alive."

Masood looked himself and saw that this was true. Hand still resting on his machine gun, Masood asked, "What do you want to do, sir?"

Jimenez asked himself, *If we warn only the vehicle leaders and just we and they open fire on that mass will the rest of the scouts catch on quickly enough? It wasn't in the plan but . . . God . . . what a target! Worth the chance. And then . . . those are our men.*

Sitting back down Jimenez keyed the mike that led to the small, short-range radios carried by each of the leaders. "On my command, I want you to blast that crowd. Try to hit only armed men . . . but don't be a fanatic about it."

Masood, who like the others heard from an earpiece stuck in one ear, looked down at Jimenez and raised one eyebrow. *You sure about this?*

Jimenez's eyes narrowed as he gave an affirmative nod. *Oh, yes, I'm sure.*

So be it. Smiling still, Masood waved his right hand, genially, acknowledging the cheers of the mujahadin and their families. The welcoming rifle fire dropped gradually as magazines were emptied. When, like a bag of almost completely microwaved popcorn, the firing had dropped to no more than an occasional pop Masood threw his head back and laughed heroically.

"In . . . three . . . two . . . one . . . FIRE!" Jimenez ordered.

The *subadar* lifted his machine gun off the roll bar, grasped it with both hands, swung it to the right to face the crowd, slammed the butt into his shoulder and pulled the trigger.

The gun was a typical Volgan model, not the newer M-26 used by the legion. This was no problem; the slower rate of fire was more than enough for such a tightly packed crowd. Cheers turned to screams of pain and dismay as Masood and a couple of dozen others swept their weapons across the crowd on both sides. The fire laid them out in windrows, cutting them down like wheat being harvested.

There were probably children in there and certainly there were women. Whatever they were, they were simply targets as the guns bowled them over.

The scouts were no slouches. Already somewhat hyped up on adrenaline, it took a mere fraction of a second for them to join their fire to the *subadar's*. Their fire lashed out into the crowd cutting down the Salafis by the hundreds. The rest ran screaming to either side, bullets in the back dropping many of them dead or screaming in pain. Mothers ran frantically to and fro trying to find children to carry to safety. The Pashtun didn't deliberately target these. Avoiding them, however, was not always possible or practical.

The Salafis returned fire, some of them. But with the confusion, the shock, and the jostling by the panic-stricken, their fire was to little effect.

Jimenez was shocked as well, half at the destruction

and half at the surprise. Leaning forward he tapped the driver, hard, on the back of the head. "Ram that central cross," he shouted. Even as he did, the cavalry—*That kid Cano is quick on the uptake, isn't he?*—began racing for the entrances to the fortress valley, Cano's men going straight ahead while Rachman's peeled off and wheeled to the rear.

Life for the crucified rarely contains any humor. Nonetheless, when he saw the fire lance out from the vehicles, Sevilla began to laugh and curse hysterically. "Die you bastards, you motherfuckers . . . hahaha . . . scream and fucking bleed, you pigfuckers."

Like some of the others, Bashir had dropped to the ground as soon as the firing from the newly arrived vehicles began. He had only a pickax in his hands anyway. This, the absence of a firearm, might have been what spared him.

Lying under the fire, Bashir twisted his head. He was surprised to see one lone sedan speed off to ram one of the crosses, eliciting a scream from the crucified man that rose even over the roar of gunfire.

They couldn't be here just to save those men . . . that man. But they intend to, even so.

Whispering, "Allah give me strength," Bashir raised the pickax, head first, to show he was unarmed. Then, when no bullets struck it, he stood erect and reversed his grip.

Still unstruck, though bullets flew all around him scything down the fleeing crowd, he began slowly to walk toward the crosses. His speed picked up as he neared them. Bashir arrived and the cross tumbled over onto its back at almost exactly the same moment.

He immediately shouted the only name he knew among the men of the legion—"Fernandez! Fernandez! Fernandez!"—then began trying to pry the spikes that went through the Sevilla's heels.

The heel spikes came out fairly easily. Both ankles were free of the cross by the time Masood joined Bashir.

"How the fuck do you know Fernandez?"

"He sent me here! Now help me get the arms free!"

The arms were tougher; the spikes had been driven farther into the wood. Still, with two men straining on the pickax handle, they came free quickly enough.

While Masood and this new convert tried to save his man from the cross, Jimenez turned the other way and walked the line of vehicles

"Up the hill! Up the hill," he screamed over the sound of the rifles. No one paid him any mind until he began walking the passageway in the bus, forcing the men to cease fire and begin to dismount. Some kept up the fire while others crawled out the left side windows or risked exposure in leaving by the door.

The trucks had less problem. From those the scouts merely grabbed a pack, their own or someone else's, jumped over the side and began to run to surmount the looming massif above. For the four-wheel-drive vehicles there was even less problem. Some of these turned left and drove at least as far as the stream at the base of the massif before dismounting. Within a couple of minutes of opening fire there was a flood of Pashtun Scouts splashing through the waist-deep stream or surging upward.

Jimenez walked the line under cover of the vehicles,

making sure the men forgot the easy targets and remembered the mission. He went first to the tail of the column, shouting and pointing, then turned around and reversed his steps.

He met Masood where he had left him, by the crucifixion site. A medic from the Scouts was already working on the saved man, who announced, repeatedly and heartbreakingly, "Sevilla, Juan B., Sergeant, *Legion del Cid*, Cazador Tercio, Serial Number Two-Seven-Zero . . . Sevilla, Juan B. . . ." The blood encrusted, oozing holes from the spikes showed on both of the sergeant's wrists and heels.

"Who is this?" Jimenez asked, pointing at Bashir.

"Fernandez's spy. And he's got a story."

"Story?"

"There's a cave over there," Masood answered. "He says we need to look in it." To Bashir he said, "Get this man to safety."

"Let's hurry then." The party of three, including the driver, trotted over to the cave. Bashir picked Sevilla up, slung him across his shoulders and headed up the mountain in the wake of the Scouts. He thought he would be less likely to be shot that way.

A bullet rang out from inside the cave as soon as the camouflage curtain moved slightly. It sounded strange, nothing like the twenty-two- to thirty-caliber favored on most of Terra Nova. Jimenez and Masood immediately fell to the ground and fired several long bursts into the cavern until they were rewarded with a scream.

When they did go past the curtain it was to see one man, uniformed, bleeding on the rocky floor and . . .

"Holy shit!" Jimenez was stunned. "The fucking

UE is here? I knew we had enemies in high places but this . . ."

The hatch to the UE shuttle was open, its integral flight of steps lowered. They looked inside and saw nothing. Then they pulled open the cargo bay doors and . . .

Jimenez ran outside, pulling a small but extremely powerful radio from his belt as he did so. "Patricio? Goddammit, Patricio, fuck radio silence. Get on the horn, goddammit!"

"Carrera," crackled back.

"Come quick, *compadre*. Come really quick. Don't spare the horses. Accept *any* level of casualties. There are eleven, I say again, *fucking eleven,* nuclear weapons here. Oh, and a United Earth transport but we machine gunned the shit out of it."

"What the—"

"Just trust me. Come a runnin'."

Cricket 4-15, 12/8/469 AC

Eleven nukes? Good God. I didn't need my little play after all.

While he was thinking this, Jimenez came back on the radio. He sounded slightly out of breath as he said, "We found our lost Cazador squad . . . *huff* . . . *huff* . . . *huff*. They were crucified. We saved one . . . *huff* . . . *huff* . . . *huff*. To do that we had to shoot up a substantial crowd . . . *huff* . . . *huff* . . . *huff*."

Jimenez continued explaining. "We really had no choice . . . But there's two effects of that . . . *huff* . . . *huff* . . . *huff*. One is that we're trying to unfuck things on top of the central hill. We got pretty disorganized in the scramble . . . *huff* . . . *huff*. The other is that the north side of the base has *got* to be weaker now. The scouts killed hundreds of men of fighting age on that side when they opened up."

"You're assuming they assembled from where they were camped, and camped on the side they were to defend, right? Makes perfect sense. Let me think on it. Yeah, despite the confusion, it may make sense to switch the side for the main effort."

"Don't think too long, Patricio. There are maybe five hundred and fifty or so of us on this hill, plus a couple of hundred cavalry blocking the entrances, and we're surrounded by thousands of the bastards."

Loud and clear over the radio came the rattling sound of incoming mortar fire, somewhere close to wherever Jimenez was.

"Roger. Artillery priority, minus the rocket launchers, is yours. Twenty-four 155mm are in range and ready. Twenty-four 160mm will be ready to fire . . . in . . ." Carrera looked up at a chart and then to a clock . . . "about seventeen minutes. Air support priority is yours. Expect nine sorties of Turbo-Finches to arrive in a few minutes followed by two more every ten minutes for the immediate future. Also three ANA-23 gunships on station continuously as per the plan. I'll be overhead in a few. Over."

"Roger," Jimenez answered. "Air and arty . . . *huff* . . . priority to me."

"Yes . . . and the Cazadors should be jumping right about . . . now. Carrera, out."

I intended to bring in one nuke as a cover and an excuse. Instead we find another eleven. Do I send that one back? No . . . I might have to blow that entire

*mountain to shit and I can't be sure of being able to
set off the captured ones. It stays in the plan . . .
for now.*

The Base, Kashmir Tribal Trust Territories, 12/8/469 AC

While *Subadar* Masood and the other leaders tried to
bring order out of chaos, Jimenez scanned the skies.
Thin antiaircraft fire was rising from the surrounding
hills, thin mostly because the bulk of the 14.5 and
23mm weapons had already been overrun with the
central massif. Even now, small arms fire was breaking
out all over the massif as Salafi air defense gunners
struggled to fight their way to their guns.

The air over the other side of one of the surrounding ridges suddenly lit up in a ball of orange
flame. That was a Finch-dropped thermobaric bomb,
intended to make as sure as possible that the jumping Cazadors weren't shot to bits on the way down.
Nothing was likely to survive such a blast, even
should the targets be bunkered in. More such blasts
followed the first.

A twin series of *pops*, one from the east, one from
the west, grabbed Jimenez's attention. He'd heard the
sound before. It was the small charge that caused the
heavy rockets, fired from almost fifty miles back, to
dispense their cargo; in this case, mixed anti-personnel
and anti-vehicular mines to help Cano's cavalry seal
off both of the entrances to the valley.

And then the small pops of the mines being laid
were lost amidst the tremendous roar of thermobaric
bombs dropped from the ANA-23 gunships. These

smashed up every known and suspected air defense position on the hills ringing the valley fortress.

The angle of the view over the ridges to the south was such that Jimenez had only the briefest glimpse of dark dots descending from the low-flying Nabakovs before they were lost to sight. He knew the men were jumping without reserve 'chutes and from a height of a mere four hundred and fifty to five hundred feet over the ground. They'd have jumped lower still except that the irregular terrain meant that while some would jump at four-fifty, others would touch down hard from as little as two hundred and fifty feet.

Deep below, in a conference room not far from where Mustafa had interviewed Bashir, the men and serving women felt and heard nothing of the turmoil above until a breathless Abdul Aziz burst in to make the announcement.

"Sirs . . . we're . . . we are *attacked*! The infidels already hold the ground above us. Their paratroopers are descending all around to seal off the base."

"What?" Mustafa asked. "How . . . ?"

"I don't know . . . panicked rumors only. Some say that a column came in pretending to be reinforcements and just opened up on our people."

Robinson turned instantly white. "The special weapons . . ."

"Damn your 'special weapons,' you infidel bastard," Mustafa snarled. "That's probably what the pigs came for."

"I've got to get to my shuttle," the high admiral insisted. "If they find those nukes we're all screwed."

Peshtwa, Kashmir, 12/8/469 AC

The office was . . . *Tasteful,* Siegel thought, looking about with approval. It was *Anglian* tasteful. There was no gilt, no tacky decorations, just simple and elegant wood with a mix of Kashmiri and Tauran art on the walls and a beautiful series of rugs covering the floor.

Siegel stood beside the ambassador from Pashtia to Kashmir. The ambassador, underpaid and, being out of the country, without any serious opportunity for graft, had jumped at the one hundred thousand drachma offered to set up this meeting. Siegel was reasonably certain that he'd have gone for less but it wasn't like he was spending his own money.

"Mr. President," Siegel apologized, "there really was no choice. You know you don't control the Tribal Trust Territories and you know that the Salafis have a major base there. We know, and we would have thought your Central Intelligence Directorate would have told you, that a nuclear weapon is coming in, possibly more than one. My principal has begun an attack by ground and air to seize that weapon or those weapons with—I hasten to add—the full backing and support of the Federated States. You can try to resist, and get in a war with the FSC or you can do the smart thing and announce that this operation is entirely with your approval. One way makes you look weak and foolish, especially when your air force goes down in flames. The other makes you look strong and decisive."

The president, Baraka, short and dark, listened attentively. His face showed only a trace of hostility. After all, what this emissary-without-portfolio said was true enough. He didn't have control of CID. He didn't have control of the Tribal Trust areas. And it was entirely conceivable, even probable, that the Salafi base could be about to play host to one or a number of nuclear weapons. It was even possible that the weapon was coming from his own country's stockpiles.

He still didn't have to like it.

Siegel understood perfectly well. To the ambassador who had accompanied him to the meeting he said, "Would you leave us for a moment, sir?"

"I am further authorized, Mr. President," he said, once the door had closed behind the ambassador, "to offer you and your family sanctuary for life, in the Republic of Balboa and to . . ." he dug into an inside pocket of his coat and withdrew a small red booklet . . . "to offer you a substantial guaranteed honorarium if you cooperate in this."

He handed the booklet over to Baraka who opened it and read without comment. Finished reading, the president placed the booklet in a desk drawer and sat, silently, for a few minutes.

"What's Balboa like, Mr. Siegel?" he asked.

"Wonderful place, Mr. President," Sig answered. "Warm though a bit wet, rather like here. Clean. Beautiful women. Low cost of living. Best of all, sir, it's very secure."

Baraka slowly nodded before reaching out one finger to an intercom. "Achmed, call the General Staff duty officer. I want every plane in the Air Force grounded. Further, I want the Army's regiments in the posts bordering the tribal lands to the south confined to barracks. Lastly, set me up a press conference for noon, to be held here."

Already he felt the vultures circling. *The important thing*, the president knew, *isn't whether or not our borders have been violated. The important thing is that I act like I am confidently in charge.*

The Base, Kashmir Tribal Trust Territories, 12/8/469 AC

Mustafa felt his confidence wilting like a desert flower— quickly and completely. His closest followers sat stunned. *This* was not supposed to happen, not here, not in the sanctuary that God, in the form of the Kashmiri government's inability to control their southern border, had ordained.

Stunned transformed to horrified when another messenger burst in saying, "The stinking President of Kashmir has come on the television. He says that the attack is with his permission. He says his air force is staying out of it only due to incompatibility between the FSC's Air Force and Kashmir's. We'll get no aid from that quarter."

Was it the nukes that brought them here? Mustafa wondered dully. *But then, how could they know? I told no one but Abdul Aziz and Nur al Deen. They wouldn't tell any one. They are the most faithful of the faithful. Robinson couldn't have told. If he had, he'd have been out of here last night. Sometimes it makes me wonder whose side God is on.*

"What are we to do, Mustafa?" al Deen asked.

"Fight," Mustafa answered, fatalistically. "What else can we do? But," his eyes fixed on Nur al Deen, "begin collecting the cadres, the most important ones, and the families. We may lose here, but that will only be

Allah's test of our faith. If we can get the key people out," his finger pointed, "along with that one weapon, we can continue the struggle."

"I'll send an advance party out now," Nur al Deen said, "to gather some of our followers further north, their vehicles and animals, to provide us a cover when we emerge."

"Excellent, my friend, except . . ." Mustafa looked at the bomb. "Not to the north. We'll take the southern route. And we will prevail yet."

Camp San Lorenzo, Jalala Province, Pashtia, 12/8/469 AC

"What is it, Alena?" Fernandez asked. "Worried for your brother and your husband?"

"I am," the girl admitted. "But that's not it. I am missing something and I don't have a clue of what."

"Maybe it's only nerves."

"No," Alena insisted. "I know nerves and I know when there's a truth staring at me from nose length away. This is the latter. *Why* can't I *see* it?"

To that Fernandez had no answer. He operated off of hard evidence, not the half mystical insights of this Pashtian witch-girl, however damnably effective those insights might sometimes be.

His father had told him to pack his rucksack—and little Hamilcar was very proud that he'd been issued the very same model the legionaries carried—and to report to Fernandez. He'd packed himself, though his father's driver had taken him to Fernandez's office in the main headquarters building. Gaining entrance was no problem; the troops were used to Ham having the run of the place.

Besides, he knew better than to ever mention a word of what went on there, not even in the thrice weekly electronic letters his father insisted he send to his mother.

Alena heard a small sound, something like an over-sized mouse scurrying, and looked towards it. A small boy, bowed under the weight of a rucksack bigger than he was, staggered and stumbled towards Fernandez. She started to smile and then looked again at the boy's face. She'd seen that face before . . . somewhere . . .

"Iskander, our Lord," she whispered, before dropping to her knees and placing her face and palms to the floor.

The Base, Kashmir Tribal Trust Territories, 12/8/496 AC

Jimenez lay beside a Pashtun Scout bearing a laser designator. He pointed at a stream of tracers rising to the sky. The tracers chased behind a Turbo-Finch, just pulling up and away from a strafing run. *Almost* they closed the gap before the Finch pulled away.

"Bring fire down on that," Jimenez ordered the scout. "Right at the base. Pulverize it."

"Yes, sir," the scout answered, aiming his designator at the target while another man on a radio called the artillery for supporting fires.

Jimenez crouched above the military crest. He was in plain view of hundreds of Salafis on the surrounding hills, but out of their range. For the enemy that were in range, he had the mass of the crest for cover. Even so, bullets from below struck the trees and branches above him steadily, sprinkling him with bits of wood and bark they had chewed off.

Crouching lower still Jimenez moved closer to the crest where the Scouts had set out a perimeter and were battling fiercely to keep the huge numbers of charging and firing Salafis at bay. As he got closer still he went to his belly to crawl forward. *A commander has to see the action; not just rely on reports of others to guide him.*

He crawled, he lay, he saw, he thought, *Holy shit.*

The hill sides and valley floor below were crawling with the enemy.

"Good fighting," Masood announced, approvingly, as he flopped down next to Jimenez.

"Maybe too much of a good thing," Jimenez answered with a smile.

Despite a pretty severe case of nerves, and the incessant shaking of the helicopter, Cruz forced a smile to his face. There was a lot of acting involved in combat leadership and he'd been to some of the best training for actors available. What, after all, was Cazador School except some hundreds of men in utter misery pretending that they *liked* it?

The helicopter would have been a little bit overstuffed if it had borne, as it was designed to, Taurans or Volgans. For the smaller and slighter Balboans who made up the bulk of the legion it was possible to cram several more, sometimes *many* more, troopers than the design had called for.

In this case, with forty-seven men of his own platoon,

a two-man and one-scout dog team, another two forward observers, the one platoon medic, a piper and Majeed, twelve men sat each side of the two helicopters carrying Cruz's platoon, and three more on each of the cargo bays' floors. The dog, tongue lolling, sat in the middle of Cruz's.

Cruz's smile almost disappeared as the helicopter crested the high ridge to the south of the target and began a rapid descent to the valley floor outside the fortress.

I fucking hate elevators.

He had a bad, heart-pounding moment when a stream of tracers passed by, visible from the passenger compartment through the pilots' windscreen. The tracers stopped abruptly mere moments before the IM-71 would have been forced to pass through them. Flying in tight formation going around the fire might have been worse than flying right through it.

Better to lose a couple of men to antiaircraft fire than all of two birds to a crash.

Again, like an elevator, the chopper stopped descending and pulled up suddenly to gain a little more altitude. Cruz's stomach sank sickeningly. It did so again as the pilot made some turns to bring the bird around to the north side of the target. Then, once again, the chopper rose rapidly.

"Two miinnuuttee," the crew chief announced, holding up two fingers and showing them to the men lining both sides of the compartment. The infantrymen in the back immediately began making last minute adjustments to their load-bearing equipment and *loricae*.

That "two minutes" was all the warning the crew chief would be able to give, Cruz knew, as the aviator turned his complete attention to the machine gun mounted on one side. This he began to fire in long bursts to the left front as the bird climbed up the side of a ridge. A bag caught the crew chief's hot, expended shell casings as they flew out the side of the gun in a steady stream.

Bad sign, Cruz thought. *Very damned bad.*

Noorzad had, he thought, no good choices. He'd lost over a third of his men just to the sudden surprise fire when the column of light trucks and buses had opened up. He'd lost some more from the aerial attack and the artillery and mortar bombardment. He thought he might have as many as fifty men left, possibly a few less.

Forget the surrounding ridges and join the attack to free Mustafa's hill? He wondered. *No . . . a few more guns there won't help much. Better to stay here and hold the ridges as long as possible, take as many with us as possible.*

There was an air defense gun, a twin 23mm job, not far from Noorzad. The crew were dead around it but, in one of those peculiar effects of large explosions, and especially thermobaric ones, the gun itself was still standing and looked fine.

"Come . . . come!" Noorzad shouted to four of his followers. Not looking to see if they followed, he raced on foot to the gun. A quick visual examination showed the gun was loaded. There was a crude metal chair to sit on and what seemed to be a sight. At least there was an assemblage that, lined up with a seated gunner's head, would define a line roughly parallel to the twin barrels.

Noorzad sat down in the chair and confirmed that the projection ahead of him *was* a gun sight. An experimental press of each of the foot pedals swung the gun left and right. He tugged on the handles and the gun's muzzles raised up. When he pushed them forward the elevation dropped.

This took mere moments. By the time his men joined him Noorzad was lining the sight up on the leading of two approaching helicopters. He thought he knew enough to lead, but he overestimated how much was required. When the firing studs were pressed, the twin cannon spit out their sixty shells in a few seconds. The electronically fired gun clicked on empty as Noorzad ran out of ammunition. That was just before the helicopter would have crossed the path of the shells.

"Get *more*!" he shouted to his men. "More shells."

The unfamiliar flexible belts of cannon cartridges, sixty per belt, caused some problem as the men tried to control them and feed them into the ammunition slots. By the time he was ready to fire again, Noorzad saw that the helicopter was on the ground with dozens of armed and armored men spilling out of it and the others that had accompanied it. The dozens became hundreds as more helicopters touched down. *Crap.*

Well . . . if I can't kill enough of the infidel infantry I can kill their helicopter.

Cruz was, per doctrine, the first man out. He stood at the edge of the rear door cursing and hustling his men off the helicopter, directing their leaders where he wanted them placed. A piper automatically took a position by the centurion's side and began playing the First Tercio's own theme, "Boinas Azules Cruzan la Frontera."

"Sergeant Avila," Cruz shouted over the helicopters and the pipes, pointing, "I want your squad there, from ten o'clock to two o'clock." Then he turned his attention back towards the inside of the just-lifting helicopter and saw the left-side wall began to disintegrate in his field of view. The crew chief, still gamely firing his machine gun, was hit by something that exploded, tearing his upper torso from his lower body at the waist and flinging the chief's remains to the right side of the compartment. Cruz had the briefest glimpse of one of the pilots being thrown across the cockpit onto the other.

Smelling aviation fuel and seeing sparks and smoke, Cruz turned to throw himself away from the bird. From behind came a loud *whoosh* as the fuel caught fire, exploded, and knocked Cruz and the piper, faces first, to the dirt.

Seeing that someone was at least trying to do *something*, more men, not all of them Noorzad's, rushed to reinforce the gun position. The column of smoke served as their orientation mark.

Noorzad and his men cheered when the helicopter began first to smoke and then to burst into flame. They saw what Cruz could not. One of the two pilots, trapped by flame behind him, tried to force his way through the strong plexiglas of the windscreen as fire rose all around.

Noorzad would cherish the open-mouthed agony writ on that pilot's face for the rest of his life.

✧　　✧　　✧

Cruz and his men were shocked, yes, by the destruction of the helicopter and crew that had bravely brought them in. More than shocked though, they were deeply angered. A red mist descended across the centurion's vision.

"Fix bayonets, you bastards," Cruz called out, as he affixed his own. "Play, you son of a bitch," he cursed at the shocked piper.

"Fix bayonets" usually meant a wild screaming charge with blood in your eye. It was not precisely a favored tactic in the legion but this was a special case, a situation where time was more valuable than lives because it *meant* lives. The men of the platoon knew that. Even so they looked at their young centurion as if he were insane.

"Fix BAYONETS!" Cruz repeated, as loudly as possible. This time the men knew he was serious. They reached to their belts and, still prone on the ground, pulled out the shiny blades (for the legion knew that a bayonet was a weapon of terror and that, thus, shinier was better) and attached them to the muzzles of their rifles, jiggling the bayonets to make sure of a secure fix.

"Now . . . you sonsabitches . . . FOLLOW MEEE. . . ."

Looking out the right side window of his Cricket, Carrera saw one of his valuable IM-71s suddenly caught by heavy fire as it tried to lift off after landing its troops. He cursed as the chopper abruptly settled back to earth and began to pour out first smoke, then fire.

His first instinct, born of hate and rage, was to bring a cohort's worth of artillery down on the gun that had just slaughtered his men. He was just starting to pick up a microphone to do that when he saw a rare thing, a remarkable thing. What looked like about fifty men were streaming towards the enemy air defense gun in a single mad rush. Sunlight glinting upward told that those men had their bayonets fixed.

Racing forward in the lead, Cruz saw the enemy heavy gun fire a brief burst. The passage of the shells created a palpable shock wave around him. No matter, possessed by battle madness he continued his charge, screaming like a demon and firing from the hip.

Nearby, charging forward with fangs bared, the platoon's attached scout dog began to howl: *ahwoooo. My pack is the greatest.*

A bullet struck one of the glassy metal chest plates of Cruz's *lorica* and bounced off, singing. With the angle of the strike and of his body, it shocked and slowed him but it didn't stop him.

Wild-eyed Salafis arose from the ground. Some were cut down by the legionaries' fire but others closed. Cruz put two three-round bursts of 6.5mm into the body of one, half emulsifying his target's innards. Wheeling to face another, this one thrusting forward a fixed bayonet, Cruz tapped the enemy rifle aside and lunged to plunge his own bayonet into the enemy's throat. Dropping his rifle to clutch at his wound, eyes rolling up in his head as blood rushed out to spatter on the ground, this Salafi sank to his knees.

Cruz put one booted foot on the Salafi's head and pushed him off of his now red-running bayonet. Again he whirled to face two more charging maniacs. He swung his butt at one and missed, but then stepped forward and reversed the motion to slam the butt into the Salafi's unarmored kidney. That one went down puking with pain. The next one up Cruz shot before spinning to plunge the bayonet into the back of his previous opponent.

"Die, motherfucker," he snarled as the Salafi screamed in agony.

By this time Cruz's men had reached him and joined the fray. The entire hilltop became a mass of lunging, shooting, screaming and dying men. The dog ripped out a Salafi throat, howled again, and bounded off in search of another. *Ahwooo; my pack is the greatest.* Not far behind the piper's playing added to the furious din.

Here the legionaries' superior training and armor—to say nothing of the pooch's—came to the fore. Even at close range, the Salafis couldn't usually get a bullet to penetrate directly from in front, though a number of the Balboans went down with wounds to face, head, limbs and torso sides. Within a few moments, all the Salafis were down and Cruz's men were finishing off the wounded with butt stroke, burst and bloodied bayonet.

There was no time, in a close fight, for the niceties. And men who had failed to surrender by the time the legion closed to three hundred meters had forfeited their right to do so.

Breathing deeply, anger still raging within him, the centurion walked deliberately to where a crusty-looking, one-eyed Salafi struggled to load the light cannon that had smashed and burned the helicopter. Seeing the look in Cruz's eye the Cyclops stopped his efforts and began to raise his hands.

"Fuck you, asshole," Cruz said, as he took aim and triggered a burst into Noorzad's head.

INTERLUDE

4 July, 2206, Cygnus House, Chelsea, London, European Governing Region, Earth

"The marquis is dead; long live the marchioness," Lucretia whispered to herself as the last of the lower class investigating officers departed the mansion. The sun was down and an ambulance had long since carted off her late father's cooling corpse.

As she closed the door behind the police, Class Fours and thus very deferential to the new Marchioness, Lucretia sighed, "Oh, Daddy, and you were such a good lay, too." She sighed, and then burst out laughing, dancing on light feet across the black and white tiled floor of the vestibule.

The police had carted off the bulk of the domestic kitchen staff, of course. They would be incarcerated in Amnesty's own dungeons and rigorously questioned by its own interrogators. *But . . . who cares? Lowers can be bought for a song. Which is a damned good thing because now, with Daddy out of the way, I intend to go through a* lot *of them.*

"Then, too," she said aloud, "perhaps I should buy

a commission in the Peace Forces. I've always fancied
how I'd look in uniform."

Lucretia walked to her father's desk and pressed
a button on the intercom. A face appeared, that of
one of the maids, Emily.

"Yes, mum?"

"I feel like celebrating. Whiskey. Ice."

"Yes, mum."

When the maid arrived, not more than five minutes later, Lucretia waited for her to pour and then
struck her across the face with her riding crop. "You
were too slow."

Weeping, the maid sank to her knees, crying and
covering her bruised face with her hands.

"That's better, Emily. I much prefer you in that
position. But . . . I think you would look even better
with your face to the floor." Arbeit used her dainty
foot to press the maid's head downward.

Lucretia left the girl there, trembling and cowering, and with blood welling from the slash across her
face. The new Marchioness liked that, the image, the
reality, the trembling fear. She picked up the glass of
whiskey and drank deeply.

Lucretia then laughed and started to sing, softly:

"Arise you prisoners of starvation . . ."

CHAPTER TWENTY-FOUR

So farewell hope, and with hope farewell fear,
Farewell remorse; all good to me is lost.
Evil, be thou my good.
—Milton, Paradise Lost

The Base, Kashmir Tribal Trust Territories, 12/8/469 AC

The two infantry cohorts peeled the edges of the fortress, one clearing east, one west. As they did, they made the valley floor below uninhabitable to the Salafis trying desperately to relieve the central massif. As they did, too, it was possible for Jimenez and Masood to shift their own troops away from the cleared portions and concentrate on the sections of the massif still under attack.

It was not possible yet for the Scouts atop the massif to delve into the lower area, the caves and tunnels. It was also, Carrera considered, unwise to pull in the wide-ranging Cazadors and cavalry scouts to assist until the outer valley floors could be cleared in detail.

Still, one part seemed clear enough. He directed his Cricket to land by that part of the massif's base.

❖   ❖   ❖

"Get us the fuck out of here, Martin," Arbeit begged. "I don't want to die here . . . or anywhere."

Robinson ignored her. He needed desperately to call his ship or Atlantis Base. Unfortunately for that, his belt communicator could not penetrate the rock above and getting up to the surface was quite problematic. His allies here held the entrances to the caves, but any attempt to emerge was driven back by a fusillade of fire. Even being near the edges was dangerous as the enemy aircraft could swoop in at any moment to deliver rockets and napalm. Burned and bleeding men were even now being carried deeper below.

"You look worried, infidel," commented Nur al Deen.

"And you're not?" Robinson retorted, then realized the retort was hollow. Nur al Deen did not look worried in the least.

The Salafi smiled. "Not at all. Not only is my faith in Allah limitless, but we have an escape tunnel."

"*What?*"

"An escape tunnel. It leads from under this hill to a main line of the local karez."

"Karez?"

"Yes, karez. They're underground . . . oh, aqueducts I suppose you would call them. About a meter wide, maybe one and a half to two high, deep below the ability of the infidel sensors to reach, and they lead everywhere. There are tens of thousands of kilometers of them in this area. It's a tight fit and, for the tallest among us it will be very uncomfortable to walk so far bent over like old women. Still, we can get out. And we will, while the martyrs above buy us time to escape."

It suddenly hit Robinson, "Those things I thought were lines of bomb craters . . . those are part of the system?"

"Yes," Nur al Deen replied. "There are none for the tunnel that leads from here to the main line. That was deliberate on our part, partly for defense and partly for deception. We are building a fire by the tunnel entrance to draw in fresh air so we can use it. Before, any enemy who tried to would have had to carry their air with them."

Relieved, Robinson ran his hand across his face, then reached into his pocket and pulled out the detonation device. He wasn't necessarily going to be captured or killed after all. "You must take me with you. I still control the nukes," he said. "Only I have the key codes."

"Of course," Nur al Deen agreed, amiably. "Otherwise we'd stake you out for the other infidels now."

Camp San Lorenzo, Jalala Province, Pashtia, 12/8/469 AC

"Karez," Alena said, suddenly, looking up from where she lay in full proskynesis on the floor before a befuddled Hamilcar. I know now. My Lord gave me the insight. Truly he is a God."

"What was that? Karez? And please stand up, girl."

Seeing that Hamilcar did not object, Alena stood and said, "What was bothering me; I know now . . . the karez. You know, the underground aqueducts?"

"What about them?" Fernandez asked.

"I think that if one passes close enough to the enemy base, they will have tunneled to it."

The Base, Kashmir Tribal Trust Territories, 12/8/469 AC

Carrera's Cricket jostled to a rough landing not far from where four crosses still stood. The pilot had a time of it avoiding the mass of vehicles still standing there, some of them burning and smoking, and which had brought in the Scouts. The ground leading from the vehicles was *littered* with corpses.

Carrera sighed, looking at the crosses. *They really did it. I suppose I shouldn't be surprised.* He got on the radio and made a call back to Camp San Lorenzo with a demand for his engineers to make something for him, a lot of somethings, as a matter of fact. Then he exited the aircraft and walked to stand at the base of one of the crosses. This one held the cold, blackened body of a young signifer he had personally commissioned not long before. *I promise you, son, they'll pay with interest.*

A half squad of Pashtun Scouts ran up, their *naik* looking at Carrera so much as if to ask, *Are you insane,* Duque? *This area is not secure.*

As if to punctuate, an almost spent bullet whined in, kicking up dust near Carrera's feet. He ignored it.

"*Naik*, can you lead me up to Jimenez?"

"Yes, sir," the Pashtun answered. "He and the *subadar* sent us. This way please."

"And leave a couple of men to guard my Cricket."

"Yes, sir."

Escorted by his two radiomen, these having pulled the radios out from the Cricket and slung them on their backs, and three of the *naik*'s scouts, Carrera began to mount the steep-sided hill to his front.

✧   ✧   ✧

The way was steep in places. Robinson nearly fell at several points. Torches were an impossibility, the air was barely enough to sustain life. Fortunately, the Salafis had a fair number of chemical light sticks to illuminate the way. Still, the point light sources were few enough that many tripped on loose rocks and slipped on the damp tunnel floor.

The people in the tunnel amounted to perhaps just over five hundred mujahadin, Mustafa's most faithful, a party of them taking turns carrying the litter on which rested the one nuclear weapon they had salvaged. There were also many times that in women and children. These last were not only those who belonged to the core of the faithful, but as many others from those staying behind as could be gathered before the tunnel behind them was deliberately collapsed.

Children cried continuously, the tunnel walls echoing with the annoying sound. This was particularly hard on High Admiral Robinson. His class rarely saw children but for grubby prole brats begging by the side of Old Earth's streets and roads. Their own progeny, few as they were, were invariably given over to lower caste governesses to care for.

"Can't you quiet your brats?" Robinson demanded. Arbeit seconded that.

"We could more easily quiet *you*," Nur al Deen answered over his shoulder. "That; or have you wailing a lot more than the children." The high admiral immediately shut up; possession of the nuke keys might, after all, not be enough to save his life. The Salafis were frequently irrational.

❖   ❖   ❖

The southern, eastern and western "walls" of the enemy fortress were cleared. Still, the Legion and its auxiliaries were shut out from entering the caves and tunnels. The fire from the defenders inside keeping them out was not less than the fire of the attackers outside pinning the Salafis in.

The call had gone out for flammables over and above the flamethrowers carried by the legion's sappers. These had seen their fuel exhausted before the defenders had been much discomforted, so deep were the excavations. Fuel, however, would not be forthcoming for hours.

Some deep excavations could be reached as they were isolated from the central tunnel and cave system. One of these, the largest, contained a UE shuttle, somewhat shot up, and eleven nukes.

Well, there's my excuse, Carrera thought, looking at the shuttle. *But do I want to give them all up? I don't think so. The Volgan weapons almost certainly didn't come in officially but from criminal channels. Those I can keep. The Hangkuk warheads are unlikely to come to light. I can keep those, too. But I have to produce at least one and if I produce one Kashmiri bomb the subsequent investigation is going to show at least three more missing. Best to turn over one Hangkuk bomb and keep the other two. Then, if I use a Kashmiri bomb someday the evidence will point at them. That might be useful. And best to send the one I brought myself back to base.*

The IM-71 that had brought that bomb waited outside the cave, rotor still turning, while Carrera inspected. A warrant officer from Fernandez's section had dismounted and accompanied Carrera on his inspection.

"I want those taken back, except that one," Carrera said, pointing out one of the Hangkuk bombs. "Have your people start loading them now and get out of here as soon as you're ready."

He considered further. *I'd love to take this shuttle back and strip it down for reverse engineering. Then, too, I don't have a lot of interest in a UEPF-FSC war . . . for now. And, if the Feds are given this, they just might go to war, given the nukes. Hmmm . . . an IM-62 could lift it, I think. There's no way the shuttle weighs more than twenty tons. We could disassemble it here and ship it home inside a plane . . . if an IM-62 can lift it so can an NA-21. Yes.*

"Drag out the shuttle, too. In pieces. We'll send it home," he finished.

Oh, Mama, I want to go home, Cruz thought as he and his lead squad eased their way further into the depths of the massif.

He broke and shook an infrared chemlight, tossing it around a corner. A grenade would have been as dangerous to him and his legionaries as to any Salafis who might be sheltering behind the corner.

The light was invisible to the naked eye. It lit up like day for the IR-sensitive monocular Cruz wore on his helmet. He flipped this down and, gulping, heart thumping in his chest, crouched low and pointed his F-26 around the corner's edge.

There *were* people there. Rather, there were a number of desiccated corpses lying on the tunnel floor and sitting with backs against walls. Cruz felt an involuntary shudder. *Bad as they are, this was a shitty way to die.*

Radio was useless down here, they'd discovered. Instead, the clearing teams laid out wire behind them, connecting their operations with the surface by field telephone. Cruz whispered his report into the phone before handing it over to his RTO.

Partly for grip and partly for silence the party imitated the generally barefoot Salafis. It felt decidedly odd to the legionaries but it did, they admitted, make a certain sense. At least one soldier asked his squad leader, "Sarge . . . if I'm killed, will you make sure they put my boots on me before they send me home?"

The sergeant slapped the legionary's helmet and told him to, "Shut the fuck up, you morbid bastard."

Cruz scanned the tunnel floor ahead with his monocular. *Nothing there to stick into feet,* he decided. "Come on," he whispered, leading his men forward along one wall.

Midway to the next twist of the tunnel Cruz stopped to pick up the IR chemlight. There were a limited number, and there was no sense in wasting one. Instead of tossing it again, he had a better idea. He stuck it in the muzzle of the rifle of one of his men and had the soldier stick the rifle out. Then, as he had before, Cruz got low and peeked around the corner.

This time the bodies at the far end were living and apparently ready to fight. Taking a deep breath, Cruz turned and walked slowly and carefully back several men. By the sniff he could tell when he had reached the right one, despite the darkness.

"Go back fifty meters," he whispered to each of the soldiers he passed until he smelt the gas. "Undo your hose here and go to the point," he told that soldier.

"Sure, Centurion," the legionary answered.

The tunnel floor sloped downward. At the juncture the soldier eased his hose out and tipped a heavy, twenty-liter, can of gasoline he carried. The gas left the can, trickled through the hose and began to flow down the sloping floor of the tunnel. The evaporating fuel was choking. Sounds of panic roared up the tunnel as Cruz bent to apply his cigarette lighter to the fluid.

"Back to air!" he shouted as the flames took hold, sucking the oxygen out of the local atmosphere.

"They'll go *where*? Carrera shouted into the microphone.

"One of the local underground aqueducts, the karez," Fernandez's voice answered. "And the system is thick up there. No telling which one they'll have used. Assuming the girl is right, of course."

Deep down Carrera knew she was right. *Fuck, fuck, fuck. They can't get away.*

Although it was only a few miles to the karez, it took more than ten miserable hours to negotiate it. In the cramped confines of the tunnel every stumble created a blockage. The air became foul and fetid. While the warmth of the bodies did cause a bit of air to rise, sucking fresh air in from the karez ahead, and displacing some of the heavy carbon dioxide down, it was barely enough to sustain life. The children too grown to be carried suffered especially. Some stopped suffering in time and were left behind. Their little bodies on the floor added to the difficulty of the journey for the others. To Robinson's discomfort, the crying didn't decrease with the dead children. Instead it increased exponentially with the wails of bereaved mothers and as the suffering of the other kids grew.

The trickle of dead and wounded out the various cave and tunnel mouths never seemed to end. Only a few of the latter were Salafi. In the close confines of the tunnels the legionaries rarely were willing to take a chance.

Above, in the ad hoc command post, a computer graphics man constructed a diagram of the interior from the reports of the grunts fighting below. Looking over the man's shoulder as he rotated the diagram on the screen, Carrera was amazed.

"Jesus, they must have been building this thing for thirty years, wouldn't you say, *Subadar* Masood?"

Masood, who had been walking up behind Carrera very quietly, snapped his fingers. It was impossible, so far as he could tell, to sneak up on his *Duque*.

"At least thirty years," he answered, "to my own certain knowledge."

At that moment an IM-71 carrying wounded lifted off from the valley floor and rotored out, heading south.

"I wish to hell I had some kind of gas that would seep down and clear the bastards out without losing any more of my men," Carrera said. "Carbon dioxide would do, if we had a way to manufacture it. Chlorine would do even better but that's against the rules."

Masood shook his head in the negative. "Wouldn't work, Legate. There are all kinds of baffles and twists down there. And then how would you get rid of the gas, even if it worked, to search?"

"Probably couldn't," Carrera admitted. Looking at the 3D diagram on the monitor screen, he said, "May not matter anyway. It appears to be mostly cleared."

He looked toward the crew manning the telephones. "You are keeping the men below informed, right?"

"Affirmative, *Duque*."

"Wait," Cruz whispered, holding up one hand to halt the second of the thirty-nine remaining men of his platoon. There was a shuffling and jangling from behind him as the men ran into each other.

"What is it, Centurion?" his optio asked.

"I heard something ahead."

"This fucking place is spooky."

"No shit."

The sound from ahead died out at the same time Cruz's men managed to quiet down. There was no need for him to tell them to fix bayonets. They'd learned early on that firing a rifle in these close confines was nearly as painful as being shot. Most of the clearing had been done with flame, rifle butt and bayonet.

"Cruz, that you?" rang out in Spanish from up ahead.

The thudding hearts slowed immediately as men exhaled with relief. If there had been anything more terrifying than closing to bayonet range in these infernal caverns the men couldn't imagine what it was.

"Yeah . . . yeah. *Dominguez*?"

"Oh, Cazador *compadre*!" came the laughing answer.

Cruz felt the fear drain away. "Christ, 'Minguez, you scared the shit out of me."

"Tell you what, Cruz; you clean my drawers and I'll

clean yours and we'll see who has the hardest job," Dominguez answered as he strode forward. "Hey, what the fuck is this?"

In the IR, using only his monocular, Cruz didn't understand at first. He pulled out one non-IR chem-light and, ·ordering his men to shut one eye, broke and shook it.

"Holy shit!" he exclaimed, looking into what appeared to be a very shallow tunnel with many large boulders blocking it a few feet in. "You don't suppose . . ."

"Buck it up to higher." In this case Dominguez meant both higher in the chain of command and higher in elevation.

"They fucking *what*?" Carrera raged.

"It looks like they got away," Jimenez explained. "Whichever direction that tunnel goes in, and I'd be willing to bet it doglegs somewhere, they'll have gotten into the karez system and that's extensive enough they could be heading anywhere."

Carrera felt his heart sink and his energy drain away. *All this, for* nothing? *All my men lost or crippled, for* nothing? *War for almost nine fucking years, for* nothing? *Why, God?*

He sat down, right on the dirt and grass. *Click.*

Jimenez sat next to him. "Hey, we hurt the bastards," he tried to cheer.

"Not enough," Carrera answered distantly. "Never enough."

"Wonder who that is?"

Carrera looked up to see an FSA helicopter, sporting a red placard with three stars on it, winging in. "Rivers," he answered, "come to claim the nuke."

"*The* nuke?" Jimenez asked. "There were eleven of them."

Carrera answered, tiredly, "I know that. You know that. He doesn't. We're going to keep ten . . . just in case. They've already gone back to base."

"Dangerous game, Patricio. I know we have the seven but those were *really* unaccounted for."

"It'll be fine."

Rivers was escorted up the top of the massif by the same *naik* who had seen to Carrera earlier. Neither said a word.

Rivers didn't offer to shake hands; he was still furious at being maneuvered as he had been.

"So there really was a nuke."

Carrera nodded. "Yes. I was always certain there would be," he answered. "But their chiefs got away. All we managed to get here were a lot of indians."

"Well, intelligence will be interested in getting their hands even on just indians."

"No . . . that's not going to happen. We'll develop our own intelligence and share it with you," Carrera corrected. "Besides, there weren't very many indians taken, either."

Changing the subject, in large part because he knew that, if Carrera said he was not going to turn over any prisoners, then no prisoners would be turned over, period, Rivers asked, "How did the chiefs get away?"

"Tunnel. We had no clue before we hit this place but it apparently leads to the underground irrigation system here, the karez."

Rivers thought about that one. "You are planning on giving me the nuke, right?" Seeing Carrera's listless nod, he continued, "Well . . . just because you share *all* your intelligence with us"—Rivers didn't really believe that— "doesn't mean we share all *our* intelligence with you."

Carrera cocked his head to one side, raising an eyebrow.

"We *might* be able to tell where they are underground. Don't bother asking how, but we sometimes can."

Hmmm. He means what? Seismic? Maybe, but probably not. Ground penetrating radar? Too deep. Carbon dioxide emissions? No . . . that wouldn't work as CO2 sinks. Maybe . . .

"Thermal? From so far underground? Some of these karez are a thousand feet down."

"It *might* work," Rivers shrugged. "I'm promising only to try."

Gunoz Karez, 800 feet down, 13/8/469

Water there was in plenty; all one had to do to drink was stoop. Since it was well above ankle-deep, one didn't even have to stoop that far. Food was another issue entirely. And, since there was none to issue . . .

"There will be food ahead," Nur al Deen promised. The word filtered up and back the long line of refugees. "Food ahead . . . food ahead."

Progress would have been slower but that the karez was dark enough that the women and older girls could lift their burkas up out of the water and away from tangling their legs in wet folds of cloth. In the light they'd have been too fearful to do so. In Salafi lands girls had been forced to roast to death rather than leave a burning building improperly clothed.

On the other hand, it was a long walk. The men and women simply *had* to go to the bathroom. Since there was no way to fully undress, no privacy at all but the darkness, they simply pissed and shat themselves. The stench made Robinson gag. Arbeit's vomit added to the stench.

I've never really understood these people, he thought, *not until now. I was a fool even to think of trying to make a world government here. All I ever really needed to do was help the Salafis to take over. They'd have knocked this world back so far into the stone age that they'd never have gotten off planet and become a threat to us. When . . . if I get back, I am going to throw all the backing I can to the Salafis. It's Earth's best hope.*

Trying to get his mind away from the stench, Robinson contemplated his flagship and his fleet. *Wallenstein must be in a panic. She would have seen the attack from space. No doubt she is frantically trying to rescue me, poor little girl.*

UEPF Spirit of Peace, 13/8/469 AC

Wallenstein had the radio traffic from below piped directly into her day cabin. She exulted with grim satisfaction at the news she received. *Cheat me, will you, you piece of rat filth?*

She pressed a button on the intercom atop her desk. "Intel, can you identify the frequency the enemy commander is using?"

"They're using frequency hoppers, Captain, but we can copy it," the Intel officer answered. "If I can ask, why?"

"Never mind that. Send the key to communications. Communications?"

"Here, Captain."

"When you get the code, patch me through to the ene—coalition commander down below. Direct from him to my cabin here with no other listeners, understand?"

"Roger, Captain. Only take a few."

The Base, Kashmir Tribal Trust Territories, 12/8/469 AC

The RTO's brown eyes went as wide as saucers. "*Duque?* There's someone on our push who says she's in command of the United Earth Peace Fleet."

Except for color Carrera's eyes became a mirror of the RTO's. He put out his hand for the microphone.

"Carrera."

"This is Captain Marguerite Wallenstein of the UEPF ship, *Spirit of Peace*. In the absence of our high admiral, I am the ranking officer in space, *Duque*. I just called to offer my congratulations."

"For?"

There was a moment's hesitation on the other end before Wallenstein came back with, "You *did* find the . . . packages, did you not, *Duque?* The *twelve* packages? You do have my high admiral in captivity, do you not."

"I found your packages, Captain," Carrera admitted. *TWELVE Packages? Shit.* "As for your high admiral, I am still looking."

"Look well, *Duque*," Wallenstein suggested. "The packages were his idea, not mine. Besides, if you find him there'll be a gap in my social schedule I'd be happy to let you fill." Though he didn't know anything about the captain, Carrera could almost see the sultry smile on the other end.

"That's all right, Captain. I think I'll be looking very carefully even without such a tempting offer. On the other hand, assuming you would prefer for your high admiral never to return, as this conversation suggests, perhaps you can help me find out where he's gone."

"Always willing to help in the 'spirit of peace,'" Wallenstein quipped. She sounded positively thrilled to help.

Some interesting politics going on above, Carrera thought. *Pity Rivers hasn't been able to deliver the location of the enemy, yet.* He asked, "Can you scan for unusual heat signature coming out of the ground in an area of about twenty kilometers around me?"

"Piece of cake, *Duque.*"

"Get me that, then, and I can guarantee your high admiral won't be coming to take command ever again. Until then, Carrera, out."

To the RTOs he said, "Not a word, ever, to anyone."

INTERLUDE

21 June, 2390, UEPF *Spirit of Peace*

The huge lightsail was deployed to brake the ship as it assumed orbit around Terra Nova. Down below the year was 334, AC.

Times there were actually pretty happy. The Federated States of Columbia, a generation past the bloodletting of the Formation War, enjoyed unprecedented prosperity. In the Volgan Empire the tsar was experimenting with the freeing of the serfs. The continent of Taurus had not seen war on its soil for *two* generations, which was something of a record. Moreover, the Moslem and Salafi portions of the globe were, by and large, under the rule of the Taurans, a result of the crushing of the last Salafi jihad. The discovery of oil on the Yithrab peninsula was still a dozen years away.

The rate of technological progress, down below, was worrisome, though. This was why, after much hemming and hawing, the Consensus had finally agreed to build the last four starships—*Spirit of Peace, Spirit of Unity, Spirit of Harmony* and *Spirit of Brotherhood*— required to bring the fleet up to the strength that had been decided on centuries before.

It isn't so much that the Consensus acts slowly, mused the new commander of the fleet, High Admiral Jonathan Saxe-Coburg, *as that it* thinks *so slowly. Something about the antiagathics seems not to help with the mind after the third century, or at least it doesn't help with a number of us. His Excellency, the SecGen, seemed particularly badly affected when last we spoke. And the caliph of Rome? Hopeless.*

Or maybe it isn't the failure of the antiagathics. Maybe it's the sheer stultifying boredom of Old Earth that slows the minds of the people who brought us to where we are today. I confess, I don't know.

And I don't know what I'm going to do about the problem of Terra Nova, either. We haven't changed, technologically, in centuries. You can watch the change as it happens down there. Sure, they're at the level of breech-loading small arms, railroads and steam, right now. Where will they be in another century?

CHAPTER TWENTY-FIVE

Bloomin' loot!
That's the thing to make the boys git up an' shoot!
It's the same with dogs an' men,
If you'd make 'em come again
Clap 'em forward with a Loo! loo! Lulu! Loot!
—Kipling, "Loot"

Gunoz Karez, 200 feet down, 15/8/469 AC

Robinson had no compass. It seemed such a primitive thing, really, that the thought had never occurred to him to bring one, even had one been available aboard his flagship. Then, too, with the twists and turns of both escape tunnel and karez, he was really quite lost. The only objective measure he had to go by was that the karez was, however gently, ascending. That meant . . .

"We're heading to *Pashtia*?"

"Yes," Nur al Deen answered. "It took you long enough to notice."

"But . . . *why*?"

"Three reasons," the Salafi answered. "The first is that they are less likely to look for us there. The second is that the enemy base, the enemy who attacked us in Kashmir, is there. The third, closely related to the second, is that there we can use the bomb we have brought to destroy the enemy in that base, in accordance with the will of Allah."

"Not without my key, you can't," the high admiral insisted.

"You will use the key as we direct," Nur said, quite definitively.

"I will not."

"Yes, you will." The Salafi sounded, to Robinson, unaccountably confident.

"There is no way you can make me."

The Salafi sighed. *Could this UE fool really believe that?*

"Admiral Robinson," he began, patiently explaining, "we *will* take the bomb to Pashtia. We will get it moved near the enemy camp. At that point you will either detonate it, as we command, or we will begin rearranging your skin."

"Torture doesn't work," Robinson countered. "People will say and do anything under torture, but you cannot tell if anything they say or do is the truth."

"This is true, High Admiral of the infidels. That is to say, it is true unless one has a way of checking the truth in part or getting immediate feedback. In this case, we will, if necessary, rearrange your skin— oh, yes, eyes and internal organs too—until the bomb goes off. Thus, since you agree that people will do or say 'anything' to stop the pain, you must agree that you will do *this*."

"You can't know if I send the key to set the bomb off or to disarm it permanently."

Nur al Deen's laugh echoed off the karez wall. "Foolish infidel, if you disarm it permanently then it won't go off at the time we demand. Then the pain will begin again and never stop."

Khalifa heard the laugh. She thought it belonged to Mustafa's number two, Nur al Deen, though she couldn't be sure; it was rare for her to be privileged to serve at the leaders' feasts. For the most part she was a woman who tended her own hearth. Still, she couldn't imagine what it might be, here, that could possibly be worth laughing over.

She was hungry, painfully so. What little food she had managed to grab before her hurried flight from the cave she had thought of as home had gone to her children, mostly to the boy, as the Holy Koran and custom commanded. The girl, younger, weaker, and hungrier, already knew her place in life and kept quiet but for an occasional understandable sniffle. It was even more understandable given than the girl was down in thigh-deep cold water while the boy, though older and taller, nestled warm against his mother's breast.

As bad as it was down here in the karez, and it was even more cramped than the narrow escape tunnel had been, there was at least breathable air and a modicum of light from the air shafts so high above.

UEPF Spirit of Peace, 15/8/469 AC

"Yes, I can find them, Captain," answered the intelligence officer. "What's in it for me?"

Like the Captain, the IO was a Class Two, almost—but not *quite*— the highest caste. Like most other

Class Twos he lived for the chance of that rare rise in caste, a rise in caste almost unobtainable outside of the Peace Force and the Clergy.

"A rise in class, of course," Wallenstein answered.

"You can't give me that."

"I can if the high admiral never comes back and I take his place and become a Class One myself."

"What proof do I have you won't just raise yourself and tell me to screw off?"

"The best of all possible reasons; I have no vested interest in keeping Class One so aloof and elite, not being one myself, and I will need friends at the same level."

The IO considered this for a moment. "Give me a couple of hours, then."

Camp San Lorenzo, Jalala Province, Pashtia, 15/8/469 AC

Carrera had found himself, over the last several years, sleeping more, rising later, and still always bone weary. He'd left Jimenez to clean up back at the enemy base, finishing the search, extracting their men, pulling back the mechanized cohort that had moved forward into Kashmir to guard the operation, and taking out the prisoners, of which there were some.

For his part he slept. He was so tired, of late, that even the nightmares generally failed to wake him when they came. Thus, the orderly had to pound on his door for several minutes before getting an answer.

"Sir, there's . . . someone . . . someone on the radio for you. Said to tell you it was 'Marguerite.' Sir, why would a stranger be calling on our tactical push?"

"I'll be there in a few minutes," Carrera answered, rising from his bed and beginning to pull on his boots. He'd slept in uniform. "Have my vehicle brought around."

"Already done, *Duque*."

"Carrera."

"Why, *Duque*, how pleasant to speak to you again," Wallenstein said, over the radio. "Do you have a map that shows the karez system near your camp?"

"Near my camp? Yes, of course but . . . near my *camp*?"

"Yes, *Duque*, near your camp. I don't know why they'd be heading there but there they are definitely heading. I mean, if they still had one of the . . . packages . . ."

Shit. "Twelve," *she'd said.*

"Give me the coordinates," he answered. "Maybe they just think we won't look so close."

"Makes a certain amount of sense," Wallenstein agreed. "By the way, I don't have your grid system. Polar coordinates from the center of your camp are . . ." And she read off a direction and distance. "They're moving continuously along that major karez."

"Thank you, Captain. Carrera out."

"Good hunting, Legate."

They've got a nuke, still. What would I do if I had a nuke and no other way to strike the people who had just chopped all my followers to dogmeat? That's a no-brainer; I'd use it.

"Get me the staff! Put the group that just returned from Kashmir on alert! Tell the Cazadors to be prepared to jump again in six hours. I want a maniple of

Pashtun Scouts ready to go at the same time. Notify the Air *ala*! Now!"

Click. This time, the click hurt.

Jebel Ansar, Pashtia, 16/8/469 AC

The karez split, one branch continuing straight ahead into the gloom while the other took a left turn that opened up after several hundred meters to a pool fed by a small stream. The pool was icy cold but the air outside was warm.

Even at the slow pace at which the column moved toward the oval of light ahead, when she finally emerged into the sun, Khalifa's eyes watered and blinked. She had to cover them with one hand to protect them from the sun until they could become accustomed to it once again.

When she could see again, Khalifa saw a half dozen vehicles, several dozen horses, scores of people, men and women both, along with over a hundred head of livestock. The air was filled with the smell of roasting meat.

As soon as he reached open air Robinson pulled out his communication device and began to call the *Spirit of Peace.* He stopped when he felt the cold muzzle of a rifle pressed against the back of his head.

"I don't *think* so," Nur al Deen said. "We can't have you calling for rescue before you have completed your task. Take it from him. Search the infidel houri," a nod indicated Arbeit—"as well, to make sure she cannot speak to her people."

While two began searching Arbeit, who huffed with

the indignity, another one of the Salafis pulled the communicator roughly from the high admiral's hand and passed it on to Nur al Deen. He saw that it was not much different from the cell phones already being produced around this world. Yes, it was a bit smaller but not all that much so. The only really distinguishing thing about it was the UE logo and the letters, "UEPF," underneath that. Nur al Deen slipped the slender device into a pocket and walked to rejoin Mustafa.

"This was well done, Hameed," Mustafa congratulated the leader of the small party Nur al Deen had sent ahead to prepare. Mustafa's eyes swept the valley into which his people had emerged. He saw that it was about two kilometers by four, lush and verdant at its floor and with tall, tree-covered hills to all sides.

"Thank you, Sheik. Our people here came to cover your emergence as soon as possible. The animals are not as many as I would have liked to provide a screen for our group, but the caves are still well stocked and we can shelter many in them to avert prying eyes. As you can see and smell, food is being prepared. The weapons, particularly those for use against aircraft, are in tip-top shape, with plenty of ammunition."

"Yes," Mustafa answered, smiling broadly. "I expected they would be. Get parties to moving them from the caves and camouflaging them."

"I will do so, Sheik."

"How do we want to set the bomb off?" asked Nur al Deen, appearing beside Mustafa.

"Move it by camel, I think," the sheik answered. "It's not that low yield a bomb. If we can get it within a mile or so, it should destroy the crusader camp."

"Very well, then. I'll arrange it. I'll also arrange some obvious punishment for the Old Earth infidel if he fails to cooperate."

Robinson swallowed hard. The Salafis had cut down half a dozen trees and made two tripods with them. They'd set the tripods over piles of wood they set alight and then let burn down to coals. The fire and the tripods were for him and Arbeit.

"We'll hang you and your houri belly down over the coals, once they're ready," Nur al Deen explained. "Then we'll lower you to cooking level. It won't be that quick, of course, because we'll start you swinging so you only cook a little at a time. It will take hours, maybe a whole day, before you die. That is, it will unless you cooperate and set off the bomb when we tell you."

"Martin, you can't let them . . . whatever they ask . . . whatever I have . . . it's yours if you just don't let them—"

"Shut up, Lucretia," he snapped. "How is this any different from the games you play back on Earth or in the dungeon Wallenstein set up for you on the *Peace*?"

"The *difference*, Martin, is that what I do I do only to lowers while what they threaten to do is to *me*."

Biting back a retort, Robinson hung his head. After a moment he told Nur al Deen, "Drown your hot coals. Take down your tripods. I'll cooperate."

"Good. I thought you might. The bomb will leave tomorrow morning and should be in position by tomorrow night."

"Can we leave then?" the high admiral asked.

"We'll see."

✦   ✦   ✦

Havaldar Mohammad Kamal saw. Six-foot-two with blue eyes half hidden by his sun browned eyelids, he smiled from his hidden perch high on the slope of Jebel Ansar. The Blue Jinn—even some of his friends called Carrera that—had promised great rewards for the scout team that first spotted the enemy as they emerged. It was the will of Allah that Kamal's team was graced with that honor. Unheard by those below, Kamal radioed in his report. He was told to continue to monitor, to spot for any enemy air defense . . . and to be careful of incoming air and artillery attack.

"Friendly fire, isn't," one of the Balboan officers had reminded him.

Jebel Ansar, Pashtia, 18/8/469 AC

There was no warning.

One moment the air in the high Pashtun pass was calm and cool with the morning's late summer breeze. Trees, tall evergreens from forests never harvested, swayed and danced in the gathering sun. Standing atop a high rock overlooking the dusty valley the muezzin called the faithful to prayer. *"Allahu Akbar; Allahu Akbar." God is great. God is great. Come to prayer. Prayer is better than sleep. God is great.*

With the muezzin's call, the women stopped cooking breakfast for the holy warriors gathered in the camp and—like their menfolk— knelt, facing generally east-northeast. The warriors and children for whom those women cooked likewise abased themselves in the direction of Makkah al Jedidah. Their compassed prayer rugs showed the direction. Their heavy assault rifles and less common heavier weapons skewed those compasses, too. Yet the Beneficent, the Merciful, the Almighty would understand that a mujahad might be off a few degrees in the direction of his devotions. The thought *did* count for something, after all.

As the people abased themselves before their God, humbly and faithfully, smoke from hundreds of camp-fires passed on the breeze, carrying savory aromas to the noses of all the hungry fugitives in the camp.

It was a moment of peace before the first of the artillery shells began to lay their minefields to the south.

Even before the coming of the shells, Abdul Aziz felt no peace. He ignored the morning call to prayer as he ignored the sounds and smells of the camp, as he ignored his own murmuring stomach—slated to be full for the first time in days from the largesse stockpiled in a nearby cave against the day of need.

Abdul's eyes wandered seeking those other eyes he felt, he *knew*, were on himself, his comrades and their families. *Damned Pashtun mercenaries. Sell their souls and their God for a little pay, the chance to loot and rape.*

But the Pashtun were as they were; nothing could change them, nothing ever had. *Il hamdu l'illah.* To God be the praise. Said differently; what could one do?

Finally, reluctantly, Abdul Aziz ibn Kalb turned to his neglected prayers. In them, he began to find a moment's inner peace before returning to his wife, Khalifa—even now preparing the morning meal—and their children.

The next moment, as Khalifa—prayers likewise finished—added a bit of seasoning to the hummus, peace ended. First came the freight train rattle of artillery shells inbound. These exploded, apparently harmlessly, to the north, near and around the exit from the karez. The shells made only dull bangs in comparison to their usual crescendo.

The shells were never intended to explode, per se. Instead, small charges pushed off the shells' bases, causing them to release their cargo. The cargo, small things—thirty-six per shell—and shaped like pieces of cheesecake, fell to ground but did no apparent harm.

Other shells, mixed high explosive and ICM— Improved Conventional Munitions—began to pepper the camp. The high explosive went off on or above the ground. It fragmented the thick steel walls of the shells—they had to be thick to withstand the stresses of firing and the spin imparted by rifled cannon tubes— sending hot, razor-sharp shards whizzing through the camp. Limbs were ripped off, bellies opened, bones shattered. Women and children, and even a few men, began to scream, some in fright, others in pain.

The ICM was more subtle, to the extent that blood, fire, and death can ever be subtle. They were somewhat like the other shells, the ones that had kicked off their base plates sending apparently harmless cargo down. Instead of cheesecake-slice shaped mines, however, the ICM sent little bomblets, eighty-eight per shell, to rain down on the inhabitants of the camp. Also unlike the mines, the ICM bomblets exploded on touching down, sending small fragments and bits of serrated wire to drench the area with pain and death.

At the first explosion Khalifa shrieked something incoherent. Her face was visible and, normally, it had its attractions, kindness not least among them. Her children froze at the shriek and at the look of stark terror on their mother's face. She grabbed the nearest of them, then ran a few steps and grabbed the other by one arm. Children half-carried and half-dragged, Khalifa sprinted for something, anything, that would shelter her and—more importantly—them from the blasts. Khalifa felt like she and her children were targets already, though actually the artillery was directed at possible and likely sites for the defenders to have posted men with guided antiaircraft weapons or—unlikely but possible, given the hasty and difficult flight of the last few days—heavy machine guns capable of engaging aircraft.

Those first shells lifted after a few disconcerting volleys. In the main, they had done their work well. Half a dozen light surface to air missile launchers *had* been posted on likely high ground. The artillery smashed them, turning the men who carried them into bloody pulp. Likewise did one heavy machine gun—it was tripod mounted but the low tripod rendered it unsuitable for anti-aircraft work—go up in fire and smoke.

The Pashtun mercenaries were clever, skilled, and persistent. Little had escaped their notice.

The artillery was followed within seconds by the malevolent whine of a dozen assault aircraft, in two waves of six, hugging the eastern ridge as they crossed it before plunging down to spit death and flame among the denizens of the camp. Rockets, cannon and machine gun fire raked out with hundreds—and in the case of the aerial machine guns, thousands—of rounds.

If the artillery had induced fear, the aerial attack created instantaneous bedlam. People ran confused in all direction. Women screamed, children cried, and men called to the Almighty for aid. Those same men, stumbling and cursing, fumbled for weapons even as the first six aircraft began their passes, harvesting before them the broken bodies of many score.

Once over the eastern side of the camp the first six attack planes released a dozen canisters of napalm, two each, one from each wing. These tumbled down from hardpoints put on the heavily modified crop dusters. The canisters hit the ground, then split, broke open, and ignited. Long tongues of fierce orange flame licked for hundreds of yards through the camp, scouring their paths free of life. The pilots aimed, insofar as they could, for groups of armed men. Still, the target area was confusing and the aircraft moved fast. Warriors died, yes, but along with them women and children twisted and shrieked and were turned to writhing human torches before being reduced to charcoal and ash.

The morning smells suddenly changed from savory to sickening as cooked human meat added its contribution to the air.

The first wave split off into two "vics" of three, one veering north, one south, to come around for another pass each from those directions. The Turbo-Finches, the modified crop dusters, could turn on a drachma.

The camp now alerted, the second wave took some fire as it made its strafe. No matter, the aircraft were armored against small arms and even had a chance against heavy machine gun fire. They were also less vulnerable to shoulder fired antiaircraft rockets than either helicopters or high performance jets. Carrying a lethal load, they were flown by men in whose hearts hate battled for dominance with the desire to be done, to finish this, to go home. These fresh, rearing warhorses had many times proven their worth in the brutal and bitter campaign.

This the second wave demonstrated as they swooped across at a higher level than the first. Not bothering to use their machine guns, cannon or rockets, they each released an aerodynamic cylinder from underneath before giving their engines full throttle and racing away. The cylinders fell a distance then, with a *pop*, broke open and kicked out three smaller cylinders and a number of glowing sparklers.

The smaller cylinders burst at a predetermined height, spreading an inflammable aerosol.

The searing tongues of napalm flame heating her face, Khalifa twisted her head and body searching frantically for the sign of a refuge. The two children now in her arms screamed and cried. Like mindless animals they twisted, trying to escape her grasp. She held them all the tighter; so tight the children could feel her own heart beating frantically beneath her breast.

Which way to turn? Which way to turn? Already Khalifa could hear the steady whop-whop-whop of the helicopters fast approaching. This was the merciless enemy who hunted without either giving rest or, apparently, taking it. She did not know what they would do to her in the event she was captured. The ignorance was worse than knowledge might have been. She *had* to escape somehow; her and the children.

And then Khalifa heard a faint series of tiny explosions overhead. She looked upward and to the east . . .

✧   ✧   ✧

Proximity fused, the thermobaric cylinders fell to a preset distance above the ground before splitting and then detonating. Their aerosol clouds spread outward rapidly, mixing with the air and growing to touch upon each other. In a short time, a moment, one finger of one cloud touched a sparkler.

Khalifa was not one of the lucky ones, those directly under the blast. They died quickly, having barely a chance to voice an unheard scream before the near-nuclear explosion obliterated them.

Instead, she and her children stood at the periphery. She felt her children torn from her grasp as she and they were picked up and thrown. Khalifa could not see them because the intense heat had burned away her face and eyes along with most of the skin on the front side of her body.

High pressure air pounded her internal organs and, forcing its way into her lungs, expanded and tore them.

Briefly Khalifa flew through the air on the leading edge of the blast wave, a human tracer trailing flame. A violent stop against a large rock broke her spine—a small mercy as at least the pain from her lower body went away with the break. Then again, with ruptured organs and lungs, and a body flash-burned, the mercy was small indeed.

Then the vacuum struck as the air rushed back in to fill the space it had occupied before the blast. Khalifa felt it ripping the air through her mouth. She felt her lungs loosen away from the inside of her chest. She, along with others who had survived so far, was pulled inward even faster than she had been thrown away.

❖   ❖   ❖

Racing back to the encampment, Abdul Aziz caught sight of the first half dozen *Shturmoviks*—some of the mujahadin still used the term they had picked up during the Volgan occupation of two decades before—sweeping across. Uselessly and fruitlessly, he fired his rifle at them as they passed overhead. Looking desperately between the swaths of flame left in their wake, Aziz caught sight of his family, still standing safe between flaming strips.

Even as he watched helplessly, his family was blasted to ruin by the second wave.

He mouthed a soundless, "Nooo."

Then Abdul Aziz ibn Kalb turned and ran.

Above and at a distance from the perimeter of the camp's smoking ruins helicopters rotored in and landed. From their bellies they began discharging troops. Some dropped off sling loads of artillery and ammunition. Some dropped off other loads of supplies.

Among those landing troops, one helicopter was distinguished by virtue of having discharged only a few men. One of these was Carrera. His face was mostly covered against the wind and the sun. A clear area had been left open, however, revealing eyes that glowed when the angle to the rising sun was just right. Sometimes, so swore both enemies and friends, the eyes glowed on their own.

The eyes glowed now. Through them the Carrera watched calmly as the heavy mortar crews struggled to manhandle the guns out of the helicopters and into firing position. He watched for a few moments before, satisfied, he turned his attention elsewhere.

Below the hill on which he stood, some fifteen

hundred meters from the camp, one of his infantry cohorts spread out to sweep across. Largely ineffective fire fell among them, bullets half spent shooting little demons of dust into the air. The advance went on regardless.

Carrera lifted a pair of binoculars to his eyes. The magnified gaze swept across the camp where some hundreds of the enemy tried to slow down or stop his onslaught. Past them, so he saw, more hundreds of women and children—and some few spiritless men—crawled, walked and ran from the carnage.

His sweeping gaze touched upon a child of indeterminate sex, tugging at the half carbonized corpse of what was probably its mother. *My children's mother was burned to death and yours warbled with glee,* he thought, without any trace of emotion . . . he could not *afford* emotion, not now. *Still, little one, I am sorry for you.*

Farther on, near the edge of the artillery-laid minefield, men, women and children who had sought that route for safety lay along an irregular line. It was much too far for Carrera to make out any details. His mind supplied them even so. *You are not so broken as my own babies were when they were murdered.*

Carrera's thoughts were interrupted by the soft padding of footsteps behind him. He recognized their source. Few walked with such near perfect quiet as his prized chief of his almost equally prized Pashtun scouts.

"*Subadar* Masood?" he said without turning.

"Sir!" exclaimed the senior Pashtun Scout, springing to attention near his side. A smile briefly crossed the *subadar's* seamed, craggy face. *You, alone of all men, can hear me coming,* he thought.

"The Scouts? All paths east and west?"

"Sealed tighter than a houri's hole, sir."

"Very good. I want as many prisoners as possible. Rewards are offered."

"Yes, sir. So my men have been told."

In the much colder air above the high pass breath gathered to frost a gray-shot beard. Hard they came, those puffs of air, pumped from struggling, bellowing lungs. They burst outward to form little horizontal pines before settling to and disappearing against the ubiquitous ice and snow.

Hard pumped the heart beneath the lungs, forcing warmth to freezing limbs, forcing blood to a brain straining to make sense of disaster.

Close to the ground, seeking to make himself invisible—one with the snow and the ice—the fugitive Abdul Aziz huddled. His eyes and ears quested for some route of escape, some way to survive to carry on the fight and avenge his family and his cause. Nothing looked very promising. Nothing sounded so, either.

In the cold, still air sound carried very well. The fugitive's ears caught easily the irregular sound of shots and screams. The fugitive cursed his enemies, then let fall a single tear which froze on his face before it had descended much more than an inch.

Ahead, the steady whop-whop-whop of helicopters told of escape routes being systematically cut off. Unseen, far above, the harsh drone of the *Shturmoviks* and the cursed infidels' gunships swept along, hunting for any who might have escaped the camp. Behind, the baying of dogs, hunting dogs with the sharpest of noses, told of other fugitives being tracked through the snow, ice and rock. From all around, at odd times, came shouts of triumph as some mercenary, apostate Pashtun Scout dragged a cowering man, woman, or child from a hiding place.

Despair crowded the fugitive's heart and mind: despair at loss, despair at ruin.

The thought of his own wife and children, now forever lost, was almost more than he could bear. "They'll pay. By the ninety-nine beautiful names of Allah, I swear they will pay for this," muttered the fugitive to himself.

The pitiless ice made no answer.

Havaldar Mohammad Kamal didn't answer either; though he heard. He pointed to one of his grinning men, then to another, and made a slight finger motion in the direction from which the sound had come.

The scouts glanced at each other. A wordless plan formed between them. Carrera would pay bounties for live prisoners. They'd take this one alive if they could.

Silently the two designated scouts began to creep forward and around. The military arts their prey had learned only partially, they had grown up with.

INTERLUDE

11/6/409 AC, Botulph, Federated States of Columbia, Terra Nova

Robert Hennessey, Senior, sat quietly on a bench in the central park of this great metropolitan city on the Federated States West Coast. In the sun Hennessey read his newspaper. More especially, Hennessey read for word of the fighting in the *Mar Furioso*, the great sea of Terra Nova, where his son, Lieutenant Robert Hennessey, Junior, led a platoon of Federated States Marines in the long, slow, bloody drive across the sea. The sooner the war was over, the sooner young Bob was safe, the better, as far as the old man was concerned.

After all, I'm not getting any younger and I need the boy to take over the chair of the firm.

There was grounds for hope now, despite the obscenely long casualty lists posted every day from the fighting across central Taurus and on the islands of the *Furioso*. Just a few days before, the papers had blared out of a second Yamatan city blasted to cinders by some new weapon developed in secret.

837

Whatever it takes to get the Yamatans to surrender short of invading the home islands, Robert Senior thought.

There was hardly a family in the entire country to be found that hadn't lost a son or a husband. Hennessey heard weeping and looked over to where a woman, formerly playing with her children on the grass, had broken down in tears.

Whatever it takes.

He heard a familiar horn beep. Folding his paper, Hennessey arose from the park bench to walk to where his chauffeur was exiting the limousine to hold open the door. He gave himself this one break, one hour every morning, to relax in the central park away from his responsibilities. The hour never seemed to last long enough.

From the corner of one eye Hennessey thought he saw a bright streak across the sky. He glanced up just as the streak became a flash that consumed him, his city, the young, weeping woman, her children, trees and buildings and park benches . . . everything.

11/6/409, UEPF *Spirit of Peace*

"Target One . . . destroyed, High Admiral . . . Target Two . . . destroyed."

Silently, High Admiral Laurence Napier, nodded his head. If ever a man looked spiritually crushed, that man was he, for he had just given the order and overseen the extinction of over one million people.

What choice had I, though? My orders from the Consensus were clear; they allowed no room for maneuver. "Any detonation of a nuclear weapon for *purposes of advancing a war effort on Terra Nova is to be met by an equivalent or greater response from the United Earth Peace Fleet." I picked the two smallest cities in the Federated States for that . . . the two smallest that had a chance of working, in any case, San Fernando and Botulph. What else could I do?*

Suddenly, Napier felt the overwhelming urge to vomit. Without another word he arose from his command chair and raced for his own quarters. Halfway to his quarters he found he could not restrain himself, emptying the contents of his stomach for some nameless prole to clean up. Still heaving, Napier continued on to his quarters.

There he sat in silent horror at the oceans of blood on his hands. He imagined it all, the young children playing on the grass, the old men reading their morning papers, the flash, the fireball . . .

In the end, the imagining was too much. Napier removed a pistol from his desk, made sure it was loaded, placed the muzzle to the roof of his mouth, and pulled the trigger.

This left another mess for the proles to clean up.

CHAPTER TWENTY-SIX

Strong wind, strong wind
Many dead tonight, it could be you
—Ladysmith Black Mambazo, "Homeless"

Jebel Ansar, Pashtia, 18/8/469 AC

They called Carrera "the Blue Jinn." He took a small and perverse pride in the title. Blue jinni were evil jinni. That his enemies thought him evil was . . . pleasant. Even more pleasant was the sight of his enemies, beaten and bleeding, captive and bound.

Carrera, the Jinn, looked over those enemies in the late afternoon sun. Sinking in the west, the sun's light was carved by the mountains to cast long, sharp shadows across the ground. Much of that ground was covered with the head-bowed, broken prisoners.

One of those captives, Abdul Aziz ibn Kalb, held his bleeding head upright. Abdul Aziz glared hate at his captors. These were a mix of Pashtun mercenaries—tall and light-eyed; light-skinned they would have been, too, had the sun not burned them red-brown—and shorter, darker men. All were heavily armed, bearing wicked looking rifles with shiny steel blades affixed.

All sneered back the hate Abdul Aziz felt, mixing with that hate a full measure of disgust and contempt.

Aziz's hate mixed with and fed on fear. Along with several hundred other male prisoners, and well over a thousand women and children, Aziz waited to hear his fate. The male prisoners' hands and legs were taped together. Not far away, the women and children waited unbound. The two groups were close enough together that Abdul Aziz could see the noncombatants as well as a small group of his enemies ascending a low hill to his front.

Leading that group, Abdul Aziz saw, was a uniformed man, medium in height, and with his face and head wrapped with a keffiyah. Another looked oriental. Three more were dressed much as any mullahs would be. A sixth wore the white dress of the Emirate of Doha. The last was another man in uniform, bearing the rank badges of a *subadar*. Trimly bearded, tall and slender, with bright gray eyes, the *subadar* looked Pashtun to Abdul Aziz.

That man in the lead partially unwrapped the keffiyah from around his head. Aziz had never seen him before, but had heard enough descriptions to recognize the "Blue Jinn."

Carrera paused and lit a cigarette. He puffed it contemplatively for a few moments. Then he sat back easily in a chair, almost a throne, which had been prepared for him by his followers out of hastily felled and trimmed trees. Even at this distance Abdul Aziz saw the eyes that gave the Jinn his name. Though it was just a trick of the sun, the eyes seemed to glow from the inside like malevolent coals.

A dark-clad, bearded mullah walked to the microphone of a portable public address set standing in front of the chair and began to speak.

"I have consulted," he announced, "with *Duque* Carrera, the man you probably know as the Blue Jinn, and whom you see to my right, concerning your fate. He, in accordance with the Sharia, has turned the general resolution of your cases over to myself and my fellow mullahs. We have pronounced sentence of death upon you, in accordance with the will of Allah, for complicity in murder."

It was widely speculated that the mullah only consulted the quarter gold Boerrand Carrera allegedly paid him for each desired "legal" death sentence he passed on. He never admitted this. Neither did he deny it.

"Your young children shall be taken back to your enemy's country," the mullah continued. "Your women, and the girls over twelve, are awarded to his Pashtun Scouts as prizes. Mr. Yamaguchi," and the mullah's head nodded to indicate the oriental man who had accompanied the party, "and Mr. al Ajami," another head nod, "represent certain interests in Yamato and Doha that might wish to buy some of these women and girls from the Scouts. Having consulted with the Jinn I have informed him that there is no religious prohibition to this, that you are all apostates and your women may properly be enslaved. For his part, he says he could care less what happens to them so long as it is within the law."

A wild and heartrending moan emerged from the cluster of women as the grinning, leering Pashtun began to prod them away to the processing area. Aziz felt a sudden relief that his wife had been spared the ignominy of rape followed by sale into prostitution.

"As for the rest of you, as I said, you shall die. But the Jinn tells me to inform you that he is solicitous of your souls."

The mullah stopped speaking and backed away from the microphone. Carrera stood and took the mullah's place. He spoke in decent Arabic, Aziz was surprised to discover, though his accent was somewhat heavy.

"Some years ago the actions of your leader and your movement robbed me of my wife and children," Carrera announced. He turned to the chief mullah. "What does Sura Eighty-one say, O man of God?" he asked.

The mullah recited aloud, loud enough for the microphone to pick up so that the prisoners could hear, "When the infant girl, buried alive, is asked for what crime she was slain—"

"What does it mean?"

"It means, *sayidi*, when Allah asks who murdered her, for no infant girl can be guilty of a crime."

"Does Allah approve of burying infant girls alive, then?"

"He does not. Sura Eighty-one, the Cessations, is concerned with the end of time, Judgment Day, and the punishment of the wicked. God will punish the murderers of infant girls."

Carrera's face twitched in the smallest of smiles. "Ah, I see. What does the Holy Koran say about those who bring disorder to the world?

"It says, O Jinn, in Sura Five, the Table, that those who fight against God or his Apostle, bringing disorder to the world, should be killed, or have the hands and feet cut off on opposite sides, or be exiled, or be crucified."

"I see," said Carrera. "Do those who kill infant girls

fight against God? Have these men brought disorder to the world?"

"They have. They do," answered the mullah, "for this is expressly forbidden under Islam."

Carrera turned back to his captives. "I loved my family, even as—one supposes—you love your own. I swore, when they were murdered, to avenge myself on all who had contributed, even passively, to my loss. Thus you shall die. I am, though, as Mullah Hassim told you, very solicitous of your fate in the hereafter. So before you die, you will be thoroughly Christianized."

Then Carrera smiled, nastily, and turned to his *subadar*.

"Crucify them."

Abdul Aziz spoke English quite well. Moreover, Carrera was close enough to the microphone for him to hear the dread words, "Crucify them."

He had not been the only one. Several others understood English, too. The group of a bit over four hundred captives began to curse and writhe on the ground, trying to free themselves of their sticky bonds. Balboan Cazadors and Pashtun Scouts then walked among them, applying boot and rifle butt until they quieted down.

Several helicopters came in shortly thereafter bearing bundles of metal stakes slung underneath. The bundles swayed in the downdraft and crossing wind. The helicopters and their load, again, caused a stirring among the mujahadin. Again, the guards dealt with it brutally.

As soon as the helicopters' loads were unbundled, some men went to work with devices—to Abdul they looked like sections of heavy pipe with end caps on one end and handles welded on—to drive the crosses (for that's what the bundles proved to be) into the earth. The steady *clang-clang-clang* went on for quite some time. When it ended, one section of the valley was saturated with crosses.

The crosses looked to have been about four meters high, with a one and a quarter meter crosspiece welded on, before they were erected. Afterwards, they seem to stand about three quarters of that above the earth.

Abdul Aziz ibn Kalb was one of the first to be taken to his death. The haughty Pashtun guards carved up the mass of prisoners, forcing lanes between them. Three of them walked up to Abdul and grabbed him by his tape-bound arms and legs. They then carried and dragged him to his cross. His arms, which had been taped behind, were cut loose. He was roughly stripped of his clothing. Then his hands were re-taped in front. Two of the guards lifted him up bodily, while the third hooked his arms over the peak of the upright. They then lowered him, none too gently, letting him fall with his back to the cross until his taped wrists reached the welded juncture of upright and crosspiece. They lifted his feet and taped them to the upright, forcing him to relax his knees by the none-too-gentle method of striking him in the gonads. Once he was in that position his hands were taped to the crosspiece so that he could not hope to wear away his bonds by rubbing them against the upright, or to free his arms by lifting them over the top.

Thus affixed, Abdul Aziz could not get his wrists over the upright even by standing fully erect by his taped feet. Still, the orders had said to do it that way and the Scouts were the sort who followed orders. Besides, what Pashtun worthy of the name would hesitate to follow the orders of a leader who gifted them so lavishly with slave women and money?

Abdul Aziz was in no pain, as of yet, even though the position was uncomfortable. He wondered how long it might take for discomfort to transform into agony. He had his first clue when, after about fifteen minutes of having his weight on his wrists, he found he could not breathe. Rather, he could not exhale and had to push up with his feet to relieve the pressure to allow him to expel the used air in his lungs to draw in new.

True, no nails were used, neither were any bones split, nor did a drop of blood flow. But this was not a mercy. The Romans knew. Of the two major forms of crucifixion, nailing and tying, it was nailing that was the more merciful.

The crosses, twenty rows of twenty, held exactly one hundred Salafis for every one of Carrera's men who had died on a cross. They faced the low hill on which he sat, watching all four hundred men affixed to the mechanism of their execution. A group of what looked to be fifteen mujahadin and two Earthpigs sat miserably at the base of the hill, at Carrera's feet, where they too could watch and feel the suffering of comrades and followers.

Masood handed Carrera three small devices. One looked like what it was, a detonator. The others looked somewhat similar to cell phones. "We took the detonator off the weasel in the United Earth Peace Fleet uniform. The old one with the beard had the communications devices."

"Bring the UE officers to me, *Subadar*." Masood

left and grabbed the bound Robinson and Arbeit by the hair, dragging them up the hill and tossing them at Carrera's feet. Arbeit squealed like a pig at the effrontery and the pain.

"You intended to give the Salafis nuclear weapons." It was not a question. Besides the eleven captured at "the Base," a Scout ambush had taken the last nuke not far from this spot as it was being moved to Camp San Lorenzo by camel.

"No, no," Robinson began. "I was only—"

Masood kicked him, hard, in the kidney.

"We've captured enough evidence and documents in the cave complex to know better," Carrera said. "You were coming to use a nuke on my people at our camp." This, too, was not a question.

"They *made* me," Robinson tried to explain, with a begging, pleading quality to his voice.

"What did they threaten? Torture? You'll soon learn a lot about torture."

Carrera looked at a cell phone-like device. It had a button on it that said, in tiny letters, "Call." He pushed it and was immediately rewarded with, "UEPF *Spirit of Peace*. How can we help you, High Admiral?"

"Give me Marguerite," Carrera said.

Carrera waited only moments before a familiar voice came back, "Captain Wallenstein, High Admiral." The voice sounded terribly fearful.

"It's not your high admiral, Captain; it's me."

"*Duque* Carrera!" One could hear the fear washing away. "How grand to hear from you. May I infer you have been successful?"

"You may. I wondered if you might like to speak to your high admiral."

"Why that would be a great pleasure, *Duque*. Thank you."

Carrera bent at the waist and held the communication device down to Robinson's ear.

"Marguerite, get us out of here," Robinson ordered, though the panic, even terror, in his voice robbed the order of all authority. "Offer them anything, give them *anything*, but don't leave us to die like this."

Wallenstein laughed. "Why would I do that, Admiral? After all, you're just an 'adequate officer, but no more than that.' You weren't much of a lay, either. And as for the marchioness . . ." She let the words hang.

Carrera took the communicator back and held it to the side of his face. "Nice chatting with you, Captain. Don't worry about your high admiral. He'll be well taken care of. Perhaps we can do business again, sometime."

"My pleasure, *Duque*."

Jebel Ansar, Pashtia, 19/8/469 AC

His troops had built a series of great bonfires around the scene of execution. More wood stood by each to light this night and the next. Two of the great, roaring fires flanked Carrera closely, their radiance keeping away the chill of the evening and early morning. The fires lit well a scene from Hell, yet were far enough away that they lent none of their warmth to the denizens of that Hell.

A bottle of scotch sat on one arm of the thronelike chair his troops had constructed for him. On the other was a glass, frequently consulted and frequently refilled. Despite the fatigue, such a tiredness as ordinary rest could never touch, Carrera refused to sleep.

Is this justice? he asked himself. *Is it justice for my family, for my men? Left to me, I'd leave them alive to suffer for much longer. But my crucified men deserve justice no less than I do. This, one hundred for one, is justice to them. My justice will have to wait.*

He glared out at the suffering men and thought, *This is what you would inflict on the world. This is the law you claimed to want. Does it please you so much now, I wonder, now when you are its victims?*

Was it justice to turn your women and girls over to my Pashtun as slaves? No matter; it was your law. "Slavery is a part of jihad and jihad is a part of Islam; thus, slavery is a part of Islam." Isn't that what one of your high clerics said? Well, we have both been in a jihad and you have lost. Thus, by your law, are your women and girls enslaved.

Of course, my Pashtun are good Moslems, most of them. They know it would have been adultery—expressly forbidden—to have screwed your wives while you yet lived. Except that those wives became slaves and a master has a right to his slaves even if they are married. More justice, I think.

For myself, I think those most deserving of slavery are those who want it for others.

Have I even paid you back? I have been suffering for four thousand days. You will all, collectively, suffer for about twelve hundred. It hardly seems fair. It hardly seems enough. Yet it is the best I can do. On the other hand, perhaps if I incinerate your holy city, Makkah al Jedidah, perhaps then we will be even.

And I can incinerate it, with as little warning as my dead wife and children had. If I kill a million for one, then, maybe then, we'll be even.

Carrera leaned forward on his rude wooden chair. He lifted his glass and sipped at it, then sipped again. He put it down to refill it from the amber bottle. The light of the bonfires reflected on the glass. Refilled glass in hand he sat back and simply watched the life leak away from his enemies like the runny shit that drained down their legs.

Jebel Ansar, Pashtia, 20/8/469 AC

The wind blew sere down the high mountain pass. It carried on it the sound and stench of four hundred men, each slowly dying in excruciating agony. That was, after all, the source of the word "excruciating:" to suffer death on the cross.

This was only the second day after the crucifixions. For a few, it would be the last. Still others would last a day or two more. If they didn't already, the living would soon envy the dead.

To the low hill from which Carrera watched came a continuous sea of moans, cresting like waves and subsiding like the tides. One man in a corner would begin moaning, then three more wretches half out of their minds with pain would pick it up. The moans would then travel from one side of the cross-studded field, reach the other and begin to bounce back. Alternatively, a shriek might begin somewhere in the middle and be picked up and transmitted to the edges before coming back to center, not unlike the rippling of a pond when a stone is tossed to its center.

Abdul Aziz felt agony in the center of his chest. He felt it, too, in the wrists and hands and feet he knew were dead and blackening from lack of blood flow.

He was also tired beyond tired. Never in his life had he gone so long without sleep. Yet the art of the cross, a part of it, was that it permitted no sleep, no rest. He had tried to sleep, oh, many times. But each time he nodded off the inability to exhale sent him gasping for air, wide awake and pushing upward with his legs, in minutes. He was hungry, too, and thirsty. He'd begged a passing Pashtun Scout for water and been rewarded with spit on his face.

That was the key to crucifixion, the thing that made it the most horrible of deaths. Even a slow hanging choked off the windpipe so that, while the dying might dance a hornpipe beneath the gallows, trying desperately to find purchase for his feet and live, at least he was not able to beg. Crucifixion allowed begging, and pleading, and all manner of personal disgraces. Indeed, it required them. Worse than being slowly killed, for Abdul Aziz, was being quickly ashamed . . . and by his own words and deeds.

He tried to let his legs go, to make himself suffocate quickly. He could not. When the air in his lungs went foul he always pushed up to breathe, to live, if only to live in order to suffer. Others, he saw, also tried and also failed. They, like he, wept bitterly, their manhood stolen. Worse, in some ways, was that their illusions about being willing martyrs to the cause were stolen from them, as well. Believe as they might that a glorious future at the hand of God awaited them, still, in their weakness, they struggled to live. That theft of faith made them weep all the more.

✧　　✧　　✧

Mustafa, of course, was not on a cross. Instead, he was "privileged," so some might say, to watch and listen as his followers died, to hear the cries coming from the Pashtun camp as his wives and daughters, and those of his followers, were forced to perform for their captors.

Shame, shame, all is shame, he mourned. *All my honor is lost with my women turned to slaves and whores.*

For Carrera had been cruel to Mustafa. He had had him brought and forced to watch the bidding as the Pashtun Scouts sold off the women and girls excess to their immediate needs to the whoremasters of Yamato and Doha. The bidding had been fierce at times as they were stripped and shown off on the rude auction block set up to one side of the mass of crosses.

Even the souls of my youngest children are forfeit as they will be converted into Nazrani. *I've lost everything.*

Mustafa glared his hate at Carrera, sitting there smug and apparently cheerful as he quaffed his sinful drink. Carrera noticed Mustafa's glare and raised his glass in salute.

"You might have won, you know, old boy," Carrera taunted, loudly enough for the Salafi to hear. "The margin of victory for the Federated States in Sumer was that close, close enough that without my legion added to the mix they probably would have lost or given up in war-weariness. You saved them from that by freeing me to help them. Congratulations on earning your place in history."

Mustafa had learned enough about Carrera's personal history to understand that this might be so. It made him sick to his stomach to think that he had caused all this himself.

Even so, he still could not see that he had created Carrera, or freed the monster within him, at any rate. Cause and effect were confused within his mind. At a purely emotional level—and in this, at least, Mustafa was intensely human—all the harm that had been done to him existed in one part of his mind as if it had always been there, while the harm he had done, in turn, seemed very small and very late. And only just.

You don't really understand do you? Carrera asked silently, looking intently into Mustafa's face for some sign of comprehension. He found none. *Oh, well; it's the common lot of humanity and always has been. In the mid to late twentieth century on Old Earth, Japanese deeply resented the atomic bombing of Hiroshima and Nagasaki. They forgot their own previous attack on Pearl Harbor in 1941, and the murders of guiltless prisoners. Conversely, Americans remembered that attack, would continue to remember it for centuries, and justified the nuking of two cities by it. The Americans, in their own turn, forgot that they had been in the process of turning Japan back to the stone age, prior to Pearl Harbor, when the Japanese had struck. The Japanese remembered the embargo, the freezing of credit, and the threat. They invariably forgot the brutal murdering, raping and thieving sojourn in China which well predated the American embargoes.*

Carrera understood, even if Mustafa did not. This was mankind's way from times immemorial. People measured right and wrong, typically, as a function of whose ox was being gored, and when. What *our* side did was good and justifiable and therefore what the other side did was evil and reprehensible. Salafis, even on Terra Nova, still harked back to the loss of Spain to the Reconquista. They rarely if ever remembered that they had stolen Spain in the first place. It was a form of Orwellian double think, but one that required no party *Pravda* to bring about.

Jebel Ansar, Pashtia, 21/8/469 AC

The sun stood up just over the mountains to the east. At Carrera's nod, Masood sent his men around with heavy steel bars. In groups of two, forty Pashtun scouts walked the lines of burdened crosses. At each they stopped just long enough to take one or sometimes two swings with the steel bars, breaking the shins of the condemned. Half the men on the crosses were too far gone to so much as scream when their bones were splintered. The loudest sound was often the grunt of exertion followed by the dull thud of heavy steel on thin flesh and thick bone.

"Never underestimate the benefits of a classical education," Carrera quipped, half drunkenly, to Mustafa.

Thereafter, all that stood between the victims and death was whatever strength remained in their weakened arms. For most, this was little enough. They hung down freely, the position of their arms forcing their chests out to where exhalation was almost impossible. Within an hour and a half all were dead and cooling. The Pashtun went around, prodding the bodies with bayonets to ensure they were indeed dead. Once satisfied, they took the corpses down and carried them to a mass grave.

With each thud, and then with each body removed, Carrera felt *himself* weakening: *Click . . . click . . . click . . . click . . . click.* Soon he was almost as drained of life and energy as his victims had been.

His chin slumped down on his chest. His breathing became labored. His eyes closed and he dreamt.

He found himself in the same chair. Now though, all the crosses were emptied. The Pashtun were removing them from the earth and stacking them in bundles. Distantly he heard helicopters coming. He thought it must be to remove the last of his troops and the few prisoners they'd kept alive.

Carrera stiffened at feeling a too-long-absent hand on his shoulder. He heard a voice say, "Don't turn around, Patricio, my beloved."

"Linda?" he asked. "What will . . ."

"Shshsh," she answered. "It's almost over now. Soon, no more war for you, not for a while, anyway. Go home, home to Balboa. Enjoy your new family. Live your new life. When the time comes, we will be waiting for you."

He shook his head and answered, "I have done awful things, Linda, here not least. How can I . . ."

"You did what you were required to do. That part is done now. You will not be well for some time, but you will recover. In time, you will come to join us. We will be waiting."

"There is one more thing to do," Carrera said. "A terrible thing."

"We know."

A second hand came to rest on the other shoulder, along with the sensation of six smaller and lighter ones . . . and, too light to be sure, maybe a seventh and eighth. Then Carrera felt a gentle kiss on the top of his head and . . . they were gone.

INTERLUDE

5/32/435 AC, Headquarters, Project Themistocles, Federated States of Columbia, Terra Nova

Deep, deep in a huge bunker buried far under the granite of the Dragonback Mountains, uniformed men and woman bent over radar screens, control panels, and communications nodes.

A woman announced, "We have liftoff . . . identified as a Class Two robotic courier vessel . . . leaving Atlantis now."

"Mark as target one," ordered a two star general of the Federated States Air Force. "Alert Launch Pad Seven to be prepared to fire."

"Target marked," said the woman. From a different section of the bunker a man relayed, "Launch Pad Seven has the target and is prepared to unmask and fire."

The two star nodded at that. *So far; so good.* "Pass on to all Themistocles assets to prepare to unmask and paint the enemy fleet."

"Target One is approaching optimum engagement range," the woman said. "Optimum engagement range in . . . four minutes."

"Commence countdown."

"General, stations one through two-hundred and forty-nine, except station twenty-nine and one-five-two, report ready to unmask and paint."

"What's wrong with twenty-nine and one-five-two?"

"Cooling leak in the missile on twenty nine . . . telemetry error on one-five-two."

"Fuck." *Well, it doesn't matter. We have plenty still.*

It would not do to demonstrate the ability to take out just one Earthpig asset. The Federated States needed to at least *imply* the ability to take out many *and* to scour Atlantis Base free of life. The nukes they had, of course.

A screen on one wall came to life. It showed the president of the Federated States at his desk. The president looked as frightened as any man might, on the verge of possibly plunging his world into nuclear holocaust. Behind him, ranged in an arc, were all of his chief advisors. They looked, if anything, more frightened still.

"Mr. President," the general said.

"General Rogers," the president returned with a slight bow of his head. "I have a message for you, General."

"I am prepared to receive, sir."

From his desk the president lifted a piece of paper. From it he read:

"By oppression's woes and pains,
By our sons in servile chains,
We shall drain our dearest veins."

The general nodded and answered, "I understand, sir. 'But they shall be free,' Mr. President."

"People! You heard the man. ICBMs, unmask.

Submarines, up to launch depth. Project Themistocles, unmask and paint that *alien* fleet," Rogers snarled.

Then, finally, "And clear that courier ship out of *our* space."

5/32/435 AC, UEPF *Spirit of Peace*

Where the uniformed woman under the Dragonbacks had seemed preternaturally calm and determined, the woman in uniform aboard the starship went instantly white. Her voice was full of panic as she called out, "Admiral? High Admiral? We've got radar and lidar illuminating us from the surface . . . dozens . . . no *hundreds* of emitters. And—oh, shit—we've got a launch. It appears that the target is robot courier 117."

The high admiral, Martin Robinson's predecessor, went as white as his crewwoman. "Red alert."

Almost immediately, red lights began flashing not only aboard the flagship, but also aboard every other ship in the fleet. Klaxons added to the sense of panic. The United Earth Peace Fleet was never really intended to fight a war. None of its crews ever really thought a war that could directly affect them was even possible.

"Message from below, High Admiral," said the communications officer. "The chief of the FSC wants to talk to you."

"Put the barbarian on," the high admiral snarled.

The president wasn't smiling when his image appeared on *Spirit's* bridges' main viewscreen. His words were icy.

"We've had enough of you," he began, most undiplomatically. "For twenty-five years we have been working, in secret, and well. We are ready now. I've ordered the destruction of one of your robotic couriers to demonstrate that you are *vulnerable*. I've also ordered my strategic nuclear forces to prepare to engage your fleet, and to scour your base on the island of Atlantis free of life if there is the slightest retaliation for the destruction of that courier.

"Try and nuke our cities again, you miserable son of a bitch."

CHAPTER TWENTY-SEVEN

The thing that hath been, it is that which shall be; and that which is done is that which shall be done: and there is no new thing under the sun.

—Ecclesiastes 1:9

Be not deceived; God is not mocked: for whatsoever a man soweth, that shall he also reap.

—Galatians, 6:7

Whatever thy hand findeth to do, do it with thy might; for there is no work, nor device, nor knowledge, nor wisdom, in the grave whither thou goest.

—Ecclesiastes 9:10

Punta Cocoli, Isla Real, Balboa, 25/9/469 AC

Though the sun was long set, still heat emanated in choking, stultifying waves from the tarmac of the airfield. Under a double-roofed hangar a Nabakov-21 transport waited for its load. With the Nabakov likewise waited a profusely sweating Omar Fernandez, along with a section of utterly reliable guards and a score of dripping men of the Tercio Jan Sobieski, seconded to Fernandez's department, who would be accompanying him on the upcoming flight.

Fernandez had reason to sweat, and it wasn't just the heat. *What Patricio told me to do? My God, does he understand the risks? This is the genie in the bottle. That . . . or perhaps he is right and it is that cap that seals the genie into its bottle. Even so . . .*

A three-ton tactical truck stopped behind the hangar and began disgorging troops who raced to surround the half of the hangar nearest the airfield. Two more trucks, hauling forty-foot conexes, pulled up to the hangar on the side away from the airfield, the side toward which the Nabakov's loading ramp faced. The trucks' air brakes squealed loudly as they shuddered to a stop. A fourth truck stopped, this one, like the first, carrying security men. Those men took up positions around the far side of the hangar from the airfield, completing the circle. Inside that perimeter, the first of the heavier trucks began to back up to the Nabakov's ramp to transfer its cargo.

Fernandez watched the transfer closely. *I hope dearly that Patricio is right and we can keep this part of the secret secret. Obras Zorilleras worked hard on these. And we will need them still to be a surprise if . . . no, not "if," when it comes to open war with Taurus.*

Open war? I'm preparing for that well enough. Whoever is in charge—we can only hope it's that Frog bastard, Janier—when the war starts he will be very surprised at the loyalty of some of the people working for him. That's for the future, though, and a lot may change. Be nice if we could ensure Muñoz-Infantes were in command on that day. We could just relax; war over and won. He won't be though. It'll be a Frog, Janier or some other one. I mean, it has to be a Frog or the mistress's quarters in Building 95 on Fort Muddville will be totally wasted.

Fernandez smiled at his own silent jest. It would never have done for him to make an open joke. And it was hard enough for him to smile at all. He pulled out his wallet and flipped it open to a small picture, that of his young daughter, murdered by Salafi terrorists years prior.

Baby, he thought to his daughter's image. *Baby, by now you know everything your father has done and does. Do you still look up to me, even as you gaze down upon me? I can hope so. What I do, I do for la Patria. And I rarely take any joy in it.*

The crew chief of the Nabakov found Fernandez deep in his reveries. "Legate," the chief said, "we're ready to board you now. The crews for the cargo are already loaded."

Xamar Airport, Xamar, 28/9/469 AC

Carrera, Hamilcar standing beside, met Fernandez at the airport. "You have them?" he asked. "They really work?"

"Tested against the best radar we could find to test them against, Patricio. They work. Mitchell and Soult came along, too. The package?" Fernandez asked.

"It flew in with me, along with my son. I didn't have all of the things in hand when I sent you the other shipment. One we took later. We'll marry up the package and the drone, here, then do the launches."

"I have a man watching the compound," Fernandez said. "He's a Sumeri, one of those who've been herding the targets for us. He's a good man, a tremendous asset. I'd like to pull him out before it's too late. I don't have to be explicit; I can tell him we think someone's on to him and to be prepared to flee at a moment's notice. Then we give the notice, maybe two hours before H Hour."

Loyalty to one's subordinates is . . . proper, Carrera thought. "You can pull him out but not more than one hour before time."

Fernandez shrugged. He'd split the difference. *Whatever it takes to keep Khalid in play.*

He'll split the difference, Carrera thought. *Fernandez is nothing if not loyal.*

"We're really not going to be able to keep this secret, you know?" Fernandez said. "Too many people are too much in the know about too many parts. At *best* we might have plausible deniability."

"At some point in time," Carrera pointed out, "we're going to *want* the word to get out. For now, only your people know. *Obras Zorilleras* only knows they had to give up two models of Condor. The aircrew that brought the Condors here only know they brought conexes. The crew that brought me and the package knew they're carrying something odd, but no more than that. And they're used to me traveling with some baggage, at least sometimes. The crew of the *Qamra* that will take me out to the *Mises* won't know anything. And if I can't trust *your* people to keep quiet then we're fucked anyway."

"You're really sure about this, Patricio? This is . . ." Fernandez struggled for words and found none.

"Horrible?" Carrera supplied. "Monstrous? Inhuman? It's all those things, Omar. Are you worried for my soul? Despite reassurances otherwise, I'm rather certain that that's forfeit anyway. And I can think of no other way to end this. We have to raise the stakes to a level the other side can't handle.

"And besides, Omar," Carrera continued, "our mercenary days are almost ended. We have another war to fight and for that we must have all the force at our disposal in Balboa. This war must end, *now.*"

Hamilcar had hardly said a word in weeks. It wasn't so much that he was in shock over what the Pashtian witch-girl had told him, though there was some of that. Nor even had he been too shocked when over a hundred of the Pashtun, apparently from the witch-girl Alena's tribe, had lined up along the road leading to Camp San Lorenzo's airfield to go on their faces as his father's staff car passed to bring them to their plane. He'd known it was Alena's tribe because she had been there, too, standing in front of them to lead them in their devotions.

His father had had the car stop and beckoned Alena and someone Ham thought was probably her brother over.

He'd spoken to them very briefly. "Upon our return, and until you are or he is dead, you are all hired to be bodyguards to my son. Is this acceptable?

The tears of gratitude and religious devotion had been answer enough.

The problem was, *I don't* feel *like a god. I don't*

believe I am a god. I don't want to be a god. I'm just a little boy.

"Remember: easy now, boys," said the warrant officer in charge of the detachment. "Take her out gently."

The conex had room, more than enough room, for the Condor frame, motor, propeller, control station, a load of fuel, three sets of wings, lifting-launch system, or LLS, all the other parts required, and a tool kit for assembly. Unpacking and assembly presented no problem to the crews; they were the same ones that had disassembled and packed them back on the *Isla Real*.

The conex doors were unlocked and opened. Inside was the body, mounted on a wheeled framework. These, the crews pulled out onto the concrete floor of a stifling hangar, then proceeded to remove the fastening straps that had held the body and wings securely during shipment. There were also a dozen cots inside, secured around the control station at the far end.

While one part of each crew went to work checking the engine, another lifted and then rotated the wings into position. These were secured in place with carbon fiber pins. A third team for each moved the lifting-launch system from the conex and trudged it out of the hangar where they checked tank pressure and began laying out the two balloons that would provide initial lift. Likewise, they unfurled the lifting and restraining lines that would, in the first case, attach to a jettisonable ring atop the Condor and, in the second case, hold the balloons to the heavy steel frameworks on which the birds rested. Still a fourth pair of teams moved out the cots and prepared the control stations inside the conexes.

The sun was up, and the air above the tarmac of

the airstrip shimmering, by the time the Condors were ready to be wheeled out and hooked to the LLS. They were left under cover for the nonce, however.

The warrant officer in charge inspected both Condors from nose to tail, along with the ancillary gear. Eventually satisfied with his inspection, he sent the men to sleep in one corner of the hangar, then stood guard himself. There would be several nights of rehearsals before the night of launch.

Hajar, Yithrab, 29/9/469 AC

In a cloth-hung room—cloth-hung the better to simulate the tents of the Bedouin ancestors—a tray of *kibsa*, lamb over rice with a yogurt based sauce, sat barely touched on the floor between the three brothers. Each man wore traditional robes, their heads covered with keffiyahs held in place by beaded cords. The keffiyahs were traditional white. The robes, however, varied, Bakr in white, Abdullah in blue, and Yeslam in red.

"This is like being in prison," said Yeslam ibn Mohamed ibn Salah, min Sa'ana, "like prison with a sentence of death on our heads!"

Bakr sighed. They'd all heard about the sentences of death, and the manner of death, of Mustafa and his followers. While the mercenaries had not advertised it, word had leaked out from the Pashtian scouts that had actually carried out the crucifixions and bore the blame, or took the credit, for them. Khadijah, inconsolable, had taken to her rooms, shrieking and weeping at the indignity presumably inflicted on her beloved stepson Mustafa. The truth was much worse than she suspected.

"I am thinking," Bakr said, "that we'd all have been

better off if someone had strangled Mustafa in the cradle. Yes, I believed we should support him, early on, but who could have suspected the kind of terror he would bring upon us."

"*I* suspected it," answered Abdullah. "You have not lived among those people. I have. There is a touch of vindictive madness about them. They keep it hidden, most of the time. But it was always there."

Yeslam shook his head. "Cursed be the day we sent Mustafa off on his grand adventure. Cursed be the money we gave him to start his project."

"*I* gave him no money," Abdullah insisted. "That was all the doing of you and Bakr. *I* counseled against it."

Both Bakr and Yeslam shrugged, eloquently. *Spilled milk.*

"Then counsel us *now,* brother mine. What do we do *now*?" Bakr asked. "How do we keep our clan's life blood from spilling *now*?"

"I would suggest a bribe," Abdullah answered, "except that we do not have enough money—no, not if we turned over everything we own—to buy our way out of this. Our enemy is implacable, inconsolable, and inhuman. He will keep us locked up here—nor would we be safe anywhere else in the world—until the judgment day."

"You mean, he's just like us," Yeslam said. He closed his eyes, hung his head, and said in despair, "Allah help us."

Xamar Airport, Xamar, 31/9/469 AC

The recon bird would go first. This was both to test Yithrabi air defense and warning radars, as well as to ensure that the secret was *still* secret, that nothing had tipped off the target and caused a mass evacuation. The other Condor, the drone, would follow in the trail cleared by the first.

For speed's sake, both crews got together to wheel out the first Condor. Just past the edge of the hangar they stopped and hooked up all five straps plus two electric wires. Four of the five straps that came from the balloon were attached to the steel frame. The fifth went to the jettisonable lifting ring atop the bird. The wires were hooked, one into a heavy duty control that would cause the balloon to cut itself away from the four restraining straps, on command, the other to the top of the *Condor* next to the ring.

These tasks completed, the crew began to fill the balloon with hydrogen. This was much cheaper than helium and, because the balloon was a throwaway that had only one mission, was not noticeably unsafe nor tactically unsound.

Gradually, the balloon filled until it had *just* positive buoyancy. At that point the crew stopped the filling and let it gently float to just above the Condor. They then resumed filling, until the restraining straps were taut.

The warrant officer in charge, holding the control box, looked over at Carrera and Fernandez. The latter nodded and the warrant pushed a green button. Instantly, all four restraining straps, plus the cable, were cut loose, falling to the ground around the Condor. At the same time, the balloon lurched upward, dragging the Condor with it, forcing its wings to bend slightly under the force of the acceleration and the resistance of the air.

✧　　✧　　✧

The pilot sitting in the control station at one end of the conex watched the altimeter and global locating system readings on his screen carefully. Sometimes, prevailing winds could help a Condor out, carrying it nearer to its target without having to expend fuel or hunt for updrafts. This was not one of those cases; the winds were crosswise to the planned line of flight. In the long run, this would cost fuel. The pilot nodded to himself, then typed in a code and pressed a button.

By the time the Condor received the signal it was several miles away from and above the pilot. It sent a further signal to the ring and the wire atop itself, which caused both to detach. Simultaneously it initiated a timer in the balloon that would cause the hydrogen to burn some hours later, after it had drifted well away from the release point and line of flight.

Freed of the balloon, the Condor initially dropped. Its wings, however, were wide and its chord nearly perfect for gliding. They immediately bit into the air, obtaining lift as the bird glided forward. Later, the pilot would use the engine to rise again, before he resumed the very fuel-efficient gliding that was really the Condor's main means of propulsion.

Back in the hangar, the pilot breathed a sigh of relief. It had happened, during development and testing, that the balloon release mechanism had failed. *Thank God it worked properly this time.*

Some distance from the conex wherein the pilot sat, Carrera and Fernandez stood and watched the package being armed and loaded into the second Condor by

Fernandez's people. Fernandez noted, *Patricio's face is just a stone mask, like he's shut himself down inside. I cannot even imagine what he's feeling. Freedom, finally, from the burden of avenging his family? Wondering what to do with the rest of his life? Or perhaps he's thinking that he has no more reason to live after this. Suicide?* Fernandez reconsidered that last. *No . . . he has a new family and he loves them. That much at least, I am confident of; he will live for them. Which is important, as* la Patria *will need him soon.*

Pier Seventeen, Port Xamar, BdL *Qamra*, 32/9/469 AC

It was almost midnight, with only Hecate—and she in her first quarter—showing. The boat was darkened to normal observation, though Chu knew that he was under satellite observation by the FSN, if anyone happened to be looking. Fosa had *wanted* them to observe the fleet, if only to get early warning of any attack. He could hardly tell them to look the other way now, even though he had stressed to Chu that he wanted this cargo moved as secretly as possible.

Chu was almost unsurprised when a four-wheel-drive vehicle, escorted by two others bearing military police, showed up at the pier and *Duque* Carrera stepped out, accompanied by several others. One of those other was, apparently, a child. *Oh, yes, that would explain the need for secrecy,* he thought.

Marta had the wheel, though the boat was tied up and stationary. Chu had been training her as a backup. The girl seemed to have an affinity for boats, perhaps because life ashore had been so seedy and degrading for her. Since the loss of Jaquelina, the larger woman had taken little interest in anything else.

Leaving her with the con, Chu hurried to the bow to greet his guest.

He saluted, of course, which salute Carrera returned. Yet Carrera didn't salute either the small standard fluttering at the stern nor the bridge. *Landlubbers,* Chu thought, with a mental *harrumph. They know nothing of naval protocol. Then again, since he owns this boat, the fleet, the entire legion, I suppose I'd best just shut up about it.*

"Captain," Carrera greeted at he stepped over the gangplank onto the deck.

"*Duque,*" Chu answered, with a head nod. *At least he knows the proper form or address.* "A cabin has been prepared below. We're past dinner but I've had the cook put a meal in your cabin." *Which is my cabin, actually, but let's not go there.* "If you would like a drink, there's scotch in a drawer in the desk. I can arrange a woman . . ."

"That won't be necessary; the woman, I mean. I appreciate the scotch, too, but I've bought my own. My son will stay with me. Billet the others. And then just take me to the *Mises*, Captain."

Hildegard Mises, 33/9/469 AC

He looks much the worse for wear, thought Carrera, looking at the emaciated body of Mustafa ibn Mohamed ibn Salah, min Sa'ana. *On him, it's plain on the outside. With me? It's all on the inside.*

Mustafa's beard, once long and flowing and rich in dignity, was shaved off. This was only fitting as he was soon to be changed into a woman. His hands were bandaged and bound. Had he not been given a robe, there would have been visible burn marks on his torso. Both of his feet looked deformed now; the guards had had to carry him into the interview room. He had his arms wrapped about his torso, holding broken ribs as if terrified of any movement. This, too, was understandable. Skevington's daughter, among her other talents, also broke ribs. Even had none of this been so, still Mustafa would not have smiled. He'd been to the dentist once too often for that.

For all that, he's still in better mental shape than Robinson or Arbeit, Carrera thought. *Those two have totally collapsed.*

"You gave up everything you knew you had to give, I think, old friend," Carrera said to him. His voice was gentle, as if he were somehow detached from his surroundings, even as if he were somehow detached from life. "Still, I wonder what more you might give up."

At a nod from Carrera, the two screens, neither of them Kurosawas, sprang to life. The screen on the left showed little but a rapidly passing desert below, with the occasional camel or goat visible only as a greenish pixilation of a slightly different shade from the sand beneath. The other screen likewise showed a night scene, taken from above. The latter scene, however, was much more brightly lit, the features much more easily distinguished. It showed a walled compound, minaret rising above the wall, and armed guards patrolling it. The images on the screens were being recorded, as was the scene on the *Mises* of Carrera chatting with Mustafa.

"Recognize it?" Carrera asked.

"Go to Hell, pig," Mustafa responded through drilled and temporarily patched teeth. One of the guards pulled the former prince of the *Ikhwan* to his feet by his hair. Two brutally quick punches to the kidney left the ex-terrorist sobbing on the floor.

It must take tremendous courage, courage passing that of men, to still remain defiant after all he's been through. I could admire him were circumstances otherwise.

"I really do insist that you look at the screen," Carrera said. "I don't want to have to have your eyelids sewn open." A shift of Carrera's chin caused the same guard who had kidney punched Mustafa to haul him back onto his chair, again by his hair. "Now *watch*. This is important . . . to you. Do you recognize the view on the right?"

Mustafa looked, this time; anything to avoid another set of blows to his already abused kidneys. *The surrounding wall . . . the minaret . . . the small mosque below . . . that's my family compound in Hajar!*

"Why are you showing me this?" Mustafa asked.

"You *do* recognize it then?"

"Yes . . . yes, of course I do. I grew up there."

"Indeed," Carrera agreed. "Did you know that nearly every child, grandchild, and great grandchild of your father is likewise growing up there? Did you know that all your brothers and cousins, all their husbands and wives, are likewise in that compound? Oh, sure . . . maybe a few distant relatives might be elsewhere. But I am pretty confident"—his tone held the very platonic essence of confidence as he said it—"that at least ninety-eight percent of your blood relatives are there in that compound. We spent . . . *I* spent much effort at making life impossible for them anywhere else."

Mustafa said nothing to that. He'd known that his family had been hunted like animals all over the planet. It was not much of a surprise that this vicious, filthy, crusading swine had wielded the guiding hand of murder.

Carrera lit a cigarette. He saw Mustafa's eyes widen with barely repressed desire. *Why not? Isn't everyone entitled to a last cigarette?* He handed the lighter and pack to one of the guards and said, "Give him one."

Mustafa took the cigarette in his bandaged and bound hands and held it to his mouth while the guard flicked the lighter for him. One it was lit, he puffed frantically, eyes closing in unaccustomed bliss.

Carrera waited patiently for Mustafa to finish the cigarette. He had time.

"You were going to use nuclear weapons on both of my homelands," Carrera said. It wasn't a question and so Mustafa didn't answer. "Did you know I've had nuclear weapons since 461? Those were small things, though. Nothing like the citybusters I captured at your base. The ones I had had other defects, too, mainly that a clever man might trace them to me and my people."

Mustafa's eyed darted to the screens. Carrera caught the movement.

"Oh, yes. One of those captured, a true citybuster, is headed toward your family compound. That's the screen on the left. It's rated at seven hundred and eighty kilotons. I am informed that we can expect one hundred percent deaths at your family compound, and anything from half a million to a million in the city of Hajar."

His face a study in horror, Mustafa shook his head in denial. "You can't . . ."

"Sure I can," Carrera said. "Moreover, why should I not? I mean, think about it. Here you are, the greatest—known—terrorist in the history of this world. You've been trying to get nukes for decades. Your chief assistant, Nur al Deen, even insisted you had them. He quoted the price you paid, did he not? And then a nuke goes off at ground zero, right inside your family compound, a place you conceivably might have stored one. That, alone, will make your movement very unappealing to the bulk of even young, idiot, male Salafis.

"But there will be doubts, too. 'Maybe,' people will say, 'just maybe it was a deliberate attack.' Now if that attack were to be from someone identifiable, then there would be a great cry for vengeance. But when the attack seems to come from nowhere? When they can't even identify a target for vengeance? No, old friend, *that* will be truly effective terror. *That* will have no focus for revenge. *That* will have your people shitting themselves at the thought of retaliation and beating their sons the first time the little bastards shout '*Allahu Akbar*' a bit too enthusiastically. It's perfect; don't you see? And *you* gave me the means. *That*'s perfect, too.

"Lastly, I think that when the king of Yithrab—whoever ends up as king, the day after tomorrow—has to spend money to rebuild his capital, he'll find he can't afford both a capital city and madrassas all over the planet."

Carrera went silent then, leaving Mustafa in torment as the clock displayed on the left-hand screen ticked down.

After that long silence, with the clock down to under five minutes and Mustafa's face showing mental agony beyond agony, Carrera said, "I *could* change the target now, I suppose. Tell me, would you rather your family die en masse or would you prefer that I obliterate Makkah al Jedidah and the New Kaaba?"

Mustafa cringed, both inside and out. "Devil!" he spat. "Spawn of *Shaitan*!"

"Which really doesn't answer the question," Carrera observed, still genially. "Would you rather I obliterate your family, your *entire* family, or that one stone building, which includes but a single stone from the original on Old Earth, should go up in smoke? I remind you that the number of civilian dead will be about the same."

Deprivation, stress, physical torture, and now *this*. Mustafa felt his heart begin to crack even as it had not cracked previously. *To lose my entire family . . . to destroy the sacred Kaaba?* He sank; physically, as he slumped and drew in on himself, mentally, as the weight Carrera had laid upon his soul bore him Hellward.

"Destroy . . . Makkah," Mustafa forced out. "Spare . . . my . . . family."

"No."

"But . . ."

"I said I could," Carrera's genial tone changed to one of pure cruelty. "I didn't say I would. Your family dies, as you murdered mine. I would kill them anyway, if only to terrorize any in the future who might contemplate going down the road you traveled. I just wanted both

God and yourself to know that your faith, your personal faith, was a fraud. I may join you in Hell, someday, Mustafa. Indeed, after this, I probably will. But at least, if I do, it won't be because I betrayed *my* God as you have just tried to betray *yours*."

Mustafa's jaw went slack, his eyes wild. As the clock on the screen wound down, he began a wordless moan. When it reached zero, and the image on the screen changed to a single enormous flash, the terrorist in the cabin aboard the *Mises* began a horrible keening. It was the sound of a man who has lost everything, in this world *and* the next.

Carrera arose to leave. "Cheer up, old man," he said. "You still have one son left. Me." To Mahamda he gave the order. "Turn him into what he despises, a woman. Then crucify him . . . her . . . *it*."

"And the Earthpigs?"

"Let's save them for a while and see what use we might make of them."

Bridge, UEPF *Spirit of Peace*, 33/9/469 AC

Life is looking up, Wallenstein thought, as she lounged in her command chair. *Robinson is gone. I am in command here, now, so it seems very likely that I shall be raised to Class One. All in all . . .*

A crewwoman at a sensing panel started back as if the panel were passing electricity through her body. "Captain, I've got a nuclear detonation on the planet's surface!"

Wallenstein's eyes grew wide in horror. Policy, long established, was that the fleet would retaliate for any use of nuclear weapons. But that would mean nuclear war with the FSC. *Oh, Annan, I don't want to die, not now, not when I'm so close to my dreams.*

"Where? Who?" she demanded, lurching straight upright.

"Yithrab, Captain. City of Hajar. Devastation is near total. There must be a half million dead. Hell . . . maybe two million. As for who . . ."

"Yes?"

"Unknown. The analysis is different from any we have a record of. All I can say is it wasn't one of ours."

"Get me a line to the president of the Federated States," Wallenstein ordered. *That son of a bitch,* she thought. *He promised he wouldn't tell the FSC that Robinson was trying to give nukes to the* Ikhwan. *And, so far as I can tell, he didn't. But he never said he wouldn't use one. And he just did. And I thought I was ruthless . . .*

BdL Hildegard Mises, 33/9/469 AC

Except for a couple of men who sat a bench near the superstructure of the ship, the small party accompanying Carrera stood in a group by its port side. In the distance, they could see *Qamra* approaching. A ladder had already been let over the side to allow them to climb down.

While waiting for the *Qamra* to come alongside to pick them up, Soult and Mitchell watched Carrera as he stood on the deck. Carrera looked, to say the least, unwell. Soult worried about the "old man's" trembling hands. To Mitchell, the major concern was the glassy, mindless stare.

If the boss said it was right to nuke a major city

and kill upwards of half a million people, that was enough for them. Still, though they, themselves, had no particular problem with the nuking of Hajar, perhaps it was bothering him.

Whatever he was feeling inside, though, could not be good. And then . . .

Ah, Jesus," Mitchell thought, *he's crying.*

It was true, not some fluke of the light nor even some bits of detritus in his eyes. Trembling, staring down at the sea; tears coursed down Carrera's face. He didn't seem to notice.

"Other side of the ship," Soult said to the other guards and seamen standing around. "Now! We'll take care of him." He looked at the boy, Hamilcar, and appended, "Stay here, son. Maybe it will help your father."

Hamilcar nodded but thought, *I don't think anything much that I can do will help.*

"He's just relieved that it's finally over," Mitchell insisted to the soldiers and sailors scurrying away. He called to their backs, "And if you mention a word of this to *anyone*, your *grand*children will have nightmares."

Both men moved in to stand close to either side. It was as well that they did; Carrera's knees buckled and he began to fall to the deck. They caught him and half carried him backwards to the bench.

"Boss? Sir? Pat?" There was no reaction, except that the tears were joined by sobs.

"What do we do, Jamey?" Mitchell asked, desperately.

"Get him to a doctor? Get him home? Hell, I don't know. We've seen him in bad shape before, but *this*?"

"I think we'd better call the sergeant major."

"And my mother," Hamilcar added.

Herrera International Airport, *Ciudad* Balboa, 2/10/469 AC

Carrera, Hamilcar, Mitchell, and Soult came in by chartered jet. The plane landed on the military side of the airport and was immediately surrounded by troops of the First Tercio, *Principio Eugenio*. Lourdes, Parilla and McNamara boarded, along with a dozen others. Inside they found Carrera stretched out on a medical litter, either asleep or comatose. Lourdes knelt before her son and hugged him tight, then turned and placed one hand against Carrera's face before bending to kiss his forehead.

"Home now, my love," she said. "Home now . . . forever."

If Carrera heard he gave no sign, but continued to stare straight up as if he were someplace else entirely.

"Doctor, what's wrong with him?" Parilla asked of the medico in attendance.

"Bare minimum, complete exhaustion," the doctor answered. "What other problems he may have will take a while to figure out and treat. A nervous breakdown is possible."

At McNamara's order, four of the men escorting picked up the litter and carried it first to the exit way, then down the long flight of debarkation steps to the tarmac below. There the litter was placed in an ambulance, which drove slowly and carefully to a legion NA-23, parked nearby.

Punta Cocoli, Isla Real, 2/10/469 AC

The NA-23 cargo plane, in the colors of the legion and with a picture of Jan Sobieski's Winged Hussars painted on the side, landed on the airstrip on the *Isla Real*, then turned and taxied to the terminal. There it stopped and lowered its ramp.

Virtually the entire population of the island—over thirty-five thousand soldiers, plus their wives and children—lined the fence at the edge of the airfield or found a spot along the road that led from there to the rest of the island.

Four of the people waiting were Jorge Mendoza, his lovely wife, Marqueli, and their two children. Another child was on the way; Marqueli's belly was impressively swollen.

Jorge's thesis was now the text for a course he taught at Signifer and Centurion Candidate Schools. The basis of the thesis and of the course was an Old Earth bit of science fiction written by a man known to Terra Novans only as RAH, a translation of which Carrera had had printed. Both thesis and course were entitled, "History and Moral Philosophy."

"This doesn't look good, Jorge," Marqueli said after the plane had lowered its rear ramp falling into her old habit of describing what he could now see for himself. "He can't walk . . . or isn't, anyway. They're carrying him on a litter, with my cousin walking beside. It looks like a funeral procession." The woman began to sniffle.

"It'll be okay," Mendoza said. "Old bastard is too tough to die on us . . . especially when we need him so badly now."

Carrera was carried down the ramp and placed on the back of a flatbed truck. Lourdes and Parilla had wanted another closed ambulance but the sergeant major had insisted, "No . . . rumors are flying everywhere. Let t'em see he's . . . basically . . . all right . . . t'at he just needs a long rest. He would want t'at."

Marqueli wasn't the only one beginning to tear up. Jorge whispered, "He was my commander. I can't say I liked him, or that many of us did. But we *did* love him."

Women began to weep as the flatbed moved away. What would happen to them and their husbands and families now? Carrera had given employment and care, had given meaning to lives. What did the future hold for them? What about the coming war? Children cried as their mothers did.

With their women and children, the men, too, began to shed tears. This was their commander, the man who had led them to victory upon victory. Would he return to them, return to continue the great war on which they had all embarked? If not, would his like ever be found again? A hard man and a harsh one they knew him to be. Did not the times themselves demand hardness and harshness?

The flatbed moved to the guarded gate to the airfield. Now they could truly see him and the weeping redoubled. Guards lining both sides of the road kept the surging crowd back. The cries grew:

"Give us our commander! Give us our *Duque*!"

Something touched Carrera. Where wife and family had not moved him, or not enough, the tears of his men and their women did. From under a draping sheet a single arm emerged and was held straight up.

At the end of the arm was a clenched fist.

EPILOGUE

The minstrel boy will return one day,
When we hear the news, we will cheer it.
The minstrel boy will return we pray,
Torn in body, perhaps, but not in spirit.
Then may he play his harp in peace,
In a world such as Heaven intended,
For every quarrel of Man must cease,
And every battle shall be ended.
—Anonymous, *The Minstrel Boy*,
Third Verse

Cochea, Balboa, 11/7/471 AC

Flames arose from torches on the green.

Lourdes had not been invited. "Love, in this one thing, you cannot be witness," Carrera had told her.

Her eldest was there, the boy Hamilcar Carrera-Nuñez. The boy was wide-eyed, half at the spectacle and half at being led kindly by the hand by his father. They walked along a path marked with the flaming torches towards the marble obelisk that marked the grave— though it was more memorial than grave, really—of his dead siblings and their mother.

883

Before moving to the memorial Carrera had shown the boy pictures of Linda and their children, explaining their names and telling him stories about them in life. He'd also told the boy how they'd been murdered.

"That's why I spent so much time away from home, Son," the father explained, "hunting down the men responsible."

"I understand, Dad," the boy said.

Perhaps he did, too. He was a bright lad, extremely so. Carrera expected great things of him. *Kid will likely be tall, too, given that his mother's 5'10"*.

Around the obelisk were several close friends: Kuralski, Soult and Mitchell, as well as Parilla. Jimenez, McNamara and Fernandez were in Pashtia, Jimenez commanding the field legion in Carrera's absence. Those present were uniformed and stood at parade rest as Carrera led the boy forward by the hand.

Soult brought out a Bible, which he handed to Carrera. Releasing Hamilcar's little hand, the father knelt down beside him, holding out the book and saying, "Place your left hand on this and raise your right. Now repeat after me."

"I, Hamilcar Carrera-Nuñez . . ."

"I, Hamilcar Carrera-Nuñez . . ."

". . . swear upon the altar of Almighty God . . ."

". . . swear upon the altar of Almighty God . . ."

". . . undying enmity and hate . . . to the murderers of my brother and sisters . . . and the murderers of their mother, my countrywoman . . . and to the murderers of all my country folk . . . and to those that have aided them . . . and those that have hidden them . . . and those who have made excuses for them . . . and those that have funded them . . .

and those who have lied for them . . . wherever and whoever they may be . . . and whoever may arise to take their places. I swear that I will not rest until my fallen blood is avenged and my future blood is safe. So help me, God."

"Very good, Son," Carrera said, handing the Bible back to Soult and ruffling Hamilcar's hair affectionately. "Now we are going to have dinner with my friends, back at the house. The day after tomorrow we go back to getting ready for the next war."

AUTHOR'S AFTERWORD

Warning: Authorial editorial follows. Read further at your own risk. You're not paying anything extra for it so spare us the whining if your real objection is that it is here for other people to read. If you are a Tranzi, and you read this, the author expressly denies liability for your resulting rise in blood pressure, apoplexy, exploding head or general icky feelings. (I am indebted to my former law partner, Matt Pethybridge, for his contributions to this after-word. Matt joins me in this dissent.)

"Do I hate cosmopolitans?" you ask. Why, no, of course I don't hate them. That would be like hating sex . . . or drugs. Cosmopolitanism is like sex and drugs, you know; it just makes you feel all gooey and great inside. It's like sex and drugs in another way, too. I'll cover that later.

Okay, I'll be serious now.

886

Imagine, just for now and just purposes of illustration, some solid geometric figure; a cube will do. One side of the cube is labeled "progressivism." Another might be "pacifism." Still another might be "multiculturalism." Then there's "humanitarianism" and "environmentalism" and "cosmopolitanism." What's inside the cube, if it is a cube, I can't tell you, but surely it's something that holds those six (or probably more) together. After all, scratch a cosmopolitan, wound a multiculturalist. Kick a progressive and set an environmentalist to screaming.

Some might say that what's inside the cube is communism. I'm not so sure it's that sophisticated. Really, I suspect there's not a lot more holding all those -isms together than a mix of arrogance, envy, hate, and rage. Oh, and greed. Greed's often very important, too. Still, I don't *know* what's inside. The cube—if, again, it is a cube—is not that opaque.

I know only what's on the outside. One of those things is cosmopolitanism. And yes, that's what I'm going to talk about right now.

There are a number of different kinds of cosmopolitanism, most of which are not really all that cosmopolitan. We have the religious versions, notably the Islamic and Christian ones. There's also a communist cosmopolitanism. And then there's what one might call "true cosmopolitanism," the kind put forth by Immanuel Kant and, more recently, Martha Nussbaum. For the most part, I'm going to talk about "true cosmopolitanism," hereinafter, just plain "cosmopolitanism." To do that, though, we need to at least glance over the others.

"All wars are civil wars because all men
are brothers."
                    —Francois Fenelon,
                    Archbishop of Cambrai[1]

Cosmopolitan religions typically allow anyone to
join in; they are open to anyone who will accept
their tenets, laws and philosophies. That's as far as it
goes, though. If one has not joined in the circle of
the given religion, and that religion *means* anything
to its adherents, one is outside it. I don't think I'm
doing any violence to cosmopolitan thought by saying
that religious cosmopolitanism is different, that drawing the kind of circle cosmopolitan religions do—us
and them, in and out—is not really cosmopolitanism.
Communist cosmopolitanism, on the other hand,
starts with the premise of ins and outs. It may cut
across nations and ethnicities, but communist cosmopolitanism cannot avoid the distinction of *class*.
It exists because of the distinction of class. Class is
a bright line circle drawn around some men, and
excluding others.[2]

---

1 If true and sincerely held, perhaps the good archbishop
  entered the priesthood to avoid committing incest.

2 Indeed, communist cosmopolitanism's circle is usually
  drawn by killing—quickly, via rope or bullet, or slowly,
  via Gulag—those who do not fit within it. It has generally
  done so with a forthright ruthlessness that even the Nazis
  could only stand back and admire. Religions do this, too, of
  course, but they're amateurs in comparison to communism.
  One is tempted to say that communism draws its circle
  with headstones . . . but this would be wrong as the mass
  graves are almost invariably unmarked.

Cosmopolitanism, on the other hand, permits no circles. It would allow no "us and them." It insists, to take Fenelon's words, that "all men are brothers." Of course, if all men are brothers then we are all part of the Family of Man.[3] To cosmopolitanism, this is so, the merest truth. Any distinctions drawn, any circle that doesn't include the entire human race, is arbitrary and illegitimate. Keep that—"arbitrariness"—in mind for later.

For now, let's look into families, shall we?

> "No matter how much I care about pro-
> gressive politics, at the end of the day, it's
> my family and their well-being that's going
> to come first."
> —Markos Moulitsas Zuniga, Kos

Kos here doesn't mean the "Family of Man." He means his own. One doesn't usually get that much honesty from anyone, let alone from the Left. (Applause—sincere applause—to Kos.) But do they act that way? Do they act as if their families came first? Of course they do, even though they usually hide behind any number of high sounding phrases: "Family of Man," "Human Rights" . . . "Progressivism."

When Kofi Annan abetted his son Kojo's tax fraud, that was putting his family and their well-being first. It was the same with the post-tax fraud cover up.

---

3 You may have noted that families have parents and children, the parents being in charge. Have you ever noticed how often people who use phrases like "Family of Man" tend to think of themselves as the parents? Guess who they think of as children.

It's there, too, in Benan Sevan's use of his aunt as a notional posthumous money launderer for his little profits from the "Oil For Food" scam. It's written in the lines of every Darien, Connecticut, mansion or Manhattan penthouse owned or rented by the head of some humanitarian nongovernmental organization.[4] It is implicit in the very generous educational benefits the fund-starved United Nations grants to the children of its bureaucrats for the sacrifice, if that's quite the word, they undergo of earning, if *that's* quite the word, fifty or one hundred times more than most of them could hope to in their own lands. It is George Soros raiding the Bank of England and doing insider trading with the French *Société Générale* for his own personal benefit. It is a highway in Africa which is never built to standard and washes away with the first hard rain because the money for material went to line someone's nephew's pockets.

---

4 And paid for by you. You know the ones: "Feed, clothe and educate poor little Maritza for twenty-seven cents a day?" It doesn't work that way. Little Maritza, if she gets clothed, fed and educated at all, typically gets it from strings-attached government grants. Sadly, for the men and women who claim to be feeding little Maritza, those strings tend to exclude things like paying for mansions in Darien. In most unenlightened fashion, when governments give money to feed little Maritza they actually insist that little Maritza be fed. Likewise stays at five star resorts for conferences are out. Likewise, flying first class to those conferences is out. That's where *your* no-strings-attached twenty-seven cents a day comes in. It can be used for the *important* things, mansions, luxury conferences, and first class airline seats. See: *The Road to Hell,* Michael Maren, The Free Press, 1997.

If there is a Third World politician who does not believe blood is thicker than water, he or she has probably been overthrown in a coup. It is the rule of Iraq, the rule of Iran.[5] It is China.[6] It is Latin America and Africa. It is, in ever growing frequency, the rule in Europe and the United States, too. Whether Third World or World Bank, that rule is "mine, first."

It's also one of the two default states of mankind. The other is *me* first." This latter occurs, for example, when environmentalist Cape Cod liberals invoke "Not In My Back Yard" to prevent the construction of energy saving windmills.

We are, each of us, descended from people who decided, generation upon generation, that their gene pool came first. The sociologists' term for it is "amoral familism." Note that that's *"a*moral," not necessarily *"im*moral." It's difficult to call something "immoral" that's in our very genes.

---

5 Oh, yes, the mullahs take care of their own. This is one similarity between religious cosmopolitanism and non-religious cosmopolitanism.

6 So do the Chinese communists. In fact, they're *especially* good at taking care of their own. They put mere mullahs and simple Tranzis in the shade. From an article by Carsten A. Holz, in *far* Eastern Economic Review, April, 2007: "Article after article pores over the potential economic reasons for the increase in income inequality in China. We ignore the fact that of the 3,220 Chinese citizens with a personal wealth of 100 million yuan ($13 million) or more, 2,932 are children of high-level cadres. Of the key positions in the five industrial sectors—finance, foreign trade, land development, large-scale engineering and securities—85% to 90% are held by children of high-level cadres."

Nor is this amoral familism by any means *arbitrary*. The connection to family is real. It is natural. It is, moreover, reinforced by close and intimate personal knowledge. It is also within the very natural human limit of what any person can really know or personally care about.

On the other hand, it's even more difficult to call the Annans' tax fraud and coverup *moral* behavior. Still less so Soros' raid on the Bank of England, mandatory kickbacks and bribes to line the pockets of dictators' and bureaucrats' nephews, and—not least—the fraudulent scamming of little Maritza's twenty-seven cents (see footnote 4). This is so, even though it may be in the genes.

Camouflage is also in the genes, for some species of predators. The predator, Man, being rather white or black or brown or yellow or red and, in any case, generally shiny and of regular shape, has to create his own. Some human predators, descended no less than we from Og, the caveman, have to disguise themselves no less than did Og, if they, the wives and the kiddies are going to eat (and live in that Darien mansion or Manhattan penthouse).

For many of these, cosmopolitanism is a cloak, the cloak behind which they can hide tax frauds and currency raids, insider trading and charity scams, graft and corruption and nepotism.

This doesn't mean that every cosmopolitan is a lying, scheming, greedy, hypocritical, dishonest predator. No doubt many are sincere, honest, selfless and, at a personal level, generally admirable in the conduct of their own lives. They sincerely believe that any distinction between peoples is arbitrary and therefore illegitimate. It may even be true, though it is no doubt rare, that they give no preference to their own little families over the Family of Man.

> "By conceding that a morally arbitrary boundary such as the boundary of the nation has a deep and formative role in our deliberations, we seem to be depriving ourselves of any principled way of arguing to citizens that they should in fact join hands across these other barriers."
>
> —Martha Nussbaum[7]

Arbitrariness appears to be one of the three core principles of cosmopolitanism; the others being, let us say, the complementary "Wouldn't it be nice?" and "Isn't it so awful?" When those for whom cosmopolitanism is more than camouflage ask those questions, in one form or another, they *do* have a point: it (life, the universe and everything) can be pretty awful and perhaps a more cosmopolitan world might be nice. Dull? Yes, probably, but that's not the worst imaginable world, is it?[8]

To concede those things, however, is not to concede much, for "Isn't it so awful?" does not mean it can't be or won't become worse, anymore that "Wouldn't it be nice?" proves that it *will* or even *can* be better.

Those we will take up later. For now, let's look into the concept of arbitrariness.

---

7 *Cosmopolitanism and Patriotism*, Boston Review 19:5 (October-November 1994).

8 After all, there are always people like me willing to spice up a dull world literarily . . . and perhaps in other ways, too.

It really *is* wrong, you know, to hate people on sight merely because they look a little different. It is as wrong to hate people just for being born on one side of a border rather than another. It doesn't follow from those, however, that it is morally obligatory to love them on sight merely because they look a little bit the same or were born on the same side of the border as you. One reason why it isn't morally obligatory to love all of mankind for looking a little bit the same is that it isn't really possible to do so. Love, if it's to mean anything, is a fairly intense emotion and there's only so much of it any individual has to spread around. Even Kos saves most of his for his immediate family.

Hate and love aren't really the choices though. Between them are such variables as like and dislike, trust and distrust. There's also indifference.

I'm not convinced that the cosmopolitan notion of arbitrariness holds any water at all. It seems to me that the accident, the one truly arbitrary factor, is *being* born. Given that, it is no accident that a particular person is born to a particular culture and gene pool, that one is of a particular family.[9] Unless people are

---

9 I'm deliberately leaving out of here the cosmopolitanism which would be justified, or at least theoretically justifiable, if people did actually reincarnate. This, of course, would presuppose that upon reincarnation we cross societal lines rather than, say, my soul having to wait, a la Druze, for another Kratman baby to be born so that I can inhabit it. It also presupposes that, unlike Hinduism, where the boundaries between men are explicit in birth, reincarnation is purely random. I know of no significant form of cosmopolitanism that has its basis in reincarnation. Such a justification would, in any case, be highly speculative.

purely fungible, and perhaps completely malleable, it is no accident that one is a product of those two factors. Really, one cannot be anything *but* a product of them. It is not accident, neither is it arbitrary, to like or dislike, to trust or distrust, based on genuine, natural similarities, acceptance of similar values, a common gene pool and a common culture.

Still, perhaps the question is not about accident, but about choice. If not quite accidental, it is true at the least that we didn't have a lot of *choice* in the nation, culture and family to which we were born. So then, is lack of choice in the matter what makes distinctions between people arbitrary? Yes, but.

Choice is a problem to the cosmopolitan ideal, as is free will. Those very things they decry as arbitrary are, in fact, the results of some very non-arbitrary choices made in the past, distant or recent. Someone said, "I like this hunk of dirt. I think I'll stay, of my own free will, and raise a family; maybe get together with the neighbors at need," and thus was born a distinction, non-arbitrary at first, that would condemn the rest of us to an arbitrary future. Just as truly, someone said, "I'm tired of this piece of dirt. I think I'll move on, of my own free will, and perhaps take a few of the more agreeable neighbors along with me," and that, too, set for some of us an arbitrary future. For still others, it was, "I like the color of that man," or "I don't like the shade or shape of that woman," and there, again, voluntary, non-arbitrary choices were made that became arbitrary for the rest of us.

And who can doubt but that—go ahead and set the clock back to zero—still more non-arbitrary choices would be made in the cosmopolitan future, unless it

were somehow possible to eliminate free will, preference and choice. But that is an inhuman future. I
believe I mentioned things could be worse.

> "Thank God my granddaddy got on that
> boat."
>
> —Muhammad Ali

The United States, Canada, Australia and some
other settler nations represent a problem for the cosmopolitan, and, especially in the case of the United
States, in more ways than one.

Our choice—more commonly, our recent ancestors'
choices—was relatively recent. Moreover those choices
are validated daily by the numbers of people who
want to come and join us. Is the Mexican's choice
to risk the border to find work arbitrary? Hardly.
Was the Soviet dissident's choice, or the Cuban dissident's choice, to come here for political or literary
or artistic freedom arbitrary? Is it arbitrary when a
young man or woman, born here, says, "I like this
piece of dirt. I like the neighbors. I believe I'll
defend it and them," and joins the military? No,
except insofar as each is rejecting the cosmopolitan
ideal and then only if the cosmopolitan eats her
own tail and defines arbitrary as "that of which I
do not approve."

To an extent, that's just what they do. When Martha
Nussbaum, in her essay, "Patriotism and Cosmopolitanism,"[10] calls for children to be educated away from

---

10 Ibid.

patriotism, to be educated into and for cosmopolitanism, she is substituting her choice for anyone else's. That, friends, is *arbitrary*.[11]

But let's not stop there. There are all kinds of voluntary, non-arbitrary choices people can make, choices, be it noted, that have no taint of nationalism. What, after all, is a member of the Mafia but someone who rejected his nation and society and opted for that non-nationalistic, cosmopolitan ideal? What of Mara Salvatrucha 13? The KKK? What of Legionnaire De Gaulle of the French Foreign Legion? All these are people who reject the nation and opt for a very non-arbitrary, tribal, even (accepting there is such a thing as a non-blood related—that is to say, a chosen—family) familial and ultimately exclusionary primary allegiance. What of the soulless, greedy, transnational Microsoft or Union Carbide or United Fruit CEO or corporate bureaucrat? Their loyalty is to the Family of Man? Their loyalty is to their

---

11 Interestingly, there's a draft declaration at the United Nations, the *United Nations Draft Declaration on the Rights of Indigenous Peoples*, Article 7 of which decries, among other things, "cultural genocide," to include, "Any action which has the aim or effect of depriving them of their integrity as distinct peoples, or of their cultural values or ethnic identities." I'd like to see that adopted, with a couple of definitions, and some criminal liability attached. Why? Well, if we define indigenous to include native-born, as we certainly might, then we could charge and try all those people who insist on forcibly inflicting upon our children foreign culture and values in place of our own for "Cultural Genocide." Be a hoot, wouldn't it?

paychecks, their stock options, and their golden parachutes . . . and, of course, to the families those things
provide for . . . and to themselves.

Thus, to succeed, the cosmopolitan *must* eliminate
free will and choice, for too many people will, left to
their own, choose something besides cosmopolitanism.
Indeed, true cosmopolitanism is the choice of a very
tiny number. Why should this be? Kos's admissions
alone seem inadequate. Rather, they are closer in
spirit to corporate greed and Mara Salvatrucha drug
running than to the cosmopolitan ideal.

> Breathes there a man with soul so dead
> Who never to himself hath said:
> "This is my own, my native land?"
> —Walter Scott,
> The Lay of the Last Minstrel

Ralph Nader, whatever else might be said of him, is a
patriot. In 1996, he wrote to one hundred of America's
premier corporations, asking that they show their support
for "the country that bred them, built them, subsidized
them and defended them" by opening their annual
stockholders' meeting with the Pledge of Allegiance.[12]

In a stunning display of cutting edge, transnational,
corporate greed, indifference and disloyalty, with no
pretense to either nationalism or cosmopolitanism,
ninety-nine declined. Ford, Motorola, Aetna and
Costco, at least, declined explicitly. (No, I will never
again buy a Ford, Aetna or Costco product. And I'll

---

12 I am indebted to Professor Sam Huntington's *Who Are
We*, Simon and Schuster, 2004, for this little tidbit.

dump my RAZR as soon as contractually possible. I'd rather buy a non-American product than an un-American one.)

I'll suggest to you, though, that Ford, Aetna, Costco, Motorola, MS-13, the KKK, and Legionnaire De Gaulle are all rational. For people give loyalty to what *matters* to them: Kos to his family, the corporate CEO to his paycheck and golden parachute (which is usually, ultimately, for his family), the KKK member to his klavern and what he thinks of as his "race," the MS-13 assassin to his peers and his pack leader. All have rejected loyalty to their entire nation, but they have not thereby acquired any notable loyalty, any transcendent loyalty, to mankind. Instead, each has picked a smaller group than the nation as the focus of their devotion.[13]

This should come as no surprise. Humanity, the Family of Man, asks nothing but it also gives nothing. It is an abstract, distant and ineffectual. People *need* the closeness and emotional support of some group they can know or, at least, think they can.

It is human to hate. For self-definition
and motivation people need enemies: competitors in business, rivals in achievement,
opponents in politics.
—Professor Samuel P. Huntington

---

13 By the way, I don't mean here to insult Juan Robles, the MS-13 drug runner and assassin, nor his organization, by invidious comparison to, say, Ford or Microsoft. At least Juan has loyalty to something beyond money and genes. And MS-13, at least, can generate loyalty that is not merely bought and paid for.

In "Patriotism and Cosmopolitanism," Martha Nussbaum wrote about concentric circles and how, having drawn one arbitrary circle at the level of nation, there is nothing to stop people from drawing ever smaller circles, from nation to religion to class, etc. Indeed she seems to make the claim that drawing the one circle practically demands that one draw ever narrower circles, excluding more and more of the human race.

Another writer, Lee Harris,[14] has pointed out that this flies in the face of the historical record which demonstrates that the nation has, in many cases, been the only thing shown capable of overcoming such narrow circles.[15]

That's both interesting and true. More interesting to me, though, is that the converse is also true. The nation overcomes interior small differences by presenting people with a set of exterior larger differences. But it is with *de*-emphasis on the nation, with a closer approach to that cosmopolitan ideal, with the decline of the legitimate nation, or in its absence, in other words with "post-national citizenship," that people define themselves and confine themselves into ever smaller groupings. We see Scotland gradually seceding from the United Kingdom. We see Quebec threatening to disassociate itself from Canada ("Good riddance," say most of my Canadian acquaintances). Yugoslavia

---

14 "If smarts were people, Lee Harris would be China."
　　　　　　　　　　　　　　　　—Jonah Goldberg

15 Lee Harris, *The Cosmopolitan Illusion,* Policy Review, April/May 2003. Other things have, too: religion, region, sect and race, for example. They all draw circles that the nation has often been able to surmount.

breaks up, bloodily. Czechoslovakia splits, fortunately without bloodshed. Arab Shiites and Sunni Kurds in Iraq want out from under the Arab Sunnis. Indeed, everywhere we have seen some close approach to *de*nationalization, we have seen just what Nussbaum informs us is the ultimate logic of nationalism. This is not a coincidence.

Consider Africa just as it was about to be decolonized. There, the European white devil provided the enemy, the outsider, the *other*, that held the locals together in a common cause. With that enemy gone, however, with that unifying phenomenon out of the picture, the overwhelming bulk of sub-Saharan Africa fell into mere tribalism and, wherever there was some power to be exploited for personal and family gain, amoral familism.[16]

Cosmopolitanism doesn't appear to lead to the ideal of Utopia, somewhere down the road, but to the miserable reality of sub-Saharan Africa, to Rwanda, Biafra, and the Congo, just around the corner.

> The world is a vastly better place because it
> contains people whose only fault is the desire
> to make all people as good and reasonable
> as they themselves are.
>
> —Lee Harris[17]

Respectfully, I disagree. For the world to be better the cosmopolitans would have to have some good

---

16 For an equally good, and perhaps better, example, consider the break-up of India following the end of the British Raj caused by that peerless cosmopolitan, Gandhi.

17 Ibid.

effect. At a minimum one would hope that things might stabilize at a level no worse than we now have. Can they? What chance?

A cosmopolitan might say, "Look, if people can be educated and trained to *die* for artificial, even abstract, constructs like nations, surely they can be educated and trained to *live* for natural, concrete humanity."

It's not a bad argument, up to a point. Unfortunately for cosmopolitanism, that point comes quickly.

Nations, and especially first class and hyper-powerful ones, have many advantages in training and education that the Family of Man simply lacks. We typically share a common, or dominant, language and a common, or dominant, culture that is, in broad terms, knowable and comfortable to most citizens and legal residents of the nation. Where is Man's common language? Not Davos Man's, which is English, but *Man's*? Where is his common value? Not Davos Man's, which is money, but *Man's*. Where is the history upon which Man can agree is important? Who are the heroes, the role models? They do not exist. They would all have to be created or recreated and imposed.

Nations have three kinds of neighbors and peers: different and potentially hostile, different and probably hostile, and different and positively hostile. These, the foreign difference and the hostility, can draw together very tightly even such linguistically differing folk as the Swiss. It is not clear that anything else can. It is unclear that cosmopolitanism can do what it would need to, in the absence of the sort of external threat that binds the citizens of a nation together. There is obviously a down side to all that hostility; I offer this *only* as an element of evidence that there are some educational advantages even an artificial construct like a nation has that cosmopolitanism is unlikely to be able to match.[18]

Additionally, a nation can give its people a sense of superiority, even if utterly unwarranted,[19] to all others that further binds them together. What, after all, binds the intellectual class of Europe and the Colleagues of the EU together if it isn't their hate for the United States and all things American?

Perhaps the chief problem with cosmopolitanism is that, while Kant may have envisioned it and Nussbaum may preach it, both are powerless to overcome those human default states of "me" and "mine," that narrow focus that allows people not only to join their efforts and affections to others, but to derive the emotional support and sense of belonging they need.

So, yes, cosmopolitanism can undermine nations but, no, it cannot then substitute for nations the Family of Man or Mankind.

There's another problem, too, a worse problem, and it's *our* problem. Cosmopolitanism is unevenly spread. Really, it exists only in the West and the West's institutions, including, of course, the corrupt dictatorships of the Third World and the World Bank and the NGOs that shunt them their graft.

---

18 Though a cynical man, which of course I am not, can hardly help but note the potential for Anthropocentric (man-made) Global Warming to fill this need for an external threat to draw people together. It would be paranoid to say this is the motive. It is not paranoid to note how very *convenient* AGW is.

19 See, e.g., the French. For that matter, see, e.g. Europe.

True, Islam has a different version of it, but that version is exclusionary. In a sense, it is *ultimately* exclusionary, as there are certain human types, atheists and gays come to mind, which Islam cannot accept but, rather, must destroy. Still others—women and those not of the Islamic faith, for example—must be subjugated. Communism, too, is a kind of cosmopolitan philosophy. Yet it draws a circle around and excludes, then usually kills, anyone who does not fit the communist cosmopolitan ideal.[20]

Being, then, a fairly local phenomenon, what can true cosmopolitanism *do*? It can't make cosmopolitans of tribalists. It can't make true cosmopolitans of Moslems. It can't stop the Chinese Communist Party cadres from looting or letting their children loot the people's wealth. It can't even get *Kos* not to put his family first.

But it can, where it is strong and accepted as logical and legitimate, undermine the faith of peoples, nations and cultures in their own worth, undermine their will to defend themselves, and leave them open to enslavement by those who still have that faith and that will. I mentioned in the beginning that cosmopolitanism feels as good as sex and drugs. Like those, it helps transmit a kind of disease. Cosmopolitanism, because it is a local phenomenon, that weakens, locally, is a sort of societal HIV, a disease that does not kill, of its own, but destroys the resistance of those who acquire it to those things that do kill. Cosmopolitanism—whatever the ideals or motives of the cosmopolitans—is doing so as I write.

---

20 There's a lesson in there, I think, about how any form of cosmopolitanism must ultimately deal with those who do not accept its teachings.

ACKNOWLEDGMENTS

Special thanks to the many people who helped with this, from concept to copy editing: Yoli (who puts up with me), Matt Pethybridge, Sam Swindell, Bill Crenshaw, Mr. William Dunnell, Mo Kirby, Barbara Johnson, Isabelle Andrews, Genie Nickolson, Sue Kerr, my brother John, Scott C, Dr. Jakob van Zyll, Toni Weisskopf and, of course, Jim Baen.

And OZ, including the crew and the design, modification and refit team of the *Dos Lindas* and the *classis*, in no particular order: Charlie Prael, Sean Newton, Peter Gold, Mike Gilson, Tommie Williams, Dick Evans, Dave Levitt, Mike Fagan, Bill Lehman, Jeff Wilkes, Bob Hofrichter, Jon Thompson, Al Hattlestad, Phil Fraering, Dave Dwyer, Conrad Chu, Dan Neely, Fionn Ryan, Mickey zvi Maor, Jason Long, Andy Stocker, Leonid Panfil, Chris French, Mark Turuk, Neil Frandsen, Gordon Gailey, Steve Stewart, Dean Sutherland, Paul Gustafson, Justin Bischel, Jose Clavell, Dexter Guptil, Alex Stace, Alex Swavely, Steve St. Onge, Andrew Gill, Rodney Graves, and Dick Atkinson. If I missed you, so far, I'll kill you off as opportunity presents. I promise.

If I've forgotten anyone, chalk it up to premature senility.

APPENDIX A: GLOSSARY

AdC	Aide de Camp, an assistant to a senior officer
Ala	Plural: Alae. Latin: Wing, as in wing of cavalry. Air Wing in the Legion. Similar to Tercio, qv.
Amid	Arabic: Brigadier General
Antania	Plural: Antaniae, Septic mouthed winged reptilians, possibly genengineered by the Noahs, AKA Moonbats
BdL	Barco del Legion, Ship of the Legion
Bellona	Moon of Terra Nova
Bolshiberry	A fruit-bearing vine, believed to have been genengineered by the Noahs. The fruit is intensely poisonous to intelligent life.
Cazador	Spanish: Hunter. Similar to Chasseur, Jaeger and Ranger. Light Infantry, especially selected and trained. Also a combat leader selection course within the Legion del Cid
Classis	Latin: Fleet or Naval Squadron
Cohort	Battalion, though in the Legion these are large battalions.

Conex	Metal shipping container, generally 8' × 8' × 20' or 40'
Consensus	When capitalized, the governing council of Old Earth, formerly the United Nations Security Council.
Dustoff	Medical evacuation, typically by air
Eris	Moon of Terra Nova
FSD	Federated States Drachma. Unit of money equivalent in value to 4.2 grams of silver
Hecate	Moon of Terra Nova
Hieros	Shrine or temple
I	Roman number one. Chief Operations Officer, his office, and his staff section
Ia	Operations officer dealing mostly with fire and maneuver, his office and his section, S- or G-3
Ib	Logistics Officer, his office and his section, S- or G-4
Ic	Intelligence Officer, his office and his section, S- or G-2
II	Adjutant, Personnel Officer, his office and his section, S- or G-1
Ikhwan	Arabic: Brotherhood
Jaguar	Volgan-built tank in legionary service
Jaguar II	Improved Jaguar
Jizyah	See Yizyah
Karez	Underground aqueduct system
Keffiyah	Folded cloth Arab headdress

Klick	Kilometer. Note: Democracy ends where the metric system begins.
Kosmo	Cosmopolitan Progressive. Similar to Tranzi on Old Earth
Liwa	Arabic: Major General
Lorica	Lightweight silk and liquid metal torso armor used by the Legion
LZ	Landing Zone, a place where helicopters drop off troops and equipment
Makkah al Jedidah	Arabic: New Mecca
Mañana sera mejor	Balboan politico-military song. Tomorrow will be better.
Megalodon	Coastal Defense Submarine under development by the Legion
MRL	Multiple Rocket Launcher
Mujahadin	Arabic: Holy Warriors (singular: muja-had)
Mukhabarat	Arabic: Secret Police
Mullah	Holy man, sometimes holy, sometimes not.
Na'ib 'Dabit	Arabic: Sergeant Major
Naik	Corporal
Naquib	Arabic: Captain
NGO	Nongovernmental Organization
Noahs	Aliens that seeded Terra Nova with life, some from Old Earth, some possibly from other planets, some possibly genetically engineered, in the dim mists

	of prehistory. No definitive trace has ever been found of them.
Ocelot	Volgan-built light armored vehicle mounting a 100mm gun and capable of carrying a squad of infantry in the back.
PMC	Precious Metal Certificate. High Denomination Legionary Investment Vehicle
Progressivine	A fruit-bearing vine found on Terra Nova. Believed to have been genengineered by the Noahs. The fruit is intensely poisonous to intelligent life.
Push	As in "tactical push." Radio frequency or frequency hopping sequence, so called from the action of pushing the button that activates the transmitter.
PZ	Pickup Zone. A place where helicopters pick-up troops, equipment and supplies to move them somewhere else.
RGL	Rocket Grenade Launcher
RTO	Radio-Telephone Operator
Sayidi	Arabic form of respectful address, "Sir."
SPATHA	Self-Propelled Anti-Tank Heavy Armor. A legionary tank destroyer, under development
SPLAD	Self-Propelled Laser Air Defense. A developed legionary antiaircraft system
Subadar	Major
Sura	A chapter in the Koran, of which there are 114
Tercio	Spanish: Regiment

Tranzitree	A fruit bearing tree, believed to have been genengineered by the Noahs. The fruit is intensely poisonous to intelligent life.
Trixie	A species of archaeopteryx brought to Terra Nova by the Noahs.
Yakamov	A type of helicopter produced in Volga. It has no tail rotor.
Yizyah	Special tax levied against non-Moslems living in Moslem lands.

APPENDIX B:
LEGIONARY RANK EQUIVALENTS

Dux, Duque: Indefinite rank, depending on position it can indicate anything from a Major General to a Field Marshall. *Duque* usually indicates the senior commander on the field.

Legate III: Brigadier General or Major General. Per the contract between the *Legion del Cid* and the Federated States of Columbia, a Legate III is entitled to the standing and courtesies of a Lieutenant General. Typically commands a deployed legion, when a separate legion is deployed, the air *alae* or the naval *classis*, or serves as an executive for a deployed corps.

Legate II: Colonel, typically commands a tercio in the rear or serves on staff if deployed.

Legate I: Lieutenant Colonel, typically commands a cohort or serves on staff.

Tribune III: Major, serves on staff or sometimes, if permitted to continue in command, commands a maniple.

Tribune II: Captain, typically commands a maniple.

Tribune I: First Lieutenant, typically serves as second in command of a maniple, commands a specialty platoon within the cohort's combat support maniple, or serves on staff.

Signifer: Second Lieutenant or Ensign, leads a platoon. Signifer is a temporary rank and signifers are not considered part of the officer corps of the legions except as a matter of courtesy.

Sergeant Major: Sergeant Major with no necessary indication of level.

First Centurion: Senior noncommissioned officer of a maniple.

Senior Centurion: Master Sergeant but almost always the senior man within a platoon.

Centurion, J.G.: Sergeant First Class, sometimes commands a platoon but is usually the second in command.

Optio: Staff Sergeant, typically the second in command of a platoon.

Sergeant: Sergeant, typically leads a squad.

Corporal: Corporal, typically leads a team or crew or serves as second in command of a squad.

Legionario, or Legionary, or Legionnaire: private through specialist.

———————

Note that in addition, under pending legion regulations, a soldier may elect to take what is called "Triarius Status." This will lock the soldier into whatever rank he may be, but allow pay raises for longevity to con-

tinue. It is one way the legion may flatten the rank
pyramid in the interests of reducing careerism. Thus,
one may someday hear or read of a "Triarius Tribune
III," typically a major-equivalent who will have decided,
with legion accord, that his highest and best use is
in a particular staff slot or commanding a particular
maniple. Given that the Legion—with fewer than fifteen
hundred officers, including signifers—has the smallest
officer corps, per capita, of any significant military
formation on Terra Nova, and a very flat promotion
pyramid, the Triarius system seems, perhaps, overkill.
If adopted, regulations may permit but not require
Triarius status legionaries to be promoted one rank
upon retirement.

APPENDIX C:
MILITARY SPECIFICATIONS
FOR THE F-26 RIFLE

From: *Janus Small Arms Review*, **Terra Nova Edition of 472 AC**

Cycle of Operation:

The weapon being set on one of its four firing settings and a round being chambered, the firer depresses the trigger (which, being nothing more than an electronic switch, has no "break point" and is thus very smooth). An electronic charge passes through the bolt face, initiating the primer, which sets off the propellant while expanding propellant and stub to obdurate (seal) the breach. The bullet moves down the barrel until reaching the gas port, near the muzzle. A stream of gas passes down the gas port, forcing the operating piston to the rear. The piston, in turn, causes the bolt carrier to begin to retract, unlocking the bolt. At that point the rearward movement of the bolt and bolt carrier causes four things to occur almost simultaneously: the VHTP (Very High Temperature Plastic) stub is ejected out the bottom ejection port, a rammer beneath the bolt—driven by a reversing cam—three-quarter feeds the next round from the magazine, a flywheel is set to spinning (recharging the integral battery until the trigger is released, at which point a brake is automatically applied to the flywheel), and a ratcheting rod is driven downward into the magazine which compresses the magazine spring from the center/rear. The bolt and bolt carrier then return forward, finishing the loading of the next round begun by the rammer. The bolt then rotates again to lock in position. At that point, and assuming the trigger is still depressed, the rifle will either fire and begin the cycle again (3 round burst), or will have a very brief, computer-controlled delay before firing (high or low automatic), or will cease fire (rounds). It is the short distance to be traveled by the bolt to load and eject that enables the weapon to attain such high rates of fire.

Note: In the event of battery failure or weakness the magazine may be removed, the trigger depressed and the bolt jacked six to ten times to build up a firing charge.

Ammunition:

The single greatest complaint about the F-26 (called, for reasons best left to etymologists and corporals, a "Zion" in Balboa and an "Arraijan" in Zion) is its weight. Between the relatively long barrel, the batteries, the integral thermal sight and range finder, and the flywheel and generator, it is the single heaviest general issue rifle on Terra Nova today. This is made up for by the ammunition.

The 6.5mm SCC round is a high ballistic coefficient, high cross sectional density bullet of 120 grains set into a hollow cylinder of cook-off resistant propellant which is capped at the base with a very high temperature plastic semi-rimmed semi-casing, with dual electrodes, referred to as a "stub." The stub is of 10.4mm in width and 9 mm in height. The electronic primer is set into the hollow of the propellant and connected to the electrodes. The stub serves to obdurate (gain gas sealage of) the explosion of the propellant and to transmit the electrical energy that detonates the primer from electrodes in the bolt face.

The ammunition comes prepackaged in sealed, generally disposable snail drum magazines containing 93 rounds. The magazines are approximately 109mm in diameter and 42mm in depth. One fully loaded magazine weighs just under 1162 grams, or about two fifths the weight of a comparable quantity of standard brass cased ammunition of similar caliber and capability. Thus, the F-26 with 465 rounds and a spare battery weighs 10.6 Kg while, for example, the lighter and somewhat less capable Abakanov with a similar sight and 465 inferior steel-cased rounds would weigh approximately 12.3 kilograms, not including the weight of the sixteen magazines required to have each round ready to fire.

The decision to pack and issue the ammunition in drums, rather than to issue accountable magazines and loose or stripper clipped ammunition to individual soldiers was a difficult one for ZMI and BAC. The cost, even when the magazines are recoverable for reprocessing at the plant, is at least twice that of the steel cased ammunition used in the Abakanov and comparable to that of the brass cased ammunition fired by the FSC's Wakefield carbine. Testing, however, revealed that the SCC was simply not up to the rough handling and exposure to weather that the more usual system entailed.

Magazines are known to come issued in at least 8 varieties, specialized but useable by all versions:

Standard: contains standard ball and tracer in a ratio of 2:1.

CQB: composed of equal numbers (31 each) of standard ball, armor piercing (tungsten), and eccentric (a particularly unstable, once it has penetrated flesh, tumbling round) in sequence.

5×1: larger magazine (17.7 cm in diameter) containing 211-213 ball and 42-44 tracer. Generally issued to machine gun crews.

Match: contains 93 rounds of match grade, 6.5mm ball

Humanitarian: match grade frangible ammunition used to engage targets mixed in closely with noncombatants. Like Match, Humanitarian magazines are normally only issued to snipers. There has been complaint from the international humanitarian community that use of the ammunition, in the hands of both Zion's and Balboa's armed forces, has not been uniformly restricted to such circumstances.

Blank: contains 93 rounds of pure blank ammunition.

Training plastic: contains 93 rounds of plastic tipped ammunition fired by underpowered propellant which, upon hitting a human target, is extremely painful but not generally deadly except at point blank ranges.

Moral training: contains 88 rounds of plastic tipped ammunition and 5 rounds of tracer, the tracer being loaded in at random. A perusal of unclassified information on the frequency of use of this magazine indicates a frightful willingness to risk losses in training on the part of the Balboan armed forces.

The magazine rear face has a key which it turned 2.5–3 times to compress the feeder spring. As rounds are fired the rifle's retreating bolt drives a ratcheting rod into the magazine (integral to the magazine not the rifle) to maintain compression.

Further, a portion of the back plate is composed of transparent polycarbonate to allow the firer to visually check available ammunition.

Variants:

Machine Gun:

The adoption of the F-26 rifle has, for Balboa at least, led to the elimination of the belt fed General Purpose Machine Gun from the inventory of its armed forces. In lieu of the GPMG a heavier version of the F-26, called the M-26, has been developed. This weapon has both a heavier, ringed barrel and a variant on the Volgan Pecheneg forced air cooling system. Both the single shot and low rate automatic fire capabilities were eliminated in the M-26 and the burst feature program modified. Thus it fires at either 6 round burst (1975 RPM) or high rate automatic (1200 RPM) only. Though it has a 265 round magazine it will feed from the same 93 round drum magazines as the F-26 (and, uncommonly, vice versa). The M-26 with 2120 rounds weighs 34 Kg, 41 with tripod. Its effective range is 1300 meters. Grazing fire range is 705 meters. It has an automatic magazine drop feature that releases the magazine when the last round is expended.

Marksman's Rifle:

Although the Balboan Armed Forces have two heavier sniper rifles, the .34 caliber LRSS and the .41 caliber VLRSS, both of which fire more conventional, brass cased, ammunition, both Zion and the Legion felt that there was a place in the rifle platoon or squad for a more than normally accurate battle rifle capable of firing the same ammunition as the F-26 and M-26. This rifle, called the F-26FT (*francs tireurs*) is almost exactly the same as the F-26, differing only in having a longer and heavier barrel and a better and longer ranged (and much more expensive) sight and range finder combo. This rifle weighs 5.4 Kg and has an effective range of 1300 meters. Match grade ammunition is available and issued.

Developmental History:

Although it is sometimes jokingly said that the F-26 began over drinks at the Zion embassy in *Ciudad* Balboa, the better truth is that it is the result of several developments, none of them major in themselves, coming to fruition in different parts of the world at about the same time. For example, the semi-cased ammunition is a clear development of two varieties of caseless ammunition, one conventionally primed and one electronically primed, developed independently in Sachsen and Ostmark. The rammer which is so critical to the very high rate of fire and effectiveness of the burst feature is similar to, albeit simpler and sturdier than, that developed for the Volgan Abakanov. The snail drum magazine clearly owes its parentage to the sturdier but much more expensive double snail drum magazine developed for the FSC's Wakefield rifle. The miniaturized computer which controls the rate of fire was a development of Nihon Teppu Jutsu, Inc, of Yamato.

However informally the project may have been initiated, very quickly a consortium between ZMI and BAC was formed to begin development.

The 6.5mm projectile was an early, and happy, compromise between Balboa, which wanted something more in the 6mm range to suit its jungle conditions, and Zion which wanted something closer to 6.8mm in caliber but of great cross sectional density to suit its more commonly found desert and urban environments. Testing and simulation showed that the 6.5 was possibly ideal for neither but certainly more than adequate for both.

Thus, the caliber of 6.5mm was agreed upon.

Development thereafter becomes a very murky and perhaps even sordid subject, with charges of industrial espionage, pirating of personnel, and illegal reverse engineering being raised frequently. Certainly it is true that some design engineers from Volga and chemists from Ostmark and the Federated States of Columbia did emigrate to Balboa and Zion in the few years before the rifle was finally prototyped. It is also true that the magazine bears a suspicious, but apparently superficial, similarity to the double snail drum in use by the FSC (some copies of which, apparently, found their way to Zion).

The following is an excerpt from:

COBRA WAR, BOOK 1

COBRA ALLIANCE

TIMOTHY ZAHN

Available from Baen Books
December 2009
hardcover

CHAPTER ONE

The warehouse stretched out in front of them, its lights dimmed, its floor and furnishings old and drab. It was obviously deserted, with a thick layer of dust that indicated years of disuse and neglect. For all Jasmine "Jin" Moreau Broom could tell as she gazed over the scene, the place might have been sitting here unnoticed since the founding of Capitalia, or even since the first human colonists arrived on Aventine.

But Jin knew better. The stacks of crates, the parked forklifts, the dangling cables from the ceiling cranes—it was all an illusion. The room had never been a warehouse. Nor had it ever been an aircraft hangar, an office floor, or an alien landscape.

All it had ever been was a deathtrap.

A shiver of memory ran through her, the goosebumps that rippled through her flesh twinging against the arthritis growing its slow but inexorable way through her shoulders and hips. Jin's own Cobra training, thirty-two years ago, had taken place elsewhere on Aventine, as befit the uniqueness of the mission she and her ill-fated teammates had been assigned. As a result, she herself had never had to deal with this room in any of its various incarnations.

But her husband had taken his turn in here. Many turns, in fact. So had both of her sons, and she could still remember the unpleasant mixture of anxiety and pride she'd felt every time she'd stood here on the glassed-in observation catwalk watching one of them in action.

The fear and pride she'd felt in them as Cobras.

Unfortunately, not all of the members of the group here today shared Jin's sense of respect for this place. "You think maybe we could get on with it?" Aventinian Senior Governor Tomo Treakness muttered under his breath from his position two people to Jin's left. "I have actual work to do."

Jin leaned forward to look at him, a list of withering retorts jockeying for the privilege of leading the charge. She picked the most devastating of the options.

And left it unsaid as the man standing between her and Treakness laid a calming hand on hers. "Patience, Governor," Paul Broom said with the mildness and assured self-control that Jin so admired in her husband. "As I'm sure your estate's chief vintner would tell you, a fine wine can't be rushed."

A flash of something crossed Treakness's face. Annoyance, Jin hoped. Politicians like Treakness, who liked to portray themselves as friends of the common folk, didn't like being reminded about their wealth. "Interesting comparison, Cobra Broom," Treakness said. "So you see this as a slow-aged *luxury* beverage?"

"The Cobras are hardly a luxury," Governor Ellen Hoffman put in stiffly from Jin's right. "Maybe you don't need them so much in Capitalia anymore—"

"Please, Ellen," Treakness interrupted, his tone cool with a hint of condescension about it. "You know perfectly well I didn't mean the Cobras themselves."

"If you disparage the Sun Advanced Training Center, you disparage the Cobras," Hoffman countered. "Without the center, there *are* no Cobras."

"Really?" Treakness asked with feigned incredulity. "I'm sorry—did the MacDonald Center burn down when I wasn't looking?"

Hoffman's face darkened— "That's enough," the fifth member of the group, Governor-General Chintawa, put in firmly from Hoffman's other side. "Save the fireworks for the Council chamber. We're here to observe, not debate."

"If there's ever anything *to* observe," Treakness said.

"Patience, Governor," Paul said again, pointing to the left. "Here they come now."

Jin craned her neck to look. Fifteen shadowy figures had appeared around the side of one of the stacks and were marching with military precision toward the section of floor in front of the observation catwalk. Keying her optical enhancers for telescopic and light-amplification, she took a closer look.

Another shiver ran up her back. The alien Trofts who occupied the vast stretches of space between the Cobra Worlds and the distant Dominion of Man had been trusted friends and trading partners as long as Jin had been alive, plus quite a few years before that. But she knew her history, and the sight of the creatures who had once been mankind's deadliest enemies never failed to stir feelings of not-quite distrust.

This particular group of Trofts were even more impressive than usual, she decided as she watched them marching along. Their gait was military-precise and as fluid as their back-jointed legs could manage. Their hand-and-a-half lasers, the size and power currently favored by the Tlossie demesne's patrol forces, were held in cross-chest ready positions. Their eyes continually swept the areas around them, their pointed deer-like ears twitching as they did their own auditory scan, and the wing-like radiator membranes on the backs of their upper arms fluttered in and out to maintain their internal temperature and distinctive infrared signatures.

They were so perfect, in fact, that they might have been real.

"They get better every year, don't they?" Paul murmured.

Jin nodded . . . because the figures marching along down there were not, in fact, living Trofts. They were robots, designed as the ultimate test of new Cobras and seasoned veterans alike.

And like all ultimate challenges, this one carried the ultimate risk.

"Finally," Treakness grumbled. "Now how long are going to have to wait for them to get to their hiding places before the Cobras can move in?"

The words were barely out of his mouth when the brilliant spear of a Cobra antiarmor laser beam slashed across the warehouse, slicing into one of the lasers in the center of the enemy formation. "Not long at all," Paul said calmly. "This is an ambush exercise."

The robots scattered madly for cover as three more Cobra lasers joined in the attack. Two of the enemy went down in that first salvo, as did a third whose laser exploded in its face as the Cobras' attack shorted out the weapon's power pack. A moment later, the remaining Trofts had made it to cover, and the battle settled into a slower but no less deadly game of hide-and-seek.

Jin gazed down at the operation, another set of memories rising from the back of her mind. She'd fought the Trofts herself once, the only person since the First Cobras to have ever faced the aliens in actual combat. She'd taken on a cargo ship full of them on the human breakaway colony world of Qasama, more or less single-handedly. Not only had she lived to tell the tale, but she'd even managed to pull a quiet but genuine victory out of the situation.

And had then returned to Aventine and watched helplessly as that victory was snatched from her fingers by truth-twisting politicians.

She leaned forward for a surreptitious look past her husband. Treakness was watching the battle closely, visibly wincing every time one of the robots was knocked out of action. With Treakness it was always about money, and Jin could practically see the calculator tape running through his brain. Fifteen robots at roughly a million *klae* each, plus the costs of the techs running the exercise, plus the maintenance costs of the Sun Center, plus the creation and training of the Cobras themselves—

"They're not actually being destroyed, you know," Paul commented.

"No, the lasers are just chewing up their outer ablative coating material," Treakness said tartly. "I *do* read the reports, thank you."

"I just thought it might be worth mentioning," Paul murmured.

"I also know that it still costs a minimum of fifty thousand for each refurbishing," Treakness continued. "That's a *minimum* of fifty thousand. If the internal works get damaged, that bill can quadruple."

"And it's worth every *klae*," Hoffman put in. "The

statistics on Cobra survival in the field have gone up tremendously since the Sun Center opened."

"You get a lot of Troft warriors in the fields of Donyang Province, do you?" Treakness asked pointedly. "I must have missed those reports."

Paul looked sideways at Jin; she rolled her eyes at him in silent reply. For some reason that she couldn't fathom, the military concept of *deterrence* still managed to elude some of the allegedly brightest minds in the Cobra Worlds. *Yes,* for most of the Worlds' existence the Cobras had served mainly as frontier guardians, policemen, and hunters, working hard to clear out the spine leopards and other lethal predators from newly opened territories so the farmers and ranchers and loggers could move in. And *yes,* the three Troft demesnes nearest the Worlds had been as peaceable as anyone could ever hope for, even if they did always tend to press their trade deals a bit harder than they should and wring out every brightly-colored *klae* possible.

But *some* group of Troft demesnes had once felt themselves capable of attacking the Dominion of Man and occupying two of its worlds. If there was one thing every Governor-General since Zhu had understood, it was that the Trofts needed to know that the Cobras were the finest, nastiest, deadliest warriors the universe had ever seen, and that the Cobra Worlds were most emphatically not to be trifled with. Why Treakness and some of the others couldn't understand that simple point Jin had never been able to figure out.

Perhaps it was simply the natural way of things. Perhaps when people were too far removed from immediate, visible threats they began to doubt that such threats could ever exist again. Or, indeed, that they had ever existed at all.

Maybe people periodically needed something to shake them up. Not a war, certainly—Jin wouldn't wish that on anyone. But it would have to be something dramatic, immediate, and impossible to ignore. A sudden influx of spine leopards into Aventine's cities, maybe, or a small but loud uprising among some group of disaffected citizens.

"Jin," Paul said quietly.

Jin snapped out of her reverie. There had been something in his tone . . . "Where?" she asked, her eyes darting around the warehouse.

"That one," Paul said, nodding microscopically to the far left toward one of the Troft robots moving around the crate stacks.

A hard knot settled into the pit of Jin's stomach. The robot had half a dozen laser slashes across its torso and head, enough damage that it should have shut itself off in defeat and collapsed onto the floor. But it was still wandering around in aimless-looking circles, its laser hefted across its burned torso, its head turning back and forth as it searched for a target. "I think I can get to my comm," she murmured.

"Don't bother—I already hit my EM," Paul murmured back. "The malfunction must have scrambled the local comm system."

And the techs in the control room, their attention occupied with other duties, hadn't yet noticed the problem. "You think we should risk trying to wave at one of the cameras?" Jin asked.

And then, before Paul could answer, the robot's head turned and tilted back a few degrees, its eyes coming to rest on the three men and two women standing on the catwalk.

"No one move," Paul ordered, his voice quiet but suddenly carrying the crisp edges of absolute authority.

"Don't even blink," Jin added, her mind sifting rapidly through their options. At this distance her fingertip lasers were too weak to do any good, especially since they'd first have to punch through the catwalk's glass enclosure. The antiarmor laser in her left calf was a far more powerful weapon, theoretically capable of slagging the robot where it stood, assuming she could hold the laser on target long enough to penetrate the layers of material protecting the robot's expensive optronics. The targeting lock built into her optical enhancers and the nanocomputer buried beneath her brain could easily handle such a task, but only if the robot didn't make it to cover before the laser finished its work. Neither her arcthrower nor her assortment of sonic weapons would operate through the glass, and her ceramic-laminated bones and servo-enhanced muscles were of no use whatsoever in this particular situation.

She was still trying to come up with a plan when the robot lifted its laser toward the observers.

"Stay here," Paul ordered, and with a sudden smooth motion, he ducked past Treakness and took off into a mad dash along the catwalk in the direction of the rogue robot.

"What the—?" Treakness demanded.

"He's trying to draw its fire," Jin snapped, her heart thudding hard in her throat. Just like a real soldier, the robot was programmed to see an enemy moving rapidly in its direction as a greater threat and therefore a higher-priority target than four other enemies standing motionless and unthreatening.

Only now that her husband had gotten the robot's attention, the only thing standing between him and death were his programmed Cobra reflexes. In the tight quarters of the enclosed catwalk, those reflexes were going to be sorely limited.

But there might be another way. Getting a grip on the handrail in front of her, Jin braced her feet against the catwalk floor, her eyes on the robot as its laser tracked along its target's vector. Paul was perhaps a quarter of the way to the distant door at the far end of the catwalk when Jin saw the subtle shift of robot musculature as the tracking laser found its mark. "Stop!" she shouted to her husband.

And pushing off the floor, she sprinted full speed after him.

For a terrifying fraction of a second she was afraid Paul hadn't gotten the message, that he would keep running straight to his death. But even as Jin dodged around past Treakness her husband braked to a halt.

And with that, it was suddenly now Jin, not Paul, who represented the greater threat. Without even pausing to squeeze off a shot at its original target, the robot swung its laser around toward Jin.

Jin clenched her teeth against the arthritic pain jabbing into her joints as she ran. *Well,* she thought. *That worked.*

Or had it? To her dismay, she suddenly realized that with the bouncing inherent in a flat-out run she could no longer see the subtle warning signs that would indicate the robot had acquired her and was preparing to fire. She tried putting a targeting lock

on the machine, hoping it might steady her eyesight.
But it didn't. She kept running, trying to coax a little
more speed out of her leg servos—

"Stop!" Paul shouted.

Jin leaned back and locked her legs, gasping at the
sudden flash of pain from her bad left knee. Even as she
skidded to a halt she saw Paul break again into a run.

Jin focused on the robot, watching as it disengaged
its attention from her and once again shifted to the
more immediate threat. This would work, she told
herself. It would work. She and Paul could just tag-
team their way to the door, get off the catwalk and
through the door into the rest of the building and
yell to the oblivious techs to hit the emergency abort.

She spared a fraction of a second to glance down
the catwalk. Only it wouldn't work, she realized with a
sinking sensation. The closer she and Paul got to the
rogue robot on their angled vector, the faster it would
acquire its new target, and the shorter the distance each
of them would get before being forced to stop again.
Worse, since Paul was closer to the robot than Jin was,
his window of opportunity would get shorter faster than
hers would, which meant she would slowly catch up to
him, which meant they would eventually end up within
range of a quick one-two from the robot. At that point,
their only two choices would be to stand still and hope
the robot lost interest, or go into an emergency cork-
screw sprint and hope they could beat its fire.

The robot twitched— "Stop!" Jin shouted, and
started her next run.

She got no more than two-thirds her last distance
before Paul's warning brought her to another knee-
wrenching halt. Two more sprints each, she estimated,

maybe three, and they would reach the dead-end killing box she'd already anticipated. They had to come up with a new plan before that happened.

But she hadn't thought of anything by the time she called Paul to a halt and started her next run. She watched him out of the corner of her eye as she ran, hoping he'd come up with something.

But he merely shouted her to a stop and took off again himself, with no indication that he was trying anything new. Either he hadn't made it to the same conclusion Jin had, or else he had and had decided their only chance was to try to beat the robot's motion sensors to the punch.

The robot's motion sensors . . .

It would be a risk, Jin knew. The chance that even a damaged robot's sensors would lock onto something so much smaller than a human target was vanishingly small. More ominously, what she was planning could easily throw off Paul's stride enough that the robot would finally get in that lethal shot.

But she had to try. Turning her chest toward the glass wall in front of her, gripping the handrail for support, she activated her sonic disruptor.

The backwash as the blast bounced off the glass nearly ripped her hands from the rail and sent her flying backwards into the wall behind her. Grimly, she held on, her head rattling with subsonics as the weapon searched for the resonance of the target it had been presented.

And with an ear-splitting blast, the glass shattered.

Not just in front of Jin, but halfway down the catwalk in both directions. Through the lingering rattling in her head, she dimly felt herself being hammered by flying objects.

But her full attention was on the robot, whose laser was even now lining up on her husband. The robot which had suddenly been presented with a hundred small objects flying through the air in its general direction.

The robot which was just standing there, frozen, its laser still pointed toward the human threats as its deranged optronic brain tried to work through its threat-assessment algorithms.

The gamble had worked, Jin realized, an edge of cautious hope tugging at her. All the flying glass had distracted the robot and bought Paul a little time. If he could get to the door and call for help, they still had a chance.

And then, the motion at the edge of her peripheral vision stopped.

She shifted her eyes toward Paul, her first horrifying thought that the shattering glass might have sliced into an artery or vein, that her move might have in fact killed her husband instead of saving him.

She was searching his form for spurting blood, and opening her mouth to shout at him to get moving, when a flash like noonday sunlight blazed across her vision and a clap of thunder slammed across her already throbbing head.

Paul had fired his arcthrower.

Reflexively, Jin squeezed her eyes shut against the lightning bolt's purple afterimage, simultaneously keying in her optical enhancers. In the image they provided, she saw that the high-voltage current had turned the robot's laser and right arm into a smoking mass of charred metal and ablative material.

But the robot was still standing . . . and with its

threat assessment now complete it was reaching for the backup projectile pistol belted at its side.

Jin could do something about that. Keying for her own arcthrower, she lifted her right arm and pointed her little finger at the robot. The arcthrower was a two-stage weapon: her fingertip laser would fire first, creating a path of ionized air between her and the robot that the current from the arcthrower's capacitor could then follow. She curled her other fingers inward and set her thumb against the ring-finger nail.

And broke off as a pair of human figures appeared, sprinting into view from behind different stacks near the damaged robot. The two men leaped in unison, one of them hitting the robot at neck height, the other at its knees, unceremoniously dumping the machine at last onto the floor. The dim overhead lighting abruptly shifted to bright red, the signal of emergency abort.

It was finally over.

"About time," someone said.

Jin turned to look at the other three members of their group, still huddled together in stunned disbelief a hundred meters behind her. She wondered who had spoken into her ringing ears, realized it must have been her. At the far end of the catwalk, behind the politicians, the door flew open and a line of Sun Center personnel came charging through.

It was only then, as Jin wiped at the sweat on her forehead, that she realized she was bleeding.

—end excerpt—

from *Cobra Alliance*
available in hardcover, December 2009, from Baen Books

DID YOU KNOW YOU CAN DO ALL THESE THINGS AT THE
BAEN BOOKS WEBSITE ?

✝ Read free sample chapters of books   **[SCHEDULE]**

✝ See what new books are upcoming   **[SCHEDULE]**

✝ Read entire Baen Books for free   **[FREE LIBRARY]**

✝ Check out your favorite author's titles   **[CATALOG]**

✝ Catch up on the latest Baen news & author events
  [NEWS] or **[EVENTS]**

✝ Buy any Baen book   **[SCHEDULE]** or **[CATALOG]**

✝ Read interviews with authors and
artists   **[INTERVIEWS]**

✝ Buy almost any Baen book as an e-book individually
or an entire month at a time   **[WEBSCRIPTIONS]**

✝ Find a list of titles suitable for young adults
  [YOUNG ADULT LISTS]

✝ Communicate with some of the coolest fans in science
fiction & some of the best minds on the planet
  [BAEN'S BAR]

GO TO
WWW.BAEN.COM